THE GHOSTS OF SLEATH

'48

Novels

The Rats
The Fog
The Survivor
Fluke
The Spear
Lair
The Dark
The Jonah
Shrine
Moon
Domain
The Magic Cottage
Sepulchre
Haunted
Creed
Portent
The Ghosts of Sleath
'48

Graphic Novels

The City
(Illustrated by Ian Miller)

Non-fiction

By Horror Haunted
(Edited by Stephen Jones)
James Herbert's Dark Places
(Photographs by Paul Barkshire)

JAMES HERBERT

THE GHOSTS OF SLEATH

'48

Grafton

This omnibus edition published in 1999
by HarperCollins*Publishers*

Reprinted 2003

HarperCollins*Publishers*
77-85 Fulham Palace Road,
Hammersmith, London W6 8JB

The Ghosts of Sleath
Copyright © James Herbert 1994
'48
Copyright © James Herbert 1996

ISBN 0 007 68304 9

Set in Linotron Century Old Style

Printed and bound in Great Britain by
Mackays of Chatham Ltd, Chatham, Kent

For Eileen, without whom . . .

*It's hard to dance with
the devil on your back*

SYDNEY CARTER

1

THERE WAS A STILLNESS about the meadows.
Insects stole nectar from flowers in the hedgerows, but their drone was subdued, their movement lazy. Cows grouped together in shady places although the morning sun was not yet full-blown; they chewed early-morning grass while their tails listlessly flicked at horseflies. Yellow and black caterpillars plagued the ragwort and here and there the cinnabar moth sleepily stretched its wings of cerise and black. Honeysuckle sprayed from wooded areas into the sunlight, its roots back among the trees where the soil was dark and moist, and the muted song of the warbler came from the deeper shadows inside the woods.

The sky, an intense blue, seemed to hang low over the distant Chiltern Hills.

Spiders weaved webs among the hedges of a lane and a carrion crow skimmed low along its dusty length. The bird abruptly soared above the treetops, then swooped down again to perch on a tilted gravestone in the cemetery beyond. It cocked its head to one side as if curious about the gathering of people there, their garb as black as its own.

An ancient church, its stonework scarred and worn by centuries of inclement weather but brightened this day by unhindered sunlight, rose high over the proceedings; uneven buttresses strengthened the square tower, and dark lancet

9

windows within the tower's walls seemed to watch the assembly with the crow.

The freshly dug grave was small, cut from the earth for a child's coffin, and the mourners' faces reflected that special grief. A woman stood apart from the others and closer to the grave itself, her head bowed, her shoulders hunched; it was as if the pain of sorrow were a physical load to bear – and perhaps it was, for Ellen Preddle's body felt weakened, her muscles shrivelled within their skin, the suffering too oppressive. She wept, but her weeping was in silence: the heartbreak was nothing new, just more cruel than ever before.

The vicar, a tall but stooped figure, glanced at her from time to time over his prayer book, anxious that the ceremony should not be interrupted by unseemly hysteria and aware that Ellen Preddle was near to breaking point. The death of her husband barely a year ago had not affected her in this way – in truth, he had been a worthless individual – but the son had always been the focus of her life. They were devoted to one another, mother and child, the lost father's wickedness soon forgotten by them, quickly erased from their thoughts and their conversation. George Preddle's death had been horrific and the vicar wondered how widow and son – the son himself now deceased – had come to terms with it. Particularly as the child had been witness. The vicar felt no shame for his less-than-godly attitude towards the late George Preddle, for the farm-worker had been too despicable to elicit sympathy even from a man of the cloth; nevertheless he did feel guilt, but this was of another kind. He returned his attention to the book of prayer, his gnarled hands trembling.

The coffin was gently lowered into the pit and for one dreadful moment the vicar thought the bereaved woman might throw herself after it. She swayed perilously over the graveside as if in a faint. Fortunately, one of the mourners stepped forward – a relative or friend, someone certainly not from the village – and took Ellen by the elbow, to pull her gently away from the open earth. She went without protest, almost as though there was no will left in her. She tucked her chin further into her chest as the man patted her back.

Soon the funeral was over and Ellen Preddle, her body even more bent than before, was led away down the thin path between the gravestones and through the lychgate to the waiting vehicles. The vicar was surprised when she climbed into the first one alone, saying something briefly to her comforter before closing the door. The black car slowly drove off, leaving the other mourners standing in a group looking after it, surprise on their faces. The man to whom Ellen had spoken shrugged his shoulders and the rest shook their heads in pity, then made towards the remaining vehicles.

I have to be on my own, Ellen told herself as the black Volvo drove the short distance to her cottage. No need for anyone else. They don't understand. They *couldn't* understand what it was like to lose your only child, the only person who could love you blindly in return for your own devotion, who never questioned your words, who was never bad, was never mischievous like other children. Simon was all she had after George had gone and had his silly accident. Just Simon and her. And that was all they needed. Just one another and no one else. Oh Simon, Simon. Why you? Why did the Almighty take you from me? As punishment for the things I did with – the things I did *for* – George, those dirty things, things you could never tell another living soul, things to be ashamed of till the day you died, shameful, horrible things. Was this the punishment? Oh Lord, he made me do them. I didn't enjoy it. But I did them for you, don't you see? Oh send my boy back, dear God, give him back to me, don't take my precious away. I'll do anything, dear Lord. Just give Simon back to me. Please. Please. *Please.*

The moan finally escaped her, a sound she had held in check all morning. She could contain the grief no longer. Ellen sobbed, and the sob became a howling.

11

The driver of the funeral car watched her in the rearview mirror and even his eyes, eyes that had witnessed twenty-odd years of bereavement pain, misted over just a little. Poor woman, he thought to himself, poor, pitiful old thing. No wake after the service, no sharing of the misery. Back to her own place to mourn alone. It wasn't the way, not the way at all. Now was the time to talk, for comfort – and a few stiffeners. A moderate amount of alcohol was no bad thing after such a tragedy, even if the deceased was a child. In fact, *especially* if it was a child. Numb the senses a bit, turn heartbreak into sentiment for a short while. Poor, poor woman.

Villagers about their business on that sunny morning paused to stare after the sombre black vehicle as it glided down the narrow lane, the older men removing their hats in respect, several of the women crossing themselves, and vicariously feeling the tiniest piece of Ellen Preddle's pain. Once the car had driven past with its lonely passenger, they resumed their routines, the sadness lingering, but shifted to one side by their own requirements. Poor Mrs Preddle, a good woman, but an ill-used one. And now a pathetically unlucky one. Death was no friend, but to some neither was life.

The limousine moved smoothly on, its speed in keeping with the solemnity of the occasion.

Why had it happened? Ellen asked herself over and over again. She had only popped out for five minutes – all right, perhaps ten minutes – to buy a stamp and post a letter at the post office and Simon was safe in his bath, playing happily, like so many other times, the tub not even half full. A few moments of the day, a few brief minutes to post the letter and yes, yes, a chat, a little gossip with Mrs Smedley, the postmistress, just a small exchange, less than three minutes – *three terrible minutes when Simon was drowning in his bath* – and then straight back to the house. But she had known something was wrong the moment she set foot on the short path to the front door; something had stirred within her, a sensing, a cold touch of fear jabbing at her heart. But he was eleven years old, for

12

heaven's sake, old enough to take a bath on his own! Everybody admitted to that. Even at the inquest, the coroner went out of his way to say no blame could be attached to Ellen (although his words had been dour, with no softness, no kindness to them), and everyone had agreed. An accident, a terrible accident. There were no marks on his body, no indication that he had slipped – nor any that he had been held under water. The coroner had surmised that the boy had either fallen asleep in the bath, sedated by the water's warmth, or that he had been playing a game, holding his breath too long beneath the surface and involuntarily swallowing too much water when his breath had suddenly given out. Perhaps that explained his open-mouthed horror.

That had been the official verdict. Death by misadventure. Why then could she, herself, not believe it?

The funeral car was drawing to a halt outside a row of three slate-roofed cottages, but it was only when the driver applied the handbrake and turned towards her that Ellen realized she was home.

'Can I help you inside, Mrs Preddle?' the driver asked.

'No,' she replied. Nothing else, just a spiritless 'no'.

Fine with him. Peculiar that she'd insisted on returning home alone, though, no relatives or friends invited back to offer comfort, no wafer-thin paté sandwiches, no tiny cakes, tea or coffee, perhaps a little sherry or something stronger, no ritual to help the bereaved accept the passing. No doubt the other mourners would find their way to the Black Boar to cheer themselves a bit. Only natural. People needed it. But apparently, not this one. Insisted on being on her own. So be it, the choice was hers. Foolish though, not healthy; you needed people around you at times like this. The driver left the car and opened the passenger door.

Her head bowed again, Ellen stepped out onto the kerbless road. A curtain twitched in the end cottage, her neighbour concerned rather than curious. Ellen hardly noticed.

She opened the gate, oddly registering that the hinges

needed oiling, their screech jarring the stillness of the day. She went through, then paused halfway up the short, paved path. On either side peonies, lilacs and primroses spread in cheerful array, flowers she and Simon had lovingly tended together, making their tiny garden the prettiest among the three joined cottages. The black car behind her stole away.

Ellen peered up at the small window over the front door, the window that belonged to the bathroom where Simon . . . She stopped the thought. *Where Simon* . . . It persisted and she drove it from her mind. She continued to look at the window though.

A peculiar sensation startled her; it was as if an icy bead of sweat had trickled down her spine.

She walked forward, her steps forced, and her gaze only left the little bathroom window when she had to search in her handbag for the door key. The chill at her back had now spread into the rest of her body so that her muscles felt tight and awkward. Fitting the key into the lock took some concentration.

The key turned, but Ellen did not push the door open straight away; instead she drew in a breath to steady herself, confused by the tenseness that had subjugated her distress. A different feeling welled inside her and she could not understand it. It was a kind of expectancy, and made no sense at all. Ellen knew there was no hope, that everything that was precious to her had been taken. There was nothing left, no joy, no future. Nothing . . .

With a neat, embroidered handkerchief she dabbed the moisture from her cheeks. Then, her eyes alight with a strange anticipation, she pushed open the door.

There was no hallway, for the front door opened immediately into the cluttered living room, with its low ceiling and stout beams inlaid on white uneven walls. A crooked staircase of worn oak led up to the bedrooms and bathroom.

There were wet patches on the stairs.

But it was the small naked figure sitting in an old lumpy armchair before the empty fireplace that she was drawn

14

towards. The boy's hair was still damp, plastered shiny and flat against his scalp and forehead, and droplets of water stippled his pale shivering body.

There was a great sadness in Simon's eyes as he watched his mother from across the room.

2

AVID ASH UTTERED a soft groan as he shifted position. The loose joints of the straight-backed chair creaked and he quickly became still again. He looked at his wristwatch, the luminous dial informing him it was almost ten to three. A. M.

God, there had to be better ways of making a living, he told himself, carefully flexing his shoulders. Nearly three in the morning and here he was, skulking in the semi-darkness between racks of towels and sheets, trying not to breathe too loudly, desperate for a cigarette . . . longing for a drink. He eased himself upright, rubbing his hands over his face to clear the tiredness. Even the scraping of his chin stubble sounded too loud at that ungodly hour.

The door of the laundry room was slightly ajar so that the night-lights plugged into the wall sockets of the corridor outside provided a dim glow. He went quietly to the door and peered through the gap. Silence out there, not a soul stirring. The smell of stale food lingered as though it had soaked into the dull wallpaper itself; he wondered if he scratched the wall with a fingernail, would the odours waft out, released as if from a magazine scent card. Ash cleared the idle thoughts and listened again. No, not a sound. The old folk were at peace.

He backed away, turning to the Olympus camera resting on a stack of towelling. He pressed its battery check lever and a

16

tiny red light glowed like the single eye of a demon. The battery was fine, but hadn't he tested it only two hours ago? He pressed fingertips against his temples, squeezing gently and willing the dull headache to leave. Was it due to tiredness or boredom? Or was tension the true cause?

Should be used to it. Endless hours of inactivity, waiting in darkness for so long that eventually even the imagination gave up. Gave up the ghost. Literally.

He allowed himself a smile, and if it could have been seen there in the darkness, its irony would have been plain.

Ash reached for the thermos flask by the chair and quietly poured himself a coffee. What the coffee needed was a measure of brandy, but no, he had promised Kate. He was always promising Kate. No booze, not when he was working. It was a rule he did not always keep.

Yes, Kate, I know I've got a problem, and yes, Kate, I know it's getting worse. Ash spoke the words in his mind, imagining her standing there before him in the darkness of the laundry room. But think back, Kate, think back three years. Could she blame him? Could she believe him?

He'd often wondered about that. She had been the only one he'd spoken to of those three nights at Edbrook, the only person who wouldn't doubt his sanity. Yet he had caught the uncertainty in her eyes – no, it hadn't been as strong as that; it had been no more than a hint of incredulity. And who could blame her? Even he had doubts when he thought back, even he sometimes wondered if it had not all been a terrible dream, a grotesque nightmare, one that haunted him to this day. His fingers rose to the faint scar on his cheek, a thin ridge of hard flesh that was only visible in a certain light, and he wondered . . .

No! He almost said the word aloud.

He took a large swallow of stale coffee and sat back down on the chair. Concentrate on now, he advised himself. Think only of the present, forget about things that happened so long ago, things that made no sense. (But they did make sense,

17

didn't they, David? Everything that took place in that old house three years ago was perfectly, though peculiarly, logical. That is, if you believed in malign spirits.)

It was as if these words inside his head were spoken by another, and they were insidious, almost sly, a whispering that did not want him to forget; yet the tone was his, they were his own words, repeated often, lest reality and time diminish their significance.

Ash shivered, though it was not cold inside this room with its warm pipes and smell of fresh linen. Maybe he should leave these night-time surveillances to others, those more stable investigators or researchers who viewed these matters less emotively. As he once had. There were enough members of the Institute to cover such work, it hadn't been necessary to take this one on alone. Yet it had been his idea, it was he who had suggested this solitary vigil to the owners of the Bonadventure Rest Home after a month's investigation had proved futile. He had discovered no paranormal activity, no haunting – and no Sleep Angel.

The Sleep Angel. Harbinger of death, portent of doom. Or so the home's old folk would believe.

A figure wearing a flowing gown that somehow glowed green had appeared before three of the oldest residents and informed them it was time for them to die. And they had followed the instructions, two of them a few days later, the third, it seemed, instantly. (One of the other residents, an elderly woman whose capricious bladder gave her cause to leave her room more than once a night, had witnessed the so-called 'angel' entering the dead man's room as she was returning from the bathroom. She, herself, had scurried back to bed and pulled the covers over her head in case the visitor noticed her and decided to pay her a call too.) It was the first two who had recounted the Sleep Angel's words to them, which they repeated until they, too, obeyed the instruction.

Claire and Trevor Penlock, the owners of the Bonadventure, had endeavoured to minimize the stories and to soothe their clients' anxieties, but the residents had little else to do with their time but gossip and exaggerate, and the Penlocks feared that rumours about the home would soon spread. While deaths in such places, given the average age of the usual residents, were commonplace – if not expected – word that unearthly forces were actively encouraging the 'passing on' would definitely be harmful to the Bonadventure's reputation. Reluctantly the Psychical Research Institute had been contacted and arrangements for a discreet but thorough investigation had been made.

Initially Ash had wondered if this seraphic spectre was some kind of contagious hallucination, first imagined by someone close to death (someone whose religious beliefs might well inspire visions of a heavenly guide to the next world), and he had spent time talking to the residents, gently probing but finding little evidence of mass hysteria, or even any great interest in the supernatural. Nor did he notice much senility among them. He also questioned the staff, from the matron, Penlock herself, to the junior care assistants and the cook, giving particular attention to the two senior care supervisors who alternated weekly on overnight duties. He checked that the building itself was secure at night and was satisfied that all windows and doors were either bolted or locked. Each night he installed tripod-mounted cameras with automatic detectors at the end of corridors and the main hallway as well as placing thermometers at certain strategic points to record any dramatic and unaccountable dips in temperature at any time. Outside the bedroom doors of the home's most elderly residents, or of those whose health was vulnerable, he sprinkled powder so that footsteps, ethereal or physical, might show the following morning. He studied architectural drawings of the building itself, including those detailing recent renovations, and looked into its history, interested to learn of any past paranormal phenomena. All to no avail. No one, apart from the deceased and the old lady, had witnessed the manifestation, nothing was disturbed during the nights of his investigation, and the cameras only took pictures of the senior care supervisors making their night rounds or certain senior citizens visiting the bathrooms.

Yet Ash was not quite satisfied. Which was why he had suggested these further night-time vigils should be in secret. And on particular nights only.

Twice the matron had smuggled him into the home while the supervisor was busy on her evening rounds administering medicine, but already Ash was beginning to suspect it was all a waste of time.

On this night, however, his patience was to be rewarded.

He heard a noise from somewhere nearby. Silence followed.

He waited a few seconds longer, then slowly eased himself up so that the chair's joints – or his own – made no sound. He tiptoed to the door and peered through the narrow gap.

. Directly opposite was the lift that serviced all three of the home's floors and to the right of this was a short wheelchair ramp, rather than steps, leading to another corridor where the central staircase was situated. He opened the door wider and stole a look outside: the corridor to his left was empty and all the bedroom doors appeared to be closed. Only the door to the bathroom was open.

He shut the laundry-room door, leaving a slight gap again, then slunk back into the gloom.

Another sound. It could be the building settling. Or it might be someone on the staircase around the corner from the ramp.

Ash moved even further back so that light from outside, dim though it was, would not shine on him. He became conscious of his own breathing.

He also became aware that the orange glow from the corridor's night-lights was changing subtly; a soft greenness was merging into it.

His breathing stopped as a shape floated by the door.

*   *   *

20

Jessie Dimple woke suddenly. In her dream her limbs had been lithe, her skin had been smooth, and her heart had been alive with passion. She had been running through a field of buttercups, their brilliant yellow, against a background of vivid green, lifting her spirit so that each step was a graceful leap that became a wonderful arc, and soon she was floating, flying, always returning to the earth, to the flowers, but easily lifting again, up towards the clear sapphire sky, to soar then sink, soar then sink, in rainbow curves that grew longer and longer, higher and higher, until eventually she hardly touched the ground at all, she really was flying, flying towards –

She gave a moan, annoyed at her awakening, sad that she had once again become an aged crone whose bones were too brittle, whose skin was too wrinkled, and whose heart and soul were too wearied with the effort of life.

She lay propped up in bed by an A-pillow, the only way she could sleep these days without choking on her own throat fluids, and tried to remember. Ah, the dream . . . such a wonderful dream . . . where gravity and age held no sway and the body played servant to the spirit. The peace the dream had brought. The freedom . . .

But what had awoken her? It was still dark outside the window.

She stirred in the bed, but her blurry eyes could not see the face of the clock she kept on the bedside cabinet. She sank back and allowed her cloudy gaze to roam around the room, trying to remember if she had taken all her pills and medicines that day, the verapamil for her angina, the Sinemet for the Parkinson's, the thioridazine for her confusion and the lactulose for her bowels. Yes, yes, the matron or the supervisor would have made sure of that. Indeed they would have teased her for knowing and demanding each prescription as though they were not up to their job. Well, Jessie had been a nurse during both world wars, when she was young . . . when she was young . . . so long ago, a lifetime ago . . . when Howard had been alive and the children . . . the children had loved her, had cared for her as she had cared so very much for them. But they had their own lives to live now, they couldn't be spending all their hard-earned time with an old thing like her who had eighty-two years of life behind her, they couldn't be visiting every day, every week, every month, when they had their work – their very important work – to see to, their own lovely families to take care of . . . to cherish . . . as she cherished . . . them.

Moisture blurred her eyes now and the dark shape of the crucifix on the wall opposite became even more indistinct. With a quivering hand, Jessie lifted the edge of the top sheet to her eyes and softly wiped away the tears.

There now, you silly old thing. Getting more and more sentimental in your old age. Getting more and more daft. Well, they'll be here tomorrow, if not, then the next day. They had busy lives. But they cared very much. Places like this were expensive, but they never grumbled. Her boys were good to her. But when had she seen them last? Had it been yesterday? No, no, the day before. Oh, you're a stupid old biddy. It had been a long while ago, yes, a long while. A month? Longer, Jessie, much longer. They came when they could, though, and the wives and the grandchildren came with them. Not every time, but often. Occasionally. Sometimes. Well, what did young children – teenagers now, weren't they, or were they even older than that? Hard to remember, hard to picture them – what did they want with horrible places like this? This was for old folk, not the young. The young didn't like the smells and the sickness and the gibberish and the forgetfulness and the reminder of what one day would be their own lives. And that was hardly surprising. Why, if she had her own way, if she were not so useless and helpless, she would be elsewhere too!

Her dry, lipless mouth tilted to a smile. Elsewhere. Oh Jessie, there was only one other place for you, my girl. That is, if He wanted you. She closed her eyes and prayed that He did, and her thoughts of heaven were not unlike her dream.

She opened her eyes again when she sensed – not heard – the movement of the bedroom door.

The Sleep Angel was standing there in the opening, a green glow shading the whiteness of its flowing gown. Its face was in shadow, but Jessie knew its expression would be kind.

The angel came towards her, gracefully, quietly, and Jessie imagined it was smiling.

It spoke, so softly that Jessie barely heard the words, and it told her it was time to let go, that there was a better place waiting for her, where there was no pain and no sadness, and all she had to do was give up her spirit, discard her life . . .

And as it leaned towards her as if to kiss her toothless mouth, Jessie wondered if the smile was not a frown, if the frown was not a scowl, if the scowl was not a grimace of loathing. Jessie suddenly felt fear and something stiffened inside her bony chest, became tight yet seemed to expand, causing a pain that was worse than anything she had felt before. The hurt was outrageous, cruel, and had nothing to do with peaceful resignation.

As she clutched at her struggling heart she became aware that light was blazing above her and that another presence was in the room. The Sleep Angel was falling away from her and it was screaming . . . was screaming . . . was screaming as she, herself, was screaming . . .

3

OU LOOK AS IF you've had a bad night.' Kate McCarrick shuffled papers together and laid them to one side as Ash took a chair opposite her. He placed a plastic coffee cup on the edge of her desk, then fumbled in his jacket for cigarettes.

'Bad morning,' he told her, shaking one loose from the pack.

'Any success?'

'Not in the Institute's terms. The Bonadventure isn't haunted.'

Kate pushed back her chair and went to one of the grey filing cabinets situated between well-stocked bookshelves. She opened the B drawer. 'I didn't expect it to be. If the sightings had been by members of staff I might have given them a little more credence. Unfortunately elderly people are not always reliable as witnesses to the paranormal. Either their eyesight's bad, or their imagination is over-active.' She thumbed through the files and stopped when she reached the one marked Bonadventure Rest Home. Opening it, she returned to her desk. 'You've done me a report?' she said, looking up from the file at him.

He smiled wearily. 'Sorry, Kate, I haven't got round to it yet.'

She removed her reading glasses and studied him for a moment: his dark, tousled hair, pale, unshaven face, his

24

rumpled clothes. 'I'm sorry if I've asked a stupid question.'

He removed the unlit cigarette from his mouth and reached forward for the coffee. He sipped it before saying: 'Busy night, busy morning. I'll get a written report to you later today.'

'No, you look as if you need some sleep. Tell me now, report me later.'

As he sipped again he wondered if Kate had a lover at present. She still looked good; her figure, although not as slim as it once was, was still seductive, her hair still had a natural sheen. Maybe the jaw was just a little less firm, and maybe there were a few more lines around her eyes than before, but Kate had an allure that not all women carried into their forties. He remembered the first time they had made love, her delicate softness then, the way her teeth had nipped at his flesh, how her lips had moistened every part of him.

'David?'

'Uh?' He shook his head, clearing the memories, and as his gaze met hers he knew she had guessed his thoughts. Her tone was brisk and her frown drew fresh lines across her forehead. 'I take it you're not registering a paranormal incident.'

'Afraid not.' Ash put the coffee cup back on the desk and reached in his pocket for matches. He struck one and held it up to the cigarette between his lips; but it stayed poised as he stared into the tiny flame. He became aware that Kate was watching him and quickly lit the cigarette, hoping she had not noticed how his hand had trembled for a moment. 'No, no ghost, although for a while there I wasn't sure.'

She leaned forward, interested.

'The residents were partially right,' he went on. 'There was a Sleep Angel stalking the corridors of the home, but it wasn't what they imagined.'

'Nevertheless it managed to frighten some of them to death.'

Ash shrugged. 'Well, they died – two a couple of days later, the last one the same night. He died of a heart attack, although he'd been diagnosed as having cancer of the bowel only a short time before. He was in his late eighties and he was very ill –

it wouldn't have taken much to send him over.' He exhaled smoke. 'A cynic might even say his visitor did him a favour.'

She let it go. 'The other two – what happened to them?'

'They were both in their eighties, and their health wasn't so good either. From what they told the matron afterwards it seemed their visitor convinced them it was time for the long sleep.'

'It told them to die?' Kate was startled.

'Uh-huh. That's why they called it the Sleep Angel. I suppose you could call it a kind of verbal euthanasia.'

'That's unbelievable.'

'Wait till you're old and tired and feel there's nothing left to do with your life anymore.'

'Every other day. So what or who was this agent for the afterlife? Did you see it last night?'

He looked around her desk for something to tap his cigarette into and Kate reached for the bin under the desk. She passed it over to him and he flicked ash before putting it by his chair. 'Yes,' he replied with a tired sigh, 'it showed up all right. It was in the early hours of the morning, still dark, and I was watching from the home's laundry room. They say old people or the very sick often pass away around that time – the body's in its deepest state of unconsciousness about then – so I had a hunch something might happen around two or three. I also made sure I was hiding on the same floor as the oldest resident. Anyway, just after three o'clock something moved past the laundry-room door, something with a greenish glow to it.' He scratched the stubble under his chin. 'It scared the hell out of me when I took a peek into the corridor.'

'Someone dressed up to frighten.' Kate said it as a statement rather than a question.

'Right. Or at least, to play the part. Flowing white gown, long, loose sleeves. And underneath the costume she'd taped those small luminous glow-tubes, you know the kind that kids play with on Hallowe'en? Clear plastic tubes filled with a chemical liquid that shines in the dark.'

'I've seen them.'

'She used them for effect, to give her an eerie kind of glow.'

'She?'

He raised a hand briefly as if in resignation. 'One of the senior care supervisors, a woman who'd been with the home for years.'

'She must be a special kind of cruel bitch.'

'I'm not so sure. The police and her employers are still trying to figure out if she frightened the old people out of malice because she was sick of them, or if she genuinely wanted to relieve their suffering by helping them on their way to something better.'

Kate sat back and absorbed what Ash had told her. 'That's awful,' she concluded.

'She frightened another choice candidate for heaven last night, but I got there before she could do too much damage. I just hope the old lady gets over the shock.' He drank more coffee, drew on the cigarette, and smiled across the table at her. 'So there you have it. I'm afraid it doesn't help the Institute's researches.'

'We can live with that. Our task is to validate incidents of the paranormal or supernatural, but it's almost as useful to expose false claims. In fact, it gives the organization more credibility when we do the latter; people might just understand we're not here to support charlatans and cranks. I'm only sorry you spent so much time on this investigation. Tell me, did you suspect at the start that someone was playing games at the home?' She instantly regretted her phrasing, for a disturbed, almost haunted look clouded Ash's dark eyes. She quickly added: 'Did you think the supervisor was involved somehow?'

He gazed past her shoulder at the window. It was bright out there, even though they were in the shaded part of the building, and street noises drifted up. Something black swept by, a bird so large that Ash thought it must have been a crow. For some reason a tiny shiver ran though him.

'I guessed someone was behind it,' he said, 'and it was easy

27

to find out who was alone on duty the nights – or early mornings, to be more precise – the apparition showed up. I offered
the Institute's services for another few nights as long as they
told the staff the investigation was over. Nobody was to know
I was still there. I suppose the supervisor thought she'd won
and could just carry on as before.'

'She really imagined she could keep getting away with it?'

'She's quite mad, Kate. She's capable of imagining anything.'

Kate closed the Bonadventure file and put it to one side.
'Well I'm glad we're done with it. It didn't seem likely to me.'

'How many of these cases do at the beginning?'

It was a remark Ash would never have made a few years
ago and Kate was puzzled. Somehow he seemed unhappy, dis-
enchanted even, with the outcome of this particular investigation, and that puzzled her too. Ash, who once had been so
cynical about psychic phenomena and the aims of the Psychical
Research Institute, had gone through a slow but appreciable
change of attitude. He no longer dismissed all paranormal
events out of hand, even though, once engaged in an enquiry,
he did his utmost to disprove the existence of ghosts or communication from the dead. The majority of cases taken on by
the Institute proved either to be hoaxes or caused by freak
conditions, and nobody was better than David Ash at exposing
fraudsters or discovering odd but real circumstances behind
bizarre occurrences. In fact, it was his very scepticism towards
all things supernatural that had prompted Kate to offer him a
job with the Institute in the first place: their researches needed
both balance and a critical eye, and who better than a non-
believer to give them that? And he had proved excellent in the
task, discounting claims of hauntings, poltergeist activity and
spiritualism time and time again with a logical, well-reasoned
argument backed up by solid evidence. There were those in
the organization who thought he did his job too well and that
he was harming the Institute's reputation with his constant
refutation of what they, themselves, endorsed; but Kate had
always resisted their arguments by explaining that Ash,

because of his impartiality – no, his positive *opposition* to such beliefs – lent them enormous credibility when circumstances involving the paranormal were proved beyond all doubt.

David Ash had been good for the Institute, and how he had relished – albeit in a quiet, grim way – his successes. That is, until three years ago. After the Mariell affair. That was the case that had shattered his confidence and driven him to nervous collapse.

What was the truth behind it, David? Did your investigation cause the breakdown, or were you already headed that way? How much of what happened there was your own imagination?

Ash was rising to his feet, draining the last of the coffee as he did so. He dropped the empty plastic cup into the bin and said, 'I need some sleep. I'll write you a report tonight and get it to you first thing tomorrow. You might give the Penlocks a ring, by the way – I think they could do with a few kind words.'

'I've got another assignment for you,' she said.

'I need a break, Kate.'

'Fine. Take tomorrow off. Sleep the whole day through after you've delivered the Bonadventure report.'

'Your benevolence is awesome. Surely someone else can take care of it.'

'I thought this one would interest you.' *Besides, I know you hate it when you're not working,* she thought. *Time on your hands frightens you, doesn't it, David? That's when you start thinking too much, that's when you start to dream.* 'Have you ever heard of a village called Sleath?' she asked.

He shook his head without taking time to consider.

'It's in the Chilterns. Not too far to travel.'

'What's the problem there – a haunting?'

'No, David,' she replied. 'It isn't just one.'

29

4

IT WAS GOOD to get away from the city, even though the
fine weather had broken and light rain was cooling the
air. Occasionally the sun broke through and the landscape
sparkled, the greens of the meadows taking on a new
lustre, the hills in the distance softening to a shimmer;
the beech woods lent darker shades while wild flowers added
glitter.

There was little traffic on the minor roads, but Ash kept the
Ford to a steady speed, enjoying the twisting lanes and the
peacefulness of this Home Counties hinterland. Now and again
he checked the map book lying on the passenger seat beside
him. Once off the main highways the route had become more
complicated and he began to understand why he had never
heard of the village of Sleath; it was one of those places made
even more isolated by the era of trunk roads and motorways,
when such diversions had become rare for most travellers. He
drove through combes and over gentle hills whose crests were
clothed in beech woods. Occasionally there were signs warning
motorists of wild deer crossing roads and once, when he had
stopped to consult the road map, he heard a woodpecker drilling
away somewhere deep in the woods. He wound down the
window and drank in the country-fresh air, relishing the different scents of the trees and plants, all enhanced by the light
rain. Birdsongs were clear and individual in the stillness, yet

in perfect harmony also; even the distant tapping of the wood-pecker was in soft accord. Ash started off again, not quite sure of his own location on the map, but trusting he was headed in the general direction of the village.

Sleath. Odd name. But then the countryside was littered with strange-sounding villages and towns, many of them amusing, a few of them sinister. This one, he mused, was of the latter variety.

He looked at his wristwatch. Should be there soon. Easy to get lost in a maze of roads like this, though, some of them wide enough only to take single-file traffic. Kate had said it was off the beaten track, and she'd been on the button with that. He hadn't even come upon a signpost with the village name on it yet. Wait a minute – one coming up now.

He stopped the car at the crossroads and peered up at the weather-battered sign, its post grey and cracked with age, the names on the pointing arms chiselled out of the wood and stained a blackish brown. He shook his head in mild frustration: the three arms told him what was to the right and left, and even what was behind him; but it failed to inform him of what lay directly ahead. He examined the map again.

Had to be the road opposite, unless he'd totally lost his sense of direction. He looked up at the signpost again, noting the villages inscribed on the three outstretched arms, then finding them on his map. 'Okay,' he mumbled to himself, 'dead ahead it is.' He engaged first gear and glanced right and left.

The car had only moved forward a matter of inches when he stabbed at the foot brake and brought it to a halt once more. A tractor had appeared to his right, its clattering engine preceding the machine itself round a curve in the road. The driver, a man whose ruddy face was in perfect harmony with the red and rust machine he rode upon, gave a cheery wave as he swung into the lane that Ash himself was about to take. The man wore an olive-green anorak with the hood pulled up over his head against the rain, and his grin revealed a sparsity of teeth, each one a dull yellow, given unfortunate importance by the gaps between.

Ash quickly wound down his window and called after him. 'Is that the way to Sleath?'

The tractor continued its journey down the high-banked lane without so much as a glance back from the driver and Ash could only watch as it disappeared round a bend. Its huge wheels left muddy clogs of earth on the road and the noise of its diesel engine faded to a low chugging. Ash disengaged gear and released himself from his seatbelt so that he could reach into his jacket pocket. He found the cigarettes and lit one, tossing the still flaming match out into the wet road. It was extinguished before it hit the ground, and the tiny curl of smoke that rose from it was quickly dissolved by the rain. He looked at the half-burnt matchstick for a second or two before resting back in the seat and closing his eyes. He drew deeply on the cigarette and remembered another time, in a different car, and someone taunted by the small flame he held, her face turning towards him in the moonlight . . .

His eyes snapped open.

Enough. Forget the past. Those kind of memories could lead to insanity.

But it seemed as though it had only happened yesterday.

He buckled the seatbelt, jerked the car into first, and stamped on the accelerator. The rear wheels squealed on the road's damp surface before gaining grip, and then the car shot across the junction into the lane opposite. Wind and rain gusted through the open window, clearing the cigarette smoke, but not the thoughts that tormented him. The car gathered speed and Ash had to make himself ease up. He soon reached the bend the tractor had disappeared round and he braked hurriedly, that reflex action bringing his thoughts back to the present, for the moment banishing those dark memories, the images that might have been recalled from a dream, a nightmare, rather than from true events. He was even grateful for the further distraction when the front right-hand wing came perilously close to the opposite bank as he steered round the bend.

He pulled the steering wheel to the left and trod harder on

32

the brake pedal, hoping the car wouldn't skid on the mud left on the road by the tractor. Vegetation growing on the steep bank swayed in the breeze as the car skimmed past.

Ash brought the Ford back into the centre of the lane and slowed down even more when he saw the red tractor up ahead. He came up behind the machine, its driver, resembling some mediaeval monk in his hooded anorak, still completely oblivious to him. There was no room to overtake and Ash had to brake again to avoid collision. Frustrated, and tempted to give a blast of his horn, he followed the clattering farm vehicle at a slow, almost leisurely, pace. The sound of the diesel engine was even worse in the confines of the bank-sided lane, the decibels only slightly lower than those from a pneumatic drill. So much for the peace and quiet of the countryside, thought Ash as he wound up the window. And the black fumes that occasionally spewed from underneath the machine did little for the sweet country air and the freshness of the rain.

Ash became aware that his hands were gripping the steering wheel so tightly that the knuckles were showing white. He flexed each of his fingers in turn, loosening the tendons, willing himself to relax. He rested his elbow on the window's edge and took the cigarette from his mouth. He blew smoke over his shoulder in a steady stream. His fingers soon began to drum impatiently on the steering wheel.

A minute went by and he decided a friendly toot on the horn wouldn't do any harm. The driver in front neither looked round nor pulled over and Ash wasn't sure if the man was playing games or really hadn't heard. Either way, there was nothing he could do: a cat could barely squeeze past the tractor, so narrow was the gap on both sides.

'Come on,' he said aloud as they approached a passing-place cut into the bank. The man in front drove relentlessly on.

They went by a gate whose muddy entrance would easily have allowed the tractor to pull in to let him through, but the other man ignored it. A little irritated by now, Ash pressed the horn button again, this time holding his thumb there for several seconds. Still he was ignored. He wound the window back down and poked his head out, ready to call after the farm-worker, but saw that the bank dipped just ahead and a grass verge ran alongside the lane for quite some way.

He flicked the cigarette out of the window and readied himself to step on the accelerator. There would be just enough room and enough time to overtake the lumbering tractor if he drove partly on the verge.

Ash waited for the right moment, then pushed his foot down, swinging the car to the right so that the wheels on that side mounted the verge. He increased speed, the front bumper almost grazing one of the tractor's great rear wheels as it passed by. The Ford lurched and rocked, but he held the steering wheel firmly, keeping it steady.

He drew level with the muddy tyre and glanced anxiously at it. He kept as far away from it as he could, but there was a ditch or deep rut on the other side of the verge that restricted his options for manoeuvre. Incredibly, the hooded man still hadn't noticed him – or at least, was pretending he hadn't. Ash thumped the horn, anger behind the blow.

But the tractor appeared to be matching his speed, the big wheels keeping him at bay. It even seemed deliberately to be moving over towards him.

With dismay, Ash realized that he was running out of space: the grass verge ended abruptly thirty yards or so ahead and the bank, tree roots entwined in its earth, reared up again.

He slammed on the brakes and the nearside wheels began to slide over the wet grass, causing the car to veer inwards.

Ash shouted something, probably a curse, as the Ford bucked and skidded and the bank loomed larger in the windscreen. He was going to hit it.

He pumped the brakes to release the lock and held the car straight, afraid of pulling over into the tractor and just as afraid of crashing into the bank. He froze –

– and the tractor suddenly swung away from him, sweeping through a gate into a field on the left of the lane.

Ash yanked the wheel round and the car shot off the grass, the right-hand tyres now gripping.

He kept his foot away from the brake pedal, allowing the car to coast, relief instantly dismissing the fear – although not the stress. But now he saw there was a narrow, hump-backed bridge ahead and there was no time to stop. He could only pray there was nothing approaching on the other side.

The car hit the rise of the old stone bridge at speed and Ash's head almost bumped the roof as he was thrown upwards at the crest. He fell back, controlling the car as best he could, his stomach still riding high in his chest.

He was over and the verges were broader on this side, leading down to the small river he had just crossed.

But a figure was standing in the middle of the lane.

Ash cried out as he swung the wheel again.

Oh, God, I'm going to hit him!

The thought screamed inside his head as the car slewed across the hard surface of the lane, its rear end swinging round, tyres squealing in concert with the screaming inside his mind. The world outside the windscreen – the trees, the foliage, the figure itself – spun to the right as the Ford mounted the grass with a violent lurch that nearly wrenched the steering wheel from his grip.

His body was rocked as the wheels hit bumps and ruts, but his foot remained pressed hard against the brake pedal as he ignored all expert advice on how to control a skid. His back pushed into the seat for added leverage, and his wrists locked rigid.

Time-expanded moments went by as trees in front grew threateningly and rapidly large. The vehicle rocked to a halt and Ash was thrown forward, then jerked back into the seat by the seatbelt.

He remained motionless while he struggled to subdue his

jangling nerves and fast-beating heart. But then the image of the figure standing in the centre of the lane – *frozen there, not even trying to escape, mesmerized like a rabbit under the gaze of a fox* – burst through the shock. With a speed that had much to do with coursing adrenaline, he released the seatbelt, pushed open the door, and was stumbling across the grass to the roadway, his eyes frantically searching for a fallen body. Rain pattered against his head and shoulders, and once he slipped, but regained his balance without going down. He was sure the car had hit him – *he must have, he was standing right in his path* – yet he couldn't remember hearing or feeling a blow. He stopped when he reached the lane's hard surface, and he whirled around, searching for the body, running to the other side and back again, his head turning this way and that.

There was no one in the road.

He hurriedly scanned the verges, but no one lay prone in the grass, no figure stood, or was slumped, by the trees. Perhaps he had staggered away somewhere, traumatized by the accident, whether he had been struck or not. Perhaps he had crawled down the riverbank.

Ash ran to the edge of the bridge and peered into the water. The river was really a fast-flowing stream, so clear and shallow he could see the rocks and sand of its bed. Dense bunches of willow moss clung to the larger stones and blue forget-me-nots sprung from shadier spots along its edges; but there was no one floating down there. Relieved but perplexed, he hurried to the other side, the idea that a body might be swept downstream never a serious consideration – the water wasn't deep enough – but reason telling him the person he'd hit or almost hit *had* to be somewhere close by. His breaths coming in short gasps, he looked along the riverbank. Leafy branches hung over its length, creating a shadowed tunnel, and here and there undergrowth crept down to the very edge of the water. Nevertheless, the stream ran fairly straight, affording him a good view for some distance. Still he could find nothing that remotely resembled a body.

He looked around again, forcing himself to take his time, studying the terrain with panic-suppressed care, scrutinizing the foliage and between the trees for a glimpse of material or an outstretched limb, anything that would indicate an injured person. And still he found nothing.

Mystified, his dread growing rather than diminishing, he ran to the brow of the short, humped bridge. He stood there, staring back down the empty lane he had just driven along; in the distance he could hear the faint clatter of the tractor he had followed.

He was taking longer and deeper breaths by now, but a sudden notion took him so violently that for a moment he stopped breathing altogether. Ash raced down the incline and made for the car.

Almost there, he fell to his knees and slid on the wet grass. One hand slammed against the Ford's metalwork and he ducked low, peering into the darkness underneath.

A sigh that contained a muted groan escaped him when he saw there was no one lying there in the shadows, and he twisted around and rested his back against the door panelling, one leg outstretched, the other bent with his wrist resting across the knee. He lifted his face up to the sky and the light rain pecked at his closed eyelids. 'Thank God,' he said in a low whisper.

There had been no one standing in the lane.

It was the only answer. He had imagined the figure.

As though very weary, Ash hauled himself up, pulling on the Ford's slippery bodywork as he did so. Once on his feet he leaned against the car, an elbow on the roof, his other hand on the bonnet; his shoulders hunched, he drew in deep, deliberate breaths, giving himself time for the tension to drain away.

He *had* seen someone there as his car had crested the old stone bridge, though. And he had been sure he was going to hit the boy as he'd desperately turned the wheel.

The boy.

A strange little boy wearing a three-button coat that was too tight and short trousers that came well below his knees. How could it have been his imagination if he had noticed details like that?

Yet there was no one around, no one at all. Even the sound of the tractor had faded away.

A cry, so sharp in the rain-splattered stillness, made him spin around. He looked for the bird – it had to be the guttural squawk of a crow – but failed to find it. It was probably somewhere high in the trees.

Ash pulled open the car door and reached over into the back seat. He unzipped the battered leather holdall lying there and delved inside, rummaging until he touched cold metal. He brought out the silver-plated hip flask and turned to sit in the passenger seat, legs outside the car despite the rain. Unscrewing the top, he lifted the flask to his lips and took a long swig of the neat vodka.

Its heat swelled in his throat and chest, then abated so that only a mild flush remained.

It helped a little.

5

E CAUGHT GLIMPSES of the village through the trees as he drove down the hill. The road curved dramatically, almost back on itself, and he concentrated on the manoeuvre, only looking towards Sleath when the road had straightened again. He just glimpsed the church tower beyond the cluster of other buildings before the woods thickened and the view was lost.

Ash tossed a cigarette butt out of the window and realized his hand was still trembling from the incident earlier. Only a few minutes had passed since then, but already reason was imposing its simplistic logic: he had imagined the boy standing in the lane. The near-accident because of the tractor had probably triggered off something in his mind, a memory perhaps; or maybe it had induced an hallucination of some kind. Whatever, he had swerved to avoid something that wasn't there. Couldn't possibly have been there. What the hell, he'd investigated enough cases of so-called phantoms or apparitions to know most were caused by over-active imaginations or trauma. He knew perfectly well that the human mind was full of tricks and he'd just been a victim of one of them. Yet the unease lingered (why else did his hand still tremble?) and certain memories endeavoured to push themselves to the fore as if in league with his mind's brief deception. No, that was wrong, he thought. His memories were stronger, they were the stimuli, and his imagination was susceptible to them. It was a logic that was far from simple, but it strengthened the original rationale and therefore was more convincing. And it was a notion that Ash was anxious, although not happy, to cling to, for anything else conjured more questions and more doubts within himself.

The road levelled out and he found himself approaching a small, rough-stoned bridge. Nearby, on the opposite bank, was an old millhouse, its wheel redundant and green with slime. The grassy banks were steep, with overhanging trees creating shady tunnels along the narrow river's length. Ash slowed down and crossed the bridge, the sound of the Ford's tyres changing tone for a second or two. And then he was in the village called Sleath.

By now the rain had stopped and the sun, when it could find an opening in the clouds, speckled the wet roadway with gold.

Ash drove slowly, looking from left to right, studying the old-world houses, many of them constructed of red brick and timber, while others were even more quaint with white wattle and daub panelling between dark-stained beams, the thatched roofs of these dripping from the recent rainfall. One or two of the chimney stacks seemed unreasonably high, particularly on the multi-gabled building on his left, a place he assumed, because of its size, was some kind of municipal centre, the village hall perhaps. The chimneys rising almost to the point of folly from its various rooftops of rust-brown tiles were constructed in oversailing courses and capped by star-shaped terracotta pots. The entrance, large oak double-doors, was closed and there were several notices pinned to the wood. Most of the houses were set close to the road, only the odd one or two maintaining tiny front gardens bordered by low picket fences.

Ash was impressed. Surprised, too, for although the village was a tourist's dream, very few people were in evidence on the main street. Situated in the Cotswolds, or the Lake District, or in certain areas of the south-west, the place would have been overrun by snap-happy sightseers, particularly at this time of year. Sleath, it seemed, was a well-kept secret.

He had arrived at a green, at the centre of which was a large, teardrop-shaped pond; its surface was murky, calm, a yellow plastic duck floating incongruously near a bank of reeds.

The road encircled the green and Ash steered the Ford to the left, passing by the small parking area that had been stolen from the grass and tarmacadamed, white lines neatly inscribed on its surface. There were several free parking spaces, but he ignored them for the moment.

Beyond the rooftops, beech-covered hills enclosed the village in a tight and, one might imagine given its unheralded location, covert valley. The sodden clouds were already beginning to drift away, their edges tattered, the breaks between them widening by the second, and the sun was confident and warming the air again, giving promise of another fine summer's day. Thin wisps of steam were rising from the road's surface.

He passed two shops, one a baker's, the other a news-agent's, both of them converted houses and in keeping with the village itself. There were customers inside, but still the street he drove along was quiet, free for the moment of strol-lers or people going about their business. He glanced at his wristwatch and saw that it was only five to eleven. Villages like this were never busy at this time of day. At least, he didn't think they were. A van approached from the opposite direction and went by on the other side of the green. It was followed by a green single-decker bus, which pulled into the kerb outside a row of three shops. Only one passenger alighted.

Two old ladies sitting on a bench beneath a large elm watched Ash as he steered the car around the green, heading back in the direction he'd come from. One said something to the other as he cruised by and after some conferring they continued to stare, their necks craning to follow his progress. Not far from where they sat passing the time of day was a combination of stocks and whipping post, the wood so aged and sturdy it appeared, like the elm close by, to have grown from the soil itself. He wondered wryly if they still used these instruments of punishment and humiliation today. Perhaps they kept them for over-curious strangers, he thought, almost smiling.

There was more to see of Sleath if he proceeded north, but he had already spotted what he'd been looking for and besides, there would be plenty of time later to reconnoitre. He drove past more quaint dwellings and the three shops – a post office, a hardware store, and a butcher's – that the green bus had stopped in front of earlier, and pulled up outside the Black Boar Inn.

A faded painting of the inn's namesake, its tusks fairly bristling along with the dark hairs on its back, its eyes glaring down at him, hung from a bracket over the main door. There were benches outside the inn, presumably for customers who liked to observe the world passing by as they imbibed; they were unoccupied, but then not much of the world was passing by at that particular hour.

Ash took a moment to study the inn before leaving the car: the façade was timber-framed with red bricks, certain sections of these laid in a herringbone pattern, infilling the close-set studs; all the windows were leaded and wisteria, with drooping racemes of purple-blue pea-flowers, climbed up from the ground to cling to the walls around them while still leaving large segments of wood and timber exposed for admiration. Again he wondered how the tourist guides had missed this place and hoped the interior wouldn't be a disappointment.

Ash stepped out onto the pavement and locked the car. The sign above him creaked as it was swung by a rogue breeze, and he took another, more leisurely look. The animal was depicted in all its natural ferocity, but time and weather had tempered the effect.

He entered the Black Boar Inn and the escape from the sun's fresh-found brightness came as a relief. Inside it was cool and shadowy, although rays of sunshine had just begun to blaze though the windows onto the worn red-patterned carpet. There were two bars, lounge and public, both attractive in their own way, the latter gloomy with wood panelling yet welcoming, the former brightened by cream walls, stout scarred beams, and the sun-filled windows themselves. In this, the lounge bar, there were high-backed settles to protect drinkers from cold draughts, and at the far end was a large inglenook fireplace fitted with leather-covered brick benches at the sides and shelves behind, presumably where food would have been kept warm in another era. Naturally there was no fire burning, but logs were piled high in the grate. The counter itself was of polished oak with brass pumps set on its top, and it stretched through both bars, a low panelled partition dividing the two. Neither bar was busy with customers at that time of day: an elderly couple sat drinking coffee in a settle by the window, while a late-middle-aged man sporting a check jacket and olive-green corduroys read a broadsheet newspaper at one of the lounge's small round tables. At a corner table sat two other men, deep in conversation until they noticed him by the door. One wore spectacles and looked to be in his sixties, while the other might have been a little younger, his dark hair greying at the temples. He was big-framed and wore a black suit and open-necked shirt; his eyes were pale and for a moment Ash felt uncomfortable under their gaze. In the public bar two gentlemen of mature years and clothing to match, their ruddy faces declaring a lifetime's outdoor toil, were playing dominoes, and at the L-shaped counter a young man in denim shirt and jeans supped a pint of beer. A dartboard adorned the wall at the end of the room, the door next to it marked GENTLEMEN. Ash had paused no more than a second or two to take all this in, and now he went to the bar in the lounge area.

Behind the counter a girl, with short blonde hair whose cut would have been severe had her face not been so engaging, glanced up from wiping glasses and walked down to meet him.

'Good morning,' she said with a smile that did not quite reach her eyes. Ash noticed dark blemishes around them, suggesting she had not slept too well lately.

He gave a nod of his head and quickly examined the range of brand bitters on the brass pumps. He pointed at what he assumed to be the local brew. 'Just half,' he said.

The girl reached for a handled glass and drew back the pump. 'Nice day now,' she said conversationally as she pulled the beer.

Ash complied with the ritual. 'Another hot one, I think.' He looked around the room again and saw that the man at the round table had lowered his newspaper and was watching him over his reading glasses. When their gazes locked the man flicked his paper and raised it again. The two men felt no such embarrassment: they continued to watch him.

Ash smiled to himself and turned back to the bar.

'That'll be –' the girl was saying as she placed the half-pint on the bar mat in front of him.

'And a vodka,' he interrupted. 'Neat. No ice.'

She regarded him with mild surprise before turning to the optics. 'No tonic?' she reaffirmed, her back to him.

'No thanks.' He lifted the bitter and took a long swallow. It was cold, tangy, a good brew. Reaching for his wallet he asked: 'D'you have rooms here?'

She returned with the vodka. 'For accommodation, you mean?' She gave a little laugh, realizing the inanity of her response. 'Yes, we do, but you need to talk to Mr Ginty, the landlord. I'll get him for you, if you like.'

He handed over a five-pound note for the drinks. 'Yeah, if you could.'

She gave him change, told him she wouldn't be a moment, and disappeared through a door at the far end of the bar.

Ash sipped at the vodka, taking it steady: it wouldn't do much for the Institute's image if their investigator was under the influence for the first meeting with a client. Still, the incident with the 'boy-who-wasn't-there' demanded at least one more stiff drink, and this was only a single. The bitter didn't count.

Still he felt eyes on him and he glanced to the left to see the youth in denims studying him from the other bar. Ash mentally shook his head, feeling like the proverbial 'stranger in town'. Did all outsiders receive this kind of attention, or had word got around that a psychic investigator – a *ghost hunter* – would be visiting the village today? But then the person who had contacted the Psychical Research Institute had insisted that the whole matter be treated as confidential, so it was highly unlikely that the client would have blabbed. If odd things were happening in Sleath, though, the residents might be inclined to be suspicious of anyone or anything new. Especially if the 'anyone' was enquiring about rooms for the night.

'Mr Ginty will be down in a minute.' The barmaid had returned and was smiling across the counter at him. She had nice even teeth, he noticed, and her long pale blue skirt and mauve half-sleeved blouse tucked into a belt at her waist complimented her slim figure. She wore very little make-up and her voice, with its soft local burr and slightly broadened vowels, was as pleasant as her manner. She seemed more like a trainee teacher than a barmaid, but maybe this was the standard in this part of the country.

'Are you on holiday?' she asked as she reached for a cloth and resumed wiping glasses.

Before he could reply a group of men entered the inn, their voices raised enough for customers in both bars to look in their direction. They went through to the other room and appeared again next to the young man who had been drinking alone. One of them slapped him on the shoulder, then ruffled his red curly hair.

'Suppin a bit early in the day, aren't yer, Danno?'

The youth scowled back at him. 'Some of us have done a half-day's grind already.'

'Listen to it,' the other man said, looking around at his companions. They laughed and he leaned hard against the youth's shoulder to say in a mock-low voice: 'Sometimes the best work gits done at night, boy.' He joined in his friends' laughter.

All three were roughly dressed, one in a fake oil-skin coat still glistening from the rain, the other two in jackets that had seen better days. Ash noted that their boots were muddy when they had entered and he assumed they were farm- or land-workers. The shortest of the three wore a maroon baseball cap, a red-Indian chief its colourful motif; he was unshaven and his hair hung long and lank beneath the headgear. 'Come on, Ruthy,' he called down to the barmaid. 'You got men dyin of thirst down 'ere.'

She moved towards them, her smile even less genuine than before. 'And I don't want to know what you've been up to,' she said, stooping for the pint glasses on a shelf under the counter.

'An we won't be tellin,' the one next to the youth replied with a leary grin.

Ash took more vodka and cooled the burn with two large swallows of bitter. A thick-bellied man wearing a tie but whose shirtsleeves were rolled up to the elbow emerged from the door behind the bar. His face was broad and not particularly friendly, the pores on his nose and cheeks puncturing his rough skin like pin-pricks; his sparse hair was slicked back across his scalp and Ash guessed he used Brylcreem rather than gel. The landlord gave the three newcomers at the end of the bar a brief scowl and they immediately became less raucous, although their bantering and laughter continued.

He stopped by Ash. 'You're looking for a room?' His manner was neither solicitous nor bluff: at the moment it was appraising.

'D'you have one available?' Ash replied.

'Oh, we've more than one available. How many nights would that be for, sir?' As he leaned on the bar towards Ash, loud laughter erupted from the other room. He turned towards the source, a flicker of annoyance crossing his features, and the laughter instantly became more subdued. 'Mouchers,' he said in a confidential tone to Ash.

The investigator raised his eyebrows. 'Mouchers?'

46

The landlord's voice was even lower. 'Part-time poachers. Rest of the time, they collect dole money and steal. Their day's work is done. No doubt what they bagged last night –' his accent made it 'las'noight' – 'or early this morning is stashed away in their garden sheds.' He gave a rueful grin. 'Steady enough work for those willing to risk a backside full of game-keeper's buckshot, I suppose. Now then, sir, how many nights did you say?'

'I'm not sure.' Ash was watching the men with more interest. The one with the cap was curling his finger for the barmaid to come closer, but she wasn't having any of it. She placed the last pint on the bar, standing well back as she did so. The youth looked uncomfortable, as if he wasn't enjoying their fun at all. Ash turned back to the landlord. 'It could be for a couple of nights,' he said, 'or it might be a whole week. I could probably let you know for sure sometime tomorrow.'

'Fair enough.' The landlord straightened. 'I'll get a room aired for you while you finish your drink. Ruth,' he called to the barmaid who came back down the bar to them, 'ask Mrs Ginty to get the main guest room ready, will you, dear?'

She smiled distractedly at Ash and went off to find the land-lord's wife.

'Now, if you've come by car,' the landlord resumed, 'which I assume you have, you can park it just 'cross the road next to the green. Only room enough for my own car round the back, I'm afraid, but yours'll be perfectly safe over there. My name's Tom Ginty, by the way, or Thomas as it says over the door, proprietor of the Black Boar Inn, as was my father before me, and his father before him.' He extended a large hand and Ash reached across to shake it. The man's grip was hard, but the greeting was perfunctory and quickly over. 'You can bring your bags in when you're ready, and I'll take them up to your room for you. We do full lunches in the bar and for dinner there's a small restaurant through there –' he indicated a door near a staircase that Ash hadn't noticed before – 'that's open to non-residents too.'

47

'Fine. Can I get you a drink?'

'Bit early in the day for me, sir,' the landlord replied without a hint of disapproval. 'Thanks all the same. So, touring, is it?'

'Uh, no. D'you get many tourists?'

'Ah.' Ginty picked up the cloth from the shelf beneath the counter and mopped up a puddle. 'We're a bit off the beaten track for too much of that, an that's the way we like it.'

It was the first time Ash had heard a landlord-cum-hotelier relish the lack of custom, and Ginty must have seen it in his expression. He stopped wiping the bar and gave a short laugh. 'We've got enough locals hereabouts to keep us busy without being invaded by grockles every spring an summer. A few ramblers' associations an suchlike visit us, o'course, but they know it's in their own interest not to blab to the whole world and its mother. I keep a room or two available for the odd occasion, but mercifully they're few and far between.'

Ash mentally shook his head in wonder, but decided he liked the attitude. Places like Sleath, where tranquillity was preferred to commercial opportunism, were rare in this shrinking domain, so good luck and God bless 'em.

'So you'll be here on business, then?'

He suspected the question was not as light as the landlord pretended. In fact, Ginty was examining a mark on the bar-top (one that had been there for a good many years judging by its polished shine) a little too intently.

'I'm here to see the Reverend Lockwood, as a matter of fact.'

Ginty's head jerked up immediately, but he looked beyond Ash's right shoulder, possibly making eye contact with someone else in the bar.

'I'll be gettin the wife to see to your room, sir,' the landlord said, some of the friendliness gone from his tone.

Maybe he doesn't like his local vicar, Ash mused as he sipped the bitter. Or maybe he's not keen on talk of hauntings going outside the village – it might attract too many curious visitors.

'Can you tell me how to get to the vicarage from here?' he said quickly as the landlord walked away.

Ginty paused in the doorway leading off from the bar. 'Straight up the village High Street till you reach a fork in the road,' he said stiffly. 'Take the right one, up the hill to St Giles'. You'll find the vicar's place a bit further on from the church. Big lodge house, you can't miss it.'

'Is it far?'

'Minute or so if you go by car, 'bout ten if you walk. Room'll be ready when you get back.'

Ash noted a hint of regret in the last words. 'Thank you,' he said, but Ginty had already gone through the door. Ash drained the last of the vodka, and then the bitter. As he left the lounge he realized that all the customers were watching him openly now. And even the three 'mouchers' in the other bar had fallen silent.

6

E STEPPED OUT into the sunshine and looked right, and then left, absorbing the village, breathing in its air, testing his own sensitivity. This was something he had learned to do in recent years for, after a long time of denial – almost a lifetime's, in fact – he had come to realize that his perception could be different from that of others, that he often had an awareness beyond normal capabilities. The faculty had always been there, but it was only three years ago that he had been forced to accept its reality. Before that, scepticism had blocked the self-knowledge. No, why did he persist in fooling himself? Fear had been the barrier. Fear had made him refuse to acknowledge this special faculty. Until something had happened, a haunting so genuine and so personal to him that all denials were swept away, all barricades breached, by a truth that was as overwhelming as it was terrifying.

Ash shuddered in the sunlight and forced memories aside.

Sleath was a perfectly normal village, a little more picturesque than most and certainly more tranquil than many. Yet still he felt an underlying tension here, a disquiet beneath the calm surface.

He chided himself as he walked to the car. Hadn't he just *thought* he'd run someone down before he got to the village, and wasn't he still a bit shaken? Added to that the innkeeper's sudden hostility, no doubt caused by a resentment towards strangers poking their noses in where they didn't belong, had enhanced Ash's unease. Such tensions could easily confuse perceptions.

He drove the car across the road into the parking area beside the green, deciding to walk to the vicarage. A few nips from his flask earlier, plus the vodka and beer he'd taken in the Black Boar Inn, would have put him on the drink-drive borderline and, although it was unlikely that the village had its own police patrol, he wasn't about to risk losing his licence again; the inconvenience was too great. Besides, the walk would do him good, clear his head, allow him to take in more of the place. And it was turning into a fine day for exercise.

To the south he saw the faint, lingering colours of a rainbow. The spectrum faded before his eyes, dissolving like an illusion dispelled by enlightenment; like a false intuition dismissed by logic.

Ash locked the car and began the walk to Sleath's church and vicarage.

He crossed the road at an angle, passing by the inn and then the small collection of shops and houses, the latter varied in style, ranging from oak beams and plaster to brick and tile. The two old ladies were still on the bench close to the stocks and whipping post and they watched him as before with forthright curiosity. He gave them a courteous nod of the head for the hell of it, together with the best smile he could muster, but received no such recognition in return. They continued to stare, following his progress along the High Street until he was well past them. Still he felt their inquisitive gaze on his back.

He continued to smile for the last two drinks he'd had, combined with the peacefulness of the village, were finally settling his nerves; he wondered if he might not actually enjoy this assignment. Too many times he'd been cloistered in dismal houses, waiting through the night and wee small hours of the morning for something unusual to happen, something unnatural

51

to stir, freezing his butt off, smoking too many cigarettes – and thinking too much of the past.

He quickened his pace, refusing to allow the familiar bleakness to temper his thoughts, its chill kindled by memories and perpetuated by nightmares. His breakdown after the Edbrook affair had sent him to the edge of insanity – there were those at the time, he felt sure, who thought he'd been driven *over* that edge – and the slow recovery had been due to a numbed acceptance rather than rejection of what had happened inside that corrupted mansion. His cynicism towards the supernatural had been checked, although he, himself, had not entirely been converted, for he still believed there were fraudsters, fabulists and fakers involved in the hereafter industry (and industry is what it had become): charlatans and cheats who extorted money from the bereaved, quacks who fooled themselves as much as their gullible disciples, and rogues who engineered, and even invented, the paranormal circumstance for their own nefarious or self-aggrandizing purposes. What would he find in Sleath? Even the fact that he had been summoned by a man of the cloth, one Reverend Edmund Lockwood, did not mean the hauntings were genuine, for Ash had dealt with neurotic or misguided clergymen before, their religion no protection against misjudgement or their own madness. Which was, as a rule, why the Church preferred to deal with such matters itself rather than bring in outsiders and risk public mockery. Ash wondered why it had been the local vicar or his representative who had contacted the Institute and not his superiors. Was the diocesan bishop even aware of his cleric's initiative? If so would he have agreed to the investigation? And wouldn't the bishop have wanted to be directly involved? These were just some of the questions the Reverend Lockwood would have to answer.

Not all of the houses Ash passed by were quite as quaint or as distinctive as those around the village green; nevertheless, with their slate roofs and rough red-brick frontages they still maintained a certain country charm. He noticed one whose huge chimney breast rose from ground to rooftop, dwarfing the front door by its side; another house close by was so thin it scarcely seemed habitable.

He reached a point where the roads branched left and right and, noticing the church tower on the gentle hill in the distance, he took the right fork.

For some reason he paused outside a row of three neat cottages with brightly painted yellow doors, their front gardens tiny but proudly kept. His attention was drawn to the middle one, as if he expected someone to appear in the doorway there. He waited, but nothing happened. Yet still he had the feeling of being watched.

He glanced up at the small window above the front door as if expecting to catch a face peering down.

There was no one. But could an observer have stepped back from view just before Ash had tilted his head?

He felt a coldness again, a familiar chill that was contrary to the heat of the day.

Voices, those of children singing, came to him, and he looked away from the cottage towards the source. Further along the road stood a building that could only have been a school, for a yard was laid out before it, this bounded by a shoulder-high fence. The children's muffled voices drifted to him in high-pitched unison, untrained yet pure, and their chant was a hymn or nursery rhyme that he vaguely recognized.

Distracted, he moved on, walking in the road, for there was no pavement here. He became aware that even the birds had stopped their song to listen to the children.

He drew level with the single-storey building: it was built of grey stone and its windows were high and light-friendly, reaching up to a roof of faded red tiles. The school door was arched, like the entrance to a church, and its green paint was chipped and puckered. A sign, this too chipped and dulled with time, by the school gate proclaimed: SLEATH PRIMARY SCHOOL FOR BOYS AND GIRLS. He listened to their voices as he walked on, the song a little ragged here and there but hauntingly sweet to the ear:

Dance, then, wherever you may be,
I am the Lord of the Dance, said he,
And I'll lead you all,
      wherever you may be,
and I'll lead you all
      in the dance, said he.

His steps became more laboured as the road's incline steepened and he was soon cursing himself for his lack of fitness. He consoled himself with the thought that at least the effects of the liquor would have burned off by the time he met the vicar. The singing behind him quickly faded. The church tower loomed above the treetops up ahead, a square-shaped structure of cobble flint. There were buttresses at each corner and a single lancet window gazed down from near the top like a wary black pupil. Ash dabbed perspiration from his brow with a handkerchief. A long row of conifers set behind a low stone perimeter wall screened much of the church grounds, but Ash caught glimpses of headstones and tombs through the gaps here and there. Something white was moving among the monuments, but when he paused to peer through branches the figure was gone. He moved on, momentarily cheered by the sweet repetition of a song thrush; a blackbird joined in, its rich call powerful in the stillness of the day. The sun glared off the road, its image reflected in a few shallow puddles.

When Ash reached the lychgate he decided on impulse to look inside the church before going on to the vicarage; there was a chance the vicar might be there. The shadow beneath the gate's canopy brought instant relief from the heat of the day, and he lingered for a moment or two to take in St Giles'. In the course of his work over the years, Ash had had cause to study the histories of several such churches and he guessed this one, with its rising buttresses, knapped-flint walls, and large oak doors guarding a projecting porch, was of thirteenth- or fourteenth-century origins. The stained-glass windows were dull on the outside and their very opaqueness gave the structure a tomb-like air, as though it were sealed tight against the world. Impressive, but hardly welcoming, Ash mused, like the village itself.

The gate was stiff when he pushed through and he was soon perspiring again as the sun beat down on his bare head. He removed his jacket and loosened his tie as he trod the pebbled path leading through the cemetery to the church porch. Several of the monuments and headstones were turgidly elaborate, one or two of them even incorporating tableaux of grimed angels as sentinels, while most were unimaginatively functional. Large areas of the church grounds were unkempt, with only glimpses of lichen-covered markers peeping over the long grass, and at the far boundary the undergrowth was shamelessly wild. Old oaks and spruce rose here and there, so close to certain graves that their roots undoubtedly intruded upon the caskets below.

One half of the porch's venerable double-door was open and Ash entered. Like some waiting predator, cool, dark air immediately slid through his clothing to claim his flesh for its own and he could not help but shiver. In that single instant the chill seemed almost parasitic, an umbrous wraith who sought to steal his warmth and freeze his senses. It was an absurd notion and shrugged off as quickly as it was imagined; yet Ash remained still for a moment or two longer, puzzled by his own reaction. Something was not right with this place. Not just with this church, but with Sleath itself. There was something here – something *hidden* – that generated a strange disquiet. Nothing obvious, nothing tangible, for the rural charm of the village was undeniable. Yet that charm was superficial. Ash felt it as surely as he had felt the sun on his face outside this shadowy portal, as surely as he had heard the school children singing, or the birds calling. This sensing was as real to him as the very stone in the walls around him.

He glanced over the notices pinned to the board on the interior door as if for assurance that all was normal here despite his unease. They told of an upcoming bazaar, a bring-and-buy sale, a Women's Institute meeting, a show, *The King and I*, in the next parish, the forthcoming council meeting, times of church services – all perfectly commonplace. Where were the times for the next Black Mass, or Satanic Rites evening? Perhaps more mundanely, but equally as sinister, where was the notice for the Sleath Paedophiles' Dinner-Dance, or the local chapter of the Ku Klux Klan's monthly meeting, or the Bestial Pursuits Society's fête? No, there was nothing out of place here, nothing extraordinary to cast suspicion. So why the doubts, why the foreboding? Was there really something wrong in this peaceful little village, or was he still disturbed by past events? The true answer eluded him.

Almost angry, Ash grasped the interior door's ring handle and gave it a twist. It turned, but the door did not open. He tried again, but realized it was locked.

The investigator was not unduly surprised. Nowadays not even holy places were safe from vandals or thieves. He rapped his knuckles against the wood on the off chance someone might be inside, but when no reply came he left the porch. He shielded his eyes against the glare as he closed the oak door behind him, but still caught sight of something moving quickly through the cemetery.

A fresh sensation washed over him, and he swayed back against the door, resting against it for support.

It had been a sudden yet subtle shock, no more than a mental *frisson*, a psychic flush that left him shaken. He blinked his eyes rapidly against the sun, but the figure was gone once more, leaving him to wonder if it hadn't been imagined.

Ash touched his forehead with the fingertips of both hands, applying soft pressure as if to ease away a pain. But it was his own agitation that he was trying to soothe. He dropped his hands to his sides and looked intently at the path.

There *had* been someone there, he was sure of it. And that someone must have seen him. Why, then, would they dodge out of sight?

Ash retraced his steps along the path, branching off where a small track led through the graves towards the rear of the church. Rain gargoyles peered down from points along the edge of the pitched roof, their grins seeming to mock. Suddenly cautious and not sure why, he slowed down as he approached the corner of the church.

He almost came to a halt, for he sensed that someone was waiting there, just out of sight.

Annoyed with himself, he picked up his step, hurrying now, as if anxious to confront whoever was in the graveyard with him. He knew he was being irrational, that this person had as much right as he to be on church ground; but then why would they try to avoid him, why hide away like this?

He reached the corner. He turned it. And stopped dead.

7

SHE WORE A WHITE unbuttoned shirt over a T-shirt and pale blue skirt, and her eyes, a slightly lighter shade of blue than the skirt, showed such abject fear that Ash raised a placating hand towards her.

They stared at each other, neither one moving or speaking for several moments.

Ash was stunned. And perplexed. It was as if an invasive energy had overwhelmed his thoughts, leaving him mentally cowed. He consciously pushed back, exerting his will against the inexplicable pressure, and in an instant his mind was free, his thoughts were his own again.

'I'm sorry,' he found himself saying.

'What?' She shook her head uncomprehendingly.

'I must have frightened you.' Or *vice versa*, he told himself.

The woman straightened, her chin lifting as though she were reasserting herself. She was slim, fine-boned, her light-brown hair swept back in a tail that curled forward over her shoulder. In her hand she held a small bunch of flowers.

'You didn't.' There was an edginess to her denial though, and her eyes betrayed her confusion.

Ash felt the same confusion. Awkwardly, he said, 'I'm looking for the vicar. Reverend Lockwood?'

'Oh.' She seemed to relax a little, although the uncertainty was still there in her eyes. 'You won't find him here at this hour.'

She looked past him and Ash realized he had boxed her in, for the church wall was L-shaped, the building continuing on for several yards. Directly behind her was a narrow door, perhaps leading to St Giles' sacristy. He casually moved aside, allowing her a psychological route of escape, and wasn't surprised when she took a few steps forward to be in clear space. It was an interesting ritual and Ash wondered if the woman was as aware as he of the behavioural dance. Her guarded smile suggested she was.

'Reverend Lockwood will be on his rounds, visiting some of the older parishioners,' she explained. 'It'll be lunchtime soon, though, so he'll be returning to the vicarage before too long.'

'Ah.' He found he had nothing more to say; he was still disturbed by the odd sensation a few moments earlier.

Perhaps sensing his confusion, the woman spoke again. 'Is Reverend Lockwood expecting you?' She surprised him when her smile broadened and she visibly relaxed. 'Of course. You're David Ash, aren't you? You're from the Psychical Research Institute.'

'Yes. How . . . ?' He let the question hang in the air.

'I was the one who contacted Kate McCarrick at the Institute on behalf of my father. I'm Grace Lockwood, the Reverend Lockwood's daughter.'

She transferred the flowers she held to her left hand and moved towards him, holding out her right. He took it and felt a mild shock of recognition.

But it was she who said: 'Have we met before?'

Somehow he knew they hadn't, despite his feelings when they had touched. Nevertheless, he took time to search his memory. He placed her in her late twenties, an attractive woman whose voice was as soft as her features. Her skin was slightly tanned, emphasizing the blueness of her eyes, and she wore little make-up. Although not glamorous, he realized she was one of those women who grew more appealing by the moment; the longer he studied her face, the more beautiful she seemed to become. He knew that if he had met her before she would not have been forgotten.

He cleared his throat and said, 'Uh, 'no, I don't think so.'

She shook her head, as though uncertain. She shrugged. 'I'm sure you're right. You looked familiar, that was all.'

Did he really? Or was she confused by the same sensation he, himself, had felt when they had confronted each other? But now even that was receding from him, becoming vague, an initial reaction that was less significant by the moment, and he knew that soon he would be wondering if the whole thing had been precipitated by his own overwrought imagination. In all probability, his sudden appearance around the corner of the church had only startled the clergyman's daughter and there had been no sharing of a psychic experience. Get a grip, Ash, he told himself, and stop imagining everyone else is as crazy as you.

Again he felt awkward and he quickly said, 'You say your father will be home soon?'

'Yes, for lunch. I'll be returning there myself in a few minutes, so we can walk together, if you like.'

'Fine. Is it far?' He was just making conversation.

'Not very. Wait for me to lay these flowers, then we'll go.'

He watched her cut through the graves, her movements appropriate to her name, her white shirt and blue skirt bright among the grey, decaying tombstones. Some distance away she came to a halt and bent down to rest the bouquet of flowers. She straightened, but remained there, her head bowed as if in prayer.

As she made her way back to him she disturbed a butterfly that had settled on a headstone and it fluttered around her, white and delicate in the sunlight. He saw her smile and her lips moved as if she were speaking to it. The butterfly circled her twice before flitting away to disappear into a clump of high grass near the edge of the graveyard.

Grace Lockwood's smile was directed at him as she drew

near and she studied him with an interest that was almost disconcerting.

'I've never met a ghost hunter before,' she said when she reached him. 'You're not quite what I imagined.'

'You thought I'd be wearing a cape, and maybe a black hat.'

'With a beard, at least. Oh, and a bible under your arm.'

'Sorry to disappoint you.'

'You haven't.' She flicked her head towards the village. 'Have you had a chance to see much yet?'

'I took in some of it on the way up here,' he told her. 'It's quaint. I'm surprised you don't get more tourists.'

'Sometimes they find us, even though we make a conscious effort to keep out of the tourist guides.'

'I can understand why. Sleath would certainly be an attraction, particularly for Americans and Japanese. They'd love a genuine slice of olde England.'

'We prefer our privacy.' She looked past his shoulder, as if disturbed. 'We're almost hidden away and the villagers do their best to keep the secret to themselves.'

'Secret?'

'I mean how lovely it is here. We're a tight community, Mr Ash, and warm welcomes aren't generally extended to outsiders.'

He gave a wry smile. 'I can confirm that. Even the landlord at the Black Boar didn't seem overjoyed with my booking.'

'You're staying there?'

He nodded.

'Tom Ginty's all right. A bit brusque at first, but friendly enough once he gets to know you.'

Ash refrained from telling her that Ginty's offhandedness only surfaced when the Reverend Lockwood's name was mentioned. He changed the subject: 'The flowers – were they for a relative or a friend?'

The question took her by surprise. 'Oh, they were for my mother. She died last year. Shall we go now?' She began to

61

walk towards the lychgate and Ash quickly fell in step beside her.

'I'm sorry,' he said, hating the cliché.

'Sorry you asked, or sorry my mother is dead?' She obviously disliked the cliché too. She turned to him and her smile softened the reproach. 'I was away from home at the time – I'd been working in Paris for two years at the *Musée de Cluny* – and arrived back an hour after she died. Father hadn't realized just how bad she was, or he would have called me home sooner.'

He resisted offering more condolences. 'What were you doing at the museum?'

'Do you know the *Musée de Cluny?*'

He shook his head.

'It was once a mediaeval monastery and now houses one of the world's great collections of arts and crafts of the Middle Ages. Spurs, chastity belts, sculptures, ivories, bronzes, jewellery – all kinds of fascinating artefacts. Unfortunately, many of the objects there had never been documented or catalogued, and it was my job to trace their history and put them into some kind of historical context. In the winter months the place is relatively empty of visitors, so it was easy to work among the treasures without being disturbed.'

'You're an expert on that sort of thing?'

'My studies concentrated on the Middle Ages. They were interesting times.'

'I'll take your word for it. But why France? I'd have thought our own Middle Ages would keep you fully occupied here.'

'Too many historians after too few jobs in this country, Mr Ash.'

'David's less formal, Miss Lockwood.'

'So is Grace. I'd been visiting the museums and galleries in Paris for years – my parents always encouraged me to travel – but when I discovered a series of tapestries – they're called *La Dame Aux Licornes* – in the *Musée de Cluny* I was hooked. They're so haunting, so compelling . . .' She broke off. 'Do you know them?'

Ash gave a little laugh and, without embarrassment, admitted he had never heard of them. 'I'll take your word for it that they're something special, though,' he added. They had reached the lychgate by now and he pulled the gate open for Grace to pass through.

'Oh, they're extraordinarily special,' she replied as she entered into shadow. 'But on my visits I realized just how far behind the museum was with its chronologizing and documentation and I offered my services. It was somewhat bold, but my French wasn't too bad and my qualifications were adequate. I was also willing to work for low wages, so after some correspondence and various references, the museum offered me a year's contract.'

'You must have been pleased.'

'An understatement – I was ecstatic. The first year went well and my French quickly improved. There was so much to do and, of course, more relics were being discovered all the time. Lots of them were sent directly to us, while others the museum had to bid for. My contract was extended for another two years but, as I told you, my mother was taken ill last year and I had to return.'

'But you could have gone back to Paris, surely.'

Her face was shaded, but he noticed the change in her voice, the quietness of her words. 'My father needed me here.'

She walked out into the brightness on the other side of the lychgate and her sadness seemed to lift with the renewed warmth. 'Are you hungry, Mr Ash – David?'

'A little bit.' Another vodka would have been more welcome.

'Well the house isn't far.' She indicated the opposite direction to the village and began to walk. 'Perhaps you'll join us for lunch?' she asked as he caught up.

'Thank you. I thought the vicarage would be closer to St Giles'.'

'It's closer than it used to be. My ancestors were the original lords of the manor hereabouts, as well as the community's spiritual guides. In fact, the Lockwood family has been part of

63

Sleath's history for many generations. Do you know what a "squarson" is?'

'Afraid not.'

'It's a term dating from the eighteenth century when the local squire and parson were one and the same person.'

'It must have been a powerful combination.'

'It was. Perhaps too much so.' She looked off into the distance and it was several moments before she spoke again. 'We're the poor generation of Lockwoods now, and my father has only the usual vicar's influence over his parish. Which isn't very much in this day and age,' she added with a smile. 'I work part-time at the community hall, so that brings in a little extra. It keeps me occupied too.'

'You said the vicarage is closer to the church than it used to be,' Ash reminded her, still puzzled by the statement.

'Sorry, I digressed. Lockwood Hall stood in the heart of its own estate, but the house burned down a couple of hundred years or so ago. My father and I live in what was once the lodge at the entrance to the grounds.'

'Quite a change in circumstances.'

'Not at all. The Lockwoods lost most of their wealth long before my father was born. I've never been used to anything else.'

He could tell by her smile there was no regret. 'I'm sure your father is just as respected by the people here,' he said. *Even if the local landlord didn't seem too keen on his vicar,* he thought.

'Oh, I don't think the old Lockwoods were very popular. They had to keep order in the parish as well as preach God's word.'

'Yeah, I noticed the stocks and whipping post down in the village.'

'There were worse punishments than that in the old days.'

'I can't imagine too many villains in a quiet place like this.'

'Perhaps not nowadays, but Sleath has certainly had its moments in the past.'

'Some of your mouchers were pointed out to me in the Black Boar this morning.'

'Mouchers? My word, you're learning fast.'

'The landlord explained the term.'

'Well, we still have our share of poachers and thieves, plus the usual village carryings-on.'

'Any witches' covens, satanists, that kind of thing?'

She laughed. 'Now what made you ask that?'

'Just a general line of enquiry – isolated community and all that.'

'We're not that isolated. True, the villagers tend to keep to themselves, but even that's beginning to change.'

They were well past the church boundary by now and the narrow lane had evened out. Woodland and hills lay ahead of them, with only a few houses in view here and there.

'How's it changing?' he asked, swinging his jacket over his shoulder and tucking his other hand into his trouser pocket.

'The younger people are leaving, looking for work in the towns or moving down to London. Even the young children are bussed to a school in the next town these days.'

He stopped walking. 'But I passed the village school on the way up here. I heard the kids singing.'

She stopped too. 'You heard them? No, it must have been a radio in one of the cottages.'

'It came from the school,' he insisted. 'The kids were singing a hymn as I walked by.'

'You're mistaken,' she insisted, and there was more than just puzzlement in her pale blue eyes: there was the merest hint of alarm. 'Sleath Primary closed down two years ago. The school is empty.'

8

NIT ONE, PURL ONE, *knit one, purl one* . . .

Ellen Preddle sat by the window, the only sound in the tiny front room the click of her knitting needles as they made contact. Her fingers worked deftly, the beginnings of the boy's jumper she was making lying across her knees, the red ball of wool on a stool by her chair.

Knit one, purl one, knit one, purl one . . .

It was an unspoken litany – although her lips moved in voiceless rhythm – a means of concentrating her mind, keeping bad thoughts at bay. But every once in a while her gaze went beyond the points of the needles to become unfocused, unseeing, and her thoughts drifted into a dark reverie of things best forgotten.

'Oh, Simon . . .' she murmured and the clicking ceased as she rested her hands on her lap. Sunlight shone fierce and bright through the closed window, causing the grey threads in her dark hair to sparkle silver. A bee's furry body made the tiniest thud against the windowpane and its drone grew to an angry buzz as it exerted pressure against the invisible barrier. Defeated, it flew off, back to the sweet nectar of garden flowers, its dance elaborate, its wrath forgotten.

Ellen sighed. Such a good boy was Simon. Such an innocent. But why hadn't he visited her for three days now? Had she done something wrong? Was he angry with her? She bit into her lower lip and her chest tightened to restrain the sob that swelled there. Mustn't cry. Crying upset Simon. Nevertheless, a mistiness settled over her eyes and she blinked, forcing a teardrop from them. It trailed down her cheek, tickling her skin, and she quickly wiped it away with the back of her hand.

She gazed at the wool spread across her lap. Simon liked red. The colour made him feel happy, he always said. Happy? What happiness had her poor little mite ever known? Only when it was just the two of them, together, playing games, tending their little garden, even shopping. And sharing childish jokes, giggling together, watching television together, together . . . The key turning in the lock soon spoilt that happiness. Simon's face would change, it would become frightened, frantic almost, the moment he heard a foot on the doorstep. He would stare at the door as the key jiggled in the lock, then sink into his mother when it began to open.

How they both hated it when *he* came into the room, filling the air with his vile stench of whisky and cigarettes and the foul odour of his unwashed body! How they wanted to run and hide from his evil, *dirty*, ways! How –

With a sharp movement, she raised the knitting again, forcing the terrible memories from her mind.

Knit one, purl one, knit one, purl one . . .

Even after his father's death little Simon was afraid. Still he watched the front door with fear in his eyes whenever he heard a sound outside, even though she assured him his father was gone, that he would bother them no more, that it truly was just the two of them now. Together . . . But still the nightmares, the dreams of footsteps on the stairway when there was really no one there, no one to creep into his room to torment him, to do those horrible things –

Knit one, purl one, knit one, purl one, slip one . . .

Put it away from you, Ellen! Forget those things. *He was gone*. It was only her and Simon now. Despite what everybody else said, what they believed. What did they know? They

67

thought Simon had left her, but no, he wouldn't do that, not her Simon. He loved his mummy too much. She had explained that to the priest, but he had chided her, told her it wasn't so, that Simon was . . . that Simon was . . .

Knit one, purl one, knit one, purl one, knit . . .

Her nimble fingers worked fast, faster, their movement difficult to follow. Stitches were dropped, the pattern began to become senseless.

But where was Simon now? Today? Yesterday? The day before? Why hadn't he returned? Did he blame . . . did he blame . . .

. . . Me . . . ?

The clicking stopped. The room was quiet once more.

Could he blame . . . his mother? Oh Simon, it wasn't my fault, I didn't know . . . didn't understand the things . . . your father . . . did . . . to you . . .

She resumed the knitting, but her action was slow, leaden.

Knit . . . one . . . purl . . . one . . . knit . . . drop . . .

A sound from the stairs.

She turned her head. She listened.

It came again. But it was from above, not the stairs. A commonplace noise, an ordinary, everyday sound.

Ellen began to rise from the chair.

The red ball of cotton slipped from the stool and rolled across the floor, unravelling as it went. Ellen looked up at the low ceiling. The sound – so real, so . . . so normal – came yet again. The sound of water. Water being quietly splashed.

Simon liked to play with water.

Simon liked his bathtime.

Until that last . . .

She dropped the knitting, the needles clicking together one last time as they hit the floor.

'Simon . . . ?' Her call was soft, uncertain.

A faint splash of water again.

Ellen took a step towards the stairs.

'Have you come back, Simon?'

A smile as uncertain as her voice played on her lips.

She continued the journey to the foot of the stairs and peered upwards as if expecting to see her dead son on the landing above. But no, of course not, he wouldn't be there. The sound had come from the bathroom. Simon would be in the bath, playing with the water like he always used to.

She trod the first step. Then the next.

More loudly this time she said, 'Simon?' and her steps became more hurried.

She stumbled and her hands held on to the higher steps to steady herself. It didn't take long to climb the rest of the stairs and within moments Ellen was at the top, on the small landing that led to the two bedrooms and bathroom.

The bathroom door was ajar.

And the sounds were even clearer now.

Someone was in the bath. *Simon* was in the bath. Where he had . . . the word was impossible for her to acknowledge . . . where he had . . .

'*Simon!*'

The splashing ceased.

'Simon.' This time she whispered the name. 'I'm coming to you.' Her smile had returned, and it was more sure.

Ellen raised her hand to push open the bathroom door, and she contained her eagerness, not wanting to startle him, afraid he would go away again, fade as he had done before.

Gently she pressed against the door.

And screamed when she saw the awful blackened thing leaning over the bath, partly obscuring the tiny white figure that it held beneath the water with its charred arms.

9

THE REVEREND EDMUND LOCKWOOD'S physical stature was diminished somewhat by his stooped shoulders and the gauntness that shadowed his eyes and cheeks. In his youth, Ash considered as he studied the clergyman standing by the drawing-room window and looking out at the woodland beyond, he would surely have presented a formidable figure, well over six feet and with a mien that indicated deep inner convictions. His hair was an uneven mixture of grey and black, swept back over his ears and accentuating his high forehead and a nose that appeared to have been broken at some time, for it was hooked and bent slightly to the right. He bore little resemblance to his daughter, save for his eyes, and even they were a shade paler. They were also piercing, so much so that the investigator had felt uncomfortable under their scrutiny when Grace had introduced him to her father earlier. Ash had looked away, perhaps afraid the cleric would see the cynicism that lay within.

He had been surprised at the lack of strength in the other man's grip when they had first shaken hands, but then realized that the Reverend Lockwood's knuckles were gnarled and the joints of his fingers were red and swollen as if from arthritis. Any pressure probably caused him considerable pain.

Ash was seated on a comfortable drop-arm sofa before a large brick fireplace, whose long grate was filled with old dry logs. The room was cool and smelled of dusty books and old leather, the latter from two worn armchairs, their surfaces scratched and even torn in parts; beams ran along the low ceiling and a stout post in the room's centre helped support the floor above.

'D'you mind if I smoke?' he asked, already reaching for the pack in his jacket pocket.

Reverend Lockwood swung round towards him with a start, as though he had quite forgotten the investigator's presence for a few moments.

'I'd rather you didn't,' he replied brusquely.

Ash stilled his hand and regarded the other man coolly. At that moment Grace Lockwood entered the room carrying a tray laden with coffee pot and cups. Lunch had been a fairly meagre affair – a ham salad with a small choice of cheeses to follow – with conversation as thin as the meal itself. Ash had the impression that the food was an inconvenience as far as the cleric was concerned, yet he refused to be drawn about the haunting of Sleath while the lunch was in progress. Even when they went through to the drawing room afterwards the vicar seemed reluctant to discuss the matter and it had been Ash who had raised the subject by mentioning the hymn-singing he thought he had heard coming from the abandoned village school. Lockwood had walked straight to one of the leaded windows and stared out, his countenance even more troubled.

Grace noticed Ash tucking the cigarette pack back into his pocket. 'Did you want to smoke, David?' She gave her father a meaningful smile, one that dared him to mind. 'I'll see if I can find you an ashtray – we keep one somewhere for visitors.' After placing the tray on a small coffee table she left the room again. The vicar scowled after her, but there was humour in his eyes.

'*Do* you mind?' Ash asked once more, emphasizing the first word.

'I suppose not,' Lockwood replied, his features softening a little. 'Forgive my bad manners, Mr Ash. I'm afraid this business has affected me more than I care to admit.' He came away from the window and slumped into the armchair opposite the investigator. The worn leather sighed with his weight. 'Do you think you might pour the coffee? My hands are clumsy nowadays.'

Ash leaned towards the little table between the chairs and poured two cups.

'Just black,' the vicar said when Ash reached for the jug of cream.

The stooped man's gnarled hand trembled as he took the coffee proffered by Ash and he gripped the saucer awkwardly between finger and thumb. His other hand helped steady the cup. 'The hymn you say you heard from the schoolhouse – did you recognize it?' he enquired as he settled back into the chair.

'I'm not up on my hymns,' Ash replied, taking his coffee black, too. 'It was familiar though. I've heard it before somewhere.'

'Do you recall any of the words?'

Ash thought for a moment, then slowly shook his head. 'It's gone. I'm not even sure of the tune now, although I know I've heard it before. Why d'you ask?'

'I wondered how old it might have been.'

'Look, I've been thinking about this over lunch. Maybe Grace was right, maybe it came from a radio somewhere. It's a hot day, somebody could have left a window open.'

The vicar smiled, but his eyes were downcast, looking into his coffee cup. 'A healthy mind will always seek a rationale. It's a way of avoiding mental anguish.'

Ash understood the truth of that only too well, but he did not respond. Grace returned carrying a glass ashtray, which she put on the coffee table next to the tray.

'Please feel free,' she told Ash, before going to the windows. 'I'll open these before Father starts complaining. Lord knows why they're closed on a beautiful day like today anyway.' She lifted the latches and swung the side-windows open. The sweet scent of honeysuckle drifted through, soon overwhelming the

72

musty staleness of the drawing room, and Ash watched Grace in profile as she drew in a deep breath. Her breasts tightened the fabric of her T-shirt and a half-smile played on her lips as she closed her eyes.

He tapped a cigarette from the pack and lit it, easily dismissing the guilt of polluting the fresh air he had just relished.

'Mr Ash is almost convinced it was a radio he heard and not ghostly voices from the old primary school,' Reverend Lockwood commented as his daughter turned to face them.

Grace directed her reply towards Ash. 'I wonder,' she said.

'It was your first thought,' Ash reminded her.

'I know, but then I got to thinking about other things that have happened in Sleath recently. If you knew you might not find celestial choirs quite so surprising.'

'Then let's make a start.' Ash produced a micro-cassette recorder from another pocket and showed it to Grace and her father. 'If you don't mind I'd like to record our conversation. It saves scribbling notes as we talk.'

Grace nodded her head, but the vicar looked dubious. 'I can't say I like these things, Mr Ash,' he said.

'It'll be strictly confidential. Anything that's said in this room will be between you, me and the Psychical Research Institute.'

'But can you be trusted?'

Grace was embarrassed by her father's forthrightness. 'The Institute has had dealings with the Church on a number of occasions, Father. Its reputation depends on its discretion – as well as its impartiality. We discussed this before I approached Miss McCarrick.'

The vicar's tone was gruff, and still reluctant. 'Very well. But I'm still not sure this is the right thing.'

'We've no alternative.' Her voice was firm, her face grim.

Ash intervened, switching on the machine as he spoke. 'Can I begin by asking you why you didn't contact the Institute through the Church authorities?'

There was no hesitation. 'I didn't want a third party involved at this stage. The Archbishop will be fully informed depending on the results of your findings. Not even the parishioners know why you're here.'

'They'll soon guess once I start making enquiries and setting up equipment. I might even have to call in back-up from the Institute once the investigation gets underway.'

'We'll face that problem when we come to it. But even then, news of why you're here in Sleath mustn't go beyond the village itself.'

Ash shook his head. 'I can't guarantee that. People gossip, and gossip spreads.'

'Rarely beyond this parish.'

'Then Sleath is pretty unusual.'

Neither Grace nor her father spoke, and Ash glanced from face to face.

'Okay, I'll take your word for it,' he said. 'As far as the Institute and myself are concerned, this is a strictly private investigation. However, we can't speak for the rest of the community.'

'That's understood.'

He drew on his cigarette, tapped ash into the ashtray and settled the micro-recorder on the coffee table. Then he announced the time, date, location and gave the names of those present in the room. 'Tell me about the first sighting,' he said, directing the question at the vicar.

'By that I gather you mean the first appearance of a ghost,' Reverend Lockwood said, and went on when the investigator nodded. 'It began soon after one of my parishioners, a dear lady who has suffered badly in life, lost her only son.'

'Could you be a little more precise,' Ash urged gently. 'When exactly did the boy die?'

Lockwood referred to his daughter.

'Simon was buried three weeks ago today,' Grace answered for him. 'Died a week before that.'

Ash's expression begged the question.

'He couldn't be buried until after a postmortem examination.

He drowned in his bath, you see. They had to see if they could find out why.'

Ash asked the boy's age, and then quickly worked out the date of death and burial. He recorded them before asking the next question.

'Were there suspicious circumstances?'

'No, no one else was involved. The conclusion that the pathologist came to was that the boy was playing in the bath, perhaps holding his breath under water – you know what children are like, especially when they're left on their own. He probably stayed under too long and blacked out.'

Ash's eyes narrowed. 'That's pretty unlikely.'

'The coroner recorded a verdict of accidental death. There was no evidence otherwise.'

'The mother . . . ?'

There was suppressed fury in Reverend Lockwood's voice, as if he had scant patience for the investigator's scepticism. 'Ellen Preddle doted on her son. She loved him beyond anyone and anything else.'

'You said the woman had suffered badly. Maybe too much? The boy could have misbehaved, upset her at a time when life was particularly unbearable. She might have just snapped. On the other hand, men have slaughtered their families and women have smothered their babies under the misguided notion they were protecting their loved ones from the wicked realities of life.'

The anger was still there. 'I'm well aware of such tragedies, Mr Ash, but the boy's death does not fall into either category. Ellen Preddle and her son, Simon, were very happy in the last year of the boy's life, far happier, in fact, than they had ever been before.' Some of the fierceness left Lockwood's voice. 'You see, the boy's father was a cruel, foul-mouthed man, who treated his wife and son abominably. I pray God will forgive me for saying this, but when George Preddle died last year his only bequest to his family was peace and happiness.'

'And how did he die?'

'A farming accident. A most horrible death.' The vicar had set the half-empty coffee cup on the table and was now leaning forward in the chair, his hands clasped together before him; he lowered his head, resting his forehead on his hands. He sighed before looking up again. 'I suppose you want the full details?' His reluctance to tell was obvious.

Ash's reply was blunt. 'I'll let you know when you're telling me too much.' When he saw the surprise on Grace's face and the annoyance on the cleric's, he quickly explained: 'Too much knowledge when investigating supernatural or paranormal occurrences can sometimes be a hindrance rather than a help – it can pre-empt some of the things the investigator has to discover for himself, or even pre-condition him. Now, having said that, because this haunting apparently involves more than one location – if I've been briefed correctly by my associate, Miss McCarrick, that is – then I'll need more background information than is usual.'

'I see,' said Grace. 'Your coffee's getting cold,' she added.

He smiled as he stretched for the cup.

Reverend Lockwood was still troubled. 'I'll help in any way I can, Mr Ash, but I should inform you that contacting the Psychical Research Institute was entirely my daughter's idea. I wanted no part in it.'

'How did you see the alternative?'

'I'm not sure I understand what you mean.'

'I assume you didn't want to inform your bishop, either. So what did you expect to happen? Did you think these activities would eventually fade away of their own volition, hopefully before too many people were involved?'

Lockwood evaded the question. 'Then you do believe they're genuine hauntings?'

'I haven't said that. And I should emphasize that nine out of ten such cases the Institute investigates turn out to be no more than exceptional circumstances or fraudulent practices, with nothing at all to do with psychic phenomena.'

'Yet the odd one . . . ?'

'Even they're not always conclusive. The cause might mystify us, but it still doesn't mean we're dealing with the supernatural.'

'We take your point, David,' said Grace as she came over and picked up her father's coffee cup. 'Shall I freshen this for you, Father?' She poured hot coffee from the pot without waiting for a reply. The vicar took the cup from her and settled back in his seat; he appeared distracted as Grace pulled a straight-backed chair over so that she could be closer to the cassette recorder.

Ash drew him back. 'You were about to tell me how Ellen Preddle's husband died.'

The vicar sipped coffee before speaking again. 'Have you ever witnessed a haystack fire, Mr Ash?'

'I thought haystacks were a thing of the past. Don't farms just bale the hay nowadays?'

'This is Sleath. A few farmers hereabouts still prefer the old methods. Sometimes a stack will burn from the inside. You might see small flames on the outside, and smoke, lots of smoke; but the real inferno is inside, burning away the very core of the stack. The heat there is incredible, just incredible, and then finally the whole thing will explode into flame.'

He paused as if imagining a fiery hell. 'George Preddle was a farm labourer – when there was work to be had. Most of the time, though, he was an idle, drunken lout who beat his wife and ill-treated his son.'

Ash was mildly surprised that a man of the cloth should talk of the deceased in such disparaging terms. Obviously this was a priest who had little tolerance for the sinners of his flock.

'He was lucky in that the cottage he and his wife lived in was passed on to Ellen by her parents when they died, otherwise the Preddle family would have possessed very little.' The coffee cup rattled in its saucer as he returned it to the table. 'He was working out at Gunstone Farm, not a mile from the village itself, and on that particular day – a day very much like today as I remember: sunny and dreadfully hot – his son was helping him. The boy earned a few shillings during his school holidays doing odd jobs around the village or working on the farms with his father. Nobody is sure how the haystack caught fire, except we do know that Preddle was a heavy smoker and he'd been drinking that lunchtime. Apparently, he was working closest to the stack so perhaps he tossed a cigarette butt or match in the wrong direction. Whatever the cause, smoke billowed from the stack and all the workers quickly formed a water-bucket chain from the nearest tap, which wasn't too far away. Foolish man that he was, Preddle dragged a ladder to the haystack and climbed up, insisting he would douse the fire from the top.'

Ash grimaced. 'It was alight inside.'

Lockwood straightened his shoulders as if to ease a pain there, and looked towards the logs in the fireplace. 'There were few flames on the outside, just billows of smoke. Whatever had lit the stack had worked its way well inside. A quirk of fate, a freak accident: our destinies are decided by such things. Preddle only laughed at the warnings from the other field hands. I'm told even his son screamed for him to come down. Arrogance or drunkenness, who knows what drove the man to it. The wretched fool fell through.'

This time Ash winced and looked over at Grace, who seemed equally disturbed even though she was familiar with the story. He soon understood why, for there was worse to come.

'It would have been more fortunate if Preddle had fallen all the way,' the vicar went on. 'As it was, he became stuck by his arms and shoulders while his lower body was in the conflagration below. He was held there, clutching at the top and screaming terribly as his legs were burnt away. They could only watch him, none of them daring to climb to the roof of the haystack and drag him out. It would have collapsed under their weight if they had tried to do so.'

Ash paled, remembering another fire in another place. He drew on the cigarette and watched the smoke as he exhaled, lost in thought.

'They said his final scream before he finally disappeared was the most horrific of all.'

The vicar's words brought him back to the present.

'There wasn't much left of George Preddle to find afterwards. The fire had virtually incinerated him.'

'Are you all right, David?' Grace Lockwood had noticed Ash's stillness, the pallor of his skin, and assumed it was because of her father's story.

He looked at her. 'What? Yes, I'm okay. That was an unpleasant way to die,' he said, almost distractedly.

'Unpleasant?' the clergyman scoffed. 'No man, whatever his sins, deserves such punishment.'

It's your God, Ash nearly remarked, but decided it would be foolish to antagonize the man – he seemed volatile enough already. 'And the boy saw the whole thing?' he said instead.

'I'm afraid so,' Grace answered.

'How did it affect him?' Ash silently cursed himself. 'Sorry, that was a pretty stupid question. He must have been severely traumatized.'

Reverend Lockwood took his time in replying. His eyes stared at Ash without seeing and finally he said: 'Oddly enough, the boy was hardly traumatized at all. Oh, I'm sure it affected him in some way, somewhere deep inside, but it hardly showed. Perhaps Simon was somewhat quieter in the weeks that followed, but then he'd always been a shy boy, always clinging to his mother, and nothing changed in that respect. If anything – and I suppose this was quite natural – mother and son became even closer.'

'As you say, natural enough. Ellen Preddle had lost her husband, the boy had lost his father: they were bound to seek consolation in each other.'

'You don't understand. They became happy. You see, they both hated George Preddle when he was alive, and nobody in the village who knew him could blame them for that. He was a vile excuse for a human being.'

Again Ash was surprised at Lockwood's lack of compassion.

This man Preddle must have been something special if even the parish priest condemned him after his death. 'Could grief have finally caught up with the boy?' he wondered aloud.

'Are you suggesting that if it had, Simon might have deliberately drowned himself in the bath?' Grace was incredulous.

'It was just a thought, no doubt mistaken. You've convinced me he would never have been that upset.' He leaned forward and stubbed out his cigarette. 'So where is this leading to? Whose ghost does Ellen Preddle claim to have seen – her husband's or her son's?' Before they could reply, he added, 'You understand, of course, that the circumstances are there for self-delusion. Two tragedies, both shocking, the loss of a loved one, leaving her entirely on her own. Her grief might make her sensitive to all kinds of things.'

'A cynical view, Mr Ash,' said Lockwood with some disdain.

'It goes with the territory, Reverend,' the investigator returned, unoffended. 'Although I'd prefer to regard it as a healthy scepticism, a sound requirement for my line of work. If I told you the stories behind some of my investigations you might appreciate why. So please tell me, whose spirit does the woman claim to have seen?'

'It was her son,' Lockwood replied solemnly. 'After the boy's funeral Ellen immediately returned home without speaking to anyone. I followed some time later to offer my condolences and to see if I could help in any way. The poor woman wouldn't let me in. She wouldn't even open the door to me.'

'But you spoke to her?'

'I called her name, but she told me to go away. Her voice sounded . . . well, strange.'

'In what way?'

'Somehow distant, and not because she was behind a door. I thought at first that she'd been drinking.'

'Maybe she had.'

'I've never known her to touch a drop in the past.'

'Sadness, shock. Who could blame her?'

The cleric shook his head. 'Not her, not Ellen. Perhaps I

described her voice wrongly. She sounded happy, Mr Ash, but preoccupied, as though there was something else on her mind. She also seemed evasive, almost secretive.'

'She was that way for the next two weeks,' said Grace. 'Ellen hardly left her cottage, and when neighbours passed by they could hear her singing. I heard her myself when I visited several days after the funeral, but she stopped when I knocked on the door.'

'Did you see her?' asked Ash.

'No. She wouldn't even answer me. She pretended she wasn't there.'

Her father interrupted her. 'Grace, would you please fetch me some aspirin?'

She regarded him anxiously. 'Is it a headache again?'

He nodded. 'It isn't severe yet.'

Grace rose and left the room. Reverend Lockwood rubbed a hand across his forehead.

'Shall we leave this till later?' asked Ash, reaching towards the recorder to switch it off.

'No, no. Let's get on with it. I don't want to waste too much of your time.'

'Waste my time? What makes you say that?'

'Isn't that what all this is? Nonsense, a complete waste of time?'

'Not if we achieve a result, one way or another.'

Lockwood frowned. 'You honestly believe you can prove the existence of ghosts?'

'Or the non-existence.'

The vicar gave a small shake of his head and the sound he made might have been a short laugh or a sudden cough. 'Then let's continue. We were concerned about Ellen, deeply so. However, each time I went to her home she either turned me away or pretended she wasn't in. But then last Sunday she attended Communion as she had regularly in all the years I've known her. I was both surprised and pleased.'

Grace returned with a glass of water and pills.

'Did you bring me three, dear?' her father asked.

'I did,' she answered in a disapproving way. 'You know you should see the doctor about these headaches.'

'Dr Stapley has enough on his plate without me bothering him with something that will go away of its own accord in due course, as these things always do.'

'It's the hauntings, isn't it?' she said, taking her seat again. 'All this has put you under too much stress.'

'If that's the case, then our psychic investigator here might solve everything, including my headaches.' There was little humour in the vicar's smile.

'You said Mrs Preddle attended Communion,' Ash prompted as he checked the cassette recorder's tape.

'Yes. She waited after the service to see me. I have to say she looked surprisingly well. Somewhat drained, perhaps, but no redness around the eyes from too many tears, and no more hunched shoulders as if the burdens were too much for her. She seemed almost serene.' He washed the tablets down with water, then dabbed at his thin lips with a misshapen knuckle. 'She shocked me by asking if it was a sin to hate someone after their death.'

'She meant her husband.'

'Of course. That she loved her son there is no doubt.' He eyed the investigator reproachfully. 'I told her she must find it in her heart to forgive her late husband and that with time, as the memories dimmed, it would become easier for her. In the meantime, because of all she had suffered with this man the sin was not grievous.' He took another gulp of water before continuing. 'She only shook her head at me, looking even sadder. I'd got it wrong, she told me. She wasn't asking for herself; she was asking for Simon, her son.'

Ash remained expressionless. He drained the last of his coffee and waited for the clergyman to continue.

'She said Simon was anxious and full of guilt. He was terribly concerned about hating his father so much, even though they were both dead. He had revealed this to his mother.'

82

Lockwood lifted a hand as if to dismiss the protest he expected from the investigator, but Ash remained silent.

'I wouldn't blame you if you suggested this was nothing more than grief-induced hysteria, and that's what I believed at the time also. Oh, I believed it fervently. Yet I humoured her, I told her I would come to her home and talk with her and although she was reluctant at first, when I indicated that perhaps I could help her son, assure him he was not in a state of sin, she agreed. Naturally I meant this in the spiritual sense, that somehow my words and prayers would reach Simon wherever he might be now, but Ellen took my promises literally.'

Lockwood was becoming agitated, one hand constantly rising and falling on the arm of the chair. 'When I called on her that afternoon, Ellen tried to tell me that her son had visited her on more than one occasion since his funeral and when I refuted this, when I told her Simon had passed over, that his soul now rested in peace, she became angry. She insisted that Simon was still here with her and would never truly leave her.'

Grace went to her father, who had begun to tremble, both hands now gripping the sides of the chair so tightly that the deformed knuckles were almost white. The pain in those arthritic joints must have been intense. She put an arm around his shoulders and urged him to calm himself, but he ignored her, his pale eyes suddenly piercing as he stared at Ash.

'And you see, then – right then – I knew she was speaking the truth.'

The investigator stiffened. 'But you implied earlier that you didn't believe in ghosts.'

'No, I asked if you believed you could prove the existence of such.'

'So tell me why you suddenly decided she was telling the truth.'

'Because, Mr Ash, I saw the boy for myself.'

10

'M SO SORRY.'

Ash was surprised. 'For what?' he asked.

'I'm afraid my father's overwrought,' Grace Lockwood replied. 'These headaches . . .' She did not complete the sentence, leaving the thought as part of the apology.

They were strolling along the centre path of the lodge's rear garden, this separated from the rest of the estate by a weathered fence and lush shrubbery. Ahead of them was a whitewood gazebo, and even before they reached it Ash could see that the paint was old and cracked, the frame splintered here and there. Nevertheless it still managed to look attractive with its backdrop of rhododendrons, and plants and other flowers on either side of the path leading up to its step. Although the sun had lost its fierceness, the air was still uncomfortably warm and Ash's jacket was draped through the loop of his arm, his hand tucked into his trouser pocket. Other perfumes mingled with the honeysuckle – lilac, rose, peony and choisia – and he drew in deep breaths to rid his head of the old staleness.

'Has he seen a doctor?' he enquired, the question not quite as casual as his tone suggested.

'He refuses to. Father has this old-fashioned notion that all ills will fade away of their own accord eventually.' She paused for a moment, stooping to examine a yellow rose by the path, and her next comment revealed she was not at all deceived. 'You think he might be neurotic, don't you?' she said.

Ash was reluctant to offend, but he was inclined to be frank. 'He, uh, he seemed quite upset.'

Grace straightened to face him. 'Upset, yes. Things are happening that he doesn't understand. I'm a little upset myself, but not neurotic, Mr Ash.'

'David.'

'David. And it isn't only my father and Ellen Preddle who have been disturbed.'

'Others have seen the boy?'

She resumed walking, less relaxed than a moment ago. 'Not Simon. But other – what would you call them? – apparitions? – other apparitions have been seen. We'd have told you about them if Father's headache hadn't got so much worse.' She glanced back at the house, looking up at a first-floor window as if she could check on her father from where she stood. 'His health has deteriorated so much in the past year or so. That's why I didn't return to Paris after my mother died; he needs me here with him. He used to be so strong, so full of vigour . . .'

'How far advanced is his arthritis?'

She turned away from the house and walked the rest of the way to the gazebo before replying. Inside she sat on an iron bench. 'He tries not to let me know how much pain he's in, but often I catch the strain on his face, in his eyes. He still works too hard for the parish, but it's my fervent hope that the Church will persuade him to retire before too long. Fortunately we have a little inherited money left, enough, anyway, for him to live comfortably.'

Ash sat at the other corner of the seat, his body angled towards her, an arm resting along the curved bench back. 'Enough to run the Lockwood Estate?' he asked.

She smiled at his bluntness, and he liked the smile. 'The Lockwood Estate hardly runs at all. Most of it is now sold off, although we've kept the grounds leading to the old manor house. That's where we spend our money – keeping those few acres in reasonable condition. But we're digressing again, aren't we?'

'Background information can be useful,' he assured her.

'I can't see how it helps catch ghosts.'

It was his turn to smile. 'We don't *catch* them. We determine if there is a genuine presence or not.'

'Are you good at your job, David?' It was a serious question, asked in earnest.

'I generally achieve results, one way or another.'

'But you do believe in this . . . this spirit world. You do believe we can be haunted.'

She wondered why he quickly turned his head as if something back at the house had caught his attention. But his eyes were not focused on the house and his thoughts were inwards.

'What is it, David?' she asked. 'What have I said?'

She saw his neck stiffen and his shoulders straighten imperceptibly as though he were gaining control over whatever had disturbed him.

'What I believe in isn't important,' he said quietly.

'But –'

He stopped her. 'No, Grace. We're dealing with what has happened in Sleath.'

'Why are you so troubled, David?' It was a simple but direct question, and it pierced through emotions he had held in check for a long time. Yet still he held back, perplexed by her intuition. 'Won't you tell me?' she urged.

Finally he spoke. 'It's too soon, Grace.'

'Is it?' she instantly replied. 'Didn't you feel something strange happen to us earlier at the church? I sensed you were there before I even set eyes on you, and I know you felt it too. Something happened between us before we even met.'

His manner became abrupt. 'Maybe. But it had nothing to do with this investigation. I'd rather we dealt with that.'

Grace was taken aback by his sudden change and she wondered what he was hiding. Why wouldn't he talk to her about the peculiar sensation she knew they had both shared at

St Giles', that sudden and almost electrifying awareness of each other even before they had met? Why did he choose to deny it?

'Grace, tell me about these other incidents.'

He had deliberately cut into her thoughts, but there was no challenge in his eyes. Perhaps it was a pleading she saw there.

'All right, David,' she acquiesced, then added: 'But how do you know that wasn't part of what's happening here? You, yourself, heard children singing in an empty schoolhouse a short time before. How do you explain that? Don't you think there might be a connection?'

He took time to consider before he replied. 'It's possible. I need a lot more information before I can make any kind of judgement. You have to help me if I'm to help you, Grace.'

'Perhaps I should apologize again.'

'No need. Just tell me about these other sightings.'

She watched him take out the micro-recorder from his pocket once more and switch it on. He placed it between them on the bench. 'Go ahead,' he told her.

Grace drew in a deep breath before she spoke. 'A young girl who works as a barmaid in the Black Boar Inn came to my father several days ago. She was very upset and looked as if she hadn't been sleeping well for some time. In fact, she hadn't.'

'Is her name Ruth, by any chance?'

'You've met her?'

'When I booked a room at the inn. I noticed she looked as if she'd had some bad nights.'

'Her name's Ruth Cauldwell. Her father's a local carpenter.'

'What was her problem?'

'She claimed she had been having terrible dreams, only they weren't dreams, they happened even when she was awake.'

'It's not uncommon to dream you're awake. She could have been in a semi-conscious state.'

'Father explained that to her, but she had insisted that she was awake. She sat up in bed and even turned on the lamp by the bed on one occasion. The man who had woken her was still there at the end of her bed.'

'It was a man.'

'It had the appearance of a man.'

'Someone she knew?'

'Someone she knew was dead. Ruth was molested when she was a child. The man's name was Joseph Munce and he worked for her father from time to time. He was jailed for what he did to her and died in prison. He committed suicide.'

'As I said, she could have been confused. Some nightmares are incredible in their intensity.'

'But she switched on the light and he was still there.'

'And he faded away.'

Grace nodded. 'That's what Ruth told Father.'

'It's possible to do such things in your sleep. Some people have left their homes and been found wandering along the streets while still asleep, others have gone downstairs to the kitchen and poured themselves a drink. The vision faded when the girl began to wake from her dream.'

Grace bit into her lower lip. 'That's too glib, David. I don't believe Ruth would say she was awake when she was really dreaming. I've known her for years and she's always been a level-headed girl.'

'She went through a terrible experience when she was just a kid, and who knows the feelings that have been pent up inside her all these years? Maybe she feels guilty about what happened, maybe she even feels partly to blame. The man's suicide while in prison would reinforce the guilt if that were the case.'

'I can't argue with you, David; I don't know enough to. Let me tell you of another incident, though.'

Suddenly he wanted to reach out and touch her hand to reassure her. For some reason she seemed vulnerable sitting there, so anxious – and so close. He wanted to explain that he was there to help, that it was part of his job to be pragmatic, sceptical even, and it didn't mean he doubted her or anybody else's story. He wanted to tell her why such a great part of his life had been directed towards proving the non-existence of ghosts, exposing the myths, unmasking the cheats, rationalizing the phenomena. And he wanted to tell her how wrong he had been all that time.

But this wasn't the moment. He let her continue.

'My father told you how Ellen Preddle's husband had died.'

'The burning haystack.'

'Yes. He visited the Gunstone farm just a few days ago – Mrs Gunstone, who helps with St Giles', has been unwell for some time. Her husband, Sam, was agitated and waited for my father to step outside the house again to speak to him. He didn't want his wife to hear, you see, he didn't want her to be upset anymore in her condition. Sam Gunstone had always been a sound, practical man, certainly not prone to flights of fancy, so the story he told my father was all the more surprising – and convincing.'

Ash heard the tape switch itself off with a tiny click. 'Wait,' he said, and quickly turned the cassette over. He switched on the machine and nodded to her to continue.

'Although it was early morning there was a heat mist over the fields. Sam was walking with his dog, carrying a shotgun and on the lookout for rabbits, when he saw a peculiar orange glow in the mist not too far from his farmhouse. He went towards it and noticed it seemed to flicker – or perhaps waver might be a better word – in the mist, and when he drew near he knew exactly what it was.'

Grace's head was bowed as she related the story. Now she raised it and looked into the middle distance as though she could see the mysterious glow for herself.

'He realized his dog had stopped behind him and no matter what he said, it refused to move. It stood there rigid, just staring at the light, making small whimpering noises. Sam went on without it and he soon understood what was causing the glow, although there was no sound and no smoke.'

'It was a fire?'

She nodded. 'A haystack was burning. But it was too early in the season for haystacks. There were none in his fields.'

Ash had already grasped the implication. 'It was where George Preddle burned to death.'

'Yes. And although there was no sound of fire and no smoke, Sam swore to my father that he could feel the heat and could smell the burning. Impossible, I know, but as I said the farmer swore that was the truth of it.'

Impossible? thought Ash. No, it wasn't impossible at all. The heat, the acrid smell. *The flames.* But no fire, no real fire.

Grace saw the disquiet in Ash's eyes. 'David, are you all right?'

He stiffened, as before, seeming to regain his composure. 'Something that happened a long time ago. What happened to your farmer reminded me of it.'

'Care to tell me?'

'It's not important. What's happening now in Sleath is all that matters.'

'Do you believe what I've told you?'

'That's not the point. These people, including your father, believe what they saw and you accept it. It's my job to gather the evidence and do some tests, then give a reasonably qualified opinion.'

'Will you be able to tell us why this is happening?'

'If Sleath really is being haunted, then there might be a reason for it. It's possible we'll learn what it is.'

'And will you be able to bring it to an end?'

He did not answer, but there was a bitterness to his smile.

11

UTH CAULDWELL CALLED goodbye to Tom Ginty behind the bar and walked out into the afternoon sun. Her bare arms warmed instantly after the relative coolness of the Black Boar Inn's shaded interior and she set off along the High Street at a brisk pace. It was a good fifteen minutes' walk to her parents' home where she lived and, had it been winter, she would probably have made the journey in her little red Mini; in spring or summer, however, she always made the trip on foot, not just because she relished the exercise and the sun on her face after the dinginess of her workplace, but because it was necessary to her, a test of her own will, an assertion over the darkness in her life.

Ruth was a pretty girl – she would have been even prettier that day had not the last few disturbed nights taken their toll – of just eighteen years of age, who dressed modestly but attractively and who was liked by both staff and customers of the Black Boar Inn. Even though her ambition was eventually to become a children's nanny, a profession that required training and a training that required financing, she worked diligently and usually cheerfully behind the bar in the knowledge that it was merely a means to an end. Once she had the money saved, she would leave the insulated haven that was Sleath and acquaint herself with the real world. Not that she craved excitement, far from it: Ruth was merely planning escape. Nothing dramatic, no sudden upheaval that would upset her parents and mystify her friends; a gentle drifting away was what she had in mind, a protracted and genial break from what she still held dear, but which would in the end only succeed in stifling her. Daddy would never understand if she tried to explain her feelings – he would only protest that his thoughts were for her alone. And so they were. But that was the problem.

If *the incident* was to be forgotten, then her life could not be governed by its memory.

Even now, after so many years, she knew that if her journey home took longer than twenty-five minutes, Daddy would be on the way to the village in his pick-up in search of her. He was the one who could not forget and because of that, nor could she. And, she firmly believed, nor could Munce's spirit.

She turned off the High Street, taking a lane that led between two houses and across a field at the back of the village. Shallow puddles caused by that morning's rain had to be avoided and she skipped over ruts caused by tractor tyres and hollows pressed by the hooves of horses. Soon she was in open country.

Ruth had once loved this picturesque route between her home and the village, cherishing the bluebells scattered around the edges of the woods, the sight of rabbits frisking through the long grass, the sudden sightings of a deer in the distance. She remembered when she was little and Daddy brought her this way to nursery school, taking time off his work to do so, carrying her over the rougher patches, the smell of wood on his hands, the light, sandy dust caught in the creases of his shirt making her sneeze and Daddy laugh. She had felt so secure then, so safe and happy in his arms. She was sure he would always be there, to love and protect her, keep away the *bad* things, guide her when she was uncertain. But he hadn't been there when . . . *Stop!* It wasn't Daddy's fault. It was nobody's fault. Except Munce's. And her own . . .

She pushed the dirty, intrusive thoughts away. It had been so long ago and the memory wasn't clear anymore. It'd never really been clear. Even his face . . . *Munce's face* . . . hardly formed in her mind these days. It was a featureless – a featureless *snivelling* – blur. Yet when she was a child she had known him so well. She'd watched him as he helped Daddy in the workshop, and sometimes he would look up and wink at her. That had made her giggle, because then there had been no harm in it. She had watched when Daddy and Munce had pulled the long ropes of the church bells, the deep and clanging sounds forcing her to clap her small hands to her ears so that the two men laughed and yanked the bell-pulls even harder, and Munce had grinned at her the special way he did, that silly, half-idiot, lop-sided grin that she hadn't understood because she was too little and Daddy hadn't understood because men didn't seem to understand that kind of thing, didn't know the signs, weren't aware of the intent, and even if she was a child and didn't understand . . . didn't *quite* understand . . . a quiet little voice inside her head told her there was something funny in Munce's globby eyes and shiny wet grin . . .

Stop! she commanded herself again. But still the thoughts persisted.

Munce had always seemed to be there, working with Daddy, eating meals with them at the kitchen table, and sometimes, when Daddy was out collecting or delivering a job and Mummy couldn't manage it, Munce would even walk her to school . . . He was almost a member of the family, a sort of uncle, and nobody realized what was going on inside his dirty head, with his crooked grin and his moony eyes and his thick soppy lips, not even Mummy and certainly not Daddy. Although she was only small, Ruth had suspected something was not quite right, but hadn't known what. But then how could she know the perversions inside a grown-up's mind, how could she really, truly, know of the filth that lurked there, hidden away, festering and boiling and waiting for the right moment to crawl out and corrupt? How could she know that?

But she had liked the games they played together.

Games when there was no one else around, when they walked along the edge of the woods to school, or in the workshop when Daddy was out. Only seven years old when it had started, but she had enjoyed that funny feeling deep down in her tummy, deep, deep, down, because it made her feel all tingly and sort of itchy and a little bit sticky. She had liked it – *no, she hadn't, it was horrible and nasty and she'd been too young to comprehend* – even though it had made her feel horrid afterwards, afraid to tell Mummy, afraid she *would* tell Daddy, because, after all, she was Daddy's girl and she loved him more than all the sweets and dollies and mummies and sisters in all the world, and Daddy wouldn't have liked it if he'd known she played games with Munce, secret games, dirty games –

Ruth stumbled over a rut in the lane and took several quick steps forward to keep her balance. Her knees bent and one hand almost touched the ground before she righted herself. Slightly shaken, she slid the strap of her open straw bag back up to her shoulder, then drew in a breath to steady herself. The unexpected jolt had knocked all those silly notions from her head. She had been a child, an innocent eight-year-old when Munce had . . . when Munce had . . . *say it, Ruth, do as the kind lady in the big place in London had told her those many years ago, the one who had given her the lovely dolly with no clothes and asked her to show the places on the dolly where the nasty man had touched her, say it and don't keep it trapped inside your pretty little head, say it as much as you want, because it wasn't your fault, it was the man's fault, the horrible man who could never harm you again because they had put him away where he couldn't do those things to anyone ever again . . .*

As she checked that nothing had fallen from the bag her eyes became moist.

Oh no, Munce couldn't harm her again, he couldn't harm anyone anymore, because in the place they had sent him to they didn't like people who hurt little girls or boys and the word had soon got around that he was a child molester.

She took a tissue from the bag and dabbed her eyes with it, absorbing the wetness in them before tears could form.

It was years later that she had learned what had happened to Munce inside prison. Daddy had told her because he thought it would help her get over what had happened, she would know the bad man had been truly punished and would never lay his filthy hands on another little person again. The pervert had been tormented mercilessly by the other prisoners – and by the wardens, if truth be told – and he had been beaten and mocked and reviled. So much so, in fact, that eventually he had done something horrible to himself to escape from it all. Escape to hell, Daddy had said with a funny and angry kind of laugh. Munce had died a sickening death, Daddy had told her, but would say no more than that. *The point is, Ruthy, he won't be botherin no tiny innocents like you ever again.* And she had smiled at Daddy when he said that, because she *had* been an innocent and this sick, repulsive creature had corrupted that innocence, had made the child aware of vile, despicable things and left her in mental torment for years afterwards, not just because she had been violated, but because when Daddy had found them in the woods together she . . . she had . . . been . . . enjoying . . . those . . . terrible . . . secret . . . things . . . they were . . . doing . . .

No! How could a child enjoy anything like that? She had been too young to understand, too pure . . .

Ruth began walking again, rapidly, her back stiff, her steps long.

It was in the past, many, many years in the past, and she was an adult now, a woman in all senses. For God's sake, she couldn't even remember what the man had looked like.

But if she couldn't remember what he had looked like, why was she so sure that it was Munce who had stood at the end of her bed in the darkest part of the night now that she was eighteen?

It wasn't him! It couldn't be him! Ruth shook her head from side to side as she walked. Munce was dead and buried and no dead person could come back from the grave! Reverend

Lockwood had assured her of that when she went to see him. She had told the vicar of her dread – that Munce had returned to continue those foul, horrible things he had done with . . . *to*, he had done *to* . . . her when she was a child, and Reverend Lockwood had comforted her, told her it was nonsense, that it was only dreams and memories that were haunting her. Munce was gone forever.

Leaves suddenly rustled in the hedgerow beside the lane and Ruth briskly stepped aside as if expecting someone to leap out. Her heart hammered even though she immediately realized there was nothing there – nothing but a startled bird or tiny animal, that is. There were no ghosts in daylight, she told herself. There were no ghosts at any time. Reverend Lockwood had repeated that to her over and over again. But how could she believe him when she could tell he didn't believe it himself? He could reassure her, but his eyes, his furtive eyes, spoke otherwise. And there were whisperings in the village. Nobody was saying it outright, nobody was standing in the bar of the Black Boar proclaiming they'd seen a ghost for themselves – nobody would be fool enough to – but there was talk, careful and discreet talk that was murmured from one to another and never in a crowd. Odd things were happening in Sleath and no one wanted to admit it.

She caught sight of something moving among the trees up ahead and her steps slowed.

She began to regret not having driven into the village, but then scolded herself. It was a beautiful day and she always walked in spring and summer unless it was wet. Even then she might don a raincoat and pull the hood up, glad of the air's freshness, pleased to be out in the open when most of the day was spent closeted indoors. She had used this route all her life, accompanied or unaccompanied, and very little discouraged her from walking. There had been the time after Munce had first been locked away, of course, when she was reluctant to take that way on foot even with Mummy or Daddy, but as the months went by, her fear had evaporated and the walk no longer held any terrors for her. And when she was a few years older, she was perfectly happy to make the journey alone. Although she never strayed into the woods, she never went into those shadowy parts where Munce had liked to take her. She preferred to stay out here in the open, even though there were shortcuts through the trees.

She kept walking, her eyes watching the place up ahead where she thought she had detected movement. Surely she'd been mistaken. There was nothing there now. She'd been jittery for days, ever since the first . . . dream? Yes, call it a dream, much better that way. No, there was no one lurking there. A breeze had stirred branches, a cloud cast a shadow.

But there was no breeze, and there was hardly a cloud in the sky.

All right, then. Someone was on a stroll through the woods, and why not? It wasn't private land. Someone had passed by and her own imagination had spooked her. No one was hiding there, no one was waiting for –

She gave a little shriek when the figure stepped out in front of her.

'Danny!' It was a strangulated sound, a gasp rather than a greeting. Ruth's hands went to her face as she tried to catch her breath.

'Didn't mean to scare you, Ruthy,' the youth said with a foolish smile. His body swayed slightly and Ruth wondered how much he had drunk back there at the Black Boar. She had served him herself, but her mind had been too involved with other things to make a count of his pints of cider.

'What are you doing here?' she demanded to know, annoyance quickly taking her from the momentary panic. 'You left the pub ages ago.'

'I was waitin for you.'

'You could be doing better things on your day off.'

Danny Marsh came towards her, one hand tucked into the back pocket of his jeans, the other brushing his shock of red tousled hair away from his forehead. He was a gangly youth with large brown eyes and a chip-toothed grin, who worked the till at the garage a mile or so outside the village. He lived in one of Sleath's smaller terraced houses tucked away behind the High Street, sharing with his divorced mother and semi-senile grandfather.

'I couldn't talk to you in the bar,' he said, offering it as a kind of excuse.

'I don't see why not; I wasn't that busy.'

'It's awkward there. Everybody listens.'

'Oh, come off it, Danny. It couldn't have been that important.' Ruth was still trembling inwardly, but she refused to let him see how nervous she was.

'We haven't had a chance to talk since las' week. We had a good time then, didn't we? I thought . . . I thought we got along well.'

She tried to move past him, but he stood in her way. She didn't like that.

'What's happened since, Ruth?' he persisted, his deep brown eyes gazing solemnly into hers.

'Nothing's happened. Now let me pass.'

He held her arm. 'Jus' tell me. I thought you liked me.'

'I did . . . I do. I have to get home, Danny, Mum's expecting me.' Her mother was in town with Sarah: dentist, then optician, then new shoes. If her younger sister had to take time off school their mother made sure it was worthwhile; in the Cauldwell household there was no such thing as a single appointment if it meant a trip into town.

'Jus' gimme a coupla minutes.'

'No!' She couldn't contain her anger any longer. She pushed by him, brushing away his hand and striding off down the lane.

Danny followed, then ran ahead, turning to face her and blocking her way again. 'Why won't you talk to me? What've I done. Is it be –'

'It's nothing to do with that!' she snapped. She turned her head aside, despising the smell of cider on his breath. Munce had liked cider, she remembered.

'I didn't mean nothin. I thought you wanted me to.' He reached out for her again, this time with both hands, taking her by her bare upper arms. She squirmed in his grip, trying to pull away, but he held on to her, drawing her close. He kissed her, at first on the cheek, then when she froze in his arms, he slid his lips – his *wet* lips – over to her mouth.

He was aware that they were in a quiet lane, fields on one side, woods on the other, and there was hardly any traffic at all at that time of day. He pressed himself hard against her, loving the soft contours of her body, her stomach squeezed against his groin, her breasts crushed against his ribs. He pushed his tongue between her lips and spittle – his spittle – drooled onto her chin.

The paralysis that held Ruth there was as frightening to her as his intentions, for although her limbs were locked tight, her mind was in a frenzy, and the scream that was captive in her throat was shrill inside her head. She could not move. No matter how much she tried, no matter how much her heart convulsed, her silent shrieks pierced her mind, her flesh crawled, she could not move one little muscle against this . . . dirty . . . drivelling . . .

One hand released her, sliding between their bodies, rising to slip between the buttons of her blouse. His fingertips touched her breast.

That violation liberated her scream. It burst from her with a fierceness that shocked her foolhardy assailant. He shot away from her and as he did, his hand, which was trapped inside her blouse, ripped away two buttons.

Ruth stared down at the opening, saw her exposed breast spilling over the top of her lacy white bra, and screamed again, and then again, and then again.

When Danny came back towards her, his eyes pleading, his hands appealing, Ruth scratched at the air between them. He came to a swift standstill, then foolishly took one more step towards her.

Ruth ran from him, not caring in which direction she went,

blinded by tears, finally released, wanting only to be away from him, out of reach of those dirty, filthy hands, those shiny, dribbling lips. Undergrowth caught at her skirt and thin branches whipped at her bare arms and face as she fled deeper into the woods, and she could hear him calling her name, telling her to come back, that he hadn't meant to upset her, and in her mind he sounded like Munce all those years ago pleading to her daddy, those same words, that same snivelling tone, the same denials.

Ruth stumbled around trees, tripping on tree roots, hitting out at foliage that sought to block her path; but she did not stop, she kept going without even looking back to see if she was being followed, crashing through the woods, looking for a place to hide . . . as she had fled when Daddy had found her and Munce in the woods together, doing . . . those . . . things. She had hidden somewhere – she couldn't remember where now, but it was somewhere safe and dark – but Daddy had found her anyway, he'd heard her weeping and he'd told her it was all right, it wasn't her fault and that Munce would never harm her again, he would never be able to because he would be shut away in a place where all dirty, disgusting men were kept so that they could be punished and never let out to bother tiny innocents again, but first she had to tell Daddy exactly what Munce had done to her, where he had put his hands and what other part of his filthy body he had used . . .

She kept running, words and images tumbling through her head, confusing her so that she had no sense of direction, her bare feet – for her shoes had slipped from her feet – pounding into the forest dust, stirring the dead leaves and breaking small twigs. Her hands and arms were bleeding, there was a gash on her chin where a prickly branch had scythed across it, and her legs were crosshatched with shallow cuts. Her feet bled too.

Ruth was close to exhaustion when she finally fell. She went down hard and fast, her forehead smacking against the lower trunk of a stout tree. Her cry was small and heard only by herself. She lay there stunned, watching a kaleidoscope of greens and blues and browns wheel around her.

Gradually the patterns began to slow and take on separate shapes. Her hand was shaking badly, but she was able to wipe moisture from her lashes. She did this again, using both hands this time, afraid of not being able to see.

She pushed herself up against the tree she had crashed into, half-turning so that one shoulder rested against it. Her forehead was numb where it had made contact with the rough bark and her senses had been numbed too. At least the blow had driven off the hysteria. Now she could only lie there, a quiet, wounded creature who was still full of dread but too exhausted and too dazed to flee any further. She noticed her blouse had opened wider, one half loose from her skirt, and her breasts bore the marks of her flight through the woods, tiny beads of blood beginning to ooze from the scratches and cuts. Ruth slowly drew the sides of the blouse together, hardly aware of what she was doing, instinct telling her she shouldn't be uncovered that way. She held the material, pressing hard as if willing it to fuse, and drew her legs up so that her knees touched her elbows.

'Oh dear God,' she murmured. 'Oh dear God . . .'

She crouched there against the tree until her trembling had become less violent and her panic had settled to mere terror.

She must get home. To where it was safe. To where no one . . . no one could . . . touch . . . her. And she wouldn't tell Daddy. No, that would be the wrong thing to do. He might look at her in that funny way. The way he had looked at her when he had found her with Munce. She didn't want him to look at her like that ever again. She hadn't liked it. It was as if . . . as if . . . as if he were . . . blaming . . . her . . .

Ruth tried to stifle the sob, but it shook her shoulders, convulsed her chest, nevertheless. She must get home. Home was safe.

The sound hardly registered at first, so soft was its stirring.

101

And then, as the sound became a gentle rustling, her attention was drawn towards it.

A nearby sapling, quite tall but rod-thin, with branches full of young leaves, appeared to be quivering. At first Ruth thought it was no more than an illusion caused by her own trembling, but when she realized that the sound was the rustling of its leaves she knew that the tree really was moving. Yet no others near or around it stirred. For there was no wind. There wasn't even a breeze here so deep in the woods. It was as if some powerful invisible hand were shaking the slim trunk to make the leaves above shiver. Yet the trunk was still.

And the leaves were beginning to loosen and fall.

It was early summer and the tiny leaves were beginning to fall and they were turning from a fresh, vibrant green to a crisp brown as they floated down and their edges were curling inwards and tearing because of their own brittleness and their lifelessness was making them lighter so that they swooped and seemed to linger in the air.

Her vision was clearer by now and Ruth watched intently, mesmerized by the display. More and more leaves dropped, so that soon it was like gazing upon a coloured snowstorm, where vivid green changed in flight into first rich, then lustreless, brown. Even as the first of the dead leaves touched the soil around the sapling the unaccountable breeze scooped them up so that they fluttered and spiralled, rising again to mingle with those still falling. The breeze that had no source grew into a wind that whipped up the leaves, sent them diving, tumbling, rearing, and rather than disperse them, drew them into a vortex so that they began to spin, faster and faster, round and round, sucking in even more so that soon Ruth was watching a diminutive cyclone of variegated greens and golds.

Ruth pushed herself hard against the tree behind her, her eyes wide, her mouth open, her heels digging into the earth. The storm of twisting leaves grew more frenzied as more were drawn in and within moments they presented an almost solid spinning shape; and still more leaves were torn from the spindly branches so that their flight and the rushing of air filled Ruth's head with their noise. She wanted to look away, but could not: she was transfixed by the sight.

The form began to change, to take on a new shape: it lost height, becoming thinner at the top, broadening, then tapering towards the ground.

The sound became a hissing. And the hissing became a multitudinous whispering, a legion of hushed voices.

Abruptly, it began to disintegrate.

To reveal a shape beneath.

It wasn't clear, it could not be focused upon; but it took the rough form of a man.

And Ruth knew who that man was.

The figure moved within the leaf storm and it seemed to Ruth that a bowed head was slowly rising to look towards her. A shudder interrupted her trembling, for she recognized that amorphous face even before the first feature, a sharp, bent nose whose tip descended too close to the upper lip, had presented itself. Her feet scuffed the soft forest wood in an eccentric pantomime of running, and her cheek crushed itself against the rough bark as she watched at an awkward angle; it was as if she really were fleeing and looking back over her shoulder at the thing that fashioned itself among the swirling leaves. A small sound, almost a mewling, came from her when a dark hole appeared beneath the crooked nose, a hole that had lips – wet, glistening lips.

It spoke, but its words, like its mass, were still ill-formed, difficult to understand. It might have called her name, it might have declared its own misery; Ruth could not be sure.

She wanted to close her eyes against this evolving monstrosity – perhaps if she didn't see it, it really would not be there – but the lure was too great, the fascination too perverse and too compelling: she could not help but watch from the corners of her eyes.

The blurred figure was stirring again as if testing its own mobility, the movement slow, minimal, when suddenly the leaves around it scattered as if blown by a fiercer wind. The shape was unveiled to her and she saw that Munce was naked.

'Oh no . . .' she said in a quiet, mournful voice.

His flesh had mouldered – *for God's sake, a voice screamed inside her head, of course it had mouldered, he'd been dead for nine years!* – and tiny feeding things nestled inside his open wounds. He gazed at her with dead, black eyes.

The deepest cuts were across his small – for Munce had always been thin – but bloated belly, although the lacerations on his scraggy arms and thighs made up for their superficiality in numbers. She was drawn back to his deadened gaze as if he willed it so and to her further horror she realized that gaping hole of a mouth with its sheeny edges was smiling at her. His head bowed again as he looked down at his own savaged body and she followed his gaze as she knew she was meant to. His marked hands moved inwards towards his groin in a macabre parody of those times long ago when Ruth was a child and they had played their secret games, guiding her attention to the wound that was the deepest of all.

She suddenly understood the extent of Munce's self-mutilation and how he had finally ended his wretched and tormented life when she watched a thick glob of black blood ooze from a ragged hole where his genitals had once been.

12

RACE LOCKWOOD KNOCKED once more on the yellow-painted door while Ash stood on the path and looked along the row of small gardens. They were all neat and the two on either side were particularly well kept; the one he was in, however, was showing signs of recent neglect, for weeds were beginning to gain the upper hand and some of the flowers were in urgent need of pruning back. He squinted up at the little window over the front door and wondered why it had interested him so earlier that day.

The door opened a few inches after a third knock from Grace, and a round face peered from the shadows through the gap.

'Hello, Ellen,' he heard Grace say. 'It's me, Grace Lockwood. I haven't seen much of you lately.'

For a moment Ash thought that Ellen Preddle might close the door again, for it narrowed a fraction before the woman's face came closer for a better inspection.

'I saw the vicar only a few days ago.' It came out almost as a statement of defence.

'I know, Ellen,' Grace reassured her. 'It was Reverend Lockwood who sent us to you.'

There was a moment's hesitation. 'You're his daughter, aren't you?'

'Of course, Ellen. You know me, we've spoken on several occasions.'

'I knew you when you were little. And I knew your mother. She was a very kind lady.'

'May we come in?'

'No.'

The intransigence of her reply startled Grace. She glanced over her shoulder at Ash before trying again. 'We're here to help, Ellen. Please won't you reconsider?'

'How can you help?' Ellen Preddle's tone was brusque. 'None of you understand what's happened. You couldn't.'

Grace stepped aside to allow a clear view of the investigator. 'Ellen, this is David Ash. I promise you, he knows about these things.'

'Knows? What does he know?'

Ash wondered why the brusqueness had turned to nervousness. He went forward, a hand lightly touching the door. 'Mrs Preddle, I'm from the Psychical Research Institute. Reverend Lockwood contacted us to see if we could discover just what's happening to you.' It seemed pointless to mention that it had been the vicar's daughter who had, in fact, contacted the Institute and it would have done a great deal of harm to point out that Reverend Lockwood hadn't been in favour.

'He said he wouldn't tell anyone, he said it was just between me and him.' There was no anger, only despair. 'He promised.'

'Yes, I know, but other things have happened here in Sleath recently. He hasn't spoken to anyone else about you, though. He respects your wishes, Mrs Preddle.'

'Miss Lockwood seems to know all about it.'

'I insisted that he told me everything after he visited you last,' Grace quickly put in. 'He was in a very distressed state. Look, can we come in and talk to you? Just talk, nothing else. And then if you want us to leave, we will. Mr Ash is . . . well, he's a sort of scientist who deals in matters of this kind, and he'll do his best to understand what's going on. Perhaps he'll be able to give us reasons.'

The door widened and the woman came into the light. Ash noticed Grace give a start.

Ellen Preddle's eyes had a strange, distant cast to them, as though her thoughts were elsewhere and the present was only registered in part. There was a darkness around them also, like the smudges of weariness that had discoloured the fresh skin of the young girl in the Black Boar Inn; the flesh beneath the woman's eyes was puffed, both exhaustion and tears no doubt the cause, and a vein beneath the finer skin of her temple throbbed visibly. Tendrils of black hair mixed with grey hung untidily over her broad forehead and her hands did not seem capable of keeping still for a moment: they clutched at her clothes, touched her face, wrung themselves together constantly. Ellen Preddle, Ash realized, *looked* haunted.

She stared directly at him. 'Can you help my Simon?' she pleaded, the anxiety in her voice as startling as her appearance.

'You mean your son?' he replied, keeping his own voice mild and as if there were nothing wrong at all with her question. 'I think I can help you both, if you'll let me.' He was uneasy with his assurance, for his function was merely to explain, disprove or verify; he was neither exorcist nor comforter. However, in these circumstances one small pretence might gain her cooperation.

Uncertainty at least brought some expression to the woman's withdrawn gaze and Grace quickly followed up. 'My father and I are sure that Mr Ash can discover the cause of all this, Ellen, and if he does we'll probably be able to put an end to it.'

Ash regarded her with barely disguised astonishment and Grace returned the look with a faint smile of apology.

The exchange was lost on Ellen Preddle, for her hands had covered her face. 'Put an end to it?' she said in a low, soft moan. 'Can you really do that? Would Simon finally be at peace?'

'Let us come inside,' Grace said gently, already moving forward.

The bereaved woman's hands fell away from her face and she turned to walk back into the room, neither inviting them in nor refusing them entry.

Ash followed Grace and scanned the interior of the little

terraced cottage. The room he found himself in was cramped but comfortable with its old furniture and bright curtains. To his right was a doorway through which he could see a small kitchen, and a staircase stood directly opposite the front door. A rose-patterned armchair was angled towards the fireplace while table and chairs filled much of the space in the other half of the room. Several ornaments decorated the mantel over the fireplace, but there was only one framed photograph, this of a young boy with large dark eyes and a mop of unruly hair, much of which covered his forehead. The boy was smiling, but it seemed to Ash there was unhappiness in his eyes.

Ellen Preddle waited in the centre of the room, her shoulders hunched, her hands never still, until Grace guided her towards the armchair. 'Sit here, Ellen, and let Mr Ash ask you some questions,' she said as the woman looked up at her for reassurance.

Ash brought over a hard chair from the table and placed it opposite the seated woman. She regarded him with a demeanour so sad and lost that for several moments he was unable to say anything to her.

Grace observed his discomfort and stooped to put an arm around Ellen's shoulders. 'Don't be afraid,' she soothed. 'Remember, David is here to help you. Just answer his questions the best you can. Now, how about I make us all some tea? Would you like that?'

The woman nodded slowly, one hand pulling at the cardigan she wore, drawing it across her chest as though she were chilled despite the heat of the day. As Grace left them and went through to the kitchen it suddenly dawned on Ash that it *was* cold in this room. Before then it hadn't registered with him that Ellen Preddle was wearing a knitted cardigan over a cotton blouse when it was a particularly warm day. He felt his own flesh contract with the change in temperature almost as though mental recognition had prompted his body.

'D'you mind if I use this recorder?' he asked, reaching into his pocket and showing her the diminutive machine.

She did not reply; she didn't even glance at it.

Ash switched on the cassette recorder and left it on the floor between them. 'I'd like you to tell me exactly what you've seen since your son passed on, Mrs Preddle.' He kept his voice low, afraid she might feel intimidated. 'Mrs Preddle?' he repeated when she failed to respond.

'I told Reverend Lockwood,' she said after a while.

'Yes, I know. But now I want you to tell me. I have to hear it in your own words, you see. Simon was buried three weeks ago, wasn't he?'

Again there was a lengthy pause. Then she said, 'Was it so long? Three weeks? Yes, it must be, that's when they buried my poor boy.'

'And you saw him afterwards?' His voice was coaxing.

'Simon was waiting for me when I got back from the funeral. He was sitting in this very chair.' She touched the arms as if to indicate the place.

'You actually saw him?' It was a necessary repetition, for often in such cases a person merely felt a presence, their own emotions making the connection between the experience and the loved one.

She nodded, the movement, as before, slow and deliberate.

'Was it a clear vision? Could you see all of him?'

This time her reply was forceful. 'Simon was here. He was in this chair.'

'Did he speak to you?'

Yet again he had to wait for an answer. 'He doesn't have to speak to me. He's just happy being here.'

The sound of the tap running came from the kitchen, then the clatter of cups and saucers. He nudged the micro-recorder closer to Ellen Preddle with his foot. 'How many times has Simon visited you?'

For the first time the faintest trace of a smile touched her lips. 'Oh, Simon was here most of the time. It was like . . . before . . . when . . .'

'When he was alive?' he finished for her.

She flinched at that, as though it were a shock, and Ash began to suspect that the woman had deep psychological problems caused by more than just bereavement. Her grief was natural enough, and her refusal to accept her loss was not extraordinary; however, the lengths she had gone to in order to convince herself her son was still alive were far from natural. Grace had already told him her father had learned that after the boy had been buried Ellen Preddle had carried on as though he were still with her, following her around, chatting with her, helping her with the housework. She had tucked him up in bed at night, told him bedtime stories, even cooked his meals (no doubt deluding herself that he had eaten the food as she wiped the plates into the bin). Yet her subconscious had told her that none of this was possible, that Simon really had drowned in the bath and was now buried up there in the cemetery, and this was why she had hardly left the house these past three weeks, for outside lay reality, outside there could be no Simon, people would sympathize with her, even weep, or try to convince her he was gone. Most importantly, they would not see him, and that would mean he didn't exist. Ellen had shut herself away so that her son could live on.

Ash sighed inwardly, depressed at the conflict that was going on inside this woman. The fact that only moments before she had accepted his use of the term 'vision' meant she was becoming more aware of her own self-deception. Eventually, and it could take years, she might even concede that Simon's ghost was nothing more than her own overwrought imagination. As for Reverend Lockwood's alleged sighting of the boy in this very house, well, that could be due to collective hysteria, the woman's strong impressions transferred to the cleric's own mind, which, in Ash's opinion, was already somewhat unstable. Then other sightings in Sleath might be part of the same syndrome too, for collective hysteria was not uncommon and, as the term suggested, could easily be spread from one to another. Multiple observations of UFOs, whole groups of people – particularly pubescent girls – fainting for no apparent reason, mass rioting in stadiums or cities: they were different forms of the same phenomenon.

Her voice broke into his thoughts.

'Can you help my boy?' She was staring hard at him.

'Why should he need help, Ellen? If you're asking me to lay his soul to rest, then I'm afraid I can't.' He was humouring her, but not spitefully: if she honestly believed her son had returned from the grave, then she would also believe he could be set at peace again. 'Reverend Lockwood could do that for you, though. Priests often perform such ceremonies.'

She shook her head impatiently. 'You don't understand. I want Simon to be left alone. I want *him* to leave us be!'

Ash was taken aback by the strength of her outburst. He leaned forward in the chair, keeping his voice even. 'Who are you talking about?'

A sudden crash and then a cry from the kitchen caused him to spin round in his seat. Grace appeared in the doorway, one hand holding on to the doorframe to steady herself, the other touching her forehead. As he watched, blood seeped through her fingers and ran down to her wrist.

He rose to go to her, but Ellen Preddle sprang forward from the armchair with surprising agility and grasped his sleeve.

'*Him!*' she hissed up at him, her pale face contorted with a mixture of fear and loathing. '*Simon's father! Don't you understand? He's come back from the dead to hurt us both!*'

13

ANNY MARSH SLUMPED on the scarred wooden bench facing the village green and pond, one arm hanging limp over the back, a bent leg resting along the seat itself. A few yards away stood the stocks and whipping post, unused but still admired by certain members of the community who thought that law and order had irretrievably broken down since flogging and hanging had been abolished. The youth was scowling, paying little attention to the occasional car, or even more occasional bus, that drove by. It was late afternoon and few people were about: it was too hot for strolling and only the odd delivery van stopping outside the shops saved the day from complete tedium. The school bus bringing the village children back from their lessons in the nearby town would arrive shortly, but nobody put out banners for that.

He stretched a hand towards his denim jacket lying over the opposite arm of the bench, worming his fingers into a pocket and pulling out a stick of chewing gum. Last one. He unwrapped it, rolled it into his mouth, and tossed the screwed-up wrapper onto the grass. He chewed, the sweetness immediately neutralizing the stale lingering taste of the cider he'd consumed earlier in the day. Why did something so welcome at the time turn so nasty in your mouth and belly later on? And why did something that made you feel good at the time make you feel so bloody awful

112

afterwards? These were important questions to ponder and he took his time over them, but when no definite conclusions were drawn his thoughts, as ever, returned to Ruth.

Shit, he hadn't meant to frighten her. There was no need for her to run off like that. He only wanted to show her how much he liked – how much he *loved* her – that was all. And he really did, he really did love her. Christ, he had spent half his day – *half his bloody day!* – in the bar of the Black Boar just so he could be near her. Didn't she appreciate that? He worked all week, Saturday and Sunday mornings, too, and he'd spent his one day off stuck inside a gloomy old pub mooning after her. He'd only wanted to talk to her afterwards. That's why he'd waited in the lane, knowing she'd be coming along sooner or later. Bloody hell, she'd liked him well enough the week before. She'd gone strange, had Ruthy, gone bloody weird. Like a few others around these parts. Loony, that's what. He hadn't meant her no harm, though. Just a kiss, a chat, that's all he'd wanted. So he'd got the wrong message. When she didn't pull away he thought she'd wanted him to touch her. Why couldn't she have just told him she wasn't interested, why did she have to run off into the woods? He might have gone after her, but not when she was in a mood like that. No bloody fear! Enough was enough. Let someone else do the chasing now. He was through with her and her stuck-up ways. Plenny more fish in the sea and pebbles on the beach. Maybe she'd get over it, though. He was sure she liked him. Maybe if he left it for a week or so. Or a coupla days. Maybe he'd call her tomorrow. He'd explain it to her. Buy her some flowers. Get down on his bloody knees and tell her he was sorry, that's what he'd do. Come on, Ruth, give us a chance.

Preoccupied with such wretched musings, Danny failed to notice the rusty grey pick-up truck that drove past the green. His head jerked up, though, when he heard the sudden screech of brakes. To his astonishment, the truck reversed back along the road at a dangerous speed to a point across the grass opposite to where he sat.

He jerked upright when the truck door sprang open and Ralph Cauldwell, Ruth's father, jumped down from the cab. He was holding something down by his side that Danny failed to recognize at first; then, as he drew nearer, the youth realized Ruth's father was carrying one of his carpentry tools. The man, shirt-sleeves rolled up past his elbows, shirt unbuttoned almost to his waist, was glaring at Danny and as he advanced, he raised the heavy-looking mallet he held in his right hand and brought it down with a resounding *smack* into the open palm of his left.

'Mr Cauldwell . . .' Danny began nervously. He half-rose, not caring for the expression on the man's face.

'Dirty . . . bloody . . . little . . . swine . . .' The words were squeezed out between the carpenter's gritted teeth. 'Dirty . . . little . . .'

'Mr Cauldwell?' The youth had frozen mid-rise, the decision on whether to remain there or run quite irrelevant, for his limbs seemed to be locked solid. His jaw dropped open.

'Touch my daughter, would you?'

Danny could barely comprehend the man's words. Touch his . . . daughter? Ruth?

Cauldwell was almost upon him, the mallet beginning a steady ascent over the carpenter's head.

'Filthy . . . scummy . . . little . . .'

Danny noticed there were shiny wet rivulets on the carpenter's cheeks.

Ralph Cauldwell blinked to clear the tears of rage and frustration so that he could see his intended victim – *the dirty little scummy bastard* – without hindrance. This lout . . . this *animal* . . . this *obscenity!* . . . had laid his stinking hands on Ruth, had tried to . . . had tried to . . . Cauldwell would not allow the picture to form in his mind. He, Ruth's father, had let her down before, had blindly permitted Munce to debase his daughter, not seeing what was going on under his very nose, not realizing, not being there to prevent that perverted beast from touching her, from sticking his vile . . . his vile *thing* . . . into Ruth's poor innocent little body. He screamed his pain and anger and outrage and despair as he brought the weighty wooden mallet down hard against the youth's skull.

Danny's arms were raised to ward off what he knew was coming and the mallet smashed one of his wrists on its way to his skull. The sound when the weapon connected with its true target was not unlike the *thwack* of leather on willow, the cricket ball against the bat, and so was not incongruous in this very English setting. It resounded across the common, a sharp, almost pleasing noise in the still summer's afternoon.

Danny did not scream as he collapsed against the bench. He could not scream, for the shell of his skull splintered and broke and pressed in on all kinds of paralysing nerves and tissues. However, his assailant screamed for him.

'You bastard! You filthy scum!'

Cauldwell brought the mallet down and down again on Danny's unresisting body, against his arms, his shoulders, his spine, his quivering legs, working up again towards the head, shattering the skull, sending splatters of red mixed with glossy clogs of matter onto the grass all around. A thick river of spittle drooled from the youth's mouth onto the wooden slats of the bench seat; it began to discolour to pink, and before long it was a deep red flow.

Tradesmen, alerted by the carpenter's shouts, appeared in shop doorways. Faces peered through open windows.

'You . . . you touched my girl . . . you . . .'

Cauldwell's revenge continued relentlessly. Poor Ruth, she'd arrived home in a shocking state, barely able to speak, her clothes dishevelled and torn, her blouse open, her forehead grazed, her arms and legs cut. He'd been in the workshop and she'd collapsed into his arms, babbling about Munce and Danny, her words making no sense, but the connection instant within Cauldwell's own mind. He had never forgotten nor forgiven the degenerate Munce, just as he had never forgotten nor forgiven himself for his own failings. He had allowed it to happen through his own ignorance and vowed that nobody would ever hurt his child again. But he had failed her yet again.

And now the little bastard – the little bastard who had been sunning himself on the village green as if he hadn't a care in the world! – had paid the price. Oh, he cared now, all right, lying there on the bench vomiting blood, his body twitching like some disgusting insect stuck on a needle. He saw the error of his ways now. He was one sick bastard who would never do anything like it again, not to anyone. No sir, not to anyone.

Cauldwell tried to control his own shaking. Someone called out from one of the nearby shop doorways. It might even have been his own name that was being called. But the carpenter took no notice. He wasn't done yet. Not by a long chalk.

He straightened, looking down at the still-twitching body as he did so. He turned and walked stiffly back to the truck whose engine was still idling. He tossed the bloodied mallet onto the passenger seat and reached across into the metal tool box he always carried in the vehicle with him. He rummaged for a particular tool that lay at the bottom of the long box and when his trembling hand found its sturdy handle he lifted it out and marched determinedly back to the bench. Surprisingly the youth was still conscious – after a fashion – and was burbling incessantly. The sounds he uttered made little sense. Perhaps he was pleading for his life.

Several of the villagers were warily, and certainly reluctantly, crossing the road, aware that they must do something, they must intervene before the lad was killed – if he wasn't dead already, that is. But they had recognized Ralph Cauldwell and were apprehensive of his strength and his temper – hadn't he half-killed that wretched pervert Munce all those years ago?

'Ralph,' the owner of the hardware store where Cauldwell purchased a lot of his materials as well as many of his tools called out cautiously. 'Calm down now, Ralph lad.'

But Cauldwell had more work to do.

He dragged the body off the bench and knelt beside it.

Danny Marsh lay on his back and stared up into the wonderfully blue sky. Whether or not he appreciated that blueness was impossible to tell, but one eye did move, flicking from left to right, right to left, as if keen to take in the whole vista. Even his lips moved, although the small sounds he made became quieter and quieter until they were almost impossible to hear.

Ruth's father lifted the new heavier tool he had brought from the truck. He had chosen it on impulse, for he had used this particular instrument many times on Munce, although only in his imagination. In fact in his mind he had used it on the deviate every time lengths of wood had to be shaved and smoothed down. He'd continued to imagine using it on Munce even when the child molester had cut off his own genitalia late one night in his cell and had bled to death by the next morning.

He poised the metal jack plane over the youth's face. 'I'll see you never want to talk to another poor innocent girl again, boy.' He lowered the tool until the cutting blade rested on the youth's cheek. 'I'll show you, boy.' There were sobs between the words. Sobs, but no pity. 'I'll . . . show . . . you . . .'

The school bus drew up at the stop just across the road from where Ralph Cauldwell's truck was so badly parked. Small, interested faces pressed against the glass as the carpenter began to plane away the skin and bone from Danny Marsh's face.

14

'KATE, IT'S DAVID.'

He took a swift nip of vodka from the hip flask as she answered.

'Too soon to tell,' he replied to her question. 'On the surface it's just another one of those idyllic little villages the tourists dream about. Funny thing, though, there are no tourists. It's a pretty tight community.'

'Have you managed to find suitable lodgings?' Kate asked.

'Yeah, the Black Boar Inn.'

'It's an *inn*?'

He grinned at her reproving tone. 'Well, it's a hotel, too. The only one here.'

'Then you take it easy.'

'Never drink on the job, boss.'

'Why don't I believe you? Seriously, David –'

'Okay, Kate.' His interruption was brusque. 'I've never let you down on a case yet.'

There was a pause at the other end. 'Sorry, I shouldn't have said that. You've picked a beautiful few days to spend in the country.'

'Yeah, glorious. Look, things have occurred here that suggest – suggest *strongly* – paranormal activity. Sleath's vicar has even witnessed one of the manifestations.' Ash, who was sprawled on the bed in his room at the Black Boar Inn, reached

118

towards his pack of cigarettes on the bedside cabinet. His suit-case lay open beside him.

'The clergy generally make reliable witnesses,' Kate McCarrick said as he drew out a cigarette with his lips. 'Did he mention why his daughter contacted the Institute directly rather than go through the normal channels of his own church elders?'

'Embarrassment, I think. They wanted an expert opinion before they took it further. There's a strange atmosphere about this place, incidentally. I've got to admit, it makes me uncomfortable.' He wedged the receiver between chin and shoulder as he lit the cigarette.

'What do you mean exactly, David?' In her office at the Psychical Research Institute Kate was frowning. She swivelled in her chair, turning away from the open window to lean forward on her desk. She put her free hand against her ear to muffle the noise from the traffic outside in the busy London street.

'Uh, I don't know – it's just weird. It's almost as if there's something waiting to happen.'

'Is this your intuition at work, David?' It was more than just a flippant remark. 'David?' she said when he failed to respond.

'Yeah, sorry. I was just thinking.'

Me too, said Kate silently.

'No, it isn't anything to do with intuition,' he went on. 'You could cut the atmosphere here with a knife.'

Anyone could, or just you, David? Again it was a thought not voiced.

'In fact, something nasty happened this very afternoon right across from where I'm staying.' He drew on the cigarette.

'Tell me.'

'Well, it seemed a young kid of around nineteen or twenty was beaten almost to death by the village carpenter. Used a mallet on him, then a jack plane.'

'A what?'

'A jack plane. One of those tools with a blade underneath for shaving wood.'

'He hit the boy with it?'

'No, he tried to plane the flesh off his face with it. Damn near succeeded, from what I heard. At least the kid was unconscious from a caved-in skull by then.'

'My God.'

'Right. I don't know the details yet, but it was the sole topic of conversation when I got back to the inn a short time ago.'

'I'm not surprised it was. I thought you said Sleath was one of those lovely little places the tourists dream about.'

'I also said there's a strange atmosphere here. Anyway, I've interviewed three people so far – the Reverend Lockwood himself, Ellen Preddle, who lost her son recently, and a farmer who lives just outside the village. Tomorrow I'll find some time to type up a report for you and I'll send it through.'

'They have a fax at the inn?'

'I'm not sure. If not I'll try the community hall – our client's daughter works there part-time.'

'Ah yes, Grace Lockwood.'

'She's proving very helpful.'

'Hmn. Neurotic type?'

'Not a bit of it. She's as sane as you or . . . well, she's sane enough.'

Kate laughed. 'Attractive? Married?'

'Yes, and no, not that that's got anything to do with anything.'

'Perhaps I really should come up there and give you a hand.'

Ash sighed inwardly. Kate's tone was light, but there was an underlying seriousness to her suggestion.

'Kate.'

'Yes, David?'

'No ties, right?'

There was a pause. 'If you say so.' She became business-like again, but Ash wasn't fooled: an undercurrent remained. 'What do you plan to do, David? Will you be able to set up your instruments?'

'The best place to start will be in Ellen Preddle's cottage. She was the first person to see a ghost.'

'Did she recognize it?'

'It was her son. The boy drowned four weeks ago. She also lost her husband some time back.'

'The poor woman.'

'You haven't heard the kicker. She now claims her husband has returned from the grave.'

'She's being haunted by *two* ghosts?'

Ash exhaled smoke in a long steady stream. 'Not quite. It seems the ghost is haunting the ghost.'

'I'm not with you on that.'

Ash smiled grimly. 'Ellen Preddle believes that the ghost of the father is terrorizing the ghost of the son.'

15

HE RESTAURANT ROOM of the Black Boar Inn was not very crowded that evening. In fact, apart from David Ash, who was waiting for the arrival of Grace Lockwood, there were only two other diners. This couple, who perhaps were in their sixties, were celebrating their wedding anniversary, the man having ordered a bottle of the inn's best champagne and invited the landlord's wife, who also appeared to be the restaurant's *maître d'*, to join him in a toast to his long marriage. Rosemary Ginty happily obliged, but Ash was aware that even when she raised her glass to the couple she was surreptitiously looking in his direction.

The dining room, with its soft wall lights, heavily beamed ceiling and inglenook fireplace, had a comfortably intimate ambience; the round tables were small, designed so that diners sat close to each other, and short candles on tiny beds of flowers glowed at their centres. Most of the leaded windows overlooked the inn's rear garden and courtyard, and as the twilight dimmed towards darkness outside lights came into play, sending starlings nested in the trees and eaves of the building itself screeching and fluttering through the air.

Preoccupied with the frantic though brief display, Ash suddenly became aware of someone standing by the table. He turned from the window and looked up at the plump, attractive face of the landlord's wife. Her expression of frank scrutiny quickly changed to one of courteous interest.

'Didn't mean to startle you, Mr Ash.' Her smile was pleasant enough, but hardly masked the unease in her eyes. 'I wondered if you'd like another drink from the bar while you're waiting.' Her hands were clasped in front of a stomach that was protesting against the corset she wore beneath her dark green dress. The candleglow lent warm highlights to the short double string of pearls she wore and deepened her lipstick to crimson.

'Another vodka would be fine.'

'Just ice, isn't it?'

'No, it's just vodka.'

'Oh yes. By the way, Mr Ginty wondered if you'd decided how long you'll be staying with us yet.'

Ash guessed that the landlord hadn't wondered any such thing and that his wife was merely trying to strike up a conversation. Maybe she was just curious because he was a stranger; or maybe the villagers already suspected why he was there in Sleath. He'd visited three locals since his arrival, so word might have got around.

'Have you, Mr Ash?'

'Uh, sorry. I was miles away. No, I haven't, Mrs Ginty. As I told your husband, it could be a couple of days, it might be a week.'

'I see. You're interested in this area, are you?' Her smile was a little too fixed, as she patted her elaborately coiffured blonde (dyed) hair.

'It's a lovely village.'

She waited, but he only returned her smile.

'Yes,' she said on realizing he was not going to give a direct answer to her question. 'Yes, Sleath is beautiful. And very quiet, Mr Ash. Well, I expect your company will be here soon, so I'll get that drink for you.'

'Thank you,' he said and looked out of the window again when she left the table.

The starlings had settled once more, probably for the night

now, and the lawns and flowerbeds were bathed in a bright blaze from the outdoor lights. The shadows, however, had deepened.

As he waited for Grace Lockwood, Ash reflected on his interview with the farmer earlier. Sam Gunstone's land backed onto the village, but it had taken a good five minutes along a winding road in Grace's car to reach the farmhouse. Gunstone, a rotund, grizzled man in his sixties whose red, veined face reflected a lifetime of open air and inclement weather, had little patience for the investigator's questions, even when Grace explained the reason for their visit. *Bollocks*, had been Gunstone's response. *All bollocks and cow dung. Whoever 'eard of ghostie 'aystacks? No such thing.* Ash reminded him that it was he, Gunstone, who had observed it. *I saw somethin,* the farmer had retorted, *but tweren't no bloody ghost thing. Memry playin tricks, that was all it was, one o'them whatcher-me-callits? – dega views. Unnerstand what I'm sayin?*

Ash certainly understood. Gunstone was a pragmatic, no-nonsense man of the soil, who might accept ancient myths and legends, but would never believe in first-hand phenomena. What was it the vicar had said? A healthy mind will always seek a rationale. It seemed that time had given the farmer second thoughts, even though his earlier account to Reverend Lockwood had been quite vivid.

He turned from the window and folded his arms on the table, gazing down into his empty vodka glass, and wondering why this sudden plethora of sightings around this particular area.

Something made him look up from the glass towards the door that led to the bar, the restaurant's only entrance. Three seconds later Grace Lockwood walked into the dining room.

Ash rose from the table to greet her and she came towards him, unsmiling. She wore a fine silk print dress with long thin sleeves, the dominant colour maroon, and this evening her hair was loose and curling inwards around her shoulders. The gash on her forehead was faint under a layer of make-up, but it served to remind Ash of the incident in Ellen Preddle's kitchen that afternoon when, according to Grace, a saucer had skimmed across the room at her from a high shelf with no apparent cause. Because of the bereaved mother's near-hysterical state at the time, Ash had been unable to investigate properly, but now he wondered if poltergeist activity might also be involved in these hauntings.

'David, I just had the strangest feeling.'

He pulled out a chair for her, and her expression remained serious as she sat down. She watched him take his own seat.

'It was like today at the church,' she said, 'a few moments before we actually met.'

'I know,' he told her, placing a hand over hers as if to reassure her that everything was perfectly all right. 'I felt it too.'

She regarded him quizzically.

'Almost like a small and painless electric shock, right? I had the same sensation. I knew you were here before you came through the door.'

'Yes, that was it.' She leaned closer when he took his hand away, shaking her head slowly. 'I don't understand what's happening.'

'Grace, have you ever had any psychic experiences before?'

She sat straight again, startled by the question. 'I don't think so. Perhaps little things, like knowing who was at the other end of the telephone before I'd answered it. But isn't that quite common?'

'It's not *that* common, but it happens. Often it's only logical guesswork – you were expecting a call from someone in particular, or no one else would phone at that time – but sometimes it can be a genuine sensing. Anything else, any other instances?'

She thought for a moment. 'I don't think – wait a minute: when I was a child my parents took me to Canterbury Cathedral. We went for a walk in the town afterwards and somehow – don't ask me how, I can't remember – we got separated. My mother and father were frantic when they couldn't find me after an hour's searching, but then *I* found *them*. I was only seven years old and didn't know Canterbury at all, but I'm certain I wasn't frightened wandering about alone. In fact, I was enjoying myself looking at all the shops and when I'd had enough I simply went to a street corner where I knew – I really knew, I remember that – my parents would be. They were there talking to a policeman and I just walked up and slipped my hand into my mother's as if nothing had happened.'

'You're sure you didn't come upon them by accident? It was a long time ago.'

'It's funny, but I still recall knowing exactly where my parents were the moment I decided I'd had enough for the day. I suppose in all those years I've never really considered it might have been through some kind of psychic ability. Certainly nothing like it has happened since.'

'It could have been nothing more than natural instinct – all kids possess a certain amount of that. But then we have to ask ourselves, exactly what we mean by "instinct".'

'Good evening, Grace.'

They both looked up in surprise at the landlord's wife, who stood over them, a small tumbler in her hand.

'Hello, Rosemary,' Grace said as the glass was placed beside the empty one in front of Ash.

'Your vodka, Mr Ash.' Rosemary Ginty took the empty glass away. 'Would you like an *apéritif* too, Grace? Oh dear, have you hurt yourself?'

Grace touched her forehead lightly as though she had just remembered the wound there. 'Nothing serious. Falling crockery, that's all.'

Rosemary rolled her eyes in mock resignation. 'I have my clumsy days too, dear. More than once Tom's banned me from the kitchen, says I'm breaking all the profits.'

Grace dutifully smiled back at her. 'I think I'll just have some of your house wine. Dry-white isn't it?'

'Not too dry, but dry enough.' She looked from face to face as if expecting to join in the conversation, but when neither Grace nor Ash offered encouragement she said, 'Right, why don't you look at the menu while I bring your wine?' She turned away, stopping to enquire how her other guests were 'getting along' before disappearing into the bar next door.

'It could be that you're susceptible to certain mental energies,' Ash said now that the landlady was out of earshot.

'What does that mean?' There was a half-smile on Grace's face.

'You're in tune with certain minds.'

'Yours, for instance?'

'It's possible. You might be a latent psychic.'

She gave a short laugh. 'I've heard of latent homosexuals, but latent psychics? I doubt it very much.'

'People tend to resist such ideas.'

She was puzzled by the conviction in his voice. 'Why should they do that?'

He shrugged. 'They have their reasons, even if they're not aware of them themselves at the time.'

'You've dealt with such people?'

His smile was humourless. 'You could say that. How's the Reverend this evening, by the way?'

She was aware of the digression, but decided not to press him further. There was something enigmatic about this man and she concluded that direct questions would only be met by guarded responses if they concerned anything too personal to him. Perhaps it was merely his professionalism – he was here to conduct an investigation on her father's behalf and self-revelation was not part of that brief. Odd how close she felt to him though, despite only having met him for the first time that day. Could it be part of this psychic thing he'd mentioned? Could their minds somehow be 'in tune', was that what he was getting at? She pushed the thoughts aside for the moment.

'Father hasn't been well for some time,' she said. 'His health seems to have deteriorated rapidly over the past year or so – even before Mother passed away, in fact. She used to write and tell me how worried she was about him. Ironic that she should be the one to . . .' She stopped, shaking her head in

127

sadness. 'Naturally her death made him worse, and now these
. . . these hauntings. He's become quite distressed by them.'
Again she leaned forward, her hands clasped together on the
edge of the table. 'David, what *is* happening here in Sleath?'

Before he had a chance to answer, the landlord's wife placed
a glass of wine in front of Grace. 'That's what we'd all like to
know, my dear,' she said, not bothering to lower her voice.
The elderly couple at the table across the room looked up with
interest. 'There's all this silly talk about ghosts and things,
everyone's walking about with long faces, and it's hard to have
a civil conversation with anyone these days.' She waved a
despairing hand around the room. 'You can see for yourself how
trade has suffered. Normally the restaurant would be almost full
on a lovely evening like this. And then there's that awful
business this afternoon.'

Her neck stiffened and she gave a little shake of her head.
'Can you imagine it, Grace? Ralph Cauldwell nearly bludgeoning
that poor boy to death.'

'My father is with Danny Marsh's mother right now, although
I don't know what comfort he can offer her. Do the police know
why Cauldwell did such a terrible thing?'

Now Rosemary Ginty did lower her voice as she leaned
forward conspiratorially. 'I heard young Danny did something
to Cauldwell's daughter. That's why Ruth isn't here at work
this evening.'

'What do you mean, Rosemary?' asked Grace. 'What exactly
did he do?'

'You know, Grace, no need to spell it out. I always thought
the boy was harmless enough – a bit dim, p'raps, but no real
bad in him. Never thought he'd do anything like that.'

'He tried to rape her?' Ash said helpfully.

Rosemary Ginty gave him a stiff sideways look. 'I'm told
that's what he'll be charged with – if he ever recovers, that
is.'

'How bad is he?' asked Grace.

'Bad as you can get with your skull bashed in.' She

128

shuddered, her clasped hands squirming against her plump stomach. 'Cauldwell scraped off most of the boy's face with one of those plane things, which hardly helped matters. Dear God, it might be a blessing if Danny does pass away now he's got no face to speak of and a brain that's probably mashed potatoes. Well then, have you had a chance to look at the menu yet?'

He had been wrong, Ash realized as he sipped the armagnac. Grace Lockwood was a beautiful woman. Maybe it was the candleglow, the wine, the brandy, maybe the flaws – and they had been few – had disappeared with familiarity. Familiarity? He'd known her for less than a day. What was going on here, Ash, what the hell was going on? Her eyes, watching him now, were soft in the low light, yet they seemed to penetrate his own as if seeking more knowledge of him than he was prepared to offer. She held her coffee cup in slender fingers and smiled across the table at him.

'You're lost in thought,' she said, and added meaningfully but with good humour, 'again.'

He apologized, returning the smile. 'There are so many different aspects to this case it's difficult to know what to focus on.'

'Oh, *that's* what you were thinking about.'

His smile broadened to a grin. 'Not really. I was wondering why you weren't married.'

If she was taken aback, she disguised it well. 'What makes you think I haven't been?'

'No rings. In fact, no jewellery at all, not even a bracelet. Husbands or boyfriends usually provide such things at some stage.'

'I've never enjoyed those kinds of ornaments.'

'Husbands or boyfriends?'

Her laughter pleased him.

'Jewellery, idiot,' she said. 'Unless it's several hundred years old, of course. As for the other two, well, I've had several of some and none of the other kind. I'll leave you to decide which.'

'I assume divorce would be frowned upon in a clergyman's family.'

'Frowned upon, but not unheard of. Anyway, that would be entirely up to me and my husband – if I'd ever had one. My father's occupation would play no part in the decision.'

'You're not religious?'

'Not in the sense you mean. I have my beliefs, but I'm not sure I have my religion. How about you? Let me guess – I'd say you were an atheist, through and through.'

'What makes you think that?'

'Oh, your cynicism mainly.'

'It's that obvious so soon?'

'You have an air of cynicism about you, David. Is that suitable for your particular job?'

'It can be an advantage.'

'But haven't you investigated cases where there can be no doubt that spirits, ghosts, poltergeists – whatever you care to call them – are involved? Surely in all your years as a psychic investigator you've met with genuine instances of supernatural forces at work? Doesn't that prove to you that there is life after death in some form or other? David?'

He was avoiding her gaze, looking down into his brandy glass. Grace noticed his shoulders had hunched slightly as though he had literally drawn into himself.

Concerned, she asked, 'Have I said something wrong?'

He lifted the glass and took a long sip. 'D'you mind if I smoke?' he said at last.

'Of course not. Won't you tell me what's wrong, though?' She shook her head when he proffered the pack, then waited for him to light a cigarette for himself. 'There is something wrong, isn't there?' she said when the ritual was completed. 'I sensed it about you the moment we met.'

'Your psychic ability,' he said flatly.

'Good old-fashioned woman's intuition,' she insisted.

'Ah, that.'

'You know, David, even your eyes look troubled.'

'And I thought they were soulful.' He pulled the ashtray closer and tapped the cigarette unnecessarily against the rim. 'We were talking about you, Grace.'

'All right. I've never been married, although I nearly got around to it a long time ago.'

'Someone local.'

'It doesn't matter. I also had a close relationship in Paris, but we broke up a few months before I returned to England. It was inevitable because he already had a wife. Now tell me about you.'

He exhaled smoke, his mind a confusion of thoughts, as well as reservations. He realized that for the first time he wanted to tell someone the full story. Of the house called Edbrook, and the family that had lived there. Of the two brothers and their sister. Beautiful . . . insane . . . Christina. God, he hadn't even told Kate McCarrick the whole story, not even in the intimacy of a bedroom, yet here he was, ready – desperate – to tell everything to this woman whom he'd only met that morning.

'Grace,' he said hesitantly. 'Do you, yourself, truly believe in ghosts?'

'You're here at my instigation, David.'

'That doesn't mean you believe what's been seen here in Sleath are ghosts. You might feel they're nothing more than mental imagery.'

'But my father, Ellen Preddle –'

'Forget what they think they saw. Do *you* believe in ghosts?'

She was startled by the intensity of the question. 'I . . . I'm not sure.' She took time to consider and all the while Ash watched her as if her answer was terribly important to him. 'Yes,' she said eventually. 'Yes, I do. I'm not particularly religious in the sense of church doctrine and ceremony, as I mentioned before, but I do believe there has to be something more than just this existence. What we do in this life has to

131

have some meaning, some relevance. I think that relevance comes afterwards, when we die. Does that answer your question?'

'Not absolutely.'

She searched for the words to voice her thoughts. 'My guess is that some part of us goes on after we die. Perhaps it's our minds, our consciousness – our psyche, I suppose you'd say. Whatever it is, it continues to exist in its own form and, who knows, perhaps it can return to this world in an image of its former self if the circumstances are right, or the will is there. It could be that it's we, ourselves, who give them that image, our own minds shaping them into something we can understand.'

He seemed to relax just a little.

'That's a reasonable hypothesis,' he said. 'Simple, but as good as any I've heard.'

'And no doubt you've heard many.'

He nodded. 'But it still doesn't explain why they come back.'

'I suppose not. There has to be a reason, doesn't there? It can't always be some freakish metaphysical accident, can it?'

'I don't believe so. I'm sure there's always a purpose.'

'So tell me why you sought my view. It seemed to be an important question to you.'

He looked away from her as if he had found a sudden interest in the garden beyond the windows. The lights outside seemed brighter, the night sky blacker.

Grace studied his profile, not for the first time that day. She was right about his eyes – they did seem to carry the troubles of the world in them. His nose was strong, as was his jaw, and although he wore a tie tonight he still appeared slightly dishevelled. Even his dark hair was tousled, as though a comb had only brought a brief order. At least he had bothered to shave before coming down to dinner, although the shadowy tone of his chin suggested the stubble was already in rebellion. She wondered about the small, thin scar on his cheekbone.

Without turning back to her, he said, 'I was haunted myself a few years ago.'

She wasn't sure how to react, for she was aware that the words had not come easily to him. But she wanted to know what troubled him, she wanted to share his thoughts, and so she said, 'Tell me, David. Please tell me.'

He turned in the chair to face her once more. 'I'm not sure.'

'You're not sure of me?'

He shook his head. 'Myself. You might think I'm mad.'

She gestured with her hand. 'After all we've told you about what's gone on here in Sleath? I was worried that you might think *we* were all mad.'

'It's . . . it's complex.'

'I'm in no hurry to go anywhere.'

Again he took his time, drawing on the cigarette, then finishing the armagnac. On this occasion, Grace realized, it was to compose himself rather than evade a question.

'Three years ago,' he said finally, 'I was sent by the Institute to a house called Edbrook. It was a huge, neglected place in its own grounds and four people lived there, two brothers, their younger sister, and an elderly nanny who took care of them all, as well as the house itself. They claimed they were being haunted by the ghost of a girl.'

He played with his empty glass, tilting it towards himself as though searching for non-existent brandy.

'And were they?' Grace prompted gently. She did not like his grin at all.

'Oh yeah, Edbrook was haunted. But there was a joke to it all.'

'A joke? They were trying to trick you?'

'Kind of. I had a reputation for proving hauntings were no more than geological disturbances, draughts, timber retraction – all manner of normal, physical things. My record was so good I was generally despised by the spirit industry.'

'But not by the Psychical Research Institute, obviously.'

'Oh, there are plenty of insiders who detest me. But it's the outsiders – the mediums, clairvoyants, and even some faith healers – who hate me most. They feel I'm undermining their credibility. Which I am.'

'And these people at Edbrook – they were trying to humiliate you in some way?'

Neither did she like his laugh.

'Yeah, that was about it. They were trying to humiliate me.'

'And did they succeed?'

He nodded slowly, his shoulders hunched again. 'They did more than that. In the three days and nights I was there they showed me the truth.'

'You mean they had you convinced there really was a haunting, and then they showed you how they'd tricked you?'

It was quiet in the dining room. The elderly couple who had been celebrating earlier had left, and the landlord's wife was nowhere to be seen.

When he spoke it was almost a whisper, and Grace had to lean forward to catch his words. 'They frightened me. God, they terrified me. And the greatest joke of all, I let myself fall in love with the girl, the sister.'

'After just three days?' she asked softly.

'The first moment I set eyes on her, I think.'

'She let you down.'

'She mocked me, Grace.'

Grace frowned. Ash hadn't struck her as the kind of man who would allow himself to be mocked.

'They were all laughing at me. Christina, her brothers, Robert and Simon. Even the nanny knew what was going on. I spent three days and nights at that place without suspecting what was going on, why they had brought me there.'

'You're sure it was you they were trying to dupe? I mean, couldn't it have been the Institute itself they were hoping to deceive?'

'No, it was me they wanted. I was their chosen victim.'

'But why? It doesn't make sense for anyone to go to such lengths just to make a fool of you.'

'I told you it was complex. In the end, you see, they did convince me there were such things as ghosts.'

'You actually saw these things? You recorded them?'

'No, I had no evidence. That's why I couldn't even tell the Institute the whole story. They'd have had me locked away.'

He looked at her steadily and she was disturbed by the darkness in his eyes, a deep depression that might have emanated from his very soul.

He spoke again, his words measured, almost angry. *'They* were the ghosts, you see. Every person in that God-forsaken house, save for the nanny, who was completely mad, was a ghost.'

He was a strange man, Grace reflected as they crossed the road to her car. How seriously should she take his story of ghostly games in mysterious houses? It all sounded so ludicrous. And yet . . . and yet there was something about David Ash that made his story credible. Or perhaps the truth was there was something about him that made *her* want to believe. He was sombre, certainly, and his cynicism created its own reserve; yet there was humour there, too, albeit of a world-weary kind. Perhaps it was the combination, or even the dichotomy, of moods that made him . . . interesting. Although his slightly crumpled appearance gave him an air of casualness, his dark, brooding eyes sometimes revealed an intensity that was almost unnerving. And then there was this odd feeling between them, this *knowing*. She couldn't read his mind, couldn't perceive his thoughts, but somehow there was an awareness of each other that should have come from understanding; yet she did not understand this man at all. She was confused, and the peculiar sensation that had struck her twice that day – it had been as though mild lightning had discharged itself into her body and mind just moments before she had met him – served to confuse her even more. A psychic experience, David had

135

begun to suggest before Rosemary Ginty had interrupted them. Could that be possible? Was that the link between them? She dismissed the notion, but it continued to trouble her.

They reached the car and she delved into her handbag for her keys.

'I'll need to, uh, talk to you again tomorrow,' Ash said.

'Sorry, what?' She drew out the keyring and looked up at him.

'I need you to tell me more about Sleath itself. The village's history, that kind of thing. Background stuff.'

'Will it help?'

He shrugged. 'It might. It's somewhere to start.'

'I have to be at the community hall first thing, but I can be back at the lodge by ten thirty.'

'That's fine.'

He watched her put the key into the lock. 'Grace,' he said. 'Your father. How well is he mentally?'

She straightened and stared at him, shocked by the question. Light from the windows of the Black Boar Inn lit one side of her face and cast the other side in deep shadow. Somewhere in the distance, perhaps up at the church itself, a barn owl screeched. 'Why do you ask that?'

'He seemed more than just physically unwell when I spoke to him this afternoon. Look, I don't mean to offend, but he was a nervous wreck. Or at least, close to being one.'

It was difficult to repress her anger. 'His village is being haunted. He's frightened.'

'Ah.'

It was a small sound and Grace wondered at its implication.

'I told you, David, we're all frightened. It's as if we're waiting for something to happen, something terrible.'

He stepped a little closer and held her arm. 'That might be some form of collective hysteria, Grace. I've witnessed it before.'

'Hysteria? You think it's that simple?'

'No, there's nothing simple about it. But when one person

136

experiences, or imagines they've experienced, a supernatural occurrence, the impression can be so strong in his or her mind that it's passed on to another, and then in turn to another.'

'Like some metaphysical virus?'

He didn't blame her for the scorn in her voice. 'No one knows how it starts, although there have been many studies on the phenomenon. Mass fainting fits among girls in the same school, crowds witnessing miracles – statues weeping or bleeding, levitation – at holy places, even spontaneous riots. It seems the mind can pass on an impulse, sometimes instantaneously, from one person to another, so that a whole body of people is affected.'

'And you believe this could be happening in Sleath?' she said incredulously.

'It's a possibility, although the form is different here. It's spreading more slowly, for a start. And those who've seen these so-called ghosts so far have suffered a trauma of some kind, which means their minds might be susceptible. Ellen Preddle lost both her son and her husband, Sam Gunstone saw George Preddle burn. Ruth Cauldwell claims she saw the ghost of a man who molested her when she was a child.'

'But my father . . .'

'I think he's still in mourning for your mother. And he was alone with Ellen Preddle when he saw her dead son. Her thoughts could have been so strong your father's own mind picked them up.'

Grace touched the small wound on her forehead. 'Then was this in my mind also?' Her anger was still there, but it remained controlled.

'Ellen Preddle was agitated. She was afraid and angry and sometimes, with a particular person, those emotions can summon their own forces. The Institute's investigated a few hundred cases of alleged poltergeist hauntings and most of them have turned out to be nothing more than released energies from pubescent girls.'

'You can hardly put Ellen in that category.'

'Of course not, but the principle stands. The mind has enormous powers, Grace, powers that we still can't comprehend.'

'You don't believe Sleath is being haunted.' It was a flat, almost dispirited, statement.

'I didn't say that. It's too soon to make any kind of judgement.'

'Then what happens now?'

'I continue with my investigation. And we wait.'

Her eyes asked the question.

'We wait,' he said, 'for something else to happen.'

16

OLDING THE BRIGHT flower-patterned curtain to one side, the gamekeeper peered out into the cloudy night.

'The buggers'll be back all right,' he said in a growl that made his wife look up from her sewing.

'Surely not, Jack, not two nights running,' she said, more in hope than conviction.

He let the curtain fall and turned from the window. 'They're that stupid, Maddy. Because they got away with a good catch las' night they think their luck's in. Take m'word forrit, they'll be back agen tonight.'

'Lenny Grover and his cronies?'

'You can bank on it.' Jack Buckler went out into the hallway and took down a pair of aged but strong walking boots from a shelf. When he carried them back into the little sitting room the Airedale, which had been sprawled before the hearth just as if the winter fire still roared there, snapped its head up. As soon as the dog saw the old boots in its master's hands it was on its feet, excited mewling sounds coming from its throat.

'Now, Gaffer, don't you be gettin into a lather,' the keeper warned the dog. He grinned when the Airedale trotted over to him, its dark eyes expectant, the pink sliver of its tongue poking between yellow teeth. 'All right, boy, we'll see what we can root out tonight, shall we?'

Gaffer quickly went through to the hallway to wait by the front door, its breathing already coming in sharp pants. Jack Buckler sat on the edge of an armchair and kicked off his slippers. He grunted as he leaned over to pull on the heavy-duty boots.

'Don't get mud on my rug, mind,' his wife scolded, although the anxiety she could barely conceal was for her husband and not the rug in question.

'Cleaned 'em earlier this evenin, an' well you know it,' he retorted good-humouredly.

'Yes, well, sometimes you forget, Jack Buckler.' Her tone softened. 'Why don't you leave it tonight, Jack? Beardsmore won't be paying you more for being out in the middle of the night.'

'Come on, Maddy, you know it's m'job to keep them bloody mouchers away. They got a good bag las' night an' they'll be after more tonight. It's happened in the past with that lot an' it'll happen agen, so I can't be takin no chances, not with the rollickin I got from the gov'nor today. Them buggers is doin too much damage. 'Sides, Beardsmore don't like strangers wanderin about his land, whatever the reason. Y'know how private he is.'

Maddy laid her sewing aside and came over to his chair, kneeling there on the rug before him. She studied her husband's face and, with a quiet sadness, realized his full sixty-three years showed in his tired old eyes, the lines around them the figurations of the sorrows and laughter of his good, God-fearing life. This gentle, kind man, while hardened to nature's cruel but pragmatic ways, cared too much for the birds and animals in his charge, and sometimes she had to coax him from a duty that took no account of age and decline.

'Call me a silly old woman, but I don't feel right about you being out there tonight, Jack. There's a funny sort of chill in my bones.'

'Don't talk daft, Maddy. Tonight's no different from las' night and the night before that, an' you can be sure there'll be those about up to no good. Chill in your bones, indeed.' He gave her cheek a tweak with thumb and finger. 'Now you don't expect me to be tucked up in bed when there's those blamed dim-witted mouchers on the prowl, do you? S'more than me job's worth, an' well you know it.'

'I know there's no arguing with you, you stubborn old fool.' She huffed at his dry chuckle and began lacing his boots for him. 'You promise me you'll be careful, that's all I ask.'

His laughter faded and he stared at the top of Maddy's head. So she felt it too. There *was* a queerness about the place lately and it was something bright days and balmy nights couldn't shift. Even the birds and the animals in the woods had the jitters. Like . . . like all those years ago, when he was a mere stripling, when his father had shown him the poachers' ways. Lord in Heaven, he hadn't thought about those days in a long time and he didn't want to think about them now. In Sleath every generation had known its own tragedy, some worse than others. Was it time again? He shivered and Maddy looked up anxiously.

'Caught yer bloomin chill,' he said jokily. 'Temperature's dropped, I think. I'll need a coat.'

His wife stood, a breath escaping her with the effort. She smoothed the wrinkles in her skirt. 'I'll fetch your jacket,' she said, disappearing into the hallway. 'Your cap, too,' he heard her call back. 'Might rain again later, like it did this morning.'

Gaffer paced in small circles while the keeper joined his wife in the hallway, its short tail erect and shining eyes glancing from its master to the door.

'Calm down, Gaffer,' Buckler said in a gruff voice. 'Don't want you tearin through the bushes scarin off the villains, do we?'

The dog immediately settled, aware it was work they were up to, not play.

Maddy helped her husband on with his jacket and he took a long Mag-lite torch from the boot shelf and slipped it into one of the deep pockets. He reached up again for a black object that resembled a complicated stunted telescope and this he dropped into his other pocket. Maddy handed him his cap and he pulled it down firmly over his grey-white hair.

'You get yerself off t'bed, girl,' he said to his wife. 'No sense in you waitin up half the night.'

'Do you think I'd be witless enough to sit here waiting for you while you're out playing cowboys and Indians? I'll be nice and snug in our lovely soft bed, m'lad. You just be quiet when you get back and don't be waking me up, d'you hear?'

She might be in bed, but she'd be lying there in the darkness, ears straining for his footsteps on the path. And she wouldn't close her eyes until she heard the key in the door and his muffled tones settling Gaffer down for what was left of the night. She knew this, and so did the keeper.

They were too familiar with each other for parting kisses, and if he had bent down to brush her downy cheek with his dry old lips, she would know that he, too, shared her unease. Instead he touched the rim of his flat cap in mock salute before lifting the door latch.

As he opened the door, she said, 'Do you want me to call anyone? Sergeant Pimlett might send someone over to give you a hand.'

The nearest police station was two villages and a town away, but sometimes the duty sergeant was willing to send a patrol car over if a catch was fairly certain. Poachers these days were not a priority for the hard-pressed county police force. 'Don't want to risk wastin their time, love. Be different if I knew for sure the mouchers will be out tonight, but I don't want to lose the goodwill of the constabulary by bringin 'em over on a wild-goose chase.'

With that he slipped into the night, Gaffer already up the garden path way ahead of him. Maddy waited until the door had closed behind him before making a tiny, from-the-wrist, Sign of the Cross over her heart. *Let him be all right, dear Lord,* was her thought-prayer. *Don't let anything happen to my Jack.* She went back into the sitting room and picked up her sewing once more. But the needle was motionless in her hand and her eyes were closed for a long time.

Gaffer bounded up to the Land-Rover parked outside the open garden gate and waited there for its master to catch up. Jack Buckler followed at a more leisurely pace, his countenance grim now that he was outside the gamekeeper's cottage. Maddy really was worried for him: never in her life before had she suggested calling in the police to give him a hand. Certainly the night patrol enjoyed the game – it was a pleasant relief from driving around concrete estates and hauling in yobs and drunks. Some of them even liked acting as beaters on daytime shoots when they were off duty – wages were poor, but fresh air, lively action and a good toddy afterwards brought its own reward and besides, it gave them the opportunity to acquaint themselves with the more rural areas of their extensive patch. But no, as a rule Maddy always left that kind of decision to him; he knew his business and she knew her place. So what had got into her tonight? Come to that, what had got into him? He'd been fidgety all evening.

He passed through the gate and pulled open the Land-Rover's door. Gaffer instantly sprung up and over onto the passenger seat, its short wiry coat brushing against his hand like a tough-bristled brush on the way. Buckler climbed in after it.

'Right then, me beauty, let's see what we can snare on this gloomy ol' night, shall we?'

Gaffer gave one thump of its short tail against the seat in response, and the keeper started the engine and switched on his lights.

He drove down the long rutted lane, heading through the woods towards an area of coverts that he knew were likely to attract the poachers, his headlights on half-beam for the moment. The hefty Mag-lite in his pocket was reassuring, although there were other gamekeepers who carried pick-axe handles for protection; worse still, there were *others* who took .440 shotguns on night patrols. That wasn't his way, and besides, he was only dealing with semi-professionals here, not an organized gang. Lenny Grover was a nasty piece of work, all right, but he was no hard man, not really. A good 'boo!' in the dark would send him scuttling for cover, as it would his drinking and poaching pal, Dennis Crick. The pair of them would be off like terrified rabbits once they knew a keeper was about. Nevertheless, no matter that neither man had any spunk, what they did have between them was garden guns – the 9mm Flobert, .360 shotgun, No 3 bore, to be precise – fitted with home-made silencers. Buckler knew this to be a fact because he, himself, had collected the empty cartridge cases from their previous night's escapade that very morning (and he knew the silencers were home-made because Grover and Crick would never spend good money on such an accessory when it could so easily and cheaply be made in their own garden shed or garage). Oddly enough, it was the third member of this nasty little gang – and he was quite aware there were three of them – that angered him the most, for this one's weapon, as well as being inefficient, was particularly vicious.

It was obvious he was an amateur, no doubt brought along by the other two for his usefulness as a carrier rather than his skill as a poacher. Young Mickey Dunn was the prime candidate, and his odious weapon was the crossbow. One of the worst situations in a gamekeeper's book was to come upon a bird or animal that had been mortally wounded by a quarrel and had managed to escape the hunter by dragging itself off into cover where it would die a pitiful and lingering death. It was at such moments that Jack Buckley would have cheerfully turned that nasty weapon on its sadistic owner. Or shot his kneecaps off with his own shotgun. Or bashed his head in with a pick-axe handle. Which was why he never carried such weapons on occasions like this. No, the Mag-lite was long and sturdy enough to use for threat or defence; no need for anything that might do permanent damage.

Thin branches whipped across the Land-Rover's windscreen as the vehicle lumbered down the narrowing track. Gaffer rocked from side to side, enjoying the motion, loving the thrill of this midnight excursion. The keeper kept the speed down, the engine revs soft, his still keen eyes alert to everything around him, both side windows kept open for any alien sounds that might come his way. An assistant would have been useful on a night like this, someone who could approach from a different direction so that the mouchers could be caught between them, but the lord and master, the magazine magnate who now owned the majority of the Lockwood Estate, had dismissed the underkeeper as soon as he had arrived on the scene twenty-odd years ago. One man was enough to look after the game on his land, Beardsmore had decreed and he'd gone on to sack half the ground staff as well. Well, so be it. If he was willing to lose a large portion of his game to poachers, then it was his own damn fault. Except, of course, it would be the gamekeeper who copped the blame.

He slowed the Land-Rover to walking pace and switched to sidelights only, trusting his own knowledge of the way ahead – plus his keeper's eyes, which were keener at night than the average person's – to get him to his destination. Soon he switched off even the sidelights.

Now the vehicle lurched along at snail's pace and eventually it stopped altogether. Buckler turned off the engine and quietly opened the door. Gaffer moved over to the driver's seat the moment its master climbed out and it waited there until the command came.

Buckler looked in every direction, sniffing the air as if for alien smells; he was absorbing everything around him, listening for sounds, watching for the slightest movement, and testing the breeze for the smell of cordite. On certain nights, when the wind was gentle and from the right direction, he might even detect the coppery odour of animals' blood. Tonight there appeared to be nothing unusual: no tiny snap of twigs as someone crept through the undergrowth, no sharp cry of a pheasant disturbed from its roost, no human murmurings as careless mouchers searched for prey. Even so, he sensed something was amiss: something was not right about the very night itself and every bone in his body and every instinct he'd acquired told him the truth of it. What was more, the quiet, dragging whine from deep inside Gaffer's throat told him the dog felt it too.

'All right, boy, jus' keep it down,' he ordered in a hushed voice. 'We don't want to be warnin 'em off, do we? Oh no, this time we'll ketch the buggers, jus' see if we don't. Can't have 'em slaughterin our friends willy-nilly, can we, boy?' His whispers were to reassure the dog, the soft tones to keep it calm. His voice still low, he instructed Gaffer to leave the vehicle and it immediately jumped down onto the track. It waited by its master's side for further instructions.

Buckler slipped the Land-Rover's keys into his pocket, making sure they did not clink together – such sounds would be amplified in the still night air. It was unlikely, but the intruders might just have been stupid enough to park their own vehicle further up the track and if so, the Land-Rover would block their way. More probably their pick-up would be left somewhere in one of the lanes that crossed the estate, the poachers travelling by foot to the covert they had in mind for that night's business.

Buckler used the Mag-lite to find a suitable path through the woods, always taking care to keep the beam low to the ground. The path he found would have been missed by anyone else, but it was clear enough to him.

'Come on then, Gaffer old boy, let's find 'em before they do too much damage.'

The dog obediently trotted ahead, quickly disappearing into the overgrown path its master's torch had found for them, but keeping well within whispering distance, alert for any further instructions. It sniffed earth and air as it went.

Buckler followed as noiselessly as the dog itself, using the swift-moving animal as a guide. Many keepers preferred Alsatians, Dobermans, or even Rottweilers – in the old days, Mastiffs were favourite – but he preferred the Airedale above all others.

Gaffer was both powerful and intelligent, and most of all it was reliable. It was a good 'sniffer' too, and would seek out injured game without harming a hair or feather on its head. Nor would it ever back down: on more than one occasion a poacher had threatened Gaffer with gun or club, but the dog had never retreated, stalking its man until the villain had either run for his life or handed his weapon over to Buckler. Such an animal would be hard to replace and he dreaded the day when Gaffer would be too old for the job. Oh, a young dog could be trained right enough, but it took time and a great deal of patience and somehow the new always seemed a little less than the old. Still, when that time came Gaffer would live out the rest of its days lolling about the house and going on short runs that wouldn't tire its creaky old bones too much. But that was a long stretch off, wasn't it, boy? Plenny of life left in you.

As if sensing its master's thoughts, Gaffer looked over its shoulder and waited for the keeper to catch up.

Buckler knelt beside the dog and laid a hand against its thick neck. 'Can you smell 'em yet, Gaffer?' he whispered. 'We on the right patch? There's one or two spinneys we can try later if we're wrong, but I've a hunch we're on the right track. What say you, boy?'

A low rumble in its throat was the Airedale's answer. Buckler felt Gaffer stiffen, and its head locked as if it were listening to something far off.

'Okay, Gaffer, let's get on. I think their luck's run out tonight.'

The dog sprung forward and Buckler lumbered to his feet, although only to a crouch. He kept the torch beam even lower and aimed no more than two feet ahead of him. At the slightest sound the Mag-lite would instantly be switched off.

He trod through the dark woodland at a steady speed, his dog just ahead of him, it, too, moving silently and easily.

*   *   *

147

Lenny Grover took a back-handed swipe at Mickey Dunn, his fingers making hard enough contact with the younger man's shoulders to draw a sharp yelp.

'Jus' keep off me bloody arse with that stupid thing,' Grover hissed.

'Weren't nowhere near you,' Mickey protested, almost tripping over a hidden tree root in his effort to keep clear of Grover's reach. He held the crossbow behind him as if afraid it would be snatched away.

'Keep it quiet, you two,' the third man whispered fiercely from the front. *'If Buckler's around we'll be forrit.'*

Grover pulled down the peak of his baseball cap in agitation. 'That bloody old fool 'asn't got a clue. He'll be somewhere on the other side of the estate tonight.'

'Whadya mean?' said Dennis Crick. 'He's bound to know we was 'ere las' night.'

''Xactly so,' agreed Grover, grinning in the darkness. 'An' he'll think we won't come back to the same place twice.' His voice became scornful. 'But thanks to that prat behind us there's plenny more to be bagged 'ereabouts.'

Mickey Dunn opened his mouth to protest again, but thought better of it when the other two moved off once more. Weren't his fault he couldn't afford one of them guns and besides, he was a crack shot with the crossbow. Well, in daylight. When the target kept still. Best to say nothing though – Grover got twitchy on night raids and a bit too bloody free with his fists.

Realizing he was alone, Mickey hurried after his companions, bent almost double and holding his weapon before him as if he were on wargames.

Even though he was poacher-apprentice to the other two, he'd managed to strike a fair number of roosting pheasants the night before as Crick had frozen the birds in the wide beam of his powerful flashlight. The only problem was, most of them had thrashed off into the undergrowth with arrows embedded in them, shrieking like banshees. All three men had chased after them, Grover and Crick ignoring for the moment the ones they managed to shoot, and Mickey Dunn had felt like puking when he saw Grover catch a wounded bird and bite it by the side of its mouth to crush its skull. He *had* puked after Grover made him do the same thing to another pheasant they'd caught. And then he'd been in more trouble when they discovered he'd brought along hessian sacks to put the dead birds in instead of carrying strings, because they said the sacks were too clumsy to lug through the woods and the carcasses would be too bloody and horrible by the time they got home – the local butchers and restaurateurs (or restraunters, as he called them) preferred their game clean and appetizing.

Something snagged on his cheap leather jacket, pulling him back so that he was almost thrown off balance. At first, and with immense dread, he thought the gamekeeper had reached out from behind a tree to grab him, but he quickly realized – and just as he was about to scream for help – that Grover had whipped back a low tree branch, no doubt with the intention of striking the man behind. He heard Grover chuckle and he cursed him under his breath. He also raised a clenched fist towards his companion's back, although he made sure he didn't make contact. You'll get yours one day, Lenny Grover, he told the other man without voicing the opinion, an' when you do I'll be there to spit in your eye. In a mood, he stomped after the two in front.

'Must be gettin near to the spinney,' said Crick after a while. He stopped, waiting for Grover to come up beside him.

'Nah, we're a long way off yet,' Grover replied.

'You sure? We've come a long way from the truck.'

Grover lifted his baseball cap and swept back his lank black hair. 'We should come to a dip first, climb up a bit, go round a pond, then we're there – *get off me, will ya, Mickey!*'

Mickey, who had bumped into Grover yet again in the dark, quickly stepped back to avoid a flailing fist. He lost his balance when his heel caught a trailer and he toppled backwards into a bush, hessian sacks and crossbow crashing among the leaves as he fell.

The other two men winced at the noise. 'Let's leave him here, Len,' Crick grumbled in a low voice. 'He's a bloody menace.'

'He'd only get himself lost and make more of a nuisance of himself,' Grover groaned. He hauled the struggling figure to his feet, then pushed his face close to the youth's so that their noses were only inches apart, and hissed, *'Shut up, you fuckin little git!'*

Mickey became still. 'Lenny, I –'

'Shut it!'

'All right, all right.' At least his whine was quiet. 'But you shouldn't have –'

'Shut IT!' This time it was nearly a shout.

'Lenny,' Crick moaned in dismay. 'Bloody Christ, *you're* at it now. If Buckler's around he'll be down on us like a ton of bricks.'

Grover thrust Mickey away. 'I told you, if Buckler's out tonight he'll be miles away. Right, let's get goin an' no more stops till we reach the spinney. You hear me, Mickey?'

There was a grumbled response and then they proceeded through the woods once more, this time Grover pushing Dunn ahead so that he was between himself and Crick. In revenge for having the crossbow sticking into his backside for the first part of the journey, he occasionally prodded the youth with the barrel of his shotgun. He sniggered at Mickey's muffled complaints.

After a while, however, the pleasure of this small torture began to wane, for the deeper into the woods they went, the more uneasy he began to feel. There was something wrong and he didn't know what. The woods were quiet enough and there were no lights twinkling between the trees in the distance, a dead giveaway for approaching keepers. It was only after they'd gone some distance further that he became aware of exactly what it was bothering him. He gave a whispered command to the others to stop.

They did so and turned round to see what the problem was.

'Listen,' Grover told them.

They did. They heard nothing.

'What you on about, Lenny?' grouched Crick. 'I can't 'ear nothin.'

'That's it,' said Grover. 'There's nothin to 'ear.'

They stood in silence, listening more intently. Crick realized his partner was right. Even in the dead of night there were sounds in the forest – small nocturnal animals shuffling through the undergrowth, the odd bird shifting in its nest, the screech of a mouse as an owl swooped from the darkness. But tonight there were no such sounds. None at all.

Yet it wasn't just the quietness that worried the three men: it was the stillness, too.

'I don't like this, Len,' Crick murmured. 'D'you think old Buckler's set a trap for us?'

'I dunno. But's there's somethin funny about this place.'

'Yer bloody daft, the pair of ya,' scoffed Mickey. 'What d'ya expect in the middle of the bleedin night?'

The other two men ignored him. 'Whadya think – get out while the goin's good?' said Crick.

'Might be the thing to do,' answered Grover.

'Oh come on,' moaned Mickey. 'We're close to the spinney now.' They heard him fit a quarrel into the crossbow.

'What you doin?' asked Grover with more patience than he actually felt.

'Gettin ready before you two frighten everything off with yer muskets.'

'I just told you we're gettin out.'

'No way. The boss told me he'd 'ave all the pheasants I could get for the weekend.' His boss was the town butcher he worked for on Saturdays.

Once more Grover grabbed the younger man by the lapels, lifting him onto his toes. 'I won't say it –'

He froze, holding Mickey there on tiptoe, as a low noise came through the trees towards them.

Slowly all three turned their heads towards the source.

*   *   *

151

Gaffer was like a statue. And then gradually, starting with its haunches, it began to tremble. Soon every part of the dog, from its long narrow head to its short erect tail, was quivering. A peculiar whining-mewling came from the back of its jaws.

Jack Buckler turned the light on the dog. 'What is it, Gaffer?' he urged quietly. 'What's it yer hearing?'

The dog continued to stare directly ahead, its small black eyes fixed on a point somewhere in the distance.

'Nearby, are they, Gaffer?' The keeper straightened, his face set in grim lines. 'Well, we got 'em this time.'

The Airedale managed a growl, a long, drawn-out sound, before the whining-mewling resumed. But this time it became more urgent, more of a cry.

'Steady there, old son.' Buckler was perplexed: he'd never known Gaffer to act in this way before. Normally the dog was fearless, always ready to leap in and mix it no matter what they faced, be it poachers, cornered foxes, or even crazed badgers (and did *they* get crazed sometimes). But never had it reacted like this in all the years it had served him. What in God's name could be spooking the dog so?

He heard the other noise then, the noise that seemed to come from the very air itself. It was a moaning, an eerie lamentation that stiffened the hairs on the back of his neck. He suddenly felt uncommonly cold, as if the temperature had abruptly dropped into the zero regions, and now it was not only the hair on his neck that stiffened, but the hair on his arms and legs and scalp also.

Coming through the trees was a piteous ululation of deep and terrible distress, the unbroken cry of those in utter despair. He narrowed his eyes, peering into the night's gloomy substance, searching for the source of such misery, of such pain. He saw nothing but shadow.

He reached into his jacket pocket and drew out the telescope-like object he'd slipped in there earlier, clicking a switch as he held it up to one eye. The image intensifier weighed no more than .6kg and was operated by a single battery; it was an instrument often used by gamekeepers when they did not want to give away their position in the darkness by using flashlights. He pointed it slowly from left to right, aiming it in the general direction of where he thought the noise might be coming from, and drew in a sharp breath when tiny floating objects appeared on the small phosphorescent screen. It was like viewing green-tinted flotsam floating in disturbed water.

He took the night-sight away from his eye and stared without it at the spot where he'd located movement. Now he detected a slight greyness there in the gloom.

'Come on, Gaffer,' he said softly but resolutely, 'let's find out what's goin on.'

But the dog was no longer at his side. He heard the rustle of undergrowth behind him as Gaffer fled. Astonished at his dog's cowardice, he almost called out its name, but stopped himself just in time: no sense in alerting whoever it was up there among the trees. More mystified than angry with Gaffer, he turned back towards the greyish light and began to creep forward, stopping every once in a while to raise the night-sight and see if he could discern any of those dancing shapes. It was odd – it was damned *peculiar* – but each time he looked with his naked eye all he could see was that shapeless grey, almost like a mist without the wispy edges, and no inner, moving shapes whatsoever.

Something told him to get away from there, to follow Gaffer back the way they had come, back to the Land-Rover; something else, though – the earthy, practical gamekeeper side of him, the man who protected the animals and the land in his charge with love as much as professionalism – told him something was amiss here and it was his job to find out what it was. He went on.

When he had halved the distance between himself and the mist, he paused to take stock. The unearthly sounds still came to him, but they were no louder than before. Raising the night-sight again, he looked through it and saw that the images, those greenish pieces of dancing flotsam, were sharper but no more discernible. Differing in shape and size, they weaved and whirled in no set pattern and with no overall form.

Buckler lowered the instrument and noticed that seen without it the mist had now become more opaque at its centre. He set off again, even more cautiously, curiosity as well as duty overcoming his trepidation. He hardly breathed, not because he did not want to give away his presence – the twigs snapping under his boots would have already done that – but quite simply because he had almost forgotten to. Although partly obscured by bushes and trees, the mist appeared to have a stronger texture as he drew nearer, as though it were a fine gauze rather than vapour, and there was more movement inside.

Oddly the noises, still no louder, were becoming clearer and as he approached he realized it was human voices that he could hear. And he was suddenly sure that they emanated from the centre of the . . . the what? What *was* it? *Haze* was the best description he could think of right then.

He was close, very close, only one or two trees and bits of shrubbery between himself and the enigma. Through the eyepiece of the night-sight the floating objects began to take on even more clarity and, with a gasp of disbelief, Buckler started recognizing those with definite forms.

One piece had three points to it, two long, one shorter and certainly thicker, and the keeper could have sworn this was part of a hand – two fingers and a thumb attached to a lump of flesh.

Another tinier piece was rounded and had a darker circle within it; a long sliver hung loose behind it like a tendril or the slender tail of some species of deep-sea fish. With a shock, Buckler realized it resembled a floating eyeball.

A solid chunk weaved into view and – or so it seemed to the bewildered keeper – another larger piece chased it. The one behind caught up and they joined together, fitting snugly, like some three-dimensional jigsaw.

Buckler jerked the night-sight away in horror as it dawned on him just what he was witnessing. The sounds were a wailing-moaning, at times a howling, and the dancing flotsam was segments of human flesh.

Without the use of the image intensifier, they appeared as faint shapes with no particular form, but now, knowing what they were, he could detect a pattern to their movements. They were all seeking each other, joining and fusing together, gradually becoming more of a mass.

Fascinated, perhaps mesmerized, the keeper inched closer, the night-sight held loosely at his side, no longer necessary as the haze grew paler and the shapes inside became more defined. Something very close to the ground stirred in there and began to rise.

A notion, albeit a bizarre one, entered Buckler's mind and it was that inside this mysterious haze was a disassembled body, its parts circling, weaving, constantly seeking the whole; only there seemed to be too many bits, for they clustered together and made no sense, too many were jostling for the same position, so that they were forced to disjoin and begin again.

The scattered parts swirled into a maelstrom, each morsel, large or small, becoming a blurred particle of light. Buckler did not remember to breathe, his instinct did it for him. He swayed and reached out to grasp the trunk of a nearby tree, his fingers curling into the rough bark to hold himself steady, the giddiness leading to an urge to vomit. He managed to control the rising bile by closing his eyes against the soft, yet somehow dazzling glare.

When he opened them again, the movement inside the haze was slowing down, taking on a more disciplined order. He realized his original notion had been right: this was a body trying to assemble itself, for the fragments were more perceptible, their shapes more recognizable.

But there were still too many parts . . .

Another, larger chunk squirmed on the earth and this too, like the one before, began to rise, sending the smaller pieces – the fingers, the eyeballs, tongues, ears and other body parts

155

– into excited flurries so that they swarmed, he told himself, like flies over dog shit.

'Good God in Heaven,' he murmured as two bodies gradually formed, ragged lines indicating where the flesh joined, an eyeball in one of the heads protruding uncomfortably from its socket, a foot twisted the wrong way round on one of the ankles, a glistening, rubbery tube of some kind flopping loosely from a breach in one of the shoulders.

The keeper felt his knees weaken and he dropped the night-sight so that he could cling to the tree with both hands. He wanted to run away, but the strength just wasn't there. He wanted to cry out, but the sound was locked tight in his throat. He wanted to close his eyes, or at least look away, but the abominations before him would not allow it.

As he watched – was *forced* to watch, the hypnotic grip too strong to break – he noticed there was more movement beyond the haze.

Grover, Crick and Mickey sprinted through the woodland, hoping they were leaving the dreadful low moaning behind; but it stayed with them, coming neither from left or right, nor from in front or behind – it was just there, all around them, only inches outside their own heads.

Through the undergrowth they crashed, heedless of their own noise, stumbling over tree roots and trailers, low branches and bushes snagging and flailing them almost wilfully it seemed, as if the forest itself was in league with the tormenting noise. They did not try to understand what it was that they were running from; they didn't *care* what it was. They only knew that never in their lives had they been so frightened. Perhaps it was the moon-hidden blackness they fled through that made the sounds so terrifying, for unseen and unknown were formidable allies. Perhaps it was the deep, heart-wrenching gloom of the sounds that sent them scurrying so, for it reached deep inside them, seeming to touch their very souls and propagate an oppressive and threatening despair. Whatever, they cared little for reasons and even less for quizzes. They just wanted to be far away from that inky woodland and as fast as their suddenly clumsy legs would allow.

Such was their fear, and such was their cravenness, that when young Mickey smashed into a tree and went down with a split lip and a startled screech, Grover and Crick stumbled on, leaving their companion to writhe among the rotted leaves and tree roots of the forest floor.

Blood trickled through his fingers as he held them to his mouth and tried to call out. *"Enny! 'Ennis! 'Um mack!"*

They were gone, though, and had it not been for the constant moaning that filled his head, now complemented by the buzzing of his brain from the knock it had just taken, he would have heard their thrashing retreat fade further and further away.

His face numbed by the collision with the tree, Mickey slowly pushed himself to his knees. He felt around the crumbly floor for the crossbow he had saved so hard for. Still kneeling, and because he was so frightened – even more so, if that were possible, now that he had been abandoned by Grover and Crick – he checked his loaded weapon, stifling sobs as he did so. *'Mastids,'* he cursed them, wincing at the pain from his lips. *"Uckin mastids.'*

Once on his feet he staggered off, clutching the crossbow to his chest, not realizing he was headed in the wrong direction. He stumbled through bushes, scraped past trees, the moaning that had developed into a wailing driving him onwards. He pulled a rolled-up handkerchief from his trouser pocket and pushed it against his cut lip to stem the flow of blood, while tears spoiled his already appalling vision.

''Enny!' he cried out again, not caring if he was heard by the keeper or whoever was making that awful racket. *''Ennnniiissss!'*

He tripped, sprawled, and his finger slipped through the crossbow's guard to release the trigger. He felt the discharge of tension and heard the quarrel *thunk* into the trunk of a tree a few yards away.

Mumbling a curse and driven by panic, he reached inside his shoulder bag for another arrow. Although he had sat inside a cupboard at home and practised loading in the dark at least a hundred times, his fingers still refused to take instructions from his brain. He even managed to drop the quarrel once and had to search through the dusty soil to find it again; eventually the crossbow was loaded and he was on his feet, hobbling through the woods with a heaving chest and sob-like murmurings.

Quite soon he blundered into a clearing where a peculiar light glowed. He blinked his eyes rapidly so that he could see more clearly. His numbed mouth dropped open and his eyes pressed against their sockets as they stared at the two pale, naked bodies inside the funny light, bodies that were not quite right because they looked as if they had been crudely stuck together with glue or invisible tape and several bits had gone wrong, like the foot that was back to front and a buttock that was hanging by thin threads and a shoulder that was too far back. One of the heads was swivelling round to look at him and he didn't want that, he didn't want this thing to see him standing there in case it decided to acknowledge him. No, he didn't want that at all.

The crossbow was already pointing. All he had to do was squeeze the trigger again, this time intentionally. It was easy. It didn't even need thinking about. He just had to do it. So he did.

And when the arrow sped through to the other side, seeming to touch nothing at all inside that curious shell of grey light, he heard a high-pitched scream that sounded much more human than the howling of the two mix-'n'-match creatures before him.

17

HE RUSHING WATERS close over his head and unseen forces conspire to drag him down into the murky depths. He screams, but the sound is muffled in an explosion of bubbles. He sinks, deeper, deeper, and his arms smash at the currents, his hands claw at the silky fronds. A shape glides towards him from the gloom, tiny, pale fingers stretched towards him. He calls out her name, heedless of the water that fills his mouth, and he sees that she is smiling as she draws near; her dark hair frames her ghostly face, the tresses curling and weaving in the turbulence. She is close and her smile festers into a grin so malevolent, so vicious, that he screams again and tries to turn away . . .

Ash twisted in the bed, one naked arm thrown across his brow as if to resist the dream's spectre.

Now this pallid vision changes: she is no longer his sister, a child, but a woman whose grin is as evil, whose glare is as insane. Her slender arms slip around his neck, the gown she wears billows in the flow, her lips move closer to his, and her eyes gleam with madness . . . and desire. Her mouth is on his and he feels her pressure, feels her draining his life as the waters have drained his breath. He ceases to struggle, he gives himself up to her embrace. Blackness consumes him . . .

Ash murmured something in the darkness of the bedroom,

but the words had no coherence; they were ill-formed, part of the dream.

. . . and mercifully, he is alone again. A small glimmer appears in that blackness – the blackness that has no weight, no eddies or flows, but is equally as oppressive as the water that sought to take him – and soon it is joined by another, and then another, so that he sees they are candle flames. They multiply, become a mass of light that fills the room he is now in with its soft, unsteady glow. Yet there is no warmth from them, no comfort, only a gradual unveiling of further horror. For the light reveals stone coffins set on tiers around the black walls. But that is not the only horror. Before him, in the centre of the mausoleum – he knows this place, he has visited here in another time – is one more coffin, this one smaller than the others and made of rich, shiny wood, its interior plush with white satin. There is movement there, a little hand on the rim of the coffin. The child sits up and seeks him out, her wicked smile never wavering, her cold eyes never blinking . . .

The bedsheets were damp with Ash's sweat. Still in sleep, he pushed the covers away, leaving his chest bare to the night.

He weeps in the dream and the tears at first blur, then dissolve the scene around him. And now he is by a broad expanse of water lit by moonlight. Its surface is calm, without even a breeze to ripple its stillness, but soon he begins to hear gentle cries, the voices seeming to be a great distance away, perhaps from the other side of the great lake. Yet somehow he knows this isn't so; he knows the cries – the moans, the sighs, the grieving – are much closer. He knows these sounds come from beneath the great lake itself. The thin, almost translucent skin of the lake stirs. It shivers. It trembles. And the first hand breaks the surface, and is quickly followed by another, this one close enough to be from the same body. The wailing rises in pitch, although it is still contained by the water. Another hand emerges, the movement swift, sudden, and the fingers reach upwards, wetness running from them. Another hand. Another. And then the surface of the lake erupts as a million hands break through together. And the cries break

through with them and the lake is a turmoil of sound and motion.
The limbs rise until heads begin to appear, and their eyes are
wide and their mouths are open and the heads turn towards him
and they attempt to call his name but their voices are distorted
as if their throats have been rotted by the water that has clogged
them for so long. Yet even this is not the worst of the horror . . .

He uttered a cry, a whimper.

. . . for all the heads that stare across in that moonlit expanse
of water are small . . .

His leg kicked at the sheet.

. . . and all those hands that claw the air are tiny . . .

He tossed, he groaned.

. . . and all those wide but little eyes still hold the terror of
their own premature deaths.

In sleep, he moaned a long, drawn-out 'Noooo . . .'

And the drowned children moan with him, pleading to be
saved, imploring him to help them. But he knows he cannot, that
it's too late, they are already dead and nothing can save them
anymore. And so they plead with him to join them in their watery
crypt . . .

Ash's eyelids fluttered. He almost awoke. But sleep held its
grip.

The scene – the waving, imploring arms, the small pale heads
bobbing on the water like spectral buoys, the silver-coloured lake
– vanishes and he is in a field of stubble. He thinks he is alone
– he feels desperately alone – but he sees a small figure in white
standing by a group of trees in the distance. The little girl wears
only one white ankle-sock and he calls her name, this calling
hollow to his own ears as if he has not uttered the sound. 'Juliet!'
She does not respond, for she is as the children in the lake. She
is impassive because she is dead, and that is her revenge on him.
He will see her – he will forever see her – but he will never be
acknowledged. That is his punishment; and his dead sister's
retribution.

The quietness of his room is broken by his mumblings. In
his sleep he calls her name again and again.

As he watches he hears the crumph *of exploding flame and her ashen face is warmed by yellow light. He seeks the source of the fire and sees the burning haystack behind him, hears the screams from within, screams that turn to laughter, distant laughter, and when he searches for the child once more she is gone and in her place is a swirling storm of crisp leaves, spinning in the air . . . and inside the storm a form slowly takes shape. When the leaves scatter the mutilated figure of a man is left behind and the man's drooling grimace is really a corrupted smile and the thoughts that came from him enter Ash's mind and they are degenerate and dirty . . .*

Ash threw himself onto his side, his fist pounding once against the mattress. But still he did not wake, although a part of his subconscious was now alert to the nightmare.

He runs from the abomination and as he runs a dry, brittle leaf brushes his cheek. He realizes the leaf, and the next one, and the next, have come from behind him as if in pursuit. He tries to increase his speed, but his footsteps only become slower, his legs heavier, his breathing harder. The leaves circle him, scratching his skin with their sharp edges, and he brushes them away from his face with his hands, continuing to flee, his movement becoming sluggish. He notices a redness spreading across his palms and fingers, and the redness is slick and shiny and he realizes it is blood . . .

His back arched and his lips drew back across his teeth as though he were in agony. Consciousness, still far away at that moment, endeavoured to haul him from slumberous depths.

He tries to swat away another leaf that has clung to his cheek like some blood-sucking parasite and this time he feels its substance is different: it's soft, and long tendrils stirred by his own motion hang from it. He tears the raw and bloody meat from his face and dashes it to the ground, all the time moving, never allowing his exhaustion to bring him to a halt. He sees the dismembered hand before it attaches itself to his wrist and with a shriek he snatches it away, but even as he does so a deep red sliver of flesh hovers before him, its end trailing behind like a long, dripping tail and, searching for a natural home, the tongue tries to enter his open mouth. His clamped teeth stifle the scream and with both hands he pulls at the slithery flesh, turning his head aside at the same time. He throws the alien tongue away from him, but more and different lumps cling to his own flesh, arriving more rapidly and in greater numbers as though it is their intention to smother him completely, to use him as the infrastructure for their own eventual shape. He pulls, tears, pushes, but still they come, and he slips on something pulpy and slimy, something that is from inside a body, an organ that glistens and steams in the grass. He goes down and his fingers curl into the soil as he hides his face in the grass. He feels the weights on his back, his neck, his shoulders, his legs, his ankles, feels them slide over him to adjust their positions, to find a part of him on which to nestle, and he rolls over to crush them and cannot help the scream that erupts when he sees the air above filled with loose meat and organs, so many pieces, so many bits. And they land on him and he wonders, as they darken his vision, as they hinder his breathing, how many bodies have been torn asunder to make up all these cuts, these portions, these segments, and he tries to rise, using his elbows against the ground, but there are too many layers, they are too heavy, yet still he tries, for he knows if he succumbs to their load they will draw his life from him so that they can live as a whole once again. He resists them, his neck strains to lift his head, his shoulders shake with the effort, and his back is off the ground. But they insist, they bear down on him, filling his eyes and his mouth, and he screams and screams again, and he rises, rises, rises . . .

And he awoke.

He was frozen there in the darkness of the room, with only a slip of light from the hallway outside shining through the gap at the bottom of the door, and it was several moments before he realized he was sitting up in bed. His naked body dripped with perspiration and his breath came in sharp gasps. Only a dream, he told himself.

'Only a dream,' he said in a hushed, frightened voice. His

breathing deepened, the trembling diminished. The dream visions lost their colour.

He was awake, and he was safe. Safe from the nightmare.

But if it *was* only a dream, and now he was awake, why was the little boy standing by the bed watching him? Why could he see him so clearly in the darkness?

Why was the boy so still, so silent?

And why was he now slowly fading . . . dissolving . . . to nothing . . . ?

18

GRACE LOCKWOOD'S EYES snapped open.

The single bedsheet that covered her was twisted and rumpled; one of her legs was exposed, bent at the knee so that the sheet lay across her hip. She stared at the ceiling, her mind a tumult of thoughts and images. The dream . . . it had been so real, so vivid; yet it had been so confused.

She pushed the clammy covering away from her breasts and lay there in the darkness, calming her breathing, trying to make some sense of the after-images that continued to tumble through her mind; but as she concentrated, so the images scattered – scattered like dead leaves in a fierce wind.

She remembered children's faces, their eyes wide and pleading, tiny hands clawing the air as if beseeching . . . someone. Not her, though. She was merely a witness, somehow an observer to someone else's nightmare. She remembered a fire so bright that in the dream she had shielded her eyes with her hands. She remembered another storm – *no, no, this had not been a storm at all, but a cascade of human flesh.*

Grace shuddered, even though the visions were rapidly fading, their impact lessened, their reality undermined by her own reviving senses. But a memory remained while these others dwindled to vague impressions.

She, the observer, was watching David Ash. Beyond him,

by a group of trees, stood a small girl dressed in white. Incongruously, the girl wore only one white sock and she, too, was watching David.

The child was smiling. But her smile was not pleasant.

Grace wondered how she knew the little girl's name was Juliet.

19

SHE KNEW IT WAS David before she even opened the door. She knew before he'd even rung the bell. Before she had heard the car draw up outside.

She knew it was him because she had been expecting him. At least that was what she told herself as she went to the door.

'David . . .'

He looked gaunt standing there on the doorstep. No, not gaunt. Grace almost smiled as she reconsidered. There was a bleakness to his stare, a darkness around his eyes. David Ash looked haunted.

'Can I talk to you and your father?' he asked.

My God, she thought, that bleakness was even in his voice. 'Of course. Father's in the garden.'

She stood aside to allow him through, but he entered and stopped beside her. Now she saw confusion in his eyes. And something else, something locked away but not quite hidden. She sensed it was fear.

'Have you heard the news in the village?'

Dread seeped through her, long cold fingers that dragged at her spirit, and suddenly, irrationally, she wanted to walk away from him, to close her ears against whatever he was about to tell her. Something more was wrong in Sleath and she did not want to hear of it, because she shared the fear that was in

David Ash. She could not comprehend it, but neither could she deny it.

'I got back from the community hall a little while ago,' she told him, 'but I didn't hear of anything while I was there.'

'It's only just breaking. The landlord at the Black Boar told me a gamekeeper was killed in the woods last night. He was shot through the heart by an arrow from a crossbow.'

'Oh dear God,' she said and Ash reached out and held her arm to steady her. 'Not Jack Buckler, surely?' She shook her head in disbelief. 'He was such a gentle man, so good with the animals . . .'

'That was the name the landlord was told. The police contacted Ginty to see if any strangers were in the bar last night, or anyone behaving suspiciously. He told me because he had to let them know I was the only guest staying at the inn. No doubt they'll want a word with me at some stage.'

'I don't understand, David. Yesterday someone was almost beaten to death, a few weeks ago a boy was drowned in his bath – and now this.'

'I need to know what else has happened here. Not just recently, but over the past few years.'

'But there's no link, there's nothing to connect any of these things.'

'Only Sleath itself,' he said.

'How could –'

He cut her off. 'I've no idea. But sometimes a place – it could even be a room, or a house – can acquire an atmosphere that's conducive to evil.'

'That doesn't make sense.'

'Believe me, it happens. Will you tell your father I'm here?'

'I'll take you to him.' She hesitated though, taking a half-step towards him instead, so that their bodies were close. 'You look . . . tired. Are you all right?'

'I slept badly, that's all.'

And did you dream, David? she asked silently. Was it his

168

dream she'd glimpsed? 'Who's Juliet?' she said, this time voicing the question.

He appeared stunned. His eyes searched hers and, for a moment, the fear she thought she had sensed earlier shed its chains and ran rampant. It was controlled within seconds and his gaze became cold, isolated.

'How did you find out about her?' His tone was so emotionless that Grace felt a shiver run through her.

'I dreamt about you last night,' she said to him. 'It was confused, I couldn't make any sense of it. I can't even remember much, but I do know I saw a little girl watching you. She never spoke, she didn't do anything, but somehow I knew her name was Juliet. Perhaps you spoke to her, or called out her name – I just don't remember.'

That cold stare transfixed her for several more moments before he lowered his head and said: 'Juliet was my sister. She drowned when she was eleven years old.'

It came as a further shock to Grace. Yes, she had seen water, someone struggling; she had almost felt the water choking her own lungs. But the girl had nothing to do with that. Like Grace, she had only been there in the dream as an observer, a witness.

She found her voice. 'I'm sorry, David. I had no idea . . .'

'No, how could you?'

She was startled by his bitterness. When he said nothing more Grace turned away and walked down the hall towards the rear of the house.

'Grace.'

She stopped and looked back.

'Look, I'm sorry too,' he said. 'It's just that, well . . . things have happened that I'd rather forget.'

'I sense them, David. I don't know how, but I can feel some of the misery you've been through. Last night I think I saw into your own dream. Your nightmare, I should say.'

'Did you . . .' He looked beyond her. 'Did you see all of it?'

'It was too muddled, there was too much happening. Falling leaves, children's faces . . .' She shook her head in

169

exasperation. 'The girl is the only clear thing I remember. She was dressed in white. And there was something else, something I can't quite recall . . . Oh yes. Yes. The girl was wearing only one sock. Silly to remember something like that.'

But Ash didn't appear to think so. He was staring at her so intensely she felt like turning away again, turning away and walking out into the bright sunshine, for never before had the house seemed so cheerless, not even on the day her mother had been buried.

Ash spoke. 'Last night you told me you weren't psychic. I think you're wrong.'

'Surely I'd be aware if I were,' she said quickly.

'It might be a gift – some call it a curse – that's lain dormant in you for most of your life. Maybe it was something you had when you were a kid, then lost it over the years. Sometimes adult things crowd out certain perceptions. Or maybe you, yourself, denied the faculty because it frightened you. Believe me, I'm someone who knows the truth of it.'

'You're psychic yourself.' It wasn't a question.

'Sometimes.'

'I didn't think it was a sometimes thing.'

'Events – traumas – can trigger it off.'

'And you think that's happening with me?'

'I can't be sure. But yesterday, when I first met you at the church, something happened between us.'

'I felt as if I'd been hit by a thunderbolt. Are you suggesting that you and I have some kind of psychic link?' She recalled the experience before she'd entered the restaurant last night and a similar feeling only minutes ago before he'd arrived at the house, a 'knowing' of his presence; neither one could be described as a thunderbolt, but they were peculiar sensations, all the same.

Ash had followed her down the hallway so that now he was close to her. She laid a hand against his chest. 'You did dream of Juliet, didn't you?' she said.

He nodded. 'And other things.'

170

'A storm of some kind? Children's faces?'

'Yes.' He had no desire to describe all those dream-visions in detail.

'What does it all mean, David? Why should I react in such a way to you?'

He touched her fingers against his chest. 'It isn't me, Grace. It's the village itself. Something's going on here that I don't understand yet. These incidents – the drowning of Simon Preddle, the boy who was almost beaten to death yesterday, and now the gamekeeper who was killed last night – those are physical manifestations. The metaphysical manifestations are the ghosts seen by your father, Ellen Preddle, Ruth Cauldwell. And by myself.'

'You?'

'I saw – I think I saw – the ghost of a little boy last night.'

Grace caught her breath. 'Simon Preddle?' she said.

Ash shook his head. 'This kid was no more than six or seven years old. I saw him yesterday, too, just before I arrived in Sleath.'

Her fingers entwined in his. Her astonishment gave way to incredulity, and this in turn gave way to concern, all in fleeting seconds.

'I'm not sure he wasn't just part of my nightmare,' Ash said as if to convince himself. 'But he seemed so real for a few moments.'

'The non-believer convinced.'

They turned together at the sound of this other voice. Reverend Lockwood stood in the doorway at the end of the hall, light from the garden beyond silhouetting his stooped figure. One arm leaned against the doorframe as if for support.

'Father?' Grace went to him, a hand stretched before her as if afraid he might fall.

The clergyman straightened at her approach. 'I'm all right, dear. Perhaps it's too early for gardening, even at this hour. If you would fetch me a glass of water, though?'

'Yes, but you find a chair and rest.'

171

'I will. Will you join me outside, Mr Ash?'

Ash squinted against the glare from the open door as he went forward, and it was only when he was three or four feet away from the vicar that he realized how unwell the man looked; his condition, which was hardly robust on their first meeting, appeared to have deteriorated badly overnight.

Lockwood noticed the surprise in the investigator's eyes and gave a weary smile. 'You seem to have had a bad night yourself, Mr Ash.'

The remark further surprised Ash. Did he look as bad as the vicar? Somehow he doubted it, for this man was *physically* ill, anxiety for his village adding its extra weight.

'It was too warm last night to sleep well,' he said.

'Ah, if only that really was the cause. For myself I found the night quite cool. There are chairs on the terrace – shall we sit there?'

Ash followed the vicar outside and Lockwood took a seat on a broad wooden chair with wide armrests, while he pulled a plainer chair away from the terrace table. The terrace itself was a modest affair with a low lichen-coated balustrade and four steps leading down into the garden. From there he could see the gazebo where he and Grace had talked only yesterday, beyond that the woodland and the old Lockwood Estate. No sooner had they settled than Grace had joined them, carrying a glass of water in one hand and a battered straw hat of the kind a cricket umpire might wear in the other. She handed both to her father.

'Must I wear this thing?' the vicar complained.

'No, you can collapse with sunstroke if you prefer.' Grace sat at the table, facing Ash; she gave him a quick smile before saying to her father, 'I want you to rest today, and later I think we'll get Dr Stapley to have a look at you.'

'You will do no such thing.'

Frail as he appeared, the vicar's objection was forceful.

'But, Father –'

'I said no. All I need is a little rest, which is what the doctor would prescribe. Rest and a sedative or two. I'm afraid that's all our medical profession is worthy of nowadays.' He regarded the investigator. 'Have you any results for us, Mr Ash?'

'It's much too soon,' Ash replied. 'But certainly something is happening here in Sleath that isn't normal.'

'And what precisely is that?'

The investigator caught Grace's anxious glance. He understood she wouldn't want her father upset unnecessarily in his fragile condition, but it was impossible to evade such a direct question.

'The hauntings, for a start,' he said.

'For a start?' The older man turned his head slightly to one side so that he was watching the investigator from the corners of his eyes.

'The other incidents.'

'The boy who was almost killed by young Ruth's father?'

'Yes.'

'And . . . ?'

Ash looked apologetically at Grace. 'A gamekeeper was shot dead last night.'

'Jack Buckler? Not dear old Jack Buckler?'

'I'm afraid so. The police are certain it was a poacher who killed him.'

The vicar was shaking his head, more in sorrow than disbelief. 'Where was he murdered?' he said eventually in a voice so low Ash had to lean forward to catch the words.

'Somewhere on the Lockwood Estate. It happened some time last night.'

'The Lockwood Estate,' the vicar intoned. 'So it continues.'

Ash regarded him with interest. 'It continues . . . ?' he said as a prompt.

Lockwood shot a glance at his daughter, his lean body stiffening. 'The tragedies in Sleath,' he said to Ash. 'They continue to plague us.'

Ash was puzzled by the look that had passed between Lockwood and his daughter. He opened his mouth to speak, but the other man cut in.

'A little while ago I overheard you tell my daughter you'd seen the spirit of a small boy: can you explain that?'

'I'd had a nightmare. Possibly I was still half-asleep.'

'Ah, and the dream went on. Are you trying to convince us of that possibility, Mr Ash, or yourself?'

It was a question the investigator could not answer. Instead he changed the subject. 'I need to do some research into the history of Sleath. In particular, I'd like to learn more about your own ancestors.' This second comment was prompted by the look exchanged between father and daughter moments earlier.

'The Lockwoods?' Grace was more surprised than indignant. 'Surely you don't think our family has anything to do with the hauntings?' Her smile, lips parted, indicated the absurdity of the idea.

'I gather that generations of Lockwoods have played an important part in the community's history. I'd like to know as much as I can about them.'

Reverend Lockwood shook his head wearily. 'I urge you not to delve into matters long forgotten, Mr Ash. They can have no bearing on what is happening in Sleath today.'

Ash was not so sure, for many hauntings – or 'psychic replays' as he liked to term them – had much to do with past events.

The vicar's irritation at his lack of response was barely concealed. 'There's no point in dredging up the ancient deeds and misdeeds of my family. Small villages like ours tend to harbour grudges from generation to generation and I tell you no good will come of such revelations.'

'I've told you before, any researches I carry out will be confidential. The Institute reports directly to its clients, and no one else.'

Lockwood's expression suggested he was far from satisfied. He rose unsteadily to his feet, bringing the conversation to an end.

'Do I have your permission to look through the parish records?' Ash persisted.

The older man's pale eyes were unblinking. 'As far as the church chest is concerned, no, you do not. Unfortunately there is nothing I can do to prevent you from looking elsewhere for information.'

With that he left his daughter and the investigator alone on the terrace, anger lending a briskness to his step.

They walked along a wide track that once, Ash imagined, must have been a finely marked road leading to the Lockwood manor house, which was situated a mile or so inside the estate itself. Now its edges were obscured by wild grass and shrubbery spilling over onto the pitted and stone-strewn surface. He had asked to see the fire-ruined mansion that had once been Lockwood Hall and Grace, although surprised by the request, had willingly agreed to take him there.

They could have driven to the gutted house, but it had been Grace's idea that they walk; the roadway was too damaged to travel comfortably by car. In truth, she wanted to spend more time with this enigmatic man, to find out more about him, perhaps even discover how his young sister had drowned and why he looked so disturbed at the mention of her name.

A bee busied itself among the wild flowers beside the old disused road, its drone a testament to the normality of the day. Ahead of them greenfinches cavorted in the clear blue sky and the distant wooded hills were softened by the sun's unhindered blaze. How, Grace reflected, could the day take no note of the violence that had been perpetrated; how could those vicious acts fail to taint the very air itself? And the dreams of last night – daylight somehow diminished their power so they became even more vague and of uncertain significance. David Ash, himself, appeared less stressed than before, as though sunshine and open air had, if not swept away, then subjugated the night fears.

The bee rose from the flowers and flew across the rough road, its flight-path hindered momentarily by the human obstruction. Grace and Ash paused while the insect manoeuvred around them.

'Why was your father so against my looking into your family history?' Ash asked as they resumed walking.

'I think he's worried about the well-hidden skeletons you might drag out from various cupboards. You know he was furious with me for contacting the Psychical Research Institute in the first place. Then he seemed resigned to your investigation until he realized this morning you'd be digging into the past.'

'I still don't understand why that should bother him.'

'It was unexpected. He thought you'd set up your monitors or whatever you use to detect the presence of ghosts, make out a report, advise us what we should do, and then be on your way.'

'It's not always that simple.'

'So it seems. His main consideration, though, is for the people of Sleath. I'm afraid the Lockwood family has a bad track record as far as they're concerned and, as he said, he doesn't want past grudges revived.' She noted his interest and went on: 'We've had some unfortunate lords of the manor for ancestors, some of them quite infamous, from what I've gathered. Frankly, I've never been that interested in Sleath's history, or in Sleath itself for that matter. I was packed off to boarding school when I was seven and even at holiday time Mother took me away, usually abroad, while Father stayed because of his duties, so I've never really felt part of the community. University and work in other countries took care of the later years.'

'I'd still like to know about these skeletons in the Lockwood cupboard.'

She smiled and he felt her warmth. 'I told you, I don't know much about them. And I don't particularly care.'

'Not even curious?'

'Well, at the risk of whetting your appetite I did learn that one of my ancestors, Sebastian Lockwood, was a great friend

176

and acolyte of Sir Francis Dashwood. I suppose that held my interest for all of ten minutes.'

'Dashwood?'

'Surely you've heard of him?' Her smile had become mischievous. 'I'd have thought the Institute would have a filing cabinet full of information on that notorious character.'

'Ah, yeah. Sir Francis Dashwood, rake and occultist, and founder of the Hellfire Club, his own secret society for devil worship. Nice company your relatives kept.'

'His family seat was not too many miles from here. He held many of his orgies and performed satanic rites in chalk caves he'd had hollowed out himself. Sebastian Lockwood was a member of his secret brotherhood and they scandalized the area in the mid-eighteenth century, by all accounts.'

'Now that's some skeleton. Was he – what was it you called it – a squarson?'

'Yes. It was my mother who told me about him and I remember she was angry at the time. I don't know why it upset her so – I found it hilarious.'

'No wonder your father won't allow me access to the church chest, especially if you've got other ancestors of the same ilk. Those records might make interesting reading.'

'Hopefully he was the blackest of the sheep. If not, then the reformation of the Lockwoods must have come along with my father's generation. I can't imagine him being involved in such activities, can you?'

He smiled back at her, though the smile never reached his eyes. 'I guess not,' he said. 'D'you mind if I smoke?'

'Even on a beautiful day like this you don't care about polluting the air, not to mention your own lungs?'

'It helps me think.'

'You only think it does.'

'Well okay, it helps me think that it helps me think.'

'Your funeral.'

'Your chance to feel superior.' He reached into his pocket, then withdrew his empty hand. 'Ahh, I don't feel like it now.'

'Good. You'll live longer.'

'Yeah, by about two minutes.'

'You might appreciate those two minutes when the time comes.'

'It'll give me time for one last smoke.'

She laughed, pleased that their banter had lightened the mood between them. Unfortunately Ash spoiled it with his next question.

'How long has your father been ill, Grace?' he said.

'That's the third time you've asked me about my father's health. I don't understand why it's important to you.'

'I didn't say it was. I'm curious, that's all.'

'There's nothing mysterious about it. Father's health began to deteriorate shortly after my mother's death, although he's had problems with arthritis in his hands for a few years now. It's only lately that he's become more debilitated.'

'Has he had a recent check-up?'

'Some months ago, when he couldn't put up with my nagging any longer. Exhaustion, mental and physical, with slightly above normal blood pressure was our doctor's verdict. The arthritis doesn't help.'

'He didn't look too good today.'

'I'll get Dr Stapley to drop by and see him before the week is out. I won't even warn Father he's coming until the last moment.'

'Dr Stapley is the village GP?'

She nodded. 'He's looked after my family for as long as I can remember. I should think he's due for retirement any day now, but like my father, he's a stubborn man. He'll probably go on until he drops on his rounds.'

A jet, so high in the sky it was merely a glint of light, was leaving a slender, and almost spectral, vapour trail in its wake. The trail swelled, then dissolved in the thin air.

'That's what's left of Lockwood Hall up ahead.'

Ash followed Grace's pointing finger and saw the grey ruins in the distance. The muted greens of the hills beyond highlighted the starkness of the scarred walls.

He shrugged off his jacket and carried it over his arm. 'The house must have been magnificent in the old days,' he remarked as they continued to walk towards it.

'In many ways it was.'

He glanced at her. 'You don't sound so convinced.'

'We still have a painting of the Hall as it was in the eighteenth century and yes, I suppose it was an imposing building. I've never liked it, though. For me there was always something cold in its architecture; perhaps it's just a bad painting.'

'I'd like to see it.'

'Fine. It's in the study of the Lodge House. Others have admired the building as well as the painting itself, so you'll probably think I'm being silly.'

'It's common enough for people to get negative feelings about places.'

'For my own ancestral home? I should be proud of its history, as well as its grandeur.'

'Maybe you're influenced by how much the Lockwoods have lost over the years.'

'I don't give a damn about what we had.'

There was no harshness to her response, merely a firmness of conviction, and Ash decided he liked that. No whingeing *nouveau* poor, this woman.

She seemed embarrassed by her outburst. 'Did I sound peevish?'

He couldn't help but laugh. 'No, just indignant, maybe.'

Her good humour was back. 'Oh, I'm a master of indignation. You should hear me when Father talks religion at me. We can both sulk for days afterwards.'

'How come you aren't religious? You, a vicar's daughter?'

'In a way it's like living in a sweetshop. You can lose your appetite when it's all around you. In the end Mother felt the same way. In fact, worse – I think eventually she grew sick of religion. But that doesn't mean I don't believe in a Supreme Being, or life after death. I suppose it's the dogma and ritual that gets me down. Besides, there are other mysteries to be solved before we worry ourselves about the meaning of Creation, things like the ghosts that have been seen in Sleath, for instance, and why you and I can sometimes see into each other's mind.'

Her last comment brought him up short, as it was meant to. She swung round at him.

'How could I be part of your dream last night, David? How could I see your poor dead sister Juliet when I didn't know you or anything about you before yesterday? And one thing I didn't mention earlier: you seemed terribly afraid of her.'

She saw her words had affected him deeply. There was an odd mixture of fear and bitterness in his eyes, but when he spoke it was with cold anger.

'I was afraid of her games, her nasty, petty little games.'

He walked on, leaving Grace standing there staring after him.

'You can't still blame her for that, David,' she called after him. 'Not now that she's gone. You have to forgive her.'

He stopped and turned, the cold anger still in him. 'You don't understand,' he said. 'She played the games after she was dead.'

20

 RASS AND WEEDS grew between the broad steps leading up to Lockwood Hall's large but empty entrance, and rust concealed the iron rail's true colour. Blackened colonnades rose high on either side of the doorway and tall, gaping windows revealed the emptiness within.

As Ash mounted the steps he could see the broken walls inside, a half-collapsed double staircase leading to upper floors that were no longer there, and rafters that were dark and jagged; the sky showed bright and clear through the open roof. Grace stood on the lowest step behind him, her face impassive.

He turned and waited for her, but she hesitated. 'Grace?' he said, wondering why she was reluctant to join him.

She looked from the open doorway to him before shaking off whatever emotion held her there. She began to climb the steps.

Ash returned his attention to the house, craning his neck to examine the upper levels and the remains of the ornate stone balustrade that ran along the length of the rooftop.

'You can almost imagine how it must have been,' he said distractedly, feeling her presence next to him.

'I don't want to think of it, David. I don't like this place. When I come here I always have the impression that it's brooding, resentful of its destruction. It's strange, but I get the same feeling when I look at the painting back at the house.'

'You're letting your imagination run away with you,' he admonished her mildly. 'There's nothing here.'

'You don't feel anything?'

He peered into the opening, his gaze sweeping the stained walls, the ruined staircase. 'It's just an empty shell.'

She hugged herself as if suddenly cold. 'I wish I could believe that. Even as a little girl I hated the place. I'd never come here alone and fortunately my mother didn't seem to like it here either. Only Father used to visit and sometimes he insisted that I came along. I remember him walking through the ground floor, moving from room to room, and often, if it was safe, his eyes would be half-closed as if he were imagining how it used to be. He'd even hum a tune, one of those old waltzes, and describe to me the social occasions that generations of Lockwoods enjoyed in this house. Holding his hand, I'd imagine them myself, the long gowns, the powdered wigs, music played on a harpsichord. I'd almost hear the laughter, the conversations, the tap of shoes on the marble floor of the ballroom as the guests danced. Romantic, I know, a young girl's idea of how it must have been; but I could almost see them . . .'

She stopped as if surprised by her own recollection, and Ash moved closer to her. Her voice faltered as she went on. 'I could imagine other . . . occasions here, too. Dark things happening . . . things I couldn't possibly understand as a child . . . things I don't even understand now . . .'

He put his arms around her and she stiffened before relaxing into him.

'How did you imagine them, Grace?' he probed gently. 'Do you recall if you actually heard music and voices? Were they that real to you?'

'I don't know – it was so many years ago. But I couldn't have, could I? It must have all been in my mind, just childish fantasies.'

'But you remember them quite vividly.'

'Today I seem to.' She left him to go to the high doorway.

Ash followed and when he stood alongside her he saw that her eyes were closed and her head was tilted slightly upwards as if she were still recalling those childhood memories. He didn't disturb her; instead he surveyed the gutted building's interior. It was easy to imagine Lockwood Hall's past grandeur, even though the walls and half-walls now were grimed black, with moss and lichen abundant in the shadier corners. The floors were littered with fallen debris, charred beams scattered here and there, masonry dust thick and clogged like mud from years of rainfall through the open roof. There were large holes in the flooring whose darkness the bright sunshine seemed unable to penetrate. He peered up at the remnants of the upper floors and was surprised to detect no birds or nests settled in the broken timbers or wall crevices, for such abandoned places usually provided ideal sanctuaries. He searched and listened for sounds, but could find no trace of wildlife at all. There was only silence and the swirl of dust motes inside this huge, empty shell.

He took a step forward so that he was just inside the doorway.

'Don't, David.' Grace had felt him move past her and had opened her eyes immediately. 'It isn't safe in there.' When she saw his uncertainty, she added: 'The floor – it isn't safe anymore. And some of the ceiling rafters are quite loose.'

He nodded, glad of the warning. 'When were you here last?' he asked, moving back to her.

'I'm not sure. A year ago, perhaps, when I returned home because of my mother's illness. After the funeral I just wanted to get away from the Lodge House, so I took a walk along the old road and found myself back here. I remember Father was angry when he learned where I'd been.'

Ash raised his eyebrows questioningly.

'Nothing sinister, David. He was concerned that the whole place might decide to collapse in on itself one day and he didn't want anyone to be near when it happened.'

'Why not have it demolished if he's so anxious?'

'It would be too costly. Besides, it's on private land – no one's allowed to come close.'

'I didn't see any warning signs.'

'They've never been necessary. Nobody seems interested enough to visit the place.'

'Not even the person who bought the rest of the estate?'

'Carl Beardsmore? He knows it's off limits. It was my grandfather, Neville Lockwood, who sold off all the lands to pay off his debts and he stipulated that the Hall was always to remain as family property, despite its condition. I suppose he wanted us to retain some kind of tradition no matter how our wealth had been diminished. The new estate owner built his own property on the southern side of the land and it was Beardsmore – I'm told he used to own a collection of engineering magazines and sold them on for millions – who took it over twenty-odd years ago. He approached my father at the time, and several times since, with offers to buy up the rest of the estate, but Father turned him down. I think Beardsmore has given up the idea of being total lord of the manor by now.'

Ash could understand the millionaire's past ambition for, rebuilt, Lockwood Hall would have made a superb residence in a fine setting, and no doubt he would have paid a very healthy price for the property. Still, in a way it was refreshing to see family tradition take pride over market forces. The Lockwoods were a dying breed.

A sudden flutter of wings startled them both and Grace quickly stepped back from the doorway as if expecting a fall of loose debris. Only dust, a million glittering specks in the sunlight, drifted down from the open roof.

Ash looked up and saw the bird that had just alighted on one of the beams high above in the cavernous interior. So I was wrong, he thought, there is life here, and as if to answer him the black crow released a sharp, jagged cry, a sound made harsher by the emptiness inside those damaged walls.

'David.' Grace had moved even further away: she was almost by the top step. 'Let's leave.'

He glanced back at the crow. It was silent now and seemed to be staring down at him. Ash shivered and suddenly realized that, despite the sun's unhindered entry, Lockwood Hall – or what was left of it – was as cold as a mausoleum.

21

H NOW, SO THIS is the place. Pleasant. No, more than pleasant: a beautiful little village. Such a pity, such a great shame.

The diminutive man on the bench crossed his legs, cupped his hands around his knee, and rocked backwards and forwards for a few moments, the movement slight, his narrow shoulders barely leaving the back of the seat. He tapped his thin, silver-handled walking cane on the grass thoughtfully.

Someone passing through might think the place was ordinary enough – well, much too pretty with its olde worlde inne and quaint houses, its village green with pond, to be described as ordinary, but to be sure, they'd imagine it was tranquil and certainly uneventful. Oh yes, and the casual visitor might assume that the villagers themselves were perfectly nice and without any special cares other than those that normal everyday living dreams up, and they'd never notice the distant but – if you looked ever so carefully – telltale disquiet behind the polite smiles, a kind of spiritual discomfort in their evasive eyes.

This is the place, without doubt. God in His great Heaven, you can feel the trembling of the very air itself, you can sniff the sour stench of trepidation. These people – look at them walking by, barely nodding to each other, avoiding eye contact – these people suspect something is terribly wrong with their village, but right now they don't know what. They're waiting for something, but they haven't a clue as to what that something could be.

Seamus Phelan scratched an itch inside his nose then, his mind on other things, wiped his finger on the red-with-white-spots handkerchief that flopped from the breast pocket of his hairy tweed jacket. He studied the ground in front of him for a little while, contemplating the dark stains in the grass, a deep frown corrugating his forehead, a shadow temporarily veiling the usual merriment of his grey-green eyes.

Now that's nasty dried blood tainting the grass there (how rank life's liquid becomes when spilt so recklessly) and spoiling the peace with its implication. Something has happened here on this very spot and very recently, something horrible and violent. Death has had its bony fingers in it, but its grip was not quite enough. Yes, yes, I can feel it. Death has not had its way here, but it stands sulking close by. There will be other opportunities.

He craned his neck to watch a red Ford drive by the green, his interest in the driver rather than the vehicle itself. His little eyes, almost merry once more, narrowed as he tried to discern the man's features, but the sun was high and there was too much shade inside the car. Nevertheless, he caught a glimpse of profile.

Hmn, strong face. Full of uncertainties, though. Now why should this man attract my attention so? Ah yes, he's part of it. Mercy, the sensing is strong. Look now, he's caught it too. He's glancing this way, searching. He sees me, but he's not sure. He looks away again, watching the road. The man's full of confusion.

The little Irishman watched as David Ash pulled into the last remaining space of the small parking area on the other side of the pond. He watched him lock the car and cross the road to the Black Boar, walking around the police car parked at the kerb, to reach the inn's entrance. Ash stopped and looked around once more before going inside.

He doesn't belong here, that's for sure. He's a stranger like meself. Yet he's part of what's going on here. Called by these terrible vibrations, I wonder? Are they what brought him to this place too?

Phelan became still on the bench. He gazed at the door of the inn.

No, this man's power was not that strong. Or, to be precise, his power was far too repressed. Still and all, we must get together before too long. Before it's too late, I mean. For the moment though, let's just sit here and absorb whatever it is I can absorb. The pond there, for instance. Horrible stagnant thing. And it's deep beyond any earthly depth, and I've decided I don't like sitting so close to it. Perhaps I'll take a walk up to the church I can see in the distance. Always a good place to start and nobody pays any attention to strangers snooping around such old places of interest.

Seamus Phelan stood and shook each leg in turn as if dislodging creases in his own flesh. Then he lifted his jaunty narrow-brimmed hat just enough to sweep a hand over silver strands of thinning hair. This done he snapped the hat smartly back into place, picked up the cane again, straightened his shoulders with a brisk jerk and prepared to move off towards the church on the hill. But something else caught his attention, something he was surprised he hadn't observed earlier. He had noticed the whipping post and stocks even before he had settled on the bench, but then there had been nothing untoward about them. At this moment, though, a dark fluid – as dark as the stuff on the grass – was running down the ancient, scarred wood of the whipping post.

He wandered over to the old monuments of torture and torment and touched a finger to the slick wetness. His finger was coloured red when he brought it away again.

Now would you look at that.

He examined the post once more and then his finger. He shook his head in wonder.

Sweet Jaisus, why would the wood be weeping blood?

22

ASH DREW UP outside Ellen Preddle's tiny terraced cottage, pulled on the handbrake, and sat there for a few moments staring through the windscreen. He felt weary and wasn't sure why. Certainly he'd had a bad night, for the dreams had been vivid, distressing; yet he'd become accustomed to such dreams over the years. So maybe the weariness was physical, rather than mental. The long walk to the ruins of Lockwood Hall in the heat of the day had been tiring enough and then, on his return to the Black Boar Inn he had been interviewed by the local police. And lying was always a little wearing.

To protect his client's confidence, he had told the two policemen that he had been engaged by the vicar of St Giles' to help collate the long-neglected church records (this inspired by Grace Lockwood's remark that she had been hired by the *Musée de Cluny* to chronologize its exhibits) and to restore them where possible, omitting the word Psychical when he'd mentioned he was from the Institute of Research. It was a small lie only, in the best interest of his client, and he doubted they would bother to check it out, for their enquiries were 'routine': because of last night's murder of a gamekeeper, any visitors to Sleath, as well as locals, were being questioned.

The whole interview had taken no more than ten minutes and had been conducted in the privacy of the inn's empty dining room, away from the prying ears and eyes of a couple of provincial journalists who had arrived in Sleath to cover both the murder and the appalling act of violence that had occurred on the village green only the afternoon before. When Ash had retired to the bar for a quick drink and a sandwich before tackling the first part of his report to the Institute, he noticed the journalists were being given short shrift by some of the inn's lunchtime patrons. Curt grunts and the occasional monosyllabic response seemed to be the order of the day, and when he, himself, was approached to be asked how he felt about the spread of urban violence to quiet rural communities like Sleath, he had brusquely explained he was a visitor, downed his drink in one and taken the sandwiches up to his room.

The rest of the afternoon had been spent there, going through his notes, listening to the taped conversations between himself and Reverend Lockwood, Grace, the farmer Sam Gunstone and, of course, Ellen Preddle, transcribing them onto paper by hand before typing them up on the compact but efficient typewriter he'd brought with him.

That completed, he'd rested on his bed smoking a cigarette, occasionally sipping vodka from the hip flask he kept on the bedside cabinet, and reflecting on what he'd learned so far from his investigations. Time and time again, though, his thoughts returned to Grace Lockwood.

It was foolish, he told himself, foolish to get involved with a client while an investigation was in progress. It was a distraction and, in a way, almost as unprofessional as a doctor or psychiatrist becoming involved with a patient: it could lead to unnecessary complications. Besides, the last time it happened had proved disastrous in every way.

Nevertheless, he was attracted to Grace and he knew she was attracted to him. This rapport, this odd but potent *frisson* between them, could not be denied. And this time, unlike before, the woman was real, she was not a deceit.

These thoughts passed swiftly through his mind as he sat there in the car and he pushed them away, aware that Ellen

Preddle was probably watching him from behind lace curtains – she and possibly one or two of her neighbours – waiting for him to come to the front door. Would she allow him to set up the equipment as she'd agreed yesterday, he wondered, or would she be having second thoughts, frightened by what had happened to Grace in her kitchen? Would she tell him to leave her alone, or would she welcome his help? One way to find out.

He opened the car door and went round to the boot. Some of the fatigue left him as he unloaded equipment for, as ever, the prospect of detecting genuine paranormal activity sent a rush of adrenaline through him.

Carrying two cases, one large, the other smallish, he pushed through the squeaky gate and walked up the short path to the cottage. The door opened before he was even halfway there.

He glanced at his wristwatch. Nearly eleven. Dark outside and as quiet as the grave inside. Ash checked the small television monitor screen that was set up on the table a few feet away from the staircase and saw only the monochrome image of the empty bathroom on the floor above. He watched the picture for several minutes, searching for something – anything – out of place. All was perfectly normal

He picked up the half-smoked cigarette from the tin ashtray he'd found in the kitchen earlier and inhaled deeply. The burning end glowed brightly in the semi-darkened room. As yet boredom had not set in, even though he had been keeping watch for hours, and that was odd, for long surveillances, no matter what the circumstances, invariably led to tedium after the first two hours.

Wires from the monitor trailed up the stairs to a video-camera on a tripod situated at the open doorway of the bathroom. Opposite, inside the bathroom itself, was a tripod-mounted Polaroid camera with automatic flash, fitted with a capacitance change detector which would trigger it off at the slightest disturbance. The camcorder had a similar device attached to it. A sound-activated cassette recorder had been placed by the bath and a light layer of talcum powder had been sprinkled on the floor and inside the bathtub itself. A greenhouse thermometer was balanced on the back of the sink and there was another outside on the stairs, this one smaller and capable of registering the highest and the lowest temperatures recorded during the surveillance. More fine powder had been sprinkled on several of the steps and thin black cotton stretched across the third one from the bottom. An ordinary camera, loaded with infra-red film, stood on its tripod by the front door, facing the stairs. On the table in front of Ash were two torches, yet another automatic camera using ordinary fast-film stock, various transparent envelopes and clear plastic containers, a spring balance and strain gauge, as well as pens, pencils, chalk and willow charcoal, notebook, and paper on which he had sketched floor plans of the cottage, both upstairs and downstairs. Other equipment was packed away in the larger of the two cases he'd brought in with him, and there was still more in the boot of the car.

Ash studied the floor plans by the light of a small table lamp while he smoked. Ellen Preddle was in her bedroom, hopefully asleep by now, under instruction not to leave the room until he called her, no matter what she heard. If anything disturbed her inside her own bedroom, then she was to call him immediately. The bathroom was not to be used during the night and Ash hoped she had made her own arrangements regarding toilet facilities. All windows were shut tight and the house had felt uncomfortably stuffy for most of the evening although it had gradually began to cool as the hour grew later.

Ellen Preddle had looked far from well when she had opened the door to him earlier. The darkness around her eyes had increased noticeably and even before he'd reached the doorstep the wildness of her expression was apparent. Perversely, the hands that had never been still on their first meeting now remained motionless by her side, and her shoulders appeared even more slouched. She wore the same flower-patterned dress and, despite the heat of the day, the same thin cardigan. Her hair was untidier, the black-grey locks tangled and dishevelled. To his surprise, she allowed him into the house without question.

As he set up various pieces of equipment he'd explained their functions, but she had sat in the armchair by the empty hearth, disinterested and barely looking at him whenever he asked a direct question, her replies mumbled, almost unintelligible. Later he'd been relieved when he had suggested she retire to her bed for the night and she rose without demur, going straight to the stairs. Ash had to call out instructions for her not to leave her room during the night and the only response had been the closing of her door. Since then there had not been a sound from upstairs.

He yawned and rubbed a hand across his eyes. Tiredness, usually enhanced by boredom, was often the first hurdle to be overcome and no matter what hour the watch had begun, drowsiness generally hit around midnight or shortly after; tonight the tiredness had probably struck a little earlier because of the previous bad night. He dogged the cigarette and resisted the urge to light another; instead he reached around to his jacket hanging over the back of his chair and drew out the hip flask from a side pocket. He unscrewed the lid and took a light sip, just enough to revive him. When tiredness returned later, as it always did, he would take another nip and so on through the night until the early hours.

Flask still in one hand, he idly picked up a pencil and began to draw a rough sketch of the kitchen, working out the apparent trajectory of the saucer that allegedly had flown from the shelf and cracked against Grace Lockwood's forehead before shattering on the tiled floor. The drawing was merely for the record, for without an independent witness it could not be registered as a paranormal occurrence; it also served to occupy his mind for a short while.

193

As he worked he noticed a vapour mist was forming each time he breathed out.

He straightened, realizing just how cool the night air had become. He felt an itch on his bare arms as the hairs there began to stiffen. It wasn't merely cooler – it had become decidedly cold.

Ash rolled down his shirtsleeves and looked around the room while he buttoned them. The temperature drop was unreasonable unless the climate outside had suddenly altered, and he started to rise with the intention of checking the thermometer on the stairs.

It was as he pushed back the chair that he heard a dull thud from upstairs.

He remained still, holding his breath and listening. Was Ellen Preddle awake and moving about? It was possible; the poor woman looked as though she hadn't had a decent night's sleep in weeks. But the noise had sounded as if it had come from directly overhead. From the bathroom.

Ash looked at the monitor screen. All was still in the bathroom. There were no extraneous shadows and nothing was out of place. Something caught his eye though, but this was not on the screen. This was on the staircase a few feet away from him.

The talcum powder he had spread on the stairs earlier was beginning to billow as though a draught had disturbed it.

He held his breath as the fine powder swirled languidly into the air. When it had risen to a height of two or more feet, Ash went to the camera containing infra-red film, his movement easy and his senses alert, all boredom and tiredness driven off.

He pressed the shutter release, the *click*, followed by the fast whir of the camera's electric motor as it wound on the film, extraordinarily loud in the quietness of the night. He took three more shots as the powder-mist spread along the steps, now dropping in height but becoming thicker, its motion growing more rapid as if impelled by something more than a draught. Within seconds it was dense. Like driven smoke, it began to take on a direction, rising again, but keeping low to the stairs, surging over each one in undulating waves. Upwards it poured, twisting at the bend, a long vaporous stream that flowed and rippled, eventually trailing off on the lower steps, leaving them clear.

Its ragged end was disappearing into the upper reaches when he decided to act. He hurried forward, pausing at the first stair before continuing, then climbing at a slower, more cautious, pace. He had reached the stair over which the thin black cotton had been stretched when a terrible, heart-stopping scream shattered the silence.

It had the sound of an animal in mortal terror and Ash reeled back against the staircase wall in surprise. The scream persisted, filling the air, reaching a shattering pitch before abruptly ending. An eerie silence followed in its wake, and then footsteps pounded along the landing over his head. Shadows shifted on the wall by the bend in the stairs and bright flashes were reflected off its surface. He shrank back.

Oh dear God, he didn't want to go up there. He didn't want to see whatever had made that awful and piteous scream. His shoulder slid against the wooden wall as he retreated a step. He hadn't been prepared for this, for even though he had been forced to confront horrors that had chilled his very soul in the past, the scream he had just heard had left him in a state of shock. But it was not only the scream, for a mood of dreadful and debilitating menace had seeped into the atmosphere as if from the walls of the cottage itself. And as it held him there, afraid, unable to move any further, the noxious stench of corruption drifted down from the floor above.

His whole body flinched at the next scream, but this time the sound was different: it was the distressed cry of a woman in terrible torment. He knew it had come from Ellen Preddle, and as a crash and more screams came to him, he knew he had to help her, he couldn't let her face whatever had manifested itself up there alone. Ash forced himself away from the wall and the moment he did so his resolve strengthened. He

195

tore up the stairs, unknowingly breaking the cotton thread as he went, stumbling as he rounded the bend and bruising a shin. He kept going, avoiding the trailing wires and quickly reaching the narrow landing. The stench struck him almost like a physical blow and he turned his head to one side, grabbing the banisters to steady himself as he retched.

Ash straightened when another crash came from the bathroom and he saw the Polaroid camera tilt on its tripod and come to rest in a corner. Square sheets of scattered film lay on the floor before it, along with the capacitance detector. Shadows danced as the ceiling light swung to and fro and Ellen Preddle, alone in the bathroom, flailed her arms in the air, screeching and clawing her hands, grabbing at nothing, eyes wide with madness, lips curled back from her teeth, cheeks wet with tears and with drool.

'*Leave him be!*' she screeched. '*Don't you touch him!*'

Ash approached the doorway more slowly, his footsteps deliberate, his body tense, his nerves screaming. He stepped over the camcorder and tripod on the floor of the landing, the wire to the monitor downstairs pulled from its socket.

'*Leave him!*' Her words were drawn out, a wail of despair.

Untouched, the thermometer that had been standing on the sink suddenly shot across the room to crack against the dark windowpane before falling to the linoleum floor. Almost immediately, the bathroom cabinet dropped from the wall and burst open in the sink beneath it, its contents spilling out, pill bottles and cardboard containers falling onto the floor to be caught up in Ellen Preddle's mad dance.

Ash rushed forward, catching the frenzied woman. But she turned on him, clawed fingers reaching for his face, his eyes. He caught her wrists and held her hands away from him.

'Stop!' he shouted at her. 'Calm down!'

Her eyes showed no recognition: they were blind with a rage so fierce he knew she would try to harm him. Spittle flew into his face and he turned his head aside, the strain of holding her there causing his arms to shake, his neck muscles to tighten.

And as he turned he saw the turbulence in the bath. He saw the faint form beneath the murky, frothing waters. He saw the face of a child, its mouth open, its eyes wide.

And the boy's filth-smeared hand broke through the scum that floated on the surface and his fingers were spread and trembling as if reaching for Ash, reaching for life itself.

23

HERE WERE FEW LIGHTS on in the village. Most people were deep in sleep; it was the others, the insomniacs, who felt the sudden coolness in the night air – an unexpected shiver, a stiffness in their bones, goosebumps on their flesh, made them aware. These unfortunates quickly hurried to their beds or, if already there, wrapped bedclothes tightly around themselves.

The main street and the small lanes leading off it were all empty. Even the bats that inhabited the community hall's various roofs had not ventured out on their usual nocturnal forage. And even the disturbance inside the little terraced cottage in the lane leading up to the church was tightly contained within its own walls. All was very quiet.

A partial moon revealed the stocks and whipping post that stood on the dulled village green, but the blackish fluid that oozed from the tiny fissures in the post's aged wood would have been imperceptible to any observer who might have been abroad that night. The pond nearby was still and impenetrable, a brooding mass that reflected nothing.

Yet now something did move across this bleak landscape. A small, lone creature glided through the grass, its pointed snout held high every few yards to sniff at the air. It was a cautious beast, mindful of the loathing it generated, and its stiffened fur bristled with tension. It reached the water's edge and it became immobile, as if mesmerized. Its sharp little eyes glazed.

With a thin squeal of alarm the rat jerked away from the water, spinning as it did so, its long tail flicking the filmy surface and causing sluggish ripples that quickly settled as they spread. It streaked through the grass and back across the road, a swift shadow among still shadows. In an instant it was gone – gone to join fellow creatures skulking in the cellars of the old inn.

Nothing else stirred. The village slept. But the dreams of the villagers were not peaceful.

Tom Ginty jerked awake. His senses took a few seconds to follow.

He lay there in the bed, blinking, his wife Rosemary snoring beside him. What had awoken him? His beefy hand slid from beneath the sheets and touched the numbness of his right cheek. That was it! It had felt like someone had slapped him while he slept! He raised his head from the pillow and looked at Rosemary.

She was just an inert lump lying next to him. A big lump and not quite so inert: the sheets swelled and fell in rhythm with her breathing. She snuffled halfway through a snore and he resisted the urge to slap her in return, even though the slap she'd dealt him had obviously been an accident. She'd probably bashed him as she'd turned over in her sleep. Hold on though – she was facing away from him, and her fat arms were under the bedsheets. She couldn't have hit him. Unless she'd been tossing and turning. Silly bloody cow. Obviously she'd had a nightcap before she'd come up to bed, a drop of port. Or two. And bet she'd had a snack, bet she'd noshed some cheese. By Christ, cheese and port! No wonder she was restless.

Something brushed against the thin strands of hair plastered down over his scalp.

He shot up in bed, raising a hand to his head as he did so. *What was that?* The bedsheets slid over his belly onto his lap. With a speed unusual for such a big man he plunged for the bedside lamp. A moment of fumbling before the light snapped on.

'Who's there?' he said aloud.

But he could see for himself: there was *no one* there.

He turned to his wife again and pulled a face when her continued snores assured him she had not been disturbed. About to prod her, he became aware of how cold it was in the bedroom and he pulled the sheets up to his bare, breasty chest, holding them there as a maiden aunt in fear of losing her virginity to a night prowler might. He looked about the room, searching the shadowy corners.

'Ridiculous,' he informed himself. Apart from Rose and himself the room was empty. He glanced up at the ceiling almost expecting to find a spider at the end of a silken thread hovering over him, as shocked as he at their contact. There wasn't one there, of course, and even if a spider had run across the top of his head it could hardly have slapped his face! He smoothed down his hair with the palm of his hand, making sure there was nothing playing among the sparse strands. Must have been a dream. Nobody had touched him. His hair? A draught, nothing more than that. The inn was full of sneaky draughts. Yet his cheek still felt numb. And he couldn't feel any draughts now, even though the room was chilly.

The end of the bedstead began to vibrate. Not much, quite gently.

He watched it quiver, incomprehension lodged on his broad face, and it was a few moments before he murmured, 'Oh my Lord, there's someone under the bed.'

He leapt out and two fast steps took him over to the cedar tallboy standing against the wall. One hand held it for support while the other clutched at his pyjama bottoms to keep them up.

'*Rosemary!*' he hissed. His wife snored on.

He stared into the shadow between the overhanging bedsheet and the carpeted floor. *Was* there someone underneath?

200

Impossible. How could anyone get into the bedroom? There was only one guest staying at the inn at present and as far as Ginty knew he hadn't returned that evening. An odd chap all right, and an acquaintance of the vicar, which made him even odder. But he couldn't have got into the room anyway, because the bedroom door was locked from the inside, a habit of many landlords who didn't trust strangers under their roofs.

The bedstead stopped quivering.

Ginty doubled up, bending as low as he could – an awkward position for someone of his build – to peer into the darkness beneath the bed. He still couldn't see anything. He got down on his hands and knees and inched closer, his nose almost touching the floor. He could smell the dust in the carpet, the mustiness that wafted out from under the bed. It was too gloomy there to make out anything at all.

He crawled even closer and with a hand that shook just a little he grasped the loose sheet. With a sharp intake of air he whipped the sheet upwards. As he did so, the whole bed began to rock violently.

Rosemary woke with a start. And when she realized what was happening to the bed she let out a shriek. And when she saw her husband's disembodied head, half of it in shadow, peering over the edge of the bed at her, his eyes and mouth wide with fright, her shriek waxed into a scream.

In a split second she was out of the bed and across the other side of the room where she wrapped the window drapes around herself as if for protection. Her husband rose from the floor and rapidly backed away from the oscillating bed. They both stared in disbelief at it and Rosemary wailed: 'What's happening, Tom? Why's it doing that?'

But Ginty had no answer. Nor did he intend to find out. He edged around the tallboy, making for the door, never once taking his eyes off the phenomenon in the centre of the room.

'Tom!'

Rosemary's hairnet had somehow snagged against the thick curtain material so that locks of unnaturally blonde hair fell over

201

her pencilled eyebrows. Her eyes were daring her husband to leave her alone in that room with the crazed bed and when she realized that was precisely what he intended to do, the daring switched to pleading. He was by the door now, his fingers fumbling behind his back for the key in the lock.

He found it, gripped it, and was about to twist, when the tallboy to his left leaned away from the wall. It balanced there impossibly, unsupported, neither standing nor falling. Only when Rosemary screamed again did it topple. The two drawers slid forward as the chest struck the bed, the first one shedding its contents so that socks and handkerchiefs jigged on the sheets. Both pieces of furniture shook and quivered, their movements becoming more elaborate by the moment, more excessive, the legs of the bedstead practically leaving the floor. Their thumping sounds almost drowned out Rosemary's moaning.

Ginty wheeled round and turned the key. He pulled open the door and as Rosemary screamed at him not to leave her, the wardrobe, which stood facing the end of the bed, joined the frenzy. Its door sprung open, clothing tumbled out.

The landlord thought he saw moving shadows outside in the gloomy corridor, but when he blinked they stabilized, became normal shadows.

From behind him came a strangulated 'Tom!'

With an expression of misery mixed with panic, he rushed out into the corridor and slammed the door behind him. But as he held on to the handle, pulling the door tight, everything became quiet once again. In fact, the silence was so immediate and so absolute it was almost as scary as the noise itself.

A muted sobbing came to him through the wood as he waited shivering in the cold corridor. Tentatively – and shamefacedly – he opened the door again and peeked inside.

The bed was still, and so was the tallboy leaning against it. The wardrobe was motionless although at an angle to the wall; fallen clothes jammed its door open. Nothing moved in the bedroom. Nothing except Rosemary's plump shoulders as she wept against the curtains.

The millwheel creaked. For the first time in many years it protested at the pull of the river even though the current was sluggish. And then it groaned, a sonorous complaint that disturbed the stillness of the night. If anyone had been about in Sleath's High Street at that hour, or on the nearby bridge that served as portal to the village, then they might have thought they had heard the moaning of someone in deep pain; but no one was, so no one heard.

The wheel shifted, perhaps a millimetre, certainly no more than that, and the cog-wheels inside the millhouse stirred. They, too, creaked and groaned and strained against the shackles of grime and rot that had bound them for so very long. Cobwebs draped from rafters moved as a chill breeze passed through the old disused building, and dust drifted in the air to settle long after the sounds had died away and everything was still again.

Dr Robert Stapley had never been a good sleeper. Even as a student doctor nearly fifty years ago, his brain and his energy had been too restless, his enthusiasm too rampant, to accommodate the calmness conducive to contented slumber. And decline, that ineludible moderator of all excesses, while dulling the restlessness and enthusiasm, had merely become an ally to insomnia; perhaps the habit was too well established for old age and its detriments to have any worthy influence. Indeed, during the past ten years he doubted he would have managed any sleep at all without the help of a half-tablet of nitrazepam taken with warm milk and a stiff shot of Grouse just before he turned in each night. Even then sleep came gradually, weariness – ever present these days – slowly succumbing to exhaustion, exhaustion eventually capitulating to oblivion. Perhaps guilt was the culprit in these latter years, memories the spur. So many things to forget . . . why didn't age and diminishing brain cells play their part in that too?

His rheumy eyes stared at the open book over spectacles that had slipped to the end of his nose and to him the words were just neat lines of tiny creatures marching in unison across the page with no purpose and no import.

He remembered. He remembered those he had allowed to die. Not deliberately, not intentionally – neglect was mostly a matter of carelessness rather than design. He remembered their names and in his mind's eye he saw their faces. One by one they paraded before him, accusation in their sad, staring eyes, pointing their fingers as if he alone were responsible and God was merely the bystander. *Not his fault, not his fault.* How could any physician be held accountable for lives that had come to their natural or inevitable end? How could every single diagnosis or response be impeccable? Doctors were human, they made mistakes like anyone else. *But there were different kinds of mistakes*, a small, tormenting voice told him. *There were blunders and misjudgements, there were confusions and lapses. But there was also disregard and failure, wasn't there? Well, wasn't there? And of course, there was murder.*

The book slipped from his lap and he let it lie there at his feet. *Yes, yes,* he replied to the tormentor that was his own guilt, *there were all these things. But murder? Could he admit to that? Could he* deny *it?* He twisted in the armchair, reaching for the Grouse bottle on the little round occasional table by his side. He poured himself another measure and contemplated the other, smaller, bottle on the table. The other half of the sleeping pill? Should he take it? It would make him so drowsy the next day if he did. But did that really matter? He slumped back in the seat. Yes, it mattered. How could he function properly if his mind was in a daze and his reactions lethargic? But other pills could take care of that. As they had in the past. As they had only too regularly. What was it they said about living in a sweet shop? You soon lost your taste for sweet things. If only that were true of the medical profession where the analogy might be apt – for sweets substitute drugs – but in truth, where availability so often led to dependency.

Leave it for now. Give it another twenty minutes or so. If he wasn't sleepy by then, what the hell, take the other half of nitrazepam. And another shot of scotch. Find oblivion, that elusive anaesthetic. No more thoughts then, no more tired remembrances to haunt the present.

He lifted the tumbler and sipped the scotch. *My, how your hand shivers, dear Doctor. How the glass rim blurs and the golden liquid agitates in your grip. Is it the coldness of the night or the bleakness in your soul that causes the trembling? Who could know the truth? Only you.*

He took another drink, throwing his head back and swallowing hard, hoping the alcohol would warm him, praying it would smother his unease. It *was* chilly in his room. He glanced towards the window to see if he had left it open: the darkness outside pressed against the windowpanes as if eager to gain entry. So dark out there, so very black. The clock on the mantel told him it was twelve minutes past one.

Ye Gods, had he really sat here that long? He had settled down in the armchair with his book around ten o'clock in the evening, the whisky bottle brand new, as yet unopened. Now the bottle was less than half-full and he was only half-inebriated. Perhaps he would need to unlock the drugs cabinet downstairs in the surgery if he was to find peace this night. A small injection, a careful dose. Sometimes it was the only way.

He wondered how Edmund got through nights like this. Badly, was his guess, for even his God would not comfort him. Solace could only come through contrition for a holy man and that was a course no longer open to the Reverend Edmund Lockwood. The poor man had severely degenerated with the burden of it all, alarmingly so since the death of his wife, and his suffering must be terrible. But then, wasn't it so for all the others involved?

Like you, for instance? You were dedicated – or were supposed to be dedicated – to saving lives and he, the clergyman, was dedicated – or was supposed to be dedicated – to saving souls: so who was more guilty then, who should carry the greater culpability? Answer me that, dear Doctor.

He drained the glass and poured another. The heat was welcome as it scorched his throat and warmed his chest, but even so his hand continued to shake.

If only Beardsmore had not come to Sleath, for he was the instigator, his twisted, deviant ways had caused the revivification of something dreadful. Something secret.

But you enjoyed the perversions, didn't you? You enjoyed the revival.

'I was drawn in, we were all drawn in!' The doctor's voice resounded around the room and for a panic-filled moment he feared for his own sanity. For the first time he had answered aloud the voice inside his own head.

He brought a hand up to his face and covered his eyes. 'Oh dear God,' he moaned.

He stiffened when he heard a noise downstairs. He listened, alert now to things other than his own thoughts. A different noise, a kind of shuffling. And voices, he thought he heard voices. Coming up through the ceiling. But it couldn't be; this sitting room was directly above the waiting room adjoining his surgery and it was always kept locked at night. As were the front and back doors to the house itself, and these were bolted too. And because drugs were kept on the premises all the downstairs windows had locks fitted; the more accessible ones even had bars on the outside. Nobody could possibly get in. It had been tried once or twice, but the house was totally secure.

So how the hell *could* anyone have got inside?

The sounds seemed to fluctuate from a murmur to a whisper, as if someone nearby were tuning through wavelengths on a radio set, or constantly increasing and decreasing the volume.

His hand still shivering, the doctor placed the glass tumbler back on the occasional table, then with an effort got to his feet, using the arms of the chair to support himself. He felt very weak that night.

The whispering-murmuring continued as he stood there by the armchair, and he listened and waited – waited for the voices to fade. They didn't. He heard soft laughter – no, more like sniggering, a dirty kind of nasal chuckling. It sounded . . . somehow . . . unearthly.

Nonsense! These voices were in his mind, or perhaps from a television set or radio from a house nearby, freakish atmospherics carrying the sounds so that they appeared to come from the room below. Oh, he'd heard the rumours insinuating their way around the village. Something odd was going on in Sleath they said. Yes, something odd was going on all right – yesterday young Danny Marsh had been beaten and mutilated to within an inch of his wretched life, and last night Jack Buckler had been murdered – but it had nothing to do with hauntings and that kind of rubbish. As the saying went, there were no such things as ghosts. And rogues like this person – what was his name? Ash, yes, something-or-other Ash – were only too ready to exploit the fears and gullibility of stupid and credulous people. Psychic investigator indeed! Sheer bloody nonsense! How foolish of Grace Lockwood to engage the services of the man. Surely her father had no part in that! Surely he hadn't become that feeble-minded. It might be an idea to call on Edmund tomorrow and have a few quiet words with him. Goodness knows, it was his duty as the vicar's doctor and long-time friend to express some concern for the man's deteriorating health. In fact, a professional call was long overdue. *(But there was a reason for that, wasn't there, a very good reason for neither one of you wishing to look into the other's eyes? How could you not be embarrassed by the deep shame you would find in each other's gaze, eh? Eh?)* He shook his head as if to dismiss this sly, inner voice. Tomorrow he would tell Edmund Lockwood that he, himself, had witnessed this man Ash making enquiries at the Black Boar and he hadn't liked the look of the man on sight. His untidiness apparently went with his shoddy profession and, if his judgement as a doctor was anything to go by, the man seemed a little too fond of a drink. It might be just as well if this so-called investigator's services were cancelled immediately.

The murmuring from downstairs swelled just enough to interrupt his thoughts. It faded, became a quiet drone again.

Dr Stapley stared at the floor as if he could see through to the room below. Was he really hearing voices? He put quivering fingertips against his temples. Or were they merely inside his mind? Had the guilt and the anxiety that went with it finally got to him? Was the lack of sleep and the illicit use of certain substances at last breaking him?

He suddenly smiled, and then laughed, a thin sound that held no humour, but which rang around the room in hollow approbation of his own deduction. Of course, you stupid, stupid fool! It *was* a radio, and it was downstairs! One of his younger patients must have left it in the waiting room some time during the day – he'd seen at least two teenagers in surgery hours and everyone knew how impatient youngsters got when they had to wait for more than two minutes. One of them had obviously brought in their transistor radio or Walkman or whatever it was they carried about with them these days and had left it behind. It made sense. He hadn't heard it earlier because it was turned low and he had been absorbed in his own thoughts all evening; naturally it was only late at night or in the early hours of the morning that the sound seemed amplified; or it might even have been a build-up of power that had increased the volume. It had been on all afternoon and evening, but it was only now that it penetrated the floorboards beneath his feet! Oh what an idiot he was.

He picked up what was left of his drink and held the tumbler aloft in toast of his own sound reasoning before taking a long gulp of the scotch; this time it tasted stale and its warmth had little effect. Still the murmurings from downstairs intruded upon his thoughts.

'Oh bloody hell,' he muttered under his breath. Have to go down and turn the dratted thing off. Couldn't let it drone away all night, or until the batteries wore out. He put the glass down and went to the sideboard where he took out a set of keys from a drawer. Dr Stapley hated the rooms downstairs after surgery hours even more than he had come to hate them when they were filled with patients: no, he didn't like sick people cluttering up the place and fouling the air with their germs, but at night (he had to pass through the waiting room to get to the surgery with its treasure-trove cabinet of opiates and anodynes – sometimes just a whiff of pure oxygen was enough to satisfy his needs) their absence seemed to emphasize not only the emptiness of the rooms themselves, but also the vacuity of his own existence, for their presence upheld his eminence among them, their need for his skills and knowledge sustained his prestige. Their illnesses gave him some substance.

He would have to go down though; besides, he could always make it worthwhile by raiding the 'treasure-trove' for something a bit stronger than the half-sleeping pill, something that might not make him sleep, but at least would help him enjoy the insomnia. He moved unsteadily to the door of his private quarters with a little more cheer than he'd felt a minute ago.

The landing was in darkness and he brushed his hand against the wall to find the light-switch. There, that was better. See what a good doctor he was? Dark one moment, light the next. A genius, no less, a god of causation. Now let's get to that damned radio and do the business there. Sound one moment, silence the next. Hah, the master practitioner (literally) at work!

He swayed as he reached out for the newel post at the top of the stairs. Oh my goodness, not enough food and too much Grouse. And wouldn't you know it? – the sleeping pill was finally beginning to take effect. No matter. Something extra would do no harm. He was the doctor, after all, and doctor knew best. He'd prescribe just enough to lift himself out of this pissing, depressing melancholy. No more, no less, just enough. Right, here we go.

He took the first step and slipped so that he had to cling to the banisters, his thin legs stretched over the lower stairs. He cursed himself for not having realized he'd drunk so much.

Well, it wouldn't be the first time, nor the last. He found purchase with his heels and let them take the strain. He hauled himself up and rested against the rail, giving himself the chance to regain his breath and settle his nerves. Could have been a nasty accident. How the word would have spread around the village – old Dr Stapley found in the morning by his nurse-cum-receptionist lying in a drunken heap at the foot of the stairs. Oh yes, a nice little story to go round and one that would have caused much merriment and shaking of more-pious-than-thou heads no doubt. How his reputation would have suffered. But what did he bloody care? To hell with the lot of them, hopeless bunch of parochial gossips! They had no idea what the real world was about, generation after generation of them stuck here in this pretty-pretty village with its thatched roofs and quaint ways. At least *he* had tasted other things; *he* had taken pleasures they could never dream of.

Bloody noise!

It was louder, seeming to surge up the stairs as if to taunt him. Voices, moanings, whispers – what kind of radio programme was it, for God's sake? He straightened, furious at the impertinence of whoever had left the machine in his waiting room. How dare they! Tomorrow he would instruct Mrs Pikings to ban any such monstrosities from the premises. Let them read the magazines he provided at his own cost.

'Damnation, I can't stand this noise anymore!'

The doctor stomped down the stairs, growing angrier by the step. It sounded as if the volume had increased of its own accord! Unless, of course, it was because he was drawing closer to the source. Or someone *was* inside the waiting room manipulating the volume control.

He hesitated on the last step and stared at the door directly opposite. He was relieved to find it closed, but only for a moment. The question was, was it locked? He almost turned about and went back to the safety of his own rooms from where he could dial the police. But then how foolish he would look if they arrived to find nothing but a transistor radio inside there and the village doctor bleary-eyed and reeking of scotch? What then?

These wretched sounds were getting inside his head! He clenched his teeth together, deep lines creasing his thin face from his eyes to his jaw. His eyes almost closed and the knuckles on one hand were white as he clenched the keys. The noise was becoming unbearable. It sounded like a madhouse in there! It was too much, too bloody much!

He took the few feet to the door in quick steps and gripped the handle with his free hand, fury overcoming any reservations he might have had. He gave the doorhandle a sharp twist and pushed. It *was* locked! Thank God. No one could be inside, this was the only way in. It really was a radio in there.

So harsh was the noise, so disorientating had it become, that the key scraped past the lock twice before he managed to insert it. He was shouting against the voices as he turned the key and twisted the handle. Confused, maddened, he thrust open the door and reached inside for the light-switch.

The noise stopped immediately.

He stood just inside the doorway in complete – deafening – silence. There was no radio and there were no people.

But there was an odious, clinging kind of smell, one that he knew quite well. For it was the smell of dead bodies.

The secretions in Nellie Gunstone's enlarged lungs precluded a decent night's sleep not only for her, but also for her husband Sam. At their worst her breaths came in laboured wheezes; at their best they were merely laboured. Furthermore, several

211

times during the night she had to lean over the edge of the bed and hawk up the mucus that had collected inside her chest into the bowl on the floor; she hated the indignity of that as much as she hated disturbing Sam. He needed his rest, for the proper running of their farm, small though it was, required early rising and working through the day, with less than an hour around midday for a snack, until late evening. He was a tough old bird, for sure, but without a good night's rest – especially now she was unable to help even with the minor chores – he would soon be too exhausted to carry on. Not that he'd complain, mind, he wasn't that sort, but she knew what was best for him – and why wouldn't she after thirty-one years of marriage. So she'd insisted he move into the spare bedroom and although he'd grumbled and resisted at first, and only after she'd complained it was *his* snoring that kept *her* awake, he'd given in. Nellie still didn't know if Sam had really fallen for her ploy – she suspected he didn't want to upset her in her poor state of health by arguing. Now, for the first time since they'd been married (except for five years ago when Sam was in hospital having a gallstone removed) Nellie slept alone. And she didn't like it, she didn't like it one bit. Illness, she had found, was a lonely occupation, and in the middle of the night or the early hours of the morning, that loneliness was worse than anything she had ever known.

She stirred, then woke, automatically shuffling her body over to the edge of the bed and flexing the muscles of her throat to bring up the phlegm that interfered with her breathing so. But as she raised herself on one elbow Nellie realized her air passages were not clogged and that her breathing was easier than it had been for several days. She slumped back onto her pillow, her grey, brittle hair framing her once full but now haggard face, and wondered what had caused her to wake.

The reason was soon apparent, for the ceiling flickered with an orange glow and a muffled crackling sound came from outside the window. It was not the noise, nor the soft reflections on

212

the ceiling, but the sensing of something wrong that had roused her. She lay there and watched the dancing light, afraid not for herself, but for Sam and the people of Sleath, for her own imminent death – oh yes, she knew the emphysema had withered the tissues of her lungs beyond repair and that she was not long for this world – had somehow drawn her mind closer to mysteries that in normal life she would not even have considered. Sleath had changed. Or regressed.

She pondered that thought and could not understand how it had come to her, or even what it meant. In close proximity to the mysteries she might be, but they were still just that – unknown and unimaginable. They could only be sensed.

She heard a noise from the other side of the room and in the wavering glow she saw the bedroom door begin to open. Nellie clutched at the bedclothes as a figure stood in the door-way, silhouetted by the feeble night-light from the passage; she let her breath go when she recognized her husband, dressed in the same old flannel nightshirt he'd worn for bed for the past twenty years or more, the one that reached almost to his ankles.

'What is it, Sam?' she asked and he knew what she was referring to.

His voice was as gruff as usual, but at least – and she guessed this was in deference to her poor health rather than any trepidation he might have – he made the effort to keep it calm. 'You know what it is, Nell,' he answered, moving to the foot of the bed.

'I want to see.'

'No, you jus' rest there. It's turned cold tonight, no sense in you gettin chilled.'

'Sam, I want to.' She was already pulling the blanket and sheet aside.

He hurried to her. 'Now, Nellie, we don't want you upset, do we?'

'Of course we don't, Sam, an' I won't be. But it's never been as bright as this before. I want to see it for myself.'

213

'Let me get your dressin gown, then. You'll need sommat aroun your shoulders.'

The dressing gown was lying over a chair nearby and Sam quickly swung it over her shoulders as she rose from the bed. Together they approached the orange-tinged window.

Sam Gunstone felt Nellie stiffen beneath his protective arm.

'Oh Sam, it's so clear. It's as though there really is somethin burnin out there.'

'There's nothin there to burn – the field's empty. No, that's the same haystack George Preddle went to hell in.' His arm tightened around her. 'What's goin on, Nell, what's happenin to this place?'

She had never heard that kind of fear in his voice before, save for when Dr Stapley had explained her illness to them both and Sam had asked if she would ever be all right again. Her arm slipped around his waist and she looked up into his face. She saw the tiny flames reflected in his eyes and shuddered.

It was when they heard the faint but eerie strains of laughter coming from the ghostly conflagration that Sam Gunstone led Nellie away from the window. He drew her to the rumpled bed and helped her climb in; then he joined her and pulled the bedclothes over their heads.

It had been a long time since they had clung to each other so tightly.

There had been no sleep for Ruth Cauldwell that night.

She lay in her bed, the bedroom door ajar so that light from the passageway could shine in. It was an inadequate light, one that created shadows rather than defined objects. The room was cold, but that was not the reason for Ruth wearing a night-gown buttoned to her neck, for the evening had been warm, sultry even, when she had made herself ready for bed; she wore a nightdress because she was ashamed of her body.

Ruth clutched a tissue that was crumpled and damp from the tears she had cried through the long dark hours, and she rested on her side, her body curled up almost into a foetal position. Her mother and younger sister, Sarah, were down the passage in her parents' bedroom, sleeping together in mutual comfort because the police had taken Ralph Cauldwell away the day before. Ruth had not wanted to join them and her mother had not pressed her. Yesterday Ruth was sure she had caught unguarded accusation in her mother's eyes just after the police had led Daddy from the house, a glare that had seemed to blame her for his arrest. It was fleeting, the accusation never voiced, and her mother had turned away, head bowed, offering no soft words of consolation or understanding. And Ruth had then, as she had since, desperately needed both.

It was her fault that Danny Marsh was in hospital, disfigured and close to death, it was her fault that Daddy was locked up on a charge of attempted murder. Her fault because it was her guilt that had brought Munce back, and her hysteria that had confused her father. When she had staggered home, her clothes dishevelled, her face and arms bleeding, forehead bruised and swollen, all he'd understood from her incoherent babbling was Danny's name and so, full of rage, he had rushed off, ignoring her pleas to stay with her. He had driven to the village and found poor, poor Danny . . .

Ruth held the tissue against her mouth to stifle her sob. Why wouldn't it stop? Why was she being punished so? No, it wasn't just her who was being punished, it was her father, and Danny . . . But they weren't to blame for what had happened all those years ago. It was her fault . . . her fault . . . *her filth* . . .

She kicked out in the bed in frustration and in hatred for herself. Her fist came down hard on the pillow. She straightened and rolled onto her back, her body stiff, rigid, her mind a turmoil of bitter self-recriminations. And at first Ruth did not notice that the room was no longer merely cold, but was freezing; if it had been lighter in there, she would have observed the mist expelled from her mouth each time she exhaled. But

215

gradually, as the chill seeped into her bones, she became aware. As she became aware, also, of the stench that had crept into the house.

It was the sickly-sweet aroma of putrefaction and rot, the stench that always came with Munce . . .

She could not move. This time the fear, this appalling limb-freezing terror, held her in its grip. She stretched her mouth to call out to her mother, perhaps even to scream, but the muscles of her throat were locked tight too. Her flesh tickled – not pleasantly though – where tiny bumps rose, and her skin stippled, hardened. She lay in the darkness, motionless and as cold as stone.

Ruth did not see him, for she did not want to take her gaze from the ceiling. At first she sensed his presence, then caught a movement of shadows in the periphery of her vision. Still she refused to look, even when a darker mass skulked around the bed towards her, for she knew that this time he was more than an apparition, more than an immaterial shape from a nightmare, now he had form, he had substance, he had strength.

And she was aware that her paralysis was self-inflicted, that if she really wanted to move – if she had the *courage* to – then *nothing* could keep her there against her will. But the undeniable truth was that Ruth chose to remain perfectly still. Because if she did move – a millimetre, an inch – then Munce would be very, very angry, just as he had been all those years ago if she moved, or struggled, when they played the game, the dirty, secret game . . .

He was close to her, she could feel the fetid air expelled from those wet corrupted lips on her cheek. Every sinew in her body tightened, every nerve tingled; her neck quivered against the pillow as the scream locked inside her throat strained to break free. It seemed as if tiny shocks were running through her in waves, every part of her recoiling. She felt a weight on the bed; she felt something slither beneath the sheet.

And then the cold, lifeless fingers touched her flesh.

Her mouth stretched wider, her lips pulling back over her

teeth, and her neck arched off the pillow; but still no scream came.

The icy hand slid across to her stomach, the mouldered fingertips rough against her skin. It lingered there.

Ruth's eyelids drooped, but did not close completely. She wanted to cry out for her mother, for her father, but she knew she could not. What was happening to her was too indecent, too squalid, too . . . too . . . secret. They mustn't know, they mustn't find out.

She felt the hand shedding skin and tiny bits of putrid flesh as it searched further. The fingers undulated slowly, caressingly, over her ribcage and paused beneath the swelling that was her breast.

His stinking breath quickened and was harsh against her cheek and neck.

The hand rose with the flesh and its dead fingers closed around her hardened nipple. She drew in a gasping breath as the hand became a claw that squeezed the softness around the erect tip and even though the pain soon became unbearable she still could not move.

The agony stopped when the hand abruptly slipped away to return to her stomach. Ruth thought she could hear his moaning, but the screaming inside her own head was so intense she could not be sure. Could a dead thing make sounds? Could a dead thing *feel*?

The weight lay upon her like some small but heavy beast in repose and for one foolish moment she thought the worst might be over. She waited and she hoped.

But the hand became restless again.

It moved down to the hairs that rose from the hollow between her legs, burrowing through them, palm flat against her skin, fingers probing and pointing the way. Munce's wrist and arm pressed into her belly, gliding on a trail of slime. His fingertips dipped and slowly, ever so slowly, sank into her body.

*　　　*　　　*

The sky was gradually beginning to brighten in the east, a widening vignette of light outlining the contours of the hills. Animal life began to rouse; birds spread their wings, readying themselves for dawn flight. Although night-chilled, the air was not refreshed; there was a staleness over Sleath that the coming day's heat would only augment. There was no breeze, nor would there be later.

The carrion crow was in flight long before its fellow creatures, for the deeper pre-dawn greys served its purpose: they cloaked its own predatory blackness.

Its prey was easy to find and the bird swooped into the cover of tall oak, to become invisible among the shadows of the tree's leafy branches. It watched a point high in the rising buttress of the old church tower, for inside a hole created up there by dislodged stones, black redstarts had built their nest of grass and feathers. Soon the adult birds left their chicks in search of food.

The crow wasted no time; it soared, then swooped down onto the buttress, squeezing its big body into the hole where the young chicks stretched their necks and opened their beaks expectantly. One by one the predator tore off their heads, killing them all before sinking its dagger-like bill into the bloody, open wounds to feed on succulent, moist flesh.

Mickey Dunn was shivering with fear and anxiety as much as from the cold. His clothes were damp with pre-dawn dew, his hair was matted and dirty, his leather jacket scratched and his jeans torn by the branches and brambles he had stumbled through last night after he had killed the gamekeeper. His eyes were bloodshot from rubbing, his eyelids red from crying.

Oh shit, shit, shit, what had he done? Weren't his fault. He hadn't known old Buckler was there in the woods. He'd shot the quarrel at the thing in front of him, the bloody mist-thing with all those other things inside. He hadn't meant to kill the gamekeeper. Hadn't hardly seen him, he was just a sort of blurry shape on the other side. But Mickey had heard him sure enough when the arrow went off and Buckler had screamed, and he'd seen him all right when the mist-thing had immediately vanished to reveal the gamekeeper staggering around the clearing like some drunken fool, with the arrow poking from his chest. Oh shit, shit. Buckler was dead, for sure. He'd made a funny gurgling-rattling noise when he'd collapsed to his knees, and then nothing when he'd toppled onto his face, pushing the arrow further in. Nothing. No groaning, no squirming, no breathing.

Mickey shuddered and drops of water were shaken from the leaves he crouched beneath. They fell onto his neck and he hastily wiped them away with a grubby hand. He drew himself in, clutching his raised knees with his arms, the loaded crossbow still gripped tightly in one clenched fist. The last two nights had been the worst he had ever known. Even worse than the time the Old Man had locked him in the bomb shelter at the bottom of the garden for the night. The concrete pit was a leftover from the war, built by his grandfather, who thought the German bombers had a special mission to kill him in particular; it had been a great joke among the villagers, but even funnier was the fact that Grandad had died of a heart attack when rejoicing the end of the war by over-strenuously ringing the church bells. Afterwards the bomb shelter had been used by Mickey's father as an apple store, and these days Mickey hid his poacher's gains in there. But one night, the night in question, when Mickey was eleven years of age, the Old Man had locked him inside the shelter – the pit, the cell, the bloody tomb! – for some mischief or other, stealing probably, and left him there till the next morning. Mickey had wailed to be let out and he had screamed when he heard the rats scrabbling around in the pitch black and he had screamed and screamed some more when one of the creatures had run across his lap. But still Dad had not come back and unlocked the door, probably because by that time he was asleep in the armchair in his usual drunken stupor (Mickey's mother had long since run off with the tally-man, who had called weekly for the payment on the living-room suite). He wouldn't have heard much anyway, nor would the neighbours, because the walls of the shelter were eight inches thick. When the door had been opened the following morning, Mickey had rushed out, white-faced, and had thrown himself into his father's arms, swearing he would never be bad again, he would never take another thing that didn't belong to him, and for a moment, just for the merest fraction in time, he had been held close against his father's chest, something Mickey had never experienced before or since. He had been quickly thrust away with a curt admonishment, but not before he'd looked up and caught the shock and shame in the Old Man's face.

Without doubt, being locked up all night inside that shelter had been traumatic – he'd suffered nightmares for years after – but these last two nights, oh these last two nights, had been far worse. For in the dark the woods were as frightening as any hole in the ground. Instead of rats there had been the sounds of other creeping creatures, and instead of total, blanketing blackness there had been deep shadows that seemed to move, seemed to come close, seemed to reach out to him. And there had been different kinds of stirrings at the edge of his vision, shapes that seemed to duck away or fade when he turned quickly in their direction.

And, of course, there was the knowledge of what he'd done, the murder he had committed, there to haunt him through the long hours of waiting. Would anyone believe his story? Would anyone believe he had seen ghosts in the woods, demons that writhed and moaned and made horrible noises inside that mist-thing? He was a poacher who had been caught red-handed by the gamekeeper – that's what they'd believe. Who would take the word of someone who had been in trouble all his young life, of a tearaway with an old soak for a father and a slut of a mother who had run off with the tally-man? *(Oh, Mum, why did you leave? Was it because I was always stealin and gettin into fights? Didn't you take me with you because I was bad and nothin but trouble since the day I was born, as the Old Man always said?)* You shot poor Jack Buckler because you knew it'd be prison for you this time, the villagers would say. You killed an innocent man going about his duty because even if you ran away you knew he'd recognized you, the police would tell him. Lock him up, not just overnight, but for good, the judge would order. *(Please, Dad, couldn't I hide in the bomb shelter till they'd stopped lookin for me and gone away? I wouldn't scream no more, I wouldn't howl, I'd stay still and quiet even if the rats ran all over me body, even if they started eatin me, nippin off one finger at a time, bitin into me belly and gorgin on me insides, I wouldn't even cry, not till the police had left, and you unlocked the door again and held me against your chest, jus' for moment like before, jus' for a tiny little second, you wouldn't have to be ashamed, you wouldn't have to feel sorry, you wouldn't even have to like me, Dad, you wouldn't even have to love . . .)*

Mickey's eyes blinked open and his head snapped up. Bloody hell, he'd almost fallen asleep. Can't do that. Not here. Got to move on.

He parted the leaves and they trembled along with his hands. He saw the dim shapes of trees and shrubbery. Then something more, something big and grey in the distance, through the trees. It was a building, had to be. But what . . . ?

He realized where he was. Still on the Lockwood Estate. He'd run as far away from the body as he could, hiding at any sounds or signs of life, sleeping rough, moving on again, and still he was on the same land, the same estate. And that place through the trees was the old burned-out manor house.

They'd never find him there, they wouldn't even think of it. And even if they did, there were plenty of little hidey-holes inside. Hadn't he done just that when he was a kid, played hide-'n'-seek in the ruins? Only once though. Hadn't liked it much and nor had the other kids. Everyone said it was haunted, that place. But that's all they were then, just kids: they believed those things. He wasn't a kid anymore, though. That ruin meant

221

shelter. He could rest up there for a while and find food –
berries and suchlike – in the woods when he felt sure it was
safe. There was plenty to eat off the land if you knew what to
look for, Lenny and Den had taught him that. He had his crossbow – he could bag a rabbit or a bird, build a small fire in the
cellar of the manor house, and cook whatever he'd caught.
Nobody'd see the smoke, not out here, not even if it came up
through the floors. Nobody ever came this way, not even the
stupid old vicar who owned the place. Nobody liked this part
of Sleath. He could hide out for a few days, then sneak back
home – the police would be well gone by then, thinking he'd
hiked it to London or up North – and get some proper food
and a bit of cash. Dad wouldn't turn him in, even if Grover and
Crick would. Oh yeah, they'd have sung all right. The police
would have known poachers were involved as soon as they'd
found his quarrel sticking out of Jack Buckler's chest and it
wouldn't have taken them long to figure out who owned the
weapon once they'd questioned two known villains like Lenny
Grover and Dennis Crick.

'*Bastids,*' he murmured, tenderly touching his swollen nose
and lip.

Mickey rose from his crouched position and, bent almost
double, shuffled out from the leafy shelter. Leaves wiped their
moisture on his jacket and a thin tendril slid across his cheek,
causing him to flinch and quickly brush it aside. Once free of
the bush, he stretched his limbs and took in great gulps of air.
He scratched an itch in his hair, his dirty fingernails raking a
tiny insect that had crawled into what must have seemed like
a safe, lush abode equipped with its own ground-floor blood
bank. Mickey squinted, peering through the breaks in the trees
to scrutinize the great grey shape in the distance.

It'd be okay in there. He could stay as long as he liked and
nobody would be the wiser. They wouldn't be sniffing around
much longer, they couldn't afford the time, not even for a
murder, and especially not if they thought he'd already done
a flit.

He started walking towards the derelict building, flexing his shoulders as he went, crossbow in one hand, its safety on.

Christ, he was hungry. But couldn't take no chances. Got to stay hidden, maybe till evening. There'd be plenty of rabbits about then. Probably kill three or four before they cottoned on they were being slaughtered. Stupid bloody animals. He kept his mind busy thinking such things, for they pushed worse thoughts to the back of his mind, if only for short snatches.

When he came to the road – a wide, hardened-mud track, in reality – Mickey moved alongside it, keeping to its bordering fringe of trees and undergrowth. The gutted shell that had once been a grand mansion soon loomed up before him and he paused on the edge of the large but overgrown clearing it dominated. He gaped up at the empty black windows and something inside him seemed to recede; it was as if a part of him – his own bravado, perhaps – had shrivelled at the sight of Lockwood Hall. He had *never* liked this place.

The open doorway at the top of the steps was as dark and uninviting as the windows, but he knew this was his only refuge. At least inside here he could light a fire and be warm for the next night or two – even if it was summer the nights had turned cool lately. He could keep the flames low and roast a rabbit or a bird without worrying about the smells and the brightness. He hesitated a while longer, then with a shrug that was strictly for his own benefit, he left the cover of the woods and ambled towards the grim sanctuary.

His soggy sneaker was on the first leaf-blown step when he heard the tinkling sound of music. At least, he thought he'd heard it for, as he paused, nothing more came to his ears save for the far-distant *kaa* of a crow. It must have been his imagination. He'd hardly slept for two nights, he was tired, hungry – and he was *scared*, for Christ's sake. His mind might be playing all sorts of tricks. A draught inside must have disturbed some broken glass or something. Hadn't sounded like glass though. More like one of them old pianos, one of them little things that played like a music box rather than a proper instrument. And there was no wind to cause a draught anyway. So it *had* to be his imagination.

Mickey continued climbing the steps and the music seemed to return with every one he took. He stopped before the high, open portal and listened again. No, there was nothing. Birds were waking up nearby, that's all it was. He was so exhausted he couldn't tell one sound from another. This place had been empty for over two hundred years, ever since the big fire the villagers still talked about. He was giving himself the jitters. Anyway, even if it was haunted – like some of them same villagers said – ghosts couldn't harm you. Everyone knew that. Ghosts couldn't do anything at all except stand around looking miserable.

Mickey tried to laugh, but his lip throbbed and the only sound he made was a kind of clucking at the back of his throat.

He raised the crossbow to his chest, holding it with both hands and pointing it at the unlit opening in front of him. He approached it cautiously and only silence greeted him as he entered.

A small, solitary figure crossed the stone bridge and walked along Sleath's High Street towards the village green. There was a deliberate purpose to the man's step, although it was by no means brisk – he had spent the night watching the village from a distance and at his age damp sank into his bones as easily as ink into a blotter. The collar of his tweed jacket was turned up and his narrow-brimmed hat was pulled down low over his forehead. The soft, sanguine flush of dawn on the undulating horizon was reflected in Seamus Phelan's grey-green eyes.

Another fine day ahead, he thought to himself as he reached the point where the short High Street branched into two roads around the green and its pond. A fine day, to be sure, but perhaps not so fine for the people hereabouts.

The night was slow in fading, despite the warm glow over the hilltops, its darkness still loured over the village like an oppressive mantle. The little man looked around him before crossing the road junction, peering at windows as if searching for signs of life. How many of you are still sleeping? he wondered. How many of you have slept at all? There were bad goings-on last night, terrible things were stirring here in Sleath. Did you feel them, dream them? Did they visit you? Yes, it would be a fine summer's day, but there would be a fatigue on the faces of the villagers. And bewilderment, no doubt. And a bit of fear. Ah, yes, there'd be some of that all right.

He crossed to the small space designated a carpark and noticed the red Ford he had observed yesterday. His attention swept towards the inn on the other side of the road.

'I'll be paying you a visit later, m'lad,' he said quietly to himself. 'We've much to talk about. But I'll not disturb you at this ungodly hour – you'll need all the rest you can get if you're to face what's to come.' Assuming you managed to catch any sleep last night, that is, he thought.

He eased his way through the few cars parked there and stepped onto the grass. He saw that the pond's surface was placid, reflecting the blackness overhead; he was reluctant to look too deeply into the stagnant waters, but his eyes were unwillingly drawn towards it. 'No,' he commanded himself sternly, determinedly pointing his face towards the bench and the great venerable elm near the other end of the green. 'I've no great desire to be gazing into your murky depths at this hour of the day,' he said as if to the pond itself, but something at the water's edge caught his eye. Ah, just a yellow plastic duck caught in the reeds. Nothing sinister about that, although there was a mystery in those gloomy waters, and its revelation would not be too long in announcing itself. For the moment, though, let it be; there were other matters to deal with. He walked on.

The curved crest of the sun glided slowly into view; it rose like some insolent and impervious curmudgeon, hostile to the night and all its stealthy malevolences. It was a grand and uplifting vision, and it almost brought a smile to his face; but he knew that the light and its warmth would not ward off the events about to unfold in this unholy place.

Phelan reached the bench and lowered himself onto it, noticing as he did so that the bloodstains on the grass were still present. He could not help but look towards the whipping post and there was no surprise in his eyes, no catch of breath, when he saw the dark crimson liquid oozing from the relic, a steady stream that swilled in the dust at its base, gradually sinking into the earth itself.

He closed his eyes against the sight, tilting his chin upwards as a sunseeker might. But the glow from the sun was behind him and as yet there was little heat from it.

His lips moved as if in silent prayer.

24

AVID ASH SLIPPED on his shirt and buttoned it, looking out of the window at the village green as he did so. It was not yet half past eight, but the heat of the sun was already drawing low clouds of moisture from the damp earth and the pond. He tucked the shirt-tails into his trousers, then rolled up the sleeves; it would be another hot day, perhaps even sultry. He spotted something yellow drifting through the thin vapour over the pond and remembered the tiny yellow duck he had noticed on the day he had arrived in Sleath.

The bed behind him was rumpled, most of the top sheet dragging on the floor where he had kicked it off during the night. He went over to the sheet and tossed it back onto the bed; he sat on the edge of the mattress and ran his fingers through his still-wet hair, trying to tidy it into respectability. A little earlier he had used the bathroom at the end of the corridor, soaking his body in tepid water to revive himself. But he still felt tired, wrung out, and it was hardly surprising given the disturbed night he'd had.

When Ash had reached the bathroom in Ellen Preddle's cottage after hearing those terrible, heart-stopping screams, he had found the woman throwing herself about in some kind of wild paroxysm. It was as if she were struggling with some unseen demon. And indeed, he learned later that that was

227

exactly what she thought she was fighting – the demon spirit of her late, hated and hate-filled husband. George Preddle still wanted the boy to suffer, she had told Ash later when the tears had dried and only the trembling remained, and she had to stop him, she had to fight his evil soul with all the strength she had. She had failed Simon when the boy was alive, but she would not fail him in his death.

It would have been easy for Ash to dismiss her claims as the ramblings of an emotionally disturbed woman had he not seen her son's ghost for himself. Without warning the bathroom light had flickered and dimmed, then left them in utter darkness. There was not even light from downstairs, for it seemed that all power in the cottage had suddenly drained. And in that darkness Ash had heard the single cry of a child in terrible torment.

Almost at once the light returned and he had found Ellen Preddle lying on the floor, eyes closed as if she were unconscious. The bath was empty.

Ash quickly examined the Polaroid shots lying scattered around the floor, but there were no images on any of them. Instead, each one showed a peculiar white effulgence, as if the camera's flash had been reflected back into the lens. He gathered them up and slipped them into his pocket for later scrutiny, then righted the cassette recorder that had been knocked over. Its battery compartment was open with only one battery left inside; the others were lying around the bathroom. By now the woman was moaning softly and he lightly shook her shoulder. She woke with a start and began to struggle again, this time with him. He quickly calmed her and soon she slumped against him as if too exhausted to fight anymore.

The strongest drink in the house was sherry and when Ash had settled her in the armchair downstairs he poured her a large one. To steady his own nerves he had helped himself to an even larger measure of vodka from the flask on the table.

Ash had stayed with her until her eyes had begun to close,

this time with natural tiredness. He had seen her up to her bed, assuring her that nothing else would happen that night (in his experience such phenomena could not sustain themselves for too long, because the drain on psychic energy was too great). Suddenly exhausted himself, he had returned to the inn to sleep, driving the short distance and using the key to the Black Boar's main door that the landlord had given him. His equipment, he decided, would be safe enough back at the cottage.

The haunting was over for one night, he had assumed, but then the other spirit child had returned.

He had almost collapsed into bed with exhaustion, and his dreams had been as confused and as shocking as the night before. And, like the night before, he had awakened to find the same apparition standing by the bedside.

There was both fear and pleading in the little boy's wide eyes, and his image was perfectly clear, as though his form held some inner light. The apparition faded within seconds leaving behind – although only momentarily – a faint aura in the shape of the boy's body, a kind of soft spectral outline. It was this that had leaned forward and touched Ash's exposed hand. Ash had felt a cold tingling where this residual energy had touched him.

As though released from a mesmeric spell, he had rolled over to the other side of the bed and onto his knees on the floor, a quick fluid movement born out of dread. He had crouched there for what seemed like a long time, but which in reality must have been no more than a minute or two.

When he had calmed himself enough to move he had returned to the bed and surprisingly, had fallen asleep. Bright daylight and sounds of life elsewhere in the inn had roused him eventually, and the bath in tepid water had helped clear his head and settle his nerves.

A sudden knock on the door broke into his thoughts.

'Mr Ash?'

It was a woman's voice.

'Yes?' he answered, rising from the bed.

'Someone to see you, Mr Ash.'

He was surprised. Who would want to see him at this hour of the morning? He immediately thought of Grace and quickly tidied the bed, working his way towards the door in the process. Before opening it he glanced around, then went back to the dressing table by the window. He slipped the hip flask into one of the drawers.

When he finally opened the door his surprise increased, for it was not Grace waiting outside.

The man standing next to the landlord's wife was small and might well have been described as flamboyant. He carried a cane and wore a russet brown tweed jacket with a spotted handkerchief protruding from its pocket, over dark green corduroy trousers and brown brogues. His waistcoat was maroon and a paisley cravat of various colours adorned the open neck of his blue shirt. His silver-grey hair was sparse on top, but thick at the sides with longish side whiskers. His grey-green eyes inspected Ash so closely that the investigator began to feel uncomfortable.

'I hope you don't mind my bringing the gentleman straight up,' Rosemary Ginty said, oblivious to the exchange between the two men, 'but he said you were expecting him.'

Ash regarded the diminutive man with astonishment, but something made him say, 'That's all right, Mrs Ginty.' He waited for the stranger to introduce himself, but the man only smiled at him.

'Well I'll leave you to it, then.' The landlord's wife moved away, her head down as if she were preoccupied with other matters. She paused, half-turning back to Ash. 'I hope you weren't disturbed last night,' she said.

'Disturbed?' He wondered if this was some kind of rebuke for his late return to the inn.

'The noises,' she went on, and for the first time he noticed the anxiety in her eyes. 'Mr Ginty and I had, er, a problem with a mouse in our room. He made a lot of noise chasing it

230

out, I'm afraid. Not that we usually have mice in the rooms, you understand.' She gave a faint-hearted laugh and tucked a dangling lock of blonde hair behind one ear. 'Bold little chap, but Tom soon saw it off. Well I'll let you get on.' She stopped again by the stairs and called back, 'Can we expect you down for breakfast fairly soon, Mr Ash?'

'I don't think –'

'Now I'm starving, meself,' said the stranger, waving his hat towards the landlord's wife. 'Why don't you set places for two?'

She gave a nod of her head and disappeared down the stairs.

Before Ash could object, the little man faced him. 'I'm thinking you might be needing a decent' – it sounded like 'daicent' – 'meal inside you to set you up for the trouble ahead.'

Ash frowned. 'Am I supposed to know you?' he said, beginning to get annoyed at the intrusion – and indeed, the familiarity. From the man's accent Ash knew he was Irish, but he was certain he had never met him before.

'No.' The little man regarded him meaningfully. 'No, you don't know me, Mr Ash, but I feel somehow that I know you. D'you mind if I come in?'

Without thinking, the investigator stood aside and the Irishman strode into the room, cane held almost as a pointer, going straight to the window opposite the door. 'Have you had the chance to look at the faces out there this morning?' he asked in his light, friendly tone. 'Everyone I passed on my way here looked as if they'd had a bad night's sleep. Did you look into the eyes of your landlady? There's a darkness over the place, Mr Ash, which is extraordinary on such a fine day, don't you think?' He looked around, waiting for an answer.

'Would you mind telling me who you are,' said Ash, 'and how you know me?'

'You're a modest chap,' came back the reply. 'You're well known in the rarefied world of psychic phenomena. Sure, haven't I read your very own book on the subject some years ago? And extremely interesting it was, if not entirely accurate.' He went to the room's single chair and sat, crossing his legs

231

and cupping his knee with both hands, his hat resting on his lap. 'I saw you driving by yesterday and recognized your face from the photograph on the back of the book.'

Ash remembered the curious sensation he'd had driving past the village green when he'd returned to the inn yesterday afternoon, a feeling of being watched. No, it was more than that – it had been a similar perturbation to when he'd first met Grace, but perhaps less powerful. 'That photograph was taken years ago,' he said, aware that the recognition had not come from that source. He closed the door and walked over to the end of the bed. 'And even then it wasn't a good likeness.'

'No, it was a very handsome photograph.' The Irishman smiled disarmingly. 'Well, it's of no importance. The point is, I know who you are.'

'But I don't know who you are.'

'Ah, forgive me. Manners have never been my greatest asset. My name is Seamus Phelan and I'm heartily glad to make your acquaintance.'

The name sounded familiar, but hard as he tried, Ash could not place it.

'It'll come to you later, I'm sure,' Phelan said, still smiling. He brushed back the thinning hair over his scalp. 'For the present, let's concentrate on the problem at hand.' Some of the lilt left his tone and his eyes bored into Ash's. 'There are peculiar things happening in Sleath, d'you not think so, Mr Ash?'

The investigator was perplexed. Who the hell was this man and what did he know about what was going on in the village? 'I'm sorry,' he said brusquely, 'but I'm here under the instructions of a client and my investigation is strictly confidential.'

Phelan gave a mild wave of his hand. 'Pompous nonsense and a typical Institute line, if I may say so.'

'You've had dealings with the Institute?'

'Not as such. I'm aware of its reputation, though. Now, David – you don't mind the informality, do you? – now, the situation here is rather grave, which isn't a suitable word to use under the circumstances, but it'll do. The fact is, it's liable to get far worse before it's over.'

Ash walked past the little Irishman and, hands in pockets, gazed out of the window. There were not many people about below – two women crossing the road, a man opening up a shop on the other side of the green, another pulling up in a dusty Metro alongside his own car in the nearby parking area – but Phelan was right: their faces were grim and they seemed to move slowly, as though burdened with some inner misery. On the other hand he might just be judging their mood by his own. Or maybe it was merely auto-suggestion, prompted by his uninvited guest. He did not bother to disguise his irritation when he spoke.

'What are you up to, Mr Phelan?'

'Just Phelan, don't bother with the mister. And I can't abide Seamus – bog-Irish, don't you think?'

Even the man's constant smile was beginning to annoy Ash.

As if guessing just that, Phelan's expression became almost solemn. 'Something unpleasant is happening here in Sleath, and I'm thinking it could be harmful to the villagers, perhaps even calamitous for them. And for you also, David.'

Ash was silent for a moment. Then: 'You're aware of the hauntings?'

The other man nodded and uncrossed his legs. 'A tremendous – and sinister – psychic energy is building up in this place. Did you know the village was built over a point where several ley lines converge?'

Again Ash was taken aback. Ley lines, so the theory went, were lines of earth energy along which high incidences of paranormal activity are purported to occur. Not being an advocate of the theory himself, his tone was somewhat sardonic. 'I had no idea,' he said.

'An inaccurate term, ley lines, but I suppose it serves its purpose. Those earthly energies are being used in this very area, together with the latent psychic powers of certain individuals. Haven't you realized this yourself, David?' It was a question put in earnest.

'Look, Mr Phelan –'

'Just Phelan. Humour me, now.'

'Okay – Phelan. I don't understand your involvement in this. I don't know who you are, or what you are.'

'I've told you who I am and what I am isn't important. But I was drawn here by the disturbances created by those energies, d'you see? I'm sure I'm not the only psychic in the country to be upset by these odd forces in the atmosphere.'

'But you're the only one to find their way here.'

'Well – there's you. You're here, David.'

'How do you know I'm psychic?'

'Takes one to know one?' His smile returned. 'Strange that you should fight it so. Why are you so frightened of your gift?'

Ash ignored the question. 'I wasn't drawn by any mysterious forces – I was invited by a client.'

'Yes, by the vicar, no less. Oh, I did some investigating in the village meself yesterday – listening to the gossip, mooching around, that sort of thing. Didn't I just spend the night watching over the place from the hill?'

It was rhetoric, but Ash countered with his own question. 'Why would you do that?'

'Oh, because of the danger I've already mentioned. Forgive me for sounding melodramatic, but there's evil about and the revenants are thriving on it.'

'Revenants?'

'They're –'

'Yes, I know what they are – those who return from the dead after a long absence. Ghosts, in other words. What I don't understand is why you should think so.'

'Feel so, m'boy. I *feel* so. And perhaps if your own gift were not so repressed you'd feel it too. You're being used, David. These malevolent forces are drawing on your own psychic energy. I thought so when I first saw you yesterday and I'm more than certain now that I've met you. You have an aura

234

around you that's depleted, and it has nothing to do with ill-health.' The Irishman was quiet for a moment, but his eyes never left Ash's. Then he said, 'You've been used before, haven't you? At some other time and in some other place.' There was concern in his manner.

Ash tried to push thoughts of Edbrook and Christina from his mind, but Phelan seemed to sense his struggle.

'Let go of it, David. We'll not talk of it just now. I understand that you've suffered traumas no man should have to endure. It's our curse, isn't it? Let's concentrate on the problem at hand, shall we? God preserve us, it's enough to be going on with.'

Crossing his legs again, Phelan leaned back and threw an arm over the back of the chair; his hat swung to and fro in one hand. 'And someone else here is being used, isn't that right? Someone else with the extrasensory power. It stands to reason, because there had to be a haunting for you to be called in, and from what I gather, there have been several sightings recently.'

Someone else with the power? Did he mean Grace? Ash was aware by now that Grace had psychic abilities more suppressed than his own, but was it possible? Could she be some kind of catalyst for these other forces?

'Ah, I can see by your expression that I've given you food for thought. Would I be right in guessing you know this other person?'

Ash did not respond immediately. He needed time to think, and he needed to know more about this man Seamus Phelan.

The Irishman unexpectedly came to his feet, a swift, energetic movement that took Ash by surprise.

'Why don't we talk about this over breakfast?' Phelan was already halfway to the door. 'Shall I go on ahead while you get yourself ready?'

'I'm not sure . . .'

The humour left the little man's eyes. 'I'm afraid it's too late for you to have doubts about anybody, my friend. It's of no consequence at all, d'you see? Whatever you decide to do, whatever action you decide to take, it's already too late. You could leave Sleath, of course, right now, right at this moment, but I don't believe you'll be wanting to do that, am I right? I can see that I am. Well, you have your reasons, but I can tell you that neither you nor I can control what is about to happen here in this place. The best we can hope for is that we'll both have our sanity when the madness is over. Oh, and our lives, let's not be forgetting that little thing. Two unfortunates have already lost theirs, I believe. The gamekeeper and the young man who was so viciously beaten.'

'The boy wasn't killed.'

'Ah well, I think you'll find I'm right. The young man is dead now, and there'll be others to follow. See you downstairs for breakfast in five minutes.'

With a jaunty wave of his hat, Phelan slipped through the door and was gone.

'Kate? Thank God I caught you.'

'Another few minutes and I'd have left for the Institute. You could have got me there.'

'Yeah, I know, but I need some information – fast.'

'Oh my. Trouble brewing in Sleath?'

A short pause. 'I think so. Can't be sure about anything at the moment.'

'Come on, David, what's going on there?'

'I wish I could tell you.'

'Have a stab at it.'

'Not now. There's something I want you to do for me, though.'

'I'm here to help. If I can, that is.'

'Have you ever heard of someone called Seamus Phelan? I think he's a medium or clairvoyant of some kind.'

She repeated the name thoughtfully. 'Sounds familiar, but nothing immediately springs to mind.'

'Yeah, it was familiar to me too. Listen, can you dig around when you get to the office – you might have something on file.'

'I'm pretty busy today, David.'

'I think it might be important.'

'Okay, I'll do my best. Do you want to give me a hint as to what this is all about?'

'I wish to God I knew. Just bear with me for a while.'

'David?'

'Yeah?'

'You don't sound too good. Are you sure you can handle this case? I mean, whatever is going on in Sleath – are you well enough to cope?'

'I'm over that last time, Kate.'

'You had a serious breakdown. Something like that isn't easy to get over. Why don't I come up there myself, moral support and all that?'

'No.'

The rejection was unequivocal and Kate jerked back a little from the phone.

'All right,' she said. 'But if you need me . . .'

'I'll call.' Some warmth was back in his voice.

'When do you need the information?'

'Today.'

'It's that important?'

'To be honest, I've no idea. But it could be.'

'I'll do my best.'

'That's all I ask.'

'Cut the sarcasm, it suits you too well.'

'Thanks, Kate.' He meant for her help.

Her voice softened too. 'You'd let me know if you had a problem, wouldn't you, David?'

'Always.'

'I told you to cut it out. I'll get back to you.'

'Thanks.'

Ash replaced the receiver. Hand still resting on it, he stared blankly at the phone for a few seconds. Then he picked up the receiver again and dialled another number. Grace Lockwood answered.

25

RACE ENTERED the empty classroom and went to the table that had once served as the teacher's desk. She laid the school keys on the table, then, thoughtfully, touched its surface, running her fingers over scratchmarks and indents. Decades of teaching had been ingrained in this wood; the walls around her had echoed with children's excited babble, their singing, even their silence. There was still faded chalk writing on the blackboard, although most of it had been wiped, and she smiled when she read the remaining lines of a poem that she and her classmates had learned in this very room all those years ago. It gladdened her that such traditions had continued here – at least, until the place had been closed – for they were reassuring in a swift-changing world where Nintendo had taken the place of hop-scotch and cheap cartoons were the new fables. She ran through the old poem in her mind:

> *Three young rats with black felt hats,*
> *Three young ducks with white straw flats,*
> *Three young dogs with curling tails,*
> *Three young cats with . . .*

Now what was it? Such a long time ago, but she definitely remembered this one. They used to chant it together here.

Timmy Norris would have known. He knew all the rhymes, as well as all the hymns. He knew them without looking at the blackboard or the book. He knew them by heart.

Her face saddened. But Timmy never went on to learn other things, more grown-up things. Timmy wasn't around to learn anything after his sixth birthday. Grace pulled back the chair from the table and sat facing the rows of tiny bench-desks as if she were the teacher now.

'With demi-veils,' she said aloud, recalling the last words of the poem. 'Three young cats with demi-veils.'

Her soft-spoken words seemed to hang in the air.

It was hot in the classroom, for the sunshine poured through the high empty windows unhindered. The windows were always opened wide in spring and summer when she was a child, Grace Lockwood remembered, otherwise the heat would have been unbearable on the sunniest days.

She checked her wristwatch. David should be here soon. He'd seemed anxious on the phone. It wasn't his voice – he disguised his feelings too well for that – but she had *sensed* his anxiety. Odd, how easy it was to judge his moods. She hardly knew him, yet . . . Yet, she knew his thoughts. Not in an explicit way; she couldn't tell exactly what he was thinking, what he was about to say, but she was *aware* of him, she felt intuitively close. And it was the same for him, she sensed that too.

Grace looked towards the middle row of bench-desks, two seats along. That was where she'd sat until she had been sent away. It had always seemed sunny in those days too. But that was only the illusion that came with childhood memories, when all summers were long and hot and it always snowed at Christmas. Life hadn't really been like that. Not here in Sleath. There had been those other times.

Grace shivered. And did not understand why. Something had bothered her, a thought, a memory; something on the periphery of her mind. She closed her eyes to assist that thought, but all she felt was confusion. Confusion . . . and a deep dread.

A shadow moved across her closed eyes and she quickly opened them. There was no one with her in the classroom. And there were no clouds to drift by outside. Grace scanned the room uneasily. Beyond the glass the sun was painfully bright, yet somehow the classroom had dimmed. She pushed the chair back, about to rise.

Before she reached her feet the voices came to her. But she did not hear them, for they were inside her head, faint, distant sounds that belonged to her perceptions rather than her physical sense. She sank back and her eyes closed once more.

Other shadows moved across her eyelids, shapes that came between her and the sunlight; yet each time she opened her eyes there was nothing there.

The voices came closer – they were inside her head, yet they came *closer*. She realized they belonged to children.

Grace swayed on the chair; her head drooped, then jerked erect again. These children were singing and as she listened to the words – the words that were only in her own imagination – she recognized them. They were from a hymn that she used to sing. In this room. When she was a child herself.

Her head bent forward and her shoulders sagged slightly; her lips began to move in time with the voices inside her head.

> *'Dance then, wherever you may be,*
> *I am the Lord of the Dance, said he . . .'*

She spoke the words as the children sang.

> *'And I'll lead you all,*
> *wherever you may be . . .'*

Louder. She really could hear them now. The voices were no longer just inside her head: they came from the bench-desks, they came from the walls, they came from the air itself. She spoke along with them, her own voice rising with theirs.

> *'They whipped and they stripped*
> *and they hung me high . . .'*

The sweet young voices were present, they were with her inside the schoolroom, and her eyelashes began to glitter silver in the shifting sunlight as a moistness seeped through her closed lids. She remembered the words as though she had only sung the hymn yesterday.

> *'. . . and they left me there*
> *On a cross to die . . .'*

But the hymn took on a darker tone as the key changed down. Although she faltered, the voices continued; and they were no longer sweet, no longer young. There was a grim hollowness to them.

> *'I danced on a Friday*
> *when the sky turned black . . .'*

The voices became deeper, less like those of children.

> *'It's hard to dance*
> *with the devil on your back . . .'*

Like adults singing.

> *'. . . But I am the dance*
> *and I still go on.'*

'Grace?'
She jumped in her seat, her hand reflexively clutching her chest. David Ash stood in the doorway, his face pale in the sunlight.

*　　　*　　　*

242

She hadn't wanted to stay inside the schoolhouse so they sat outside in his car, the side windows open wide to keep them cool in heat that was steadily becoming oppressive. Mist curled from grass verges and the road's surface shimmered. They could see the church tower further up the hill peeking over treetops; the sky behind it seemed almost bleached.

'What happened in there?' Ash asked, his body twisted towards her, an arm resting on the steering wheel.

'I was thinking of a hymn we used to sing in school when I was a child.'

'I heard you. You were speaking the words.'

Her hands fidgeted with the small brown-leather shoulder bag on her lap. 'Did you hear the other voices too?'

'Yes, I did. And it was the same hymn I heard just before I met you at the church two days ago. The one I told you about.'

'At first it was children's voices singing, then they seemed to change. They became . . .' She looked desperately at him. 'They became unnatural, not like children's voices at all. They frightened me.'

His hand dropped over hers and she did not pull away. 'Some parapsychologists believe sound can be absorbed into the walls of certain places, perhaps even into the atmosphere itself, stored there to be released at some later time, in the right conditions, by certain people.'

'Then why has it never happened to me before?'

'Until now you haven't even acknowledged any extra sense you might have. But circumstances have changed. Tell me – what made you come here this morning?'

She managed a weak smile. 'Nothing mysterious about that, David; I wasn't drawn by paranormal forces, if that's what you're insinuating. As part of my work for the community hall I have to check on the school building from time to time, then send in a report to the local authority. They own the premises so I suppose they want to make sure it's kept in a reasonable condition. Eventually it will be sold off to a property developer, or someone who wants it for a private conversion. When you

243

phoned you said you wanted to see me urgently, so I thought this was as good a place to meet as any. Now tell me – why was it so urgent?'

'Someone called on me at the inn this morning. A colourful-looking Irishman who said his name was Seamus Phelan. He reminded me of a leprechaun.'

'You didn't know him?'

'Never met him before in my life. But he seemed to have an idea about what was going on here in Sleath.' He quickly told her of his introduction to the diminutive Irishman. 'We even had breakfast together after I phoned you, although I must admit my appetite wasn't up to much. While he finished his breakfast and half of mine, Phelan told me he believed there was some kind of immense spiritual upheaval taking place in this locality. That's how he put it – "spiritual upheaval".'

'If I hadn't heard those voices inside the school for myself, I might have said he was exaggerating. All the same – "upheaval"? Hauntings, yes, but as you said yourself they're confined to certain people who've undergone traumas at some stage.'

'These hauntings might only be the beginning.'

'Oh God, surely not? There couldn't be more.'

'He said the very atmosphere is being corrupted by what's happening to Sleath.'

'The two killings.'

'What?'

'He's right, don't you see? Sleath *has* become tainted some-how, can't you feel it? The gamekeeper who was murdered, and then the boy, Danny Marsh, who was beaten to death. How else could such sudden and violent acts happen in a peaceful place like this?'

'Danny Marsh is dead?'

'The police rang my father this morning. As the village priest they thought he might want to talk to Danny's family.'

'The Irishman told me the boy had died.'

'Perhaps he'd already contacted the hospital himself.'

'Why should he? Besides, he wasn't a relative – they wouldn't have given him the information.'

'Then you think he might be credible?'

'If I hadn't witnessed a manifestation myself last night, and another early this morning, I might easily have dismissed Phelan as a crank. As it is, I'm not so sure.' He told her what had taken place in Ellen Preddle's cottage the night before, and then in his own bedroom at the inn around dawn. 'Ellen believes her son's soul is still in danger from his father and on both occasions when I saw this other boy he appeared to be reaching out for help. Phelan feels these spirits are not alone, that there are others seeking help. And possibly others with more malign intent. He advised me to look into Sleath's past records as quickly as possible while he carries out his own researches.'

'Why should you take advice from a complete stranger?'

'I'm not. I'd intended to examine the records anyway – it's part of my job. And that's why I wanted to see you.'

'I'll help in any way I can, David, you know that.'

He squeezed her hands. 'It means going against your father's wishes. I need access to the church chest where the records are kept. I have to know where it is and if it's locked, I'll need the key to open it.'

He looked at her askance, and her reply was to lean forward and kiss the small scar on his cheek.

26

E PULLED UP in front of the lychgate and turned off the engine. Through the opening he could see the flint walls of St Giles' and, for some reason, the sight disturbed him. It was only when Grace touched his arm, prompting him, that he put uncertain thoughts aside and reached for the door-lock.

As he stood beside the car waiting for Grace to come round from the passenger side he felt a trickle of sweat run down his back. He loosened his shirt collar and flapped the opening a few times, allowing cooler air to circulate beneath the soft material. Despite the mounting heat, Grace looked as fresh as ever; she wore a light blue chambray shirt tucked into a thin, summer skirt. Her hair was loose around her face, its curled ends resting on her shoulders. He caught her giving a nervous glance towards the school down the hill before she joined him.

'Try not to think about it,' he told her, only too aware that the advice was absurd.

For an instant she looked confused, but recovered with a faint smile. 'It's hard not to. I don't understand what's happening to me, David.'

You and me both, he wanted to say, but kept his own confusion to himself. 'Let's go in,' he said, walking to the wooden gate.

The rusted hinges resisted as he pushed it open and the

shade beneath its canopy brought temporary relief from the morning sun. He allowed Grace through, then followed her along the gravel path towards the church porch. As they walked through the graveyard Grace slipped her hand into the shoulder bag and brought out a set of keys. She reached the big double-door, twisted its iron-ring handle, and stepped inside the porch, a particular key from the set already poised in her other hand. She looked round at Ash as he entered and he saw for himself that the inner door to the church itself was ajar.

'It should be locked,' she told him as she dropped the keys back into the bag. 'Father or his curate must be here.'

The coolness inside the porch wrapped itself around Ash as it had on the first occasion, but this time he found it even more disconcerting; its mantle was too enveloping, the chill too deep.

Grace opened the inner door and they both went through. Ash stopped as if held there by some unseen hand, for the stillness inside the church was almost as palpable as the cold that had gripped him a moment ago.

Although by no means a large church, the interior of St Giles' was modestly impressive. A series of arches on each side led towards the chancel and its raised altar, an ornate rood screen separating them from the nave; the space over the chancel arch was taken up by a depiction of Christ's Transfiguration. Behind and above the altar itself a wheel-rose took the full glare of the sun, so that its stained-glass images were vividly illuminated. Their fused, mellowed reflections shone through the rood screen onto the high stone pulpit that stood to one side of the nave. A centre aisle divided the rows of pews and led back to the other end of the church, where a pipe organ and choir stalls were positioned opposite each other on either side of the arch to the turret area. Through the arch Ash could see the ends of bell ropes; they swayed slightly, perhaps disturbed by the opening of the porch door.

Grace gripped his arm and spoke in a tense whisper: '*Did you hear that?*'

Ash listened, then shook his head.

'I thought there was something . . .' she began to say and then they both heard the sound, a low and indistinct moaning. Grace's fingers tightened on his arm.

'It's coming from that direction,' said Ash in a hushed voice, pointing towards the altar.

Grace retreated a step, but Ash moved forward, taking the side aisle, his steps cautious. He walked towards the altar, peering ahead, searching between the pillars of the arches as he passed them. Grace reluctantly followed, her steps even quieter than his.

The soft moaning continued.

Ash snatched a quick look back at Grace and he saw that her face was pallid, her steps halting. They both stopped dead when the moaning erupted into a shrill wail, its sound amplified by the stone walls and high ceiling.

Suddenly Grace had pushed past him and was running towards the source. He called her name, afraid for her, but she ignored him, reaching the end of the aisle and crossing the nave to another smaller archway.

Ash hurried after her as she disappeared into a side chapel.

Although tiny, the chapel contained a small altar and credence table, as well as the stone effigy of a supine figure in ancient garb. At the base of the plinth it rested upon lay the slumped body of Reverend Lockwood, scattered around him a debris of torn books and crumpled parchments.

27

ASH STUDIED the painting of Lockwood Hall and decided Grace had been right: there *was* something cold in its architecture. Oh it was grand enough, palatial even, with its Corinthian pillars and pilasters, its high windows and ornate roof balustrade, but there was an austerity to that grandness, as if the architect had been more concerned with exactitude than elegance. On the other hand, the fault might lie with the artist's interpretation rather than the architect's vision, for there was a preciseness to the rendering that left scant leeway for the beholder's romantic interpolation. Even the tiny figures of horsemen cantering across a field beyond the house were painted in fine but prosaic detail, and indeed, the woodland trees in the distance were almost too clearly defined. Yet – and perhaps it was because of its very precision – the picture was fascinating.

Ash found himself absorbed, his eyes focusing on particular features – the long drapes behind the windows, the ornate rail of the stairway leading up to the huge entrance door, the bright costumes of the riders, the diminutive figure in white standing beneath a evergreen oak in the middle-distance . . .

Voices outside the study distracted him. The door, already slightly ajar, opened further and Grace Lockwood entered, followed by a dour-faced man who was somehow familiar to Ash;

he quickly remembered him as one of the Black Boar Inn's patrons when he'd first arrived in the village – the man and his companion had seemed particularly interested in Ash. Grace was preoccupied with their discussion and she regarded the investigator with momentary surprise, as if she had forgotten he was waiting.

'David,' she said, indicating the man who had followed her into the room, 'this is Dr Stapley.'

There was a deep weariness to the doctor's rheumy eyes behind their thin-framed spectacles, as well as a general fatigue about the man himself: the doctor's flesh tones had an unhealthy pallor, as though he had spent too many years in shaded rooms rather than enjoying the lush countryside around the village he served. Retirement seemed long overdue for this general practitioner.

Something prevented Ash from offering a hand in greeting – certainly none was offered to him – and he became aware that he, himself, was under close scrutiny from the doctor. 'How is Reverend Lockwood?' he enquired, puzzled by the distinct coolness in the other man's demeanour.

'He needs rest.' Stapley's reply was curt. 'I've explained to Grace that her father should spend at least one night in hospital, under observation.'

'He won't hear of it,' Grace quickly explained. 'Father insists he should stay close to the village.'

Ash's curiosity was aroused instantly. 'Why would he think that?'

The doctor cut in. 'The poor man's suffering from severe exhaustion. At this moment he has few coherent thoughts, but I'm afraid he does have certain fixations. Unfortunately Edmund's health has steadily deteriorated since his wife's death and, frankly, I'm surprised he hasn't collapsed long before now.'

'He's had a nervous breakdown?'

'I didn't say that.' The reply was sharp, almost a reprimand. 'Edmund is both mentally and physically exhausted, no more than that.'

250

'He fainted in church, David,' came Grace's quiet voice. She had moved to the study's small, worn oak desk and was staring unseeingly at its scratched leather top with its jumble of papers and books. Her arms were folded beneath her breasts, her shoulders slightly hunched. 'Father told us upstairs that he was examining the church records when he suddenly felt dizzy. Then he just passed out.'

'But he wasn't unconscious – we heard him moaning.'

'Obviously you caught him as he was reviving,' said the doctor. 'In such a semi-conscious state he would have been disorientated, and probably very frightened.' He addressed his next remarks to Grace. 'I've sedated him, so please leave him to rest for a few hours. I'll pop by later to see how he is, but should there be a change for the worse – and I doubt there will be – call me straight away.'

Grace turned and gave him a worried but appreciative smile.

The doctor stood by the open door holding his black bag in one hand, the other tucked into his jacket pocket. Perspiration dampened his forehead and Ash wondered if it was only the sultry weather that was sapping the man's strength. Behind the lenses, his eyes darted from Grace to Ash as though he suspected they might not carry out his instructions. 'Please make sure the Reverend is not disturbed,' he reiterated before leaving the room.

Grace hurried after him and Ash heard their muffled voices on the doorstep. While he waited for Grace to return he took in the study, cursorily examining the books lining the walls, many of them old and leather-bound editions, the shelves sagging under their weight. Because the room was on the dark side of the house, sunlight held little authority here, and the smell of dust and aged leather contributed considerably to the stale sobriety. His eyes came back to the picture of Lockwood Hall and he remembered something had caught his attention just before Grace and the doctor had entered the study. As he was moving closer to the painting he heard the front door close and Grace's footsteps along the hallway.

Ash turned as she came back into the room and before he could say a word she was in his arms, burying her face into his chest. He felt her tears seep through the material of his shirt and for a moment his hands hovered inches from her back, as if he was unsure of what to do. Then they dropped and held her close.

'I'm so frightened,' she whispered against his chest.

'He'll be okay,' he soothed. 'You heard the doctor – your father's only suffering from exhaustion. He needs rest, that's all. It might be an idea to get him away from here for a while.'

Her body pressed against him, she looked up into his face. 'Leave Sleath? You heard what I said earlier. He'd never do that, not when there's trouble here.'

'There's nothing he can do.'

'He's their spiritual leader. He has to help them.'

'The villagers? Most of them aren't even aware of the hauntings.'

'Are you really so blind, David? Haven't you looked into their faces, haven't you seen the fear in their eyes? They *know* something bad has come to Sleath.'

The little Irishman's words earlier that morning came back to him: *There's a darkness over the place.* Phelan was right, and so was Grace. The darkness, this *foreboding*, was pervasive and it touched everyone who lived in or around Sleath. He didn't have to see their faces, he didn't have to hear their stories – and probably there were those in the village who preferred to keep their hauntings to themselves, either out of fright or embarrassment – nor did he have to run tests with cameras and thermometers to be aware of this. He could sense it now as clearly as he could feel Grace in his arms.

'I believe it, Grace. Something is going on here that I don't understand and my instinct is to get as far away as possible.'

He felt her stiffen. 'You'd leave . . . ?'

'If you'd come too.'

'You know I can't do that.'

'There's no defence against this kind of thing.'

'Why do you say that? Is it because of what happened to you in that house called Edbrook?'

He fell silent and she persisted.

'That's in the past, David. Besides, you were burdened with guilt at the time, you were vulnerable.'

He held her away so that he could look at her. 'How did you know that?'

'You told me the other night, in the restaurant.'

'No. No, I didn't. I never mentioned anything about . . .'

'Juliet? Then it's another thing I sense about you, something to do with the dream. The guilt involves your sister and it's still there with you, isn't it? Please help me understand why.'

'It isn't important right now. There's enough to deal with here.'

'You'll stay?'

'I didn't say I'd go.'

She closed the gap between them and once more her head was against his chest. His hand slipped beneath her hair and his fingers caressed the nape of her neck.

'There's something else that concerns me though,' he said. 'I have to know why your father tried to destroy the church records.'

Again she tensed. 'I don't think –'

'You saw them,' he interrupted. 'The papers were ripped, the books torn apart.'

She gave a small shake of her head. 'He couldn't have known what he was doing. Dr Stapley said Father must have blacked out; perhaps it happened then.'

'I doubt it. I think he was afraid of what we might find.'

'That's nonsense. What could there be to hide?'

'That's what we need to discover.'

She gripped him tighter. 'I'm glad you're helping us, David,' she said.

Ash put his fingers beneath her chin and brought her head up. With his thumbs he wiped away the tears from the corners of her eyes, and then bent down so that his lips were close to

253

hers. The move was tentative, unsure, as if he were afraid of rejection, but she completed it for him. Grace slid an arm around his neck and pulled his head down further so that their lips met.

Their kiss was full and Ash tasted her moistness. He pressed harder, his body firm against hers, and her softness accommodated him. She returned the pressure, her lips parting just enough to steal his breath, and his senses reeled crazily, unexpectedly, so that his thoughts became disordered, tumbling into hers. It was an alarming yet wonderful moment, one of confusion and rapture, and it was mutual. The kiss, the intimate contact, had become something more.

A sensation of lightness swept through him as their embrace tightened and their minds, with their bodies, seemed to meld.

He soared into her, and she into him; their thoughts and their sensations intermingled, became part of each other's. He explored her depths, her feelings, her secrets, and he was as aware of her as she was of him. He touched her emotions, her passions, and was overwhelmed by her desire.

And Grace welcomed him in, confused but delighted by the invasion and she in turn explored his consciousness, roaming free, absorbing his thoughts and his feelings. She plunged deeper into his subconscious, wary of the darkness there but unafraid. She passed through veils that were merely shadows of the psyche, shuddering at each impression, but unable to turn back, unwilling to. *And suddenly she found herself inside the dark brooding walls of the house he had called Edbrook.*

Two men presented themselves, ethereal spirits that floated across her mind – and his mind! And a girl, a beautiful vision with long, dark, curling hair and eyes that held mockery as well as passion. This thought *drifted by and beyond it, firmer than all the others, stood a young girl, a child whose smile was malicious and whose skin was alabaster. Young yet so old, so degenerate in soul, and Grace knew that this was David's sister, this was Juliet. With that perception she understood David's deepest secret.*

As if in a dream, she felt the girl's rage, and she saw her stagger away, she saw her slip, she watched her fall into the pitchy black river. Swirling waters rushed around the child as she was tossed by spumy currents and the boy, the boy who was David, tried to reach her but was hurled and pitched by the terrible forces; his mind was filled with shame and he screamed with terror.

They both watched – Grace and this young boy – as Juliet lost her fight against the furious water, and her eyes, so wide, so frightened, slowly became opaque with death. And Grace sensed that the boy felt the guilt of the other child's death, felt that it was he who had killed her. But he was wrong! The girl had fallen and he had tried to save her!

Juliet floated away, flotsam on the stormy currents, one shoe and one white sock gone, torn away as her life had been torn away, leaving David to be pulled clear – and to die Juliet's death a thousand times over.

They stood in the room, their bodies steady, while the walls around them seemed to spin and weave. Their lips were still joined for, in truth, it was only moments since their lips had first touched; but then time had no value in this conjunction of minds.

Ash became lost in a kaleidoscope of perceptions and images, and he gloried in them even though trepidation also played its part, for never before had he gained access to another's mind in this way. He flinched at her emotion, so strong, so enveloping, but gave himself up to it. He sensed her probing and gave himself up to this too, for its delicate intrusion was exquisite; and while she searched his thoughts so he delved further into hers.

As he sank deeper he became aware of a small voice, one that belonged to Grace, but not as she was now. This was a child's plaintive entreaty and its source was not clear; somehow he could not direct his own thoughts towards it.

His lips pressed harder against her, physically striving to reach the voice, and Grace leaned back under his force, her hands moving up his back to grip his shoulders.

He found the direction. Inside her mind he located the source of the tiny, frightened voice and he swept towards it. But something dragged at him, hindering his progress, and he found himself drifting aimlessly. Yet he was nearly there, he could hear the voice so clearly. And soon he was before a huge blank area and as he drew near he saw – he perceived – that it was grey and uneven, like a murky cloud that filled this special space in her mind. He knew he would never penetrate its mass, for this was Grace's secret and it was one that even she did not know, at least, not in the conscious part of her mind. He reeled back, stunned by the force of the opposition, and hurtled upwards as a drowning man might rush from the depths of the ocean.

They both recoiled, each taking a step away from the other. They stared at each other in consternation, bewildered by this singular experience.

But before either one could speak they heard a scream, and then a crash, from upstairs.

28

SH GRABBED HOLD of Grace's arm as she made for
the door. She spun round, alarm, fear, bewilderment
in her eyes.

'Wait,' he said over his own confusion.

'Father . . .' She tried to pull away, but he held
her firm.

'Let me go first.' He drew her aside, roughly, because she
resisted at first, and then headed for the door himself. Grace
followed close behind.

Ash took the steps two at a time, but paused at the top,
realizing he had no idea which was the vicar's room. Another
wailing cry told him.

The door was closed and for a moment he thought it might
be locked, so stiff was its handle. He took a tighter grip, using
both hands, and the door opened. He rushed in and came up
short, taken aback by what he saw.

Although the curtains were closed, there was enough light
to make out the figure of the Reverend Lockwood on the floor
of the bedroom, his back pushed into a corner, bedsheets
clutched to his chest. He was staring at the opposite corner,
abject horror dragging at his lower jaw so that his mouth was
agape; saliva glistened on his thin lips, a stream drooling onto
his chin. His white hair was wild around his face and the pupils
of his eyes were so wide and black the pale irises around them

257

had almost disappeared. The vicar was shaking as if in a fit and he gazed only at the empty corner.

Ash felt Grace enter the room behind him. Then her hand was grasping his shoulder as she looked past him at her father.

'*Keep away from me!*'

The shout erupted from the vicar so suddenly that they both gave a start. They realized that the warning was not directed at them, but at whatever false vision lay in that empty corner of the bedroom.

'Daddy!' Grace cried, unaware that it was a term she had not used since she was a child. She tried to step around the investigator, but once more Ash held her back. Struggling to free herself, she called out to her father again. Never had she seen him look so old and frail, so deteriorated; even his months of ill health had not prepared her for this. She gasped when his frightened gaze wandered to her and Ash felt her sag against him.

The Reverend's voice was as decrepit as his appearance. 'Leave here, Grace. Go from this room, this house . . . leave now . . . please . . .' The words grew softer, then failed him completely as the effort of speaking became too much. His attention slowly returned to the empty corner, and he moaned, the sound degenerating to a long sigh that ended in a wretched sob. His trembling arthritic hands lifted the bedsheets and his forehead sank into them, his face hidden from view.

'Forgive me . . . please forgive me . . .' he pleaded.

They thought these faint words were directed at whatever he imagined was in that corner until he whispered Grace's name again.

'Forgive me, Grace . . . it's you . . . it's you they . . .'

Ash caught her as she swooned and began to fall. He held her to his chest as his own legs buckled and he sank to one knee, his arms around her waist and shoulders, her face pressed against him.

He heard the laughter then, a low, mocking sound that seemed to come from the empty corner.

29

T WAS GOOD TO BE OUT in the open air, sultry though it was. Ash hurried away from the Lodge House, relieved to be beyond its cooler yet no less suffocating confines. It concerned him that he had left Grace to tend her distraught father on her own, but there was no other choice: Ash had to look at those church records, or at least, those that hadn't been too badly damaged. Besides, once she had recovered from her shock, Grace had insisted that he go to St Giles' alone.

By the time he reached his car the back of his shirt was damp with sweat and his step had already lost its initial briskness. He quickly switched on the engine, and then the air cooler. He sat there for a few moments before driving off, brooding on what had occurred inside the house. Just what manner of demon had presented itself to the Reverend Lockwood in the corner of that shaded bedroom? If he, Ash, had not heard that cruel, mocking laughter emanating from the other side of the room, then he would have concluded that the vicar, in his distressed state, had been hallucinating.

He reached over to the back seat for his discarded jacket and rummaged in the pockets for cigarettes. He lit one and tossed the match out onto the dusty road.

Demon was the wrong word – maybe he was becoming overwrought himself. Demons were the stuff of cheap novels and even cheaper movies. Spirit manifestation was better. Yes, he could accept that, and he could accept the malignity of such an entity, too. He touched the thin scar on his cheek as he exhaled cigarette smoke through the open window.

But why had Lockwood begged his daughter's forgiveness? What the hell had he done to her? Ash remembered what had happened between himself and Grace in the study before they had heard the scream from upstairs. Somehow they had been able to enter each other's inner consciousness, their minds had joined in some kind of extrasensory embrace, a telepathic melding of perceptions and sensibilities. It had been a powerful and almost overwhelming experience, and he knew he had given away secrets long repressed in the deeper levels of his consciousness. Yet his own delving had been blocked by some kind of barrier, one that was instigated by something within her subconscious. Now he wondered if there was a connection between Lockwood's plea for forgiveness and whatever it was in Grace's psyche that blanked truths not only from others but from Grace herself.

And was this part of the Reverend Lockwood's secret? Why *was* the man so afraid? Why had he attempted to destroy the church records? Just what the fuck *was* going on here in Sleath?

Angrily Ash engaged gear and jerked the wheel so that the car shot over to the other side of the narrow road. He quickly executed a three-point turn, swinging round over the grass verge so that the car was pointing back towards the village. He glanced towards the Lodge House one last time before putting his foot down and heading down the hill towards St Giles'.

Within seconds he was at the church and he had to resist the urge to drive straight past and keep going until he was out of the village, beyond the hills, back in the grubby city where lunatics and thugs were the only threat. Instead he pulled over to the lychgate and stopped the car.

The cigarette was half smoked and his anger contained before he climbed out and went through the cool portal where long

260

ago coffins were rested before being taken into the church itself. Only when he was at the porch door did he drop the butt and grind it into the dirt with his foot.

He surveyed the old, leaning headstones of the graveyard and wondered why death did not always mean conclusion.

The familiar coldness clung to him as he went through the porch and opened the inner door to the church. Inside, he paused once again, immediately aware that he was not alone in the sepulchral gloom. There was no sound, no voice and no movement other than his own as he turned his head, searching for whoever shared the quietness with him. Unlike earlier when he and Grace had arrived at St Giles' there were no murmurings to warn him; yet he was certain there was someone else there in the church – his senses were too cruelly stretched to lie to him.

It was almost with relief that he detected the faint sound.

With a feeling of *déjà vu* he walked quietly down the side aisle, listening intently with every step. The sound grew louder, although it was still soft. It had a kind of cadence to it, as if . . . as if someone were humming a tune. And it was coming from the small chapel where they had found the slumped body of Reverend Lockwood.

Much of his nervousness left him when the sound took on a more tuneful and less threatening quality. He became aware of other noises as he drew closer to the source – the riffling of papers, a muffled cough, the scraping of something across the stone floor.

'Is that yourself, David?'

The brogue was unmistakable.

'Phelan.'

'Come and join me, there's a lot to talk about.'

Ash leaned on a pew and allowed himself to breathe again before going on. 'You scared the hell out of me,' he said, crossing the nave.

'Ah, I didn't mean to do that. As a matter of fact, I thought I'd find you still here.' The humming resumed.

261

Ash stood at the entrance to the side chapel where the stone effigy shared space with the tiny altar and credence table. Seamus Phelan had found a small plain chair from somewhere and was sitting on it surrounded by sheaves of yellowing papers and aged books. Among them were old parchments, most of which were crumpled or torn. Earlier Ash had not had time to realize the damage dealt to these old documents, but now he saw just how destructive the vicar had been. The books, themselves, were also in poor condition, either through wear or vandalism; loose leaves spilled from them and one or two had ripped covers. He bent down to pick up a creased sheet of vellum, on which handwritten text was faded and barely legible.

'I'd be grateful if you didn't touch anything, David. I've spent some time piecing things together here.'

Although the banter was still in the Irishman's voice, Ash realized there was also a degree of tenseness. He took a closer look at Phelan and saw there was a grimness to his smile.

'I was surprised you weren't here at the church when I arrived,' Phelan said as though unaware of the investigator's scrutiny. 'After all, that was part of the plan, wasn't it? We'd make separate searches?'

'I didn't know you'd be back so quickly.'

'The microfiles at the library soon told me all I needed to know. I wanted to consult with you before I went on to the archives.' That grimness had travelled to his eyes. 'It might be worse than I feared, David. Much worse. But tell me first, who's the scoundrel responsible for this vandalism?' He indicated the mess on the floor.

Ash quickly explained how he and Grace had found the vicar semi-conscious in the chapel, the church records in disarray around him.

'So it was the Reverend Lockwood himself,' said Phelan thoughtfully when Ash had finished. 'Now why would a man of the cloth, the very pillar of the community, wish to destroy the day-to-day history of his parish?'

'Because he didn't like the story it told?'

Phelan regarded him with interest. 'A story of his own ancestors,' he added.

Ash knelt before the paper debris. 'You've had time to examine all this?' Ignoring the previous warning he picked up a torn piece of parchment.

Phelan made a weary scoffing sound. 'It would take a week to go through this lot, much more to study them properly. But I have already found something of particular interest.' He leaned forward and carefully picked up a bound volume which, although obviously ancient, appeared to be in better condition than most of the other tomes it had laid amongst. 'I found this fellow at the bottom of the chest under a lot of other stuff. Fortunately our pernicious vicar hadn't quite got to it before his collapse.'

Carefully balancing the book, with its cracked leather cover and gilt-edged vellum leaves, on his knees, the Irishman opened it up. 'Much of it is indecipherable, and even more reads like gobbledygook. I'm afraid its author was no scholar, judging by his use of Latin. But what I can discern makes fascinating reading. This fellow might be of interest to you, by the way.' He half-turned, nodding his head towards the stone knight lying on the plinth behind him. 'Sir Gareth over there was the first Lockwood to come to Sleath. I don't suppose it was much of a place back in the thirteenth century, but the village and all the land around it was given to the man as a reward for his services to the Fifth Crusade. D'you know your history, David?'

'I can just about tell you what happened yesterday.'

Phelan raised his eyebrows. 'I'm sure you're having fun with me. Well, no matter. It seems Sir Gareth took part in the Christian army's somewhat illogical attempt to conquer Egypt – I suppose they were all full of their own glory after the Fourth Crusade had led to the capture of Constantinople a dozen or so years earlier and the setting up of the Latin Empire of the East.' He gave a bemused shake of his head. 'Now you'd think our knight would have returned a chastened man after defeat, but not a bit of it. From what I can make of these somewhat perplexing notes here he came back from the war with some strange – and to him, exciting – ideas in his head. Unfortunately for the villages and the landsmen hereabouts, these were not very Christian ideas.'

'There's evidence in the book?'

Phelan smiled. 'There's some, but I've had to read between the lines here and there, venerable though those lines may be. He was certainly an enthusiast, I'll say that for him. Unfortunately again, that enthusiasm – no, let's call it what it was: an unhealthy obsession – was for the dark practices.'

'But his descendants became ministers of the church.'

'Yes, very odd, isn't it? I presume it made their power over the villagers absolute.'

A breeze that had found its way into the old building lifted the edges of the papers by Phelan's feet. He took the cane that had been leaning against the back of his chair and laid it across them.

'Y'see, several passages appear to be direct quotations from the Egyptian Book of the Dead. Through your own knowledge of the occult I'm thinking you'll have some idea of what that particular potboiler was designed for.'

'It was meant to be read to the dying to give their subconscious-self control over their spirit when they passed on.'

'Well, a certain control over the weird and wonderful experiences to come, shall we say? Quite a prospect, don't you think?'

'I imagine Sir Gareth was pretty pissed off when he died and discovered it was all hokum,' Ash replied drily.

'Ah, but is it? What d'you suppose ghosts, shades, wraiths, revenants, spirits – whatever you'd care to call the poor divils – are all about? Aren't they the souls of those who have not been allowed, or indeed allowed themselves, to pass on to the greater glory? Perhaps Sir Gareth had discovered the secret for himself and sought to share that knowledge or even to govern with it.' He stopped and gave Ash a smile that was resigned rather than weary. 'But I can see you're not convinced, David. Ever the cynic, eh?'

'D'you blame me? It's all a bit absurd, isn't it?'

'No more so than ghosts terrorizing a little village in the Chilterns. But let's not get into that particular debate for the moment – we've a lot more digging to do before we can draw any conclusions. Still an' all, I think Sir Gareth's journal here is a good start, much better than we could have hoped.' He slowly turned other pages, lost in thought for a while.

Ash rose from his kneeling position and walked over to the recumbent effigy. He ran his fingers along the cracked stone and felt its coldness seep into his own flesh. Alarmed how swiftly the chill spread through his whole body, he snatched his hand away.

The sound of Phelan closing the book and muttering under his breath distracted him.

'Did you say something?' Ash asked, unconsciously rubbing at his arm to bring back some warmth to it.

'Thinking aloud, m'boy, one of the more irritating habits of the aged.' He hummed a tune for a few moments, drumming his fingers on the thick cover of the book on his lap as he did so. Then he fixed Ash with eyes that held no humour and now precious little weariness. 'As I said, there's much work to be done and we've not much time.'

'I can help you sift through some of this lot. Maybe I can read the later records, those not written in any obscure language.'

'I've a feeling it's the earlier stuff that will provide us with the answers we're looking for, though I'll scan through everything to be sure nothing's missed.'

'But what good will answers do?' Ash said with something approaching exasperation.

'Well now, they might help us understand what's happening in Sleath, why these revenants are frightening the folk. And then perhaps we can convince those involved – the living, I'm meaning – to stop whatever practices are attracting these unnatural forces.'

'Wait a minute – you think there are people here responsible for the hauntings?'

'I believe so, although if it's consciously or subconsciously on their part I haven't a clue. Y'see I doubt these forces have the power to present themselves without some kind of encouragement, or even invitation. In most cases it's either spiritualists or receptive minds that draw such entities, but in this case – well, who knows? It'll be interesting to find out.'

Phelan shook his head as if saddened and began to rise, the effort, apparently, not easy for him. He turned to place the book carefully on the chair, then flexed his short legs, working the stiffness from them. 'There's a peculiar iciness to this church, don't you think?' he remarked casually as he peered up at the walls and into the chapel's vaulted ceiling. 'I feel there's evil in Sleath and it's been here for quite some time. In fact, I'm prepared to believe it's been here for centuries.'

'Why would you think that?' Ash demanded.

Phelan looked quizzically at the investigator. 'D'you not sense it yourself? D'you not *feel* the badness in this place? Good Lord, it's almost palpable, you can almost touch it. Oh, it's here all right, and so it has been for longer than either one of us has trod this earth, and I've a notion its power waxes and wanes depending on certain factors. What they might be, I've no idea at present, but as our American friends say, "We're in a learning process here".'

With a grunt, Phelan bent down and picked up his cane. He presented an odd figure in his tweed jacket and paisley cravat, leaning on the cane with the knuckles of his other hand resting against his hip. Around him lay the piled documents and papers, and a shaft of sunlight, softened by the stained glass it shone through, coloured his white hair in mellow tones. In contrast the stone knight behind him seemed ominous in its adamantine contemplation and grey dourness.

'One thing I do know,' he went on, fixing Ash with his penetrating gaze once again, 'and it's something I discovered in the microfiles of those old local journals.'

Another breeze ruffled the papers on the floor and Ash glanced into the main body of the church to see if anyone had entered by the porch door. There was no one there.

Phelan was oblivious to the sudden gust, even though a parchment had lifted and now rested over one of his brogues. 'It seems sudden disappearances and unnatural deaths are not unusual in this neck of the woods. I mean, over a long period of time, of course, perhaps a hundred years or more, and for all we know, a lot longer than that – the local gazettes only go so far back. In a shorter span of time, no doubt such incidents would have been noted for their regularity, don't you think?'

A dark shape fluttered against the stained-glass window above Phelan's head and they heard the muted *kaa* of a crow. The shadow was soon gone from view, but not before its wings had flapped against the glass a few more times.

Phelan hardly glanced round. He tapped his cane on the stone floor to gain Ash's attention. 'And the thing of it is, David,' he said gravely, 'the *terrible* thing of it is, that most of those who have disappeared have been children.'

The cry of the crow came to them again, this time as a bleak, distant sound.

30

ICKEY DUNN WIPED his sleeve across his face, spreading the dirt there rather than shifting it. He shivered, although it was only cool and not cold in the shadowy room in which he had hidden. 'Must've dozed,' he mumbled to himself, the sound of his own voice odd and echoey in the silence of the ruin. His outstretched legs disturbed rubble when he drew them up and he worried at the noise he'd made. No need to, he told himself, no need at all to worry. No one else was in this place and no one knew he'd come here. Nevertheless his fingers scrabbled around the floor and when they found the armed crossbow Mickey hugged it to his chest, making sure its arrow was pointed away from himself.

The room was brighter than when he'd first crept in, but still gloomy. He could just make out large porcelain sinks under the blackened windows and there was a big square block in the centre of the room, probably used for chopping and preparing food in the olden days before Lockwood Hall was reduced to a gutted shell. Leaves and branches outside pressed against the grimy windows, intruding here and there where the glass had broken, reaching in as if searching for shade rather than sunlight. Was it only dirt on those panes, Mickey wondered, or were they stained by smoke from the big fire all those years ago? Then again, who gave a toss? They made a good cover, and that was all that mattered. No bugger would find him here.

Fragments of his dream came back to him and at once he felt less secure hunched there in the semi-darkness. He remembered being shut away in the dream, the stench of rotten apples poisoning the air, the bomb shelter's door locked tight, even though he pounded and pounded against it. Strangely, the smell of those mouldering apples lingered in his nostrils still, as if he hadn't really woken up, as if the dream was continuing.

Mickey pushed himself up to a squatting position, sliding his back against the wall and brushing dust from its surface. Bits of plaster cracked and fell away, exposing the brickwork beneath.

Nah, weren't no smell of rotten apples; that was just in his mind, left over from the dream. All he could really smell was dirt and dampness. What was this place? Lockwood Hall, yeah, but what was *this* place? He'd wandered in in the early hours of the morning, shit-scared, dog-weary, shuffling through wasted rooms, feeling his way along corridors that had no ceilings, wary of creaking floorboards beneath his feet, finally finding this huge square room with its nice safe stone floor. What was it? Easy, now there was a little more light. Sinks over there, walls partly covered with charred old cupboards, the big burnt centre block – easy to see it was the Hall's great kitchen. Bloody rich people with loads of bloody servants and skivvies – they'd've needed one as big as this. All their money didn't do them much good in the end, did it? Bloody place still went up in flames.

He managed a feeble smile. Can't fight fire with boodle, that was for sure. Can't buy off fate, neither. His smile, what there was of it, disintegrated. Bloody right, you can't. Weren't his fault last night, he didn't mean to kill nobody. Fate bloody did it.

A sob escaped him, a short barking sound. Its echo snapped his head up again.

Mickey pushed himself all the way to his feet, scraping more blackened plaster and dust from the wall. Clutching the

269

crossbow in one hand, he wiped the back of his other hand against his eyes, smearing more dirt.

They weren't going to get him. Oh no, they could blame him all they liked, but they weren't going to send him down. It was Buckler's own fault, he shouldn't have been roaming around in the middle of the night. Besides, he hadn't aimed at the gamekeeper, he'd shot at the . . . thing . . . the thing that made no sense, the spooky thing.

'Oh shit, shit, shit!' he moaned, banging the flat of his hand against the wall behind. More plaster fell away and this time dust trickled down from what remained of the ceiling too, powdering his lank hair and floating into his nostrils. He stopped banging, gripping the loaded crossbow with both hands instead.

Bloodyell, this place was ready to cave in. He squinted at the bare beams above his head, blinking away dust that was still settling. Weak sunlight filtered through the broken floors, and he could make out parts of what was left of the roof. A bloody good sneeze and it'd all come down, he told himself, and his giggle was like a hiccup.

It wasn't really funny. He didn't like it here, didn't like it at all. There was something weird about this old ruin, there always had been. Everyone knew it was haunted, that's why nobody from the village ever came here. All the better for him, though. *He* knew there was no such things as ghosts – that was just kids' stuff – but if the idea kept nosey bastids away, so much the better. Noises had rattled him earlier when he was dozing, but Mickey was smart enough to know they were only the sounds of the place settling, breezes sifting through woodwork, pieces of stone breaking loose, little animals mooching about. And even when that funny music, that faint old-fashioned tinkly sound he'd heard hours ago as he'd climbed the steps, came back to rouse him from his dozing, he knew it was just part of his dream, because it stopped as soon as he opened his eyes and his wits returned. Stupid to think otherwise, and he certainly wasn't stupid, even if Lenny and Den sometimes called him that to his face. If he was stupid he'd be banged up in jail by now like those two probably were, and here he was, free as a bird, nobody knowing where he was hiding. He could stay here for days, weeks. If he had to – if he *really* had to.

Mickey flexed his shoulder muscles, pushing himself away from the crumbling wall, then walked over to the charred block in the middle of the room. Pieces of fallen masonry and wood crunched beneath his sneakers as he made his way through the debris and he jumped when a long splinter of wood snapped, the sound ricocheting off the walls like rifle fire. After that, he made his way more carefully, using the mote-filled shafts of light for guidance, even though he knew there was no one else around to hear.

He reached a scorched doorframe and peered through it. The light was a little stronger out there and he remembered this was the wide corridor he'd crept along in the grey dawn hours; it led from the great hall where the main entrance was situated and where the remains of the two staircases swept down from the floor above. The fire all those years ago must have been worse at the front, although no part of Lockwood Hall had gone unscathed. He sniffed the dank air and it seemed to him that the acrid taint of smoke was still there, locked in with the ghosts that were supposed to haunt the place. Bloody daft. Weren't no smoke, weren't no ghosts.

Mickey gingerly stepped over piled rubbish into the corridor and as he did so a sudden and distracting pain squeezed his stomach, almost causing him to lose balance.

'Bloodyell!' he gasped, one hand clutching at himself. *That hurt. That bloodywell hurt!* He knew the cause, of course, because it wasn't a new pain; it happened most times when he was out on a 'job' with Lenny and Den. In part it was due to hunger – he never could eat before a night-time jaunt with his two companions-in-crime – but mainly it was anxiety that brought it on (which he would never admit to his cronies). Lenny Grover always laughed at him when he complained of gut-ache, but it was no bloody joke. Mickey's doctor, old Stapley, had explained about acids eating into the stomach walls when certain people got over-anxious, especially when there was no food inside them. The doctor – creepy old git – had warned him off booze and greasy food and not eating at the right times, but what the fuck – life was for doing what you wanted, when you wanted. Right? Yeah, right.

Another spasm, a nasty one again, and then it eased off. Must get something to eat, even if it was only berries from the woods. He might even find a nice plump bird or rabbit to shoot. Had to be careful, though, mustn't be seen. Christ, it was shivery in here.

Mickey moved along the corridor, carefully picking his way over the rubble, the crossbow held tight against his chest. A floorboard bent and creaked beneath his foot and he paused, alarmed at the noise as well as the possibility that it might give way completely. He snorted. He was doing it again, worrying about someone hearing him when he knew the old ruin was deserted. But that floorboard had sagged badly under his weight. Go careful, he warned himself, most of the wood was rotted or burnt through.

There were two doorways next to each other immediately on his right, and curiosity made him peep into the open one. Nothing but charred wreckage beyond, yet oddly, the door next to the open room was made of metal. It was scorched, but looked solid enough, and its handle was smooth and dulled, as if it had been used a lot. No way. No one came here anymore. No one was interested.

He reached for the handle and gave it a twist. It turned easily enough, but the door was locked. Maybe just jammed. He put his shoulder against the flat metal and shoved. Wouldn't budge.

His attention went back to the other room. Nothing much in there, just fallen rafters and brickwork, a few gaps in the floor, too. Lighter than the one he'd dozed in, though, because its two big windows were not only glassless, but were frameless too. The fire had done a lot more damage here. Could be a better place to hole up in – it still stunk, but not so much.

272

Mickey took a few steps inside, felt the floorboards sag and was about to make a hasty retreat when his stomach bit him again, the pain even more intense than before. He doubled over, reflexively pulling the crossbow into his belly, the momentum taking him forward rather than backwards. His foot shot ahead to steady himself and the sudden weight caused the floor to give way.

With a yelp, then a scream, Mickey crashed through.

Dirt, rubble and wood fell with him and for a moment – an eternity for him – he experienced fear worse than the night before and worse even than the night in the bomb shelter. It was the not knowing that did it: the time-expanded drop into unknown darkness, wondering how deep the fall would be and what might lie at the bottom to break his bones or pierce his flesh, as well as the thought that the rest of the ceiling might cave in and crush him to death when he landed. There was another possibility too, but even though the descent seemed inordinately long to his dread-stimulated mind, there was not enough time for it to occur to him.

The fall ended, but the clamour went on. Mickey was deafened by the noise, his own scream contributing to this, and blinded by the swirling dust and denser darkness. He was stunned, too, and not just by the awkward landing. Through the confusion of falling debris, the splintering of wood, his own screaming, Mickey had heard – *felt?* – something like a spring being released, and instantly his open jaw was snapped shut by something thudding into it from below. His scream was immediately plugged as that something continued on its way into the roof of his mouth to burst into the open again through the cartilage and bone of his nose.

The short quarrel lodged there, its slickened tip protruding from the bridge of his nose, its feathered end pressed against his neck.

Mickey writhed like some stuck animal, suddenly comprehending what had happened, yet still not believing it, while debris and powdered dust fell on and around him.

273

It took some time for the downfall to settle, although Mickey, himself, did not. He couldn't scream anymore, he could only gag and retch because of the blood pouring down the inside of his throat. His screams were nothing more than restrained gurgling sounds.

He pulled at the metal arrow, trying to grip its sticky stiffened feathers, but the blood that ran down its exposed shaft made it impossible. Soon his grubby hands were completely red as the thick liquid oozed between his closed lips and flowed from his nostrils; the blood poured from orifices, natural and rendered, to mix with the filth his fall had released.

Mickey's agony took him on a frenzied journey across the rubbled floor as his body rolled over and over. Incredibly, he managed to raise himself to his knees and he carried on tugging at the quarrel, his soaking hands constantly slipping away. The pain and shock soon drove him to his feet and he staggered around in the night-darkness, his legs bent in an ape-like swagger. He crashed against the staircase – one that led down from the corridor's locked iron door – then tottered across the basement chamber, stumbling over debris he had created, sliding on his own trail of blood, burbling and squealing his hurt and distress in alternate bursts.

Blood soon drenched his clothes and each time he spun round in a fresh frenzy blobs of it speckled the walls. His hands and arms were a deep ruby red in the gloom, and his lungs soon began to fill with liquid. Gradually his movement slowed, became weaker, less erratic, and his body began to sag. But by then his maddened trip had taken him to the other end of the dusky room.

As he finally sank to his knees, the lightness in his head defying the dull heaviness of his limbs, Mickey found himself staring into another chamber. His mind was confused and frightened enough, but now it soared to a new level of hysteria as his wild eyes took in the bizarre sight before him, one that was lit entirely by candles.

An expulsion of remaining air drove a huge spurt of blood

through the narrow parting of his lips and dark, bubbled liquid stained the clean stone floor inside the opening.

Mickey followed that arc of blood, falling onto his face with a dull, fleshy *smack*. His eyes remained open, although vision swiftly faded. The image of those bright-burning lights and the person they revealed lingered longer in his mind, however, almost, but not quite, following him into his miserable death.

31

SH PAUSED BENEATH the hanging sign of the Black Boar Inn. Although he had paid it little mind before, he now craned his neck to take in its faded detail. The black fur and yellowed tusks of the huge wild-eyed beast depicted there seemed to quiver with rage. Although a crude work, its paint cracked and flaked away in places, the picture still conveyed the ferocious strength of its subject. Perhaps it was the madness in the boar's reddened eyes that gave the painting its potency, or perhaps it was because of the animal's stance, shoulders hunched, one hoof raised and pointed as if to paw the ground; or perhaps it was merely the contrast between the fearsome image and the tranquil setting it glowered over that startled the observer. But then, it seemed Sleath was a village of contrasts.

He dropped his gaze to look around him. The pond, with its overlay of rising mist, no longer appeared so placid to him: somehow it was too still, too deep. Further along the stocks and whipping post presented a stark and shameful reminder of Sleath's more sinister past rather than the interesting relics he had thought them when he'd arrived. Even the windows of the old houses and the community hall opposite looked darkly brooding, and the few people he had passed on his short journey from St Giles' seemed weighed down by their own cogitations – when one of them had raised his head to watch Ash drive by and the investigator had acknowledged him with a brief nod the man had quickly and almost shiftily averted his eyes.

Ash turned towards the narrow, hump-backed bridge leading out of the village and was surprised to see a mist there also, its wispy tendrils reaching over the low stone walls from the river below. He realized a less perceptible haze was drifting along the High Street itself. It was too hot, too humid, and his head ached, his throat was dry. He badly needed a drink.

The inn door was stiff when he shoved against it, as if reluctant to allow him entry, but he gave it a firmer push and it swung wide. With some relief he stepped into the shadowy coolness of the saloon bar.

The place was empty of customers and, on first inspection, appeared to be devoid of staff also. However, he soon picked up the sound of voices coming from the open doorway behind the bar as he made his way across the worn carpet. Although it was long past lunchtime, he was mildly surprised at the lack of drinkers, particularly on such a sweltering day. Maybe those who were not working wanted to stay inside the coolness of their own homes. He decided not to drink at the bar himself – he was in no mood for small talk – and quietly strode towards the back stairs. There was vodka in his room and that was all he needed for now; food had no appeal whatsoever.

He made it to the stairs without alerting the voices in the back room and quickly went up. The stale odours of beer and cooking permeated the wood-panelled corridor as if the heat had drawn them from the walls and carpet; the musty aroma of time itself. It was almost cloying and he was relieved to reach his room where the window had been left open. The bed had been made, the room tidied; best of all a fresh jug of water had been left on the bedside cabinet.

He was unbuttoning his shirt and pulling it free of his trousers even as he closed the door with his shoulder. He flapped the sides to create his own draught as he headed for the flask on the dressing table near the window. He picked it up and settled on the edge of the bed with a weary sigh; he used a shirt-tail to wipe sweat from his stomach and chest. Closing his eyes, he sat there for a few moments and tried to breathe in air from the open window; he soon opened his eyes when he realized precious little fresh air was entering the room – the curtains were perfectly still, not a single breeze wafting through to disturb them. Raising the flask to his lips, he took a quick nip of vodka, then poured water from the glass jug into the tumbler by its side. The water was tepid, but it tasted good as it soothed the alcohol's burn and quenched his thirst at the same time. Thoughts crowded in as he stared sightlessly at the window and minutes passed before he reached for the jug to refill the tumbler. Vodka, then water. Again: vodka, then water. Ash began to feel a little better and his thoughts began to assemble into some order.

Seamus Phelan wasn't the fool he appeared. Eccentric he might be, flamboyant too; but there was a sharp intelligence to the man that wasn't evident on first appraisal. Whether or not he was psychic was another matter, although he was certainly perceptive: he had judged Sleath's mood well enough. His knowledge of the dead language Latin was also impressive, as was his grasp of history – he was easily able to fill in historical background to the church records as they went through them. There was still much to learn from these old record books and documents, but after a couple of hours of piecing them together, finding some kind of order, and then painstakingly combing through every separate item of information that might be relevant to their searches, the two men had begun to feel fatigued.

There was more to do, but eventually Phelan had urged Ash to return to the inn and rest while he, himself, continued the work and Ash, still wearied by lack of sleep, reluctantly agreed. Besides, he wanted to check on Ellen Preddle, to see how she was after last night's 'disturbance', as well as collect film from the cameras he had set up inside her cottage. He also needed time to take stock of what he and Phelan had learned so far for, unless parts of those church records had been transcribed by madmen, Sleath had a secret history that was as horrific as it was repellent. With some misgivings, Ash had left the Irishman to continue alone.

Ellen Preddle had either not been at home – unlikely, he thought – or was refusing to answer the door – much more likely – when he called. He'd knocked on the door for several minutes, then tapped on the window, peering in and calling out her name. There had been no sound from inside and no movement that he could see. He decided he'd return later with Grace, who might be able to persuade the widow to let them in again. His uneasiness increased, he had driven slowly back to the inn.

Ash jiggled the flask against his ear to estimate how much vodka was left. It was almost empty. He took a last swig, then reached for the cigarette pack he'd tossed onto the bed. There was a gentle knock on the door as he lit one.

'David?'

It was Grace's voice.

Ash was up and moving round the bed as the second knock came and he had the door open even before she could lower her hand. Although the light was poor outside in the dark-panelled corridor, he could see the agitation in her pale eyes.

'Grace? Your father . . . ?'

'Dr Stapley is with him.' She looked beyond him into the room and Ash stepped aside so that she could enter. 'I came straight up,' she said as she walked past him. 'There doesn't seem to be anyone about downstairs.'

She stopped by the bed and faced him, her hair loose around her face. A light sheen of perspiration glistened on her forehead. 'I had to see you, David. We had no chance to talk earlier.'

He remembered their kiss, the overwhelming freedom it had unleashed in them both, the exploration of each other's mind. Those images, those sensations, were still with him, but now there were more urgent matters to deal with.

279

'I have to tell you about Sleath, Grace,' he said to her. 'Your father –'

'He's all right, Dr Stapley is taking care of him. We need to talk about you first, David, don't you see?'

'Christ, I'm the least of all this . . .'

'Don't you understand? I know about you, I know about your guilt. But you're not responsible, don't you see? Your sister's death wasn't your fault.'

He was stunned. What the hell was she saying?

'I entered your mind, David. I knew your thoughts, I experienced your memories. I was with you when Juliet died.'

He turned his back on her, closing the door as an excuse. He needed to think. 'You couldn't know about her . . .'

'But I do. We became part of each other for a few minutes, perhaps just seconds, and our thoughts merged. We do have that link, that psychic link. We both felt it on the day we met.'

She took a step towards him, but he lifted the cigarette to his lips as if to ward her off.

'Why are you afraid?' There was pleading in her voice. 'I know your sister's death wasn't your fault even though you blame yourself. Hasn't that been your problem all these years, that you feel responsible for Juliet's drowning? And in your mind Juliet has haunted you ever since. That's why you worked so hard to disprove the existence of ghosts. If there were no such things, no spirits wandering this world after death, then Juliet could never be there, she could never truly haunt you, or seek revenge, she would just be in your own imagination. Isn't that how you thought of it?'

He found he could not reply, but Grace had continued anyway.

'Then something happened at that place called Edbrook, that was where finally you were forced to accept the existence of ghosts. The two brothers and their younger sister, Christina – they revealed the irrevocable truth to you. As they were meant to, because they and Juliet belonged together. They were evil, David, evil spirits who conspired with your dead sister to make you suffer not just for Juliet's death, but for your rejection of the supernatural itself, for your work, your book, your efforts to dissuade others from believing in the spiritual world. And dear God, you were so vulnerable.'

His emotions were in turmoil, but he kept his voice level. 'You realize how ridiculous this all sounds?'

She came back instantly. 'Then deny it, tell me it isn't so. You can't hide from me, David, I know you too well now.'

Her smile was not mocking . . . not like Christina's had been . . . not like Juliet's . . . On Grace's lips it was meant to tell him it was all right, she was telling him his own secrets because she cared, she cared for him . . . Her eyes softened and again she tried to reach out for him.

He held her hand before it touched him. 'Grace . . .'

'Don't you understand how I feel about you, David?'

He was lost to her. Everything he had wanted to tell her, all the bad things about Sleath and the Lockwood family were gone, swept away for the moment because she had revealed a truth to him that his own beleaguered conscience had always denied. Through their psychic joining, Grace had entered his subconscious where there could be no lies, no untruths, only incorruptible testimony to reality, the place where even Juliet's malign spirit could not intrude, and there she had been eye-witness to the memory of that day so long ago on the river-bank, where his sister had perished and he had rendered himself culpable.

He drew Grace to him, and she came into his arms willingly.

'I need you,' she said in a low voice and all other thoughts were driven from his mind, for it had been a long time since such words had been spoken to him. He held her close and suddenly her face was tilting, her lips seeking his. They kissed and a lightness pushed through him, a euphoric charge that banished all weariness and concerns. At that moment, he knew only her.

She pulled away slightly, ending the kiss, but the elation remained within him.

281

'The cigarette . . .' she said.

He was confused for a second, then realized the cigarette was still burning between his fingers. Quickly he crushed it in the ashtray and turned back to her. She had moved closer to the bed.

'Please . . .' she said quietly.

Ash went to her and they both sank down onto the sheets, Grace lying back so that he was over her, his lips only inches away from hers.

He tried to speak, but her fingertips touched his mouth. There's no need, her eyes told him.

Her hand moved to his cheek and he pressed his lips to hers once more, relishing the soft, warm moistness he found there. He felt her hand slip behind his neck, pulling him down so that their kiss became hard, a swift passion rising from their closeness. Her lips parted when their embrace tightened, and their bodies grew rigid, the pressure almost desperate. The tips of their tongues touched and Ash felt his muscles quiver as if with mild shock. He heard her faint moan and became lost in her, bearing down even harder so that her head was pressed into the mattress beneath them. Her legs parted and he slid his leg between her thighs; her hips rose to meet his hardness.

For the briefest of moments, an inner voice warned him that this was foolish, that the time was wrong, there were things to tell her; but already it was too late, for they both shared the same hunger, their passion was equal, and even if he chose to stop, then her need alone would easily overwhelm him. He gave himself up to her, casting aside any other thoughts, lost to a desire that was now beyond control. Their kiss became less fierce and instead, more exquisite; they were sinking into each other, their physical bodies no barrier to each other's consciousness.

Her hands roved down his back and under his open shirt, her fingers curling into his flesh, and he murmured with the pleasure of it. He lifted his upper body from her so that he could run his fingers along the line of her soft, graceful neck, slipping the tips beneath the collar of her chambray shirt to touch the hot skin beneath. The feel of this concealed flesh, his first tentative exploration of her body, was more sensual than he thought possible; it was the initial moment of mutual discovery, that sublime point when two people understand they are to become lovers. His hand, trembling slightly, moved down, following the line of her shirt, fingertips hidden beneath its cloth. The first three buttons were undone and he traced the nascent rise of her breast; the fourth button undid easily, as did the fifth.

She was naked beneath and his hand closed over the small point of hardness at the centre of her swelling. He felt a tiny shiver run through her. She spoke his name in a low, breathless sigh as his fingers stroked the nipple, causing it to become even more erect from the softness around it. Grace's hands became still as she savoured his caress, her breathing shallow, her body tight with desire.

She held her breath as his hand pushed away the covering material and his lips brushed against the smoothness of her breasts, his tongue moistening the nipple that had become so firm yet so wonderfully sensitive. She shuddered as he drew it into his mouth and smothered its very tip with his own juices. She gasped as his tongue pressed into her, then coaxed the nipple forward again with soft, wet strokes. Her hands could no longer remain still and she clenched them into the flesh of his back, kneading his skin, reaching for his spine and following its rigid line into the waistband of his trousers.

Ash raised his head to find her lips again and this time their kiss was frantic, their mouths crushing each other's, teeth clashing, their tongues probing, fluids mingling, their senses spinning, their hands never still now, but pushing, squeezing, gripping, hard, then soft, firm, then tender.

Abruptly, he broke away, leaving her beneath him to stare up into his eyes, her chest heaving as she struggled to draw breath. The room might have been in darkness so unaware were they of anything around them. A light sheen covered her skin, and the tenderness of her gaze, tinged with the hunger of her passion, was almost mesmerizing. His thoughts began to sink into hers.

Suddenly weakened, Ash lay down beside her, his sensory confusion fighting briefly with his physical need. Only seconds passed before he reached inside her shirt again to find her breasts and expose them for his own private view. Her eyelids closed and her lips tilted in a smile that Ash found as erotic as the naked breasts he fondled.

The smile became desperate as his hand wandered down her stomach to fall into the cleft of her thighs, there to press the thin material of her skirt against the delicate, most intimate, opening of her body. Grace gave a little cry as she writhed beneath his touch, and her hand held his shoulder, pulling down so that the pressure of his fingers would be increased. He felt her dampness seep through.

She breathed his name once more, an imploration that was unnecessary, and he shifted his hand, searching beneath her skirt to feel the velvety smoothness of her thighs; to the blindness of his touch they seemed so beautifully long, his journey deliberately slow, cherishing rather than teasing as her faint murmurs urged him on. Her hair splayed on the sheet beneath her as her neck arched and her shoulder blades almost touched; her breasts stood bare and proud in the light from the window, their tips pink and swollen.

His fingertips found the line of her panties and slipped beneath. Ash thought it impossible to be aroused further, but when his fingers slipped into the full, creamy wetness between her legs he felt a surge of excitement that seemed to awaken every sensory nerve he possessed. And now she helped him by reaching inside her skirt and hooking her thumbs over the elasticated waist of her panties and tugging them down over her thighs so that she was completely free to him; she raised her knees to slide the silky material over them, allowing the panties to fall first past one ankle and then the other. She waited, eyes closed, her mouth open slightly, the tip of her tongue resting between her teeth.

Grace wanted him inside her, she wanted his hard, lean body to smother hers, she wanted his legs tight between her thighs, she wanted him filling her so that their bodies were joined, locked together with nothing between their flesh except their own heat. Aroused so deeply that she was almost in torment, she waited for her lover to enter her.

But Ash was not yet ready for that.

She felt his hands on her thighs, spreading them further; she felt the sensuous trail of his tongue as it left its silky trail along her soft skin. She moaned and turned her head aside so that her temple pressed into her own hair and the bedsheets beneath.

Ash caught her scent, that woman's issue that was so potent. He needed her badly – he ached at his centre for her – but he could not resist this tantalizing prelude, for it had as much to do with homage as it did with lust. He wanted to please her, and he wanted to taste her.

She shuddered when his lips reached her and his kiss there was as tender as any kiss could be. When his tongue stabbed gently into her, opening her, wetness joining wetness, her arms spread outwards and her hands clutched at the sheets. He explored the outer edges, probing the fleshy folds that protected her, titillating nerve endings, moving higher to find the inner nipple, curling the tip of his tongue around the tiny, hard swelling, arousing it as he had aroused her breasts, making it come alive, erect.

And as he made love to her in this most intimate of ways, an abstractedness filled his mind; his thoughts gently began to dissolve and melt into hers as they had when he and Grace had kissed earlier that day. It was a brief flow for, like a sea tide, his thoughts withdrew momentarily to wait for the next surge.

Grace was helpless, pinned there by a muscle that had scant force but great power. Her legs opened wider as she drew in a breath that wheezed in her throat, and when he glided deeper

285

into her, his tongue flexing against the inner walls that themselves were moving with rhythmic restlessness, her hands
uncurled from the sheets and held his head, fingers sliding into
his untidy hair to take grip, using him. She cried out, a sound
that had nothing to do with pain but all to do with pleasure,
and she knew she could not take much more of this, that juices
inside her were beginning to flow too freely, her movement
was becoming too vigorous. She needed him completely when
that dam of ecstasy was breached, she wanted his rapture to
arrive with hers. She pulled at him, calming her own motion
as she did so, and he understood.

Ash rose, his belt undone and clothing quickly discarded as
Grace shifted across the bed so that only her ankles and feet
were off the edge. The sight of her lying there – her perfect
breasts free from the dishevelled shirt, the skirt pulled high
over her parted thighs, but shadowing the small, dark mound
of hair that fell between her legs – left him breathless. She
watched him from the bed, an alluring, heavy-lidded haziness
in her eyes, and raised a hand towards him.

He went to her, lowering himself gently, pushing himself
into her, slowly, smoothly, feeling little resistance, deliberately
taking time with the intrusion so that there would be no pain
for her, penetrating until he had no more to give, his hips were
tight beneath hers. Her hands were like claws at his back as
she writhed beneath him and her breath was hot against his
cheek as he thrust and withdrew, thrust and withdrew.

'David, oh David . . .'

A new, heightened delirium took charge of his mind and
his consciousness sped into hers in emulation of his physical
penetration; but with this mental ingress there was no with-
drawal, no pulling back, there was only a forward thrusting into
a place of few boundaries. It was as before, when they had
probed each other's mind in her father's study, yet so much
stronger now because Grace had given herself up to him, physically and emotionally: she was content to allow him into her
consciousness, for she was too lost in the pleasure of their

lovemaking, too absorbed by its wonder, to send her thoughts into his. He floated in her psyche while their bodies created the mutual joy.

Ash glimpsed the images, the memories, he experienced her exquisite joy of this moment, all the turmoil that was inside her consciousness, and he travelled on, without lingering, aware of his own physical sensations, but never distracted by them. The vast grey, cloudy area he had viewed earlier that day loomed up before him, so familiar now with its tumbling vapours of denial. A small child's voice came to him from beyond that gaseous barrier and this, too, was familiar, for he had heard it before. It was Grace's voice, and it was frightened, appealing for release. Once again, he felt that dragging resistance, as if ethereal hands were holding him back; but he was stronger this time and Grace had given herself up to him. He went onwards.

Wetness had gathered at the corners of her eyes and a tear, disturbed by her movement, spilled over to glide across her cheekbone into her hair. She was frantic, almost unable to draw breath, for never – *never* – had she known such agonizing bliss. A long, shivering moan escaped her and her whole being began to clench tight. Every tendon, every muscle, seemed to be drawing itself inwards, and the secretions inside her flowed, became a torrent, all rushing to that one point in the centre of her body, the place she now shared with this wonderful, extraordinary man. The moan diminished to a thin, drawn-out, euphoric cry.

The tenseness in Ash's chest stretched to the rest of his body, seizing his muscles so that they were rigid in his limbs and stomach. His hips worked even more forcefully and he buried his hands in her hair as her head tilted backwards and her neck arched in the final throes before ecstasy. She collapsed away from him as if all her muscles had suddenly loosened, but immediately came back at him, almost lifting his body. He stayed with her, matching her motion, their rhythm perfect, falling, rising, falling, rising, her feet now on the edge of the bed to give support. This union between them began to peak and together they soared to a new level of rapture, reaching, it seemed, towards a blinding white light.

And the part of Ash that was remote from this – although it heard her cries, it felt his pleasure – plunged through the barrier that stood between her conscious and subconscious and he saw – his mind *saw – the memory that Grace had kept hidden from herself for so very long. And as the final paroxysm of complete glorious fulfilment swept through their thrusting bodies, he discovered her secret, he understood her own self-duplicity . . .*

32

HE IRISHMAN'S SHADOW was cast long and black across
the chapel's stone floor, and the colours around it, the
blended reds, greens and blues that were reflected
through the stained-glass windows high in the wall
behind him, were now less vibrant as the sun sank
lower in the hazy sky outside. Phelan lingered there among
scattered papers, his brow furrowed, his body shaking.

So, he roared to himself, the whole business started with
the monstrosity entombed in this chapel, the first Lockwood
to govern Sleath! A knight of the Crusades, venerated by
fools and feared by those who were wise to his unholy course.
Phelan breathed a tremulous sigh and turned his attention to
the stern countenance of the sculptured warrior; he considered
the black soul once held by the husk that now lay beneath its
own stone image. No soldier of God, this one; more a mer-
cenary of the Devil. A scholar, undoubtedly, and someone
who had studied not only the black arts of the Egyptians, but
also the occult ideologies of the Chaldeans and Babylonians,
such knowledge to be used on his return from foreign wars
when he had been rewarded with lands and governance of his
own.

Phelan picked up his silver-handled cane and hurriedly left
the tiny chapel, entering the main body of the church. He
walked along the side aisle, his steps wearied, his senses

shocked. He paused by the fifth row of pews, turning to look back at the altar. *In the name of God,* his mind cried out, *how could these things happen? How could they be allowed to happen?* There came no answer. He rested in the nearest pew, placing his cane against the seat in front.

The colours of the high window behind the altar were now subdued and the altar itself seemed bleak, almost sterile, in its simplicity. How apt, he thought, for this temple was no more than a vacant shell that mocked the Lord's glory rather than honoured it.

He drew in a long, shivery breath and as his thoughts ranged over the history of this place called Sleath, so the shadows grew deeper around him.

The jumbled writings of Sir Gareth Lockwood were full of obsessions; they hinted at strange rites, ceremonies designed to corrupt rather than enhance, rituals that only the degenerate could perform and endure. This depraved knight boasted of how he had brought the Mysteries back with him from Egypt, after the thwarted Fifth Crusade, of how he had shared that forbidden mysticism with others of his kind – or others he had persuaded to his ways – and of practices that more than once had caused Phelan to slam the journals shut in disgust, only to go back to them when his nerves and his anger had settled. One of the basic tenets of this clandestine order created by Lockwood was that the dead, through certain evocations and rituals, could encounter the living. One particular rite learned from the Egyptians was the rejoining of a severed head to its body so that the person could live again, and Phelan could only wonder how many times this had been practised, and how many wretched victims had given their lives to this worthless and insane cause. Just as worrying was the insinuation in those crazed writings that occasionally the exercise had indeed been successful. How had the man deluded himself so? Was he so mad he truly believed in the impossible? Beyond doubt he had many followers, so how could they be witness to this ridiculous miracle of regeneration? In his journal Lockwood also claimed to converse with the dead and in particular with those spirits specially indoctrinated into his ways before their departure from this world, those still susceptible to his influence. And worse, he considered children to be the ideal 'agents' for such communion, for he professed that their souls were more vibrant and their will more malleable.

Phelan leaned forward, his feet on the pew's cushioned kneeler, and rested his head in his hands as he thought of the slaughter perpetrated by Sleath's first lord. These innocents had had their throats cut, had been starved, poisoned and subjected to all manner of perversions so that their master could pursue his bizarre purposes. Surely villagers were aware of the evil in their midst? Could the disappearance of children and loved ones have been so common in those troubled times – or at least, not so uncommon – that it was accepted? Only a few years before Lockwood's arrival thousands of young ones had been led away to foreign parts on the Children's Crusade to the Holy Land, many of them dying from malnutrition or sold into slavery on the way, never to return to their homes. Had this dreadful episode in history contributed to the sanction of such losses, or were the people of Sleath merely too afraid to voice their suspicions? An even more sinister notion struck him: Could the villagers themselves have cooperated with their lord and master? What value had human life in that harsh century when food, warmth, and the means to stay alive were all that mattered?

The disordered writings defeated clear analysis, but the Irishman, against his own better judgement, wondered if Sir Gareth truly had achieved his goal, this communication with and the direction of the dead, the knight presumably gaining some kind of divine – or diabolic – power by doing so. Oh, he implied his success, but was that merely the false bragging of a lunatic, the demented scribbling of someone whose own madness led to grandiose self-deception; or was there genuinely some value to his cryptic claims? If the latter, then why veil his own dubious accomplishment in coded ramblings?

Perhaps secrecy was a prime rule of the Mysteries, the cabalistic nature of the occult.

Phelan straightened in the pew, then relaxed his spine against the seat's backrest. He noticed that the church was growing darker around him, the shadows more subfusc. And was it cooler than before, had the old building retained none of the day's heat? He rubbed his bony knees, more for the sake of activity than blood circulation.

Working through the afternoon, and helped earlier by David Ash, he had managed to bring some order to the disarranged and, worse, ravaged papers and ledgers, and had organized the journals into successive historical periods. Much was missing in terms of progression down the centuries, and even more had been rendered illegible, or beyond repair, by the vicar's vandalism. But time and time again, Phelan had been drawn to particular stages in Sleath's development, a puzzle even to himself until he realized his own psychic ability was guiding his mind towards details relevant to his searches. It was as if certain passages in the texts exuded a dark energy which his own extra sense had become attuned to and on each occasion that this happened he took extra care to decipher the awkward writings. Ash had been perplexed, but soon accepted the Irishman's strange ability as more elements of Sleath's past had been unravelled.

Sir Gareth Lockwood's outpourings had ended abruptly and Phelan assumed that this signified the man's death or chronic ill health, perhaps the final decline into utter dementia. By then his script had become completely illegible and even Phelan's psychic ability did not enable him to pick up any more than a sense of tortured confusion from the faded pages. Unfortunately the evil had not ended with this ungodly knight's passing, for it seemed that other generations of Lockwoods had continued with the Black Arts, no doubt inspired by their ancestor, his base corruption carried through in the bloodline.

However, it was not until almost a hundred years after Sir Gareth's apparent demise that the wickedness became evident once more, the outrages then chronicled by the depraved lord's descendant, Hugo Lockwood. How opportune for this heir to evil when the Black Death had swept through the country, devastating cities, wiping out whole villages, and allowing him to use its terror for his own ends. The plague, carried by the fleas of black rats, had spread from Asia to China, and on through mediaeval Europe, wiping out millions in its wake, eventually reaching England, bringing with it a new order called the Flagellants, men and women who literally whipped themselves into a frenzy, using metal-tipped scourges, to atone for the sins they believed had brought God's wrath down upon them. Like the pestilence itself, these Flagellants had proliferated throughout Europe, although their influence in England was limited. Whether ideology or cunning caused the lord of Sleath to embrace their masochistic ways, the writings gave no clue, but embrace them he did.

Phelan gave a slight shake of his head in despair. How easy it must have been for this new Lockwood, now the village's spiritual leader as well as its master, to convince his people that punishment meant appeasement to their Lord God, and how easy to snatch the living when death was at everybody's door. At the first sign of illness – *any* illness – the sufferer was whisked away, never to be seen again. And who could complain, what relative or loved one could protest, when the country's entire population was so cruelly being decimated? How the author had gloated over the deceptions, and how lovingly he had detailed the manner and improper purpose of each victim's death. A shudder ran through the Irishman as he considered the damnable passages of text he had been forced to read through, those tortures, slayings, defilements and sexual violations therein recorded as if testament to something prodigious.

After a while he had insisted that Ash return to the inn to rest, aware that the investigator had hardly slept the night before. Besides, there was not much more that Ash could do here in St Giles' now that the records had been sorted through and laid out in some semblance of order, those papers and books dealing with the mundane accounts of village and church expenditure and announcements of births, marriages and deaths set to one side. Reluctantly, the investigator had agreed, leaving Phelan to continue his work with the arrangement that they would meet later at the inn to confer. Never had the Irishman felt quite so alone as when he heard the porch door close behind Ash.

There were many gaps in Sleath's history – the Reformation apparently had meant little to the village folk here, or their lord – but the English Civil War around the mid-1600s brought with it a renewed programme for secret activities and foul play. Again and again, Phelan mused, history had conspired with generations of Lockwoods and their sinister objectives. In this particular era of unrest, young men were sent off to fight an internal war that few would have had stomach for. How many of those reluctant conscripts from these parts failed to reach the separate armies of the King or the Parliamentarians, disappearing without trace, casualties not of war, but of something even more insidious? Who would know, save for the person who had organized their conscription, the master these unfortunates served?

Phelan's head tilted back and he stared into the church's high, vaulted ceiling. Images of script and events weaved before him and he realized there was too much to take in, too much to comprehend. His temples throbbed with the effort of it all. It wasn't just a matter of reading or translating words, for his sixth sense had picked up far more, revealing to him confused scenes of terrible malevolence. He began to wish he had bid the investigator stay, for each new horror unearthed deepened his own dread; Ash's presence might have strengthened his own resolve to remain in this iniquitous place.

It was so peculiar that generations of Lockwoods should feel obliged to log these outrages, as if they represented an inventory of wickedness, their sum total adding up to . . . what? It was beyond him. Could such an accumulation have any purpose, or any consequence? Unless they served as a guide – perhaps even as some warped kind of inspiration – to future Lockwoods.

He reflected on another tragic episode, this some twenty-odd years after the Civil War and around the time of London's great fire. It had been recorded by possibly one of Edmund Lockwood's vilest ancestors, Robert Guy Lockwood. London was rife with violence, prostitution, law-breaking – and bubonic plague; only the fire that swept through its squalid streets had purged it of its own degeneration. Retribution for its sins, this Lockwood had proclaimed to his followers, the Almighty's vengeance on the profane and the diseased, the sick of mind and imperfect of body. Aberrancy of soul had manifested itself in abnormality of health and limb, this pious hypocrite had declared, and a visitation of fire and plague would be on Sleath itself if they themselves did not cleanse the corruption.

Such inglorious cunning! Such guileful distortion! He had led his gullible cohorts on a purging of all that was 'bad' in the village and its surrounds in what he described as 'the night of purification'. Sick infants, children maimed by accident or deformed from birth, the unsound of mind – these unfortunates who perhaps were the results of Sleath's own iniquities and perversions – were dragged from their homes or snatched from their cots, their families, those with courage enough to resist beaten into submission. The victims were carried or dragged to the black pit at the village's centre: the pond of unnatural depths. There they were drowned, their pitiful cries dashed from their lips by cudgels as they desperately tried to cling to the banks.

Phelan had moaned aloud, for the vision raged in his mind. He had thrown the journal from his lap, the loose papers scattering over the stone floor as he had found them. Then he had sunk to his knees, unable to continue, and his prayers had been both for those lost innocents and for the future of Sleath itself.

Eventually, when the images of screaming children and youngsters disappearing beneath those unsettled black waters, their little hands grasping at the night air before sinking from sight, had been forced from his mind – or at least, suppressed enough for him to pull himself together – he had taken his place back on the solitary chair in the chapel.

The horrors were not yet over, and would not be for him until he laid down the last Lockwood journal; but he had steeled himself against whatever else lay ahead inside those tainted pages. Mercifully, Sleath appeared to have gone through a period of normality – or disguised normality – under the control of succeeding Lockwoods. The evil had been either subdued or entirely covert in the more civilized years that followed and the records were like any others that might be found in old church chests throughout that part of the country: parish accounts, baptisms, weddings, deaths – all commonplace for this type of rural village.

Yet . . . Yet as he continued to comb through the faded texts he could not rid himself of the revulsion. No matter how ordinary, how mundane, the documentation, dark undertones seemed to permeate the very pages under his gaze. He wondered if his thoughts, his imaginings, were still influenced by earlier revelations and, in truth, he couldn't be sure anymore. He was wearied, he was sickened, and by then his extra faculty, his sixth sense, was dimmed. But the inner coldness that had gripped him throughout his searches took firmer hold when he reached journals and records dealing with an extensive period in the eighteenth century.

These records were neatly kept, their script tidy, almost fastidious. He soon discovered, however, that the mind behind these later chronicles was as unhinged and as deviant as that of the earlier Lockwoods. Sebastian Lockwood was squarson to Sleath, both minister and squire, governing his parishioners with a fist of iron and also, like his predecessors, seeming to take special delight in listing all punishments meted out to wrongdoers, or to those who offended him. In one instance two poachers had been caught on the squarson's land in the early hours; Lockwood had the intruders beaten, then set his dogs on them. Their bodies had been ripped to pieces by the pack while Sebastian Lockwood and his cronies had watched and made wagers as to which poacher would fall first. Merciless enough behaviour for a so-called man of the cloth, but to record the event with such relish was more than just eccentric. *'The beasts had their fill,'* the script informed, *'and greatly enjoyed the human flesh.'*

Phelan's hand had trembled on the page as he read the line. What kind of master would order, then take bets on, such a cruel punishment? Clearly the Lockwood 'sickness' had prevailed through the centuries.

Other poachers had been treated in similar fashion, although only a few were allowed to be killed by the dogs. Instead survivors were locked into the stocks on the village green and left there to bleed to death as an example to the rest of the community. Another miscreant, a miller called Samuel Bridgestock, whose crime was to declare false accounts – apparently a small part of his ground corn was being sold for private profit rather than for the benefit of Sebastian Lockwood, who owned all rights to the water mill and its produce – was lashed to the millwheel itself while his family and villagers were ordered to watch. 'Ten revolutions,' was Lockwood's sentence on the miller, 'and if he doth live, then so shall his sin be atoned for.' It was gloatingly recorded that Bridgestock had drowned beneath the waters on the fifth turn of the wheel.

And so it went on, this list of names and punishments, as if Lockwood took delight in each 'crime' as well as its discipline, as if their sum was the inheritance of future generations of Lockwoods. Phelan wondered how such atrocities could have been perpetrated with apparent immunity in what was supposed to be the Age of Enlightenment, when reforms such as equality before the law, religious toleration, the abolition of serfdom and the reduction of noble and clerical privilege were being advocated and even accepted by many despot monarchs on the Continent. Was Sleath so remote from the rest of the world? Or was Lockwood rule so powerful that no one dared whisper against it?

He went on to find references to Sir Francis Dashwood, a familiar name to him and, so it would seem, a close associate of Lockwood. That hardly came as a surprise, for the Irishman was aware that Dashwood was notorious in this area in the 1700s as an occultist and founder of the infamous Hellfire Club, a clandestine organization that engaged in satanic rites and aristocratic dissipation. A suitable friend and ally to one such as Sebastian Lockwood.

A cloud must have passed between the high windows behind the altar and the dying sun, for the colours of the stained glass darkened, became a dull mix of browns and greys. Phelan looked around to see that other windows had dimmed. He hadn't realized the day had gone.

Sebastian Lockwood's journals and lists had filled many books, but in the last few the writing had degenerated to an untidy, erratic script. In places it seemed that the squarson had stabbed at the pages with his pen, for there were indents and even holes in the paper itself, with ink blots rendering certain words illegible. Jagged lines crossed out whole passages of text and often sentences were garbled, incomprehensible, as if his fevered brain was no longer able to translate his own thoughts. Phelan could only wonder if madness as well as cruelty was inherent in the Lockwood genes.

These latter journals aroused such fresh repulsion in him that he was almost physically sick, for they disclosed Sebastian Lockwood's necrophilic obsessions. Difficult to understand though the scrawled handwriting had become, Phelan quickly realized that this madman, like the first Lockwood of Sleath, had conducted experiments on cadavers in order to regenerate them; but, unlike his forebear, Sebastian Lockwood had gone even further, in fact copulating with the dead bodies, be they those of adult male and female, or – and this was where Phelan had retched and almost vomited over the open pages on his lap – with children.

Worse than the reading of the words were the sensations that leapt from them. He tried to close his mind against the dreadful images, but still they invaded, spreading like a virulent infection, pushing rejection and all other thoughts aside. He had terrible, abhorrent visions that caused his stomach to heave once more and his body to shake as if he were in seizure; then he was on his feet, the journal slipping from his lap onto the chapel floor where it lay with other scattered papers.

He had whispered, not shouted his outrage, the harsh hissing sounds loud enough within the confines of the chapel. And after a while he had left that place and all the depraved works it contained.

He faced the modest altar, his shock, his anger, his exhaustion, his despair, all conspiring to drain him of resolve. Had the sickness ended with Sebastian, was he the last in the line of Lockwood degenerates? Or was there more evil to come?

It was a tiny sound at first, the scraping of stone against stone. He inclined his head, wondering where the noise had come from.

The church had become dark – had he really been here that long? – but no one else had joined him, that was perfectly clear. He took a peek at his wristwatch and blinked his eyes several times to focus; it was no good, he'd spent too much time peering at almost impenetrable handwriting and his eyes were blurred with fatigue. Glancing up at the windows he realized either the sun had sunk behind the hills, or the sky had become completely overcast.

He reached for the back of the bench seat in front to pull himself up and as his fingers curled around the edge he thought he noticed the shadows around him perceptibly deepen. That couldn't be so. Nightfall was a steady, creeping thing – at least it was in this part of the world – and shadows obeyed its rule. It must be his tired old eyes, too much reading in poor light, and too much squinting at scrawled handwriting. Had to be the answer. But why was it so cold? Not just cool in the way all stone buildings were, despite high temperatures outside, but tomb-cold, the kind of cold that chills a person's innards, stiffens and tingles the spine.

This was nothing new, though, was it? He'd felt this kind of cold in certain locations before. Haunted places. Rooms or houses that needed exorcizing.

Stone grated against stone again. This time the sound was louder. And longer.

Oh dear Saviour. He knew where the sound came from.

He felt the stiffness in his spine, that tingling stiffness, travel up to the back of his neck where the small hairs themselves became rigid. Well, isn't that in the best tradition? he asked himself. Aren't the sphincter muscles supposed to loosen now, wasn't that the way of these things? They seem firm enough to me, so I don't suppose I'll be soiling the underwear, thank you.

His smile, raised to reassure only himself, was little more than a twitch of his lips.

The twitch was replaced by a grimace when the next sound was a grinding of stone against stone, as though a slab were being pulled away from its base.

'Oh dear Saviour.' It was not a thought this time, it was a spoken plea.

He stared towards the open archway to the little chapel where the husk of Sir Gareth Lockwood lay.

Oh no, this was not possible. This sort of thing did not happen outside the tales of Edgar Allan Poe. All his experiences with the paranormal and psychic phenomena, gained over many years, reliably informed him that corpses – especially bits of dried skin and bone – did not try to leave their resting place by their own efforts. A spirit might return, but the dead most definitely did not get up and walk, nor push aside great slabs of stone.

The sound stopped.

And Phelan began to rise to his feet.

This was all in the mind. He'd scared himself witless with

the reading of those accursed journals. The sounds were his own imaginings, just like the darkness inside this place. He'd allowed the lunacy of the writings to influence his own mind.

And what was that now? A dragging of a foot across the floor? Get a grip on y'self, you ol' fool.

Eyes still watching the opening to the chapel, Phelan stooped slightly to pick up his cane. He began to edge his way along the pew towards the centre aisle.

Of course it was his own imagination, but no point in staying here. There was much to be done this night; leastways, much to be *undone*. It was by no means an excuse, there really was someone he needed to see.

Phelan never once glanced away from the dark – *the pitch black* – entrance to the chapel.

So if you'll pardon the impoliteness, I'll be on my way, he found himself silently saying, as if by keeping this whole experience within the realms of light-hearted banter it would make it unreal.

Nausea clutched at him again, this time fear the instigator and not disgust. Almost at the end of the pew, he bent forward, grabbing at the back of the seat in front for support. He held himself there, doubled over and swallowing bile, reluctant to vomit inside a house of God. To reaffirm it *was* still a house of God, he made the Sign of the Cross.

'. . . Father, Son, Holy Ghost,' he murmured.

A dizziness kept him there.

'I'm creating this meself,' he said in a whisper. 'It's me own fright that's the cause.' The thing in there is dead, eedjit, and nothing on this earth could bring it back. 'Eedjit,' he reiterated, this time in a whisper. He'd opened his mind to all manner of aberration and atrocity that day, and this was the result: over-tired, over-anxious, and as the youngsters might say, over-the-top. Get a grip on y'self, man.

He pushed himself upright. And saw a shadow within the blackness of the chapel opening. How a shadow could be seen within pitch blackness was not a question he wished to ask himself at that point; rather, he felt it better just to be on his way.

The shadow moved, as if emerging from a cloak of its own substance, and the Irishman stumbled into the aisle.

It was more of a hobble than a trot when he turned from the front of the church and headed towards the main door, but at least he was moving. If he lacked dignity in his haste, then who was to know, who was to see? Nobody but that . . . thing . . . behind him . . .

He soon reached an interruption in the rows of pews, a cross-aisle that led to the arches and the porch door beyond. He almost tripped, and the cane cracked against the floor ahead of him, helping him keep his balance. He wanted to look over his shoulder, he had a great desire to see what was emerging from the chapel; but he refused himself permission. If there was something following him, best not to know, better to get away from there just as quickly as he could. After all, the dead did not walk, so there was no point in looking anyway, no point at all.

He lurched round the last pew in the row, still refusing to look over his right shoulder even though . . . even though . . . there in the periphery of his vision . . . something was . . . something really *was* . . .

. . . *moving* . . .

. . . *shuffling* . . .

. . . *coming after him* . . .

He plunged into the greater gloom beneath the arches and, dark though it was, the big door that opened into the porch was visible, a black mass in the shade, a good, stout shape, solid, protection from the hordes, guardian of God's keep . . .

Phelan realized he was gibbering, if in mind only, but what did it matter as long as it kept his thoughts from what was there in the church with him, the thing that surely was a figment of his imagination, yet somehow, in some way, had followed him from the old knight's tomb.

He reached the door, practically blundering into it, a hand smacking against the rough wood. His palm numbed, he felt for the iron ring that needed to be twisted to turn the lock.

He found it – and it would not turn.

Dropping the cane so that he could use both hands, the Irishman tried again. Still it seemed stiff, unturnable . . .

Ridiculous. He'd had no problem with it when he'd entered St Giles'. Panic was doing this. It required a knack, a special way of twisting the ring.

He felt the presence behind him, a slow, deliberate movement along the cross-aisle. He heard the shuffle, feet dragging across stone, and he heard . . . *couldn't be, couldn't be, the dead had no need* . . . he heard air being drawn in and exhaled, a rough, uneven respiration as if disintegrated lungs had too many holes in them and the rotted throat was too dry, too coarse, too flaky . . .

He half-turned his head – only half-turned, because he didn't want to see the black shape, the centuries-old husk preserved by its icebox of stone, didn't want to confirm his suspicions that this dead creature from his imagination was truly behind him – and caught sight of something – *something*, nothing definite, nothing you could call a *real* thing – lumbering after him.

No! Impossible!

He fumbled with the iron ring. It gave an inch or so and he twisted harder. It turned all the way and he heard the click of metal. He pushed against the door, stupidly, foolishly, feeling whatever it was behind him drawing closer, and closer. He used all his strength, his wrists shaking, his shoulder against the wood.

The dead don't breathe, his mind silently screamed, *so why can I hear it, why can I feel it, why can I smell its fetid scent?*

And why could he sense a bony hand reaching towards him, scraps of thin, crispy flesh falling like sparse confetti from it to litter the floor?

'Oh Mother Mary . . .' he whined and then remembered the door opened inwards.

He pulled, cracking the door against his knee, then slid through, slamming it shut behind him. He thought he heard something scrape against the wood on the other side.

Phelan did not wait inside the porch. The cold here was as deep as a freezer's and he had the irrational fear – as irrational as being chased by the dead – that his limbs would be too rigid to move if he remained much longer. Besides, there really was no incentive to stay.

Two steps took him to the outer door and this time there was no fumbling with the handle. The door opened easily and he staggered out to collapse onto the gravel path outside. Still he did not stop; he crawled through the graveyard, scraping his knees and hands against the gravel, all the while telling himself that this was madness, that there really could not have been any ghostly stalker back there in the church, it was entirely in his own overwrought imagination, a sudden aberration of the psyche brought on by the horrors he had subjected himself to that day. Spirits, evil or otherwise, did not come in this form – they did not move tombstones, they did not breathe, they did not give chase. Madness. Madness. *Madness!*

His mind being on other things, he failed to notice the mist around him.

33

THE TRANSITION FROM sleep to wakefulness was abrupt. One moment Ash's eyes were closed, the next they were wide open and staring up at the ceiling.

He lay still, regathering his senses, for a second or two his mind a blank sheet. And then it came to him, a sudden recognition of events and circumstances. He shut his eyes again, raising a hand to cover them, struggling to bring some order to the thoughts that flooded in.

He began to understand.

Ash uncovered his eyes and wondered why the room was so dark. How long had he slept?

Rising from the bed, he went to the window and drew back the curtains. His body tensed when he saw the fog outside, a yellowish, curling mist that all but obscured the houses and village hall on the other side of the green. It turned and drifted, lazy in movement, somehow sinister in texture. Its unearthliness was heightened by the absolute silence out there, a total lack of normal activity. No footsteps or voices, no birds calling to each other, and no traffic; even the inn itself was bereft of the usual muffled tones of customers in the bar below.

Ash turned away from the window, perturbed by the fog and the hush that came with it, and caught sight of the figure asleep on the bed.

Grace lay on her side, one knee bent, her skirt high over a

smooth thigh; her shirt was open, the curve of a breast revealed. Shadows veiled intimate parts he had kissed, caressed, and he felt himself stir at the sight of her, his own nakedness contributing to the arousal. But with the desire came the memory of his journey into her consciousness, the discovery of a secret she had hidden even from herself. He went to her, kneeling by her side on the bed.

'Grace.'

It was said too quietly to awaken her.

He touched her shoulder, shook it gently. 'Grace,' he called again, louder this time.

She stirred, a slight lifting of her chin, a parting of her lips.

'Wake up, Grace.' He brushed her hair away from her cheek with his fingertips.

A frown disturbed the smoothness of her forehead and he saw the twitch of her eyes as they moved beneath their lids. Grace mumbled something, perhaps his name, and her eyes slowly opened. A smile touched her lips at the sight of him and a hand reached out, sliding along his thigh. She twisted, unbending her leg so that the dark hair between her legs was no longer in shadow. He wanted to touch her, wanted to slide his hand between the flesh of her thighs and again feel the moistness of her inner body.

Instead, he said, 'We have to go.'

She stayed her hand, her frown harder this time.

Ash leaned forward to kiss her and her lips eagerly met his. Once more desire almost drove other thoughts, other purposes, from his mind, but a deeper concern strengthened his resolve. Even so he wondered at the intensity of his feelings for her. It should never have happened, he shouldn't have allowed it to happen; he had remained immune for so long and now he had let this woman, this sweet, vulnerable woman, slip through his guard and become part of his life as if the lesson had never been learned. He craved to hold on to her, he wanted to crawl beneath the bedcovers and keep her there tight against him, away from the dread and discovery that lay beyond this safe, protected room. Yet he was aware that this was a false hope and that Grace's release from the sickness inside her could only be through revocation. They both shared a rejection of the past, his own misguided guilt confusing the memory of his sister's tragic death, while Grace was tormented by something concealed even from herself. Perhaps her conscious mind was unaware of that inner turmoil, but her subconscious understood it only too well.

She clung to him as he attempted to draw away. 'Please, David,' she whispered.

He gripped her wrists to take them from his neck. 'It's happening, Grace,' he told her. 'Take a look outside the window.'

She pulled back to look into his eyes. 'What are you talking about?'

'Can't you feel it?'

A smile of misunderstanding broke into her frown, but it faded almost instantly. He saw her stiffen, her eyes searching the room.

'What is it?' She clutched at herself as if suddenly chilled.

When he didn't answer she slid past him and made for the window. He heard her faint gasp.

'It could be a natural heat mist,' he offered lamely, not sure why he was trying to rationalize the phenomenon. Could he be hoping she'd agree with him? Would a mutual assessment *render* it normal? Such hope was quickly dashed when she turned back to him with fear in her eyes.

'*What does it mean, David?*'

Because he had no answer he ignored the question. Instead he reached for his clothes and began to pull them on. 'I want to take you back to your father,' he said.

She appeared surprised, then slowly began to button her shirt. 'He knows, doesn't he?' Her hands were still for a moment. 'My father has something to do with all this.'

'I think he may be one of the causes.' He moved towards her, his hands reaching out to touch her shoulders. 'He hasn't

307

been honest with you, Grace.' She broke away as if angry and went to the bed to find the rest of her clothing.

She suspects, he thought as he watched her. But she has no real idea of her own involvement. Ash slipped his shirt on, then reached for his shoes and socks while Grace sat on the bed and waited for him. She seemed numbed and he wondered what turmoil was going on inside her head. He busied himself tying his laces, realizing that for the moment he could not help her, that in all probability she would not believe him anyway. Not for the first time he cursed the psychic aberration that sometimes allowed him to understand the thoughts, hidden or otherwise, of others.

When he was ready, he took her by the hand and led her from the bedroom.

As they made their way along the musty corridor and then down the stairs, Ash resisted the urge to break the silence and call out for the landlord or his wife. When they reached the bar, they found it empty.

It was an odd sensation crossing the large vacant room towards the open doorway to the street, for the hush was almost a sound in itself. Ash could not help but imagine how it would have been a century ago, with its stout oak beams and large open fireplace, the room filled with tradesmen, farmers, labourers, even the local gentry, mingling and swapping yarns, laughter over there in the corner, the landlord remonstrating with a farm-worker a little worse for ale at the bar . . .

'David . . . ?'

He blinked, startled.

'You stopped,' Grace said. 'You were listening for something.'

He gave a small shake of his head as if dazed. 'I thought . . .' He wiped his hands across his face. 'Never mind. Let's get moving.'

They continued their journey through the apparently deserted inn and Ash concentrated on the doorway ahead, unwilling to be distracted again by activity that existed only inside his own imagination. When they reached the large entrance door they stopped again, this time deliberately.

'It's so eerie,' Grace said quietly as they gazed out into the yellow-tainted mist. 'And its smell . . .'

The various colours of the cars parked opposite were lack-lustre seen through the drifting clouds and the grass of the village common appeared dull, almost grey. Ash narrowed his eyes, peering intently into the haze when he thought he discerned darker shapes moving through it. It was impossible to tell if there were figures out there for, once focused upon, the shapes seemed to dissolve into the fog itself.

Reluctant though he was to leave the sanctuary of the inn, Ash knew they could not stay there. Something – he guessed it was a kind of anger, a rage at the things that had already occurred in Sleath – was compelling him to go to the Lodge House and confront Grace's father.

He stirred himself. 'No point in taking my car,' he said to her. 'I think it'd be quicker to walk in this.'

She nodded and rubbed at her upper arms.

'You cold?' he asked, and she nodded again.

He felt it too, the same kind of chill he'd felt inside St Giles'. Briefly he wondered if Phelan was still searching through the records up at the church.

Grace hesitated as Ash stepped out into the street and he had to take her hand once more to coax her. She followed, keeping close to him, her hand tight in his.

'Do you see them, David?'

At first he wasn't sure what she meant, then realized she was referring to the vague shapes moving in the mist.

'They're nothing, Grace, just odd patches of darker fog.'

But he knew he was wrong, he knew they were something else.

'They're people,' Grace said.

One was close, on the other side of the road, close to the common. Determinedly, Ash strode towards it, leaving Grace behind. He could make out the shape of a head, shoulders, the rest of the figure obscured by a low swirling of denser fog, and he opened his mouth to call out, anxious to make contact. As he approached, the figure – or what he could see of it – simply evaporated, became nothing.

Stunned, Ash came to a halt halfway across the road and stared at the spot where the partial figure had been. The mist blustered as if disturbed by a sharp gust of wind. He felt Grace by his side again.

'I saw it,' she said, catching at his arm. 'It just vanished.'

He continued to stare into the mist. 'It isn't possible.'

'You know it is, David. Haven't you learned anything about this place?' Before he could respond she raised a hand. 'Oh dear God, look . . .'

Ash followed her pointing finger and saw that the yellowish clouds had thinned out over the village pond, the water there as placid as usual. Yet there was a difference now, for there seemed to be a peculiar sheen to its surface. And the grass around its edges was stiffened and white as if . . . he blinked his eyes to clear them . . . as if frosted.

'It's ice, David.' Grace was still pointing. 'The pond is frozen over.'

A cry from somewhere in the distance startled them both. It was a bleak, isolated sound, like an eagle's call across a lonely moor. Grace's grip on his arm tightened.

Ash shifted his gaze from the iced pond and peered into the sluggish mist. There were more grey shapes out there, some perfectly still, others moving slowly.

'Let's go,' he said, taking Grace by the waist.

She resisted. 'I'm frightened, David.'

He faced her, pulling her close. 'They're apparitions; they can't harm us.'

'Can you be sure?'

'Only our own fear can hurt us.' It was glib, unconvincing, but the best he could do under the circumstances. 'It's important that we get to your father, Grace,' he added, perhaps to motivate her.

'You haven't told me why.' She searched his face as though she might find some answer in his expression alone.

Ash began to speak, changed his mind, and started again. 'There are certain things I think he can explain,' he said simply, hoping to leave it there.

Grace persisted. 'Why shouldn't he have explained them to me before? He's my father, for God's sake.'

'You have to ask him that yourself.'

It was a cold reply, and one that visibly shook her.

'What do you know, David?' The question was asked quietly, but there was an intensity about it that unsettled him.

'You sensed things about me, Grace, memories and traumas that only I could be aware of. Earlier I sensed them about you too. All I can tell you is that your father has deceived you for a very long time.'

She shook her head, refuting his words.

'Then let's go to him, let's confront him,' he urged.

'He's sick, Dr Stapley said he shouldn't be disturbed.'

'Then you'll never know the truth.'

He could see her confusion, sense the shock inside her. But soon a resolution took hold of her.

'You'll help me, won't you?' she said to him, and Ash quickly took her in his arms. He kissed her hair, hugged her close.

She drew away and, after another searching look into his eyes, turned to face the road ahead.

They kept to the centre of the High Street, listening for any approaching traffic but, save for the scuff of their own shoes on the roadway, there was only a deep silence all around them. The fog, or mist, was patchy, sometimes obscuring the buildings across the green completely, at other times allowing them to see white picket fences, small hedges and verges, and the houses beyond. The houses were unlit, but they knew there had to be people inside, that the whole village could not have been evacuated while they, Grace and Ash, had slept. So where were the villagers? Were they so frightened that they were staying behind closed doors? Could they, too, sense the threat?

A thicker cluster of shadows was gathered beneath the tree at the end of the common, but again, as they approached, the shapes dimmed, then faded into the mist itself. But a pitiful moaning came to them as they drew level with the old stocks and whipping post.

'Keep walking,' Ash urged calmly.

Grace allowed herself to be taken along, but could not help glancing at the weathered wooden relics, almost as if expecting to find them in use. To her relief they were empty, although something dark and slick seeped down the whipping post, forming a spreading stain at its base as it sank into the earth. It looked like blood, but she had no desire to confirm the impression. Neither did Ash, who had noticed it too.

They kept moving, reaching the end of the green, and when Ash looked back over his shoulder, the shapes had re-formed around the stocks and whipping post. He did not mention it to Grace.

A scream came from one of the houses off to their left, a human cry this time, muffled by the walls around it. It was followed by another, this one further away, from a different house. They heard a door slam, then running footsteps which faded into the distance.

Silence descended again, broken only by their own steps. The tainted fog drifted around them, offering glimpses of the empty street one moment, concealing the way ahead the next. The few shops they had passed appeared empty, with no lights on against the gloom, and their doors closed. At one stage Ash touched a hand to his face and felt a cold dampness there.

A door to a cottage on their right suddenly opened and an elderly couple stumbled out. They caught sight of Grace and Ash and froze for a second or two, then hurried around the side of their house onto a path leading to the fields beyond. Ash made to follow them, but they were quickly lost to the mist.

He returned to Grace, shaking his head at her, and they resumed their journey. Something smashed inside a house nearby and they heard a raised voice, then nothing more. Ash thought he caught a curtain flicker in the window of another house, but a sound distracted him. A car was starting up somewhere behind them.

It was surely foolish to drive in conditions like these, but apparently someone was desperate enough to do so. They heard the engine fade away, the driver obviously heading out of the village over the small bridge. Good luck, Ash thought, beginning to wish that he and Grace had taken the same direction.

Soon they arrived at the fork in the road and for one brief second Ash considered taking the route to the left, for it led away from the church and the Lodge House beyond, away from Sleath itself. This time it was Grace who did not hesitate; she went to the right, beginning the gradual climb up the hill, unaware of his moment of indecision. Ash, himself, barely broke his step.

A row of cottages drew their attention and Grace said, 'Should we see if she's all right?'

Before he could answer they heard voices from up ahead. Both instantly forgot about Ellen Preddle and listened intently.

'It's the children,' Grace breathed softly.

Although the hymn was now familiar to him, it sounded no less sinister, for he was aware that it was the chant of discarnate voices. Their steps quickened as he and Grace made towards the small schoolhouse.

They paused outside the gate and Ash imagined the children assembled in their classroom, little mouths wide and eyes shining as they sang out the hymn. He reminded himself that the building was empty and these voices were from another time, that he and Grace were hearing the ethereal singing of the dead.

> *Dance, then, wherever you may be,*
> *I am the Lord of the Dance, said he.*
> *And I'll lead you all,*

> *wherever you may be,*
> *and I'll lead you all*
> *in the dance, said he.*

Yet he was puzzled, not just by the unearthliness of the phenomenon, but because Grace had told him the hymn was not that old. Most, if not all, of the children who had sung it here would still be alive, so why should it be adopted by the spirits of those who had passed on? Unless, as he'd suggested to Grace before, it was merely a memory, a sound retained by the atmosphere, the very walls, of the school, an uncanny kind of recording released now by his own and Grace's psychic power. The hymn changed in tone, somehow became darker.

> *I danced on a Friday*
> *When the sky turned black;*
> *It's hard to dance*
> *With the devil on your back.*
> *They buried my body*
> *and they thought I'd gone;*
> *but I am the dance*
> *and I still go on.*

'Don't you see?' It was as if Grace had been reading his mind. 'Don't you see?' she said again. 'It's a warning of some kind. It's their way of letting us know what happened here in Sleath.'

He shook his head. 'I don't get it.'

The voices became louder and the mist in the tiny playground became disrupted, curling and billowing as if blown by a fierce wind.

Grace was still, staring beyond the swirling vapours at the schoolhouse itself. 'They need our help, David,' she said. 'Can't you understand? They need our help.'

34

ST GILES' HAD BEEN EMPTY.

Grace, anxious to return to the Lodge House, had waited by the lychgate while Ash hurried along the path between gravestones to the open door of the porch. As before, the sensation had not been pleasant inside the small covered entrance, its tomb-like oppressiveness sending a shiver through him as he struggled with the inner door. At first he thought it was locked, but the door gave when he twisted the ring handle and used his shoulder to push. To his discomfort, the dispiriting chill seemed to have graduated to the old building itself and he felt no desire to venture into its forbidding, unlit interior. From the doorway he called Phelan's name, and when there was no response he closed the door again and hastily left the porch.

Grace's impatience was evident when he reached the lychgate and told her the Irishman had presumably completed his researches and left St Giles'; she immediately set off for the Lodge House, leaving him standing alone wondering why Phelan had not come to the inn as they'd arranged. Still puzzled, he caught up with Grace.

The fog was not quite as dense further up the hill and the Lodge House soon came into view. There was something wrong and they both sensed it.

Grace gave Ash a swift, anxious look and quickened her

pace, almost running the last few yards to the front gate. It was open, just as the door to the house itself was open.

'Grace, wait!' Ash shouted as she ran to the front door, her hair loose and flowing, and disappeared inside. Slightly out of breath from the climb up the hill, gentle though it was, he raced after her.

The dusky gloom closed around him as he entered the hallway and he heard footsteps on the landing above. He listened as Grace called for her father, her steps suddenly coming to a halt. She called again and Ash realized the vicar was not in his bedroom. Without waiting for her, he opened the door to the nearby drawing room and peered in. No one there. Grace's voice came to him again as she searched other rooms upstairs. He walked along the hallway, looking ahead through the open kitchen door; as far as he could tell, it was empty also. He paused outside the study.

Grace's footsteps were on the stairs as Ash opened the study door. He stood there transfixed.

'David, he's not –'

Grace had joined him in the doorway, but her words faltered when she looked past his shoulder into the room. He felt her draw in a sharp breath as her eyes set on the picture over the empty fireplace.

The painted canvas was turning a deep brown in parts as if exposed to a naked flame, and its oils softened and blistered. The paintwork began to crack as small black curls of smoke rose into the air.

They watched in horror as the picture of Lockwood Hall was consumed by a fire they could neither see, hear, nor smell.

35

ATE MCCARRICK CHECKED the signpost through the window of her Renault.

My God, she thought, it's as if whoever puts up those bloody things doesn't really want you to find the place you're looking for.

She consulted the map book on her lap. Yep, Sleath had to be somewhere in this direction. Must be to the right, had to be.

Engaging D, she steered the car through the junction and took the right-hand turn.

The drive from London had not been pleasant, all thoroughfares north, west, east and south congested as hell. Friday evening was a bad time to be heading out of town. When she eventually reached it even the motorway had been chock-a-block, making the journey to the Chilterns not only longer, but extremely frustrating. Dusk was falling and Kate, having taken time only to pick up some things and an overnight bag from her flat, was feeling both tired and peckish. How on earth could *all* the phones be out in Sleath? She had tried calling the Black Boar Inn several times during the late afternoon, and then the vicar's residence, to no avail. The operator had informed her that there were problems with the lines for the moment, but service would be back to normal as soon as possible. Okay. A trip into the hills was fine by Kate, and the information she had concerning this man Seamus Phelan might be useful to her investigator. Besides, as much as she disliked to admit it, she was missing Ash.

Love was no longer involved – probably never had been as far as he was concerned – but she still had strong feelings towards him despite his moodiness and irritating world-weary manner. They'd had some good times together – all right, fraught times mainly, but David Ash was still an intriguing person. His breakdown three years ago had taken some of the edge off his cynicism, made him less sure of himself, and if anything, that new vulnerability had somehow increased his appeal. Theirs was always a casual relationship at best, even if intense in passion at times, but Kate had been prepared to commit herself more deeply during his illness; Ash hadn't allowed that closeness, drawing even further into himself. It had taken at least five months – and then some – for him to overcome his inner demons, and the change in him, oddly enough, was an improvement. He still fought just as hard to expose the charlatans of the psychic world and remained wickedly contemptuous of certain spiritualists and healers; yet there was a new tolerance in him, he was less inclined to dismiss all paranormal and supernatural phenomena out of hand.

By now the sun was no more than a fiery red crescent peeping over the dark, distant hills and Kate hoped she would reach Sleath soon. She needed a good stiff drink, followed by dinner and then – well, she'd play it by ear. Perhaps she'd stay the whole weekend and maybe, just maybe, she and Ash would recapture some of that old magic – or at least, some of that old lust.

She smiled to herself. Oh yes, she missed that. For an enigmatic, self-contained man, David Ash was surprisingly demonstrative where passion was concerned. Until three years ago, that is. The events at Edbrook, the Mariell house, had changed him completely – and no wonder.

The road had inclined steadily for a mile or so and suddenly a stunning scene was offered her through a break in the trees.

She pulled over onto the grass verge, not to absorb the panoramic view, but because something else had caught her eye.

Only the very tip of the sun now peeped over the faraway hills, and darkening clouds had begun to gather as if they had been waiting for its demise. The atmosphere was humid, close, the threat of thunder in the air. But it was the valley between the nearest hills that had attracted her interest, for it was filled with a thick yellowish cloud. At least, it looked like a cloud, but it had to be a heat mist or fog. She could just make out a hazy church tower poking from it on the far side, but that was all.

Was the village of Sleath beneath that lot? According to the map it was somewhere close by. How very peculiar. There was no other fog in the region as far as she could see, so why this small pocket of it? No doubt there was some geological reason for it being trapped there. She stood watching it for several minutes, entranced by the weird beauty of the scene.

Eventually, Kate returned to the car, shaking her head wryly. Not what she'd expected for the weekend. Perhaps the fog would have drifted off by tomorrow, or dispersed with the rain clouds, leaving the village open to the sun and all its glory. It was certainly a wonderful location, far removed from the dreariness of the city. She buckled her seatbelt and set off again.

The road soon began to descend, a winding course that kept her alert and her attention away from the brief glimpses of the valley through the trees. The road wasn't very wide, but thankfully she met no other vehicles travelling in the opposite direction. As she rounded yet another sharp bend near the bottom of the hill she saw the fog bank stretching across the road a few hundred yards up ahead.

Slowing the car, Kate regarded the great opaque barrier with dismay. It looked so impenetrable at that distance. And so . . . she chided herself for the thought, but it was there anyway . . . so forbidding.

Two vehicles were parked a short distance away from the

wall of fog and Kate pulled in behind them. The drivers were standing by the lead vehicle, a grey Ford van with the red and blue logo of British Telecom emblazoned on its side and rear doors. They stopped talking to look her way.

One of them, the younger of the two, whose hair was pulled back into a lank ponytail, gave her a grin. 'You won't be driving through that, love,' he announced. He leaned an elbow on the roof of his van and rubbed round the back of his neck.

The other man, who, unlike his companion wore a tie with his neat blue-striped shirt, nodded his head in agreement. 'It's a freak fog,' he informed her, adding, 'I've never seen anything like it.'

'Surely if I use my lights . . .' she replied hopefully.

The ponytailed Telecom engineer shook his head. 'Tried it,' he said. 'Didn't get beyond ten yards using dipped beam. I've never seen nothing like it neither.' He looked back at the slow-swirling mass. 'They don't pay me enough to risk driving through that sort of thing,' he remarked defiantly.

'I'm going to find another way round it,' said the other man, who Kate guessed was a businessman or sales rep. 'No need to go through Sleath anyway.'

'Then Sleath is up ahead?' Kate enquired.

'Coupla miles.' The telephone engineer clucked his tongue in mock frustration. 'Don't know what they're gonna say back at the ranch. All the lines from the village are buggered and they think the distribution box is out. I was suppose to suss it out, fix it, or report back. No chance of that this evening.'

'Would that upset all the phones?' Kate asked, realizing now why she had been unable to get through earlier.

'If the damage is bad enough. Last time this happened was in town when a lorry crashed into one of our green boxes. It knocked out half the town's lines in one go.'

'But I have to get to Sleath,' she insisted.

The engineer shrugged. 'Can't help you, lady. If you don't believe how bad it is, take a walk into it. But don't go far . . .'

he winked at the other driver '. . . or we might never find you again.'

Kate decided to do just that. After all, how thick could a fog be? Perhaps it was denser at the edges and this idiot couldn't be bothered to try too hard. She walked away from the men and they eyed her appreciatively.

'Be careful now,' the man with the tie called after her quite sincerely. She was no spring chicken, but he wouldn't mind.

The engineer gave him a knowing wink.

Kate paused at the edge of the fog, amazed by its opacity and surprised by the odd yellow tint of its particles. There was a rather nasty odour, too. It followed a ragged course to the left and right of her, yet did not appear to be drifting in any direction, although it swirled and moved within itself. She took a step forward and immediately felt the fog's coolness; a further two steps and it was impossible to see the road ahead. Craning her neck round she could just make out the dim shapes of the vehicles and their drivers behind her. Although anxious, she faced ahead again and advanced a few more steps.

The coolness became a chill and she halted again. This wasn't right. This bloody fog wasn't natural. She began to feel disorientated.

Quickly she searched for the grass verge by the side of the road and was relieved to find it, even though it was faint. The coldness seeped into her and with it came a sense of foreboding. She didn't like this, she didn't like it one bit. She began to retrace her footsteps, for some reason walking backwards as if afraid to turn her back on whatever lay ahead inside that fog. It was irrational, it was crazy, but she didn't care. She searched the mist as she retreated, expecting something to loom up before her, something from deep inside those swirling clouds. Nothing came for her, but still she would not turn round. She could hear her own shoes on the roadway and it seemed to be taking longer to leave the fog than it had to enter it. Surely she should have been clear by now? She would run in a moment. She would take a chance and turn and run and not stop until . . .

The telephone engineer's sarcastic handclap greeted her reappearance; the businessman gave her a sympathetic smile when she spun round. Kate shivered and kept walking, calming herself mentally so that she would not break into a run.

'You'd think Brigadoon was in there,' the businessman said as if a light remark might reassure her.

No, she thought, looking over her shoulder at the inscrutable wall of lazy-moving mist, it was nothing so romantic. In fact, it was downright bloody sinister.

Kate climbed back into her car and sat there catching her breath. The two men got into their own vehicles and executed several-point turns in the narrow road to face back up the hill. The businessman gave her a small wave and the engineer tooted his horn as they drove by, leaving her to sit there alone watching the great blankness through the windscreen.

So what to do now? How the hell could she get to David Ash with the information she had? Although not pertinent to the case he was investigating – at least, she didn't *think* it was – her discovery might be interesting to him. And suddenly it began to bother her, for it was curious that this man Seamus Phelan seemed to show up only when major disasters occurred. No, not quite correct: he showed up just *before* the disasters occurred. She had recognized the name when Ash had first mentioned it to her, but it had taken quite a few enquiries to find out about the Irishman, and even then knowledge of him was scant.

His presence had never been recorded officially in any of the subsequent investigations into the catastrophes – obviously he was regarded as nothing more than a crank by the authorities – but there were people who knew of him, the police, a few journalists, and those in her own field of work who had made studies into the metaphysical nature of such horrendous events. It was from the latter sources that she'd learned of Phelan.

His first appearance had been noted about thirty years ago when at Aberfan, a small mining village in Mid Glamorgan, a tip of coal waste had slid and overwhelmed a school and houses, killing a hundred and forty-four people, most of them children. Nothing more was heard of him until the mid-eighties when a fire had engulfed London's King's Cross underground station, incinerating thirty-one passengers and staff. Phelan, along with several other unconnected individuals whom the public were never told about, had been taken into custody for suspected arson and later released without charge.

He seemed to have gone to ground again until 1988 when he had resurfaced warning people in a small Scottish borders town called Lockerbie just before an American Boeing 747 from Frankfurt had been blown from the sky by a terrorist bomb to plough into the little housing estate below. More recently – and this was only rumoured, Kate's sources had emphasized – Phelan had directed police to a house in Gloucester where twelve bodies had been found buried beneath the cellar and garden area as well as in a field nearby, all of them of women and young girls who had been reported missing years before. This was the first time Phelan had turned up *after* the event – in all the other cases he had managed to be on hand *before*, apparently warning people of the danger to come. It was hardly surprising that no one had listened.

And now Seamus Phelan was in Sleath.

Kate thumped the steering wheel and cursed the fog that barred her way to the village.

Why was the Irishman here?

And what did he want with David Ash?

36

HE RIVER WAS SLUGGISH, yet it pushed against the millwheel with irresistible force. The blocks that had held the wheel in place for more than half a century began to crumble, slivers breaking off, pieces turning to dust. A high-pitched squealing, as if some creature were in terrible pain, pierced the night as the wheel juddered, then slowly began to turn.

With its first dragging revolution something bloated and white emerged from the river, a putrefied carcass that once might have been human. Rusted chains bound it to the millwheel's green-slimed slats and from the open pit that should have been a mouth there came a wailing sound, the pitiful lament of a soul in torment.

For once Sam Gunstone did not bother to pull off his dirty boots and leave them on the doorstep. He hurried down the passageway leaving a trail of mud and dust behind him and climbed the stairs, using the banisters to haul himself upwards. Winded though he was, the farmer kept going when he reached the top. Something was wrong. He didn't know why he was so sure, and never once had doubt dragged his step. The strange-coloured fog enveloping the fields around his farm, a throwback from the filthy smogs of yesteryear, had initiated his alarm, and for the life of him he couldn't explain why. The great blank wall of rolling mist that had swept across the fields as he returned from a rabbit-shoot had disorientated him at first, for it was difficult to see more than a yard in front. Its smell was nasty too, and the drifting clouds seemed to cling, making his flesh cold and damp even though it was summer. He had almost been afraid to breathe it in.

Out there in the fields his immediate concern had been for Nell. She was too ill to be left alone for long and if he should get lost in this . . . He tried to remember if he had shut her bedroom window before he'd left the house. This foul stuff wouldn't do her poor old lungs any good and she might be sleeping, unaware it was creeping in.

He had dropped the sack of warm dead rabbits he was carrying and waved at the vapours in front of him as though to clear a path. The effort was wasted, of course, but at least he was familiar with the land and as long as he could see the ground beneath his feet he should be all right.

Fortunately, as he progressed the fog became less dense – it was as if there was a thick outer ring to it – and soon he was able to increase his pace. He plodded on, his shotgun, barrel 'broken', over one arm, and it wasn't long before he could make out the first outbuildings of his farm. Quickly the farmhouse itself came into view but, because he was approaching from the front and Nell's bedroom was at the rear, he could not tell if her window was open. He was being a silly bloody fool, he knew that, but he couldn't shake off the feeling that something was wrong and Nellie needed him badly. Discarding the shotgun, he had broken into a trot. Oh Lord, don't let me be too late, he silently prayed.

Through the front door, up the stairs, and then he was on the landing and rushing to the open bedroom door. He gave a brief exclamation when he saw that the window was closed, the fog outside filling the panes, but the cry caught in his throat when he noticed the empty bed.

The sheets were trailed across the floor as though dragged along as Nellie had made her way over to the window. The window . . . Gunstone stared hard at it.

An orange glow flickered through the fog.

No, not that, he thought, not again, not that dratted spook fire. How could Nellie know, how could she have seen it from her bed? He moved closer to the window and peered into the mists, watching the ill-defined flames as they swelled and danced, their flicker muted by the drifting veils.

'Nell?' His nose was almost touching the glass. '*Nellie?*' He called her name aloud because he could vaguely make out a dim silhouette standing before the dim blaze. The figure was short, bulky, wearing something shapeless that could only be a nightgown.

Gunstone exhaled a long, fearful groan before tearing himself away from the window and lumbering out to the stairs. He descended them awkwardly in his heavy rubber boots, but his pace never slackened. At the bottom he turned towards the back of the house, calling his wife's name again and again as he ran. The door there was open wide and he hurried through, crossing the yard to the gate in the wild hedge. Unable to see his wife anymore, he came to a halt. Although the fire was reaching high into the sky and flushing the mists with its glow, Nell was nowhere in sight.

He lumbered off again, his breathing laboured, his chest tight with the effort. Where was she, where was his Nell? He let out an anguished yell. 'Yer silly ol' fool, why'd yer come out here, why'd yer leave yer nice safe bed? It weren't genuine, this bloody fire. God 'elp us, it's only a ghost thing, it don't really exist!'

But if it wasn't real, why was he beginning to feel its warmth? Why was the skin on his face prickling with its heat, and why were his eyes beginning to hurt just looking into its glare? Why, if the fire didn't exist?

The exertion was finally becoming too much for him, and he slowed to an exhausted lope. His chest pounded and he could hear his own scratchy gasps. He was a tough, hardworking man, had been all his life, but he was getting on now, his stamina wasn't what it used to be. The lope had become a sluggish, clumsy hobble.

He saw her then. Nellie was lying in a heap on the ground before the fire. She looked almost like a mound in the earth itself.

'Oh Nell . . .' he said. 'What have yer done, girl . . . ?'

Sam Gunstone dropped to his knees beside his slumped wife, already aware that she was dead: he could *feel* her absence. He touched her shoulder and the warmth he felt was not from her but from the conflagration nearby, from the flames of a fire that did not exist.

He roared then. He confronted the ghostly fire and screamed his outrage and pain.

And when finally he turned his wife's face towards him, perhaps to kiss her one last time and in a way he had not kissed her for many a year, he saw the horror frozen there in her dead eyes.

Ruth Cauldwell stirred the coffee without realizing she had not put sugar in the mug. She stared at the miniature whirlpool she had created with the spoon, her thoughts drawn into the vortex, swilling round and round, moving faster with the descent, becoming confused, jumbled, disappearing into the dark centre, becoming . . . nothing.

Her slumped head snapped erect and she dropped the spoon onto the kitchen table. The coffee continued to circle, but the whirlpool flattened and was soon gone; it seemed to Ruth that the thoughts that had been drawn from her were returned in an instant and she gave a faint moan as she leaned back in the chair. Her neck arched and for a moment or two she gazed at the ceiling.

The light bulb above the kitchen table was like an eye

watching her, studying her every move, every expression, every nuance of speech. It spied on her, as did all the light bulbs in the house, but she never let on she knew. She wasn't stupid, she wasn't some dumb bitch who didn't know what was going on. She'd caught her mother watching her out of the corner of her eyes. Even Sarah, her little sister, had been told to spy on her. They wanted to catch Ruth out, they thought they could discover her secret.

But Ruth wouldn't turn on the lights, even if the house was growing dark. The light bulbs couldn't see her then, could they? Not if they had no power. They wouldn't be able to report back, and nor would the mirrors, because she wouldn't look into them. She hated seeing her own reflection anyway, because then *she* could see the secret in herself so plainly, and if it was so obvious to her, it would soon be obvious to everyone else. They would see her sin, her filth, the horrible dirty things she had done with . . .

She slumped forward again, elbows cracking against the table's surface, her head over the coffee cup so that rising steam warmed the chill from her face. Bubbles swirled around the mug's rim like tiny floating eyes and these, too, were watching her, keeping a check on her while her mother was visiting her father in jail. She knew her mother had given the house instructions to mind her daughter while she was gone, see if she got up to her filth again.

It isn't my fault, Mummy! It's him, don't you see? He makes me . . .

Careful. Almost screamed aloud just then. Mustn't do that, mustn't let the house know. Nor Sarah.

The sleeve of her blouse had worked loose and she hastily did up the button again, covering the flesh of her wrist. She checked the neck button, reassuring herself that this, too, was secure.

Mustn't show anything. Mustn't let Munce see any bare parts. Oh please, don't let him come again tonight.

Her skin seemed to crawl at the very notion.

Think of something else! Think of poor Daddy. Mummy had said it would help his case if Ruth agreed that Danny Marsh had attacked her out there in the woods. Why was she being such a daft, obstinate girl by denying what had happened? The marks were all over her body, and her clothes had been torn when she had staggered home that day. Just tell the police and Daddy's lawyer the truth so that Daddy wouldn't be charged with murder. He might not even be convicted of manslaughter if a jury knew how horribly she'd been attacked. All through the day Ruth's mother had persisted, never giving her a moment's peace. And at night, in the quietness of her own bedroom, when Ruth was alone . . .

She shuddered, the spasm jolting her from tip to toe. She didn't want to think about that . . .

Her sister's voice wafted down the corridor from her room, the song off-key as usual, but Sarah's enthusiasm undiminished. The sound almost brought a smile to Ruth's lips. Sarah didn't understand any of what was going on. She was lost in her own innocent world of dollies and Disney. She was sure the policemen would let Daddy go as soon as Ruth told them about the silly boy who had tried to kiss and cuddle her.

Ruth stole a surreptitious glance at the ceiling light again. You can't see *inside* me. No one can. Not you, not Mummy, not Daddy. And you couldn't see *him*, either, you couldn't see *Munce*. If you could, then you'd let Mummy and Daddy know, and then they'd understand, they'd know the secret, they'd know what he does . . .

She hunched her shoulders even more and clasped her hands under her nose, thumbs pressing against her lips. A wisp of white steam rose from the coffee. The singing from her sister's bedroom stopped and the house became very quiet.

How shadowy it was in the kitchen. And how gloomy outside. The windowpanes were no longer clear; they looked as if they had been smeared a dirty grey-yellow colour. She ought to turn on the lights now. They couldn't really see her, that was only in her own imagination. Honestly, she was aware of that; but

it made no difference. She supposed it was like being hypno-
tized: a person could be conscious of their ridiculous actions,
yet unable to change them; in a trance they seemed entirely
natural. That's how she felt. She knew perfectly well that the
light bulbs were not spies, but she could not stop her mind
from telling her they were and then acting accordingly. It was
the same with Joseph Munce. She couldn't possibly have met
him in the woods the other day, because he was dead, and he
couldn't visit her at night to touch her, feel her, do those *filthy*
things . . .

Ruth laughed, a nervous cackle brought about by both embarrassment and fear. It was only a short laugh.

The coffee was still hot, but she forced herself to take a sip.
The pain was good for her. She sipped again, welcoming the
burn. *That* was reality, she told herself. Sharp, unpleasant, but
fact. The coffee was hot so it burnt her lips. No dispute, no
deception, no mind games. The light bulb was a light bulb,
nothing more than that; the mirrors reflected images, they
didn't make x-rays of your secret self.

Munce was dead, he could *never* come back.

Munce was dead, *he could never come back*.

Munce was dead, he could never come back.

Then why was he here at this moment?

Why was that familiar coldness shrinking her skin?

What was that shuffling she could hear through the partly
open kitchen door?

What was that stink if it wasn't body corruption?

What was that phlegmy murmuring if it wasn't from a rotted
throat?

What were all those things if Munce wasn't outside in the
passage?

Ruth swivelled slowly in the chair so that she could see the
gap in the door. The shuffling was coming closer. Although it
was dark, something even darker filled the opening. Something
was waiting there. Something was watching her.

Ruth opened her mouth to scream even though she was

aware that no scream would come. It never did. It always stayed locked inside her chest whenever he came to her. He even challenged her to cry out, but it was never ever any good – her throat was paralysed.

Wide-eyed, Ruth stared at the narrow shadow, one hand gripping the back of the chair, her body shaking, but so imperceptibly that an onlooker might have thought she was perfectly still. She wanted to plead; no sound came. She wanted to flee; she could not move. She wanted to kill; he was already dead.

But there was an answer to all this, there was a way of preventing his vile, putrid hands touching her body. Or at least, there was a way she could prevent herself from feeling his touch. She cast her gaze around the kitchen, looking for a knife. Her wrists first, and then her throat. It would be easy. And this way no one would ever know how she had allowed Munce to touch her so. Or how his touch had aroused her.

No knife was in view, but she knew where they were kept. Her attention went back to the open door.

The shadow was gone.

But she heard the shuffling once more.

He was going away. *Munce was leaving her.*

Her body sagged. She wanted to weep, she wanted to sink to the floor and thank God for this mercy. She listened, wanting to be certain. She could still hear the movement, but it was definitely receding.

And then it stopped, and she heard a door handle rattle.

A door opened. And she heard Sarah scream.

Ruth understood.

'Nooooooo!'

Her own scream had finally broken free as her chair tipped over and she lunged towards the kitchen drawer. She yanked it open, pulling it too far, tipping its contents onto the floor. Falling to her knees and ignoring the barbs of pain that stung her flesh, Ruth swept her hands through the cutlery, finding the broad-bladed carving knife. She gripped its wooden handle and staggered to her feet. Her legs felt stiff, uncoordinated, but she forced them to take her to the kitchen door. Sarah's second scream sent Ruth stumbling through and then she was running down the passage, knife held high over her head, her own scream wilder, more fearful even than her young sister's.

Ellen Preddle waited. And her dead son waited with her.

Simon sat in the lumpy armchair by the empty fireplace, his frail naked body as pale as alabaster, while his mother had drawn up a chair opposite him. Although directly in his line of vision, Ellen was not sure if her son really saw her, for there was no recognition in his eyes. By facing him this way she could at least pretend he was aware of her. She exhaled a small white cloud each time she breathed and now she pulled the knitted cardigan tighter across her chest to keep out the chill. No such breath-clouds came from Simon's mouth, and even though he was unclothed, she had not seen him shiver.

Fresh tears seemed unavailable to her, although the handkerchief clasped between her fingers was sodden from those shed earlier. Perhaps she had cried them all; perhaps even grief could wear itself out. The tears would come again when the pain resurfaced.

Simon, *her* Simon, was gone. She realized that at last. The little figure that sat there was not her son, it was not his *flesh* and *blood*: it was his ghost. Simon was dead. She had finally accepted the fact. And nothing would ever bring him back. But if she could just have this – his spirit, his soul, whatever it was that sat opposite her – so that she knew there was something more, that death didn't mean oblivion, then perhaps she could be satisfied. This was better than being without Simon entirely.

She remembered the moment a few hours ago when she had come down from her bedroom, having wept the afternoon away, and had found him there, hands in his lap, his narrow shoulders hunched forward. Simon had always huddled that way when he was afraid, and there was only one thing he had ever truly feared, and that had been his dad. She had rushed towards him, meaning to take his naked body in her arms and soothe away the dread, but something had held her back; somehow she knew that if she touched him she would discover he was not really there, he was visible only in her mind, and that would mean she'd be alone again, and the truth forever more would demean the dream.

Other truths had come to her as she had taken her place opposite him. Thoughts had plagued her during the night, notions that worried her, tormented her, but were never fully realized. During these last few hours they had taken on more certain form.

Simon was dead, and his father had killed him.

George Preddle, himself, had died as he had lived: miserably. The wretchedness of his own life had been inflicted on those around him, so that she and Simon had suffered years of his abuse. He had hated them both, but for some reason that Ellen had never quite understood, he had hated his son more than his wife. Only on the night before George's death did she discover why it was so, for it was then that he had taunted her about their *bastard* boy. How he had come to regard Simon as such she could not fathom, but his jibes were as relentless as they were malicious, and eventually she had understood it was the sickness of his own soul that made him believe in his own words. Probably he couldn't understand Simon's goodness, his innocence, his love of all things, especially his mother, and how different he was from George himself. In looks, the son favoured his mother, but Simon *was* George's child, for she had never as much as looked at another man since their marriage. No, his insistence that Simon was not his son went much deeper than misguided belief in her infidelity: it was because of his own sexual abuse of Simon that he repudiated any blood-tie, for in his evil, twisted mind that would make his offence against the boy incestuous and that – oh, the sickness of it – *that* just wasn't natural.

Sometimes she had suspected what was going on, but because Simon never complained, never even hinted at his father's attention, she pushed the suspicions away, for to know for sure would have been too painful and the shame too hard to bear. She had remembered Simon's unaccountable moods, the times he hid away in his room, withdrawn and tearful, particularly after he had been left alone with his drunken father, and now she wondered what threats from George had sealed her son's lips. Yes, she had suspected and often – especially when Simon had regarded her with those dark, reproachful eyes of his – she had determined to do something about the situation. Indeed, at one time she had.

Ellen had gone to the vicarage and confided her fears to Reverend Lockwood. How shocked her pastor had been by the allegation and how he had assured her she must be wrong, that although George Preddle was a foolish and idle man – yes, yes, a drunkard even – he would never act in the way she suggested towards his own son. She was surely mistaken. Certainly he would talk to her husband, remind him of his duty towards his family and, if she insisted, confront him with her suspicions. Leave it to him, he would sort out old George, but mention her concerns to no one else. Remember, social workers and local authorities were only too eager these days to break up perfectly good homes at the slightest hint of child abuse, and the last thing Ellen would want was for young Simon to be taken into care. Think of what happened to all those poor families in the Orkneys.

The thought of her son being snatched away from her – it seemed that every week you read about that sort of thing in the newspapers – filled her with a worse dread than before. She only *suspected* what was going on, and Simon had never actually spoken of it. He knew how much his mother loved him, so surely he would have told her, even if he was afraid of his father. Unless, of course, he was not afraid for himself alone, but for his mother too . . . No, no, she couldn't let herself think that, it would have been too horrible. Besides there were no marks on Simon, no bruises. Reverend Lockwood had promised to speak to George, and George might bluster, he might rant and rage, but he was a craven half-wit outside the home and he would pay heed to the vicar's words.

One evening shortly after, George had returned to the cottage even more drunk than usual and in a furious temper. He had cursed her, and shook her so badly that she had collapsed to the floor. The vicar had spoken to him all right, her husband had told her sneeringly, oh yes, the high-and-mighty, holier-than-thou Reverend Lockwood had had a few words to say to him, but there was no problem, was there? Y'see, he and the squarson saw eye-to-eye, didn't they? The reverend understood old George. So don't you ever forget it, you stupid fat sow.

The leer on his face had been sickening, and when he'd kicked her for good measure as she lay on the floor, he had sniggered and announced that the boy would get what was coming to him before too long and nobody would do anything about it.

Ellen had crawled up the stairs and into Simon's tiny bedroom and she had cuddled her son while they listened to George vent the rest of his anger on the furniture downstairs. Occasionally they heard him laugh aloud and call out, his words incomprehensible, but he had not come up after her. And he had not touched the boy the next day, or any day since.

But sometimes, when Simon was in the bath and she sat on the stool by the side, telling him stories, helping him wash his hair, George would appear in the open doorway, not *always* drunk, and just watch the boy with a peculiar expression on his face. Simon would cover himself by curling up, chin against his knees, while she would push her husband from the doorway and along the landing into their bedroom. More than once on those occasions, to appease George, to keep him away from the bathroom door, Ellen had to do things with him that shamed her, dirty, bestial things that no woman should ever be forced to do by another person. If it kept Simon safe, though, if it kept

335

those filthy, leering eyes off her son, then what did it matter?

Unfortunately, although George did not lay a finger on his son again, somehow his menace grew worse. Sometimes he mumbled strange, incoherent things; other times he was full of dark hints and threats that would make him chuckle to himself. It affected Ellen so badly that even when she left the cottage to take Simon to the bus for school, or to do some shopping, or visit the church, she felt a dark, ominous gloom over the village itself. It was as if something nasty was pending.

Then George had died in the fire.

The release – and the relief – was overwhelming. Instead of sorrow, she and Simon had felt deliverance. And joy, such blissfully sweet joy.

When they had brought Simon home after he had witnessed the death of his father in the burning haystack, her son had not wept and he had not been in shock. He had thrown himself into her arms and when those who had brought him to the door, their own faces sombre with the bad news, had left, Simon had looked up into her face and smiled.

How happy they had been together because the threat – and her guilt – had been removed. How much they had enjoyed life, their bond so much stronger than before, and what good times they'd had in this new-found freedom. Almost a year of perfect contentment.

Until George had returned.

She hadn't known it then, but she knew it now. For a complete understanding of her son's death had come to her as she sat with him earlier that evening. Simon hadn't spoken, he had not even acknowledged her presence, and images had not appeared in her mind. The understanding had simply arrived without warning, without announcement, without mental pictures.

Ellen had left Simon alone on that fateful afternoon. He was in his bath, quite happy, quite safe, but his small heart had stopped – *literally* stopped – from shock for a moment when he saw the ghost of his father standing at the open bathroom

336

door, watching him with that loathsome, leering expression that Simon remembered so well. Her son had collapsed in the water and, because his body had relaxed into unconsciousness, his lungs had automatically tried to draw in air. Simon had drowned within seconds. Murdered by his own father.

As she sat there Ellen wondered why, if she could not hold his thin, naked body, if she could not offer comfort, was Simon here? Why hadn't his poor little soul gone to God? Why was he waiting in the chair?

It was not until she heard the noise from upstairs that Ellen began to have a glimmer as to why Simon had returned again and again. The sound was that of water being disturbed, as if a hand was scooping through it, testing its heat, just as she used to when it was time for Simon's bath.

Simon continued to stare at her – or at least, at the space she occupied.

Someone called, a low gruff summons.

And Simon was rising.

Fighting her panic, she said his name quietly, but he ignored her and went to the stairs.

'*Simon!*' she screamed when he began to climb them.

Ellen ran to the stairs, pleading with him as his small, white body turned the bend. She swayed, her senses reeling, both fear and revulsion attacking her like conspiring demons, draining her strength, her legs becoming weak, unable to bear her weight. Simon was gone from view and she thought she heard a different sound from the bathroom. It was the deep-throated chuckling noise that George used to make when he forced her to do those horrible, disgusting things.

She uttered a warning, but it had no strength, no authority. She began to pull herself up the stairs, crawling on hands and knees. She screamed again when she heard the splashing of water.

*   *   *

337

Shadows wandered through the mists around the worn relics that in another age had served as Sleath's instruments of correction and torture. A whispering could be heard – *if* there had been anyone on the common to listen – and as darkness drew in, the shapes grew firmer, became more resolved, and the discarnate murmurings became louder.

Still the blood seeped from the whipping post, gradually becoming an outpouring from every cleft and fissure, from every fine crack, spreading to the stocks where it dripped onto the earth below. Soon the ground was soaked with the deep-red effluence and a pool was formed, the pool becoming a stream that flowed further, eventually spilling into the road itself . . .

. . . Where more shadows, the ghosts of Sleath themselves, moved through the mists . . .

The crockery on the table began to rattle, one of the teacups dancing around its saucer as if in a bid to escape.

Rosemary Ginty clamped a hand to her mouth to stifle a cry and her husband, Tom, glanced over his shoulder at the commotion. His beefy hands still held the curtains he had just drawn against the foggy night outside, but he let them drop when he saw the dancing chinaware.

The teacup finally toppled over the saucer's brim and continued its agitation against the tabletop. They watched in numbed silence as it jiggled its way to the table's edge and fell to the floor. The thick rug that stretched almost to the walls of the Gintys' upstairs parlour prevented the cup from breaking, although it bounced, then twitched a few times before coming to rest.

'Tom!' Rosemary finally managed to call out as if accusing him of some transgression.

If she expected a response, it was not forthcoming. Instead, the landlord of the Black Boar Inn cautiously approached the table and its rattling crockery, a hand held before him as if to pacify a distraught household pet. For the sake of space, the table was pushed up against a wall with two chairs on either side (apart from breakfast, the Gintys rarely dined in their private quarters, preferring instead to use the inn's small restaurant directly below), and the parlour, itself, was crammed with unmatched furniture and Rosemary's overflowing collection of cheap curios. A television, only occasionally switched on, stood in one corner of the room, with a lamp and framed photograph on its flat top, while opposite was a low coffee table and comfortable armchair which Rosemary currently occupied. A sideboard, sofa, glass-fronted cabinet stocked with Rosemary's ornaments and bric-a-brac, and an antiquated radiogram filled the remaining space.

Warily, Tom Ginty reached out for the nearest cup and saucer and with a last-second rush clamped down on the jittering cup. It submitted to his pressure, remaining perfectly still under the considerable weight of his palm, and even stayed motionless for a short while when he took his hand away again. Then its tremors resumed, joining the general oscillation of chinaware. The teapot lid clattered against its rim, and the sugar grains hopped in their bowl; even milk in the fine china jug tossed in its own miniature storm.

The silence when they stopped was almost as startling as the clatter they had made when the vibration had begun.

As Ginty spun round to his wife, his mouth open to speak, one of Rosemary's ornaments, a mock-eighteenth-century figurine, burst through the glass cabinet and shot across the room.

This time Rosemary could not hold back her screech, for the piece missed her head only by inches and glass fragments lodged in her stacked, blonde hair. The figurine smashed into the wall beside the drawn curtains and fell to the floor in pieces. Ginty cringed at his wife's shrill outburst, then looked in amazement at the broken pane in the cabinet.

After drawing a breath, Rosemary rounded on her husband. 'You caused this!' she yelled, and his amazement was replaced

339

by dismay. 'You and those . . .' she flapped a hand frustratedly at the window '. . . those others!'

'What're you talkin about, woman?' He shook his head in wonder.

'You know! You bloody well know!'

Ginty's round face paled, throwing the tiny mauve veins on his cheeks and nose into sharp relief. Oh Lord, could she be right? Those things they had done up at the Hall . . . Oh Lord, no, it was all nonsense. He'd gone along with it, but he hadn't *believed*. It was just a sort of village tradition, a covert one, admittedly, but with no real harm to it. He'd always been pissed anyway, he could never remember what had happened the day after, only bits and pieces, parts of the stupid ceremonies, the silly chanting, dressing up in old robes. It was only like the Freemasons, nothing more harmful than that. But how did Rosemary know? *What* did she know?

He covered his face as another ornament flew from the broken section of the cabinet. Rosemary ducked her head against the cushioned arm of the chair, her hands clasped over her hair, as the statuette, two lovers entwined on a loveseat, hit the curtains and broke the window behind.

'*How could you?*' she shrieked as she risked raising her head again.

Why was she blaming him? She couldn't *know* anything. 'Don't be bloody daft!' he yelled back at her.

Rosemary slid to the floor, afraid of other flying objects. Why did he pretend so much? They had spent the last few hours locked inside their private quarters in the inn because something bad was happening to the village and they both knew it. But he knew more about what was going on than her and he wouldn't admit it! As soon as that horrible fog had blanked out Sleath, Rosemary had sensed something was terribly wrong. Somehow it was like a warning – no, what was it they called it? A portent! Yes, a portent! – that something nasty was going to happen. And the funny thing was, it had been on its way, this nasty thing that was about to happen, for a long, long time and it wasn't only she who was aware.

No staff had turned up for work that day and no customers had set foot in the bar. Later in the afternoon she had tried to phone round the village, and a horrible cold panic had chilled her through and through when she realized the lines were dead. She had become too afraid to step outside and knock on doors. Tom was just as anxious – no, maybe even more so, because he was part of it, he was bloody well part of it! – and had hustled her upstairs and locked the door after them. Even when they'd heard movement outside in the corridor some time ago, he hadn't let her unlock the door to investigate, and to be honest, she hadn't been *that* curious. She remembered the night before, the disturbances in their bedroom, and Rosemary gave a shiver.

'Bastard,' she said to her husband.

Something tickled her plump stockinged legs and when she glanced down she saw that the rug that covered most of the parlour's floor was undulating as if a series of breezes were rippling through underneath.

Rosemary hauled herself to her feet and stumbled from one section of the rug to another in an effort to avoid the mysterious rolling waves.

She could feel the thick material trying to rise beneath her feet, her weight too much for it; the undulation merely spread around her, rippling outwards, bypassing furniture to find the rug's outer edges.

Tom Ginty was rigid, his brain rebutting everything that was happening around him, but his eyes insisting it was all very real. The curtains flapped as if a wind was forcing its way through the broken windowpane. Incongruously, the clock on the mantelpiece began chiming the hour, even though neither hand was close to any numeral. A picture on the wall, a hunt scene print full of red coats, horses and hounds, inexplicably fell to the floor. The stale contents of the teapot began to slurp from its spout, while another cup, this time with its saucer,

341

toppled off the edge of the table. The parlour's flower-patterned sofa began to rock to and fro, spilling its cushions onto the rug. The lamp and framed photographs were suddenly swept from the top of the television set.

By now Rosemary had lost her balance and was on her knees once more. It turned out to be fortunate for her, for without warning all the remaining glass in the cabinet and the window opposite exploded outwards, the pieces, large and small, scything across the room from both directions. The curtains were shredded and tossed aside, while statuettes, glassware and ornaments were blown with the shards from the cabinet. Lethal shrapnel met and passed through each other at the room's centre, which was precisely where the Black Boar Inn's landlord was standing.

The glass inflicted the worst damage, although the china and porcelain did their share. Ginty's surprised shriek became a splutter as a glass shard cut into his throat. The wound was not deep enough to kill him instantly and his hands had automatically protected his eyes, but when Rosemary raised her head she saw her husband's upper body pin-cushioned with tiny, sharp daggers. The ceiling light swung like a pendulum above them and reflections glinted from Ginty's clothes and flesh, bright one moment, dimmed the next. Hysteria bubbled from Rosemary, while Ginty, himself, remained perfectly still, as if traumatized, pierced hands still raised to eyes, the noises from his throat becoming a gurgling drone.

Pain quickly bit into the shock, causing him to move in a stiff, almost robotic way. He lowered his hands and stared unbelievingly at his wife. Rosemary's scream had already begun, but now it gushed with renewed vigour, for this grotesque, punctured version of her husband, blood swelling from his wounds, frightened her more than the kinetic disturbances of her household furniture. Of late, intuitions, perhaps even vague but upsetting premonitions, had come to her, as she knew they had to others in the village – oh, no one mentioned them, they kept them to themselves, afraid that they were alone in those thoughts, that it might be some kind of creeping dementia; but she had seen it in their faces, their troubled eyes, their constrained manner – and the dread had deepened with every passing day. Bad, hidden things were festering like some sneaking disease and now it was here, the cancer had revealed itself. A part of it stood before her with a million glass splinters sticking from its bloated body.

Tom Ginty took a tottering step towards his wife and Rosemary screeched afresh as she scrambled away from him. There had never been an honest love between them, only initially a joint need soon followed by a tolerance of each other, and this was eventually replaced by a mutual loathing, so there was no guilt when she fled from the bleeding monster that was her husband.

The ornate clock, a cheap imitation Bamberg, slipped from the mantel and shattered in the hearth. The mirror that had hung above it cracked into a crazy pattern of fractured glass. The sofa, which had become increasingly violent in its rocking action, finally overturned onto its back.

Rosemary gave voice to and flinched at each new shock as she put the armchair between herself and her advancing husband. She suddenly made a dash for the door, clambering over the back of the up-ended sofa. Glass and broken china crunched under her feet as Tom Ginty tried to follow her.

At the door, she frantically scrabbled at the key. The door opened and Rosemary all but threw herself into the corridor beyond. She almost collapsed when she saw the small shapes skulking in the swaying shadows cast by the unsteady light of the parlour. The rats scurried away, keeping close to the narrow walls, long tails slithering behind them.

Rosemary forced herself to follow them, aware of the mutilated stalker close behind. She had lost a shoe somewhere in the room and could only hobble along, a hand occasionally touching the wall's wood panelling to help her keep her balance. Shadows before her pitched crazily, confusing her, until darkness suddenly filled most of the corridor; she realized Tom must be in the doorway, blocking the erratic light. She thought she heard him call out, but it came as an odd, incoherent snuffle and she refused to halt; Rosemary had no sympathy, only fear. An idea flashed into her mind to seek help from the inn's solitary guest, but she realized she was too uncertain of this man David Ash. There was a coldness about him, an inscrutability; besides, she was not sure if he wasn't involved in the hauntings, too. A glow from up ahead encouraged her to hobble even faster.

Someone had switched on the lights to the stairs and the floor below, but Rosemary did not begin to descend immediately, despite footsteps behind her. She and Tom had always been aware that there were rats down in the inn's cellars and occasionally one or two had had to be chased from the kitchen and bars; but never before had the vermin been bold enough to venture further, and certainly not in these numbers. The rats littered the stairway.

Gripping the handrail tightly, Rosemary made herself take the first step, issuing shooing noises as she did so. Most of the creatures fled before her, but one at the bend of the stairs bared its teeth and hissed at her approaching figure. She stamped her foot and, reluctantly, the rat slipped away; she heard the scrabbling of its paws on the wood of the steps.

'Ro . . . Rose . . .'

It was a liquid moan and her head jerked round at its sound. Tom was on the landing above, his body swaying and prickly with protruding glass. He began to lean forward and Rosemary ducked away, losing her footing at the bend in the staircase and plummeting downwards, yelping as she went. Her plump body slid over the worn edges of the steps with painful bumps, and she came to a slithering halt near the bottom. Even before she had regathered her wits she heard stumbling footsteps from above. Something nipped her hand and she recoiled from the rat she had nearly squashed.

Rosemary struggled to her feet, her other shoe gone now, and padded across the floor of the saloon bar, her hands flailing

344

the air, her wailing screech filling the big room. She made for the open door where tenuous, yellowy fog curled into the bar.

Tom called out once more and she glanced over her shoulder to see him still lumbering after her, walking like a zombie, his whole body stiff, his face, arms and shirt by this time drenched in blood. *Why wouldn't he leave her alone? What did the rotten shit want from her?*

She ran through the open door, out into the High Street, out into the fog. Rosemary pulled up with yet another scream when she saw two bright-glowing spectres emerging from the swirling mists, moving fast, bearing down on her.

Lenny Grover giggled inanely. 'Can't see a fuckin thing,' he remarked to Dennis Crick, who occupied the pick-up's passenger seat.

'Well slow down then, prat.' Crick was grinning himself. He all but pressed his nose against the grimy windscreen. 'It's a fucker, this one,' he remarked, his words slightly slurred from the few jars he and Grover had had earlier at a roadside pub.

'Chemical gas, if you ask me,' observed Grover. 'Look at its colour, an' jus' take a whiff.'

'I already did, an' didn't like it.' Crick screwed up his face to emphasize the point.

'Been a spill somewhere, take me word for it.'

'You do talk crap, Len. It's fog, that's all. Hold up, it's gettin thinner already.'

'Thank Gawd for that.' Grover giggled again.

His companion hadn't wanted to drive into the fog they had come upon so suddenly on their way back to Sleath through the country lanes, for it had been impossible to see more than a yard in front of them. But Grover had insisted that they go on, because they had a spanking-new lawn mower in the back of the truck, as well as a smart electric hedge trimmer and a few outside pot plants, all of which they'd collected on one of their regular 'round-ups'. At least once a fortnight they cruised the country roads keeping an eye out for unattended garden equipment or anything else left standing in front gardens or drives. The owner of the lawn mower, a still-gleaming Hayter Harrier 56, had taken the grass collector back to his dump or compost heap at the rear of his house, an exercise that probably would take no more than two minutes, giving Grover and Crick the opportunity to lift – literally – the machine from the front lawn. They had already driven past twice and were only waiting for the right moment. It had taken less than thirty seconds to stop the truck, nip out, hoist the mower over the tailgate, and be on their way. They'd had an even bigger laugh when only ten minutes later they saw the electric hedge trimmer lying on top of a hedge, its owner no doubt having popped inside the house for a pee or a drink, and Crick had jumped from the cab, given the trimmer's long lead a hefty tug to pull the plug from the point in the open garage, then dropped the whole thing over the side of the truck next to the mower. Grover could hardly steer straight he had laughed so much. A few pot plants swiped from windowsills and outside front doors, a pint of milk that turned out to be curdled by the heat, and their afternoon's work was done. Nice and easy and a lot less risky than creeping through the woods in the middle of the night waiting for a blast from a gamekeeper's double-barrelled.

Once they had hit the blanket fog they had proceeded more cautiously, both men sticking their heads out of the side windows to check the edges of the road. Grover had alternated the headlights between full and dipped beam, with Crick complaining constantly that they ought to turn back.

Grover took a swig from the can of warm lager he held between his thighs and Crick reached down for one of the unopened cans rolling around the floor. He pulled the tab and aimed the spray at his partner-in-crime.

'You silly fuck!' Grover bellowed, lager tippling from his own can into his lap because he'd raised the wrong arm to protect his face. The pick-up swung to the right and scratched its way along a hedge for several yards. He took his time bringing the vehicle back into what he estimated to be the middle of the road, splashing lager from his can onto Crick's shoulder as he did so. Both men considered that hilarious.

'Watchit!' Crick had broken off laughing and clutched Grover's wrist.

Grover, who had tucked the beer can back between his legs and was using his baseball cap to wipe his face, jammed on the brakes. Although the brakes were inefficient, the truck had been travelling reasonably slowly despite Crick's protests to the contrary, and it slid to an easy halt.

'What?' demanded Grover, squinting through the windscreen. *'What?'*

Crick looked from right to left. 'Thought I saw someone crossin the road.'

'Well I can't bloody see no one.'

'We must be in the village, so take it easy.'

'Yeah, yeah.' Grover indicated the back of the pick-up with his thumb. 'Soon as we get them tucked away we'll have a few in the Black Boar.'

'I dunno. The pigs might still be askin questions aroun' the place about Mickey. I don't much fancy talkin to them agen.'

'Nah, they'd've packed up for the day.'

'Maybe. I'm jus' sayin we oughta keep out the way a bit, y'know, till it blows over.'

'Bad idea, pal. Y'carry on like nothin's 'appened, that's what y'do.'

Crick was unconvinced. 'Anyway, let's get the stuff stashed.'

Grover rammed in the gear and the truck crept forward again. It began to pick up speed as he grew more confident. 'Not as bad now,' he remarked cheerfully.

'Yeah, still ain't good though. Take it steady.'

Grover deliberately pressed down on the accelerator.

'Lenny,' Crick warned meaningfully.

Grover snorted and kept the pressure on.

They reached the junction where the two roads leading to the High Street, the one they were on and the one that went up to St Giles', converged and Crick gawped through the window on his side. He repeatedly blinked his eyes, even wiping a hand across them, unsure of what he saw.

'Lenny, can you . . . ?'

Grover was singing as he drove along. No other traffic was around – nobody would be stupid enough to drive in this – and there was a reckless thrill in speeding almost blind. He belched, enjoying the renewed taste of lager on his tongue.

'Lenny,' Crick said again. He was sure he'd seen people moving about there in the fog. And he could hear a funny sound, like voices, although he couldn't be certain, what with Lenny's singing and the noise of the truck's engine. What was that in front of them? It looked like oil spreading across the road from the green. He was afraid the vehicle might skid and opened his mouth to warn Lenny, but they had already passed through the flow before he had the chance. He thrust his head out the window again and wrinkled his nose at the smell. Nasty . . . Wait! There *were* people in the High Street, only he couldn't quite make them out, they were just shapes . . .

He looked to the front, but the pick-up's lights were reflecting back from the fog, making it difficult to see. There were no other lights, not in the shops, nor in the houses. It was bloody weird . . .

'*Lenneeeee* . . . !'

Crick only saw the figure that had dashed from a doorway when they were almost on top of it. Grover had spotted it too and was jamming his foot down hard on the brake pedal, shouting a curse as he did so.

He yanked the steering wheel to the left to avoid the blonde woman and the truck mounted the curb with a fierce lurch. The wing struck the second figure emerging from the doorway the woman had come from, sending it flying back into the room behind, its scream no louder than their own. With sickening force the vehicle crashed into one side of the stout doorframe

348

and wall behind it. Both men, who had always scorned seat-belts, smashed through the windscreen together as the truck was brought to a sudden and violent halt.

Because of the angle of the truck, Crick's body was fortunate enough to land inside the inn, but Grover's smacked straight into the wood and brickwork around the doorway. Ultimately, neither one was lucky though, for the impact killed them both: Crick just lasted a little longer.

They were here again. Downstairs. Murmuring. Whispering. Moaning. Trying to drive him crazy. Well, he wouldn't stand for it any longer. Enough was enough. He was sick of their voices, tired of the haunting.

The doctor poured the last of the Grouse, then let the empty bottle drop to the floor. He held up the tumbler and peered into the amber liquid. Oblivion was your game, wasn't it? Well that's fine by me, because oblivion meant protection. They couldn't get at you when you were out cold. His fingers tightened around the glass and the whisky inside shook.

Lockwood could go to hell. Beardsmore could travel with him. And the rest of them, those small-minded fools – initiates, Beardsmore called them – who enjoyed the rites and the corruption that went with them without comprehending their meaning, well *they* could rot in hell too!

Dr Stapley drank the whisky, no longer appreciating its quality, using it only to blank his mind. Then, with some resolve, he returned the tumbler to the small table beside the armchair, straightened his tie, stiffened his shoulders, and stood erect; or as erect as he could manage given the amount of liquor and pills he had consumed over the past few hours.

His hand held the back of the chair to steady himself. Dignity, he assured himself, could be afforded by any man.

As could degradation, the inner voice, which had become a constant companion of late, reminded him.

349

He strode towards the door, an affected firmness to his expression.

A guise, the voice immediately mocked. *The real doctor is weak and panic-stricken. You don't honestly want to go down there, do you, my friend? What might you find? Think now . . .*

At the door he paused and closed his eyes. The doctor is real enough, he assured himself in his other, less-chiding voice, but the sounds from the waiting room below were not. They were merely the mutterings of conscience, and conscience was a consequence of intellect, which itself had no physical substance. It was a fact that *nothing* in the mind was real.

But when you draw closer, won't those voices be louder? And when you open the door downstairs . . . ?

The mind can fool itself, was his perfectly rational reply.

Then no reason at all to be afraid.

None at all.

Yet your hands tremble, your palms are moist; and isn't your heartbeat just a little strident?

Tiredness. Stress. And . . .

And . . . ?

He wrenched the door open.

He descended the stairs, his steps brisk, bold even. Yes, it was good to feel anger – it overwhelmed so many other emotions, particularly fear. He would not become a gibbering wreck like the craven Reverend Lockwood, who hid in his bedroom clutching bedclothes around him like some old maid imagining a rapist at the door. Edmund's decline into madness had been no sudden thing: the process had begun a long time ago. Perhaps centuries ago.

Beginning with Sleath's first Lockwood?

Yes. And subsequent Lockwoods. Edmund followed in a long line of psychotics.

As the dead doctor followed in a long line of acolytes?

Yes, yes, it was in the bloodline, if you like – if you *insist.* Perhaps to be born in Sleath was to be born into bondage.

So you are not to blame.

Once more, Stapley hesitated. He stood in the darkness of the stairway, his resolve waning. If only it were that easy to deny culpability, to blame his father and his father before him. Unfortunately, to do so would be to deny free will.

Ah, yes, free will. Was that enough to oppose the impulses of your own insanity?

But *I* am not insane.

Yet you hear voices from empty rooms.

Not empty.

Empty.

Three more steps took him to the foot of the stairs. Opposite was the closed door to the waiting room.

It couldn't be empty.

Empty.

Listen to them, listen to their voices.

The *inner* voice, the one inside his own head, was silent for a while, then:

What do you intend to do?

Make them leave.

If they're there . . .

I *can* hear them.

If the room is empty, will you accept your own madness?

But it *isn't* empty. Look, I'll show you . . .

The doctor took one stride forward and threw open the door.

There was no triumph in the discovery, no gloating that he had been right all along. He staggered backwards, falling against the stairs he had just descended.

With the door now wide open, the noise from inside was a babble, a hellish cacophony of wails and moans, of implorations and appeals, of rage and reproach. He raised his hands to block the sight of the horrors gathered in the tiny waiting room, but their images had already entered his mind and they could not be erased. Still he saw them –

– *the screaming woman thrusting the bloody foetus of her dead baby towards him, the umbilical cord still wrapped round its tiny throat, its birth having killed them both – the old people, clustered together, too many to count, gaunt and wasted even in their spirit form, reviling him for the misery of their deaths, for his uncaring, his disdain, his negligence – the child, incorporeal tears glistening on a translucent face, bitter because a wrong diagnosis, influenza rather than bronchial pneumonia, had led to his death – the AIDS victim to whom Stapley had administered only perfunctory treatment, and that with contempt, the victim's huge ghostly eyes staring at the doctor from within the shifting clutter of inconstant wraiths, his cheeks sunken to dark caverns – the girl, exposing her scarred, breastless chest to him, mutilated by a cancer that could have been dealt with sooner and with far less severity had the doctor not dismissed the early signs, the death that followed horribly compounding the mistake – the monster in the corner, once a newborn whom the doctor had considered too hideous to be allowed to live, matured now in its alternate world of phantasms –*

– and there were others, spectral faces he hardly remembered, unfortunates who had fallen prey to his neglect and inadequacies, peripheral victims of his own drug and alcohol abuse –

– others he most certainly did not know, faintly visible in the mass, shades from a past that was beyond his time –

– and still others, their forms bolder than the latter, some of whom he could identify, for they had been used in the rituals . . .

. . . among these, little Timmy Norris, barely seven years old, standing in the doorway, his shape the clearest of them all, for he was almost real, almost of substance . . .

Dr Stapley slowly lowered his hands when he heard the murdered boy's quiet song. Somehow the words, soft though they were, could easily be heard over the clamour that came from behind. Timmy was singing a hymn, one that Stapley recognized, one that he had heard in his dreams, his nightmares . . .

The doctor began to understand.

'Nooooooo!' he screamed.

He slid away from the stairs, his gaze fixed on the boy who stood in the open doorway; he was almost at the front door

352

before he pushed himself erect, his back still sliding against the wall, all the while shaking his head as if to reject the growing awareness.

The cries, the babble, the *ululation*, from the waiting room continued, and the boy's quiet voice was distinct above it all.

It took Dr Stapley several fumbling seconds to release the various locks, but finally he pulled the front door open. The tainted mist drifted through as if attracted by the sounds inside and he turned his head away from its smell; it reminded him of those houses he had been called to where bodies had lain dead and undiscovered for several days, a not infrequent occurrence in these fuck-thy-neighbour times, for this mist had the stale-sweet aroma of decay. He clamped a hand over nose and mouth before dashing outside.

His car was parked on the paved frontage to the surgery and, as he hurried towards it, the doctor dug into his trouser pockets for the keys. He moaned aloud when he discovered they were not there. He couldn't go back inside, he *wouldn't* go back in there. He could still hear the commotion coming through the open front door, fainter now, but the boy's voice still unearthly and clear.

. . . danced on a Friday
when the sky turned black . . .

He almost sobbed with relief when he saw through the car window that the keys were already in the ignition. He was not surprised – only grateful – that they were there, for it was typical of his forgetfulness over the past few months, the strain he'd been under for so long having led to fatigue of both mind and body. He all but fell into the driver's seat and found at first that his fingers were too shaky and too damp to grip the ignition key. Using both hands, one clasped over the other, his body hunched into an awkward contortion, he managed to turn the engine on. It rumbled into life and he quickly snapped on the headlights.

Only when he looked through the windscreen did he realize how difficult it would be to drive through the fog. It swirled across his vision in lazy drifts and he could see darker patches wandering through it like . . . ghostly . . . figures . . .

. . . it's hard to dance . . .

Even through the closed car window he could hear the hymn.

The doctor engaged gear and stabbed at the accelerator with his foot. The tyres screeched for grip as the vehicle shot forward. Here and there were clearer patches in the fog, making it easier for him to find his way – or at least, to keep on the road. His teeth, blunted and yellowed with age, pressed into his lower lip. Lockwood had to help him. After all, he was responsible, he was the one who had instigated everything. But he was now nothing more than a cowering wreck. Beardsmore, then. He was stronger. And he and Lockwood were the same . . .

. . . with the devil on your back . . .

Stapley pressed even harder on the accelerator and the car lurched as it picked up speed. The child's voice was still with him although he had left the surgery far behind. It was almost as if . . .

He snatched a look over his shoulder, almost expecting to see the figure of Timmy Norris sitting in the back seat. The back seat was empty, of course.

He turned to the front again and caught sight of two lights careering through the fog. And too late he saw someone rushing across his path.

His car struck the person, even though he pulled hard to the left. The body struck the windscreen, sending lightning fissures through the glass. He heard the woman's scream as the vehicle skidded, saw her body disappear from the bonnet. A jarring knock as he struck another vehicle parked at the edge of the village green shot him forward in his seat. His car spun round, disorientating him, and then a peculiar floating sensation followed, a sense of gliding smoothly through the air itself. The car continued to spin, causing a dizziness in his head that oddly was not unpleasant.

The motion slowed to a halt, easily and without collision, the engine stalling. Everything became still and quiet. Even the hymn had stopped.

The doctor leaned against the steering wheel, his spectacles tilted on his nose. He gasped for breath.

Then heard the cracking. Impossibly, it sounded like ice breaking.

The car jolted. It plunged down, but only a foot or so. It began to slide forward.

He gave a sharp sob when the car plunged downwards again and he heard the splash of water against the sides. The water began to rise darkly over the windows and his feet and ankles were suddenly wet.

More of the pond filled the car's interior as it sank, a deep, deep greyness pressing against the windows, seeping through the cracks in the windscreen, the seeping soon becoming a streaming. The lights went out, but even in his terror, the doctor had noticed the darker shapes out there in the murk, all floating towards him as though attracted to this new element in their dingy aqueous world.

Something tapped on the passenger window and his head jerked round. He thought he saw a small hand pressed against the glass. Except there seemed to be no flesh on its fingers.

A thump on the glass next to him caused him to turn in that direction.

It was difficult to see clearly at first, for it was dark everywhere, inside and outside the car; but even so, his eyes adjusted and the face had pressed closer to the glass. Inexplicably – for the gloom had not brightened – he could see more clearly as another face joined the others, it was as if these

355

ghostly mirages were lit from within; other hands pressed against the glass.

At first he thought the faces were grinning at him, and then he realized the pond's foul waters had eaten away the flesh of their lips.

Freezing liquid constricted his chest and it became difficult to breathe. He could not move. He *would* not move. Where would he go? Out there with those ghosts?

The faces seemed to nod as if in answer to his unvoiced question. There were more shapes, more lipless faces, more eyeless sockets, filling the windscreen and side-windows.

The water lapped over his chin.

Although the flesh had been worn away in this watery grave-yard, he realized that the faces belonged to children, for they were mostly small, just as the fleshless hands that tapped at the windows were small. And they were lonely here, the children told him. They had been without comfort for too long. They needed someone to take care of them. Someone older. Like him.

Water poured into his mouth, rushed up his nose. His spectacles floated away.

The last words of the hymn came to him. A single child's voice that seemed to make those outside grin even more.

> . . . *I am the dance and I still go on.*

The water closed over his head.

Maddy Buckler sewed while she waited. Earlier she had placed a small lamp in the window, foolishly perhaps, but feeling it might serve as a beacon.

Gaffer was by her side, snuggled up against the armchair, as close to her as it could get. The dog had followed her every-where since it had returned alone two nights before and howled at the front door. That was when Maddy had known for certain that something bad had happened to her Jack. She had phoned the police immediately, but they had refused to come over to the estate and look for him. Give it till daybreak, they had told her, when – *if* anything had happened to her husband – he would at least be easier to find. Besides, he would probably turn up under his own steam at any moment, cursing the dog for having run off. She failed to convince them that something was wrong and they should start a search right away; when she tried to coax Gaffer into taking her to Jack, the dog had refused to leave the cottage, backing away from the front door and cowering under the table in the kitchen.

The police had found Jack's body later that morning and their apology, with their sympathy, had not helped. Nor had their assurances that they would soon find the person responsible for shooting him through the heart with a metal arrow.

Last night Maddy had waited for Jack to return. Tonight she waited for him again.

He would come. She knew he would come. He would find his way back through that nasty fog and the light in the window would guide him.

Oh, they might have pronounced him dead, they might have taken his body away, but that didn't mean her Jack wouldn't return to her.

Because they were *all* coming back.

Didn't anyone understand that?

They were all returning.

So she would sit here and sew until Jack arrived. Maddy began to hum a tune.

But stopped when Gaffer's head shot up. The Airedale began to whine softly.

'S'all right, you silly old thing. You know who it is.'

The dog stared fixedly at the sitting-room door, the keening in its throat becoming more urgent.

'Hush now, be a good dog.'

357

Maddy laid a hand on its long flat head and the dog became quiet. It remained alert though, its head cocked to one side, an ear lifted.

Soon, Maddy, too, heard the footsteps.

They were on the path outside the cottage.

They were coming closer.

37

ORE THAN ONCE Grace rushed ahead of him, forcing Ash to quicken his pace to catch up. The fog was patchy now, thin and wispy one moment so that the wide track ahead and the trees on either side were clearly visible under the half-moon, so dense the next that he was afraid of losing sight of Grace, only the torch she carried guiding his way. The smell, that sickly odour of decay, was still prevalent, but he had become used to it and no longer felt like retching each time he took a deep breath.

Beginning to tire, he caught Grace's arm. 'Can we slow down a bit?' he suggested.

'We might be too late if we don't hurry.' She had barely glanced at him, her concentration on the rutted track before them.

'For what? Why the hell are we going to the ruin?'

'You saw what happened to the painting in Father's study.'

They had both been stunned by the phenomenon, all the more extraordinary because although the picture of Lockwood Hall had virtually been consumed by invisible flames, the frame around it and the wall on which it hung had not even been scorched.

'We –' he began to say, but she cut him off.

'Father is there,' she insisted. 'I know he's there.'

He kept silent, searching the way ahead. A thick cloud bank rolled across their path, obscuring everything, the cloudy night sky included. They walked on, Grace keeping the torch beam on the ground a yard or two in front. They emerged from the worst of it and Ash thought he glimpsed the burnt-out shell of Lockwood Hall in the distance before it was swallowed up once more by the roving mists. Grace had caught sight of it too and she broke into a run, giving him no alternative but to chase after her.

She could not keep up the pace for long for, like Ash, she was becoming wearied by the journey. The fog and the roughness of the track combined to make the going difficult, and at times they had walked along almost blind, the torch light merely reflected back at them by the mists. The shell that was Lockwood Hall came into view again as they drew nearer and for a while, as the haze around it thinned, they saw the gutted mansion almost in its entirety. Under the light of the half-moon Lockwood Hall appeared more bleak than ever.

Ash felt a compulsion to turn away from this cheerless place – even the black pits of its windows seemed forbidding – but Grace would have gone on without him, and that he couldn't allow. Their lovemaking that afternoon had not merely been an insentient coupling – their passion came from something much more binding, a deep understanding of each other's nature and a mutual recognition of each other's vulnerabilities; and of their separate burdens.

As if sensing his thoughts, Grace suddenly took his hand. She did not look at him, but kept her eyes on the ravaged building that loomed so close now. Together, they advanced, and the mists closed in.

They arrived in the wide clearing where once, a long time ago, carriages had drawn up before the steps of the mansion, where horsemen had assembled with pack hounds milling around their mounts' legs, where guests had arrived for grand balls and social events. Grace pointed the light at the dilapidated façade.

The upper reaches of the old building were lost in the fog, the walls seeming to vignette into oblivion, a vaporous void that might have led on to infinity. Ash felt its desolation, and something more – there was a canker here, a black virulence that had not revealed itself on his first visit. Perhaps only darkness could bring forth the purulence of its troubled soul, or perhaps it was time's cycle that governed such unholy effusions, for he sensed that the things that had been unleashed on Sleath were a culmination of some kind, perhaps even a fulfilment. He shuddered at the thought, unsure of how it had come to him.

'Father's inside.'

He looked sharply at Grace. 'How can you know?'

'The same way you can,' she replied, shining the torch towards Lockwood Hall's entrance. She began to cross the stony, grass-strewn clearing and by the time he joined her she had reached the steps leading to the colonnaded entrance. He took the torch from her as they started to climb.

'Listen . . .' She had stopped behind him and he turned to look back at her, one foot on a higher step. The music was faint, and it swelled and ebbed, so that he had to listen intently to make sure of what he was hearing. It sounded like a distant harpsichord.

Grace stepped up to him and held on to his arm. 'I used to hear it when I was little,' she said in a hushed voice, adding, 'when my father brought me here.'

'Was he aware . . . ?'

'I . . . can't remember. I'm sure I must have asked him why he didn't hear it too.' She touched her fingers to her temple as if the effort of trying to remember was causing pain there. 'I would dance to those sounds inside my head and he warned me that the floors inside weren't safe.'

'Then why did he bring you?'

She could not answer and he wasn't sure if it was because her memory failed her, or because she was reluctant to probe her own mind further. He suspected the latter.

Rather than persist, he said simply: 'Let's find him.'

They climbed the rest of the steps together and, as they reached the large open doorway, the music stopped. It was as if their presence had been noted. Ash shone the torch into the vast, gutted interior.

Nothing was different to his first visit: the sweeping but half-collapsed double-staircase, a pitiful indication of past splendour, rafters jutting from broken walls, mounds of debris, some piled like small hillocks – all was exactly the same as when he had looked inside on that first day. Yet he could now feel an uncertainness about the place – no, a precariousness – that wasn't there before. He sensed that the damaged structure had become even more frail and, as if to mock his trepidation, the building let loose a shower of dust and rubble from somewhere high above.

They both stepped back and Ash swung the torch beam towards the source of the fall. The fog had invaded the shell so that the light barely reached beyond the first floor. They waited in the doorway until the last pieces of masonry had clattered to the littered floor.

When the echoes had died away, Ash spoke. 'It's too dangerous, Grace. We can't go inside.' He had kept his voice low, as if afraid of being overheard. 'Besides,' he went on, 'we've no real proof that your father is here.'

Grace did not bother to answer. She entered the building, forcing Ash to follow with the light.

She pointed. 'Shine it along the hallway.'

He did as she asked.

The hallway entrance was between the two arms of the curving staircase, directly opposite where he and Grace stood. He shone the torch along its length but, although thinner at this level, the mists restricted the beam's penetration.

Grace startled Ash by saying excitedly, 'I know where he is, David. I remember a place.'

She started off again and this time he kept with her. He aimed the torch low, checking each step of the way ahead, afraid that the flooring might collapse beneath their feet. Dead

362

leaves that had been blown through the openings were piled everywhere. With Ash now leading, they continued their way through, soon passing between the pincer ends of the stairway. The hallway beyond appeared to be even more hazardous.

Parts of the ceiling had fallen in to leave gaping holes above and below, so that Grace and Ash had to skirt their way carefully around the breaks in the floor. The going was so narrow at one point that Ash was forced to brush against the wall. He placed his hand against the discoloured plaster and looked back at Grace.

'Feel it.' he told her.

She did so and, with a small gasp, pulled her hand away again.

'It feels as if it's vibrating,' she said.

'But its surface is steady,' he replied, almost touching the wall with the head of the torch. 'Look, the dust there is perfectly still, it isn't being disturbed at all.'

The music came to them again, its distant, hollow sound joined by others, by voices, laughter, footsteps. Their eyes met, light reflecting from the wall onto their faces. They stood there rigid, and only when the noises faded again did they think to breathe.

'I've always thought I imagined it,' Grace whispered. 'Those sounds were real when I was a little girl, David, they weren't figments of my imagination at all.'

A crash from somewhere nearby sent her into Ash's arms. He aimed the torch over her shoulder, towards the direction of the crash, but there was nothing to see other than the swirling wraps of fog.

'This place is going to come down,' he said, keeping her close against him.

As if in confirmation, they heard another shifting of masonry and rubble. This time it was further away, possibly from one of the upper floors.

'We'll find him soon, I know we will.' Grace drew away and her eyes looked pleadingly into his.

'Try calling him,' Ash suggested. 'Maybe he'll come to us.'

Grace turned away and called her father's name, softly at first, as if afraid of disturbing the unstable building further, and then more loudly. The only answer was another fall of brickwork from somewhere above their heads. For a few panic-filled moments, Ash thought the whole section of ceiling above them might cave in and he pulled Grace into the relative safety of a nearby doorway. The hall ceiling held, although dust floated down in great choking clouds.

'We can't stay here.' He held her wrist tightly, ready to drag her away. Both of them coughed with the dust, trying to clear their throats.

'There's a door further down,' Grace finally managed to say. 'I think it leads to the cellars.'

'And you think your father might be down there? For God's sake, why?'

There was only confusion in her eyes when he shone the light into her face.

'All right,' he said resignedly. 'We'll take a look, but if we don't find him in the next few minutes, we get out. Okay?'

The confusion was still there.

'Okay?' he repeated, giving her a shake.

Dust had settled in her hair, and her cheeks and forehead were smeared with dirt. She gave a quick nod of her head and looked past him into the darker reaches of the hallway.

He kept hold of her as they made their way over rubble and piled leaves, avoiding sections of flooring that were visibly unsafe and, in parts, completely gone. Much of each wall was blackened and here and there doors were completely burned away. Each time they passed an opening, Ash shone the light through: all the rooms appeared to be empty except for wreckage. The fire two centuries and more ago must have been horrendous, for no room they passed had gone untouched, and the smell of burnt timbers and scorched brickwork was somehow still an element of the overall stench. Even the rank scent of the mists that drifted through was overwhelmed by the general odour. Each time Ash brushed against the wall or touched a charcoaled doorframe, he felt the same strange oscillation as before, and his unease increased with every step they took. He began to wonder if, in truth, the tension was within his own body and not the building around them, but then remembered Grace had felt it too. A new thought struck him: Perhaps there were tremors from deep below, in the earth itself, a seismic trembling that was sending pulses to the surface and through the old building. It wasn't an uncommon phenomenon, and it provided a logical explanation which at least assuaged some of his fears. Unfortunately the rationalization did not make the building any safer.

'Here it is.' Grace had come to a halt and was staring at a dark opening in the wall opposite.

When Ash swung the light that way he saw a large, half-open door, its surface scorched black. Together they stepped over debris to reach it, Ash noticing another open doorway close by as they did so. He briefly flicked the beam through the adjacent opening and saw a large black pit. While his attention was diverted, Grace pushed at the scorched door. It grated noisily against the floor and when he leaned against it to help her he discovered it was made of iron.

Beyond was a steep stone staircase leading down, it seemed, to the very bowels of Lockwood Hall.

38

HEY HAD OBSERVED the warm flush emanating from a breach in one of the cellar's walls even before they had completed the descent, and their last few steps had become hesitant. Ash had also noticed a gaping hole in the ceiling: obviously the fall-in was from the room he'd glanced into a moment or two before. The atmosphere was musty, dank, and everything was filthy with dust.

They reached the last step and Ash swept the light around the room. There was no fire damage as far as he could tell, although the reek of burnt timber was prevalent and rubble had collected beneath the hole in the ceiling. The walls were lined with shelves and empty wine racks, but surprisingly there were no cobwebs; Ash wondered if even spiders had abandoned this godforsaken place. His attention soon returned to the large opening, a soft, unsteady glow emanating there. Something lay at its entrance, a heap that from the staircase he had assumed was more rubble. Now he realized it was a body, legs curled up, hands tucked beneath its chin. It lay in its own dark grume of blood.

With a signal to Grace to follow, he skirted the debris and examined the body more closely. The dead person – impossible to guess his age with his face so bloodied and the tip of some kind of spike protruding from the bridge of his shattered nose – had lank curly hair and wore filthy jeans and a cracked-leather jacket; his mouth was locked shut, caked blood providing the seal, and his stained hands death-gripped the end of the shaft that jutted beneath his jaw. His neutral eyes bulged as if pressured from within.

'David, have a care now.'

Both Ash and Grace jumped, for the silence before the words were spoken had been intense, and although the investigator recognized the voice immediately it took him several seconds to regain his composure.

'Phelan?' he said, peering into the opening.

The great chamber beyond appeared to be lit entirely by candles, hundreds of them of all sizes and thicknesses. Shadows at the furthest edges of the room wavered in the unsteady glow, and he could just make out arched recesses and alcoves cut into the walls all around, their interiors as dark as sable. Faded tapestries and curious archaic instruments adorned the walls, while a long table, its surface made of stone, stood near the centre. Large, carved-wood chairs, a dozen or more, sat between the vaulted cavities and many of the stouter candles were mounted on tall, coiled posts of black metal. The smell of burning wax overwhelmed any other odours, although any warmth from those myriad flames was impalpable in the glacial chill of this inner sanctum.

The Reverend Edmund Lockwood was slumped forward in a large carved chair, his chin almost resting on his chest, his gnarled arthritic hands clasped over the armrests, while Seamus Phelan stood behind the chair, his small, almost dainty, hands resting on its high back, cane discarded on the floor beside him.

'How –' Ash began to say, but was cut off by the Irishman's urgent explanation.

'When I left St Giles' I went straight to the vicarage and persuaded Reverend Lockwood to come with me to this place.'

'But why?' Grace had already entered the candlelit room and was moving towards the two men. 'My father's unwell, he shouldn't –'

'Stay back!' Phelan was holding up a hand as if to ward her off. 'David, please take her away from here, now, this instant.'

It was too late: Grace had already reached her father. She knelt before him and tried to look into his downcast face. The vicar stirred at the sound of her voice, swaying in front of her as though drugged. She spoke to him, but there was no response.

Phelan's voice became softer. 'I'm afraid he's in a bad way.' He came from behind the chair and put his hands around the clergyman's shoulders, gently pulling him back into an upright position.

Slowly Reverend Lockwood looked up and when he saw his daughter he attempted to speak her name. Only a dry whisper came from him.

'What have you done to him?' Her eyes blazed at Phelan.

The Irishman addressed Ash rather than the girl. 'Please, David, do as I ask. Take Miss Lockwood away from here. You don't understand.'

But Ash was distracted. As he'd followed Grace into the huge room, he had noticed shapes inside the shadows of the vaulted recesses. He shone the light he was carrying into the nearest opening and the shock of revulsion that ran through him caused the torch to slip from his fingers. It hit the stone floor with a clatter, its beam instantly extinguished.

Although the niche was in darkness once more, the image he had glimpsed remained in his mind's eye. Despite its misshapen appearance, the thing was human – or at least, had once been human – he was sure of that. The desiccated skin of its head was brown and leathery, clinging closely to the shrunken frame-work, stretched tight across a diminished skull from which brittle threads of white hair hung; its black shrivelled eyes stared from sunken cavities, and a portion of its nose was missing or eaten away, discoloured bone pushing through, while its ears were no more than twisted lumps of gristle. A tattered rag, left colourless and begrimed by the passage of time, hung loosely from one frail shoulder, mercifully shrouding much of the skeletal body, its ragged hem reaching to ankles and feet that were mere grey-yellow joints of bone to which strips of dark carcass clung. Its stumped-tooth grimace seemed to be taunting Ash.

'Dear God,' he said slowly through the dryness of his own throat. 'What was that?'

There was a resigned weariness in Phelan's voice. 'They're Lockwoods,' he said. 'The one you've just seen, and others around this room have been embalmed and preserved here by successive generations of Lockwoods. Like this old ruin itself, they're mere shells with no life, no soul, having only black, degenerate histories. Ah, David, if only you hadn't come to this place . . .'

'Tell me why you brought my father here.' Dread edged the fury of Grace's demand.

Phelan studied her face before replying. 'Atonement,' he said eventually, as her eyes continued to burn into his. 'And I thought perhaps salvation, his, and others'. Now I fear it's too late for either one.'

They heard something move at the far end of the long room. Ash squinted, but Phelan did not even bother to turn his head. Grace rose from her kneeling position and she, too, narrowed her eyes against the unsteady shimmer of the candles.

Something was emerging from one of the alcoves into the light.

Ash caught his breath. Phelan had said these things had no life. They could only be husks, ancient cadavers preserved by fluids. They couldn't possibly move . . .

A glint, a reflection of light, preceded the black shape that was emerging from the darkness, and then the figure itself entered into the light.

He wore mostly black and he was tall, big overall, his dark hair, grey at the sides, sleeked back from a high forehead. In his hands he carried a shotgun, one barrel above the other, the type of weapon preferred for precision game-shooting

Somehow the man was familiar to Ash, although he couldn't

remember ever having met him, and there was something disconcerting about his eyes – in the flickering light they seemed almost pupil-less. Only when the dark man drew closer did Ash realize they were of the palest grey or blue, the pupils strangely contracted despite the chamber's gloom.

He had reached the stone table and was circling it, the shotgun trained on Ash.

His nose was prominent, hooked, and only the absence of a definite jawline undermined the strength of those features, for his chin was tucked into the pouchy flesh of a broad neck. The paleness of his eyes was emphasized by the thick, black eyebrows; his hands were large and steady on the weapon.

It was only when he stopped a few feet from Phelan that Ash realized where he had first set eyes on him: when he had arrived in Sleath three days ago, this man had been sitting with the village doctor in the bar of the Black Boar Inn, both of them watching him. And suddenly he also knew the identity of the dark-clothed gunman.

'You're Carl Beardsmore,' he said.

The tall man smiled. 'How perceptive,' he said.

'Have you heard the term "psychopomp", David?'

Phelan had put the question mildly enough, almost as though the weapon aimed at them was of no consequence.

'I'm not sure . . .'

Beardsmore jerked the barrel of the shotgun, irritated by the Irishman's manner. 'There's no time for that,' he said.

'Doesn't the man deserve an explanation?' Phelan responded. 'What harm can it do? Besides, it greatly concerns the young lady here.'

Grace, crouched by the inert clergyman again, glanced from face to face.

Phelan maintained his composure, only he aware of the true danger they were all in. He had tried to warn Ash, but now it was too late, they were all at the mercy of Beardsmore. And there were other concerns also, such as the condition of the old ruin itself; he could feel the disturbances in the very atmosphere. In the village the portents were now so strong that even those without the 'gift' had become aware of the signs, for the hauntings were no longer confined to the intuitive. Something dreadful was happening to Sleath and a terrible price would be paid before the night was out.

Keen to gain time, he ignored Beardsmore's objection. 'A psychopomp is a conductor of souls to the other world, a sort of guide or usher, if you like.' He waved a hand towards the recesses in the walls. 'Generations of Lockwoods, these monstrosities foolishly preserved for a time that will never come, believed they were such people.'

'Oh, they were more than that.' Beardsmore was smiling again, although his pale eyes remained lacklustre. 'They were visionaries, men who achieved the incredible.'

'As you say,' the little Irishman condescended. Beardsmore had moved around to the other side of the large chair, standing a few feet away from the main group, and Phelan noticed Ash take a surreptitious step forward while his attention was diverted. 'As a matter of fact,' he quickly continued, 'at St Giles' today we learned for ourselves some of the, uh, well now, how should I put it . . . ? Diverse practices? It'll serve for now. We learned of the diverse practices indulged in by the men who have governed Sleath over the centuries, although my friend here . . .' he nodded towards Ash . . . 'did not stay for the complete lesson. Miss Lockwood, I'm afraid your predecessors used the Black Arts to secure the souls of poor wretches that they, themselves, had murdered. It was their purpose to control those very souls through the transient stages of death, a skill refined if not perfected from one generation to the next.'

'That was their genius.' Beardsmore's smile was more like a sneer.

'That was their madness.'

The barrel of the shotgun singled out Phelan, and Ash

371

wondered if the Irishman's comment wasn't a deliberate ploy to upset Beardsmore. He took another small step towards the gunman.

'You wouldn't be the first to mock the genius of those who are unique,' Beardsmore said.

'Nor would you be the first to use such a cliché.'

Ash thought Beardsmore might shoot Phelan there and then. The big hands gripped the weapon so tightly the knuckles showed white. Surprisingly, though, Beardsmore suddenly laughed. 'Another step towards me and I'll shoot your fucking head off.'

He had not so much as glanced Ash's way, but the investigator knew who he was talking to. He became perfectly still.

Phelan hastily bridged the silence. 'Y'see, Miss Lockwood, your forefathers believed if they could control and communicate with the spirits of those they killed then they, themselves, would learn of death's mysteries. And by gaining that knowledge they hoped for their own immortality.' He sighed and regarded the vicar, whose chin rested on his chest once more. 'The worst part of all is that the quest for such wisdom involved experiments and rituals practised upon young innocents, many of them mere children, because it was they who possessed the strongest, the most vibrant, life-force. I suppose you might say that the energy of their spirits was more easily captured and manipulated when they died.'

There was a barely repressed anger in Grace's voice. 'This is sick,' she said. 'Utterly and totally sick.'

'Unfortunately, it's also true.' Phelan returned her stare.

She shook her head vehemently. 'My father wouldn't –'

Laughter interrupted. Beardsmore appeared to be enjoying the discourse. 'Your father is part of it,' he said. 'Haven't you even understood that? It was left to him to carry on the tradition.'

'You're lying!' Grace's eyes blazed through the grime on her face. 'He would never carry on such wickedness, even if it were true. He's a priest, for God's sake!'

'Not for God's sake – for his own. Who could be closer to the souls of mankind? There were many Lockwoods who were both priest and squire, masters and shepherds – why don't you ask him yourself?'

The suggestion was made with such confidence that Grace looked from him to her father, and then for some reason, to Phelan.

The Irishman nodded. 'I'm afraid it's so, Miss Lockwood. The affliction your father has finally succumbed to is no more than the physical manifestation of the sickness in his own soul. An inherited badness, if you like, something he struggled against for most of his life. A battle, I fear, that eventually he lost.' He leaned against the chair, the lines in his craggy face softened by the candleglow. 'David told me of your father's condition today, but when I went to your house Reverend Lockwood was reasonably coherent. We talked and I managed to convince him we should come to Lockwood Hall. He was full of repentance, y'see, he wanted to make amends in some way. Oh, it isn't his guilt alone, there are others involved, villagers who, I imagine, are at this very moment in conflict with their own demons. But the fault is mainly his. He's a Lockwood, do y'see?'

Grace shook her father's arms, as if to rouse him into awareness. 'It isn't true,' she cried, 'it can't be!'

'He brought you here when you were a child.' Ash had moved again, but he made it appear that he was moving closer to Grace rather than Beardsmore.

She spun round to him. 'I know that, David. I told you that.'

'No. I mean he brought you down here, to this place. That's why you knew about it, don't you see? You led me here, Grace.'

'Not you as well, David. Please tell me you don't believe in this nonsense.'

'I saw it in your mind, Grace. I broke through that barrier to your subconscious, one you'd erected yourself. You've never wanted to know the truth, don't you understand? It's too painful for you to remember.'

373

Her eyes were incredulous. 'What are you saying?' She was shaking her head.

'He brought you here when you were a child and they used you.' He hesitated. How the hell could he tell her? 'The ceremonies . . .'

Phelan helped him. 'You were part of their perverted rituals. You, and other children. You were the more fortunate; they took the lives of others.'

Grace continued to shake her head, and unconsciously her hands went to her face, covering her ears.

Phelan went on: 'Your mother discovered the truth just before she died. Your father confessed, although I'm sure she suspected something over the years. How could she not? That's why you were sent away from Sleath when you were a child, to get you away from this place and all its evil. Your father told me it was his idea that you go, so maybe there was still some goodness in him.'

Tears were trickling through the dirt on Grace's face.

'She suspected, but your mother never truly knew the extent of the activities that went on inside this secret room. But when your father eventually told her – out of guilt, remorse, perhaps he was seeking her help – then her heart became exhausted by it all.'

Grace began to rise, and her face was towards her father so that Ash could not see her expression. Was she beginning to understand? Was contempt, disgust, now in her eyes?

'You made yourself forget,' he said gently, desperately wanting to go to her and offer comfort, but only too aware of the twin gun barrels aimed directly at him. 'For the sake of your own sanity your mind blocked everything out – the rituals, the indecencies, the sickness here – because you believed you were part of them. And because you loved your father your mind wouldn't let you admit his depravity.'

She whirled on him and there was neither comprehension nor disgust in her eyes; there was only anger.

Before she could speak, Phelan intervened, for there was a

further truth this girl had the right to know; it might even lessen by some small degree the hatred she would surely feel for her father once she accepted – as eventually she must – these odious revelations. 'At that time,' he said, 'there was someone who wanted you killed, but your father convinced him to take the life of another in your place.'

Confusion stifled the anger. 'They would have murdered me?' Grace said slowly.

'*I* would have killed you.' Beardsmore sauntered closer to the group. 'You were the weak link in the chain, I'm afraid. Even at that tender age I could tell you were not a true Lockwood. Not like your father, not like me. You weren't the first weakling in our lineage, there were others in the past who could never be part of the Lockwood ideology, and they had to be dealt with too.'

'She was a mere child,' Phelan said as if keenly interested. 'How –'

'How could I know?' Beardsmore was scornful, although he smiled. 'One senses these things.'

Ash was staring at the tall man, wondering at what he had said a moment or two before. 'You?' he said, comprehension dawning on him. 'You're a Lockwood?'

'Look at him closely, David,' said Phelan. 'Can you not see the likeness? The eyes, the sweep of the forehead. Doesn't he bear a passing resemblance to Edmund Lockwood himself? God only knows what accident of birth presented him to this world.'

'No accident, my friend.' Any trace of amusement had disappeared from Beardsmore's manner. 'Would you seriously be surprised to learn, knowing what you do about the Lockwood history, that the sexual activities of the males of the family – not to mention their particular proclivities – were not confined only to their own bedrooms? And have you not bothered to wonder why someone such as I, someone of wealth and a regard for things that might be considered anomalous by the rest of society, should be drawn to a dreary place like Sleath?'

'I'd be interested to learn,' Phelan replied drily.

'I'm sure you would. But then I imagine all this pointless yatter is your way of buying time. What it will gain you, well, that I *can't* imagine. Perhaps you think a sudden attack of remorse, something like the one that appears to be afflicting my distant cousin, the fallen priest, will cause me to throw down this gun and beg you all for forgiveness. Or perhaps my attention will wander, giving this fool . . .' he indicated Ash '. . . a chance to attack me. What say I cripple him now?' He aimed the shotgun at the investigator's legs. 'Hmn? It'll give us a chance to talk without worrying about being interrupted by heroics.'

'And have all that groaning distract us?' Phelan kept the banter light, despite the horror on Ash's face.

'Ha! Good point. Dispense with him entirely then? No, I think not. Too much hysteria from Grace. Well then, let's have you on your knees, Mr Ash. That'll do for now.'

'Do as he says, David.' Tone still mild, Phelan looked warningly at the investigator.

Reluctantly, Ash knelt down. But he moved forward a little as he did so.

Phelan raised his silver eyebrows. 'Well, now, you were going to give us a hint as to your connection with the Lockwood family. Which one had the bastard who was to be your progenitor?'

Beardsmore seemed delighted to tell. 'None other than Sebastian,' he said. 'Quite renowned – no, no, notorious, I should say – in his time.'

'Ah yes. A member of the Hellfire Club no less.'

'A member? Not at all. The reverend would tell you, if he were able. Sebastian Lockwood was the *founder* of the Hellfire Club and Sir Francis Dashwood, who has always taken the credit – or the *blame* – was merely one of his acolytes. And let me add this: nobody at that time, nor this, knew the true extent of their activities, but I think at least you might now have an idea.'

'Yes, I suppose I have.'

Phelan seemed reflective, but Ash noticed that he, too, had closed the gap between himself and Beardsmore. While the tall man was watching Phelan, Ash pressed the fingers of one hand against the stone floor and raised a knee in a sprinter's stance. He tensed his body, ready to spring.

'No doubt they were a shoddy lot,' the Irishman went on. 'Like the Lockwood family itself, I should say. Yes, indeed, a depraved bunch of lunatics, one an' all.'

'Be extremely careful,' Beardsmore advised.

Ash wondered at Phelan's change of tactics. Was he deliberately needling Beardsmore because he realized the situation was drawing to a conclusion and a move against the gunman had to be made soon? The Irishman's eyes flicked this way and that, as though something other than Beardsmore was worrying him. A vibration ran through Ash's fingers, and he remembered when he had touched the walls upstairs. Was this what Phelan was waiting for? Did he sense that something was soon to happen to Lockwood Hall?

The Irishman obviously had no intention of letting up. 'And d'you not think that madness has been passed on to every generation of Lockwoods? Yes, I suppose it's well ensconced in the family genes by now, the insanity and the wickedness. Now, who would have been the slut involved with Sebastian? A maid to the manor house? One of his society ladies? No, probably a cheap whore from the town or, knowing the man's baseness, some mindless and toothless hag from the village, someone of no account, you can be sure. But then, you'd know the answer.'

'I think you should be very quiet, little man,' Beardsmore warned again, levelling the shotgun at Phelan's head.

Dust drifted from the ceiling, causing candles to gutter and smoke.

Phelan was relentless, his tone wheedling. 'Didn't you pay someone to trace your family tree? I'm sure your wealth could have afforded the finest genealogist. Isn't that how you discovered your true identity? I bet the whore even kept her own records just to make it easy for some future person to trace his or her ancestor. Or d'you wonder if she intended to blackmail Sebastian? He would probably have laughed in her face. Or had her horse-whipped. What would he care about some slut and her offspring? Fornication with the woman wouldn't entitle her bastard to call himself a Lockwood. If Sebastian were alive today, sure wouldn't he spit in your face?'

'*Shut up,*' Beardsmore hissed.

'No, he'd not allow any old riff-raff to join the clan. And that's what you are, after all. Someone just pretending to be what he's not and could never be. In their own deviant way the Lockwoods were special, maybe – as you, yourself, pointed out – maybe even brilliant. And isn't that what you really want to be a part of, a cut above your fellow man? Eh? Am I right?'

Beardsmore raised the shotgun to his shoulder. But he smiled and pointed it at Grace's head.

Phelan faltered. 'Not . . . not the girl. She's a Lockwood, man. You can't kill your own kind.'

Beardsmore grinned and took a step towards Grace, the weapon still at his shoulder. 'You've just spent an awful long time telling me I'm no relation. Besides, she should have died years ago, when she was a child. Even then I could tell she would never be a true Lockwood. As I said, she was a weak link, but still one that could be used. She could never be like her father. Like me . . .'

He touched the gun to her neck.

Ash launched himself forward, but Beardsmore had been expecting the move, for even as the investigator was rising he had turned to face him.

The stock of the shotgun struck the side of Ash's head and white light exploded in his vision. He felt himself falling, his senses numbed.

His eyes closed when he hit the floor and when he opened them again nothing in the room was steady. He blinked, opened them again.

And saw the end of the shotgun resting against Grace's neck once more. He heard the first click as Beardsmore's finger pulled back one of the twin triggers.

But he also heard something else.

39

HEY ALL HEARD IT.

Beardsmore, the twin muzzles of the shotgun still pressed against Grace's neck, scanned the chamber with suspicious eyes, while Grace, herself, waited with her eyes closed, her body rigid, chin slightly raised. Phelan watched only her.

The Reverend Lockwood became restless; he flinched and shifted in his seat like a man whose nightmare was beyond tolerance. His chest began to heave and his shoulders twitched; slowly his head lifted and a dazed kind of consciousness returned to those pale, vapid eyes. This new dream he found himself in offered little comfort.

The sounds were distant at first, but approaching, and soon they could be recognized as voices raised in some discordant anthem. The advance brought with it other strains, sibilations, footsteps, a gabble that rose to a tumult; a dissonant counterpoint joined the loudening chorus, music from another era, heard by Ash and Grace when they had entered Lockwood Hall, but played with vigour rather than skill. It seemed to come from the corridors and halls above, from the ruined grand rooms themselves, and it seeped through the black ceiling and from the shadowed walls around them.

They heard the hymn too and its plaintive line was distinct from all other sounds.

Seamus Phelan had strayed from the rest of the group, his head cocked slightly as he listened.

Beardsmore's reaction was more frantic. The gun was lowered as he turned in one direction, and then another. 'What is it?' he said, and there was fear in his voice.

'Listen to the words,' the Irishman spoke as if mildly rebuking an inattentive pupil. 'I recognize that hymn, don't you?'

'We heard it at the empty school,' Ash told him.

'Ah.' Phelan spoke the words they could hear: '"They buried my body and they thought I'd gone, but I am the dance and I still go on." D'you see what they're telling us? It isn't an old hymn by any means, but the spirits have learned it from the newer ones. Quite fascinating.' He smiled, looking from face to face to see if they shared his appreciation. 'It tells their story, do y'see? "It's hard to dance with the devil on your back." D'you understand what they're saying? It's the reason for the hauntings.'

'You're mad.' Beardsmore shook the weapon at Phelan.

'Ah, mebbe so, mebbe so.' The Irishman seemed almost amused. '"I am the life that'll never, never die",' he said along with the hymn. 'It's damn appropriate, I'll give 'em that.' His expression altered. He swung round to Ash, who was now half-crouched on the floor. 'It's time we were leaving, David. I've a dreadful fear of what's about to happen.'

The clamour rose to a deafening pitch and Grace clapped her hands to her ears again, this time deliberately. Tears reflected the soft lights.

The walls pulsed and dust burst from them, billowing out into the room.

What do they want?' Beardsmore's mouth remained gaping as he continued to wheel about, the gun now raised defensively.

Phelan's reply was calm enough, but he had started to make his way back to Grace and her father. 'Retribution, I should think,' he said over the commotion.

The walls shuddered violently as if giant battering rams had punched them from behind. The movement was accompanied

381

by a thunderous crash, and everything in the chamber shook. Tapestries fluttered, candles juddered and toppled.

Grace sank to the floor and Ash saw her father reach forward to touch her hair. He watched helplessly, his head still reeling from the blow he'd taken, as Beardsmore stepped towards her with the shotgun held low at his waist.

'*You can have her!*' he yelled into the air. '*She's a Lockwood. Here, I give her to you!*'

'*No!*' Ash shouted as the end of the shotgun was jabbed against Grace's temple. He started to rise.

But Edmund Lockwood had understood Beardsmore's intent, for he had seen the hatred and the panic in his distant kinsman's eyes. And he knew why the ghosts of Sleath had come to this place. He understood so much now. It had all been so wrong, this interference in God's way, but neither the sins nor the proclivities could be passed on, each generation to its own; every man, woman or child possessed self-will, and the corruption of a soul could only begin by choice. Grace, unlike her mother, would not pay for an election he, himself, had made.

He weakly raised his hand against his daughter's assailant, aware that the sickness of his soul had led to the atrophy of his flesh. Nevertheless, he gathered whatever strength remained to him and levered himself from the chair.

No longer stooped, his bearing as straight and as tall as the man who stood before him, the clergyman grasped the gun barrel and lifted it from his daughter's face, pulling it towards himself as he did so.

Beardsmore's finger jerked against both triggers, and the blasts unified, became one, the noise overriding all other sounds.

Grace felt the heat from the fire-bursts that bloomed from the weapon, and her eyes blinked against the sudden glare. She did not see the disintegration of her father's head, nor did she feel the bloodied lumps that splattered into her hair. She screamed because there could only be one outcome to the gun's roar.

Edmund Lockwood's gnarled and crippled hands remained locked around the heated double-barrel, even though there was no brain left to instruct them, and it was the gunman, himself, who released his own grip. Beardsmore watched in horror as his unintended victim slowly toppled backwards. The heavy wooden butt of the weapon clattered against the stone floor.

Like driven steam, clouds of vapour poured into the room and candle flames flickered, tapestries flapped against the walls. The noise renewed itself, filling the space with its insistent chanting, its wailings and whisperings, its music and its footsteps. The walls began to tremble, their pulse occasionally broken by a furious juddering; even the floor quaked as if picking up the resonance from some seismic disturbance far below.

Ash hauled himself to his feet and hurried to Grace, who appeared to be in deep shock. Phelan joined him and together they pulled her up.

'We mustn't stay here any longer,' the Irishman said close to Ash's ear.

'What in God's name is happening?' Ash yelled back, slipping an arm around Grace's waist.

'Not in God's name,' came the barely heard reply. 'Their power is drawn from another source. And you and the girl are part of it. You're both psychic catalysts, like others in Sleath. When you arrived, you only added to their force.'

'What are you talking about?' Ash shook his head incredulously.

'No time to discuss it now, boy. Let's be on our way.'

They started to drag Grace towards the entrance, but a hand swiped at Phelan's neck, shoving him aside. Ash winced as his hair was caught from behind and he was forced backwards. A clenched fist struck him on the side of the head.

He dropped to the floor once more, but this time rolled over onto his back, and then over again. A foot stamped the space he had just vacated and as he came up on one knee he saw the huge bulk of Beardsmore looming over him. Without waiting to be felled again he threw himself forward, the top of his head aimed at his attacker's midriff. Beardsmore staggered back, his legs taking fast, retreating steps, and Ash drove onwards, his hands grasping the other man's clothing.

Tall candles on thick posts were sent toppling, and Ash's shoes dug into the dusty floor for leverage. The long stone-topped table was at Beardsmore's back and he collapsed onto it, sprawling there while Ash struck at him with a torrent of blows that were as unrelenting as they were desperate. Despite the punches raining down on him, Beardsmore was aware of a peculiar vibration running through his shoulders, coursing down his spine. Frightened by the sensation, he pushed Ash away.

Ash stumbled back, managing to keep his balance and startled by the big man's strength. He swooped up a fallen candlestick holder and raised it as a weapon, ready to launch himself into the attack again. But he stopped mid-step.

Beardsmore was staring past Ash at the entrance to the chamber, his mouth agape, his eyebrows raised in a look of almost comical surprise. Tenuous drifts of mist swirled around him and powdered dust continued to float from the ceiling so that his hair and shoulders were covered in a fine grey layer.

Ash turned to find Grace and Phelan also watching the wide opening to the chamber.

The mists had become yellow-tainted clouds, the fog that had smothered the village now invading these secret cellars, as if earlier tendrils had been no more than antennae for the mass. Amidst the rolling, tumid vapours were odd shapes, configurations of dust and shadow and mist itself, umbras that sought to resemble the human form, but never completing the image, misshaping and melding into other conformations, never still, always moving. Their advent had been announced by the continuing clamour – the ululation of voices and music and stampings – the disordered declaration now given tenuous and disarranged portraiture. Inchoate faces presented themselves inside the tumult, loose shimmerings that soon lost their arrangements and dissolved amorphously back into the broil. The vision lay awesome and grim before them.

Steadily the accumulation began to surge into the chamber, following its flimsy harbingers, flowing over the curled body, the dead thing whose soul was not among their legions but secure in another place that was neither hell nor paradise, spreading into the great subterranean chamber to purl and sweep, touching the walls, dimming the candle flames, circling the people who stood transfixed, its incoherent callings persisting all the while in their outrage. The gloom began to fill with chimerical spectres, their likeness to earthly form still tentative, their patterns sheer, without substance, but nevertheless more delineated than before, the assembly swelling so that it seemed all the ghosts of Sleath had been assigned to this sanctum.

A nebulous veil brushed Ash's cheek, its feel so glacial his skin prickled as if with sudden frost, and he saw Grace recoil, as though she, too, had been touched.

Beardsmore flailed his arms to disperse the mists that swarmed around him. His large hands dispelled emerging faces, scattered transparent hands that reached for him. But more shapes took their place, clamouring around him as though he were chosen, peculiar to the others, the wailings increasing, the sibilation of their breeze like a harsh sighing.

A hand, this one real, heavy with substance, clamped on Ash's shoulder.

'Come, David,' Phelan shouted above the uproar. 'No more time to lose.'

'Grace . . . ?'

'More bewildered than you, I'm thinking. And in deep shock.'

She was standing as before, watching the mists and the wraiths within them pour into the room. Her dirty hands were held to her face and when Ash drew near he saw her lips were moving. He could not hear her words, for they were as nothing against the cacophony of other sounds.

Even when Ash called her name and pulled her to him she seemed lost to something else, no recognition in her eyes, no acknowledgement of his embrace. Her gaze followed the flow, her head craning round to look past him. A force pushed at the three figures, a power as invisible as the wind, causing them to lurch. Both men steadied Grace as she almost went down.

'Oh, God help him . . .' Phelan was looking back at Beardsmore, who leaned against the stone table, one hand gripping the edge, the other still swiping at the busy air before him. A flap of skin hung from his forehead.

The whole chamber began to tremor violently. Candles toppled, dust fell in great showers from the ceiling. A grating of stone rumbled around the room.

A fallen candle, still burning, lay at the foot of one of the alcoves and its light caught movement inside. Ash watched mesmerized as something shuffled forward from the darkness. His hold on Grace made her gasp.

The mummified cadaver that had been propped up inside the recess, giving it the illusion of strength beyond death, was emerging into the flickering light. Another, close by, toppled out, its shrunken head breaking loose as it struck the floor.

Phelan had also witnessed the spectacle and he quickly assured Ash. 'It's the shaking of the building, that's all it is. It's causing them to move!'

One candle had fallen against a tapestry, igniting its dry weave. The fire billowed out, catching the grotesque in its parody of life, and it too roared into flame. And now the husk did seem alive, for its absurd head lifted from its chest and its torso twisted as its leathered skin shrivelled and tightened. Its arms twitched, then curled, and its maw stretched, the black pit of its mouth yawning wide as if to protest the assault. Purple flames engulfed it and it fell writhing to the floor, blazing crisply with no sizzle, for its meat was juiceless and brittle. It burned for the waste it was.

A fearsome scream, a high screech that Ash thought had come from the fiery husk itself, rang round the chamber and he felt Phelan's fingers tighten on his shoulder. Blazes danced in the little Irishman's eyes and his countenance was grim. A draught, carrying with it a mist trace, ruffled through his silver hair like country air on a windswept day, and he faced away from the burning carcass, his gaze fixed on the frenzied figure at the core of a crowded maelstrom. Grace sagged against Ash, as if her strength – or perhaps her resolve – had left her.

The mists, with their shadows and ambiguous forms, circled the screaming Beardsmore so furiously he seemed to be at the centre of a nubilous whirlwind. He lashed out wildly and his fists passed through immaterial conformations of limbs and featureless heads. But even as Ash and the others watched, these phantoms took on definition and substance, the limbs evolving clawed hands, the heads acquiring character, blurred faces with dark mouths that screamed at Beardsmore as he screamed at them. And the claws struck at him from that encircling storm, plucked at his clothes so that they became ripped and opened, scratched at his face so that it, too, became ripped and opened. The spectral bodies dissolved, reformed, became absolute, dissolved again, all the while picking at the man who was flesh, striking him, tearing his skin.

Beardsmore roared as a layer was torn from his cheek, from lower eyelid to jaw, revealing the blood-spotted pinkness beneath. The flap of skin that dangled from his forehead was ripped away, the exposed flesh glistening in the candle- and firelight. Shadows passed over it, the spinning continuing. A sliver was stripped from his defensive hand, from wrist to third finger, and he would have hidden both hands inside his clothes had he not needed to protect his head and neck. Like paper tissue, skin shed from temple to cheek, bubbles of blood unveiled by the peeling. The storm wraiths wheeled about him, snatching, seizing, tearing and tugging his casing from him, laying bare the raw meat of his face and hands. His jacket and shirt became shredded so that they hung like rags, and then the skin of his arms and belly was sheared, the pieces that hung down becoming his tattered clothing. Beardsmore lay back on the stone-topped table, his body thrashing, his screeches maddened, and still the demon mob attended him, never relinquishing their claim on his life, on his soul, clawing and pulling, their howling the understudy for his screams, their torture merciless and unrelenting.

'Dear God in Heaven . . .' Phelan crossed himself, and crossed himself again. He seemed mesmerized by the spectacle and it was Ash who shook *him* this time.

'*Why?*' he shouted over the babble. '*Why are they tearing him apart?*'

Phelan turned his head slowly, but his eyes remained gaping at the horrifying display. 'He's a Lockwood,' Ash thought he heard him say.

The Irishman blinked rapidly and Ash could not be sure if it was to clear his eyes of dust, or to expel the terrible vision. As if with effort, Phelan focused upon Grace.

'Help me get her away from here, David,' he said, and although his voice was not raised, Ash heard him perfectly well.

Together they dragged Grace towards the chamber's entrance, the wind tugging against them as it funnelled through, skeins of fog carried with it, twisting mists that seemed to whisper as they passed by. The hymn had become faint, a distant counterpoint to a raging theme, and images rushed with the flow, their composition travesties of the human form. More drapes were burning, ignited by candles hurled against them, and more grotesques flamed inside the cavities that were their open graves. The fires illuminated the great chamber, revealing ancient and mouldering volumes, arcane and cabalistic scripts, all stacked on shelves within deep alcoves at the far end of the room; there, too, were bottles of various colours and sizes, containing liquids, potions, poisons, mixtures that had the power to prolong life long after death was due, but not the sway to halt the withering and the pain. The flames disclosed, then torched robes that hung from racks, fanciful costumes of clandestine ceremonies. Other relics that were more like instruments of torture than divine paraphernalia began to burn.

The recumbent body of the clergyman, an abdicated shell that continued to twitch as if life yet loitered, lay on the stone floor with blood pumping from the viscous pulp that had once been its head, while crepuscular formations, dim and indeterminate, hovered above and around it like inquisitive spectators. On the table nearby the bloodied and skinless hulk that was Beardsmore convulsed and screeched in the agony wrought by ultimate denudation, his raw limbs beating at the stone beneath him, his protests in voice and movement growing weaker, becoming shivery spasms that eventually reduced to a rasping of breath and a flinching of arms. And still his tormentors were not satisfied: they raked him with phantom claws, popping his eyes from their sockets, burrowing beneath the bones of his stripped breast to reach his failing heart. His last feeble whimpers were pleading that this persecution would soon be over and that the demons would not follow him into whatever domain he was bound for. Or that others of their kind would not await him there.

It only occurred to him as his last rattling gasp was squeezed from his lungs by the host of wintry hands rummaging inside his open flesh that death for him, as it had for other Lockwoods, might mean complete and utter extinction.

Something thundered, and it seemed to be from all around. It felt as if the whole building, from collapsed roof to the cellars below ground, had quivered. Fissures appeared in the walls and masonry fell from the ceiling. There were more jolts, as if after-shocks were rumbling through, and more crashings, these spilling brickwork and falling timber, resounding from above.

Ash and Phelan helped Grace to her feet, for all three had lost balance with this fresh jolt, the girl falling to her knees, Phelan lurching to one side. Grace tensed, as though some alertness had returned with the impact.

She pulled back, trying to wrench herself from the two men. 'My father . . .'

'He's dead, Grace, you can't help him!' Ash shouted as he tightened his grip.

She turned in his arms, struggling to break free. 'No, we can't leave him here!'

'Listen to David, girl,' Phelan told her, holding her fast from the other side. 'There's nothing we can do for your father now. He sought some kind of redemption, that's why he allowed me to bring him here. He understood, d'you see? He knew the price that had to be paid.'

She shook her head fiercely. 'He wasn't part of this . . .' she began to say, but memories were no longer impeded and they flooded her mind with their ugly truths. She sagged again, but Ash was there to catch her. 'David, I'm so sorry.'

'You're not to blame, Grace. You didn't know.'

'I'm so sorry . . .' she repeated.

A strip of dirtied skin tore from her cheek.

'David, we must get her away from here!' Phelan pulled at them both, directing them towards the antechamber.

Something struck Ash's back, a brick or timber, he couldn't be sure which, and he ignored the pain. He pushed Grace ahead of him, one arm around her waist, a hand at her elbow, Phelan leading the way. Streamers of mist skimmed against their faces, searing like sharpened ice, and the conflagration behind them spread. At the chamber's far end the old books exploded into flame, creating their own inferno.

It was Phelan who faltered this time, for amid the turmoil of vague and mutable apparitions that crowded the opening in the wall, among that inconsistent pattern of human semblances, was a small figure more corporeal than the rest. The boy stood before the curled dead thing that littered the entrance floor and he watched them gravely as if unaware of the turbulence around them, his pellucid eyes on them alone.

Grace gave a start and Ash was not sure if he heard her say, 'Timmy,' or if his own mind had picked up the thought. She shrunk back and he had to hold her firmly.

The image began to fade almost immediately, the swirling mists claiming it for their own, the vapours swelling, then dispersing around them into the chamber.

Phelan hesitated no longer. With a shout of encouragement and a tightening of his grip on the girl's wrist, he led them on.

They stepped over the corpse, itself vague in the mists that now poured like dry ice into the room behind, and made for the stairs leading to the metal door above. The reverberations continued, rumblings that shook the very floor beneath them, loosening shales of rotted cement and plaster, making their way treacherous; and all the while the howling persisted, driving them onwards so that they quickly reached the staircase. Phelan went first, hauling Grace up behind him, with Ash keeping her steady from behind. They could hardly see the steps because of the fog that streamed over them like some fouled waterfall, rippling through the doorway above as if sucked down by some subterranean whirlpool. Grace did not resist, but neither did she assist their passage; a peculiarly livid strip scarred the grime that covered her face.

Phelan reached the top step and paused only to dip into his jacket pocket and bring out a slim, black torch. He twisted its head and a pencil-thin light sliced through the gloom; he turned the head again and the beam broadened, filling the hallway beyond the door.

'Careful, now,' he told his companions. 'We have to hurry, but it's dangerous out there – the floor isn't safe. Watch where you tread.'

Ash did not respond – he was already aware of the hall's dangerous condition – but came through the door behind Grace, his hold on her never relaxing for a moment. The bedlam from below quietened and he was at least grateful for that. White light suddenly strobed from doorways and ceiling holes along the wide hall and a second or two later there was a boom of distant thunder.

'Follow me, quickly,' Phelan ordered, grabbing Grace's wrist again. He journeyed the torch beam along the floor, searching out the hazards ahead, wary of the pits he knew were beneath the fog flow, then started off, following the course he had set with the light. They listened to the cracking of timber and the rending of stone as they made their way along the cluttered hallway and each time one of them touched a wall, they felt the trembling of the house itself. They took large, careful steps over debris, the Irishman testing each footfall ahead, stopping when he was unsure to probe the mist with the light before continuing. Grace was ushered along like some blind person, for once again she had retreated into the trauma of her own memories and imaginings. Occasionally one of them tripped, but never did they linger to nurse any pain. They kept moving, lightning dazzling them each time it invaded the gutted mansion, its ensuing thunderclap closer on every occasion and making them cringe, so afraid were they that its roar would bring down the fragile shell around them. Once, when Ash lost his balance he struck at the nearest wall and its surface crumbled at his touch. It was as if nothing was firm here, that all had become pulp beneath a decaying skin, the vibration that ran through its substance abetting the disintegration. He wiped his hand against his trousers as if afraid it might be contaminated.

He lunged past Grace when the flooring beneath Phelan suddenly sagged and the Irishman began to pitch forward. He caught him in time and yanked him back, all three of them frozen there while they listened to the creaking of boards and the falling of invisible objects. They moved to the opposite wall and, with their backs against it, edged past the danger area. A shower of dust fell in front of them and when Phelan pointed the torch at the ceiling they saw that it, too, was beginning to bow.

Grace gave a small cry and Ash couldn't be sure if it was because of the danger overhead, or because she had hurt herself against something in the dark. There was no time to find out.

'We'd better make a run for it,' he said, leaning close to Phelan.

'I'm thinking you're right. I'm sure the worst of this is behind us, anyways.'

Without further word, they moved ahead, pulling Grace along with them, hurrying their steps, breaking into a trot when the way ahead seemed clearer. With a great grinding and screeching, this joined by thunder outside, the ceiling behind them caved in, almost as if their clattering footsteps had been the final influence. Noise and billowing dust chased them into the great hall, and they kept running, leaping over debris and fallen timbers, making for the big open doorway. As lightning flared once again Ash glanced up and saw something so terrifying his knees almost buckled under him. His throat constricted so that he could not cry a warning to the others.

The night sky was clearly visible through the jagged floors and rooftop as the lightning flooded the interior of the gutted shell, and in that bleached fulguration the whole of one wall, almost from ground to roof, had seemed to lean inwards with a deep and ominous groaning.

Grace fell in front of him and with a strength born out of panic, he picked her up, half-carrying, half-dragging her towards the entrance. Her body jerked and tiny screams escaped her, but Ash kept her going, never loosening his grip, no matter what pain was caused. She tried to pull away, but he forced her on, no time even to be puzzled at her resistance. Phelan was already at the doorway, just a few paces ahead, shouting something, urging them on. He was reaching a hand towards them.

Lightning flared, the thunder boom instantaneous, and in that blaze Ash saw that the Irishman's face was set in an albescent contortion of horror. He was staring at Grace.

All three of them went through the door at once, too fast, too disordered. They stumbled out onto the terrace area before the steps, their legs finally giving way, their exhaustion asserting itself, so that they fell in a heap.

Ash rolled over onto his back, gasping great lungfuls of tainted air, his chest heaving, a dull ache in his head from the blow he'd received earlier. The fog flowed over the stairs into the building through the doorway, low to the ground, elsewhere creeping up walls, pouring over the sills of glassless windows. The half-moon had broken through clouds that boiled and furled in the night sky, momentarily casting its eerie sheen over the landscape and the broken façade of this once-grand place.

'Thank God,' he said breathlessly, his eyes closing as if in prayer. 'It's done, it's over.'

More concussions rumbled deep inside the ruin and Ash felt tremors run through the stone he lay upon. Lightning stutter-flashed overhead again, its thunder cracking the air so fiercely it seemed the earth itself shook. The clouds were bulky and black with unshed rain, their silver edges twisting raggedly, fusing and separating, never still. His breathing slowed, his heartbeat steadied, and he forced calmness upon himself. They were safe. As long as they did not linger here, the ghosts and the perversions of Lockwood Hall could no longer harm them. The price of retribution had been terrible, but it was paid. The Lockwood evil was finished. Grace was free from a burden she had never realized was hers.

He propped himself up on an elbow and looked towards her. She lay with her back to him and he could see the rise and fall of her shoulders, her outline defined by the moonlight. The Irishman lay just beyond her, his torch gone now, discarded or broken. He was very still.

Ash reached towards the girl.

And stopped, his fingers outstretched, when her body jumped and she gave a sharp cry.

'Grace . . . ?' he said, his voice low, uncertain.

She cried out again, a kind of agonized yelp.

He pushed himself up onto one knee, his hand still reaching towards her.

This time she shrieked, her legs kicking out as if in spasm.

He hurried to her side, half-crawling, half-crouching, and he spoke her name again.

Her scream rang through the night.

'*Grace!*' He tugged at her shoulder, pulling her round to face him. Her body jumped beneath his hand.

Just a few feet away, Phelan was sitting upright, his head turned in their direction.

Grace twisted violently, her cry full of pain.

'Grace, what's wrong?' Ash felt helpless as he knelt beside

394

her, his hands close to her, but no longer touching, afraid any pressure might cause more pain.

Her arms struck out, hitting his, and she squirmed and flinched, sucking in sharp breaths. *'David!'* she screamed. *'David, help me!'*

He held her shoulder and tried to pull her to him, but she twisted away, her body bending double, her head touching her knees.

Phelan's shadow, cast by the moon, fell over them and he, too, tried to hold her. Clouds reeled across the light and they were in darkness once more; but still they heard her moans and felt her writhing. Ash clung to her, desperate to help, afraid she would hurt herself in her frenzy.

'What's happening to her?' he demanded of the Irishman, as if he surely must have the answer.

'I thought she'd be safe out here.' There was grief in his words, grief and pity. And his own desperation. 'I thought we'd got her away in time. Lord Jesus, don't let this be so!'

Her screams had become unremitting and they tore through Ash's senses. He had to do something, he had to help her, he couldn't let her suffer this way. He tried to lift her, his hands trembling with panic, but she wrenched herself away from him, falling back onto the stone and lying there, her body arched, her fingers curled into claws, gripping the night itself.

Lightning blazed, a fitful coruscation that washed everything in its glaring, sterile light. He was oblivious to the thunder that so quickly followed, for in those brief moments of utter illumination he was aware only of the wounds of her open flesh and saw only the peeling of her skin, the delicate tissue strips ripped from her face, from her neck, from her breasts, and heard only her screams, her pleadings, the calling of his name.

Darkness once more, but the sight had fused into his brain. He pressed his hands against her face as if to hold the skin there, to prevent its tearing, and he felt the slivers, light and flimsy, brushing past his own flesh, his efforts useless against the unseen hands that ripped her body. She beat at him, as though he were the assailant, and screamed her suffering, her terror, and she squirmed beneath him, trying to rise, perhaps to run and hide, to escape this ruthless mutilation.

A prayer was being said, an incantation repeated over and over, and he knew it was the Irishman imploring his God for help. But there was no help. Even when Ash lay over her, shielding her body with his own, the scaling continued, and he knew – *oh, dear God, he knew* – it would not stop until she was rendered as naked as Beardsmore, exposed and bloodied, her flesh raw, peeled, her body scarcely human. His screams joined hers, and when the moon showed through again, his tears blurred the sight of her.

He tried to keep her there, but her agony was too intense and it had made her too strong. She slid from beneath him, one of her flailing arms catching the bridge of his nose, stunning him and knocking him aside so that for a few precious moments he lay helpless on the terrace. She stood over him, hands to her face, her head raised as if to howl at the moon, and he thought it was the rags of her clothing that fluttered in the night breeze, but realized instantly that she was almost naked and that it was her skin that flapped and fell away in rags.

Phelan, who knew she was beyond the help of any mortal, remained kneeling in prayer.

Then she was gone. She had returned to Lockwood Hall.

'*David, no!*'

Phelan tried to grab Ash as he started after her, but the investigator easily pushed him away. Ash plunged through the doorway.

The Irishman was old, and he was wearied, but he was still fast: he followed Ash close behind.

Lightning deluged the great hall and both men saw Grace standing quite still among the debris. She appeared to be frozen there, her raised arms glistening in the light, her breasts bloody and raw protrusions, her eyes white against the dark, jellied meat of her skinless face. Her hair flew out as if charged, and mists gathered round her, swirling and weaving in some mystic dance. There was a cold silence within the old, broken walls now – no whispers, cries, music or crashing of masonry – and Grace no longer screamed. But her scoured lips moved and she seemed to be beseeching something beyond their vision.

This time the thunder was distant from the lightning and when it came the ruin's very foundations shook. Ash was scrambling over the rubble to reach Grace when dislodged brickwork showered down on him, striking his head and shoulders so that he staggered backwards, his senses once again reeling.

The deep rumbling that followed the thunder was more ominous than anything that had gone before, and Phelan looked up instinctively to see that one massive section of wall was bending inwards, the momentum at its top, at the very roof itself, increasing. He only caught a quick glimpse, for the half-moon was soon obscured, but the rumbling increased to a great roar . . .

With a warning cry, he reached for Ash and pulled him back over the debris. The injured man's resistance was weak, for he was dazed, ready to collapse, and as Phelan dragged him back he shouted at him, telling him that they could not help the girl, that she was lost to them, but her pain and her torment would soon be over.

The noise increased, a great rending of wood and stone, a shrieking that overwhelmed all sounds and all senses, and the two men stumbled back, almost falling through the doorway, Phelan never easing his grip on Ash, nor allowing him to falter. They lurched down the steps, and *still* Phelan would not let Ash slump. He dragged, shoved, coaxed the investigator away from the crumbling building and only when they were across the clearing did he release his grip.

Ash turned, his hands to his temples, and as he sank to his knees on the mist-covered track he saw the final collapse of Lockwood Hall, enormous clouds billowing out, its mighty roar a worthy match for the thunder that pounded the night.

His consciousness ebbed, then stole away from him. He slipped to the ground, the soft grass welcoming his battered body.

The first raindrops dampened his cheek.

40

INY EXPLOSIONS RUPTURED the river's surface as the dark, mountainous clouds released their load. The fog was driven off by the downpour, its mists retreating through the village, dispersing, thinning, becoming nothing.

The millwheel groaned to a halt, its cargo of putrid flesh left beneath the river to dissolve there, to fade to the nothingness it really was. Old wood creaked inside the millhouse and cogs settled with moaning sighs. All became quiet once more.

The inferno was suddenly gone.

Its light no longer brightened Sam Gunstone's face as he cradled his wife's dead body, and when he looked up he saw that the field was dark and empty. He wondered if the rain had doused not the fire, but the vision itself.

He bowed his head, murmuring a prayer, and when he stooped to kiss his wife's forehead and lightning seared everything white, he noticed that the horror that had been frozen in her gaze was gone too. There was no expression at all, and he felt that was good.

Nell had found her peace.

*   *   *

Ruth stood in the bedroom doorway, the knife poised in the air. Her sister was on the narrow bed, her legs drawn up, her back against the wall. She clutched her dolly, Sally Rags, to her chest, as if it, too, were in jeopardy. Sarah's eyes were wide with terror.

Munce – this thing that *was* the dead Joseph Munce – was at the foot of the bed, watching Sarah, its back to Ruth. It moved slowly at Ruth's presence, from the waist only, swinging its shoulders round, turning its leprous head towards her, and it grinned – that sly, *dirty* grin that she knew so well. Its elbows were tucked into its sides, hands out of view, clutching at the mutilation of its groin.

Munce sniggered, and she was enraged by its familiar guttural sound. Shamed, too, for once, many years ago, she had laughed with it. Ruth ran at the repulsive figure but, even as she plunged the knife, Munce was disappearing, fading fast like Alice's Cheshire cat, the legs, then the torso, the head – and its grin – last.

The knife blade struck empty air and Ruth, startled at first, began to laugh. And began to cry.

Sarah leapt from the bed, Sally Rags discarded, and threw herself into her sister's arms. The knife fell to the floor.

They hugged each other, and after a while Ruth told Sarah to hush, the creature had only been a nightmare and, like any bad dream, it had gone away. It would never, she assured her little sister, it would never *ever* come back again. And though Ruth cried as she spoke, she was smiling too.

When she reached the bathroom, he was holding Simon beneath the water, one hand gripping the boy's hair, the other on his frail, naked shoulder. Simon was struggling, kicking out, grasping the edges of the bath, fighting for a life that was already lost. And George was laughing while he pushed, unable to kill something that was already dead, but his black soul enjoying the parody of it all, relishing the misery it wrought.

Ellen screamed at George to stop, but even as she did so, small flames lapped around his ankles, quickly rising, claiming his legs, roaring up his back. Only when the fire reached his shoulders and enveloped his head did he relinquish his hold and crash back against the bathroom wall. He wheeled about inside the peculiarly vapid flames and his screams had a hollowness to them, sounding as if they came from a long way off.

Simon had risen from the water, his skinny arms wrapped around himself, his pale, wet body shivering.

Ellen could just make out her husband's dim form inside the inferno as he backed into the bathroom's small window, and she ran forward, giving it a push, her hands and arms not even scorched – it was like dipping into a deep-freeze. George went straight through the glass, his body folding to accommodate the small windowframe. He disappeared into the night and when she looked there was nothing to see on the ground below. The path was wet with rain and trails of thin fog straggled across it; but of George, burning or otherwise, there was no sign.

And when she drew her head back inside the broken window, Simon had vanished too. But she didn't mind. She had the feeling – so strong inside her that it had to be right – that her son's soul had finally been laid to rest.

And George had gone back to his hell.

The breeze and the rain continued to disperse the fog, its threads and drifts roaming across the village green, some of the vapours curling around the whipping post, where the blood had ceased its flow. It wasn't long before the storm had washed away the final dregs of mists, and with it, its malodour; and it wasn't long before the rain had cleansed the bloodstains from the grass and from their spread across the road.

*   *   *

The rain had also roused Rosemary Ginty. It fell on her crippled body, a new torment for her.

She tried to pick herself up, but couldn't: something was broken inside her and it hurt, it hurt like bloody hell. And something was wrong with one of her legs, too: she couldn't move it, it wouldn't bend. And her head . . . oh, how her bloody head ached.

She lay there for quite some time before managing to turn herself over onto her stomach, by that time sick of the rain pounding her eyes. When lightning lit up the High Street she saw something odd poking out of the Black Boar Inn over the road. It looked like a truck or a lorry. Now who would do a stupid thing like that? And where was Tom? Why wasn't he out here helping her? Well she would have a few words to say to him when she got back inside.

Rosemary began to crawl, furious with Tom and deeply annoyed at the rain that was doing its best to ruin her hair.

Crick looked up just once, and wished he hadn't: it hurt too much. He let his head loll sideways and again wished he hadn't: the figure lying close by with its face smashed in and its fat belly and arms porcupined by shiny bits was not a pleasant sight.

At least the voices had left him in peace. Couldn't understand it: the bar was empty – apart from the fucking truck sticking through the front door – but for a while all he could hear was the gabble of voices. Fuck 'em. And fuck Lenny, whose fault this was.

Crick closed his eyes and went back to sleep, a sleep he would never wake from.

*   *   *

The broken ice on the pond melted under the rain and for some time its murky waters stirred and eddied. Eventually the surface settled, only rainfall disturbing it. Occasionally, though, a flurry of bubbles broke through from below, but soon even they stopped.

Maddy reached the door, but Gaffer had not accompanied her. The dog cowered behind the armchair back in the sitting room, white showing around the edges of its bulging, fearful eyes. Small whimpers came from deep inside Gaffer's throat.

The footsteps on the path outside had stopped. Maddy knew he was waiting there, waiting for her to open the door.

'It's all right, Jack, I'm here,' she called out as she reached for the bolt at the top of the door. Jack insisted she keep it locked and bolted when he was away – never knew who might come knocking these days, he always told her.

Just for a second or two her fingertips lingered on the bolt's cold metal. A quiet sob escaped her. I know it's you, Jack, she said in her mind. I know you've come back to me. It is all right, isn't it? This is the proper thing? She could hear the rain drumming on the stone path.

Maddy shot back the bolt and lifted the latch. She threw open the door.

Lightning flared, momentarily dazzling her. And when the distant rumble of thunder came and she had blinked several times, she saw the path was empty.

Maddy stood in the doorway for a long time that night, the rain blowing in to soak her clothes, the breeze ruffling her loose, grey hair. She watched the path. She listened for footsteps.

But her husband never did return.

41

HE SUN DREW VAPOURS of steam from the earth, its
glare hard, unrelenting, even at that early hour, and the
rutted, grassy track had lost its firmness, the surface
slippery and full of shallow puddles. Ash's clothes were
damp, his shirt heavy on his back.

He walked as if still in a daze, no longer looking back, the
collapsed building by now lost in the distance. Bird calls came
from the woods around him and occasionally there was the
rustle of some foraging creature in the undergrowth. Not a
single cloud blemished the sky that morning and, even looking
away from the sun, its azure hurt the eye.

He wiped a hand across his cheek, smudging the dirt there
with his own tears, and his mind fought to subdue the images
from the nightmare. His foot slipped in the mud, but he recovered and kept walking.

When he had come to some time before, he had found himself
lying by the side of the track under the cover of trees. He
vaguely remembered having been dragged there by Phelan during the night to escape from the worst of the storm, the
Irishman talking to him, telling him something, the words difficult to recall. Something about being too late again . . . but at
least some were saved . . . and now it was finished, it was
over . . . It made no sense to him, but maybe it would when

the ache had left his head and his thoughts had settled. He wondered why Phelan had left him.

His shirt and trousers already beginning to stiffen as they dried, he went on. At times his steps were uncertain, his mind confused, and when visions of Grace finally overwhelmed him, he dropped to his knees, and clawed his fingers into the moist earth. He wept.

The front door of the Lodge House was still open and for a wild, irrational moment, he wondered if he would find Grace inside. It was a madness, and he did not even pause outside the gate; she was gone, lost to him forever, and the time of madness had gone too. He turned into the narrow road that led to the village.

The tower of St Giles' rose above the treetops, but he averted his gaze. Only when he reached the lychgate and the sharp *kaa* of a crow startled him did he look through the opening at the old church. The carrion crow was perched on a headstone not far from the porch, its dagger-like bill stabbing at the air in short, jerky movements. It became still, its black eye observing the observer.

Then it was gone, powerful thrusts of its wings taking it high over the tower, its cry becoming remote, a faint echo without resonance and of no significance.

Ash went on, descending the hill, passing the silent school. When he walked by Ellen Preddle's cottage, tucked in between its neighbours, he noticed a small upstairs window was broken. He did not stop, even though he glimpsed a shadowy figure watching him from behind a lace curtain in a window on the ground floor. He gave no thought at all to the equipment left inside the cottage. The village was very still and very quiet, his own soft footsteps the only sound to be heard. Windows in other houses were broken too, and the wall outside one was smoked black, its door open wide as if its occupants had fled.

He reached the deserted High Street, where thin wisps of steam rose from the roadway, the sun, although not yet high, beating hard on its surface, drying the night's dampness. Here and there were other open doors, broken windows, and there was no traffic, nothing passing through. On the empty village green the stocks and whipping post seemed strangely isolated, relics of a bygone age, of no relevance here anymore.

A column of smoke from beyond the nearest buildings rose listlessly into the air, but only the birds gave Sleath any semblance of real life, and even their chitter seemed chastened.

Ash continued his journey and had no interest in the pick-up truck that had wrecked the entrance of the Black Boar Inn, the sign above hanging loose from its bracket; nor did he as much as glance at the yellow plastic duck that drifted through the mist rising from the murky pond. His concern was only for his car parked at the edge of the green, for as he drew near he could see something was wrong.

His footsteps slowed when the damage became clear. All along one side the metal was scraped and bent, the wing itself completely buckled, the nearside wheel beneath twisted, its tyre flat. He was conscious of the skid marks that veered across the road and continued over the grass to the pond's edge, but he gave them no thought; nor did he linger to examine the harm done to the Ford – the twisted wheel told him all he needed to know.

Ash made for the bridge at the end of the village, never once looking round, concentrating only on the road ahead.

He crossed the stone bridge, the millhouse on his left quiet, dormant, another defunct memento of a distant era. He began to climb the hill that led away from Sleath.

Sweat ran down his neck and he could feel its clammy coolness on his back; his breathing became laboured, his steps more wearied. But he did not rest. He wiped his eyes with trembling fingers, his mind gradually growing numbed to the events of the night, the memories becoming dulled. The trauma was still with him, and perhaps it always would be, but for the moment all that concerned him was to get as far away from Sleath as possible.

A car passed him, heading towards the village, its two occupants staring curiously as they went by. Another car a few minutes later. And then a police car, its siren silent, but its speed urgent. The policewoman in the passenger seat craned her head to watch the lone figure, but the vehicle did not reduce its speed. It disappeared around a bend in the road and soon even the sound of its engine was gone. Two more vehicles went by, and then an ambulance, with its siren shattering the quietness of the country lane. Its blare lasted some time before it, too, faded. Ash trudged on, putting distance between himself and the village, his head aching, the muscles of his legs stiff after the ascent of the hill. Trees closed over the lane and the air became cooler.

His eyes were downcast, seeing only the sunlight-dappled ground before him, and when the sound of yet another vehicle approached he did not look up. He heard the car slow down, its tyres crackling on the road's surface, but still he ignored it. The car drew to a halt, and Kate had to call his name before he came to a standstill.

'David?'

Slowly he turned and looked at Kate McCarrick.

'What is it, David? What's wrong?'

He waited there, his chest heaving, unable to respond, and it was Kate who had to leave the Renault to go to him.

She touched his arm carefully, alarmed at his state. 'You look dreadful,' was all she could say. Then, in a rush: 'I tried to reach you last night, but the fog stopped me. Did you know the phones were out of order all evening? I stayed the night in a hotel so that I could be here first thing. Oh God, David, what's happened? You look so . . .' She could only shake her head.

'Get me away from here, Kate,' he said, slowly, deliberately.

'But –'

'Just get me away.'

407

'All right, David. Of course.'

Without another word he walked away from her, going round to the other side of the car and climbing into the passenger seat. She quickly joined him and restarted the engine.

'Do you want me to take you back to Sleath?' she asked.

'*No!*'

She flinched, then stared into his face. He looked so haggard, more tired than she had ever seen him. And his eyes seemed distant, as though his thoughts were on something that had nothing to do with the here and now. She wondered how he had become so dirty, not just his clothes, but his face and hands too. Even his hair was thick with caked dust. And was that dried blood on his shirt?

'Just drive, Kate,' he said, looking straight ahead. 'Turn the car round and drive.'

By reversing onto the grass verge, almost touching the trees there, she soon manoeuvred the Renault so that it faced the opposite direction. As they headed away from Sleath another ambulance raced by, its siren deafening them for a few seconds. Kate resisted asking Ash if he knew where the ambulance was going, wary of his grimness.

Ash leaned back and closed his eyes while Kate talked. She was saying something about Seamus Phelan, her words not penetrating, making no sense, no sense at all. Lockerbie . . . Aberfan . . . it meant nothing to him. Sunlight played on the windscreen, leaves overhead casting patterned shadows; the blazing ball of the sun seemed to be following them through the trees, always level, never shrinking or changing course.

Up ahead a narrow, hump-backed bridge came into view and Kate slowed the car in case another vehicle might be approaching from the other direction. The change in speed caused Ash to open his eyes again, and as he did so he caught sight of a small figure standing by the roadside.

He started to say something to Kate, but she was concentrating on the road ahead and the car had passed the boy in an instant. Ash wheeled round, his elbow resting over the back of the seat, his eyes searching the lane behind through the rear window.

The boy had moved to the centre of the lane and was watching the car. Watching Ash.

He wore a three-buttoned jacket, tight even on his slight figure, and short trousers that reached past his knees. And Ash recognized the boy he had thought he'd run down on his way to Sleath, the day he had almost lost control of his car when speeding across the bridge.

The one who had appeared to him in his bedroom at the inn.

The same little boy who had stood among the other ghosts at the entrance to Lockwood Hall's secret chamber.

The one Grace had called Timmy.

Who had died in place of her all those years ago.

And even as Ash watched, the apparition began to fade.

The car rose over the bridge, descending the other side, so that the boy was out of view. But even if they stopped and went back, Ash knew the lane behind them would be empty.

He turned and faced the front. Once more he closed his eyes.

JAMES HERBERT

'48

For Kitty, who knew more than one Tyne Street.
Love and appreciation from us all . . .

1

WHAT THE HELL WAS THAT?

My eyes snapped open and my head lifted an inch or so from the floor; a mess of thoughts stalled any sense.

I pushed the quilt I'd borrowed off my chest and an empty beer bottle rolled across the dusty carpet when my booted foot (I'd learned to sleep with my boots on) knocked it over. The glass made a dull *clunk* as it struck a tiny centre table. I raised my head another inch, my body tense, hearing now acute; I looked right, I looked left, I even looked up at the fancy ceiling. Early-morning sunlight flooded through the open half of the balcony doors, butting in on a gloom caused by boarded windows. A slight breeze tainted with the musk of decay drifted through with the light.

I listened.

Cagney, who'd found a dark corner to nest in – he liked the shadows; survival came with low profile – gave a mean growl, a soft rumbling that was warning rather than alarm. I brought up a hand to silence him and he obeyed; I could just make out the shine of his eyes as he watched me.

The quilt slid away when I leaned on an elbow and a sharp knife punctured the general ache inside my head, punishing me for the insobriety of the night before. There were plenty more brown bottles littering the floor around me, empty soulmates to the one I'd kicked over and counter-testimony

7

to my long dislike of English beer. Skin scraped against jaw bristle as I wiped the back of my hand across dry lips.

Full consciousness arrived in a rush and then I was up, moving swiftly towards the light, crouched and quiet, ears and eyes alert for the slightest disturbance. I skirted the little round table and paused beside the open door to the balcony, keeping out of sight behind glass darkened by rotting blackout boards. Despite the early hour a dry summer heat maundered through the opening, its soft breeze carrying dust motes from the damaged city outside along with its sourness. I snatched a quick look into the sunlight, ducking back again straight away. Then I took another, extended look.

The last barrage balloons hovered over the battered landscape like bloated sentinels. Much closer, directly opposite, the grey and grimed trio on the memorial plinth bowed their heads as if in shame, the words Truth, Charity and Justice now irrelevant.

Save for metal litter, the broad, tree-lined avenue behind them was deserted.

What then? I'd chosen this billet because the balcony room offered a good view of anyone approaching the main entrance; it also gave me plenty of places to play hide 'n' seek in. The building was a warren of rooms, halls and corridors, a honeycomb of hideaways. It suited me fine.

But someone had discovered my sanctuary; the mutt wouldn't have growled for no reason. Maybe it was rats, skulking through the passageways, hardly afraid of humans any more. Or another dog, a cat maybe. But I didn't think so. Instinct told me it was something else. Instinct and Cagney I'd learned to rely on.

I didn't waste any more time.

The motorcycle was where I'd left it last night, carpet rucked up around its wheels. That was another thing I could rely on: a single-cylinder Matchless G3L, this one painted buff for desert warfare, only never shipped out. A survivor. Like me and the dog.

I moved fast, scooping up my fly-jacket from the floor and shrugging it on as I went. The added weight in the lining provided a small comfort. Out the corner of my eye I saw that Cagney was on his feet, ready for action, but waiting for me. His stubby mongrel tail was erect, expectant. Within seconds I'd pushed the bike off its stand, mounted it and was switching on. I kicked down on the starter, hard but smooth, sensing the machine the way you can if you 'know' them, if you love every working part, and the engine roared into life first go (I'd given this baby a lot of care and attention).

The wheels burned carpet as I took off, heading for the closed set of doors at the end of the room, doors that were just beginning to open.

I hit them hard and someone on the other side squawked blue hell as the heavy wood struck him. Paws grabbed at me as I shot through, but the Matchless was already too fast and all they found was empty air. Now I could smell 'em and believe me, it wasn't pleasant. One fool standing further back in the room jumped in front of me waving his arms like some demented traffic cop, so I swerved the bike and raised a boot. Groin or hip, I'm not sure which I made contact with, but he doubled up and swung round like a top, his whooshy grunt affording me some pleasure. Short-lived though, because the angle of the bike caused it to slide along the room's big rug, ruffling it up in thick waves. A few years' dust powdered the air as I fought to control the skid.

I lost it, though. The machine slicked away from me and I let it go, afraid of catching a leg underneath if we both went down together. I rolled with the fall, tucking in a shoulder and staying loose the way I'd been trained. I was up, crouched and ready before the bike had slithered into a fancy chest of drawers halfway down the chamber, ruining painted panels and gold carvings.

One of the intruders, his face ugly with dirt and aggression, came lurching towards me while his two pals behind the crashed doors tended their hurts. Cagney trotted into view and stood in the doorway, interested in how things were working out.

The Blackshirt, almost on me now, clutched an M1 carbine across his chest. Now either he was too crocked to aim the rifle, or he was under orders not to shoot me. I figured the second was most likely, because I knew by this time that his chief, Hubble, would prefer me alive – my blood would be better warm and runny. You see, he had a crazy use for me. Real crazy. But then I guess only the crazies were left. The crazies and me. And who said I was sane?

Well fuck you, Hubble, you and your goons. Satan's hellhouse would be cooler'n a penguin's ass before you took me alive.

Hubble's stormtrooper caught the glint in my eyes and changed his mind about following orders. He began to swing the weapon towards me.

His action was sluggish though, as if he had to think about the move rather than just react, and it occurred to me he wasn't only dazed by the slam he'd taken, but by the effects of the Slow Death itself: there was a darkness around his eyes and smudges beneath his skin, bruisings that were never going to fade; and the ends of his fingers were blackish, as if the blood had jellied at his body's extremities. That didn't make him any less dangerous though, just a little slower.

My own weapon, a Colt .45 automatic, standard US issue, was in the holster I'd stitched into the lining of my leather jacket. Buck Jones might've made the draw, but I was no gunslinger. So I made the only move open to me.

I took a dive, rolling forward under the rifle barrel, head tucked in, legs curled up. As soon as my back hit the deck I kicked out with both feet, catching the goon in the lower belly and doubling him up. He almost fell on top of me, but I used my legs again to push him to one side. He gave a

10

kind of honk and collapsed. I was on him before he had the chance to get his breath back, pushing the rifle towards him instead of pulling it away as he'd expected. The breech cracked against his jaw and his grip relaxed. In one swift action I wrenched the carbine from him and smacked the stock against the side of his face. His head snapped to the right and his body went limp.

I tossed the weapon aside and sprinted towards the Matchless. Cagney decided things were going pretty well and scampered from the doorway to join me, yapping his approval as he skirted the injured Blackshirts. I ignored his licks as I hauled the motorbike away from the wrecked cabinet, angry that my cover was blown, my regal refuge now useless. There'd be more of them around, searching for me, combing every room, every corridor, every damn nook and cranny, no matter how long it took.

I pulled the bike upright and swung a leg over. Voices came through from the balcony room I'd been using as a bivouac and I guessed Hubble's screwball army had been applying a pincer movement, working through the place from both sides. How the hell did they know I was here? I had the whole goddamn city – and there was plenty left still standing – to hole up in, yet he'd zeroed in on me. Shit luck. Someone must've followed me or caught me sneaking in. With anger as much as fear I hit the starter hard, but this time the engine didn't kick in first time. Those voices were getting louder and the men I'd already tangled with, 'cept the one I'd poleaxed with the rifle butt, were rising to their feet and regarding me with hate in their hearts and caution in their eyes. I tried again, adding a cuss for luck, and the engine caught, the machine roared into life. Music to my ears.

Running footsteps next door; they'd heard the music too. Cagney took off without me, heading into the blue as if he were the prey. Well maybe he had a point – they'd shoot him just for the pleasure.

The motorcycle's front wheel almost reared up as I took

off; I had to lean low over the fuel tank and use my weight to hold the bike to the floor as I fled the bad guys. There was a crack of gunfire from behind and the cobwebbed face of a tall pedestal clock ahead of me imploded. Sculptured figures, all dusty gilt, clung for dear life as the old timepiece reverberated with tiny jangly explosions. The marksman was either a shit shot or he wanted to unnerve me; maybe he was only warning others I was on my way.

I hurtled through the open doors at the end of the room and had to brake hard to avoid crashing through windows dead ahead; this was where the east face met the north wing. My left foot dragged floor as I brought the bike round in a skid that sent a small table and the ornate and no doubt priceless (but nowadays worthless) vase on its top flying. The vase shattered on the floor, but no one was going to complain.

Because of the blackout precautions, everywhere inside this place was gloomy, but enough light shone through chinks and cracks for me to find my way. I'd just entered the complex of private apartments and bedrooms so knew there was a stairway close by. Unfortunately it was too steep and narrow for the bike and I had no mind to try it on foot: speed was my ally, had been for some time now, y'see, and I had to stick to the escape route I'd already worked out. Besides, I'd be an easy target for anyone waiting to ambush me in the stairwell.

Another bullet whistled through the doors and thudded into the wall next to the windows; but I had the bike under control again and shot into the long corridor that would take me through the north wing. Fortunately the place had been cleared of corpses and evacuated as soon as the main tenants – God rest their poor souls – had taken flight, so I didn't have to worry about rotting carcasses getting in my way. I opened up, roasting rug, spewing up dust, the engine's roar shaking the walls, filling the air. It didn't take long to reach the west wing and that's where the real fun started.

I'd been making for the main staircase, which I knew the Matchless could take easy enough, reducing speed along the way only to negotiate the trickier twists and turns, and I'd arrived at a long picture gallery where I could change up a gear, make better headway. I'd zipped past Rembrandts, Vermeers, Canalettos (I'd spent some time in this museum with its glazed arched ceiling and low viewing couches set around the walls, enjoying the brilliance before me but bitter, I guess, that these works of art now counted for zilch), when a figure leapt out from one of the several openings, halfway down on my left.

He only clipped my shoulder as I went by, but that was enough. I lost balance and slewed off at an angle, careering into one of the gallery's small tables, knocking it aside before running into a couch. I recovered enough to keep going, my right leg trapped between bike frame and seat, yelling as my pants ripped and my skin burned. I pulled away, picking up speed again, the gallery no more than a dirt track without soil to me.

But again I had to brake as three men appeared in the little lobby at the end of the hall, using the handbrake a split second ahead of the footbrake pedal and leaning hard so that the bike screeched to a clean sideways halt.

I sat there one or two moments, fists tight around the handgrips, holding the clutch lever, sweat soaking my forehead, running down my back. Vibrations from the machine's simmering engine ran through my body. The three Blackshirts watched me from the lobby, one of 'em grinning, knowing they had me trapped. They all carried firearms, but no one bothered to take aim. Their hair was short, cut military-style, and their shirts – black, naturally, although the effect spoilt by dust and creases – were tucked into loose black pants, the grimy uniform of arrogance, the cloth of annihilation. These sick degenerates still hadn't learned the lesson.

A shifting in the shadows behind them, and then another

face, a woman's face, appeared at their shoulders. She grinned too when she sized up the situation.

I glanced to the left and saw the sap who'd tried to ambush me pulling himself up, disappointment souring his mug. Through the same entrance came another Blackshirt, this one thumping what looked like a pickaxe handle into the open palm of his hand, the dull *thwack* it made amplified by the long room's acoustics. The gleam in his eye and the twisted leer he beamed my way were anything but pleasant. Just to confirm the odds really were against me the sound of running footsteps came from the far end of the picture gallery. The vermin who'd started the chase arrived at the opening down there and they also took time out to consider the state of play.

I turned back to the four who were creeping out of the lobby. They stopped, as if my look had caught them out, and now all of them grinned as I sat there revving up the engine. They had me, they were thinking.

And then I grinned too and theirs faded away.

I took off, spinning the bike, swerving close to the wall, aiming straight at the luckless ambusher who'd only just picked himself up. His eyes widened, first in surprise, then in panic, as I hurtled towards him, the bike's roar deafening as it bounced off walls and curved ceiling. He managed to jump clear, throwing himself into the arms of his slack-jawed buddy, the axe handle trapped between their bodies. I was long gone before they'd had time to disentangle, veering left and disappearing through the opposite doorway to the one they'd used (luckily for me the gallery had more than its share of entrances and exits).

I was in a room whose main wall was one huge bowed window that, if it hadn't been for the blackout shades, would have overlooked acres of overgrown lawns and weed-filled gardens. Tall black pillars on either side of individual windows reached up to a vaulted and domed ceiling and over white marble fireplaces were big arched mirrors in plaster

14

frames. (I'd taken all this in, you'll understand, on another day when my time was less occupied.) I kept the bike turning in a rough elongated semi-circle from my starting point, tyres screeching off a parquet flooring of rich woods, speeding up into the adjoining room, sure of the layout even in the dusky light. I straightened up, whipping past Corinthian columns, long velvet drapes, the breeze I was creating causing low-hanging crystal chandeliers smothered in cobwebs to sway; past blue and gold chairs, large paintings of ancient monarchs mounted on blue flock walls; past a marble and gilt bronze clock with three dials, a dark blue porcelain vase, a set of elaborate side tables, again all marble and gilt bronze; diverting round a circular single-pedestal table, before zooming through the open mirror doors into the next state room. (I knew exactly where I was headed because I'd had plenty of time to check out the whole set-up during my stay and, being naturally cautious, I had more than one escape route planned should the need arise, with certain doors deliberately left open to give me a clear run.)

What I needed was for those lunkheads to follow me rather than try to cut me off, because I was continuing the semi-circle, the blue room itself parallel to the picture gallery they'd chased me from. I'd snuck a quick look to my left just before going through the doors into the grand dining room and observed that the small lobby which served both the gallery and the blue room was empty. Good. It meant they'd taken the bait – the Blackshirts were chasing instead of waiting.

Vases of withered flowers, an oval tureen, and tarnished silver ewers with cobweb sails trailing to the huge lacklustre tabletop said it all: Grandeur given over to decay. The dusty red walls and carpet gave me the sickening feeling of passing through a festering, open wound, and the cold eyes of long-gone royals framed by dull gold followed me all the way. These crazy notions were brought on, I guess, by adrenaline overload; but what the hell, they kept my senses kicking.

I began to brake again for the sharp turn I was gonna have to make, and almost stopped completely inside the smaller antechamber filled with large tapestries I found myself in. Shoving one of those over-elaborate kneehole desks out the way with my front wheel, I went on through to a short passage room, then foot-wheeled a left into another gallery. A wide descending stairway was at the far end and that was my goal. I gritted my teeth and tightened my grip as I raced past the usual collection of masterpieces, aware I was travelling too fast to take the stairs but disinclined to slow down – I knew my pursuers would second-guess me as soon as they heard the bike coming back their way. I braked hard at the last moment.

It was a bumpy ride, despite the fact that the Matchless G3L was one of the first British motorcycles to be built with hydraulically damped telescopic forks and the stairway itself was fitted with a plush red carpet all the way down; my arms were rigid fighting the acute angle, my butt barely touching the seat, every bone in my body jolted as I kept the rear wheel almost locked. Head juddering, bones rattling, I vented a staccato kind of wail (I'd never taken the stairs at that speed before), and then the bike was level for a piece and my wail pitched to a whoop of relief or triumph, I'm not sure which.

On either side, two arms of the grand staircase swept up to a balcony overlooking the next set of steps I was about to take, the doorway at the top leading to the long picture gallery where they thought they'd had me trapped; the Blackshirts had cut back and were pouring through that doorway. The lead goon just had time to raise his gun over the bronze balustrade and fire a wild shot before I opened throttle and took off, sailing over the second set of steps without touching one. My extended whoop came dangerously close to a scream as a bullet clanged off the bike's pannier rack.

The shock of landing nearly threw me off, but I rode the bounce, tyres scorching carpet as I braked and fought to keep the machine in a straight line. We screeched (yeah, bike and I) to a stop inches from the opposite set of rising steps in the great entrance chamber.

I grabbed a breath, then dug my heels into the deep pile, hauling the Matchless back to give me room to swing round. Shouts and footsteps behind told me the mob was descending the curved staircase. Someone released a burst of fire that could only have come from a Sten gun and as I turned I saw holes puncturing paintings around the walls. Maybe the shooter was trying to scare me into surrender; or maybe he was just pissed off, as the British say.

I'd cleared enough space when I heard a yap from close by. I did a quick scan for Cagney, but he was nowhere in sight. Well the mutt could take care of himself – hadn't he let me grab all the attention while he'd sneaked down another way? I opened up again, and the Matchless spun a smart turn, scuffing the bottom step of the four leading to a marble hall beyond the entrance chamber. That was where Cagney finally showed, loping along the royal gathering place, avoiding the marble on either side of the red carpet which presumably was too cool or too smooth for his dainty pads. He lingered to wag his stumpy tail at me and I yelled at him to get the hell out. He took the hint and streaked past me towards the entrance doors.

My circle was taking me close to the staircase I'd just sailed over and the sight I caught was not an encouraging one: three of my pursuers were leaning over the stair rail aiming their weapons at me while still more scurried down behind them. The angle was too awkward for the marksmen and anyway, I didn't wait for them to get a bead on me. Their shots chewed carpet and chipped marble columns, but I was out of there, hunched over the handlebars, already passing through the entrance doors to the classy porch outside.

With my right foot scraping concrete, I skidded around the double portico's stone columns and was soon out in the open; left again and a quadrangle surrounded by the four blocks of the ancient building itself spread out before me.

Across the broad expanse of concrete and directly opposite the portico was a narrow archway, with even narrower pedestrian passageways on either side, leading through to the forecourt and open gates. In better times the ceremonial coach had used that archway, but now it was going to accommodate just one man and his dog. Cagney was already halfway across and I was catching up fast when I spotted the Bedford OYD tucked away in the far corner of the square. The army truck hadn't been there the night before, nor the night before that, so I figured the Blackshirts had arrived in it earlier that morning – a military vehicle suited their martial games just fine.

One of them, on his own and presumably the driver, straightened from the snub-nosed hood he'd been leaning against, his jaw dropping open, cigarette falling from it. His weapon must have been inside the cab of the truck, because he was soon pulling at the driver's door. He'd guessed my intention and by now I was too committed to change direction. He heaved himself up into the driver's seat.

Cagney had already disappeared into the shadows of the arch (which, incidentally, was beneath the balcony room I'd holed up in for the past few days – I'd run full circle, you see) and I accelerated, anxious to join him.

The Bedford quivered as the driver started her up, and then began to roll forward. Yeah, he'd guessed my game plan all right and now I understood his: he was gonna plug the exit. Just to tighten things an arm appeared through the open cab window and the black metal of a gun barrel pointed my way.

Maybe I could have tried for a different route at the last moment, through a courtyard behind me on my right and out into the street beyond (the two other archways directly ahead were sealed by sandbags), but like I say, I was committed. Besides, that would've meant slowing down, then offering my back as a target; even if he'd missed with the first bullet, he'd have taken me with the second. No, there really was only one choice and anyways, I was already two-thirds across and going a pretty fair lick.

A bright flash of gunfire came from the truck and even over the noise of the bike's 347cc engine I swear I heard the *thiddd* of displaced air as the bullet passed by.

I rocked a little to spoil his aim, mighty glad that driving and shooting at the same time wasn't this particular hero's speciality. That small pleasure lasted no more'n a heartbeat – it was plain the truck was going to reach the archway ahead of me. Another shot cracked out, just as wild as the first one, but it struck metal; the blackout shield over the front light whipped away. I tried a fancy swerve, but with every second our common objective was drawing us closer together and soon he'd have a target he couldn't miss. I hissed a curse – I mean, the beginning of one – when the Bedford's hood moved across the first passageway; that curse changed to a rage-roar as the truck stole some of the archway.

The rattle of gunshots from behind reminded me the truck driver was not the only contender. A hail of badly aimed bullets flailed the wall ahead. The Blackshirts chasing me were too far away and maybe too excited to get off any decent shots as they came out of the double portico, but they sure as hell didn't help the situation any. Luckily they were keeping their fire to the right to avoid hitting the moving Bedford and from their angle truck and bike must've seemed pretty damn close. More puffs of plaster powdered off the wall beside the second passageway and at any moment – we're talking split seconds here – I expected to feel bullets thudding into my back.

Goddamn, the truck had covered the archway and the driver was slamming on his brakes to keep it that way. It slid onwards though, bellying across the passage. Another gunshot, the *crack* clear as a bell this time – hell, I was close enough to see the joy in the driver's eyes – and I felt leather rip at my shoulder. No numbness, no pain – no real damage.

I twitched the handlebars, no more'n a shrew's shrug, as

the hood closed the gap, knowing I couldn't stop now even if I'd wanted to.

I kept up the roar, jaw straining, eyes narrowed, hands clenched tight around the grips, bullets spewing into the wall above and beside the passageway, truck still sliding, the hand with the gun waving at me, the gap closing down, tighter, tighter –

And then I was through, elbow skimming along the truck's hood bar, leather sleeve on the other side scuffing plaster. I was in the cool shade of the short passageway, my roar hollow-sounding, and then I was out again in bright, glorious sunshine, tearing over the wide forecourt for the open gates, their gilded ironwork rotting to rust, the tall railings on either side worthless protection against the death that had claimed almost all, bloodline having no privilege over blood type.

Through the gates I sped, and around the old queen's memorial, past the statues of women and children I'd gazed at from the balcony room less than ten minutes ago, round to the other side where Victoria herself sat facing the long, elm- and lime-lined Mall. I swear I could feel her mournful eyes on my back as I fled Buckingham Palace, heading for another sanctuary in the dead city. Half a century ago she'd been proud mother to a fabulous empire and a great country; now there was nothing left of empire and precious little of country. Better then those eyes were only of stone.

Gunfire broke the thought that was fleeting anyway. I had a straight run ahead of me and I took full advantage: the Matchless approached seventy and I knew I could coax more out of her.

If I was gonna lose those bastards behind me I'd have to.

20

2

ST JAMES'S PALACE and Clarence House to my left, the over-grown park and lake on my right. Sally and me, we'd fed the swans in that park and laid together on the moist spring grass. But that was another lifetime, a different age, and this was now. Crazy that memories should override all other considerations, even at moments like this, choosing their own time, it seemed to me, with a mercilessness that suggested self-torture. But they were my link with the past, and the past was all I had left.

I avoided the few cars parked along the road, some of them askew, doors wide as if the drivers had skidded to a halt and attempted to flee before the Reaper finished his job. Probably there were bodies – rotted corpses or loose suits of bones – still inside some of them, but I wasn't looking, I had other things in mind.

The mutt, his sandy-brown coat glistening damp gold in the sunlight, looked over his shoulder as he heard me coming up. He didn't break pace any, but seemed pleased to see me.

'*Lose yourself, stupid!*' I yelled at him as I drew level. '*Get off the road!*'

I swerved into him to give him a fright and he veered away, making for a flight of stone steps leading off the main hike. I watched him go and returned my attention to the road just in time to avoid a Wolseley parked sideways across the Mall's centre. Its passenger window suddenly shattered inwards and the metalwork of its doors punctured as bullets tore into it. The shots were wild, but that didn't mean they couldn't get lucky. I straightened up, keeping the Wolseley at my back, using it as a temporary shield. Those Blackshirts were acting like good ol' boys from down South out on a nigger hunt, rednecks on a roust, the local sheriff one of 'em. Back home we'd pretended that kind of bigot didn't exist – theirs was another state anyways, a foreign country almost – and when the news informed us otherwise, we'd be pretty damn certain some black buck had raped another white girl so he, along with all his blackass cousins, was getting exactly what he deserved. You might say these days my opinion on such things has changed a little, 'specially now I'd kind of taken the place of that black boy.

Admiralty Arch loomed up, sandbags piled high in front of the doorways and windows of buildings around it, red London buses and other vehicles clearly visible in the square on the other side. I kept the Matchless on a set course, building speed, putting distance between me and the truck behind. The roads through the arches had been narrowed some by barbed wire and guard boxes, but that was no problem for the bike – I was through in the blink of an eye and into the great square beyond.

With its loose jumble of immobile vehicles, Trafalgar Square looked like one of those frozen pictures you used to see sometimes on a movie screen, as if at any moment the action would start right up again and everything would get going, engines rumbling, car horns honking, people jerking into life. Last time Sally had brought me here – she was like an excited kid showing me the sights – the square and the sky above it had been full of grey pigeons; now even they were gone. The dry fountains with their silent sirens under Nelson's Column were surrounded by wooden barricades and where sections were broken or had fallen flat I could see brick shelters inside. I had it in mind to take refuge in one of them, or even hide behind a barricade, but as I dodged between cars, taxicabs and buses, something moving caught my eye.

I'd never quite worked out how many survivors Hubble had recruited into his Fascist army – the Blackshirts had always appeared in small groups before now – but had figured their numbers to be maybe a hundred or so, and today they seemed to be out in force. Right then another vehicle was heading towards me and from its camouflage marking this one also had to be military. I paused long enough to establish it was a Humber heavy utility, a four-door station wagon that could carry at least seven passengers over heavy terrain. Like the Matchless I was riding, it was probably intended for the North Africa Campaign but never made it overseas. The Humber was entering the square from the Strand and as I watched it nudged a black cab aside, then swung round a double-decker bus.

I took off in the opposite direction, weaving through the still traffic and catching a glimpse of the Bedford pushing its way past the barbed-wire barricades of Admiralty Arch as I did so. The Humber and the Bedford had to be in contact with one another by radio, maybe by one of those walkie-talkies, but I was confident I could outrun 'em both, the bike ideal for slipping through blocked roads and over debris. If it hadn't been for gasoline rationing during the war years, the roads would've been a lot more crowded, which would've suited me fine. No matter, I still had the advantage.

A bus poster wanted to know if I'd Macleaned my teeth today, while a board at the base of Nelson's Column said that England expected me to enlist today. I went on my way, steering around a quaint little English taxi that looked like an upright piano on wheels, its headlights masked to narrow crosses, and past a Dodge van with a loudspeaker mounted on its roof, then squeezing by a platform truck carrying huge

23

casks of God-knows-what, all of these vehicles abandoned by their drivers and passengers three years before, Blood Death victims who had not understood what was happening to their bodies, why their arterial veins were suddenly hardening and swelling, becoming rigid beneath their skins, why their hands were darkening, extremities filling, why smaller veins were becoming engorged, bulging then popping beneath the surface, blood beginning to trickle, then stream, from every orifice, their ears, their eyes, their nostrils, their mouth, from their genitals, their anus, from the very pores of their body, not realizing that their main arteries had begun to coagulate, their body's clotting factors all used up by their major organs, the brain, the heart, the kidneys, causing instantaneous haemorrhaging and necrotic bruising elsewhere, their chests and limbs cramping with agonizing pain until their skin split and everything vital stopped functioning, their curiosity, their awe, their fear and panic lasting mere minutes because the Blood Death held no patience and no pity, each of them dying wherever they happened to fall.

Yeah, and they were the lucky ones – their horror was short-lived, literally, and their suffering only transient; although few in number, the *really* unfortunate victims took longer to die, some even years. And then there were the rest of us, the minority, those left to grieve.

I kept pushing on, blocking thoughts, concentrating on escape. The idea was to get lost in the dead city, then hole up in some dark place and wait. That was the idea. The reality was something else.

A black Ford was heading towards me from the direction I'd intended to take, making me wonder if Hubble had every exit to the square covered. It seemed in no hurry, but was making good progress anyway, dodging in and out of frozen traffic as if the driver was enjoying the caper. It disappeared behind a bus marked EVACUATION SPECIAL, then its roof appeared among the jumble of other car roofs, threading its way through, coming closer all the time. Someone behind

24

me blasted their horn hard and mean, a signal to the others maybe that I was outflanked. It was easy to picture their grinning faces.

But the game was a long ways from over. I had two choices: I could either evade the approaching Ford, using other vehicles as shields against the potshots they were bound to take at me; or I could cut across the square itself.

There were no breaks in the barrier closest to me, but those boards looked fragile enough – several winters of wind, rain and snow, with no one around to maintain them, must have left them rotted and feeble. It didn't take long to make the choice.

I stood loose-legged on the footrests, helping the bike hop the kerb, then sat firm, shoulders hunched, head low, as bike and I flashed past the bronze lions guarding the giant column holding the old one-eyed sailor. I hit wood and it offered minimal resistance, splintering into mouldered pieces, my speed taking me through too fast so that I only just missed the waterless fountain on the other side. I zoomed around one of the redundant brick shelters behind the barrier and, hardly slowing, I made for the broad set of steps that led up to the square's higher level, a road that ran past the great art museum, praying the Matchless would be able to take them, an insistent little voice inside my head telling me I was crazy, that those steps might not be steep, but they were *hard*, bone-breaking *hard*, with no carpet this time to soften the impact.

I stood on the 'stirrups' again, pulling at the handlebars, trying, I guess, to coax the bike to fly. We hit the steps . . .
. . . too fast, too hard . . .

The Matchless rose up several of them, but the front wheel reared out of control, the handlebars bucking and twisting in my grip. We toppled backwards, machine trying for a backflip with me doing my best to dissuade it. I had no real choice though, I had to let go. The engine whined as I slid down the seat and tumbled back, away from the steps and falling machine, arms raised over my head to protect myself.

The bike keeled over, falling at an angle and hitting stone with a crash of metal. I rolled clear as it bounced down after me and, with a moan of engine and a jingling of busted parts, the bike settled in the space I'd just occupied. I knew better than to try and start it up again – it was finished and I was in even more trouble.

I forced myself to a kind of crouch, groaning at fresh pains in my left leg and back, but wasting no time on them. I hauled myself up those steps, using hands as well as feet, then round and up the next, lesser, flight, standing upright only when I was at the top.

More screeching of brakes told me what I really didn't want to know. The station wagon had turned up from the Strand, going the wrong way round the square, aiming to cut me off. Even as it rocked to a halt, doors were opening and black-garbed figures were piling out. One of them raised a rifle in my direction and I ducked back behind the parapet wall beside the steps, reaching inside my jacket as I did so.

I whipped back again, kneeling though, offering a smaller target, and sent off a shot towards them. They scattered, two of 'em taking cover behind a St John Ambulance van, three more scuttling back to the other side of their own vehicle. I broke cover, running low, gun hand pointing in their direction just to give them something to think about. They knew well enough not to take chances, so they kept out of sight, a head bobbing up occasionally to check on me. I sent another bullet their way to let 'em know they were behaving sensibly.

I didn't have much of a plan 'cept to keep moving, using all the cover available to me. A bullet whanged off metal close to my head and I almost dropped to all fours. Another shot shattered the windshield of a nearby taxi. Traffic on this side of the square was thin and I knew I'd soon be running out of cover. Some of the Blackshirts were growing bolder, slinking through metal alleyways like beads of oil through conduits.

A wide expanse of emptiness opened up ahead of me, beyond it the steps to the National Gallery, a museum that at one time had contained some of the world's finest and most valued works of art. Most of the paintings and sculptures had been shipped out to less vulnerable places than a building in the heart of war-torn London, although some had been returned when the battle (or so it was thought) was almost over, and I'd been in and out of there plenty of times, so knew it was a maze of rooms and corridors, just like the palace. I'd thought that one day it might come in handy as a means of escape; it looked like that day had come.

So there was my plan: get inside, lose these neo-Nazi clowns, find a way out on the north side. No problem – as long as I could make it inside without having my legs shattered by enemy gunfire when I sprinted across open ground.

I waited until the Blackshirts had discharged another volley before setting off again, firing back at them just as wildly, but maybe a bit more effectively. They kept out of sight, aware that any kind of wound could prove serious without the right medical attention, and medical attention was just what the whole fucking world lacked.

I pounded road, running towards the flight of steps leading up to the gallery's entrance, which was behind a façade of high pillars (the English liked their pillars). A ragged line of bullets raked the wall ahead of me and I fell back, losing balance and going down on my butt. I swung the Colt round, holding it with both hands, and returned rapid fire, sweeping the area from a sitting position, trying to at least scare the bastards if I couldn't kill 'em. Again, the ploy was effective – they hid, afraid to show an inch of flesh as glass exploded and metal punctured around them. Effective, that is, until the firing pin hit empty.

The clip was all used up and I couldn't reload sitting there in the middle of the road. I had to get into the shelter of the gallery before they realized I was theirs for the taking.

Ears deafened by gunfire, I scrambled to my feet and rushed the last few yards to the steps.

Stopping dead when I saw the figure watching me from the top.

Hubble had never been handsome, but I guess he had that arrogance of features that had some allure for the weak-minded. Pencil-thin moustache, beaky nose, he could have been a shorter version of his own hero, Sir Oswald Mosley, the leader of England's very own Fascist party, a megalomaniac who'd spent most of the war years locked away in Holloway Prison. No, Max Hubble – *Sir* Max Hubble – was never handsome, but on this summer's morning he looked a thousand times more unattractive, as though he were only a short distance from death. His stance, once stiff-backed, shoulders squared, chin jutting, was now bent, shoulders hunched, jawline sunken into a loose neck. The swagger-stick he had once used for Field-Marshal effect had been replaced by a stout walking cane, which he used like a third leg, and the uniform – black shirt and jodhpurs tucked into knee-length boots – seemed two sizes too big for him. The smudges beneath his eyes, the drained paleness of his skin emphasized by patchwork areas of broken veins, the swollen darkness at the ends of his fingers, confirmed what I'd already guessed. The disease in him was accelerating.

We exchanged looks but nothing more. I understood the all-out effort to capture me that day.

I was Hubble's last-chance saloon. His final throw of the dice. His only hope. That is, my blood was his only hope.

One of his men stepped from behind a large poster advertising a Myra Hess piano concert (a regular event at the gallery during the grimmest days of the war), just outside the entrance, carrying with him a portable radio transmitter. I guessed that Hubble had used the gallery as his HQ that

28

morning, directing operations from there, trying to drive me in this direction. Well, it couldn't have worked out better for him.

Others emerged from the entrance and from behind pillars, a ragbag army of the damned. Jew-baiters, nigger-haters, corrupt in their minds and now corrupt in their bodies. These days they had someone else to hate. Me. I was their Jew and their Black all rolled into one.

Okay, I was stunned seeing Hubble standing there, sick and hunched up, but I hadn't lost all sense. I pointed the gun at them and they all ducked, including their leader, who practically sank to his knees. I hadn't forgotten the Colt was empty, but it seemed they had – unless they hadn't even noticed. Waving it in the air gave me the chance to start running again. I managed no more'n three, maybe four, steps though.

Bullets from a Sten gun bit into the road before me, forcing me to leap back, a hasty two-legged hop, arms in the air as if in surrender. I just caught sight of a Blackshirt launching himself from between two pillars of the entrance terrace above me, swooping like a bat from rafters, expecting me to cushion his fall. I sidestepped, but he caught my shoulders, bringing me down with him. He must've winded himself, but even so, he managed to get me in a neck-lock. He squeezed tight, attempting to choke me into submission.

First I used an elbow, driving it hard into his stomach, then, with the same arm, I clipped his face with the gun barrel, bringing it up like a smart salute. Spittle dampened my cheek and neck as he blew a forced breath, and his grip relaxed just enough for me to break free. I twisted, swiping him with the gun barrel once more so that all opposition left him. He collapsed sideways and I scrambled to my feet.

His friends were hurrying through the vehicle alleys and more poured down the gallery's steps, all of 'em hollering banshee-like, eager to get at me and teach me a lesson or

29

two. So what if Hubble wouldn't let them kill me right off? I'd be dead sooner or later, and all in all, I think I preferred sooner. It looked like I'd have to force the issue.

I reached inside my jacket pocket for another clip, ejecting the used one from the automatic in my other hand as I did so. I noticed some of the Blackshirts were already pausing to lift their weapons and take aim. This was it, then, I told myself. The moment had been a long time coming, but I was more than ready. What was so good about living anyway?

A goon had already reached me as my hand came out of my pocket with the spare clip, screening me from the others. I regret to say it was a woman, hair cut nastily short, face and teeth smeared with grime, eyes red with shot blood vessels; regret, because I whacked her hard, fist wrapped around the metal clip, and I don't like hitting women, never have. Hell, I never *had*.

Her teeth broke under my knuckles and she crumpled without a murmur. Her place was immediately taken by another Blackshirt and I knew it would take more than a punch in the mouth to deal with this mean-looking bruiser. Yeah, we'd tangled more than once before and one time he'd even introduced himself. McGruder was his name and he was Hubble's first-lieutenant or captain of the guard, or whatever fancy and meaningless title Hubble had bestowed upon him. He was tall, six-three or more, built like an ox and, as far as I could tell, a long way off from the Blood Death. Big hands reached for me.

I moved back against the terrace wall, afraid to take my eyes off him, Colt and new clip of ammo still separated because of the previous distraction. By staring into his eyes I seemed to be delaying the final rush; taking my gaze away to reload would break whatever goddamn spell we were both under. He, and the others, drew closer.

The black Ford I'd seen earlier came out of nowhere, tyres squealing, brakes screeching, one of its four doors open wide so that it hit the big man with a force that sent him sprawling. I caught sight of two faces peering out at me from the open car door and a female voice yelled:

'*What are you waiting for? Get in, you daft bloody ape!*'

The passenger, a man, had already slammed his door shut again but was indicating the rear door through the open window. The scattered Blackshirts were already moving in, some of them thumping on the Ford's triangular hood with their guns and fists.

'*Get bloody well in!*' came the woman's voice again and I guess it was her cursing that shocked me out of my stupor.

I yanked open the rear door and the Ford immediately took off, giving me a split second to hop onto the white-painted running board. I looped an arm through the lowered front window, gun still held tight in that hand, the other quickly tucking the clip into my pants pocket before grasping the top of the open door, and hung on for dear life as the Ford's rush dispersed the Blackshirts again. A hand reached out from inside the car, grabbing my belt and trying to pull me in. That became more difficult as the Ford gathered momentum and the open door pressed against me, trapping me on the running board.

One of the goons had decided to stand his ground and I groaned when I saw him raising his Sten gun as we sped towards him. It was a stupid move on his part, taking his time to get a bead on me when he should have shot from the hip, because the car was on him before the gun was even chest-high. Self-preservation gave me the strength to push the door wide again and it caught the Blackshirt straight on, lifting the Sten and sending him spinning round, bullets spraying the air and busting the top windows of a nearby bus. The door's recoil crushed my chest, the sudden pain causing me to drop my right arm and lose hold of the Colt. It fell somewhere inside the car.

'*Will you get in here!*' came the woman's voice again, frustration more than anger giving it its pitch.

Instead I almost lost my grip and tumbled into the road

31

as she steered onto a kerb to avoid a truck blocking the way. I forgot my own manners, aiming a cuss at her that would've turned her cheeks red under any other circumstances. I hauled myself up and threw myself onto the back seat, the door slamming shut behind me of its own accord. Wheezing from the pain in my bruised chest, I sprawled across the lap of the other person sharing the back seat with me, the owner of the hand that had grabbed my belt moments earlier.

I noticed her sweet scent first, and then her gentleness as she tried to hold me steady. Breathing hard and shaking some, I looked up into her shadowed face. Her smile was as sweet as her perfume, and kind of, well, *demure* too. Leastways, that's how it struck me. A line of sunlight through the window on her side shot sparkles of gold through her light brown hair.

The car bumped again as it left the kerb and I was jolted against her small breasts. Just as quickly I was pitched back into the other corner. The girl held on to the front seat, looking ahead over the driver's shoulder, her face anxious.

As I steadied myself I took note of my fellow travellers. Oddly, the man in front of me wore a brown trilby and a tweed jacket despite the heat of the day. His attention was on the road ahead too, so there was no chance to catch his features. I noticed, though, that his straggly hair (with no barber shops around any more we all had bad haircuts, although I kept mine reasonably short with sharp scissors and guesswork) did not quite manage to cover the burn scars that fingered their way up the back of his neck from beneath his shirt collar.

My angle was better to take in the woman – the girl – driver, and as I studied her she threw a quick glance my way.

'Who are you?' she said, her voice raised, but no longer shouting. Her accent was pure London, but not from the smarter end.

Before I could answer, something – debris of some kind,

I guess – struck the windshield, cracking the glass. The girl wrenched the steering wheel round, hissing something tight and nasty as she did so, and the Ford executed a squealing curve into the broad, littered and ruined street that was the Strand. Past taped shop windows we sped, avoiding small craters or foetal bundles that were carcasses in the roadway. Bullets *thunked* into metal behind us and I felt the girl beside me flinch. I took a peek out the rear window and saw the Bedford truck was back in the game; the Blackshirts in the rear section had lifted the front flap of the canvas roof so that they could lean on the cab's top and take potshots at us. Luckily, the metal-encased spare tyre fixed to the Ford's trunk was taking most of the strikes.

'And just who the hell are *those* people?'

The driver wasn't looking my way – she was too busy avoiding a Griff Fender removal van and a Shank's open-back truck that had collided with one another years before and had remained locked together ever since, blocking most of the road's centre – but there was no doubting who she wanted answers from. Before I could say anything a bullet shattered the rear window, whistling between the heads of me and the girl I shared the back seat with and finishing the job on the windshield in front. I pulled her down into my lap and crouched over her. The driver let loose some more curses as fresh air rushed through the car.

'We'd have pinched an open-top if we'd wanted the wind in our hair,' I heard her shout over the noise.

'*Keep going!*' I advised, my own voice a little louder than hers.

She said something that I didn't catch.

'*I said, any idea where we should go?*' she yelled when I leaned close and pressed her.

'Keep heading east. We'll lose 'em if you can pick up speed.'

'Hey, you a Yank?' She risked a glance over her shoulder, and I got a better look at her face.

Her eyes were a hazel-brown and she was pretty enough, although the thinnest of scars cut diagonally across her cheeks, rising over the bump of her nose. Her lips were unrouged, but still nicely shaped, and her jawline was firm, indicating some stubbornness in her nature. Her dark hair, curling over her forehead, was tucked neatly into a snood at the back of her head. Why I was noticing these things about the two women at this point of time, I had no idea; maybe I'd spent too long on my own and their effect on me was overriding more urgent considerations. I don't know; but that's how it was though.

'Watch the road,' I told her and she turned away, only just managing to pull round a two-toned Austin.

When she'd straightened up again, I said, 'D'you have any weapons?'

At that time I had no idea of what had happened to my Colt.

Now the man with the trilby, its brim slouched low and shading his eyes, craned his neck to look at me. He shook his head, saying nothing, and his appraisal was cool.

'Why would we need weapons?' the girl driver called out. 'The war ended three years ago.'

I didn't answer her. We were passing the narrow street that served as forecourt to the Savoy and I was tempted to tell her to pull into it. We could have left the car and run through the hotel to its riverside entrance, easily picking up another vehicle parked on that side (I kept several there, keys in the ignitions). It might have been too risky though: our pursuers were close and probably would've caught up with us on foot. Besides, the Savoy was one of my 'home bases' – I had my own grand apartment right up there on the third floor overlooking the Thames – so I was reluctant to bring the enemy so close to a sanctuary. Better to lose the Blackshirts before going to ground.

We passed blitzed buildings, some of them destroyed by the *Luftwaffe*'s bombs, others ruined later by gas explosions

34

and electrical wires burning, still more by fallen cigarettes, lighted candles, or any manner of domestic accidents caused by victims of the Blood Death dropping dead in their tracks. The damage to the city was not yet over: gas mains still blew, waterpipes continued to burst, and bomb-hit buildings still toppled long after they'd been struck. London was a dangerous place, even without this army of lunatics roaming the streets.

Strangely, no epidemics had spread after that black day of *Vergeltungswaffen* – vengeance – despite all the rotting corpses left lying around, but maybe that had something to do with the nature of the Blood Death itself and its effect on human and animal body systems. An attempt to clear up the place had been made by those who had the Slow Death (and didn't realize it) until eventually even they were gone. Leaving just the crazies behind.

Oh, and there was one other danger, but that hadn't happened for a little while, so maybe it was over.

We entered the Aldwych, the gutted shell that had been St Clement Danes just visible beyond the logjam of traffic ahead.

'Swing left!' I ordered, checking on our pursuers as I did so. The Humber station wagon was catching up with the Bedford truck, but both were having a tougher time than the smaller Ford finding their way through the tangles behind us. The girl did as she was told, sweeping round into Kingsway, tyres bumping over tramlines. She had to reduce speed to work round a huge crater in the road.

I turned in surprise as the girl next to me spoke, her voice quiet but easily heard now that we were travelling more slowly.

'Are you the same as us?' she said.

I knew immediately what she meant. The man in front looked at me again, his eyes full of interest beneath the brim of his hat, and the driver stopped muttering curses for a moment to hear my reply.

'AB negative? Yeah, I'm one of you,' I said.

'Well, welcome to the club.' The driver tossed me a quick grin. 'And how about these loonies chasing us?'

I shook my head. 'Slow-dying. They're finished, but they won't accept it.'

'Is that why they're pissed off with you? Y'know – why them and not you?'

Once more I was a little taken aback by her language – girls in Wisconsin are not, *were* not, quite as loose-lipped – although it didn't seem to bother her companions. Probably they were used to it.

'They seem to think I can do them some good. At least, their leader does. When you come to the traffic lights up ahead, go right. Keep heading east.'

'He wants you as a guinea pig, to do tests?' It was the girl next to me who spoke.

'No. He wants me as a refill.'

'Blood transfusion?' It was the man in the hat and I thought I detected an accent. Polish? Not French. Maybe Czech.

'Yeah. He's a fool.'

'But they tried, they proved it could not work. Blood types do not mix.'

'He refuses to believe it.'

The foreigner shook his head in pity, in disbelief, I don't know which. The car lurched and I wedged myself in, one arm against the back of his seat, the other against my own.

'Where you've come from,' I said to the girl next to me, 'were there many of you?'

She wore plain utility clothes. A pale blue dress with puffed shoulders, brought in by a belt at the waist, no stockings, brown shoes that were sensible rather than stylish. On her it all looked good.

'Not too many. AB negative is rare.'

Yeah, I know it, I thought. Too goddamn rare.

The driver, still carefully guiding the car around obstacles, cut in. 'They took us away to a secret location after the plague struck and they discovered our type wasn't affected. It was down in Dorset, a sanatorium of some kind. They did tests, all kinds of things, trying to find an antidote for everyone else, but they failed. I suppose they were doing the same all over the country – all over the world.'

I watched her profile. I guess I expected tears, but none appeared.

'Most ABnegs took off,' she went on, 'when what was left of the medical staff started dying.' For a few moments she concentrated on squeezing through the middle of two tramcars stopped adjacent to each other on the broad street, then she said, 'Hey, what's your name? As we seem to be saving your life it's only right we be introduced.'

'Hoke,' I told her.

'Hi, Hoke. Anything to go with that?'

'Eugene Nathaniel.'

'Christ, you Yanks. Okay, I'm Cissie and the beauty sitting beside you is Muriel. Muriel Drake.'

Despite her anxiety, Muriel managed another smile.

'And the chap in front of you is Willy,' she said. 'We picked him up when we found him hiking along a lane after we left the sanatorium. Only it's not really Willy, is it, Willy?'

He, too, managed a smile, but it was stiff, no warmth to it. He had a strong face, a prominent nose that I think must've been broken at some time, and eyes that looked beyond your own, eyes that kind of rummaged around *inside* a person's head, maybe seeking out their own information.

'No,' he said. 'My name is Wilhelm Stern.'

The *w* sounded like a *v* and there was almost an *h* between the *s* and the *t*.

'German?' My voice was soft.

He nodded, and now his scrutiny of me had retreated, had drawn back swiftly, a flicker of alarm in his eyes.

I lunged forward, grabbing his neck with both hands, thumbs digging in, trying to join with the fingertips on the other side. He pulled away and I went with him, leaning over

37

the back of his seat, jamming his head against the dashboard. His own hands tried to grab my wrists, but the angle was awkward, and I felt the girl called Muriel tugging at my shoulders, trying to haul me off him.

The driver, Cissie, struck out at me, battering my head with her fist. *'Leave him be, you bloody fool! It's all over now, there's no point!'* she yelled.

It was no use though – in my hatred I was oblivious to either blows or entreaties.

Stern fought back, but I had the advantage. He pushed at me, but could get no leverage, while Cissie continued to beat my head and arms, now with the heel of her fist.

In her rage Cissie was paying more attention to me than the road ahead and the Ford hit something, something solid and immovable – maybe another tram – and we were spinning round, screeching a dry skid, engine whining while the tyres burned off rubber. Then we struck something else and the girls screamed and I shot forward, losing my grip on the German, hurtling through the broken windshield, taking whatever glass was left with me. I sprawled on my back on the Ford's long, triangular hood, the rest of the world spinning round me, too soon to know if I was hurt and too dazed to care. Then I slithered off the hood and down the white-painted fender, a slow-motion drift that ended on the road's hard surface. I was vaguely aware of doors opening and legs gathering around me. One of them kicked me, but it wasn't vicious enough to do any damage; more likely it was meant to rouse me. I blinked, more than once, and saw Cissie glaring down at me.

'You stupid bastard,' she said, more in pity now than rage. 'I told you, the war's over. We can't go on killing each other any more.' Her eyes were softened by the beginning of tears.

The other girl, Muriel, knelt close to me. 'Are you all right?' She touched a hand to my shoulder.

Stern, the goddamn *Kraut*, was pointing my own gun at me.

I struggled to get up, anger beginning to replace dizziness. I feebly attempted to reach for him, but Muriel shoved me back down against the crashed car. Her voice was quiet though.

'It isn't worth it, don't you see? Your kind of hatred brought us to this.'

My hand was shaking as I stabbed a finger towards the German. 'No, it was his kind of madness.' My words seemed to be squeezed from my chest.

'My friend, if we do not get away from here right now, it will be *their* kind of madness that will kill us all.' Stern waved the gun in the air, indicating the general area behind us.

'Oh my God, they're almost here.' Cissie bent down and started pulling at my arm. 'We ought to leave you here, you big dope.'

Muriel tugged at the other arm and I was up, looking over their shoulders at the advancing vehicles. The Humber was having difficulty squeezing through the gap left between the two trams further down the road, while the Bedford truck was closer, but having problems with a lamppost on the kerb it had just mounted. The truck scraped by though, and began to gather speed again, the gunmen leaning on the cab roof pointing excitedly when they saw we were easy prey.

Parts of me were beginning to hurt like hell, my body by now having accumulated a fair share of cuts, bruises and plain hard knocks; no bones broken though, nothing seriously torn – even where the bullet had ripped the shoulder of my leather jacket there was only grazed skin – so I knew I could function okay. I was still a little dazed, a bit numbed, but it wasn't a problem. I quickly scanned the immediate area, searching for another vehicle to get us away from there, and all I saw was a jumble of snarled wreckage. There'd been a mighty accident here at some time, no doubt caused by panic when the population of London had tried to flee the Blood Death. We might have made our way through, found a car on the other side, hopefully with the key still in the ignition, but the Bedford was almost on us, its occupants whooping with glee. We were shit out of luck.

And then I knew what we had to do. And I felt the blood drain from my face. And my hand was shaking a whole heap more than before when I raised my arm and pointed.

MURIEL WAS WATCHING ME as the others turned in the direction I was pointing. Our eyes locked and a faint line appeared in her otherwise smooth brow. There was a question in her gaze.

It was Cissie who put the question though. 'The Underground? You want us to go down there?'

Stern was looking puzzled too.

'They'll never follow us,' I said, already moving towards the entrance.

'Of course they will,' Cissie snapped back. 'And then we'll be trapped.'

I paused, taking in all three of them. 'Believe me, they won't come after us.'

A crash of metal against metal as the Bedford barged past a black Austin, tearing off the little car's white-painted fender in the process.

'If you want to stay alive, get moving!' I yelled, and I guess the urgency – and the fear – in my voice convinced them. A single gunshot from the approaching truck was the only other encouragement they needed. They ran, following me.

Although limping slightly, I was in no serious pain, and was soon inside the cool, twilight ticket hall of Holborn Underground Station. I let the others pass me and took a peek out into the street. The army truck was only twenty yards or so away, now pulling to a screeching halt.

I ducked back into the shadows and made my way towards the ticket office, stepping over dark shapes lying there in the half-light, ignoring them and hoping my new acquaintances were doing the same. The ticket office was a solitary booth erected in front of the opening to the escalators and as I reached for the door I called out: 'Grab a mask each. You're gonna need 'em.'

The two girls just gawked at me as I yanked open the door, but Stern had caught on; he'd already picked up a small cardboard box from the floor and was busy opening it. He pulled out a gas mask and handed it to Muriel. As I went into the booth he was looking around for more.

A suit of bones sat slumped on a high stool inside the ticket booth, the skull with its leathery skin and empty eye sockets resting sideways on the narrow counter in front of it, thin, mummified hands stretched towards the small pay-window as if reaching for fare money. Long strands of greyish hair hung loose from the tan-coloured head and yellowed dentures lay on the shelf at the entrance of the open mouth, this itself guarded by the few remaining teeth, exposed and gumless, like crooked tombstones before a black vault. I was glad the light was poor, everything muted, hard to see.

I'd expected the stench to be worse, but I guess the corruption had run its course long before, the smells of that decay slowly fading, escaping through the ticket window and vents, until only a staleness remained, unpleasant, cloying, but no big deal. I'd say this ticket clerk had been one of the lucky ones: the Blood Death had hit him fast, killing him where he sat while others fled around him, so that the booth had become his personal mausoleum, his solitary, unviolated sepulchre. His mouldering had been his own private affair.

It didn't take long to find what I was looking for. I knew the clerk would have kept a flashlight or lamp close at hand for emergencies and, of course, the Blackout itself. It was a

42

heavy chrome flashlight and I found it in a small corner cupboard just inside the door. I wasn't surprised when I flicked it on and nothing happened. Okay, new batteries. I started pulling out drawers, opening more cupboards, and soon found a whole box of unwrapped Ever Readys. It took only seconds to eject the old ones from the flashlight and push in the new, and I held my breath as I switched on. A dim circle of light appeared at the other end of the ticket office and I let my breath go in a quick sigh of relief: the batteries were weak, but they'd do. I was out of the booth and shoving the flashlight into the German's hand in an instant.

In the street outside I could see the Bedford truck, Blackshirts jumping down into the road from its back.

'Gimme the gun,' I barked at Stern and for a second he pulled away, holding the Colt out of reach, the flashlight in his other hand.

'It's not loaded, for Christ's sake!' I grabbed it from him.

By the time the first Blackshirt had reached the kerb just yards from the entrance I'd inserted a new clip and fired off a warning shot. The Blackshirt, and the others following him, ducked instinctively and changed direction, spreading out to take cover behind the walls beside the entrance. Because the Underground station was on a corner there were two accesses, and I hoped they wouldn't have the sense to use the second, smaller one to our right. Two flanks I didn't think I could handle.

'Take the girls down!' I shouted, indicating the escalators behind the barriers. *'Get 'em in the subway and wait for me there.'* I gave the Blackshirts another blast to keep them occupied.

'Come with us,' begged Cissie as Stern began pushing her and Muriel towards the escalators.

'Soon as I can!' I shouted back, then dodged behind the booth to fire off another couple of shots. The Blackshirts started to return fire, but they weren't taking time to aim,

43

afraid of exposing themselves for more than a split second. Funny thing when you're living on borrowed time, as these goons outside were – life becomes even more precious. I knew they weren't going to rush me, that I could hold 'em there for a while; but sooner or later they'd figure a way to flush me out.

I took some well-spaced potshots, just enough to keep their heads down without wasting ammunition, giving the German and the girls time to get downstairs (hoping they'd have the nerve to carry on once they realized what they were descending into). After that I'd have my own problem: making a break for it with no one to cover me.

Well, that problem kind of solved itself.

It happened fast, and it happened without warning. One minute the Blackshirts were keeping out of sight, taking turns to spray bullets my way, filling the ticket hall with thunder, the next the black Humber Estate was roaring through the entrance, hurtling towards me, guns blazing from its side windows like in one of those gangster movies.

I backed away fast, firing from the hip, turning when the Humber crashed into the ticket office and limping towards the barriers, leaping over the nearest rail, using my left hand for support, barely breaking stride on the other side. The Humber had lurched sideways when it hit the solid booth, swinging round and throwing its passengers against one another. Its bodywork hid me from more Blackshirts pouring through the entrance after it, giving me time to reach the top of the frozen stairways.

I didn't need to look to know what lay on those stairs – I'd used another subway as a means of escape almost three years ago and had never wanted to repeat the experience. I also knew the Blackshirts wouldn't follow me down there – they didn't have the balls for it. But the human debris that littered the escalator – all those dead, rotted corpses of men, women and children who'd tried to flee the Blood Death, thinking that the disease, the toxins, the chemicals, the goddamn *visitation*, whatever it was that Hitler had sent over in his revenge rockets, would never reach them in the tunnels beneath the city – I knew they'd be blocking the stairways, that they'd perished as they ran, and their skeletal limbs would now snag me as I went by, their heaped bodies would bar my way, forcing me to stumble through or to climb over them, giving the gunmen above time to find me in the darkness with a lucky bullet, or a hail of lucky bullets, and slow me down for good. So I forgot about taking the stairs.

I leapt up onto the centre ramp between the escalators and slid down on my butt, kicking aside any stiffs slumped over the rail as I went, gliding down like a kid on a sleigh, slowing myself by grabbing the middle lamp columns, controlling the descent just enough to keep me from taking a tumble.

Below I could see the dim light of the flashlight, the others waiting for me, the German having horse sense enough not to direct the beam at me. Glass from one of the dead lamps exploded as I swept by, showering me with fragments, and the light at the bottom of the stairs instantly vanished. I hoped Stern hadn't been hit (I had my own plans for him), but had taken the two girls into the safety of one of the platform entrances. I lost control then, plummeting faster than I could cope with, my trunk trying to overtake my legs so that I began to turn. More bullets split the air, keeping me company, but I must have been just about invisible as I slid further into the blackness. The automatic was back inside my jacket holster, where I'd shoved it before the ride, and I clamped a wrist against it as I began to spin off the ramp. The next thing I knew I was falling, toppling off the slide and onto the stairs, soft (but brittle) things there breaking my fall, cushioning the rest of my uncontrolled descent.

Probably I cried out – I don't recall – as I tumbled down, rolling onto things that seemed to collapse at my touch, until I arrived at the bottom in an avalanche of corpses.

I lay there, breathless and dizzy; and horrified. Something

scratchy brushed against my cheek and I didn't like to guess what. The thought came to me anyway and I panicked, thrashing out at the darkness, pushing the dried husk away and kicking at anything within kicking distance. The smell whacked me then, and I choked, gagged, fought back the swelling nausea. Until I realized it was all in my mind.

Sure, the air down there in that huge mausoleum was foul, but it had more to do with staleness than rotting bodies. The corruption had run its course, you see, and the corpses had deteriorated as much as they ever would under these dry and stagnant conditions. When I'd first ventured into one of these places it had been in the early months after the holocaust and the dead were still decomposing, the stench unbearable; I should have understood by now that once the organs and internal body tissue have putrefied and finally disintegrated, there's little else that can happen – the body can only become a mummified shell. No, the stench had been in my mind, what I'd expected. And the horror was not in the atmosphere, but in the *presence* of so many cadavers gathered together in this black void.

'Hoke. Can you hear me? We are over here.'

It sounded like the German's voice, but it was muffled, distorted by the gas mask the speaker was wearing. The light, dim and comfortless, was coming from a passage not far away.

'Are you hit?'

Ignoring him, I picked myself up and, still crouched, peeked over the curved stair rail at the light from the top of the escalators. Bright flashes and ear-deafening explosions sent me scrabbling towards the light, the sounds amplified by the tiled walls. Vague heaps on the floor did their damnedest to trip me as I went and other bundles I knocked into, carcasses locked tight in sitting or kneeling positions, toppled over to lay there in those same attitudes of rapid death. Bullets ricocheted off walls or found softer targets around me and, with only a few feet to go, I took a desperate

46

dive into the passageway where the German and the two girls were hiding. I lay there sprawled and gasping bad air and would have stayed that way a lot longer if Cissie hadn't knelt beside me and pulled at my shoulder. She said something, but it was difficult to understand because of her mask. She tried again and I shook my head.

'No, they didn't hit me,' I told her. I heaved myself up and the effort seemed to be getting harder each time I made it.

The light, weak though it was, hurt my eyes and I pushed the flashlight away. In its beam I could make out more bodies filling the passageway and I wondered if the girls would have the nerve to journey among them. Even though the stench was nowhere as bad as I thought it would be, I decided not to tell them they didn't need the masks. Their vision would be restricted through the lenses, especially in this poor light, and the gas masks might even make them feel insulated from what lay around them. I had no idea if my thinking was correct, but what the hell, it didn't matter.

'Let's get away from here, fast as we can,' I said to Stern, taking the flashlight from him. Like before with the gun, there was some resistance, but it was minimal and quickly over.

'Are they following us?' he asked, his mask, with its stubby filter unit and big circular eye-pieces making him resemble a creature from another world.

'No, they won't come down here,' I said, looking at the two girls.

'How can you be sure?' His voice was distant behind the mask, but his anxiety was plain enough.

'Maybe they're afraid of ghosts,' I replied. Stupid. The girls clutched each other. 'Come on,' I added hastily, 'let's get away from the noise.'

In fact, the Blackshirts had already given up shooting, although we could hear their shouts, hollow and mocking, drifting down and finding us where we hid. I moved on, the others in tow, negotiating a passage through the tangled

47

heaps and ignoring the noises from behind us. We soon came to a steep stairway, more bodies strewn over the steps.

'Where are we going?'

The question might have come from Muriel, but it was difficult to tell with the masks. Besides, I was ahead of them, concentrating on finding space for my feet on the steps. For the moment I didn't want to answer her.

When I reached the bottom I shone the light back at the trio, keeping it at their feet so they could find a way through. A leathered head, shrunken and brown, seemed to follow their passing with empty eye sockets; an arm, only remnants of dried gristle clinging to its hand and wrist, slithered down a step or two, disturbed by their progress, a single grey finger pointing the way. I tried to keep these sights from them, but they needed the low light so they wouldn't trip, wouldn't fall headlong into the human garbage around them.

Cissie was in the lead, sensible flat-heeled, crêpe rubber-soled shoes shifting through the debris, arms raised and fists clenched for balance. For the first time I noticed she was wearing dark slacks – blue, I think – and that while not as slim as the other girl, her figure was trim enough, attractive even. Jesus, I *had* been too long on my own – this was hardly the moment for that kind of appreciation. I guess I must have lost concentration, because the light wavered and Cissie lost her footing. With a tiny yelp she came toppling towards me.

I caught her easily and held her there in my arms until her panic subsided. She held on to me too and seemed reluctant to let go.

She touched my face. 'Why aren't you wearing a mask?' she asked, voice muffled and eyes vague behind the misted glass of her own mask.

I made a decision. It'd be tougher for them, but we'd all make better headway if they could see more clearly. 'You can take your gas masks off,' I said, pulling her aside so that

48

I could direct the beam back onto the stairs. I still held on to her with one arm.

'What did you say?' Muriel was frozen there in the light.

'I said you can take off the masks,' I repeated more loudly.

'But the . . .' Cissie shook her head.

'It isn't so bad. These bodies decomposed a long time ago.'

She pulled off her mask and stiffened when she breathed in the stale, tainted air. The snood at the back of her hair had come loose with the mask and she pulled it away entirely, shaking her head so that her locks swung free around her face. By the time Muriel joined us, Cissie had become more used to the atmosphere; or at least, had become less tense. Fortunately, beyond the circle of light from the flashlight it was too dark for her to take in very much. Muriel tugged off her mask as well and I watched her face wrinkle as she gasped in the air.

'Some light would be helpful.' The German, his gas mask already removed and hanging by his side, was watching us from midway down the stairs. He came down swiftly when I swung the beam in his direction.

Close to me, he said: 'What is your plan? Do we wait here until they are gone?'

His English was almost perfect, but again that *v* instead of a *w*, so aggravatingly consistent, had the muscles in my chest tightening, my anger boiling towards eruption. I barely held it in check.

But it wasn't only hatred for this German, this relic of the Master Race, that kept me silent. I didn't want to make decisions for these people. I was too used to being on my own, making choices for myself (Cagney was of an independent kind of nature). I didn't want anyone depending on me.

'Hoke, come on, tell us what we should do.' Cissie was tugging at my jacket.

I mentally cursed them for coming into my life, even though they'd saved it. 'We could wait them out,' I said finally, 'or we could go into the tunnels.'

'*No!*' Muriel's reaction had a lick of hysteria to it. 'We can't go any further. I won't. The platforms . . .'

We all knew what she meant.

'I'm with her,' Cissie agreed. 'God, this is bad enough, but what else could be in there?' She indicated the platform entrance.

Only plenty more of the same, I was about to say when something happened that took away any choice. From a distance, up the stairs and back along the passageway, there came the sound of breaking glass instantly followed by a kind of muffled *whoomph*. Then another: same sound, smashed glass followed by that shushed explosion of air. As soon as a bright orange glow lit up the top of the stairs I knew what those sounds were.

'They're using gasoline bombs,' I said almost to myself.

The Blackshirts had tried to flush me out before with these home-made bombs of bottles filled with fuel, a rag stuck into the neck, then set alight, but I'd always been lucky – and too fast. They'd either made them quickly, scavenging bottles from the street or shops, syphoning off gasoline from fuel tanks of vehicles, or they'd brought the cocktails ready-made with them. I thought I heard their taunts, their voices carrying easily down the funnel of the stairway, but the fire had already taken on its own life, passing from one dried husk-like body to the next, incinerating each one as it went along, its muffled roar coming our way. Popping sounds reached us, sharp, explosive reports, as bones cracked and gases ignited. The fire had an abundance of fuel to feed on, a trail of kindling that led directly to us.

'Okay, there's your answer,' I told them. 'We can't stay here.'

'But where can we go?' Cissie wasn't fooling anybody – we all knew where.

'Like I said, into the tunnels.'

I turned away, tired of the argument. It was their decision now.

A huge billow of black smoke swept down the stairs towards us and as I glanced up I saw the flames were not far behind. Reflections flickered on the walls and waves of heat washed over us. Almost as an afterthought I checked the big enamel route map at our backs, the flashlight hardly necessary, and it told me what I needed to know. The girls began coughing as more smoke spilled down the stairway, rolling off the ceiling and curling down the walls.

'Put your masks back on,' I ordered, and they did as they were told, following me as I backed out onto the platform. But the German had dropped his mask on the stairs and instead of finding another – there were plenty of masked corpses around us – he went back to retrieve it. A few strides took him halfway up the stairs, and as he grabbed it the first real flames appeared above him. Bodies around him appeared to twitch and flinch in the unstable light, as if the advancing firestorm was making them uneasy. An illusion, though; macabre, and scary, but no more than a trick of the light. Their clothes began to smoulder.

I gave Stern a warning shout, but it was already too late. As he straightened, pulling on the gas mask as he did so, there was an explosion of fire behind him, trapped gases and flammable material joining forces to give the inferno a special boost. I'm not sure if the German jumped instinctively, or the blast of scorching air threw him forward, but suddenly he was airborne, arms outstretched, back arched.

He was lucky – the flames never got the chance to engulf him completely. He landed on the floor, his jacket alight, and I rushed forward to roll him over, pinning him against the tiles and smothering the flames. Stern didn't struggle; he seemed to know exactly what I was doing. If he hadn't been a *Kraut*, I might have admired his nerve.

The heat from the stairs was unbearable as I dragged him over bodies out onto the platform, the flames above us spreading under the roof, rolling down like a raging river of fire, the ceiling its bed, its torrent of boiling yellows and

51

reds and blacks fierce enough to scorch the eyeballs. It had a kind of terrifying beauty as it hit the wall at the bottom of the stairs and curled to the floor, devouring the dead things lying there before rearing up again in a huge fireball that ballooned outwards.

'Get back!' I yelled, and we all hit the deck together as the flames poured out at us.

I felt my hair crackle as I sprawled among the corpses filling the platform. Smoke created its own menace, blinding and choking, billowing from the opening as the flames retreated for the moment, falling back to consolidate, to feed before progressing. Now it was Stern helping me, pulling me up and away from the worst of the smoke, his mask giving him the advantage. I was retching, lungs filled with the black stuff, eyes streaming, and I felt other hands grab me.

A gas mask was tugged over my head and, although still coughing smoke dust, I caught the faint whiff of old disinfectant under the stink of rubber. I blinked my eyes rapidly and saw the blurred image of Cissie standing in front of me. She was pointing down the platform, her other hand on my arm, and I nodded in an exaggerated way, bowing my shoulders as well as my head. We moved off awkwardly, me still limping, going as fast as we could, like survivors of a subterranean battlefield, the conflict long over, only smoke and the dead left behind. We passed by cots pushed close to the curved platform wall, and bedding laid out on the concrete floor itself. Among those rumpled rags, filling every space, was all kinds of domestic stuff: kettles, fold-away chairs, suitcases, books, even a wind-up gramophone. A small wooden clotheshorse still stood, its hanging rags once a screen for some modest family and probably, like other carefully placed items along the platform, a marker for regular users of the shelter, a sign of territorial claim. A kid's doll, eyes wide as if still terrorized by the carnage around it. A crushed bowler hat, a single boot lying on its side, a pair of spectacles, lenses still intact. There were even one or two tiny portable gas or paraffin cookers, the kind used for 'brew-ups' or warming babies' bottles, smuggled in by families who enjoyed their home comforts. An accordion propped up against a cot bed, a baby's gas mask, oversized and ugly, like a deep-sea diver's helmet, lying empty on a blanket next to it. Newspapers strewn across huddled bodies, faded headlines as irrelevant as the advertisements for gin or Brylcreem they shared the page with.

And the corpses. Avoiding them, stumbling over them, pulling them aside when they blocked our way. Thousands of them it seemed, there in the flickering light. Empty shells that had once been living beings, most of these people fleeing here when the rockets fell from the skies and others around them – in the streets, the cafés, the offices, the buses and trams and cars – started dying before their eyes. A good many had probably neither seen nor heard the vengeance weapons fall, but the Blitz had conditioned them to seek shelter whenever the sirens sounded. Yet when they did, when they sought refuge in the street shelters, the park trenches, and even deep down in the subways, the Blood Death had followed, hunted them out, touching every one and poisoning their life's flow so that it hardened, congealed, became like concrete in their veins.

Only a special few escaping. Others living on, but for a limited time; succumbing, just taking longer to do so.

We hurried through all this, each of us holding on to our emotions, following the dim white safety lines painted along the platforms, four feet and eight feet from the edge, all of us observing but cold to the horror, more than just panic over-riding our compassion. Skull faces, eyes long since liquefied, the skin tight and dark like stretched parchment, torn in places – we saw it all, but quickly learned to focus on nothing.

I led the way, never allowing the weak flashlight beam to linger in one place too long, moving it away from the worst sights, finding a path through the slaughter, always aware

53

that the fire was stealing up on us, progress helped by the body heaps. Its advance scout, foul, swilling smoke, threatened to overwhelm us despite our gas masks and I quickened the pace, aware that the train tunnel was not far. The smoke would follow us into the tunnel, but there would be fewer corpses to slow us down (and less material to burn). The flashlight showed more bodies lying on the tracks below and I quickly gave up the idea of using that level as an easier route.

Right about then a scream grabbed my attention.

I turned, swinging the flashlight around, and found Muriel on the floor, body stretched out but head and shoulders raised, supported by her elbows. She wrenched off her mask and began to scream even louder.

I was an idiot, but I guess it was a natural reaction: I shone the light on the cause of her hysterics.

The small body was lying beside a suitcase – I think the case must have concealed the child as I'd walked by, Muriel's outstretched arm knocking it over when she fell – and only tattered rags still clung to what was left of it. It was easy to tell that the little girl's eyes had been pulled out rather than dissolved, because hard ridges that were the remnants of tendrils trailed down her sunken cheeks; and where her belly should have been there was only a gaping, empty hole, all the organs gone, and although I didn't look too hard or too long, I couldn't help but notice that other parts of her were missing too, only stained bone left behind. I closed my eyes for a second or two, but the sight was replaced by a memory – *a terrible, sickening memory* – and I opened them again.

Oddly – *Jesus Christ, bizarrely* – Muriel reached forward to touch the long dull, hair that lay around the remains of the child's face, as if to stroke it, a gesture of pity and regret, I guess. But the hair came away in Muriel's hand and that was when her screams became wilder and her body began to shudder.

Taking her by the arm, I eased her away, lifting her so that Cissie could hold her, comfort her, and as the cries echoed around the Underground station I tore off my mask and quickly ran the light over the mounds of human remains nearby. I saw what I had dreaded.

Partially consumed corpses were nothing new to me, yet revulsion – and yeah, hatred, sheer bloody *hatred* for the scavengers who'd done this thing – filled my gut and set my own body shaking. I controlled it though, controlled my emotions and my shivering limbs, despite what lay around us, despite those torn and mutilated victims, their wounds – *their ruptured skins and absent parts* – not at first obvious in the altering light of the fire and swirling smoke, so easily missed among the shifting shadows.

Shifting shadows . . . At first I thought that's all they were. Little movements among the human remains and the litter. But they were too furtive, sometimes too brisk. And here and there tiny bright reflections shone back.

'Come on, we can't stay here!' I shouted at the others, jerking the light away, aiming its beam towards the end of the platform. *'D'you hear me? The fire's getting closer! Let's move on!'*

I grabbed Muriel's wrist and pulled her away from Cissie, leading her onwards, not gentle at all, but let's say determined, channelling my horror into anger. I held the flashlight high, keeping its light off the floor, stumbling through the wreckage, but still catching those little, scurrying movements in the corners of my eyes. The girl was limp, so I had to drag her along until Cissie caught up with us and supported her, making the going easier. Soon the smoke was blurring my vision, its acrid smell scraping at the back of my throat. Behind me, Muriel was choking, her body bent over, but I wasn't gonna ease up, I wasn't gonna hunt around in that mess for more gas masks.

I threw a hasty look over my shoulder, but there was too much smoke and my eyes were too teared-up for me to see any more than a blustering hellfire filling the station. By then we were nearly at the end of the platform and obstacles were fewer. Dense smoke curled against the facing wall, but I could see the black hole of the tunnel next to it, a ramp leading down. Letting go of Muriel I wiped my eyes with the grimy fingers of one hand, then squinted into the dark. There were bodies blocking the ramp, more of them lying between the tracks below.

'Help me with her,' I shouted at Cissie as I stood at the platform's edge. I shone the weak light into her face for a moment, and beyond the windows of the mask her eyes widened. I thought hysteria might overwhelm her too, but she just nodded, steering Muriel closer to the tracks, then holding her there. Hand on the platform's lip, I hopped down, trying not to land on anything mushy, wincing when I landed on my damaged leg. There was less smoke at that level and, before reaching up for Muriel, I aimed the beam into the tunnel. The light didn't stretch very far, enough only to reveal more victims scattered there, dim heaps that were more rags than human remains.

Cissie guided Muriel into my upstretched arms and I lowered her onto the tracks. She leaned against me, her slim body racked by coughing, as I turned back for Cissie, who followed without hesitation, first sitting on the platform and swinging her legs over before dropping down next to me. The German was crouched on one knee, looking even more alien behind his mask, and he held something towards me, something he'd found among the platform clutter.

I took the oil lamp from him, a red thing with four windows and a stiff hook at the top to hold it by. It must've belonged to a station guard or someone who used the place as a regular shelter during the war, and the question was, would it still function or was it dry and useless? Although charred a dark brown, the wick looked okay, and I gave the lamp a shake close to my ear, listening for oil. Liquid slurped around inside.

Okay. No time to try it now, but it'd come in handy later. Stern had joined us and as I returned the lamp to him the station brightened and sharp, fresh heat washed over us. We all ducked, but the flare-up was short, as if maybe one of those portable cookers had exploded, adding to the conflagration. The smoke went crazy for a while, billowing down the curved walls in murky waves, swirling around us so that Muriel and I were left blinded and reeling around in its choking thickness.

Something caught hold of me and started pushing, and it took a moment for me to realize it was either the German or Cissie, both of them protected from the worst of the smoke by their gas masks. Bent double and half-suffocated, I allowed myself to be led. We staggered into the tunnel, using the rails at our feet as guides, the hand at my elbow firm, supporting, keeping me upright when I stumbled, dragging me onwards when a coughing fit threatened collapse. From the strength of the grip I guessed it was the German holding on to me and would've shrugged him off if I hadn't been too busy retching.

Then the smoke thinned out and I could see again. I rubbed my eyes and realized it was darker, much darker here, and cooler too. We were well inside the tunnel and up ahead it was so black we could have been on the slip road to Hades. It was damp too, as if water was seeping through the old, neglected brickwork, the dank, musty smell strong enough to compete with the drifting smoke and fumes from the station.

I leaned on my knees and coughed up the dust I'd swallowed, blinking my eyes to get rid of the sting, wishing I had a gallon of beer to soothe my raw throat.

'Are you ready to walk on?' The German had removed his mask once more and was squinting anxiously at the tunnel's arched entrance and the advancing flames beyond.

'Sure, I'm okay,' I said, running a sleeve across my mouth, no gratitude implied.

Cissie ceased tending her friend for a moment to say something. She, too, took off her mask when she realized we hadn't understood a word, and tried again.

'I said, where does this tunnel go to?'

'What the hell does it matter right now?' I replied. 'You think we should wait for the fire?'

The light was shining right on her and I watched her lips tighten, her eyes blaze.

'Who the –' she began.

'Cissie, he's right. We must keep going.' Muriel was still sagging slightly, one hand on Cissie's shoulder for support. She held a tiny handkerchief, not much bigger than a Wills cigarette card, to her mouth, and she was still shaking, little cough-spasms hunching her shoulders.

Cissie clamped her jaw tight, but the annoyance was still there in her eyes. When she spoke again, she barely parted her teeth. 'All right. But, mister, you and me are falling out fast.'

I couldn't help it, it wasn't the time, but I grinned back at her. She looked good and mad, her face all sooted up, big hazel eyes glaring, but I saw now she was young, maybe twenty, twenty-one, and at that moment she had the angry-stern look of a mother whose kid was gonna get one hell of a beating when she got him home. I guess my grin got her more riled, because she stomped off into the shadows ahead without waiting for any of us.

Muriel threw me a reproving look and set off after her. The German followed without comment, lamp in one hand, mask in the other.

My shrug was for my own benefit – there was no one else around – and I limped after them, shining the dismal light into the darkness ahead to help them find their way. I was soon in the lead again, warning the others of the 'obstacles' laid between and across the tracks whenever I came upon them. The atmosphere this far along wasn't healthy, but it was breathable, and I assumed some of the smoke was escaping through airshafts that we couldn't see. The ground began to dip and it wasn't long before we were treading through puddles, and then what felt like a shallow, stagnant pool, the water filthy black and oily in the light from the flashlight. A lot of these tunnels had been flooded during last year's awful winter and I guess we were lucky most of the water had drained away from this one. In the distance behind us we could hear the muted *rumple* of the fire, but when I looked back I could only see a dull, reddish tinge to the darkness, a soft kind of hue that pulsated almost benignly; somewhere along the way we had rounded a slight curve in the tunnel.

Abruptly, the flashlight dimmed even more, revived, then settled at a weaker level than before. The batteries were fading fast. I brought my little troop to a halt.

'Let's take a look at that lamp,' I said to the German.

'By all means.' Stern came forward and passed me the square-shaped oil lamp. 'And perhaps you will now tell us where this tunnel leads to and how long our journey will be.'

His English was almost perfect, but the *will* sounded like *vill* and the *where* like *vare* – he spoke like Conrad Veidt in one of those Nazi spy propaganda movies – and it steamed me up plenty. I held tight though, biding my time.

Lifting one of the glass windows at the side of the lamp I shone the light directly at the wick inside. It looked okay, enough there to burn. As I passed the flashlight over to Stern and searched for my Zippo with my free hand, I told them about the tunnel and where it would take us.

'And how do you know these people who chased us will not be waiting there for us to emerge?'

Vaiting there. My jaw muscles clenched.

Cissie surprised me by speaking up. 'They wouldn't know which tunnel we took. Plenty of Tube lines run through Holborn – we could come up anywhere.'

'She's right.' I found the lighter and flicked it on. 'Besides, they probably think they got us with the fire.' I held the small flame up to see their faces. Muriel looked about ready to fold.

'But how long is this tunnel?' she said in a quiet voice. 'I don't know if . . .'

'You'll make it. It's the shortest route we could've taken.'

'For a Yank you seem to know your way around.' There was still some resentment in Cissie's voice, as well as some breathlessness.

'I had a good guide once. Someone who was proud of her city.'

Silence then from the girls; I guess they'd caught something in my tone. But the German was becoming agitated.

'Then, as you say, we must keep moving. This place is not good.'

I ignored him, tilting the lamp and touching the lighter flame to the wick. Before it had the chance to ignite, faint sounds came to us, too distant to make out what they were. The sounds were growing louder though.

We all looked in the direction of the fire.

I'd heard this kind of noise in the past, but couldn't remember where or when. The volume was turning up, as if the source was drawing closer. A hand closed around my arm and I found Muriel beside me, body tensed rigid, the whites of her eyes shining dully in the gloom. Then it came to me, where I'd heard such a racket before.

Although there were fewer animals kept in the London Zoo during the Blitz years of the war, the more dangerous kind even being put down in case they escaped while an air raid was in progress, Sally had taken me there more than once when I was on leave, enjoying the sight of some of those exotic creatures more than I did, I think. One time we'd wandered into an aviary and something had set the birds off – a low-flying aircraft, as I recall. The explosion of noise was incredible, all those different species of bird splitting the air with their gabble – a bedlam medley of panic, anger, fright, and maybe just plain comfort calls to their partners, who knows? We'd clamped our hands over our ears, but the hullabaloo had still come through, so we ran out of there laughing – we laughed at a lot of things in those days – leaving the birds to their riot. Even from a distance we could hear them, kicking up hell, screeching their tiny lungs out.

And that was the kind of sound I was hearing now. Not the same, because birds didn't live in underground passages, never did, never would. No, these sounds were similar, but different. Someone ran an ice cube up my spine.

Muriel pressed against me and I felt her draw in a sharp breath. Cissie moved closer to the both of us.

Squealing, that's what it was. Not birds' chittering. Squealing. Like high-pitched screams. Hundreds, maybe thousands, of them.

The light down the tunnel grew brighter. Fluttered, kind of. And then the first few appeared.

Small fireballs coming our way. Little units of run-amok blazes. Lighting the darkness as they came.

4

'WHAT ARE THEY?'

Muriel's hold on me was painful, but I ignored it.

'Move back!' I yelled, following my own advice and dragging the girl with me. It was hard to take our eyes off the fiery horde – there was something mesmeric about these miniature infernos, some of them rising up the walls and falling back when they got so far, others spinning in the air to land on the tracks where they burned like tiny beacons, but most streaking towards us as if launched from some ancient war machine – and soon we were tripping over the human remains hidden in the darkness. That's when we wised up and ran like hell, with Cissie and the German in the lead. An anxious backward glance told me it was a race we could never win – the fireballs were nearly on us. I'd thought we could outrun 'em, that they'd be consumed by the fires that rode their backs long before they could catch up with us, but I was wrong, they kept coming and we kept running.

Dirty water splashed at our feet as high-pitched squeals mocked our flight. In the unsteady and almost useless light of the flashlight carried by the German I could see shadows here and there along the tunnel walls; it didn't take long for me to figure out they were safety recesses used by Underground workers to slip into whenever a train went by. Stern had noticed them too; he suddenly stopped and threw himself into one.

It would have left us almost blind if the other lights hadn't closed in on us. I reached forward for Cissie, caught hold, and pushed both her and Muriel into the nearest opening, crowding in with them and pressing them against the back wall. I could feel them trembling, and Christ, I was shaking some myself.

The little burning creatures sped by, screeching their agony, the water they rushed through too shallow to douse the flames on their backs. Some of them rolled over so that steam and smoke hissed from their hides; they squirmed in front of us, shrieks echoing around the brick walls, until their roasted bodies gave up and lay still, the occasional twitch nothing more than their final death-throes. Muriel turned away and Cissie buried her head into my shoulder when they both realized what these creatures were.

But I took pleasure in watching the rats burn. I may have even smiled there in the flickering shadows as their fire-ravaged bodies writhed and their thin screams tore through the darkness, and their sharp, ugly snouts stretched and their jaws yawed, exposing razor teeth, and their clawed limbs quivered until they crisped and flamed and became twisted, blackened stumps. Yeah, I'm sure I smiled, and I remembered too, remembered what these surviving scavengers had done, what they'd fed on all these years . . .

Some died in front of us, others scurried onwards, still aflame, dying as they ran, lighting the tunnel ahead as if showing us the way. I kicked out at one that came too close, sending it toppling backwards, flames turned to smoke by the black water, but extinguished too late to save it. The rat spasmed, twitched, and I wanted to blast it with the Colt – I wanted to blast all of them – not out of mercy but out of revulsion, loathing, hating the creature in the way I hated

63

the German, both of them species of the same kind, vermin who'd lost the right to walk this earth.

But I held still, closing down my emotions. It wasn't easy – it never had been – but I coped.

Pretty soon the rats' death-wails became fainter, faded altogether, and their thrashing lessened, finally stopped. Their bodies lay scattered along the tracks, small funeral pyres that slowly dimmed, burning themselves out until only a few feeble blazes sputtered there in the dusk. We could still hear the distant sounds of those which had fled further into the tunnel, but eventually only the stink remained. Hell, the air down here was foul enough, all ventilation systems long since quit and no trains left to push out the staleness as they passed through; now, with drifting smoke and the stench of cooked meat, the atmosphere was almost unbreathable.

I felt Muriel sobbing behind me, the sounds suppressed but the body jerks uncontrolled, and the other one, Cissie, lifted her head from my shoulder and leaned back against the side of the alcove.

'It's all right, Mu,' she said, rubbing her friend's back with a comforting hand. 'We're safe now, it's all over.'

There was no point in persuading her otherwise.

The German stepped back into view, the flashlight in his hand not much more than an orange orb, its beam barely penetrating the darkness. I heard him coughing and watched as the dull ball of light danced in the air.

Joining him on the track I fumbled for the Zippo, found it and crouched, balancing the lamp on a rail as I did so. I lifted the lamp's glass side and flicked on the lighter.

'We cannot linger here,' the German said between coughs. 'We shall be overcome if we do not find a way out soon.'

'There's only one way, and that's straight ahead,' I answered, putting flame to wick. It didn't catch at first, so I held the lighter there, concentrating hard, as if serious contemplation would encourage the waxed cord to kindle. Eventually the flame took and the light grew bright. I grunted, glad that *something* was going my way; it'd been an untidy day so far.

The sound of Muriel's weeping distracted me and I held the lamp towards the nook where the two women still sheltered. Cissie was holding her weeping friend in her arms, patting her back soothingly and murmuring comforts.

'Please tell them there is no time for this.'

The German obviously believed they would take more notice of an ally than a foe. Probably – I wanted to think so – he was right.

'Listen,' I said, calmly as I could, 'we gotta go. The fire might not reach us here, but smoke's gonna draw through the tunnel like a chimney, despite any unblocked airshafts along the way. It's not far to the next station – twenny minutes' walk at most, I figure, maybe less – so let's get going and save the bawling for later.'

I hadn't meant that last remark to sound harsh – really – but I guess it came out that way. Cissie fixed me with a stony look.

'Can't you see she's had enough?' she said to me and I nodded in agreement.

'Lady, the whole goddamn world's had enough, but still it goes on. Now you can decide for yourselves – stay here and choke to death, or follow me. 'S up to you.'

I turned away and stepped over a smouldering rodent in the water at my feet, passing by the German, who stood there, stiff-faced and hard as rock. I soon heard his footsteps splashing after me.

'You bastards.'

It was coldly said, no anger and scarcely a trace of resentment in Cissie's voice. Just a statement of fact, I suppose you'd say, and not far wrong at that.

I kept going, holding the lamp high, eyes fixed on the way ahead, or at least as far as I could see. There were still small

65

flames moving away from us in the distance, some of those vermin refusing to lay down and die, and I couldn't help wondering how many of these creatures had survived the Blood Death, living on to enjoy the easy pickings of the aftermath. The medics and scientists had known the blood groupings of animals were not the same as humans, yet still the death rate was comparable to that of mankind's; some research on our differences might have helped, but there'd been no time, no time at all.

I snapped back into the here and now when I heard the two women plodding through the water behind us. To my relief the sobs had stopped and Cissie was keeping her opinions of me and the *Kraut* to herself. The flashlight finally gave up the ghost, its light fading to nothing, and Stern tossed it away with a muttered comment that was probably a curse in German. The clatter the metal flashlight made as it bounced off the wall caused us all to jump and although the thought of shooting him there and then was appealing, I kept the Colt tucked inside the jacket holster and waded onwards.

Pretty soon the water level had dropped away and only separate puddles spread before us, but the atmosphere itself had become even more foul. Smoke had been with us all the way but in the main had stayed close to the roof; now it was curling downwards, even coming back at us as if something was blocking the tunnel up ahead. It became harder to breathe and I told Stern to give his gas mask to Muriel, advising Cissie to put hers on too.

'I lost it back there,' she informed me stiffly as though really it was none of my business. 'I don't think they help very much anyway,' she added, just to let me know she felt no remorse.

Well, they were pretty handy when we were in the station, I thought, but I wasn't going to argue. I didn't have the energy.

Stern waited for Muriel to catch up, then handed her his

mask. 'If the smoke becomes too much . . .' he said, and she nodded gratefully.

I looked to the front again and had gone no more'n a couple of yards before I saw what was blocking the tunnel. Some of the smoke was rising over the top of the train, more seeping around its sides; but a lot of it was coming straight back at us.

Waving a hand in front of me in a vain attempt to clear the way a little, I told the others about the blockage. It took a few seconds to reach the train and I stood on tiptoe to peer up into its closet-sized cab, debating whether or not to climb inside and use the carriages themselves to travel through the next part of the tunnel. The others gathered behind me and I went round to the side, holding the lamp high enough for me to see into the windows.

Nothing should have shocked me by now – three years of living among sights that were the stuff of nightmares should have conditioned me – but the skull-head that returned my stare, with its black hollow eyes and gaping grin, made me jump back in fright. Stupidly, I'd expected the train to be empty. Of course passengers had been travelling on the Underground network all over the city when the disease had struck, the Blood Death drifting down into the tunnels, seeking out its victims like some predator roaming the burrows of the earth, and the Dead Man's Handle had jammed on as soon as the train driver had slumped over, cutting the circuit so that the carriages had come to a halt, to remain locked there in the darkness as one by one their occupants keeled over. How many had escaped? I wondered. How many of the ABnegs – if there'd been any on board – had managed to crawl out into the tunnels and make their way back to the surface, only to wish they'd died with their fellow travellers below?

The skull resting against the window still wore a driver's cap, its peak tilted by the glass to a rakish angle so that, with its unrestricted grin, the skeleton appeared to have kept its sense of humour. I didn't get the joke though, and was ready to unravel as I went back to the others. I was about to tell 'em to keep their eyes low when they passed by the carriages, but I never got the chance.

The flash that swept through the tunnel was like sheet lightning, its glare bleaching everything white before blinding us with its brilliance, the thunderclap that followed a split second later shaking the walls and deafening us all. Searing air blasted around us, but we were protected by the carriages we cowered behind, only our legs feeling a deflected part of the heat. The world may have become silent to us as we fell to our knees, but it continued to spasm and shake, causing us to sprawl between the tracks, bodies stretched, hands over our heads.

I'm not sure if I felt or sensed the train lurch, but an instinct sent me scrabbling forward onto the girls, using my weight to hold them still until the wheels shuddered to a stop. As I blinked to clear my dazzled eyes, I became aware that the air was suddenly cleansed, the smoke and filth pushed back by the blast; but even as I rubbed at my eyes and my hearing began to return, grime and dust, along with brickwork, started to fall from the ceiling and walls. Head still reeling, senses floating, I guessed what had caused the explosion further down the Tube line, but now was not the time to mull it over – although we'd been shielded from the full force of the blast, we were now in a worse predicament than before. And unfortunately our chances of survival were getting slimmer by the second.

I staggered to my feet, grabbing the fallen but still-burning lamp as I rose, then swung round to squint into the flickering shadows behind us. The shadowy figure of the German was leaning against the train, his head jerking from left to right as if he were trying to shake some sense back into it; and beyond him the train itself was burning, the flames further along the carriages contained by the walls and ceiling of the tunnel, but spreading fast towards us. Stern was swiftly lost from sight as great clouds of smoke swept between us.

The very air felt scorched, dried out, and suddenly it was hard to draw breath.

'Back!' I managed to squawk, but I doubt any of the others heard me.

I pushed the girls, herding them away from this new threat, and Stern wasn't slow in figuring it out for himself. He was soon alongside us as we staggered through the smoke and falling dirt. He held Muriel's arm while I hung on to Cissie, and as a tight group we stumbled back along the track, not thinking ahead, fear and heat forcing the retreat, the thick, choking smoke swilling around us, increasing our panic, until it was exhaustion, not common sense, that slowed us after a hundred yards or so. Muriel dropped to her knees first and Cissie followed her down.

Stern attempted to drag Muriel up again, but she was bent double, gagging on fumes, her body a dead weight.

I crouched close to Cissie. 'Come on, we'll choke to death if we stay here.' Even to me my voice sounded faint after the explosion, kind of trapped inside my own head, but I think she heard me. She tried to tug herself free.

Her voice was distant too, but I caught what she was saying. 'Where can we go?' she asked. 'We're between two fires, you bloody fool, and it's your fault. You made us come down here.'

She had a point. But hell, what other choice had there been?

I looked around, up the tunnel, down the tunnel, and wasn't encouraged. Out of the fire and into the inferno, I told myself. Some days were like that.

The German, his back against the wall, was coughing so violently I thought his gut might burst, and Muriel's arched figure was heaving, her throat rasping as she fought to draw in poisoned air. Back there the whole tunnel was alight, clouds of rolling smoke softening the blaze, and in the other direction, towards the station, even more smoke tumbled towards us, a thick, curling torrent of it, so dense it looked solid.

I hauled myself up, but my legs barely supported me. My energy was sapped and my head was dizzy from lack of pure oxygen. A veil seemed to be drawing over my mind, and it wasn't unpleasant; no, it seemed like an escape, a retreat from the horror all around us in this black stormy hell. I fought it though, because fighting against things that were not right, legal and fair was in my nature, always had been. That was why I'd gotten into the stinking rotten war before most of my compatriots in the first place. Sure, I was a fighter – life, and death, had made me that way – but this looked like the final battle.

I raged against it, even lifted a weary fist in defiance, but I knew I'd lost. There were no options. Like the girl said, I'd led them into a trap of my own making, and the price of that foolishness was death. We were gonna die alongside the scorched vermin.

And as the black smoke closed in and that flimsy veil floating across my mind thickened, something happened that sent a last reserve of adrenaline rushing through me.

5

EVEN THROUGH THE SMOKY mists this new light was bright enough to dazzle. It seemed to come straight from the tunnel wall itself, only a few yards away, and it swept over us, taking us all in, its beam defined by the smoke. The speaker was invisible behind the glare, but his voice was clear enough.

'You're a sorry sight, the lot of yer.' The voice was low, gruff, a little peppery, as if the guy wasn't excessively pleased to find us. 'You'd better get yourselves inside,' it went on in that growly way, 'unless you want to choke to death. Come on, in 'ere, ladies first.'

The German was on his feet, but the two girls remained sprawled across the tracks, heads raised and looking towards the light. I figured we were being offered sound advice so I dragged Cissie up by her armpits, croaking out to Stern to help Muriel at the same time. Every muscle in my body ached and my shoulder stung from the nick it had taken earlier, but I managed to haul Cissie over to the light source, the lamp I'd been using left by the tracks. We must have looked quite a sight, covered in filth, clothes a mess, faces blackened and tear-stained, all of us coughing so much smoke we could hardly speak. Blasts of heat swept over us in waves and we could hear the sound of popping glass as the train's windows fractured. There were other noises too

71

– the roof over the train falling in, old brickwork crumbling with the heat, and a deep rumbling, like an earthquake, going on way below our feet. Between coughing fits, the girls were crying out, floating ash and smoke creating a storm around us, and I swallowed hard before lending my own voice to the racket by shouting at the man behind the light to quit blinding us.

When we didn't seem to be getting any closer I realized the light was pulling away, its spread becoming confined and outlining a doorway in the tunnel wall. I realized the door must have been in shadow when we passed it before and we'd been too busy running from those fireballs to notice. Possibly it'd been locked from the inside anyway, so it would have been useless even if we had spotted it. None of that mattered now though: the door was open and this surly guardian angel was inviting us in.

The light retreated along a bare-bricked corridor and we tumbled after it, collapsing inside the doorway in a tangle of bodies, too exhausted and overwhelmed by our escape to move another inch. As we lay there gasping air like decked flounders I felt something, *someone*, shuffling around us, back towards the entrance. I caught a glimpse of baggy, dark-coloured overalls before the iron door clanged shut behind us.

Although there was still a faint rumbling somewhere off in the distance and a weak vibration running through my hands and knees from the concrete floor, it suddenly became quiet, peaceful, as though the mayhem had been left far behind. I could barely move, and thinking was too much effort; I just wanted to lay there and convalesce. The others were coughing up smoke, their breathing scratchy and difficult, and I wasn't much better off: my throat was raw and my thoughts were disassembled. It took a great effort of will to roll over from my knees and press my back against the wall so that I could look around.

The corridor was long and narrow, and at the end of it was a stone flight of stairs leading upwards. A softer light than the one carried by our guardian angel came from a paraffin lamp set on the second step, and when the flashlight switched off I turned my attention towards the door and the man standing before it.

I guessed him to be in his late fifties, maybe sixty even, a stocky little guy wearing dark blue overalls and a flat, white tin helmet with a large black *W* painted on it. It was the uniform of an Air Raid Precautions – ARP – warden, and I wondered why nobody had bothered to tell him the war had ended three years ago, back in '45. His face was kind of flabby and hard at the same time, a working-man's, used to fresh air and tough labour, a network of purple veins colouring his jowly cheeks; bushy eyebrows, stubby nose and small, gimlet eyes completed the picture. He looked us over and didn't appear happy with what he saw. He gave a disapproving shake of his head.

'All right, you lot,' he said, 'on yer feet. I don't know what you've gone and bloody well done, but even this place ain't safe any more.'

As if to reinforce the message, a muffled explosion came from somewhere close by.

'Oh, good Gawd,' he said, more to himself than us. He stepped over our legs, making his way towards the concrete stairs, but pausing when he reached me. He bent closer, squinting his eyes, then nodded as if confirming something he already knew.

'Always reckoned you'd be trouble one day,' he murmured before moving on to the steps. He scooped up the lamp and turned in our direction again. 'Listen, I can see you're all done in, but you can't stay 'ere. You're still in danger, see? Somethin you set off in the tunnel has ruptured gas mains that feed into this bunker, an' that's caused fires that're spreadin right through the place. We're safe where we are for the minute, but that won't be for much longer. So unless we get movin right now, we'll be stuck. Understand? Get me? Stuck.'

He was talking to us as if we were sapheads, but I guess we were all wearing dumb expressions, relief and exhaustion taking its toll. I was still wondering why I'd been given the double-take. The little guy was getting impatient. 'When somethin blows under the streets, it can cause an upset somewheres else. Then that starts a nuisance in another place, a fire or explosion or somethin. Chain reaction, y'see. Build-up of gas, pipe gas or sewer gas, all bleedin lethal. It's a wonder the whole city's not in ruins by now.'

'It was a gas pocket in the tunnel.' The words hurt my throat.

'What's's'at?' His beady eyes set on mine again.

'Burning rats ran past us in the tunnel. I think they reached some trapped gas further along the line.'

He sniffed and brought out a grubby spotted red handkerchief from his overalls pocket to mop his face and plump neck. 'Yeah, that was probably it, not that it bleedin matters right now.' He nodded his head a couple of times, considering me. 'So you are a Yank then? Thought you was from the Yank flying jacket you always wear.'

'You know me?' My brain was beginning to function again.

'I've seen you about, son. And this mornin I saw yer bein chased by them Blackshirts, you and these others 'ere. Yer didn't see me though, none of yers did, I made sure of that. I watched you duck into the Tube station and reckoned on where yer'd be headin if yer got the chance.'

I struggled to my feet and gaped at him, one elbow resting against the wall, every muscle in my body stiff. The German and the two girls were beginning to stir themselves, but I wasn't sure if they'd been following the conversation.

'How did you know which tunnel to find us in?' I asked the warden, curiosity overriding the tiredness.

'Like I says, I thought I knew where yer was headed. It

74

was a chance, but yer struck lucky, son. Now then, yer got the strength to help your friends?'

I barely had the strength to stand upright, but I nodded anyway.

'Right, follow me.' He began climbing the stairs, boots noisy on the concrete.

'Who is he?' Cissie asked in a hushed voice as she used my arm to drag herself up.

'No idea,' I replied, giving her some help. 'But I could kiss his little fat head.'

The German helped Muriel to her feet and she caught my anxious look.

'I'll be okay,' she said quickly, her voice strained. 'Once I get into better air I'll be fine.'

'You lot comin?'

We could only see the glow of the lamp shining down the stairs, the corridor we were in now darkened, full of our own shadows, and without another word we set off after the warden, the girls behind me, Stern following at the rear. The old guy was waiting for us by another door at the top of the stairs, this one also made of iron.

'What is this place?' I asked when I reached him.

'Civil Defence shelter. There's a whole complex of plannin rooms on the other side of this door, all underground, too deep for any bombs to reach. They never counted on the poison though, never thought anythin could touch 'em down 'ere. All very hush-hush and all bloody useless.'

'If it was so secret how did you find it?'

'It was on my beat, son. As a warden it was my job to make sure none of the street entrances was blocked.'

He peered over my shoulder to make sure we were all together, then twisted the handle and pushed open the door. It was heavy, judging by the effort he put into it.

I touched his arm, moving closer. 'You said you knew where I was making for. I'd like to know how.'

My hand stayed on his arm and he looked down at it, then

up at me. 'I know where your base is, so it stood to reason you'd use the Tube line going back to the Aldwych, which is near the hotel you've been usin. I've watched yer goin in and out of the place plenny a' times. Sometimes yer disappear for a while, but yer always come back to it. Yer like yer bit of luxury, don't yer?' He even gave a little chortle.

'You've watched me?'

Any humour vanished from his broad, ruddy face. 'Yeah, I've watched yer, son. And I know what yer do.' He turned away, but not before I'd caught the unease in his eyes.

'Hoke?' Cissie was pressing against me, her breathing shaky, coming in gasps. 'What are you two –?'

'Forget it. Let's just concentrate on getting outta here.' I took her hand and surprisingly – I thought she was still mad at me – she allowed me to guide her.

Once through the door we found ourselves inside another corridor, this one wider though, with openings along each side. Water covered its concrete floor and at the far end a carbide lamp burned, its white glare harsher than the warden's paraffin lamp but more effective. On the wall outside one of the open doorways was a yellowing poster, an upper corner drooping over, and as I passed by I saw there were two pictures of Adolf Hitler on it, front and profile, WANTED writ large at the top, smaller headline type explaining why. FOR MURDER . . . it said. FOR KIDNAPPING . . . FOR THEFT AND ARSON. It should've added FOR WORLD GENOCIDE. Our breeze caused the opposite corner to curl over so that the paper folded and the mad *Führer* was out of sight. The floor shook beneath our feet and Cissie's grip tightened in mine.

I took a peek through a doorway and saw a plain square room inside, pipes running round the walls close to the ceiling. One of the smaller pipes was leaking in a couple of places, thin jets of water arcing onto the bare floor. The only furniture was an iron table with four straight-backed chairs around it; a black telephone sat on the tabletop. It was a relief to see there were no human remains in there.

Other rooms were similar but with more furniture; two or three tables, green filing cabinets and cupboards. The pipes ran through every room, and there were more leaks, some pretty bad. There was another stairway at the end of the corridor, broader than the last and turning back on itself as it rose to the next levels. We used its iron handrail to drag ourselves upwards, the warden urging us on and getting mighty agitated with the ladies for holding us back. We'd just reached the next level when an explosion beyond a set of doors to our left shook the walls.

The warden clung to the stair rail until the world had settled down a little. 'It's the gas cylinders!' he shouted at me accusingly, as if it were my fault, I'd arranged the whole thing. 'They're kept 'ere for emergency power and now your bloody fire's got to them!'

My bloody fire? Yeah, sure. But you had to wonder what kind of genius built an underground bunker vulnerable to explosions *beneath* the city streets. We were both distracted by smoke curling through the gap beneath the heavy double doors.

'Which way do we go?' I asked as Cissie sank down next to me. Muriel stood with her back resting against the wall, the German supporting her, his impatience to get moving plain in his quick-shifting eyes.

'Upwards!' the warden shouted back at me. 'There's sleepin quarters and plannin rooms on the next floor, and we can get out through there.'

'Doesn't this stairway lead to the street?'

'It does, yeah, but the buildin over the exit collapsed and blocked it a long while ago. Thank Gawd there're others.'

'No point in hanging 'round then, right?' I kept my voice calm – shouting would have only hurt my throat even more anyway.

'You're not wrong there, son.' He'd calmed down a little himself, but he still looked scared. Letting go of the rail he bustled round to the next flight of stairs.

'*Hey,*' I called after him, the stab to my throat making me wince. 'What's your name?' I finished more quietly.

'Potter. Albert Potter, ARP warden for the Kingsway and Strand area.' He seemed proud of the title and I almost expected a smart salute. He started climbing again, but I just caught his added remark. 'Can't say I'm pleased t'meet you at last.'

My limp was getting worse as I followed him, but I knew I'd only bruised the ankle – anything more severe and I wouldn't have been walking at all by this time. But tiredness was slowing us all down, I guess only our last reserves of adrenaline keeping us going. I'd learned a lot about that during the war, because flying a Hurricane at more than 300 miles an hour with a couple of superior Me 109s on your tail, it's the old energy-juice that takes over, overrides the fatigue that comes with too many sorties and not enough sleep, keeps your brain razor-sharp, until maybe a Spitfire can get to you and cover your back. Even if you got shot up, it was the adrenaline pumping that got you through the shock, helped you function until you'd baled out. Yeah, I'd learned a lot about what adrenaline could do for you in times of crisis, and I also knew that eventually it dried up, it could only take you so far . . .

The German surprised me by drawing level and taking me by the elbow. 'Do you need help?' he asked. His face was black with dirt – hell, all our faces were black. 'Cept the warden's – his was just getting redder by the second.

I paused just long enough to pull my arm away. 'Take care of the girl,' I told him, my voice low and full of warning. I climbed on, leaving him there, but he was close to me again, this time with an arm around Muriel's waist, her own arm over his shoulder. I let them go on past and then it was Cissie who was by my side.

'You're slowing down, Yank.'

'It's been a busy morning,' I managed.

Her teeth flashed through the dirt, and I appreciated the smile.

'If you need a shoulder to lean on . . .'

'You're not sore at me any more?'

'Anyone can make a mistake. Besides, if those Blackshirts are as nasty as you say –'

'You had a taste of 'em.'

'Trying to roast us alive wasn't very civilized. As for wanting our blood, well, we only have your word for that. I mean, for all we know you could be a criminal of some kind and they could be the only law and order left.'

'You got a point. When you see 'em next, march right up and introduce yourself. Tell 'em about your blood type. They'll be pleased to get acquainted, wait and see.'

She gave me a long look, then grinned again. 'I'll take my chances with you – for the moment. Not that I have any other choice.'

The banter might have continued – we were both dog-weary and this was a way of keeping each other going – but the next explosion that ripped through the underground bunker was the fiercest yet.

Although the blast was somewhere deep within the complex, the walls around us shuddered violently and debris began to fall through the stairwell from above. Brickwork caught the rail and shattered, throwing out pieces like shrapnel. Cissie yelped as she was struck on the forehead and she fell back against the wall. I grabbed her when she staggered down a step, and pinned her there while rubble and dust rained down.

'It's the ceiling at the top!' I heard Potter shout back at us. 'The whole lot's gonna break loose in a minute!'

With Stern and Muriel just ahead of us, we clambered up to the next landing, spitting dust and blinking grit from our eyes.

'This way – quick!' The warden was holding one side of a double door open and we scooted through, the deluge behind us increasing, becoming a cascade of bricks, masonry, timber and powder. Once inside the door we could barely see, even though there was another carbide lamp on the floor – the warden must have placed these lamps in strategic places along our escape route – because it was like running into one of those famous London fogs the guide-books told you about, 'peasoupers' I think they called them in those days. The fog was smoke, and it swirled everywhere, thicker in some parts than others.

Potter hurried past us, his tin helmet knocked askew, and we followed after him like lost souls, afraid of losing sight of his broad back. Luckily, the smoke soon thinned out and we were able to see our way more clearly, although every so often we had to wipe our blurred eyes with sleeves or knuckles. We found ourselves in a huge open room filled with desks and large tables with street maps set on them, the maps marking out various divisions of the city and outlying areas. There were more maps around the walls, coloured pins indicating what could only have been other Civil Defence centres and contact points; metal lightshades, disturbed by the eruptions, swung low over the desks and map tables. As well as a phalanx of telephones, still in neat formation along the desktops, I glimpsed a whole battery of radio transmitters against a side wall. Only one thing was missing, but now wasn't the time to ask the warden.

We reached another set of doors on the far side of the room and beyond them was a broad hallway. But even as we staggered through, yet another blast rocked the floor, sending us stumbling forward. On my knees, I watched great cracks snake across the long expanse of concrete before us.

I had no idea what had gone up on the floor below this one – more ruptured gas pipes, drums of fuel stored there for emergencies, chemicals, who the hell could guess what was stored away in places like this? – but I realized this whole complex was now on self-destruct. Potter had been right about chain reactions. German bombs had inflicted the initial damage, but the demolition had continued long after the war had ended, a fault causing a fire in one building, which spread to the next, one explosion kicking off another, then another, a collapsing building bringing down its neighbour, that one in turn wrecking or weakening the building next to it. And so it went on, with no one left to contain the damage, or repair the faults. Like the man said, it was a wonder the whole city wasn't in ruins by now.

I had a nasty feeling about that floor ahead of us, and I guess that was what made me hesitate while the others picked themselves up and sped on. I saw a whole section shift, kind of tilt, and I knew what was going to happen next. So I moved, I moved so goddamn fast I could have been shot from a cannon. But it wasn't fast enough.

Even as I gained on the others, who by now were almost at the far door, I felt the ground beneath me start to give. For a second or two it was almost like racing downhill as the floor inclined, and I picked up speed, despite the limp. It was a curious sensation, the world falling away from me in slow motion, and I think I may have screamed or yelled or whined to showcase my terror as I began to slide. Then came a massive and sudden lurch and the section of floor I was on dropped away from me.

Instinct rather than calculation made me throw myself to one side, towards the nearest wall and the sturdy old iron radiator fixed to it. My hand caught the valve pipe at its base and my fingers wrapped around it. The pipe loosened in the wall, jerking out at least an inch, and for a moment I thought the whole thing was gonna dislodge itself; but it held and I hung there as the broad section of floor crashed down to the level below, sending up a huge cloud of smoke and dust and a sound like thunder.

Flames and sparks followed, licking at my heels as I dragged myself up, and someone far off was screaming. My hand curled over the top of the radiator, but I could feel my strength slipping away, the effort of holding myself there becoming too great. I groaned, too feeble to pull myself towards the jagged ledge where the others waited, their hands stretched towards me, their voices raised over the crackle and fire rending noises.

I took a look down and didn't like what I saw: if the fall didn't kill me, the fire below would. Already I could feel the soles of my boots heating up and I guess the thought of a nasty death, one way or the other, encouraged a last burst of energy. I slid my left hand across the curved top of the radiator, taking the strain with my right. But when I tried to grip with my left hand again, the sweat on my palm caused it to slip, slowly at first, until it fell away completely, leaving me hanging there by one hand, my body swinging round helplessly.

Then Stern was peering down at me, his face only a couple of feet away, smoke billowing around him so that for a moment his head seemed disembodied, floating in space. I realized he was leaning forward from the ledge, one hand on the end of the radiator, the other reaching out for me. It was a dangerous move on his part, but I saw no fear in those colourless eyes of his. For a split second though, a moment gone by so fast I may have imagined it, I thought there was a shift in those eyes, a kind of cold mocking that vanished as soon as I'd noticed it. His hand stayed just beyond my reach, then edged forward an inch or so as if he'd only been tormenting me. Maybe I'd got it wrong, maybe I'd misread his expression; that look might have been his own fear, because now he was risking his life even more by leaning closer. I just couldn't be sure.

'Take it,' I heard him say over the roaring from below and the shouts from the others behind him. There were no hints in that gaze right then, only a blank – and equally as unnerving – coolness.

I hesitated. Would he let me go, pretend to the others I'd slipped from his grasp? There was no way of knowing and anyway, I didn't have time to consider. My hand slapped into his.

Then he was pulling me up, the movement strong and smooth, as though it was hardly any effort at all for him. I managed to hook a heel over the ledge, and then other hands were dragging me to safety. I rolled over onto what was left of the floor at that end of the hallway, my rescuers shuffling back to give me room, and I lay there on my back, drawing in great lungfuls of filthy, broiling air. They wouldn't let me rest though; I was pulled to my feet even as I choked on the smoke I'd sucked in, and the two girls stood on either side of me, steadying me until my head stopped reeling and some life returned to my arms and legs.

'Yank, you've got enough lives to keep a dozen cats happy.' Cissie was thumping my back, helping me get rid of some of that smoke.

'Are you all right?' Muriel's touch was more gentle as she cleared soot from my eyes with her fingertips.

The warden had no patience for any of this. 'Yer can make a fuss of him later, ladies. If we don't leave right now all our gooses'll be cooked, and I ain't kiddin yer.'

He ushered us towards the door and when I gave one last glance back at the pit they'd hauled me from, it was filled with fire, the flames touching the ceiling above. Potter hauled open the iron door and we piled through into a welcoming coolness. The door made a satisfying *clunk* when the old warden pulled it shut behind us, and because of its metal flanges everything suddenly became hushed. The girls collapsed on the narrow concrete stairs that disappeared into the darkness above and the German went down on one knee, his shoulders heaving as he gasped in the cold dank air. It gave me some satisfaction to see he was as pooped as the rest of us, even if he'd disguised it a few moments ago. I watched those deadpan eyes, eyes that had seemed to be looking inwards rather than out, and wondered why I felt no gratitude.

Leaning back against the rough brick wall, I slowly sank to a crouch, wrists over my knees, eyes closed, taking deep breaths to control the trembling that ran through me.

Potter interrupted the moment of peace. 'Sorry to disturb you folks, but we're not in the clear yet.'

He sounded angry, as if he still blamed us for the destruction of the Civil Defence shelter, and when I opened my eyes again I saw his mouth was set in a grim line across his round reddened face. Then I understood.

'You lived down here, didn't you?' I said.

'What?'

'I said, you lived in this shelter.'

''Course I bloody lived 'ere. Safest place in London with you and those Blackshirts runnin all over the place, shootin off guns at each other. I just got on with me job and kept well away from lunatics.'

His job? I let it go for the moment. 'Why did you rescue us today, then?' I said, keeping my voice mild, just making conversation.

He gawked down at me in surprise, as if I'd asked something dumb. 'You had those two ladies with you, didn't yer? I couldn't see them come to any 'arm. What kind of bloke d'yer think I am?'

I liked that about the British. I'd learned a lot about old-style manners and chivalry from the English pilots I'd flown with, and I can't say it'd come as too much of a surprise – I'd spent most of my life hearing stories about England and its people. Sure, much of it was romanticized, I knew that, but the person who taught me was someone you could believe in, someone who missed her home country but allowed nostalgia to colour her memories only a little. She was one of the reasons I'd come over at the beginning of the war, when England was crying out for trained pilots because the *Krauts* were kicking at the door. And if she'd still been alive at the time, she'd have been proud, proud as hell.

I didn't realize it, but I was smiling at the warden.

'Nothin funny about it, mister. Yer could've got these young ladies killed takin them down into the tunnels. The most precious things we've got left and you go riskin their lives.'

He was still riled, but his eyes had softened, become tear-blurred. I didn't know what he was talking about and my expression must have shown it.

It was the German who put me in the picture. 'Women are now the world's most precious commodity, my friend,' he said.

Vimmen and *vorld*. That just irritated me (and I noticed Potter giving him an odd, sideways look) but the 'my friend' bit really got me hopping. If I'd had the strength I would've been at his throat.

But it was Cissie who was really stomping. 'Oh, sure we are! Who else is going to give birth to more chumps like you two so they can grow up and start a whole new war just to finish off what's left of the human race?' She'd been sitting upright on the stairs, stiff as a board, and now she pushed herself to her feet. 'I don't want to stay here any longer. I want to see sunlight again.'

The warden hurried over to her, his face big and anxious. 'Don't you worry, miss, we'll get you out of here. Once we've climbed these stairs we'll be safe.' He stooped to help Muriel rise, but held on to her when she turned to climb. His other hand gripped Cissie's wrist. 'Look now, you ladies,' he said almost apologetically. 'You're not goin to like what we'll find up there, but try and close your minds to it. I had to put 'em somewhere, y'see, and I couldn't bury 'em all. 'Sides, there was others out there already, people who'd tried to get away from the poison. There's hardly any smell now, so that won't bother yer, and you can keep your eyes closed if yer like . . .'

'What are you talking about?' Muriel was shaking her head, too tired to understand.

I picked myself up and walked over to them, explaining as I went. 'He dumped the dead bodies from this place outside the back door. I wondered what was missing from inside the shelter.'

'I had to, you can understand that,' said Potter, appealing to me. 'I had to make this place fit enough to live in.'

'Listen, you did right,' I·reassured him. 'And nothing could be worse than what we found inside the Underground station.'

'At least there were no flies,' he said as if it made a difference. 'The bodies just rotted away, like. No maggots and not much stink after the first few weeks.'

Yeah, no flies and no maggots. In fact, hardly any insects at all. I suppose we had to at least be grateful for that small mercy. God knows what kind of diseases could've wiped out the rest of us in the aftermath.

Distant rumbling from beyond the iron door and dust drifting down from the stairway's slanted ceiling got us moving again. Potter went first, lighting the way, and Cissie and Muriel followed close behind. I guess both were eager for that sunlight. The German, who'd remained on one knee, stood erect, the motion almost fluid, as if his steam had already been restored. I let him go on ahead of me – enemy at my back, and all that – then got going myself. Something heavy slammed against the door behind us, but none of us bothered to look back.

Christ, it hurt to climb those stairs – every muscle in my body was now stiffening up – and I favoured my injured leg, using the rough wall to lean on. My shoulder didn't bother me that much but the rest of my arm felt like a lump of lead. Nothing was broken though, I was sure of that, so considering the punishment I'd taken that morning, I figured I'd gotten off lightly. If these strangers hadn't picked me up in the square when they did I'd've been not just dead, but *dried* meat, by now. And if the old guy, Albert Potter, hadn't rescued us from the burning tunnel, we'd all be cooked meat – yeah, choked, smoked and goddamn coked.

At the top of the stairs Potter was dipping into his overalls pocket, the others squeezed up behind him, so I waited further down, rubbing some life back into my arm. I heard a clink as he drew out a large metal ring, at least a dozen keys attached to it. The one he chose unlocked the door immediately and he pulled it inwards so that a gust of air rushed through. He disappeared outside and I wondered why it was still dark up there. I soon knew the answer.

The almost pitch-black place we stepped out into was bigger, much bigger, than the Tube tunnels further below, and huge, monolithic shapes loomed over us in the gloom. When the light from Potter's paraffin lamp fell on the nearest one, I realized those shapes were passenger vehicles, tramcars that ran on embedded iron tracks with electric cables overhead supplying the power, and the hangar-like place we'd escaped into was a large tunnel, a kind of under-passage beneath the city streets. It occurred to me as we stood there that those trams would be full of withered corpses.

There were hints of daylight coming from what must have been overhead airshafts along the tunnel's length and at the far end we could just make out a greyish hue that might have been the sloped entrance/exit. As our eyes grew accustomed to this new level of darkness we began to discern other forms lying in the roadway and across the sunken tracks, small black mounds, hundreds of them, and we were aware that they could only be the remnants of those who'd perished down here. Many, we assumed, were the remains of Civil Defence workers, laid there by Potter, himself.

Stern and the two girls lingered in the oasis of light, as if frozen there, afraid to move on. One of the girls – Muriel, I think, began to weep. What lay around us was no more horrific than anything we'd found inside the Underground station and tunnels – far less so, in fact – but the quietness of the place must have stirred something deep within them – sorrow, dread, an interweaving oppression of emotions – that held them there, shocked and grief-stricken. I guess the fact that they suddenly had time to reflect had a lot to do with their paralysis, but it was nothing new to me, nor to the old warden.

His gruff East End voice cut through the mood. 'It's as good a tomb as any,' he said, no pity, no remorse, in his tone, only a sepulchral hollowness caused by the high walls and ceiling lending any reverence to his words. 'I've said a prayer over 'em,' he went on, 'which is more than most of the world's dead ever got, I expect.'

'Let's just find our way out of here,' said Muriel quietly, and the calmness in her voice surprised me. In the dim light I could see the glistening of tears on her cheeks.

Cissie, on the other hand, had channelled her sadness into anger. 'Bloody well right! I can't breathe down here!' She looked towards the distant light and took a fierce step towards it, ready to march off in that direction. I caught her arm.

'No. It's too close to Holborn Station that way.' I'd figured it out, finally got my bearings. The incline had to be the northern approach to the under-passage and I remembered how near that was to the station. 'The Blackshirts could have left the entrance guarded, just in case we came out that way,' I explained quickly as Cissie tried to pull herself free.

'He is right,' Stern agreed. 'They will be waiting.'

Cissie ceased struggling and turned her head, looking in the other direction, towards a stifling blackness that seemed to go on forever. 'Wait a minute,' she said warily. 'You're not suggesting . . .'

'There's no choice,' I told her, not for the first time. And when I followed her gaze towards that eerie inkiness, I knew the day's nightmare wasn't over yet. Not by a long shot.

6

SO WE WALKED through that nightmare, keeping close together, a tight bunch, the lamplight defining the soft borders of our world, none of us caring to look beyond and none of us focusing on what lay within. The warden kept us to a narrow sidewalk and every now and again we had to step over rag bundles, clothes that had become shrouds. There were other doors set along the wall, but we weren't curious about them, not even a little bit – we'd got to the stage when all curiosity was numbed and we were only interested in getting to the end of that goddamn tram tunnel. If Potter knew what lay beyond those doors, he wasn't saying. As a matter of fact, he'd fallen into a sulky silence since we'd started off, his way of letting us know he wasn't happy about our continued association. To tell the truth, he'd wanted to leave us right there outside the bunker door, deciding he'd done enough for us already and that he would go in the opposite direction, towards the light, Blackshirts or no Blackshirts. He'd easily sneak past 'em, he assured us, but I wasn't willing to take that chance. As far as the goons were concerned, we were either dead or still trapped down there in the Underground, and I didn't want anybody persuading them otherwise. Potter might be gabby if he got caught and anyway, he was more useful leading us out of that place. The barrel of my Colt pressed against his plump belly won the day, and he figured it'd do no harm to stick with us a little longer.

We passed more trams with death cargoes and soon learned to avoid looking at the windows. It was weird though, because although we didn't look at them, each one of us felt those corpses behind the glass were watching *us*. We felt like intruders in some private purgatory, a kind of halfway stage where the dead passengers waited for the current to be switched back on so they could continue their journey towards oblivion. Okay, so maybe now and again our eyes strayed towards skeletal arms hanging over the sides of open-top trams or eyeless skulls leering out at us, but mostly we fixed our gaze on the warden's light, following the beacon like pilgrims following a cross.

We'd travelled some distance before we started to notice shadows moving along the opposite wall, a black shifting against black, and it was the German who brought us to a halt by raising his hand and pointing. Potter, in front, realized we had stopped and when he saw Stern indicating he raised the paraffin lamp, stretching his arm out. Tiny yellow lights shone back at us.

Muriel, close to me, whispered, 'What are they?' The reflected lights were quite still now and I guess she thought if she spoke too loudly she'd set them moving again.

I'd already realized what was out there, but it was Stern who gave them identity. 'Dogs,' he said quietly. 'I have witnessed' – *v*itnessed – 'such packs roaming the ruins of Berlin, scavenging for any morsels they can find in the bomb debris. Often they would turn on their own weakest, then devour it. I have' – *haf* – 'even seen them attack a lone child. If these animals are hungry we must be very careful.'

I stared at him for a moment before turning back to those strange yellow globes that glowed like twin moons in a black velvet sky. Neither they, nor we, moved.

Without warning us, Potter produced the flashlight he'd used before from his overalls pocket and aimed its beam across the broad roadway, bleaching the mangy pack with its powerful light. They remained motionless under the glare, the sorriest bunch of skin 'n' bone curs you'd ever see outside a Bowery soup kitchen. They skulked, shoulders hunched, heads bowed, their coats dry and matted, and returned our gaze, those eyes now mean, jaws open just enough to show us their ochre teeth.

There might have been others hidden out of sight in the shadows or behind a couple of nearby trams, but I counted seven in the light. The closest one began swaying its shabby old head to and fro, near to the ground, and a low keening came from its throat. The dog wasn't pleased to see us and, considering what mankind had done to the planet, I couldn't blame it. One of its pals took up the note, only this one didn't wave its head around; no, it wrinkled its snout and showed us some more of its discoloured teeth. Its keening descended to a growling and a thick stream of drool sank from its jaw onto the concrete floor. But it was the frothy liquid that bubbled between its teeth that bothered me more.

These animals were sick, and it wasn't from starvation. Sure, they were rangy, bones jutting like iron tools in canvas bags, but they'd been on a poor diet, eating the wrong things – and I didn't want my mind to linger on what. I could see the madness in each and every one of them, a catching thing that came from living in the new wilderness.

'Let's walk on,' I suggested to the others, keeping my voice calm and the gun aimed at the pack. 'Just slide away, smooth 'n' easy, no noise and no running. Let's not get 'em riled.'

We started to file away, one by one, Potter leading, me taking up the rear, half-turned so that the Colt was still levelled at the animals, a veil that was shadow coming down on them as the light drew away. But that first mutt crept back into the light, following it, crazy old faded eyes never leaving mine. Was it salivating because it was hungry? I wondered, or was that just madness drooling out? It gave a long growling moan and another dog joined it in the retreating light, this one all bristling fur and quivering ears. Then another came back into view, padding past the first two almost to the centre of the road. It sat on its haunches for a moment or two, sized me up, then trotted even closer. It looked as unhealthy as its companions, but was bolder, hardly scared of me at all. Only a couple of yards away, it began stalking me.

I caught more disturbances among the shadows as others sneaked forward. Maybe they wanted a better look. Maybe they were working up the courage to charge. More padded footsteps, still quiet but swifter now, and when I looked to my left I saw a dog descending the winding stairway of a tram just three or four feet away.

I was walking backwards now, gun arm extended, and Potter and the others had made some distance on me, so that I was barely within the wide circle of light, the dogs on the soft fringes. Every time I took a step back, so the lead dogs took a step forward.

I'd come upon packs like this before in my travels across the city, starving creatures made wild by circumstances, and more than once it had been Cagney who'd frightened them off, standing his ground and ready to take on the leader if not all of them. By comparison, he was pretty fit, you see, and a lot stronger than his half-starved city cousins, so a few ferocious barks and a couple of threatening lunges were enough to see them off, no matter how many were in the pack. I can't say he was braver than those other curs, because some of those wild things had guts born out of desperation; but he was kind of arrogant, like he was superior, you know? Not because he was with me, he had a human and they didn't; no, my guess was that he'd always been that way.

First time we laid eyes on each other was a year and several months after the first V2s landed. I'd spent the morning working on my back-yard allotments – these little suburban crop plots had always been popular in England, small pieces of land or gardens used for growing fruit and vegetables, becoming almost necessary during the war years when the authorities had even allowed a few public parks to be cultivated for food – and was boiling up some tinned sausages for my lunch on an open fire. Tinned food was my usual diet – easy to find, easy to cook – but I needed fresh vegetables if I was going to stay healthy. When I looked up from my digging to check on the sausages, I found the dog watching me from a bomb-site across the street.

Maybe I was feeling more lonely than usual on that particular day. I'd kept to myself after the Blood Death, you see, avoiding the crazies I met roaming the city, aware that the normals – those that were left – had abandoned the place for fear of epidemics breaking out, or just to get away from all those dead bodies, but there must have been something about that mutt that appealed to me. Sure, there were plenty of strays around, and not just dogs. Cats, chickens – unfortunately for the chickens, they didn't last long once I'd set eyes on them – pigs – yeah, same thing if I could catch 'em – horses, and I'd even observed a cow or two wandering along the roads. 'Cept for releasing horses from carts, putting any injured creature I came upon out of its misery, and slaughtering those mentioned for food, I'd ignored any surviving animals or birds, and mostly they'd ignored me. Oh, and there was one I'd hidden from. From a distance I'd watched a leopard loping along Regent Street – just once, I'd never seen it again – and I'd stayed out of sight in case it got hungry for warm flesh. Like I said earlier, the London Zoo had evacuated most of its dangerous animals, even put some down, at the beginning of the Blitz, so I had no idea where this cat had come from, and still don't.

Well, I *must* have been feeling pretty lonesome that day, because I called out to the dog. It was wary, though. Cocked one ear, angled its head, and kept well away. I guess it became a kind of game then, a challenge, me and the boiling meat against the canine's canniness. It looked interested enough, squatting there amid the debris of flattened houses, blackberry and elder poking through the dry earth and bind-weed adding some colour to the greyness of it all, but the interest was in the sweet smell of cooking rather than me. I'd noticed by then that all the animals who'd survived the holocaust had become 'un-used' to humans, suspicious of us – or at least, of me – as if somehow they knew humans were responsible for the big foul-up. And who could blame 'em for that? But this run-down, red-haired mongrel's belly was ready to forgive all, because although it kept its distance, its nose was sniffing the air and one paw was raised as if to take that first step towards me of its own accord. And then an odd thing occurred.

It was a warm day, early in the year, May, I think. The winter of '46 had been real nasty (but nowhere near as bad and as scary as '47's), killing off most of the allotments and weaker wildlife, and it was obvious that this mutt had had a hard time of things. Ribs protruding, coat kind of threadbare, this old boy looked pretty beat up, and when I dipped into the can and pulled out a steaming sausage it became even more fascinated. And as I tossed the meat from hand to hand to cool it, then broke it in half, that timid paw touched the ground, taking the first nervous step towards me. I allowed a grin, but it froze on my face when something black and awful fell from the sky to land on the dog's back.

The heavens had been unblemished, not a cloud in sight, a gentle breeze the only interruption, but I'd neither seen nor heard the bird overhead and, so it seemed, neither had the dog. This was a huge bird, dark and ugly, with a wingspan of three feet or more. A goddamn great carrion crow, with claws like hooks, and a long powerful-looking black bill, sharp as a knife. Those claws dug into the poor mutt's flesh, while the beak stabbed at its head. The dog howled, but fought back, twisting and turning and snapping all at the same time. Blood was already beginning to flow from its wounded back, though, and it yelped between howls.

The Colt .45 wasn't always the only weapon I carried

around with me; nearby, propped up against the curved roof of a half-buried Anderson shelter, was my other weapon, a Lee Enfield sniper rifle, picked up from a military barracks in another part of London. It was handy to have around for whenever I caught sight of one of those pigs or chickens – I'd even bagged the odd squirrel in the parks – and I made towards it. Before I'd even picked up the rifle, three more crows had joined in the attack on the dog.

I was surprised and shocked: where the hell had they come from, and why were they picking on this poor old boy? Exhaling my breath, I took a bead on one of the newcomers through the telescopic sight, the original crow too mixed up with the victim itself for a clear shot. It was clinging to the dog's leg with its beak, yanking and twisting, trying to bring its prey down, while its friends swooped in when they got the chance, pecking at any exposed dog-flesh they could find. I squeezed the trigger nice and easy, aloof from all the excitement, and felt the rifle recoil against my shoulder.

The bird I'd targeted thudded to the rubble without a squawk and one of its companions fluttered away, screeching some kind of alarm, heading back to wherever the hell it'd come from. The other two were too absorbed in their work to take any notice.

By now the victim was rolling through the dirt in an effort to dislodge the crow on its back, biting and snarling, no longer howling. It had guts, this skinny hound, but needed all the help it could get.

My next shot clipped a wing and scattered black feathers into the air, stunning the bird but not seriously wounding it. It hobbled around for a few seconds, and that's when I got an idea of these birds' true size. They weren't carrion crows and they weren't rooks. These were the giants of the species: Ravens. I'd always thought these creatures lived on mountains and moors, or sea cliffs, but I guess I shouldn't really have been surprised: *nothing* was the same after the Blood Death. Maybe all the small mammals, frogs, lizards, or even dead sheep that these birds usually feed on had all been used up in their natural territory. Then I remembered I'd seen this kind once before in London, long before the Blood Death rockets had fallen, but I was too busy at that moment to remember where.

I aimed again and took off the injured raven's head with the next bullet.

That left one more to deal with, and this would be the trickiest shot of all. I moved closer, going to the road's edge.

The dog was putting up a brave fight, but not quite giving as much as it was taking. I knelt on the cobblestones, looped the sling around my upper left arm to take the rifle's weight, breathed out, and took steady aim, knowing it was gonna be tight, but what the hell, if I missed the bird and hit the victim, it would be doing the mutt a favour. Without hesitation, I squeezed the trigger with the pad of my index finger.

It was a true shot, square in the chest, and the bird, still clinging to the dog's back, flapped madly for a few moments before flopping to the ground, dead meat before it even landed. But the dog wasn't satisfied: it pounced on the carcass and broke the raven's neck with its jaws, then proceeded to drag it through the dirt, shaking it like a rag doll and tossing it into the air until exhaustion set in. The mutt wandered off a few yards and slumped to the ground, chin resting on its paws, weary eyes watching what was left of the bird.

Leaving the rifle on the cobblestones, I approached the panting dog to see if I could do anything about its wounds, but as soon as I drew near it rose and shied away, watching me all the time over its shoulder. It settled again immediately I retreated, this time keeping its eyes on me rather than the feathered carcass. I went back to my lunch and I guess the aroma of those boiled sausages was too much to resist, because the next time I looked up the dog was in the middle of the street, standing on all fours, bloodied but undefeated, nose twitching again. Tossing a whole hot sausage towards it, I went on with my meal, and when I glanced the mutt's way again, the scrap of meat was gone.

This went on for some time, one morsel following another, each throw a little shorter than the last, until the scraggy-haired dog was sitting across the fire from me and we were finishing the meal together. Later I took it into the nearest house and bathed its wounds (there was plenty of water in this row of houses, although elsewhere pipes had been fractured by bombs during the war, or had frozen and burst over the last winter). I found quite a few old scars on its body, proof, I guess, that survival hadn't been easy for it.

So that's how we met. Eventually I called the dog Cagney, because of the red hair (amazing what a scrub-down had produced) and a certain wise-guy attitude, and 'it' became 'he' because now the mutt had a personality. Cagney was a cross between a retriever and God knows what else, and he stayed independent, coming along with me only when he felt like it, disappearing for days, sometimes weeks, always finding me again at one of the several safe places I used all over the city once he knew where they were. I guess we were company for each other, and if he got offended whenever I got soused and ranted at him and the world in general, he never sulked for long. And if I got maudlin and shed a few self-pitying tears, he just let me get on with it, taking himself off to avoid mutual embarrassment. I didn't know his history, and he didn't know mine. We maintained a cool reserve between us most of the time, afraid, I guess, that tomorrow the other might be gone for good. Now I'd have welcomed his company in the tram tunnel as the mangy, slavering dog-pack crept up on me from out of the darkness.

'Hoke? Are you okay?' At least Cissie hadn't forgotten about me. Her voice echoed around the walls and the dogs hesitated.

'Keep walking,' I advised her.

And in a short while I was following my own advice,

catching up to the others as they held their hands to their ears, pained expressions on their faces.

The dogs? Oh yeah, the dogs. I'd taken out that first and meanest-looking one with two bullets to its head, the gunshots reverberating like thunder around the confines of the tunnel. Taking my old instructor's sound advice, I'd followed the first shot with a rapid second just to make sure. You didn't need to do that with a rifle, but a handgun is less powerful so you could never be sure if the first bullet had inflicted enough damage.

It'd leapt into the air, then dropped stone dead, without a twitch, without a murmur, and the rest of the pack had vanished into the void, running like hell from the thunderclap. I knew they'd return, and soon, because now they had a warm meal waiting for them, one of their own kind.

My own ears were ringing with the gun blasts and although I saw Cissie's mouth working I couldn't hear a word she was saying. Suddenly I was lit up by the full blaze of the warden's powerful flashlight, so not only was I unable to hear, but I was blind too.

Shielding my eyes with a raised hand I told him to get the light off me.

If he was deafened too he must have got the idea from my angry expression. The light blinked off and we were left in the softer glow of the paraffin lamp again. By the time I reached Muriel the ringing had toned down and I could hear voices once more.

'Surely those dogs wouldn't have attacked us,' she said in her very correct manner.

'Things have changed,' I told them all, not just her. 'You can't trust the animals any more. Most of them are half-wild, the rest all-wild. And they're pretty hungry.'

Cissie was pulling at her ear lobes. 'You could've warned us you were going to shoot.'

'Yeah. Sorry. I'll make a formal announcement next time.' I brushed past her and, taking the flashlight from the warden's hand, kept going, switching on the light again to play the beam along the road ahead. I didn't care if they followed or not, I just wanted to be out of that place and breathing fresh air.

The tunnel swept round in a long gentle curve and soon we came upon many other kinds of vehicles, cars and trucks, cabs, bicycles, even a wheelchair (we didn't examine the slumped bundle inside it too closely), their drivers and riders mistakenly thinking they'd be safe underground, just like the people who'd fled into the Tube stations. Well, they'd been wrong. We'd all been wrong. Every son-of-a-bitch who thought Good always conquers Evil and who'd gone to war to prove the point had been wrong. I couldn't help wondering – then and many times before – how that squared with a so-called 'benevolent' God.

I trudged on, limping badly by now, exhaustion, mental and physical, exaggerating the effects of my injuries and bruises; I remained oblivious to whether or not the others were keeping up with me, just set on reaching daylight before my legs gave out. And gradually I closed my mind down, shutting out all thoughts that had nothing to do with getting to the end of the tunnel.

Save one, that is. I couldn't stop thinking of when and how I'd kill the German.

7

WE CAME UP on the approach road to Waterloo Bridge, battered, bruised, and shielding our startled eyes against the harsh sunlight. We were all filthy, black from head to toe, even Potter, and although the ramp leading out of the tunnel was gentle enough, our lead-weight legs found the going tough. Our breathing was laboured and old Potter was wheezing badly by the time we reached the surface road.

The girls sank to the ground at the top of the incline, faces turned up towards the sky, like sun-worshippers after a long, hard winter, while the warden took off his helmet and mopped his brow with his crumpled red spotted handkerchief. He muttered something under his breath, complaining about 'lumbago', I think, and he rubbed the small of his back so's we'd get the message. Stern stood aloof from the others, taking in deep, purging breaths, getting rid of the rank, sooty air he'd swallowed back there in the tunnels. I left them to it, going over to the corner of the ramp and peering round the railings back towards the big intersection where the Strand met the Aldwych. The tram tunnel had been built to avoid the traffic congestion at that point, beginning its descent in the middle of the broad bridge road and curving round below ground before straightening again to emerge in Kingsway. Everything looked peaceful enough at the intersection, with only the jumble of motor vehicles we'd weaved through earlier creating its own silent chaos. I sagged then, going down on one knee, shoulder resting against the railing's end post, my face, like the girls', turned up towards the clear sky.

My eyes closed for a second or two, and when I opened them again I saw a solitary seagull sail across the blue, heading downriver, its haunted call as lonely as its image. With a weary grunt I pulled myself up again and crossed the road to the bridge's parapet. Although small craft and floating debris littered the wide River Thames below, its waters sparkled in a way they never had during the war; the old river had cleansed itself and from where I stood I could see shoals of silver fish, swimming free of human effluent and, so it seemed, untouched by the great disease. The breeze was cool here, and somehow placating, soothing the dread that had travelled with me these past hours; only the sagging barrage balloons hanging lazily above reminded me that all really was not well with the world. I went back to the others.

'Listen up,' I said to them. 'We need to get off the streets for a while, at least 'til the Blackshirts have given up on us. The place I've been holing up in isn't far from here, so you're welcome to join me there for a while. When the heat dies down – say, in a day or two – you can do what you like.' I meant that for the girls and Potter; Wilhelm Stern I wasn't gonna let out of my sight.

Muriel's face broke into a tired but almost radiant smile. 'You mean the Savoy, don't you? That's the hotel you've been using, isn't it?' She brought her hands together as if delighted by the surprise, and even dishevelled she looked a princess.

I frowned though, because even if I had decided to let the German go – which wasn't likely – mention of the hotel's name had sealed his fate. He and the Blackshirts were of the same mould, brothers-in-arms, comrades-in-creed, and if I allowed him to wander off, chances were he'd find his British allies and lead them back to me. My fingertips played

101

along the teeth of my zipper, close to the shoulder-holster inside my jacket.

Almost as if he could read my mind, Stern said quickly: 'I would be happy to go with you to this place. I think we all need to rest and perhaps make some plans.'

His expression was serious, stiff even, the good volunteer. His eyes might have flicked towards the hand still lingering close to the gun butt just out of sight under my jacket, but if so it was too fast for me to catch. I knew he'd noticed though.

'It would be so lovely to return to the Savoy,' Muriel was saying, unaware of the tension between myself and the German. 'Even during the war it was a wonderfully exciting place to wine and dine. Do you remember the Lord Woolton Pie?' She had swung round towards Cissie, the brightness in her grey-blue eyes hinting at the sparkle that must have been there in better times. 'You remember, Cissie – potatoes, carrots, mushrooms, leeks. The Savoy's chef created it specially for the Ministry of Food when rationing was so severe.'

'Oh sure,' her friend replied drily. 'I used to hobnob there all the time. You know, with Clark Gable when he was in town, or Douglas Fairbanks Junior. Even good old Tyrone Power used to lie to his wife Annabella just so's he could spend an evening with me dancing to Carroll Gibbons and his band. Now let me see, what were they called . . . ? They were on the radio all the time.'

'The Orpheans.' Muriel hadn't caught the weary sarcasm. 'Carroll Gibbons and the Savoy Orpheans.' There was something edgy about her delight, as if it might break at any moment, leaving only bitterness to take its place.

'For God's sake, Muriel,' Cissie snapped. 'You know where I'm from. You know I would never have dared set foot in a swanky place like the Savoy, even if I could afford to!'

'I only meant . . . The recipe was used by housewives all over the country.'

'Oh yes, what a wonderful example you toffs set for us commonfolk. My-oh-my, if you lot could survive on Spam and powdered eggs quaffed down with only the scummiest vintage wine, then the rest of us peasants could easily get by on good old Lord Woolton's bloody pie. God bless you, ma'am, if I had a cap, I'd doff it.'

The shine in Muriel's eyes dimmed. She looked down at her knees, her weariness returned. In a softer voice she said, 'My father used to take me to the River Room for lunch whenever he could find the time. We used to toast Mother's memory with a glass of champagne before we even looked at the menu ...' Her words trailed off, but she remained in that position, head bowed, distracted, as if memories were continuing inside her head; and then Cissie was kneeling beside her, telling her quietly that she was sorry, hadn't meant to be a cow, her arm sliding around her friend's shoulder as she apologized.

I was impatient to get moving again. 'The water's still running,' I told them, and Cissie raised her head, scowling at me, wondering what the hell I was talking about. 'The hotel,' I said. 'There's plenty of water. And the tubs are big enough for hippos.'

The thought of a bath, cold or not, soon changed Cissie's mood. She examined her filthy hands and arms for a moment, took a token swipe at the dust on her slacks, then beamed a pure white grin from her sooty face.

'Now you're talking,' she said, straightening up and bringing Muriel with her. 'Come on, Mu, snap out of it. I'll let you scrub my back if you promise not to go all ritzy on me again.' She hugged her companion, then looked at me expectantly. 'Tell me there's tons of food, and not just Woolton Pie. I'm starving.'

'If you don't mind tinned stuff.'

'So what are we waiting for? My tummy's already screeching at me.'

I glanced across at Potter, who was still pulling in short,

103

gasping breaths and looking unreasonably hot in his dark blue overalls. 'You coming with us?' I asked, and he returned my look with some sourness in those broad, sweaty features.

'You mean I don't have to? I can go on me own way if I want?'

'Sure. It's every man for himself.'

'Oh, is it? That's good to know, son. I'll remind you of that next time yer stick a gun in me belly.' He mopped the inside rim of his helmet with his red rag, then, with some dignity, placed it back on his head, tucking the strap under one of his plump chins. 'Well, since my little hideaway has gorn up in smoke, I think I'll indulge in a bit of luxury meself. The hotel was on my watch durin the Blitz, so I know a bit about the place. I was quite pally with a few of the staff in there too, 'specially the volunteer ARPs and Red Cross nurses. Even had mugs a tea on the rooftop with the fire spotters. They were quite a bunch, I can tell yer. Heroes, the lot of 'em. Old William Lawes from the Works Department use'ta ponce about in a two-hundred-guinea raccoon coat to keep out the chill when he was patrolling the roof. Left behind by an American guest in the Twenties who couldn't pay his bill, so I was told.' He gave a short nostalgic chortle, then became serious again. ''Course, we can duck down the basement to the Lincoln Room when the mad bomber comes over next.'

Before I could say anything more, Cissie cut in. 'What are you talking about? What mad bomber?'

'Eh? You know who I mean.' Potter looked at her, perplexed.

'They've been out of London for a while,' I explained quickly, anxious to be on our way. Nostalgia and sunshine was okay at the right time, but this wasn't it: we were still in danger. But Potter had become rattled.

'D'yer think I'm in uniform for the fun of it?'

Both Cissie and I stared at him. Behind Potter I could see Stern was also taking an interest.

'I'll carry on me duty until it's all over,' Potter went on.

'Nobody's stood me down yet, and until they do I'll keep on with the job I was given. We old 'uns have got our uses, y'know. We can serve King and Country as well as anyone.'

Maybe I shouldn't have been so surprised – this old boy had been living in an underground bunker for the past three years, getting rid of the dead bodies that filled the place to make room for himself, when he could have chosen to live anywhere in the city. He could even have followed other survivors and fled to the hills around London, or beyond, away from the worst of the holocaust and constant reminders of what we had done to ourselves. This guy had gone crazy all right, but only mildly so; he seemed harmless enough – so far – and anyway, I hadn't forgotten he'd saved our lives.

'Okay, let's get going,' I said, unwilling to waste any more time.

Cissie was more than ready and Muriel seemed to have taken a hold on herself. 'You'll stay with us?' she asked Stern, who still stood apart from the rest of us.

His pale eyes took us all in. 'Of course. That is, if no one objects.'

Potter shuffled round to regard the German. 'This feller's foreign, ain't he?' he said suspiciously.

'Forget it,' I snapped. There was no time for a new debate. I did my best to sound neighbourly. 'Okay, Willy, you stick with us' – (like he had a choice) – 'for now.' Then to all of them: 'There's a stairway opposite that'll take us down to the Embankment. The hotel's one block away.'

Our footsteps sounded hollow inside the covered stairway and I think none of us liked being in the gloom again. But it wasn't for long and at the bottom I brought them to a halt.

'What is it?' whispered Cissie, her eyes wide and searching the road outside over my shoulder.

A finger to my lips quietened her. I stuck my head out and did a swift recce of the way ahead.

Warm air shimmered above the metal roofs of the scant

105

traffic stuck there in the broad thoroughfare that ran alongside the Thames, but that was the only thing that moved. No noise, only our own breathing. Everything was abnormally normal. I stepped out, gesturing to the others to keep close.

We could see the modest riverside entrance to the Savoy a few hundred yards away, the narrow street it was located in rising gently, a small overgrown garden park opposite; a zigzag wall built during the Blitz to protect the hotel's rear access and river restaurant windows ran along the frontage. Several of the vehicles in the street had been parked there by me, their tanks full, keys in ignitions, batteries fully charged. The MG two-seater was for speed, the black Austin taxi for manoeuvrability, the Bentley for comfort (never used so far), and the flatbed truck, a Foden diesel which took up most of the street's width further down – well, that was for other purposes.

As far as I could tell, nothing had changed since my last visit three days ago – there were no new vehicles in sight and the single board I'd left leaning across the opening to the trench between the barricade and the hotel wall was still in place. But that didn't mean the enemy wouldn't be lurking inside the building itself, waiting for me to return. Until this morning the Blackshirts had never discovered any of my havens, so now I was extra wary. Hubble was stepping up his search, no doubt about that, and you didn't have to be an Einstein to figure out why: I've said it before – time was running out for him and his bunch of blood scavengers. Today, of course, he had even more reason to intensify the hunt: he'd discovered there were three more possible walking blood banks in town.

The sun's heat seemed raw after we'd spent so much time underground and soon the back of my shirt was sweat-soaked. I felt exposed and scared out there in the open, which may have added to the perspiration, but it didn't take long to reach the cover of the barricade. Lifting the plank of wood aside, I indicated to the others to go through, and with one last look around, I followed. The revolving door into the entrance hall was stiff with disuse and while Cissie struggled with it I let myself in by the glass side door.

The others crowded in behind me, nervously looking around the compact, low-ceilinged entrance hall, Muriel walking straight to the short flight of stairs leading to the floor above and peering up them. Cissie finally emerged from the revolving door, her glare telling me I should have advised her. From the relief on the faces of the others I guessed they were pleased to find there were no shrivelled corpses cluttering up the place, and I wasn't about to tell them otherwise, at least, not right there and then. Sure, there were plenty of guests still in residence, all of them dead, but I'd tucked them away out of sight along with members of staff as far as the rooms, stairways and corridors I used were concerned. Like the warden, I preferred them out of sight and out of mind. I had to give these people some warning though, because certain areas I'd left untouched.

'Stay with me and don't go poking your noses into any closed rooms,' I said. 'You wouldn't like what you'd find. And hey . . .' I paused, making sure I had their full attention. 'There are some parts we have to go through that are gonna upset you. Unfortunately there's no other way . . .'

Muriel shuddered and turned from the stairs. Cissie held her own upper arms as if a chill breeze had followed her through from the street.

'I thought the hotel would be empty,' murmured Muriel. 'I didn't realize . . .' Her voice sharpened and there was enough daylight inside the entrance hall to see the astonished curiosity in her eyes. 'Why would you choose to live in a . . . in a . . . *morgue* like this? There must be so many other places.'

I brushed past her to reach the stairs. 'This is just one of a few safe places, lady, and one I was already familiar with.'

'I don't understand.'

On the third step, I turned to look down at her. 'Did you ever hear of the 1st American Eagle Squadron?'

She nodded slowly, but it was Potter who spoke up. 'Yanks and Canadians who couldn't wait for their own countries to come off the fence.'

'We joined in your war early, fought with the RAF when you needed all the pilots you could get,' I said, too weary to explain fully, but ready to satisfy this girl's curiosity if it would get her moving again. 'We made our unofficial HQ in this hotel. Suite 618–619. We drank, we caroused, we played poker, we did anything to take our minds off killing and being killed for a coupla hours. The American Bar became our watering hole, though I don't remember any of us ever paying for a drink. Hell, we even got into Tich's Bar with the war correspondents.' I didn't tell them about Sally, how I'd courted her here, my turn to impress her after she'd shown me all the good things in her town, bomb damage or not, how I'd loved her, and yeah, one year before the last V2s had landed, had married her here in the Savoy Chapel. 318–319 was our honeymoon suite, but the hotel had only charged us room rate and had thrown in champagne and flowers as a wedding gift. I didn't explain because there wasn't time and there was no point. Besides, these people meant nothing to me – I didn't owe them a thing. 'Cept maybe the German. Yeah, he had something coming, and that was why I wanted them *all* to stay with me for now. I wanted him to suffer just a little before he took his last breath, but I was too beat up to play it out right then. When I put the *Kraut* away, I wanted to enjoy the moment. Heck, I wanted to *celebrate* it.

'So why are we hanging around?' Cissie said, looking from me to the others, then back to me again. 'You mentioned the water's still running, didn't you? And I bet the bar's open all hours, isn't it? So what are we waiting for?'

She joined me on the stairs and when I failed to budge because my thoughts were still otherwise engaged, she prompted me with: 'Mine's a large gin and tonic, easy on the tonic, heavy on the gin. Hey, Mr Fighter Pilot, did you hear me? A girl could die a thirst aroun' here.' Her attempt at Mae West was pretty cruddy – maybe it was the hint of hysteria that spoilt it – but it changed my mood. For a short while, anyway.

I took them up to the next level, through an art deco foyer with dusty chandelier and fountain-etched mirror, then up more stairs into twilight corridors, past doors with fancy names – Iolanthe, Mikado, Sorcerer, Gondoliers – and over thick carpets that smelled of mildew. The further we ventured, the gloomier it became, until after a sharp turn the way ahead radiated a palish grey again. Soon we'd entered that grey.

'Oh dear God.' Muriel's fingertips covered her lips.

'How could . . . ?' Slowly Cissie had turned her eyes on me, away from the spectacle that spread out before us, away from the vast front foyer where the rich and the gracious and the businessmen on expenses had taken late-morning or afternoon tea, or evening cocktails, in elegant easy chairs or sofas set between brown marble columns and exotic potted palms, surrounded by tasteful murals and high mirrors, ormolu clocks and knee-high tables laid with finest chinaware and tiered cake-stands, served by waiters in tails, with reception clerks in morning dress bustling through it all with courteous calm, the war outside an inconvenience but never a hindrance to the Savoy, service as normal even if the building itself had become a little battered and the menus reduced to basic (if stylish) fare; where now rotted figures slumped in those same elegant easy chairs, or sprawled across those knee-high tables amid broken crockery, or lay on carpets thick with dust, the foyer nothing more than a vast emporium of horribly macabre tableaux, each one solidified in death, the plants merely dried stems, the chandeliers grey with dust, and the humans only desiccated husks. And beyond this, through the open doors to the grand restaurant overlooking the park and river, opened only for lunchtime custom in the dark days, the scene was repeated, but rendered even more grotesque by the sun's brightness through the high, broad, taped windows. Cissie had diverted her eyes from this to look at me with ... with what? Not with Muriel's astonished curiosity when we'd first entered the building. Horror, then? Yeah, horror and something more. Dismay would come closest. Her sentence might have finished with, 'How could you live in a charnel house like this and remain sane?'

Well, lady, I hadn't claimed to have all my marbles.

I didn't say that, though. I just couldn't be bothered any more. I ignored those bewildered hazel eyes and her unfinished question.

'The stairway's along here,' I said instead, moving off to the right towards the Savoy's stately vestibule and entrance hall, sensing their eyes on my back, their disgust. I kept walking and knew they'd follow me anyway, like frightened stray sheep in need of a leader.

Up a broad set of steps I took them, past a balcony over-looking the vestibule, then down a high-ceilinged hallway towards the stairs next to the defunct elevator. On the way, but without changing pace, I took a quick peek into a half-open doorway, checking on the Velocette Mk II motorbike I'd hidden away in there. It nestled in the shadows like some great black and fabulous insect, tank full, parts greased and free from rust, spark plugs clean, all primed and ready for a swift start, and just a glimpse of it stirred something deep down in my gut. It was the sudden urge to get away, I guess, to climb aboard that machine and roar out of the hotel and free myself from these people and the liability that went with knowing them. Involvement was something I neither wanted nor needed, because that kind of burden only brought more grief.

My own exhaustion smothered the impulse no sooner than it was roused (besides, I hadn't forgotten Stern and why I wanted him here) and I kept going, heading towards the staircase beside the elevator.

It was a sluggish climb and by the time we reached the third floor our line was strung out. Without waiting for the others I left the stairway to walk down a long gloomy corridor, coming to a halt and waiting for the others to catch up only when I reached the sharp left turn at its end.

The German was the last one to reach me and briefly I wondered why. He was much stronger than the others, so had he taken time out to explore possible escape routes while trailing behind, investigating rooms close to the stairway on the landings we passed, looking for doors to the fire escape? What the hell – he had a right. None of it would help him, though, not when the moment came.

I turned my back on them and unlocked the door to Suite 318–319.

8

TO THEM IT MUST have looked like an Aladdin's Cave – an Aladdin's Cave of junk, canned food, cardboard boxes, and weapons, all kinds of stuff that came in handy when you lived in a city where shopping was free but nobody produced any more; and where blood-bandits roamed the empty streets, so that shopping was sometimes a risky business.

My suite in the Savoy had lost some of its elegance because of the clutter, no doubt about that, and there was a whole lot less room than when I'd first moved in. We were crowded inside a tiny vestibule between the bedroom and sitting room, the jumble spilling into both, and to our right was a marble bathroom with a stirrup pump that fed from the half-filled tub standing in the doorway in case of sudden fire (what good the pump would do in a real emergency was debatable, but it might at least buy me time to escape into the hallway). The pastel-coloured walls of both rooms were easily overwhelmed by the flashy labels of canned foods and mixed jars, and only the king-size bed was free of clutter in the maze that was my refuge; the mess was everywhere, things piled high on easy chairs and mirrored dressing table, a selection of handguns and cartons of ammo on the lounger, a shotgun leaning against the writing desk. Boxes full of items I couldn't even remember poked out of the half-open closet. A radio that would never broadcast again stood on a small occasional table by an armchair heaped with magazines and books, and on the fancy Louis-Seize escritoire was my wind-up gramophone, a stack of dusty records next to it, Bing Crosby still on the turntable.

The two girls had already wandered into the sitting room and were gawking about – ration-book kids in an overstocked candy store. I didn't know what they'd been living on the past three years, but from the wonder in their eyes I guessed their cuisine had been pretty dull. Muriel glanced back at me, gave me a smile, then went to a cabinet set against the near wall where a mountain of canned stuff was piled high. She picked one can out and the mountain threatened to topple; it steadied itself, though, and she read the can's label.

'Creamola Custard Pudding,' she said in awe.

Cissie giggled and put a finger against another label. 'Fancy Quality Fish Roll,' she read aloud, and her interest instantly moved on. 'Mrs Peek's Puddings. Batchelors Peas. Oh wow, peaches . . .'

'Ostermilk for Babies?' Muriel said questioningly from another stack.

'Look.' Cissie again. 'He's got coffee. Three whole bottles of Camp Coffee.'

'Handy eggs.' Muriel. 'Ugh, dried whole egg.'

'All I can get hold of,' I put in, beginning to enjoy their enjoyment.

'Spam. Oh dear, lots of Spam.' Muriel sounded disappointed, but I could tell she was joshing.

'And Weetabix,' said Cissie, a grin spread all over her face as she scanned the rest of the room. 'Bovril, Ovaltine, Peek Frean biscuits, marmalade. My oh my, you're determined not to go hungry, Yank.' She drew in a sharp breath. 'Are those fresh vegetables over there?' she asked, pointing.

'A week or so old,' I assured her. 'Grew 'em myself on one of my allotments. It wasn't easy after last winter.'

She was already picking up potatoes and examining each one individually. 'After everyone had gone or died at the sanatorium we tried to grow our own, but somehow it never worked out. I suppose we'd both have been useless as land girls, but that's the problem when one of you has been brought up in a London pub and the other's the daughter of a lord.' She indicated her friend, and it was easy to figure which one was the lord's daughter.

'Didn't you get supplies from the nearest town?' I asked, surprised.

'We were too scared to go far,' replied Muriel, her interest still on the gold mine of food around her. 'The nearest houses were the furthest we strayed. Mostly we ate from the centre's own stores. We were afraid we'd catch some disease off the dead, or even be infected with the Blood Death itself. Nobody knew anything, you see, not even the scientists in charge of research. Are those cabbages I see?'

She hurried to another box on the floor. 'Oh, and Brussels sprouts, and onions. You must have worked hard to have achieved all this, Mr Hoke.'

'Just Hoke,' I told her, then shook my head. 'All I've done is kept a few things going. It isn't much, considering.'

'May I?' Stern had followed us through to the sitting room and had lifted a single pack of Camels from a carton on a straight-backed chair.

I nodded and he quickly broke open the pack. He put the cigarette between his lips, then searched around for matches.

'Over there,' I pointed to the mantelpiece above an extinct electric fire.

As he took a box of Swan Vestas from my stockpile of matches, he studied himself in the dust-dulled mirror over the mantelpiece and frowned. He was filthy, but it must have come as a slight shock. Maybe he'd always thought his kind didn't pick up the dirt like the rest of us.

'I need to wash,' he said, more to his own reflection than to me. 'You say there is plenty of water in this hotel?' Now he was looking at me, but only through the mirror.

'The Savoy has its own artesian wells, but the pumps are out of action. The tanks are still pretty full, though.'

'Me first,' Cissie insisted quickly. 'I can't go another minute stinking like this.'

I guessed stinking wasn't a word Muriel used a lot, especially when it applied to her own body, but she was nodding in agreement. 'Yes, I'd like to get cleaned up too. Then perhaps we can enjoy some of this lovely food; I'm beginning to feel quite faint and it's not just from fatigue.'

I addressed them all: 'You're in a building full of bathrooms, so you won't have to take turns. But stick to this floor, don't go wandering off.'

I noticed the German, now puffing away at his cigarette, had strolled over to the M1 carbine leaning against the writing desk and my hand went inside my jacket when I thought he was going to pick it up. Instead he passed by the rifle and went to the tall window overlooking the park and River Thames below. The drapes were open, but a lace curtain covered the glass.

When he raised a hand to draw the lace aside, I said, 'Leave it alone. I close the curtains at night if I'm using light –' I indicated the candles and lamps set around the room '– and in the daytime the netting is always kept in place.'

'In case someone looks up and wonders?' he mused, and although I couldn't see his face, I knew there was a half-smile there. 'Quite unlikely, wouldn't you say?'

'Unlikely or not, I don't take chances.'

'I could do with a stiffener.' Potter had sat himself down on the edge of the sofa and was eyeing the array of bottles crowding the low coffee table in front of him. Gin, vodka, and several brands of whisky – Famous Grouse, Haig, Johnnie Walker, and even good ol' Jack Daniel's, as well as bourbon and rye – all of them severely rationed during the war, but not nowadays. Hell, there was even the Savoy's own special blend to drink, a Scotch as fine as any I'd tasted, and I'd tasted a lot during my lonely nights in this city. Then there were the wines – hocks, moselles (yeah, German, old stock, I guess), clarets and burgundies, even some vintage stuff – sharing space on the edge and underneath the table with cartons of cigarettes – Lucky Strike, Camel, Wills Capstan, Churchmans No 1, and some I hadn't even taken note of. Genocide had turned me into a heavy smoker as well as an inebriate.

'Help yourself,' I said to Potter as his roving gaze took in all that was on offer. 'I'll get you a clean glass.'

'No need, son, no need.' He gave a satisfied grunt and reached for the Grouse. 'Plannin to drink an' smoke yerself to death, was yer?'

He didn't wait for a reply, nor did I bother with one. His plump fist closed over the neck of the bottle and he gave the top a twist.

'Yer know, I was always scared to come inta the Savoy after those last V2s dropped.' He paused to hold the bottle up and examined the golden liquid before he drank, the loose cap in the palm of his other hand. 'Even though I'd seen you comin and goin a few times, I was still frightened of what I might find in 'ere. I coulda raided the American Bar easy enough if I'd had the spunk to come inside, but nah, somehow it wasn't in me.'

He took his first swallow, the whisky glugging into his throat.

'You weren't afraid of entering the Civil Defence shelter,' I reminded him.

'That was different. I knew most of them people. I wasn't as funny about it. But this lot in here – toffs, rich people, even some of our own leaders, members of the War Office an' that – well, I didn't feel it was my place to intrude.' He took another, longer, swig from the bottle, wiped his mouth with the back of his hand and eyed me again. 'If yer know what I mean.'

116

I didn't think I did, but I was in no mood to think about it. I faced the others. 'You can have your own separate rooms along this hallway, but don't go any further. All the suites on this side of the third floor interconnect, though the doors are locked right now.'

'You are a cautious man, Hoke.' Stern had remained by the window and the light shining through the nets revealed how spoilt his tweed jacket and pants, so neat and clean when we'd first met, had become. A sleeve and a pocket were torn, his shirt collar crumpled; yet as he drew on the cigarette, his arm across his chest, hand holding his other raised elbow, he still had that air of superiority about him, that icy arrogance we'd come to expect from the Master Race. Movies and propaganda had told us this was how they were, how it was part of their Aryan nature, and I'd never doubted it for one moment.

'A cautious man . . .' he went on, and I wondered if it was mockery I saw again in those colourless eyes '. . . yet today you were almost caught by those Blackshirts, as you call them.'

'Sometimes it happens,' I said by way of explanation. Going to the coffee table, I picked up a Johnnie Walker, one-quarter full, its cap missing. 'But it won't happen again,' I added before taking a long, long drink.

That evening, using two of my three portable gas cookers, I made them all a meal. It was only Spam, tinned peas and boiled potatoes, followed by peaches and custard, but they made ecstatic sounds as they wolfed it down.

Earlier I'd shown them other rooms they could use as their own sleeping quarters, the two girls moving in to a suite next door to mine; Potter and Stern in separate rooms further down the corridor, the old warden at the end of the line. I kept all the interconnecting doors locked. They were surprised to find that these rooms were used as store rooms as well, although none of them was as cluttered as my own suite, but there were no complaints. Not that I cared one way or the other. I left them to settle in and went back to my rooms where I threw off my filthy, ripped clothes and showered – the reduced water pressure still allowed a Niagara Falls soaking under those big Savoy shower heads. Although goosebump cold, the water freshened me up a whole lot. A fast shave was followed by some attention to my injuries. The wound where the bullet had passed through the shoulder of my leather jacket was only skin deep and iodine (Christ, that *hurt*) with padding held in place by sticky plaster took care of it. My ankle was puffy and soft, but I knew no bones were broken, so the swelling would go down within a day or so if I bandaged it tight. The bruising on the same leg was just beginning to show through and was already looking ugly; it stretched from calf to mid-thigh and the muscles underneath were stiff and painful. For a while walking would be a problem, but no big deal. Cuts and grazes were soon dealt with and the rest of the bruises could take care of themselves. My hair was singed – the front looked like scorched corn – and the skin on my face and the backs of my hands was puckered and flaky; likewise, though, no serious damage. Oh yeah, and the knuckles of my right hand were scraped raw. All things considered, I'd been lucky that day – more lucky than I deserved – and I'd also been taught a lesson. Lately I'd become complacent, figured myself too smart to be nailed by the crazies. Well, I'd been wrong. Stupid and wrong. And the booze was taking over. Like I'd told the German, it wouldn't happen again.

Before I pulled on chinos and T-type shirt (Lord knows why, but I'd stuck with military underwear, and this under-shirt with short sleeves had been washed a hundred or more times) I checked all the guns in the room, making sure they were oiled and loaded, even though they were always kept that way. Still shaky after nearly being caught out that morning, I guess.

Taking the .45 from its jacket holster and tucking it into my waistband, I left the suite and limped barefoot through the third-floor corridors and hallways, checking stairwells and windows all round the building. Because the Savoy was really in two parts, I couldn't look over the main drag outside, the Strand, without going down and up again, but that didn't bother me. I was certain the hotel was secure, otherwise there'd have been a reception committee waiting for us when we returned. I scouted the place pretty well though, and didn't go back to my rooms until I was satisfied there was no hostile incursion. Ankle throbbing like hell along with other parts of me – the bruise over my chest felt like a thick sheet of lead had been bolted there – I poured myself a whisky, using a glass this time, but still taking it raw. It did me fine.

Still tired, but feeling a little better, I washed some glasses and the accumulation of plates and dishes I'd collected over time in the bathroom sink, then began to prepare chow for myself and my unwelcome guests. I think I would have slept twenty-four hours solid if I'd closed my eyes, so I didn't allow it. I kept going because that was the only thing to do, and besides, I was so hungry a horse would've only made first course.

The German showed up first, politely rapping on the door and waiting for me to open it. He'd found fresh duds from somewhere – white shirt, dark slacks, but the same brogues he'd been wearing that morning – and if they looked a little snug on him, it didn't matter, he still wore them well. He'd shaved too, and his hair was slicked back with water so that it looked shiny, kind of sleek. Although he looked nothing like the German actor Conrad Veidt, the image kept coming back to me; maybe it was his manner, stiff, watchful, arrogant, and yeah, even charming in a snake-like way. I wasn't gonna admit it to myself then, but all that propaganda had worked on me as it had on most people on our side of the conflict, and I didn't want to be persuaded otherwise. Hatred has its own fodder, and I was a pig for it.

Inviting him in, I told him to help himself to a drink. He opened a bottle of wine.

We hardly spoke a word to each other, but I felt his eyes on me as I got on with cooking and he sipped the wine. Albert Potter appeared next, shuffling in without announcement, still in his blue overalls, helmet tucked under his arm. Making straight for the coffee table, he poured himself the same brand of hooch as before. The conversation didn't exactly flow even then, mainly because of the tension between myself and the German.

The girls arrived ten minutes later, both of them looking a whole lot prettier than when they'd emerged from the tunnels. The wife of whoever had once occupied the suite next door had great taste in fashion, and it looked like the husband hadn't been mean with her dress allowance. The girls' outfits were simple but classy.

Muriel wore a light green knee-length skirt, cream square-shouldered blouse tucked into the waist, the ensemble a little looser than Cissie's who was, well, a little more upholstered. Don't get me wrong – both girls were slim, but Cissie had been given more curves. Her pleated skirt fell just below the knees and she wore a matching jacket, despite the heat (I think she wanted to make the most of what she'd found in the closets), with a white blouse underneath. Neither one wore stockings, though I was willing to bet the previous tenant had plenty – that was their one concession to the climate, I assumed – and both balanced on high heels that did a lot for the shape of their legs. I had to admit it was swell to see the female form looking so goddamn good again, although it went no further than that for me. Not at that time, anyway.

Their hair gleamed from fresh grooming, Muriel's light-brown locks curling round one cheek, Cissie's darkly vibrant curls resting over her shoulders. The thin scar line across her face was barely noticeable as she smiled at us three men.

The German, who'd cleared an easy chair for himself when he'd entered the room, stood to attention. 'It is wonderful to know that such beauty still exists,' he said to them with oily sincerity.

Cissie ignored him, following the warden's example by heading straight for the cocktail bar – the booze-laden coffee table where Potter was holding fort. He tipped his glass at her in greeting.

'Give me something strong, long and life-preserving,' she begged. 'Something I can regret tomorrow.'

'Well there's gin, but I can't see no tonic,' said Potter, lifting bottles and scouring the collection in front of him.

She looked at me accusingly and I said lamely, 'There's no call for it.'

'All right,' she said. 'Open a tin of peaches and use the juice. I'm a girl who's used to roughing it.'

For the first time that day I grinned. I quickly found the right can and punched a hole in its top with the opener, then handed it to Potter, who'd already worked on the gin.

'Ice would have been perfect,' Cissie complained jokingly, 'but I suppose the Savoy isn't what it used to be. Mu, I expect it's champagne for you?'

It was as if a shadow had darkened her friend's face. 'A glass of wine will do,' she responded quietly, and I remembered she and her father had toasted her mother's memory with champagne in this very hotel.

'Vino it is,' piped Potter, picking up the bottle already opened by Stern. 'And a very sensible choice, if I may say so. Leave the hard stuff to reprobates like me.'

'And me,' piped Cissie.

They drank and watched me cooking over the small stoves on the floor, no one saying anything for a while. I think that initial coolness between us all was due to something more than just unfamiliarity: I think it was because there was no trust between us yet, despite what we'd been through together that morning. Even though we were the survivors of a scourged world, we weren't sure of each other, we weren't comfortable in each other's presence. It was different between the two girls – they were already friends – but the rest of us were strangers. Heck, one was even an alien, a *Kraut* at that. Just sharing the same blood type wasn't enough, not by a long chalk. Part of the problem, for the girls I mean, was that in a depleted society, our gender roles took on a whole new significance, and they weren't quite ready for that just yet. None of us were. And to add to the girls' discomfort, they couldn't be sure if any of the men they were with were quite sane.

The ice only began to break when I started serving up the food.

9

THE INFORMATION didn't come out like this; it was in no sense as concise and dispassionate. The evening developed in its own easy way, you see, after a while people just gabbing when they felt like it, their bellies a little fuller, their heads a little mellowed by the booze; a person could be maudlin one minute, cold-blooded the next, emotional after that, a real mixture of sentiment and hard fact. Regret figured a lot, nostalgia for the good things now gone even more; but grief, having had three years to settle, was pretty much subdued. Here's what most of that evening's parley amounted to.

First Cissie, her whole name Cicely Rebecca Briley. Like me, she was of mixed parentage, her father English, mother Jewish. Her folks had run a public house in Islington and she had helped out behind the bar (illegally, of course) until old enough to find herself proper employment, one that might help the war effort. That was back in '41 and she was sixteen at the time. With most of the able menfolk off fighting the war, the country was crying out for women to fill the men's jobs, so Cissie began her working life on a lathe in an engineering company.

On the same day the factory was bombed and a flying piece of metal scythed across her face, her parents' pub was demolished by another pilotless plane – these were the doodlebugs, the flying bombs, the first German V1s to be used on England and Belgium in June '44. Henry Briley was dead when the Heavy Rescue squad dug him out of the rubble, but his wife, Rachel, Cissie's mother, survived almost another three days with both legs and pelvis crushed, and one arm missing. Cissie's stay in hospital was only overnight – beds were needed for the seriously ill or injured – and when she left there was no home to go to. It took her two days to locate the hospital they'd taken her mother to, and by that time Rachel was dead. Home gone, parents gone, job gone, there wasn't much left for Cissie. She moved in with relatives and joined the ambulance service, channelling all her anger and grief into the work and quickly realizing hers was not the only tragedy of this devastating war. Within a year and with Hitler losing, the V2s replaced the V1s; and then everything changed.

Naturally she couldn't figure out why everybody around her was dropping dead even though the rocket bombs were falling in other parts of the city; but then, nobody could at first, not even the military or the government itself. All hell had broken loose, but the panic was short-lived, as short-lived as the people themselves. It was horrific, a hideous nightmare, the deaths so sudden and so gruesome to watch; and not knowing if they were going to be next added to everyone's terror. Soon, because Cissie remained healthy while everyone else was dead or dying, she was taken into hospital and blood-tested. Before she knew what was happening she was in the back of a truck with a bunch of other ABneg blood types being driven down to the special sanatorium in Dorset, and it was in the truck that she made friends with Muriel Drake, a fellow passenger and blood kind.

All manner of tests were carried out on the ABnegs at the sanatorium, but still no scientist or medical officer could figure out why they were immune from whatever it was that had been released by the V2 rockets. To make progress towards a solution even more difficult, those very same investigators were falling dead themselves, and it was only when a couple of medics with the immune blood type were found that any sustained research was achieved. Another problem was that it was only in the last decade that truly extensive research was being carried out on blood groupings, so very little was already known. Now they were learning fast, but it was too late.

It seemed the disease, gas, poison, virus – the military still didn't know what had been inside those last V2s – worked on the blood system, stimulating the chemical reaction that caused coagulation so that, within minutes in most cases, the blood hardened inside the large veins of the bigger muscles, this leading to – and it was Muriel who remembered the term – thromboembolism. The veins in the heart, lungs, brain, as well as other less life-threatening areas, were completely blocked, while minor veins became engorged. It meant that because of the blockages, the excessive free-flowing blood had nowhere to go and nowhere to return to – 'venous occlusions', Muriel called that effect – so massive swellings and leakages occurred all over the body. The cramping pains victims suffered because of this were excruciating, rendering many unconscious before death itself claimed them.

So, they realized anti-coagulant therapy would be ineffective, because it would only promote further haemorrhaging, and clotting drugs would only intensify the thrombosis. And they still hadn't discovered why AB negative blood refused to react to the Blood Death, why they themselves, and their human guinea pigs, were immune. You have to remember that all the advanced nations of the world were desperately working on a solution, an antidote, any kind of cure, the Allied countries keeping in close contact with one another, but none so far had come up with an answer. Time had run out swiftly, and eventually the remaining doctors in the sanatorium ran out too. One day they just walked, leaving no note, no explanations, no excuses. They'd realized it was hopeless.

For the guinea pigs left behind it was almost a relief. No more tests, no more blood drained from their bodies to be taken away in glass tubes, no more tissue samples cut out, no more needle jabs – and no more vanishing into the sanatorium's special, restricted wing where, it was believed but never confirmed, because no patient ever came back, operations were performed on the ABnegs (the rest suspected that experimental blood transfusions were being carried out). When those principal doctors fled, all order went with them. First the soldiers guarding the 'inmates' – no ABnegs had stayed on voluntarily after the first week – had absconded, soon followed by all the remaining staff and researchers. These people knew by then that death was hanging over every one of them, and they could think of better places to be when it happened.

Soon after, the guinea pigs, about a hundred in all, went their separate ways. Cissie and Muriel decided to stick together.

Muriel Drake was from a higher branch of society than Cissie, although even as a daughter of a lord she had been treated no differently from anybody else at the sanatorium (panic is classless, I guess). For whatever reasons, the two girls got along and did a lot to keep up each other's morale in those terrible days. Like everybody else, they'd lost family and friends, and at the sanatorium they never knew when an amiable nurse or guard was going to cash in their chips right in front of them. Now that the place was emptying fast, they made their plans together.

Muriel's mother, Lady Daphne Drake, had been struck down in the first year of the war, but not by anything the mad *Führer* had sent over. A No 14 bus had knocked down Lady Daphne as she'd tried to cross Piccadilly Circus during the Blackout, after she'd enjoyed Jack Hulbert singing for the conga and outwitting Nazi spies in *Under Your Hat*, the bus killing her instantly and leaving Muriel pretty much alone with her father, Lord Montague Drake – Muriel's two older brothers, who had joined the Forces as soon as war was declared and much against their father's wishes, were in other parts fighting the Germans, one with the navy, the other with an RAF squadron based on Malta. Muriel had not heard from either of her brothers since the Blood Death outbreak and, not knowing if they shared the same blood type as her, assumed they were both dead. Although the family home was in Hampshire, most of the time she had lived in their Kensington apartment; at seventeen she had joined the ATS, the Auxiliary Territorial Service, and was soon serving as a subaltern. Nothing heroic in that, she'd assured us: it was a natural role for any patriot. And hadn't Princess Elizabeth herself joined the ATS just before her nineteenth birthday?

On the day the first Blood Death V2s had rained down, Muriel had been having lunch with her father at Simpson's-in-the-Strand when the waiter, who had just served them with mulligatawny soup, which was to be followed by cold roast gosling and salad – strange, she had told us, how she had never forgotten that day's menu despite the horror that had accompanied the lunch – had keeled over onto their table, his skin turning blue, the veins in his hands and temples protruding as if about to burst. His eyes had started to bleed.

Muriel, not unreasonably, had proceeded to scream the place down, while her father, who was attempting to help the distraught waiter by opening his shirt collar so that he could breathe more easily, suddenly clutched at his own heart. Her attention now solely on her father, Muriel hadn't noticed that virtually everyone else in the restaurant was going through the same paroxysms, and when Lord Drake's skin began turning blue, his hands and cheeks ulcerating at an unbelievable rate, his veins swelling like the waiter's, she fainted. When she had eventually come round again, every person who had not fled the restaurant, including her father, was dead. She had run out into the street, out into a dying

127

city, and only later did it occur to her that she hadn't even heard the bombs drop.

Like Cissie, she was rounded up within days, blood-tested, then taken down to the Dorset sanatorium.

Even while this secret medical establishment was slowly being abandoned, she, Cissie and a few others had been reluctant to leave the security it offered, afraid of what they might find in the strange new world outside. But three years was a long time to be cooped up anywhere; also, rations were finally running low. Neither desperation nor bravery took them back to the capital though: it was homesickness that had done that.

And as they'd driven one of the few vehicles left behind at the sanatorium through the country lanes they had come upon Wilhelm Stern.

As we listened to the German tell his story, the sun sinking low over the Thames outside, flushing the walls of the suite a soft red and deepening the shadows, it seemed to me he was a little light on detail. Sure, he told it convincingly, but there was something about the guy that made me unwilling to trust him. The fact that I still regarded him as the enemy had a lot to do with it, right? Yeah, no doubt about that. But he'd said something back there in the tunnel that firmed up my suspicions.

That evening Stern said he was a navigator on one of the *Luftwaffe*'s medium-sized bombers, a Heinkel He 111, which had been dropping mines along the east coast of England in April 1940, when the plane had been hit by ack-ack. With his clothes on fire he'd parachuted from the blazing bomber, and the rush of air had extinguished the flames, although not before his back and neck had been severely burned. The He 111 had crashed at Clacton, a few miles away, killing (he'd learned later) two civilians and injuring a hundred and fifty others, and he and the rest of the crew were captured and shipped off to Island Farm POW Camp down in Wales. That, he told us with an almost apologetic smile, was the extent of his personal war on Britain, although in March '45, a week or so before the fatal V2s were launched, he and sixty-five other German POWs had escaped from the camp (I vaguely remembered reading something about the breakout in the British newspapers at the time). It was while Stern, who had become separated from his *Kameraden*, was trying to make it to the Welsh coastline, where he hoped to steal a boat that would take him across to neutral Ireland, that the world about him changed.

The dead were everywhere and he couldn't comprehend why. Deciding to keep away from the towns – now for two reasons: as far as he knew his country was still at war with Britain and America, and he was still a prisoner on the run; and he thought the plague that had killed everyone, including most animals he'd come upon, must be contagious – he scavenged from farmhouses and empty cottages. He survived almost a year that way until the harsh winter of '46 forced him to venture into a town.

He told us he must have gone into shock because of what he found there, since he'd lost all memory of those first weeks. When reason eventually returned he left the town, heading east, travelling in cars and abandoning each one when it ran out of gas, finding another to continue the journey in, determined to make it to the opposite coast, there to find a boat and cross the English Channel to mainland Europe. From there he would return to his homeland, perhaps to die, for at that time he did not know how widespread the plague was, whether the Continent itself had been devastated. On his journey he had come upon an army base and had steeled himself to enter it. With nothing more than a scarf covering his mouth and nose, Stern had located a battery-operated radio transmitter and, using fresh batteries, had tried to contact his own base in Germany. There had been no response. All night he sent messages, praying for some reply, from anyone, from anywhere, but still there was no contact.

Giving up all hope, he'd sunk into deep despair, unable to understand what had caused the disease and why he had survived it. The whole of the next day he had contemplated ending his own life – not only did there seem nothing to live for, but his personal guilt at having lived while everyone else appeared to have perished was crushing. That thought evaporated with the next dawn when he realized it was his duty to live on, he owed it to his people and to his *Führer*. He made no mention of the Master Race, but it was in my mind. I figured Stern thought the fittest had survived, so affirming Hitler's attitudes on breeding and the natural order. Stern was living proof of his leader's theories and to die now, especially by his own hand, would refute all that.

So, he wandered on, looting grocery stores for food and sleeping in empty houses. And then he had chanced upon other survivors, a kind of community living in a tiny village. They'd treated him with suspicion and, on hearing his accent and learning he was German, they'd driven him off, almost killing him in the process. It seemed they blamed him in full and personally for what they called the Blood Death, and he was lucky to get away with his life. For a long time after that he had lived on a remote farm near the New Forest, first clearing it of its corpses, then cultivating a few crops as best he could. The winter of '47, even worse than the previous year's, had put an end to that.

His food had to come from village stores and shops, and so he lived on the fringes of these places, alone and, he admitted to us, 'somewhat insane in the head'. With the summer of '48 the desire to return to the 'Fatherland' returned and his journey began again.

The vehicle he was travelling in soon broke down – lack of maintenance rather than shortage of gasoline – and it was while he was trudging down a country lane looking for another means of transport that the two girls came upon him in their Ford.

Their greeting was different from the kind he'd received two years before, and he was grateful for that. As far as Cissie and Muriel were concerned, well, they were just overjoyed to find another live and healthy human being. His nationality meant nothing to them, not after all this time, and he certainly felt no enmity towards British civilians. He agreed to accompany them to the capital, although he told them that from there he would continue eastwards, possibly using the River Thames to reach the estuary and the English Channel. Stopping only once to refill the Ford's tank from a garage handpump along the way, they soon reached London. And hit trouble. Namely, me.

I put the question to the two girls, not the German. 'Like Cissie said before, for all you knew, I could've been the bad guy, and the Blackshirts the only law and order left. So why help me?'

'It was Cissie's decision,' Muriel replied, indicating her friend. I stared at the dark-haired girl.

She shrugged. 'I didn't like their uniform. I had bad memories of Mosley's Blackshirts before the war and that lot this morning didn't look any different.' Another sip of gin and peach juice. 'I told you my mother was Jewish. Besides, you looked desperate and I like desperate types.' She grinned at me.

It wasn't enough, but I didn't push it. Before Oswald Mosley, founder of the British Union of Fascists and Jew-hater, had been interned at the beginning of the war and his vicious party of bigots broken up, he'd led marches into the very heart of Jewish ghettos in London's East End just to provoke the people into riots. He was one bad man and later, as the Allies were taking back Europe, grim stories of the Nazis' attempted extermination of the Jewish race reached the rest of the world and the British public finally understood the full horror of the ideals Mosley – along with his more discreet ally, Sir Max Hubble – had aligned himself with. Those ragbag black outfits had meant only one thing to Cissie and, as she'd been driving the car at the time, her companions could only go along with her. She was a gutsy lady.

A little juiced by now, they had begun to ask questions about me, but I ducked them. We still hadn't heard the warden's story.

Albert Potter, his nose a deeper shade of red by this time, was only too pleased to gab, three years of loneliness and a good few measures of Grouse loosening his tongue some. Too old to join the British army, he'd volunteered as an ARP on the very day Neville Chamberlain had mournfully declared war on Germany, and he had dutifully served through both Blitzes on London, twice being buried beneath rubble himself. His home was in an LCC block of flats in the Covent Garden area and when this, itself, was eventually demolished by the *Luftwaffe*, he and his family had moved into the basement of a school that was being used as a Civil Defence HQ. (It was here that he first learned of the secret bunker beneath Kingsway, where he later became 'door watcher'.)

He had won three commendations for heroic action during the war years, we were proudly told, once for single-handedly clearing an entire building of office workers when a DA (delayed action bomb) was discovered on the rooftop, the second time for reviving an unconscious woman who had choked on a stale (she later claimed) piece of Battenburg cake in the Lyon's Corner House on the Strand, and thirdly for preventing a bus carrying several passengers from toppling into a bomb crater during the Blackout by dashing in front of it waving his flashlight at great risk to life and limb. He'd served King and Country as well as any man could, despite the taunts and jibes from the public, who tended to regard all ARPs as jumped-up little Hitlers, mad with the tiny powers given them. Well, that had never bothered him. Like Stern, Potter knew his duty, knew it then, knew it now. And when his wife died of the blood disease, 'Gawd bless 'er', and his daughter, Katie, thirty years of age, still single, and serving as a gun site operator near Cheltenham, had never got in touch so was presumed dead too, he had only one purpose left, and that was to continue with the job he'd been given. Only when the war was finally over would he hang up his helmet, collect his medals, and retire to the countryside.

We'd looked at each other uncomfortably, but none of us felt like breaking the news. At least believing the war was still raging had given Potter a reason for carrying on, misguided though it was. Besides, the war never had been officially declared over. Sure, it had ended when those last V2s fell, but there had been no one in high office left to say, 'Okay, enough is enough, let's call it a day.' Or if there was, they were off somewhere, either living away from the cities or deep down in some secret Blood Death-free bunker. That got us onto other topics, like what had happened to the governments of the world, why hadn't the scientists or medical profession been able to contain the disease, and what the hell was in Adolf Hitler's mind when he released such destruction (assuming he still had some kind of rational mind left after his dreams of world domination were shattered)? Had the *Vergeltungswaffen* been one cataclysmic mistake? All big questions, to which we had no answers.

Perhaps the biggest question though, because all the others meant nothing as far as the future was concerned, was this: How many of us were left? Just how many ABnegs were there in the world? Muriel said someone at the sanatorium had told her that AB negative blood types amounted to only approximately three per cent of the global population, and it might be that their Rhesus Factor (whatever that was) was hostile or non-submissive to the virus or gas released from the rockets. The problem, this person had gone on to say, was that not enough was known about different blood types and time itself was running out too fast for new research to be mounted, intensive though that research might be. The truth was, doctors and scientists were a swift-dying breed, along with the rest of mankind, and no matter how concentrated their minds, oncoming death brought about certain disabilities.

There was a silence for a while after that, all of us lost in our own thoughts. Cissie collected the dirty plates and dumped them in the bathroom sink; then she was back in the doorway, yet another question in her eyes. She voiced it: 'Does anybody know what happened to the Royal Family?'

Potter made a sound, a kind of heavy rumbling sigh, as he poured the last of the Grouse into his glass. His rheumy eyes watched the liquid, but I don't think he saw it; his mind was on other things. We waited for him to speak, aware he was preparing to tell us something that we wouldn't like. Well to me one tragedy was as bad as another, and they were all part of the grand catastrophe; all except my own, that is. The German was of the same mind, because there was only interest in his cold expression and none of the fearful apprehension revealed in the eyes of Cissie and Muriel.

It was Muriel who prompted the warden. 'Did they die of the disease, Mr Potter?' she said.

'I suppose so,' he replied, 'but not in the way yer might think.' He took a long swallow of whisky and wiped his shiny lips with the back of his hand. 'Yer know, Queen Elizabeth, Gawd bless her poor soul, was never more pleased than when the bombs fell on Buckingham Palace durin the Blitz. She could look them poor people who lived down by the docks in the eye and say, "We're takin it too, we know what it's like."'

He let the empty whisky bottle slip to the floor as he drained the glass. Shaking his head as if in both admiration and regret, he continued, 'Do y'know, them little girls, them little princesses, used to knit socks for the Red Cross in the evenings. Princess Elizabeth – Lilibet she was called by the family – she joined the ATS, like this lady said.' He gave a nod towards Muriel. 'Worked as an engineer, got her hands dirty on engines and suchlike. And King George, he spent evenings makin parts for RAF aeroplanes, just like a common man. The King and Queen never left us, not even when the Blitz was at its worst, never even thought of sendin their youngest, Margaret Rose, out of the country to some safe place. They stayed together and stuck it out, an example to us all.'

I studied the faces around me, curious to see their reactions. Muriel's expression was rapt, a mixture of emotions like the warden's; both pride and sorrow shone in those grey-blue eyes as she waited to hear the tragedy that was about to unfold. Cissie's eyes were a little unfocused, as if tears were about to roll.

'The public didn't know for sure,' Potter went on, 'but the rumours spread almost as fast as the plague itself. Some said the Royal Family was dead within the first hour of those rockets landin. Others said the whole lot of 'em, includin old Queen Mary, was given cyanide pills by the King's Physician when reports came in of how horrible the Blood Death was and how fast it was spreadin. But I'd got into the Kingsway shelter when I found out what was happenin out there, and I heard the true story first-hand, because even though the Civil Defence personnel were droppin like flies all round us, reports were still comin through on the wires.'

'You really know?' Muriel was leaning forward, hands clasped over her knees.

'Yes, miss, I think I do. On that terrible day the Royals was rushed down to Windsor and as soon as the authorities knew what was goin on, a single-engine aeroplane was sent to take 'em out of harm's way. There's a wide and very long road that runs through the park up to Windsor Castle itself; the public was never aware, but it was there as an emergency runway in case the country was ever invaded.

'They got on the plane all right and, so we heard, they even took the Crown Jewels wrapped up in newspaper with 'em. But the plane had barely took off when it came crashin down again, explodin into houses outside the town.'

There was a tiny, shocked gasp from Muriel and I saw that Cissie had closed her eyes.

'Radio contact broke off just as the pilot was reportin a safe take-off, and the authorities reckoned he'd been struck down by the disease right at that moment. No other explanation, y'see. 'Course they was all killed, bodies burned in the wreckage, but there was no public announcement. Hell's bells, there was enough occurrin without demoralizin the people completely.'

I could've smiled, I could've wept, at the absurdity of his last remark. But it was Stern who broke the silence that followed.

'Do you know what happened to your Winston Churchill?' he said, and I could see the '*V*inston' annoyed Potter as much as it did me. He glowered at the German.

Then he raised his empty glass in salute and said, 'Old Winnie.' He shook his head, looking down at the floor. 'They say he topped hisself, shot hisself dead. All too much for him in the end, y'see. He'd put everything into winnin the war for us, and he'd finally done it, it was almost finished. Then Hitler sent his secret weapon over and had hisself the last laugh. It would've been too much for any man.'

And that quietened us a whole lot more. Tears were running down Cissie's cheeks and Muriel had her head bowed. Potter rummaged among the bottles on the coffee table for fresh whisky and Stern sat stiff-backed, his face a mask. Me, I just poured another Jack Daniel's.

Grief is only finite, you know? Sure, over the past years I'd thought a lot about death and those I'd lost, about the major players, the little guys too, friends, acquaintances, kids I'd gone to High School with, good pilots I'd fought battles with. You don't forget, but you hold down the memory; or at least, the emotion that goes with the memory. After a while it fades, the emotion, because the soul can only take so much. The numbness eventually sets in, although, if you're really lucky, that can happen right away. Generally though, it'll take months, maybe years, before you begin – and only *begin* – to pull through and start to think straight again. In my case I only had two people to really grieve over, because my folks were dead before the war even started, Ma in '38 of cancer, Dad soon after in '39, of heart disease. I had no brothers or sisters, and other relations were too distant to cause much concern. Those two people closest to me, wiped out by the Blood Death, took up most, if not all, of my mourning.

As I looked at the strained faces around me, I realized my new and unwanted companions were still in a state of shock. The girls had been cloistered from the worst excesses of the disease for some time, and the warden had taken his own mental route for dealing with the situation. Now Cissie and Muriel had ventured beyond the confines of the sanatorium and local villages to witness the full horror of the V2s' legacy for themselves, and Albert Potter had finally come into contact with other survivors, and *their* sanity, such as it was, had to be nagging at his own delusions. As for the German, well, even he had to have had family, people to weep for, so he had to be suffering too. Maybe guilt – it was his countrymen who had unleashed the final holocaust – figured in his emotional state also; race responsibility for such annihilation would have to lay heavy on any man. Unless, of course, the only person he really mourned over was his *Führer*, whose actions he considered to be both appropriate and heroic.

I watched Stern and tried to guess what was going on behind that mask; he remained inscrutable though, despite hitting the juice and chain-smoking along with the rest of us. Funny thing is, he never got soused, nor maudlin, no matter how much he drank. But then, neither did I that evening.

10

DIVING, DIVING, DIVING . . .

The two Fw 190s had chased me to thirty-eight thousand feet, and the air was thin up there. I'd had no choice, there was only one way to get away from them, because they were like angry hornets on my tail, relentless, dogged, and out for revenge. They'd watched me shoot down one of their buddies at twelve thousand feet, and that'd made them pretty sore, because their buddy, in his superior plane, should've finished me. I'd been in his sights, sure enough, but had flipped over just before he'd fired and gotten behind him, winging him with my own guns. I'd followed him down, giving him another burst, and the Fw 190 had gone into a spiral, an entrail of white smoke marking his descent. He didn't bail out and I'd hoped he was already dead.

His two friends came steaming in, angry – hell, they were insulted – because I was on my own, one against three, and they'd thought they'd have some fun with me.

They'd assumed they had me when I levelled out. A Spitfire might have gotten away from the Focke-Wulfs, but my Hurricane, with its eight Browning machine guns in its wings, was a clumsier animal and I knew I'd have to take desperate measures. There was only one way to outfly the Germans, but they'd have to follow me. I headed upwards, into the blue, taking the Hurricane to the limits. And the Focke-Wulfs came after me.

Thirty-eight thousand, cockpit rattling around me, and I levelled, took her into a dive. Thirty-seven thousand feet, thirty-six, -five, and my belly's pressing against my spine. Picking up speed, though, control column vibrating in my hand. Can't hear them, but I feel the bullets tearing into my left wing. Diving faster. No more gunfire – the Krauts are beginning to have problems controlling their aircraft as all three of us pick up speed.

Thirty thousand feet and my speed's up to four hundred miles an hour, considerably more than the Hurricane's limit. Diving, faster, faster, everything shaking around me, engine's screaming, my goggles are fogging up, sweat's beginning to blind me.

Twenty-five thousand.

Twenty.

I manage to twist my head, look behind me. Can only see one pursuer, and he's pulling out of the dive, giving up the chase. Where's his pal? Can't see the other Focke-Wulf. Have to assume it's still on my tail.

Nineteen, then eighteen.

Too fast. Christ, much too fast. I tear off the goggles. Can't believe it when I look at the instrument panel. Everything's quivering, but still I can see the speedo's needle. Not possible. I'm approaching six hundred miles per hour. Nobody's gonna believe this. If I ever live to tell the tale.

And now it happens, the thing I'd dreaded. They call it compressibility. It's when everything gets dampened, nothing works as it should. The plane is out of control, the stick's all over the place.

Jesus H, I'm down to twelve thousand.

I grip the control column, try to pull the Hurricane out of its dive, but it won't listen, it won't obey. Pulling harder, both hands clamped around the stick. The plane won't haul up. Oh dear Lord . . .

Eight thousand feet.

Seven.

Six.

That's it. I'm done. I'm locked into that seat by pressure, no
way can I get out of the cockpit. Not giving up though. Too
much to live for. I pull harder.
Five.
I begin to pray.
But forget the prayer and start to scream.
Everything becomes white, like the centre of an explosion . . .

And I woke up. Thank God, I woke up. And as I sat there,
bolt upright in the bed, body wringing wet, limbs trembling,
I realized it wasn't the imminent dream-death that had awakened me. The light knocking on the door came again.

Moonlight flooded the room so that the walls, the furniture, the rumpled bedsheet, were bathed ghostly white. I
stayed where I was, still in shock, my mind completing the
dream that was, in fact, a memory: Coming out of the dive
at the last moment, skimming over the treetops, the Fw 190
which had remained in pursuit not so lucky; it'd hit those
same trees and exploded into one huge fireball. The German
pilot's screaming face, imagined by me as I sat there in the
moonlight, resembled Wilhelm Stern's. Fortunately for me
on that day almost seven years ago, the rest of my squadron
hadn't been far away, and the wing commander himself had
hurtled towards me along with two other Hurricanes and
chased off the surviving Focke-Wulf, giving me hell over the
radio for wandering away from the main battle as he did so.
It wasn't the first time I'd had that dream, but it was no
worse than any of the others that disturbed my sleep almost
every night, drunk or sober.

The rapping on the door came again, still light, but more
urgent this time, as though the person outside were becoming impatient. Or desperate. The doorhandle turned, but with
no effect – I always kept the door locked at night.

Tossing back the sheet, I snatched my chinos from the

foot of the bed and pulled them on. Before going to the door, I picked up the .45 from the bedside cabinet and cocked it. Index finger outside the trigger guard, barrel pointed at the ceiling, I padded barefoot over to the bedroom door.

As if sensing me on the other side, a muffled female voice called softly: 'Hoke, please let me in.'

Quickly turning the key, I opened the door a few inches. I could see only a shadow outside in the hall.

'Please,' she repeated, and I could tell she was close to tears.

I stood aside, pulling the door open a little wider, and Muriel slipped through the gap. The moment the door was shut tight again and I'd turned to face her, she was in my arms, her slender body shivering despite the night's warmth.

I resisted at first, remained stiff, unyielding, gun hand still raised towards the ceiling, the palm of my other hand wavering inches from her back. Then I smelt her sweet perfume and I remembered what a woman's embrace was like. My hand closed against her back, pulling her towards me, and I lowered the gun to my side. I breathed in the aroma of her freshly washed hair, then the scent she'd used on her skin, on her neck, her breasts. I even enjoyed the faint taint of wine still on her lips. A pressure inside me was released, the tightness in my chest loosened. I held on to her for a moment, maybe a few moments, and closed my eyes. My mind reeled in her presence.

It had been so long, so very long . . .

But the numbness within returned, the rejection of true feelings that was my only defence against the terrible thing that had happened to the world and to me overrode those stirring emotions: I stepped away from her. In the silvery light from the window, I saw the glistening of tears on her cheeks and I saw the confusion in her eyes.

'Hold me,' she asked in a hushed voice.

I couldn't. I didn't want to. I knew if I took her back into my arms I'd lose something that had kept me together these past three years, the detachment I'd come to wear like a suit of armour. I did not want to become vulnerable again.

Her bare shoulders were trembling still and the moonlight shimmered off the silk slip she wore. She watched, her tears catching that same light so that crystals seemed to shine from their trails, then slowly lowered her head.

'I'm so afraid,' she said.

And I gave in, so easily, so goddamn willingly.

Her weeping dampened my naked chest and I felt tiny spasms jerk her whole body with each sob she uttered.

'Take it easy,' I said to her quietly, at a loss for any other words of comfort. 'We're safe here.'

Her hair was sensuous against my skin. 'I saw them, Hoke,' I heard her say. 'There were so many.'

'Who? Who did you see?'

She lifted her head to gaze up at me. 'I saw their spirits. The people who died in this hotel – I saw their spirits wandering the hallways and corridors. I saw them on the stairways, lost souls, just drifting, with nowhere to go. It was so sad, Hoke, so pitiful – and so frightening.'

'I told you all not to leave your rooms tonight.' My anger was false, a diversion from what she was telling me, because I didn't want to hear such things. Memories were enough to cope with.

'I had to get out. I needed to see more of this place, perhaps only to revisit better days. Can't you understand that?'

I shook my head. 'It was a stupid thing to do.'

She wasn't listening. 'I went as far as the main stairway, the one by the lift. They were just shadows at first, a shifting in the dark, until they began to emerge, slowly at first, as if my own concentration was helping them take form. Then they were all around me, drifting, floating, and oblivious to each other. Even for those who were together, elegant women in long, flowing dresses on the arms of men in dinner jackets and winged collars, there appeared to be no contact between them. But the anguish in their eyes, the misery in their features . . .' Her head rested against my chest once more. 'Was it only my imagination, Hoke? Or were they real . . . ?'

'A dream, that's all,' I told her as I held her tight, my arms pressed against her back, the gun now awkward in my hand.

'But I wasn't sleeping,' I heard her murmur.

'Illusions, then. Don't you get it? The shock of seeing all those corpses earlier today is still messing with your head. Believe me, I know about it, Muriel, I've been there myself. You, me, Cissie, old Albert Potter, and the German – we're the only living, breathing things in this hotel.'

'I didn't say they were living –'

'There are no ghosts.' She jumped at the anger in my voice. 'The dead are dead. Anything else is fantasy. You understand, Muriel, you understand?'

My free hand was gripping her upper arm and she flinched at its sudden pressure. She tried to pull away.

'Okay, okay, I'm sorry,' I soothed, annoyed at myself for letting her wild talk get to me. 'Just relax now and try to put those thoughts out of your mind. They'll fade away eventually, I promise you. They'll fade away for good.'

Her body seemed to sag and she leaned back into me, her hands down by her sides, her weight against my chest. I let her weep, my hand stroking her hair, and soon I became aware of the hardened tips of her small breasts through the thin silky slip, nudging my skin, arousing feelings I'd long since subdued. I fought against it, against yearnings that had been denied for so many years, aware that it was wrong, the wrong time, the wrong circumstances. And afraid she would be repelled.

Her weeping had stopped and she suddenly became taut once more, as though aware of what was happening. But instead of pulling away, she relaxed into me and the contact between us took on a new intensity. The very air around us seemed charged, as though an electric storm was gathering inside that cluttered bedroom. Impossible, but it seemed so real, and I soon realized that energy was building inside our own bodies and not in the atmosphere outside them. For me it became a kind of agony, an ecstatic craving that battled against other emotions, feelings and memories that would not be cast aside, not just for this, not just for – *the image appeared stark and horrifying in my mind, her body lying there on stone steps, her belly torn open* . . . I tried to block the thought, but still the horror of it lingered.

'Hoke?'

Now I was the one who trembled, the one who fought back tears and turned away.

Muriel held my arms and shook me gently. 'What is it? What's wrong?' she said.

'It's okay,' I lied, suppressing the dread inside. 'It's nothing.'

'For a moment I thought you'd seen the ghosts too.'

'I told you, there are no ghosts.'

'Then why were you afraid just now?'

'It wasn't fear.'

'No?'

'No.'

'So why are you shivering?'

There was only one way to stop her questions. I kissed her. Hard. Angrily.

And she responded, pressing her lips just as hard against mine, as if there was a fury in her longings also, a fierce aching that had been there for a long time. We fought against each other in a battle that was for fulfilment, not conquest, each of us clinging so that flesh touched flesh and desire met with desire. It was a struggle that required an outcome and we both knew it.

She drew her head away and whispered something. I became still and looked at her questioningly.

'I need more,' she said, her voice barely audible over our gasps for breath. 'I need to lie next to you.'

I hardly hesitated, because any resistance was gone, lost in those first few moments. After wiping away the rivulets of tears from her cheeks with the thumb of one hand I led her to the bed and lowered her onto the wrinkled sheet. She kept her arms around my neck as I left the gun on the bedside cabinet and I took in her scent, not the perfume she'd found in her suite, nor the soap she'd used on her hair, but the aroma of her womanhood, of her arousal. The sheet beneath us was an unblemished white in the moonlight and her skin was of that same whiteness; the slip she wore was a shade darker, its reflections soft and silvery. Only by closing my mind to the past could I release myself to the present, and the vision of Muriel lying there, her arms outstretched to receive me, her legs slightly parted, one knee raised, helped me banish that other time. We needed each other badly and any reservation was swiftly put aside.

I sank down onto her, taking most of my own weight on my elbow so that I could gaze into her moon-bleached face and into those eyes that sought more than just passion. There was an urgency there, but also – or so I told myself at the time – a need for some kind of security, maybe a commitment.

My fingers, still trembling, slipped beneath the strap on her pale shoulder to ease it aside. Resting my hand there, curled around her shoulder, I lowered my face so that our lips brushed against each other. The touch was deliberately delicate, unlike the bruising kiss of moments before, and it excited us both; still we kept the encounter tentative, moistening each other's mouths with tiny stabs of our tongues, resisting the impulse to crush, to give ourselves completely, the restraint soon becoming unbearable, the years of abstinence heightening the tension, increasing the pleasure.

It could only last a matter of seconds and when finally we pressed into each other, teeth clashing, our lips hurting, I felt a roaring inside my head, a rush of charges surging through each limb, each part of my body. My hand left

145

her shoulder to find her small, firm breast, and my fingers tightened on its solid core. I heard her gasp at the sudden pain, but the sound became a moan, and this was of pleasure.

Her hands slid round my neck, kneading its flesh and the hard ridge of my spine, her fingertips retreating so that they could come between us to work themselves against my chest, digging into the muscles there, smoothing over the ridges. It was my turn to gasp when her fingers probed the bruising. She quickly took her hand away, afraid she'd hurt me too much, and I felt those fingers flatten against my stomach, causing the muscles there to shudder involuntarily.

Our kisses were equally wild, our breaths equally as desperate, and when her tongue entered my mouth and pressed against my own tongue, I became even more aroused. One of my hands tugged at the slip, pulling it down, away from her breasts, and I took time to drink them in with my eyes, because they were so naked, so bare, so sensual, like delicate spheres carved in marble; and then I drank them in with my mouth, taking each nipple in turn between my lips and drawing them in so that they stood wet and proud as Muriel squirmed beneath me. I heard the quiet rustle of the sheet as her legs parted and when I rose from her again, I saw that the smooth material of her slip had ruffled up over her thighs, leaving a deep, alluring shadow between them. It was another flawless sight, an image that set my mind reeling as all control, all reason, slipped away from me.

Muriel's chest was rising and falling with her own breathlessness and her hair framed her sweet face on the pillow. Her hands suddenly busied themselves with the waistband of my pants, and then I was free, her fingers closing around me and drawing me towards her so that I cried out with the wonderful shock of it. Her thighs opened wider as she guided me down between them and her cry was louder than mine when I entered her body, the resistance only slight, the hesitation only minimal. Again her cry turned to a moan of pleasure as I travelled further, the journey now smooth and easy, like gliding through warm butter, and her narrow hips rose up to meet me, her hands, her arms, pulling at me fiercely, urging me on, never, it seemed, wanting that journey to end. But quickly I reached the furthest point, and we clung to each other, her tears dampening my chest and shoulders once again.

Only then did we pause, and my own tears fell into her hair. She felt the wetness and held me tightly, but now with a tenderness that had nothing to do with passion. It couldn't last though, that moment of caring and compassion – our physical demands were too great, our sexual needs too critical. We began to move against each other again, each thrust becoming wilder, our senses rushing towards that point in our bodies where our juices could fuse and our energies meld. When my flow finally streamed from me I buried my face against her shoulder and groaned, and I stayed that way until the fluttering spasms grew less in intensity, ebbed away, left me exhausted.

Slowly my body and my mind relaxed. And for the first time in three years I found a temporary peace.

I lit another cigarette with the one I'd just finished and settled back against the bed's cushioned headboard. The shadows in the room had altered as the moon beyond the high windows had drifted upriver, and it was hard to make out Muriel's form as she lay beside me beneath the single sheet, her hand resting lightly on my thigh. The scent of spent passion lingered between us, a sweet-sour musk that was both calming and sensual at the same time, and I remembered how Sally had called it 'love-fragrance', believing it was some kind of invisible shroud that enveloped lovers after the act, bonding them for a little longer. Yeah, I'd laughed at the time, laughed like a hyena, making her mad at first, until she'd joined in the laughter, but punched my

147

arm all the same. I'd liked the idea though, despite my teasing. At least, I'd liked it with Sally in the picture. Now the thought only stoked up my guilt.

'Hoke?' There was a quiet huskiness to her voice. 'Are you all right?'

I could just see the outline of her hair and her arm in the darkness, the vague glint of her eyes. As I drew on the cigarette she was briefly bathed in its warm glow.

'Sure, I'm okay,' I replied.

'You were telling me about your parents.'

Lighting the fresh cigarette had interrupted the flow; the aroma of our lovemaking had rekindled a memory.

'Like I said,' I went on, 'Ma was English, with a touch of Irish thrown in. Peggy. "Peg o' my Heart" Dad liked to call her, naturally enough. They first met when he was over from Wisconsin for an agricultural fair – he dealt in farm equipment, bought 'n' sold anything from machinery to fertilizers. Had a fair little business going just after the Great War and he was kind of anxious to get a head start with all the new technology for farming.'

'That's where you're from – Wisconsin?'

I nodded in the dark, and added a 'yes' for Muriel's benefit.

'Peg was a maid in one of your small, country hotels Dad was staying in, and when I was growed up enough to be interested he told me it was her "sparklin eyes" he first fell in love with, the rest of her 'bout two days later.'

'And your mother – did she fall for him so quickly?'

'Guess she must have, because when he left eight days later she went with him. Just took off, the pair of 'em, bill paid, notice given, but no explanation to anyone. Back to Winona, Wisconsin, USA. They got hitched right away and a year later I arrived.'

'Wasn't she afraid? A new country thousands of miles away from her own family?'

'Ma had none to speak of. Her old man had been an Irish immigrant, who hadn't treated Grandma too well. Peggy was

148

his only daughter. When his wife died, he returned to Ireland where he probably killed himself with booze, according to Ma. Oh, he'd found his kid a job in a wash-house before he'd left, so I guess he figured he'd done his duty. And that was fine by Ma – at fourteen years of age she figured she was better off without him. When she married Dad, she didn't know if her old man was dead or alive, and she told me years later she hadn't cared.'

Muriel's fingers moved to my arm and she stroked it, elbow to wrist.

'She was never bitter about it though. Hell no, she was too thankful for her new life with Joseph, my dad. But y'know, although she never had a family to miss, she had something else to hanker after. Ma never got tired of telling me about her home country and I never got tired of listening.'

Muriel couldn't see me, but I was smiling at the memory. It felt good to talk about my folks after all this time and, for a while at least, it was holding down thoughts of Sally.

'She regretted leaving England?'

'No, I didn't say that. She'd found her happiness in Wisconsin, but that didn't mean she didn't get homesick now and again. She read me books by English authors all the time, and when I was old enough, got me to read 'em myself. Got me interested in the country's history, too. Maybe the only regret she had was that I wasn't getting an English education and I wasn't being brought up the British way. She took a lot of pride in the traditions and manners of this country of yours, even though she was only from working stock, and sometimes I wondered if those funny wire-framed spectacles she wore later on in life weren't just a little rose-tinted. Her dream was to bring me over here for a short while, show me all those things she'd told me about, but the cancer put a hold on that.'

My smile was gone and I took time to inhale smoke. Muriel's hand was still on my arm.

'She passed away in '38, and Dad followed her eight

months later. His ticker, the doc said, disease had worn it out. I always believed it was heartbreak that did it, though; or at least, hurried it along. I think he just didn't want to go on without his Peg any more.'

My smile had come back. It gave me some comfort, the thought of Dad going after his Peg, darned if he was gonna let her explore the great unknown on her own. 'Your ma's got no sense of direction,' he'd always joked with me. 'Lose herself in the parlour if she didn't have me around to call her.' Well, wherever she'd gone, I hoped he'd caught up with her. And I was kind of glad they'd both missed the horror that was to come.

'You were left alone?' Muriel's hand tightened around my arm.

'Alone ain't so bad,' I lied. Alone was hell on wheels. Alone was a slow trip to insanity. Alone was the worst thing any man, woman or child could live with. My smile was gone again, wilted away in the shadows.

'By that time I was living away from home anyway,' I went on before self-pity set me blubbing again. 'I was in Madison, attending the University of Wisconsin, studying engineering. Dad's company was in bad shape by the time he died, and his brother, a wiseacre even Dad didn't like, offered to take it off my hands, lock, stock and barrel, for no money at all. Well, that suited me just fine – what did I want with a pile of debts and a head full of problems when I was barely scraping eighteen? My uncle was welcome to 'em. Besides, I was supporting myself well enough by bike racing and some barnstorming at weekends.'

'What's barnstorming? I've never heard of that one before.'

'Air acrobatics, I guess you'd call it.'

'You were flying at eighteen?'

'Sure. When I was ten years old, Dad took me over to a barnstorming show in a field just outside town. Gave me a dollar to spend while he looked over a couple of crates he had in mind for crop-dusting, something that was becoming pretty popular about that time. I wandered off towards an old airplane I'd spied soon as we drove in, a beat-up Fairchild, as I recall, and when I handed its pilot the dollar and asked for a ride, well, he sized me up, bit the dollar, and lifted me aboard. 'Course, I told him Dad said it was okay, and that was good enough for this flyer, whether he believed me or not. And once I was up there in the clear blue air, high over the whole goddamn world, everything below shrunk into insignificance, well, I never wanted to come down again. I knew flying was the thing I wanted to do with the rest of my life.

'But Ma – 'specially Ma – and Dad didn't agree with my ambition, though when I kept ducking school so's I could wander around our local airfield we came to an arrangement. They'd pay for me to take flying lessons if I promised to stay in school and study hard. Anyway, I think Dad had an idea floating around in the back of his mind even then, because by the time I was sixteen I was crop-dusting for his farmer friends and acquaintances in our own second-hand plane.'

I leaned forward in the bed, wrists resting over my raised knees, cigarette butt warm between my fingers. I kept perfectly still, ears keen, eyes straining at the reflected moonlight on the opposite wall.

'What's wrong?' Muriel sat up next to me, the sheet falling around her waist.

I shushed her, listening still. I felt her body go tense beside me.

'Thought I heard something,' I said eventually. 'Must've been wrong.'

Relaxing against the headboard again, I reached for the cigarette pack on the bedside cabinet. This time I remembered to offer one to Muriel, but she shook her head, a movement I barely caught in the darkness. Lighting one for myself, I stubbed out the old cigarette in the full ashtray by the bed, and dropped the pack into my lap. Smoke drifted

151

across the room, thin spectres that caught the light by the windows. Muriel rested her head on my shoulder, her hair tickling my flesh.

'Tell me more,' she urged, as if my story reminded her of a different reality, a better time than the present.

'There's not much more to it.' A second lie, but there was only so much I was willing to tell. 'When war broke out in Europe, I knew immediately what I wanted to do. All those tales Ma told me, about her life in England, the places she'd worked and lived in, about the kings and queens, dukes and duchesses, all those books she'd read to me and the ones I'd read myself when I was older – hell, I even knew the rules of cricket. Dad had always kidded me I was more British than American, and I kind of liked that, made me feel different, something special. I guess that was because I thought Ma was so special. Huh, sometimes when I was little I even copied her accent.' I gave a shake of my head. 'Y'know, she never did lose that accent in all those years she was married to Dad.'

I exhaled smoke, enjoying its taste, its smell. It'd been a long time since I'd felt so relaxed and I figured it was due to the talking as much as the lovemaking. The booze at dinner had loosened me too and I was almost – only almost – beginning to feel glad of the company. I should have known it was dangerous to let others into my life once more.

'You've stopped talking again.' There was no impatience in Muriel's voice, only amusement.

'Yeah. Just thinking.'

'You said when war broke out you knew what you wanted to do.'

I blew smoke away from her face. 'I wanted to help the Brits fight their war with Germany any way I could. So I began flying aircraft, bombers mainly, up to the Canadian border. Because of the Neutrality Act, America couldn't export planes direct to the UK, not even over to Canada, so we used to fly 'em as close to the Canadian border as possible, then tow 'em across the line by rope and truck. It was a crazy way of getting planes to you, but it worked. No rules broken.'

She laughed, a soft fluttery sound that did us both some good.

'It wasn't long before I got another bright idea. I hitched a ride on a bomber out of RCAF Training Station Trenton to the 1st American Eagle Squadron over here and they let me sign up as a pilot officer. I had the flying hours and they needed the men, it was as simple as that. So I became part of your war, long before my own country decided to get involved.'

I closed my eyes, feeling some relief. But that was it, I was done, I didn't want to tell her any more. Anything else would dredge up memories I'd fought too long to keep down. Fortunately, Muriel didn't press me further. She must have sensed my change in mood, realized that more questions might arouse too much pain in me, release the bitterness I was holding in check. I liked her for that. Yeah, at that moment I almost loved her for it.

Opening my eyes, I leaned over and dogged the cigarette, then turned towards her. Her hand moved across my chest, her touch as sensuous as before, though less demanding, both of us at ease with one another. She shifted her body, offering her lips to me in the dark, and I accepted, my own mouth brushing against hers, the kiss tentative at first, but soon becoming firmer as fresh desire began to climb. Our tongues probed, we tasted each other's juices. Her hand slid down my chest, over my stomach, dipping beneath the rumpled sheet, finding my hardness and causing me to gasp as her fingers encircled and gripped me tight. I pulled her to me, one hand cradling her hip, and she turned her face towards the ceiling as my lips pressed against the softness of her neck.

Now she was gasping, and she squirmed her body so that she was beneath me, her legs parting once again as she murmured words I couldn't hear. Her breasts rose into me as her breathing became more uneven and her grip went to my waist, her hands pulling at me, her murmuring taking on a new urgency, her passion revived, her hunger just as desperate as before. I felt the familiar rush inside me, the incredible surging of senses, blood pounding in my chest so that I could hear its sound ... could hear ...

She cried out as I abruptly turned away from her, wheeling round in the bed to stare at the big windows. The pounding ... somewhere in the distance out there. Lighting up the night sky. And drawing closer by the second.

'Oh my God,' said Muriel, panic rising in her voice. 'What is it, Hoke?'

'Bombs,' I told her flatly.

'But –'

'We'll be okay. Don't worry about it.'

My back was to her and she slid closer, her hands reaching for my shoulders. I winced as her fingers touched the covered graze the bullet had left along my right shoulder earlier that day.

'Who is it, Hoke?' she pleaded. 'Who would be bombing London now? Is it those people who chased us?'

'Listen,' I said, my eyes still watching the windows.

The deep drone of engines came to us between the sounds of bombs exploding.

'An aeroplane?' she asked incredulously.

'You got it.'

The windows suddenly lit up and rattled in their frames as a bomb fell somewhere across the river.

'I don't understand. Why would any–'

I cut her off curtly. 'They're German. Possibly just one man, still fighting his own personal war. He's insane, d'you understand that?' I didn't know why I was angry at her; maybe it was because suddenly I had to explain things that I'd gotten used to.

She flinched as another bomb hit the other riverbank, the

blast shaking the hotel's windows, this time with more force.

'He comes over every once in a while, usually when you think things have quietened down again and he's given up. Given up or dead.'

'It's madness.'

'Like I said.'

Another explosion, this one on our side of the Thames and fierce enough to make the whole building tremble. Muriel pulled me round so that she could squeeze between my arms, and I was about to suggest we take cover on the other side or beneath the bed when another noise came to us, a harsh, demented rattling from the corridor outside our room. She tried to burrow into me and I wasn't sure which was scaring her most. The rattling grew louder, a terrible cacophony that resembled a stick running along iron railings, only a thousand times more piercing.

Then we heard the old warden's voice. *'Air raid warning, everyone under cover, please go to your nearest shelter!'*

The door burst open and Potter's bright flashlight lit us up on the bed. We shielded our eyes and the light dropped. I blinked away the dazzle and when I looked back at the doorway I saw there were two figures standing there.

Another blast outside – this one mercifully further off, the German bomber moving onwards – diverted my attention for a moment or two, and when I turned towards the doorway again, only Albert Potter was standing there, flashlight in one hand, his air raid warning rattle in the other. The second figure, Cissie, had gone.

11

I BROUGHT THE FLATBED truck round, a hard left from the Embankment into the gentle rise that ran between the park and the Savoy's rear entrance, and was surprised to see Cissie sitting on the kerbside opposite the hotel. I grinned when I saw who was keeping her company and I wondered at it too.

They both looked up when they heard the chug of the truck's diesel engine and the girl's concerned frown switched to a guarded smile of welcome when she realized I was the driver. Cagney quickly rose from his haunches and gave a pleased yap, then chased after me when I drove on by. I headed towards the end of the narrow street where there was room to turn the long vehicle round so it faced the right direction, easy to get away in a hurry should the need arise. Another road ran beneath the buildings at the end of the street, but it was blocked by other vehicles, its first few clear yards only good for manoeuvring. A few hundred yards away one of the buildings of London's law courts was still smouldering from last night's bomb damage, but I couldn't see any other wreckage. The crazy German bomber pilot was unpredictable, but I hoped he'd had his fill of laying waste for a while: sometimes he came over several nights in a row, sometimes he wouldn't appear for a few months; I guess it all depended on his disposition. I hoped some day a bomb would jam in its bay and blow him and his Dornier to smither-eens. After completing the laborious parking procedure, the truck's left wheels cracking pavement stones, I jumped down from the cab and made a fuss of Cagney, who'd been waiting for me.

I ruffled his ears, something he didn't like, never had, and he growled low and menacing, so I did it some more. Before he got too riled I hugged him to me and got a face full of tongue for my kindness. The taste of dust didn't seem to bother him and he would have slobbered me to death if I hadn't stood and pushed him down when he reared up with me. Taking the hint at the second shove, Cagney trotted off back along the street, making, to my surprise, straight for Cissie, who was still sitting on the kerb observing us.

Cissie averted her gaze before I reached her, studying some point in the distance, her neck and shoulders kind of stiff-like. I sat next to her, laying my leather jacket with its added weight of Colt .45 on the ground between us.

'Hyah,' I ventured.

'Hello,' she responded without much interest.

Cagney settled in the middle of the road, facing us, head resting on his paws. He yawned as he watched us.

'Hot day again,' I said, making conversation.

The back of Cissie's head bobbed in agreement. Today she was wearing a dark-brown dress that matched her hair, puffed at the shoulders, slim at the waist. No stockings and, when she finally turned my way, I saw she wore no make-up. She eyed the dust in my hair, on my hands, on my face, but ignored it for the moment.

'Is that *your* dog?'

'He's nobody's dog.'

'He was waiting outside when I came down for a breath of fresh air. I thought he was a stray.'

'He didn't run away?'

'He was wary at first, so I just sat there and talked to him and after a while he came over and sort of slouched down next to me. Wouldn't let me pat him though, moved away every time I tried.'

'Cagney doesn't like people very much. Seems to think they're to blame for everything that's happened.'

'Did you say Cagney? His name's Cagney?' At last her face cracked into a smile. 'After James Cagney?'

'Well his real name's probably Rex or Red, but he wasn't saying when we met up. I decided on Cagney and the mutt didn't seem to mind.'

'Has he been with you for long?'

'Coupla years, maybe.'

The sun beat down on the dusty roadway and pretty soon Cagney's eyes drooped shut. I took a rumpled rag from my pants pocket and wiped sweat from the back of my neck and underneath my chin.

'D'you have any idea what time it is?' Cissie asked, a coolness still there in her tone.

I looked over my shoulder and squinted up at the sun. ''Bout four, I'd guess. Busted my watch way back, had no use for it anyhow. Hell, I got no appointments to keep.'

'So where have you been all day?' She was looking directly at me now and I wondered at the suspicion in her eyes. 'You left before any of us were awake. Even before Muriel was awake, apparently,' she added meaningfully.

This time I looked away, staring up at the hotel's taped windows. The thought that so much death lay beyond them was depressing. 'I had things to do,' I replied eventually.

She must've understood that was all I had to say on the subject, because she didn't push it any further. I liked her for that.

'How've you survived, Hoke? How have you lived on your own like this for three years?' Curiosity, and maybe some concern, was edging aside her coolness.

'It's easier to get by when you've only got yourself to take care of. You can move faster and make your own decisions. It's a lot simpler this way.'

'You sound bitter.'

I gave a small, dry chuckle. 'Really? Well now.' I left it at that.

'The aeroplane that came over last night . . .'

'A Dornier Do 217. German medium bomber, the Flying Pencil they used to call it. Whoever's flying it doesn't realize the war's over, or doesn't care. And there's no way we can communicate.' I tucked the rag back into my pocket. 'Maybe one night I'll be waiting for him in a Spitfire or Hurricane and finish it once and for all.'

'No. No more killing, Hoke. Hasn't there been enough?'

'Try telling it to that guy.' I indicated the sky with my thumb and I could have meant the mad German pilot or the Creator Himself. It didn't matter which.

'What's the point of continuing the hatred? Look what it's already done to us.' She lowered her head and I could see the beginnings of tears glittering in her eyelashes.

I could stand my own self-pity, but not somebody else's. I pushed myself to my feet and reached down for my battered and torn leather jacket. 'I'm gonna clean up, then get a bite t'eat,' I said.

She joined me, brushing dust from her seat, and suddenly I was the one who was curious.

'How d'you get out of the hotel? Past all those dead people, I mean. Weren't you afraid?'

'Of what? Empty shells? You think I'm scared of ghosts too?' From the glint behind those unshed tears in her eyes I guessed Muriel had offered some kind of explanation, maybe even some excuse, for last night. 'No, I'm more afraid of maniacs still dropping bombs or lunatics trying to steal my blood.'

'I can ease your mind as far as one of those threats is concerned. Let me show you the safest place to be in the hotel when the bomber comes over again.'

I led her across the street and through the brick, zigzag barrier protecting the Savoy's River Room windows and back

159

entrance, Cagney immediately rousing from his doze to follow us. Inside the gloomy entrance hall I picked up the flashlight I always left in a corner by the stairway in case of emergencies or my own late-night arrivals, then took her downstairs to the hotel's vast basement area. We entered a long room on the left of the hallway and I played the flashlight over pink-curtained bunk-beds, all of them numbered.

'Sleeping quarters for the rich and famous,' I explained. 'At the first sound of an air-raid siren, Savoy guests were ushered down here for their own safety.'

I moved the light on, showing Cissie the discreet alcoves, heavy drapes across them turning their interiors into small but private chambers. 'For your royalty, big shots, even princes and princesses. If they were gonna shelter from the bombs, they were gonna do it in comfort.'

I picked out a bust resting on a pedestal at the far end of the room. 'Abe Lincoln,' I told her. 'This place is dedicated to him. The Yanks who came here looked on it as another tiny state of the Union wedged between the Strand and the Thames. A lot of work for the US was carried out down here, and a lot of bridges built between your country and mine.' I shone the light up at the ceiling and around the pillars. 'It's reinforced with thousands of feet of steel tubing and timber beams, all strengthened by concrete. The place is bomb-proof, Cissie, so if you get scared next time that damn crazy starts blitzing us again, just get yourself down here. Safest place in town.'

I felt her shiver beside me.

'Thanks for the tour,' she said, 'but can we leave now? There's something horrible about this room.'

I turned the flashlight on her and saw her eyes were wide and constantly moving, as if she expected something to jump out at her from the dark at any moment.

'I thought you weren't afraid of ghosts.'

She was already backing away. 'I'm not, but it's like

the Underground station down here, it feels like a mauso-leum. Hoke, have you looked behind those curtains?'

She had a point. It was one thing to be surrounded by the dead, but another to be enclosed with them, especially in the dark. I began to feel uneasy myself.

I followed her from the Abraham Lincoln Room and we climbed back to ground level. She became calmer standing in the light from the entrance doors, but I could tell she was still agitated. Could be I'd made a mistake taking her down there, because it had only underlined the fact that we were holed up in one huge tomb, and whether Cissie believed in spirits or not, the idea had to be a mite unnerving. Y'see, I'd forgotten how accustomed I'd become to living with the dead all around me. These people, save for Potter, weren't used to the new cities yet.

'How long have we got to stay here?' Cissie demanded to know.

I'd been trying to make things easier for her, so I guess I got a little irritated by her tone. 'Lady, you can leave when-ever you like.'

'But . . .' she started to say, 'but surely . . .'

I was stone-faced.

'Surely we'll stay together.' Her hands were held towards me, palms facing, more in exasperation than pleading. 'We need each other, Hoke, can't you understand that? Could you really go on living by yourself, with only . . . only a dog for company?'

Cagney, who'd stayed in a sunny spot by the entrance, cocked his head. He looked from Cissie to me, as if waiting for the reply.

'Cagney's been enough so far,' I shot back. 'He doesn't gripe and he doesn't need nurse-maiding. Yeah, I'll stick with the mutt.'

She left me then, stomping up the stairs, head and shoul-ders stiff with suppressed – outrage, resentment, good old-fashioned pique? I didn't know which – and I had to resist the urge to call her back. Cagney made a noise deep in his throat, a kind of drawn-out groan, and rolled his eyes at me.

'Quit it,' I snapped, and went back out into the sunshine.

Muriel was waiting for me when I eventually got back to the suite. She was standing by the window, a hand parting the net curtain so she could watch feeble strands of smoke rising from somewhere across the river, another piece of real estate damaged in last night's explosions. She dropped the curtain and hurried towards me as I closed the door.

'I've been so anxious,' she said and stopped a few steps away when she saw the dust in my hair and clothes. 'My goodness, what have you been up to? You look so . . . dirty.'

I'd left Cagney outside where he could guard the corridor, a position he was well used to by now, so I didn't have to contend with his growling suspicion of this stranger in the room. Again I wondered at his swift acceptance of Cissie, particularly as I hadn't been there to make the introductions in the first place. I remembered I was still rankled with the girl, so any credit I gave her was limited. Tossing my jacket onto the bed and ignoring Muriel's question, I headed straight for the bathroom. She followed me in.

Muriel started the shower for me as I tugged off my undershirt and I heard her gasp when she saw the massive bruising on my chest and the inflamed edges of the gunshot nick showing around the dressing. She took in some of the other cuts and bruises on my arms and body, shaking her head in sympathy as she did so.

'Does it hurt badly?' It was a dumb question and she knew it. 'Do you have any pain-killers that I can get for you?' she added quickly.

I shook my head and took her by the elbow. 'I'm gonna take my shower alone,' I told her.

162

'Let me help. You must be sore all over.'

Yeah, I was sore, and I ached too, some of that from the day's work I'd just done, but I didn't need anybody's help to wash myself. 'I'd like some privacy, Muriel.'

Disappointment, hurt – I guess both were in those grey-blue eyes of hers. 'Can't I stay and talk to you? Last night –'

I cut her off. 'Last night was last night. You needed me, and I wanted you – last night. Today's another day, kid.' Bogart couldn't have put it better.

Now she looked stunned. 'I don't understand,' was all she could think of to say.

'Look, you came to me for one thing last night, and you got it.' I'd never spoken to a girl like that before and I think I was almost as shocked as Muriel, although my anger covered it. Not only had the world changed, but I had too. I didn't back off though, and the English Rose before me wilted under the blast. 'You think you fooled me with all that stuff about seeing ghosts? Christ, I knew what you wanted soon as I opened the door. You and your friend, you just want a man around to look out for you, keep you out of danger, keep you fed. Well you picked the wrong guy, y'hear me? Maybe you better start cosying up to your friend Vilhelm. Sure, he'll take care of you. Didn't you know he's the new Master Race?'

'Why are you so angry?' she pleaded. 'What have I done?'

Why? The heck of it was that I didn't know myself. Maybe I was scared of getting involved with other people after I'd spent so long looking out for myself. Was I angry at their intrusion, the sudden burden of having all these people around me? Or in truth, was I plain ashamed of myself for taking this girl to the same bed Sally and I had first made love in? I felt my face redden and it wasn't through rage. Yeah, that was it, or at least a big part of it. Maybe it was foolish, but I felt I'd betrayed the one love of my life, someone I'd sworn eternal love for, no matter what. Stupid kid's stuff?

No, not really. Despite the war going on, and both of us knowing that we could die the next day or even that night, we'd made promises to each other that we vowed to keep. Not only had I broken my part of the deal, but I'd done it in the very bedroom Sally and I had honeymooned in. Although I'd had pangs of guilt at the time – all of them easily overwhelmed by the moment itself – the real sense of what I'd done had hit me with its full force when I'd opened the door to Suite 318–319 and found Muriel standing there. Sure I was mad, madder than hell, but not at Muriel, not at Cissie, not at any of them ('cept Stern, but that was different). I was mad at myself. And I was ashamed. The combination was bad.

But I couldn't say all this to Muriel. No, instead I spun away from her and smashed the heel of my hand into the mirror over the washbasin, cracking the glass and fragmenting my image. I heard her give out a small scream and when I glared at her over my raised arm, my palm still pressed against the splintered glass, blood beginning to drip into the sink below it, she seemed about ready to run. I felt stupid, but I must have appeared insane.

I was ready to make some comment – it could've been an apology or a cuss – when Cagney started barking up a storm outside in the corridor. We heard shouting, more barking; something thumped against the bedroom door.

I moved fast, pushing Muriel aside and taking time to snatch the Colt from its holster inside my jacket. Then I was at the door, yanking it open. I stopped dead, gun hand extended.

Cagney was upset. He was damn-near rabid. Crouched low, snout wrinkled over yellow teeth, haunches quivering, the dog was getting ready to launch itself at something or someone standing beside the door I'd just thrown open.

'It is wild.' Shit – *v*ild.

I took a step forward into the corridor so that I could see him. The German had his back pressed against the wall and there was real fear in those pallid eyes of his. Like mine, one of his arms was outstretched, at the end of it the muzzle of a small automatic. He was pointing it at Cagney.

My reaction was almost instinctive, the thought and the movement instantaneous: I smashed my own weapon down hard on Stern's exposed wrist. Spittle shot from the German's open mouth with the shock and his gun clattered to the floor. He bent forward, clutching at his arm, and I brought my gun hand up again, catching him on the forehead so that he straightened and his head slammed against the wall behind. He slid to the floor and I went with him, grabbing the lapel of his jacket and jabbing the Colt's muzzle into his scarred neck.

'Please stop.'

His jaw must've been numbed, because the two words weren't that coherent. I understood them though.

'The animal...' he managed to blurt. 'It was ... it was going to attack me ... when I tried to enter your room.' That's what he tried to say, but it didn't come out quite that well. I couldn't have cared less anyway – I was ready to blow his brains out.

'Hoke!'

Female's voice, but I wasn't taking enough notice to decide whose. It was time to settle the score with the German and I was just mad enough to do it right then and there. Blood oozing from my cut hand made the gun's grip slippery, but still I pressed it into the flesh of his neck. A scream then and I glanced round to see Muriel standing in the doorway. It was Cissie who attacked me though.

Her knee connected with the side of my head, knocking me aside. Then her fingers tangled themselves in my hair and she pulled me backwards, so that I sprawled onto my back. She followed through by kneeling on my chest and grabbing at my gun hand, while Cagney leapt around us, yapping and too excited to figure out which one of us to attack. With a quick swipe of my other hand, I knocked

Cissie away and raised my shoulders off the carpeted floor, the Colt finding its target once more.

'Don't shoot him!'

Now it was Muriel who was getting in the way. She positioned herself between me and the stunned German and screamed down at me.

'Stop it, stop it now! We can't go on killing one another, don't you understand?'

To complete the picture, Albert Potter came lumbering along the corridor from his suite. For some reason he still had the warning rattle he'd used last night in his hand and for one bad moment I thought he was gonna blast our ears with it again. Instead he shouted: 'What the bleedin 'ell's goin on? Can't a fellah get a decent kip around 'ere?' Mercifully, he tucked the rattle back into one of the large pockets in his overalls.

Cissie, a leg still across my chest, finally got both hands around my wrist and pulled the gun away from its mark.

'Please, Hoke, give it up,' she pleaded and there was a sob at the end of her words.

I glanced at her, saw the tears beginning to roll, and I guess it was that that took the wind out of me. I was still full of rage, but some of its energy had left me. I let my head slump back onto the carpet, and as I lay there, staring up at the ceiling, I relaxed my grip on the gun, let my arm go limp. Still Cissie clung to my wrist, not trusting me.

'Okay. I'm done,' I assured her. 'Just get him outta my sight for a while.' They knew I meant Stern and not the dog who, now that the commotion was over, was trying to lick my face.

I heard someone helping the German to his feet, and then he was standing over me, looking down. There was no wariness in his eyes, no fear, only a simmering anger.

'You are a fool,' he hissed. 'There was no need for this. I am not your enemy.'

166

I ignored him, then suddenly remembered the gun he'd been aiming at Cagney. I sat up, fast, Cissie's grip instantly tightening on my wrist. With relief I saw that Potter had picked up the German's weapon.

'What's this then?' the warden mused, as if he'd never seen a gun before.

'It's a US military issue Colt 380,' I informed him, and he nodded his head like he knew all along. 'Don't let Stern have it,' I warned.

'Do you really think I would shoot you?' Stern sounded almost regretful. 'After all that has happened . . .' He waved his hands around as if indicating the world outside. 'I found this weapon in my room and kept it for my own protection. I believe I was wise to do so. But do you honestly believe I have the desire to kill again? If you do, then you really are insane, Hoke. The Blood Death has made you so.'

With that he walked away from us, one hand held to his injured forehead. He disappeared inside his room and we heard the door close quietly behind him.

Supper that evening was a miserable affair. No one felt much like talking and Stern didn't even join us. Let him sulk, I thought, it didn't bother me none. Potter did his best to get things going by reminiscing, relating stories of the Blitz, some of them funny, some of them not so. He told us how one night when he was on his rounds, he'd found Ed Murrow, the famous American war correspondent, lying in the gutter outside the Savoy, not rolling drunk, as Potter had first assumed, but picking up the sounds of wailing sirens and enemy bombs hitting their targets with his microphone, these authentic noises of war to be broadcast across the Atlantic. He told us about the authorities' grand idea of turning gas masks into Mickey Mouse faces so the kids wouldn't be afraid to wear them; how once he'd chased a couple of looters through Covent Garden only to see them both blown to pieces before his eyes by a land mine, one of the looter's legs landing on his shoulder as he'd stood there surprised; how on a cold, frosty dawn he'd come upon an elderly, white-haired lady sitting up in bed, totally bewildered as to why she was in the open, one floor up, two walls of her house completely demolished. He told us about the fireman he'd witnessed breaking down a warehouse door across the street, the poor man sucked inside by the firestorm when the door collapsed, to be burned to nothing, not even his bones left in the ashes; the warning whistle Potter always carried but which got stuck in his throat when a nearby explosion caused him to suck instead of blow, only a hefty blow on the back by a Heavy Rescue worker, who wondered why Potter was turning blue, saving his life when the whistle popped back into his mouth; the effigy of Adolf Hitler, wearing baggy grey bloomers, hanging by the neck from a crooked bus stop sign in Whitehall; the milk-cart horse painted with white stripes so that it wouldn't get knocked down on dark winter mornings.

Potter rambled on, amused and saddened in turn by his own stories, while across the room Muriel gave me an occasional long meaningful look, which I ignored, and Cissie, who'd taken over the cooking, shot me an angry glance from time to time, which I also ignored. We ate mostly in silence, Potter finally giving up the chatter, and both girls left the suite as soon as pans and plates were washed. Muriel's 'good night' was kind of stiff, and Cissie didn't bother. So the warden and me, we cracked open another Jack Daniel's and finished it between us.

He was a mite unsteady when he left me that night, and he said a funny thing. He swayed in the doorway and laid a stubby finger against that beetroot nose of his, giving me a wink at the same time.

'I know what yer business is, son. And it's okay by me. Bloke's got to do what he thinks is best, even if it is 'opeless.

I won't tell another bleedin soul, seein as 'ow yer keepin it secret yerself.'

He shook his head, his eyes bleary with the booze.

'But it can't be done, boy. It can't bloody well be done. There's too . . .'

He just shook his head again and walked away.

'Too bloody many . . .' I heard him say as he tottered down the corridor.

12

I'D CLEARED THE STREET. This was the last carcass. Any others were out of sight, inside the buildings. Like they say – *said*: Out of sight, out of mind. Only they weren't; I could still see them in my mind's eye, slumped in chairs, sprawled across tables, curled up on floors – dried-out, feather-light shucks, dusty, brittle refuse. My mind could always see them inside shops, restaurants, offices, dwellings, factories, stations, vehicles ... Christ, the list went on forever. But I couldn't take them all. As Potter had remarked: 'There were too bloody many ...'

I lifted the bag of bones onto the back of the truck, oblivious to its shrivelled eyes, like black raisins above its yawning, meatless mouth, and it slithered down at me from the pile, a reluctant evacuee. Its bony fingers snagged against my sweatshirt as I pushed it back and I was too tired and too seasoned to feel any revulsion. When the desiccated corpse was settled, I picked up my jacket lying on the kerbside and the rifle leaning against the truck's rear wheel, then climbed into the cab.

Once this had been an ordinary city street, its houses untouched by Hitler's worst, the corner pub still open for business; but weeds now grew between the cracks in the pavements and vehicles rusted away in the road. But it was the silence that got to me. After three long and lonely years,

I still hadn't become used to that eerie hush, not in undamaged streets like this where everything seemed so normal. It was as if the place was ... well, haunted. I thought of Muriel's ghosts back at the Savoy and got angry with myself.

Slamming the truck's door after me, I tossed my jacket onto the passenger seat and settled the rifle in the footwell on that side, its muzzle leaning against the open window opposite, pointed away from me but within easy reach. The girl had been wrong, she was haunted by memories, not by spectres. Even I'd imagined the sound of voices, laughter – music, too – drifting up to me as I'd lain awake nights in that grand rotting mausoleum. Couple of times I'd even gone to the door and listened, opening it when I was sure there really was something going on downstairs, the noises always vanishing the moment I stepped out into the corridor. Just night-notions, that's all they were. Dreams when I hadn't even realized I'd been asleep. Muriel would soon get to realize that imagination had a way of playing tricks on you when you were in a low frame of mind. They weren't just dreams either, they were *wishful* dreams, dreams you hoped would be true, cravings for life to return to normal, to the way it had once been. Daybreak always put things right again; as right as they were ever gonna be.

I turned on the engine, took one last look at the deserted street out the side window, and drove off. Although weary from my labours and a little hungover from the night before, I kept alert, constantly on the lookout for the unexpected. One time about a year and some months ago, a crazy had jumped out at the truck I was using, an Austin 5-ton, as I recall, its flap sides and back easy for loading. He was waving a butcher's meat axe over his head and hollering gibberish at me. Maybe I should have stopped, but it was the middle of winter and this guy was stark naked. And oh yeah, around his neck under a long greasy beard he wore a ragged necklace of severed, blackened hands. When he realized I wasn't gonna stop, he threw the axe at me. Luckily, his aim was

171

poor and it broke through the windshield on the passenger side, so I kept going, heading straight for him, figuring he wasn't in the mood to discuss his complaint. Well, he didn't even try to dodge me, just kept coming forward, screaming and shaking his fists; and I didn't try to avoid him either. I ran right over him, and when I stopped further down the road and looked back, I saw his naked body was still twitching. By the time I'd climbed out and walked back to him, he was trying to crawl along the gutter, his back broken, both legs crushed. It wasn't out of mercy that I put the gun to his head and fired, nor was it out of spite: those feelings didn't come into it. No, I was just carrying on as usual; I was just tidying up.

When his body finally lay at rest, I added his corpse to the rest of my cargo and took him with me.

There were other creatures I had to keep a lookout for, mainly cats and wild dogs who'd lost any road sense, but mostly I kept my eyes open for Blackshirts, who had a nasty habit of appearing when I least expected it. Although it was a big city, it was inevitable that our paths should cross from time to time. Our battles were usually short and sharp, and I always had the advantage that their sickness had slowed them down considerably.

Today was a good day though, the summer making up for winter's severity, when there were twelve-foot high snowdrifts along the streets. The sky was clear again, but a slight breeze coming in from the east was keeping things a little cooler. With my full load, I avoided craters, debris and any other wreckage along the route, heading north, the way well known to me by now. Within twenty minutes I'd reached my destination.

I drove straight up the ramp into the stadium whose stands had once held over a hundred thousand people at a time. I passed through the tunnel and emerged inside the vast arena itself. Driving past stacked gasoline cans and boxes of explosives, I headed into the centre aisle whose banks were formed by piled-high rotted corpses, turning at its centre into a narrower lane, the stink hardly bothering me these days. Occasionally I spotted movement among the heaps, the vermin disturbed but not intimidated by my presence. I used to waste time taking potshots at them, at the scavenging dogs too, but nowadays I didn't bother: when the time came, they'd burn along with the corrupted things they feasted on.

Soon I reached a clearing, the grass there long and unhealthy-looking, and I brought the diesel flatbed to a halt. I stood on the running board for a while, just listening, checking around me. As I gazed over those great mounds of human debris I wondered how much more I could accomplish. Almost three long years I'd been filling this huge arena with the dead, always aware it could be no more than a token gesture. Lime pits and thousands of cardboard coffins had been made ready in the early days of the war in case they were needed, but nobody had predicted the Blood Death. Most of the population had remained where they'd dropped. 'Cept for these people. At least they were gonna receive some kind of burial.

It didn't take long to unload this, my last haul of the day, and soon I was on my way back across London, leaving the grimy walls of Wembley Stadium behind, a place where once crowds had gathered to roar their excitement, but which was now just one huge and silent burial vault.

One day, when I was satisfied I'd done all I could, it would be their crematorium.

13

I'D CLEANED MYSELF UP and was sprawled half-naked on the bed, a glass of Scotch held on my bruised chest, cigarette in my other hand, when there was a knock on the door.

'Hoke? It's me, Muriel. Can I come in?'

I inhaled, exhaled, lifted my head and took another sip of the Scotch.

'Hoke.'

She sounded impatient. The doorhandle rattled.

With a groan, I rolled off the bed, placed the glass on the cabinet, and grabbed my pants. Cigarette drooping from the corner of my mouth, I unlocked the door and opened it a few inches. Smoke curled out into the corridor.

Muriel was wearing a different outfit, a cream blouse and loose, brown slacks, her hair drawn back on one side with a slide. She looked good – even *grubby* she'd looked good – but I didn't let that affect me.

'You've been gone most of the day again,' she said, and there seemed little sense in replying to the obvious. After a pause: 'Can I come in for a minute?'

Leaving the door open so that the option was hers, I picked up a shirt lying across the back of an easy chair and shrugged it on. I didn't bother with the buttons, hoping her stay would be short; I sat on the edge of the bed, close to the Scotch.

Muriel closed the door behind her and stood in front of me.

'No point in asking where you went to, I suppose?' Her neat, pencilled eyebrows were raised.

'Had things to do,' was my response.

'Why so surly, Hoke? The other night . . .' She left it there, waving a hand in exasperation.

What could I tell her? That guilt was busting my head, making me feel Sally's presence all around me in that room? It was stupid; I knew it then, I know it now. Three years dead and I was still grieving for her, mourning for the life together we'd been denied. The whole fucking world gone to damnation and I was still focused on my own loss. And now I not only suffered the guilt of survival, but of betrayal also. It was morbid and it was irrational; but when I closed my eyes I still saw my young bride in this room with me, breathed in her perfume, heard her whispers. And I had closed my eyes.

I opened them quickly.

'We . . . I . . . made a mistake,' was all I could think of to say, and in truth, I wasn't sure if I was addressing Muriel, or someone long since dead.

'A mistake? My God, man, don't you realize we're living in a whole new world with a different morality? I wasn't asking for love, just comfort, compassion. I was frightened, don't you understand?'

Or staking a claim? I wondered, then hated myself for the cynicism. I dragged on the cigarette, confused, maybe even disgusted with myself. Anger was burning me.

'All right,' she said in a resigned, kind of stiff-backed voice. She was tired of reasoning with me and I couldn't blame her for that. 'I only wanted to let you know that Cissie and I have arranged a dinner party for us all downstairs in the Pinafore Room.'

I stared up at her as if she were the wacky one here.

'Hoke, we've got to put the past behind us. It's unreasonable of you to carry on despising Wilhelm Stern just because

175

he's a German. Gracious, not only did he not personally start the war against us, but he actually played very little part in it. He was shot down and captured in 1940, for God's sake!' Her tone changed and she looked at me appealingly. 'We've got to forgive and forget, don't you see? How else can we build a new life for ourselves? Some order has to come out of all this and that can only be if we cast past grudges aside.'

She strode to the writing desk and leaned back against it, arms folded, eyes intense. 'It's time for those of us who are left to come to our senses, to introduce some kind of order to our lives. What else is there otherwise? Lawlessness? Chaos?'

Calmer now, I swung my legs up onto the bed and rested my back against the headboard so that I could watch her across the room. She was *serious*. The planet had gone to blazes and she was talking law and order. Resting my cigarette hand on my raised knee, I cocked my head at her.

'You don't see it's all finished?' I was genuinely surprised. 'You don't see that our so-called civilization has gone AWOL? Jesus Christ, Muriel, there's nothing left for any of us.'

'We're alive, blast you, and there are many more like us, waiting to make a fresh start, waiting for the survivors to come together again, perhaps even hoping for a new leader. It can be better than before, we can avoid the same age-old mistakes.'

Maybe she was right. That's what I thought as I smoked the cigarette, my gaze never leaving hers. Someone had to start things rolling again and probably – *no doubt* – it was already happening in other parts of the globe. So why not here, in what used to be one of the world's greatest cities? I studied Muriel in a way I hadn't before. She was a slight, almost fragile, kind of girl, but I could see the resolve in her, a steeliness that I guess came with her breeding. Lord knows, as a kid my head had been filled with literature

176

depicting England's upper classes as people of fine character and great purpose (although Ma had warned me it wasn't all true), and at that moment I was beginning to glimpse those qualities in Muriel. I'd witnessed the good old British stiff-upper-lip style in plenty of the RAF types I'd flown with, so I shouldn't have been surprised to see the same trait in a lord's daughter. Okay, a romantic view of the English – at least, of their gentry – but I'd had plenty of evidence to back it up since coming to these shores, and looking at Muriel across the room, that intensity still in her eyes, her jawline delicate but determined, I suddenly thought she might just have the backbone to see it through. Another thing I realized, though, was that my kind of cynicism could play no part in her vision of a bright new future. But that didn't mean I'd discourage her. Truth was, I didn't care one way or the other.

'*Will* you join us this evening, Hoke?' Her tone softened, her arms had unfolded. 'Stern and Potter cleared some of the rooms downstairs and even raided the hotel's foodstores. We've set up a makeshift kitchen in the private dining room next door to the Pinafore, and Wilhelm even went out and found us two portable oil cookers bigger and a touch more sophisticated than the ones you've been using.'

'He left the Savoy?' I didn't like the idea.

'We've all been out today. What did you expect us to do – remain cooped up all day in this place waiting for your return? For myself, I travelled across town to Daddy's Kensington apartment.'

'By yourself? Christ, woman, why?'

'Are you really that dense, Hoke? I wanted to visit our old home, is that so unreasonable? After all, it was why we returned to London. I have certain things of sentimental value there, photographs, diaries and, yes, even jewellery. Things I want to keep to remind me of better times. And clothes, my own clothes. Yes, I know I could choose from any fashionable Knightsbridge shop, but I wanted certain

177

items I already possessed, is that so difficult to understand? Cissie would have done exactly the same if she'd still had a home to go to. Instead she stayed behind and helped get everything ready.'

'But –' I started again, then let it go. 'Okay. How did you get there?'

For the first time since she'd entered the suite she smiled. 'I was going to use any motorcar I could find still working. Instead I found a bicycle that wasn't rusted completely – it was inside a shop – so I used that. It squeaked a lot and the tyres need pumping up, but it got me through all the parked traffic in the streets.'

'D'you have any idea where Stern went to?'

'I told you, he found us some better cookers, so obviously he got those from one of those big camping stores nearby. Potter went off on his own too, probably patrolling the streets looking for UXBs and incendiaries. He's quite dotty, you know.' She moved from the writing desk and stood at the end of the bed. 'Why so pensive, Hoke? What's troubling you now?'

Dogging the cigarette, I replied, 'The city's a dangerous place.'

'The Blackshirts, you mean? I didn't catch a glimpse of one. But then, it *is* a huge city. Anyway, I'm sure they assumed they'd killed us all when they set fire to the Underground station.'

I wondered. Would Hubble and his Looney-Tunes army think we were dead by now? The notion that he'd lost four valuable blood donors would have sent Hubble into a frenzy and I pitied the fool who'd broken the news to him that they'd fire-bombed the station. If only that were the case, if only Hubble believed we were gone for good ... On my own travels that day I'd seen neither hide nor hair of any Blackshirts, although that wasn't unusual; as Muriel said, it was a big city. Besides, I always kept off the beaten track, taking side streets rather than main thoroughfares. But heck, it was a pleasant enough thought on an otherwise grim day. Muriel took advantage of my sudden smile.

'You'll come, then?'

I blinked.

'Our little celebratory dinner,' she persisted. 'You'll join us downstairs?'

'What're you celebrating?'

'Just being alive. Isn't that enough?'

Sometimes I thought it was too much, but I didn't say that. 'Okay, I'll be there. But don't get the idea I'll be making any new friends.'

'All I ask is that you be civil to Wilhelm.' She left it at that.

They'd found hundreds more candles from somewhere and had filled every nook and cranny with them so that the Pinafore Room resembled some holy shrine. They were supplemented by two or three oil lamps in strategic positions around the room, and the heat and waxy smell took some getting used to at first. Behind the thick, rich drapes daylight was fading and, despite the candleglow, there were dark shadows in the room, especially in its corners. Warm scintillas of light reflected off tall glasses and cutlery set around the long table, and cedar panelling, studded with silver buttons, on the walls and central square column lent a soft ambience to the proceedings. It was a ritzy setting for a dinner party, an evocation of more pleasant times.

I paused in the open doorway, Cagney at my side, his nose in the air, sniffing out food.

Muriel was chatting to Wilhelm Stern before a tall mirror over an empty fireplace at the far end of the room, and an elegant couple they made, she in a slim floor-length gown that shimmered silver, cut high from shoulder to shoulder, with long tight sleeves, her hair once again held to one side but this time by a decorative comb, while he wore a dark evening suit, white handkerchief, probably silk, peeping from his breast pocket, his tie a deep grey worn against a white shirt. They'd made an effort for this evening's *soirée* (clinging to the wreckage?) and I was relieved to see that Potter, who'd suddenly appeared at a double door on my left, hadn't bothered to fancy himself up at all: he still wore his warden's all-in-one outfit, although he'd brushed it down and his helmet was nowhere in evidence.

Spotting me, he called, 'Grub's up soon, son,' and pointed a stubby thumb over his shoulder at the room behind. He gave me a broad, yellow-toothed grin. 'There's time for a pair o' teeth first, though. What can I get yer?'

I frowned.

Muriel wised me up. 'Albert means an *apéritif*. As I'm sure he knows,' she added, looking meaningfully at the warden and smiling. She turned her smile on me, but it had an uneasy edge to it, as though she was a little nervous.

As I walked the length of the table towards them Cagney trotted before me, his excuse for a tail wagging in anticipation of the food he could smell. He disappeared through the opening behind Potter and I heard Cissie's muted cry of welcome. The mutt was getting used to people again too fast and that concerned me: I didn't want him to lose his usual caution in case eventually it proved dangerous for both of us.

'We're using the Princess Ida Room as a makeshift kitchen,' Muriel told me, and I remembered that all the names of the private dining rooms along this floor had something to do with Gilbert and Sullivan operas. 'Cissie's in there playing chef and I must get back to help before she starts getting cross.' She eyed me up and down as she sipped her drink. 'Thank you at least for putting on a fresh shirt.'

I checked her eyes for sarcasm, but she quickly looked away. My pants were a little wrinkled, my boots none too clean, and my torn leather jacket was thrown over one arm, pistol tucked inside. The shirt *was* fresh though, one of a bunch I'd picked out of a Regent Street menswear shop's smashed window, none of which I'd gotten round to wearing until now. I guess it would've looked better with a tie, but ties never had been one of my things, even in peacetime. Muriel moved closer to me, away from the German.

'What would you like to drink?' she asked, but again she averted her gaze when I looked directly into her eyes. 'Gin and tonic, a Martini, sherry . . . ? We're well stocked, as you can see.'

'Scotch'll do.'

'Good boy,' approved Potter. 'Think I'll join yer.' He bustled over to a small, round dining table that was loaded with the hard stuff. Rubbing his fleshy hands together he cast his eye over the wide selection. He spied the Scotch, another bottle of his favourite Grouse. 'Lovely,' we heard him mutter.

'Hoke . . .'

It was the German and there was a wariness in his approach. I laid my jacket over the back of a chair at the head of the long table, folded so that the concealed holster would be easy to reach, before facing him.

'It is extremely foolish for us to regard each other as enemies,' Stern said, his manner relaxed, but still that appre- hensive cautiousness in his eyes. 'In the war I was merely a navigator doing my job, as were you as a fighter pilot. I mean you no harm now and would' – *v*ould – 'hope you no longer wish me any harm. We were airmen loyal to our own countries, but all that is in the past. We can no longer live that way. We should endeavour to live in peace and, as the British themselves say, let bygones be bygones.' Speech finished, he offered me a hand to shake.

Unfortunately, I didn't take to the idea of shaking the hand of someone I would eventually kill, so I ignored the offer. His pale eyes momentarily hardened, and then he smiled as he let his hand fall away.

'So be it,' he said coldly. 'I have made an effort to be civil

– or indeed, civilized – and I shall continue to do so. You will make up your own mind about how you regard me, but I must warn you, I shall always defend myself.'

'Please, Wilhelm.' Muriel looked anxiously from me to Stern. 'This isn't necessary.'

'Have I not just tried to make that very point?' He never took his eyes off me. 'I will behave honourably, but Mr Hoke must decide for himself. I have offered the hand of friendship and he has rejected it, but still I will not be the one to make trouble.'

Potter arrived between us with two tumblers of Scotch in his hands, one of them held out to me. 'Bottoms up,' he said cheerfully, as if he hadn't noticed the exchange between myself and the German.

'Yeah,' I responded, taking the tumbler and tipping it against my lips, my gaze still not breaking from Stern's. We all turned when another voice called from the far end of the room.

'Dinner's coming along nicely.' Cissie was in the doorway to the Princess Ida Room, wiping her hands with a cloth. 'So I'm going to socialize for a bit. I think a large g-and-t would go down very nicely right now.' She tossed the cloth onto something behind her and headed our way.

'You've earned it.' Muriel quickly busied herself at the drinks table, glad to turn her back on the tension between Stern and me, I guess. 'I think I'll have another one, myself.'

Fumes from the portable oil cookers kept drifting through from next door to mix with the smell of melting wax, but they didn't spoil our feast any. We kicked off with oatmeal soup and dumplings, followed by 'brisket of beef', as Cissie announced, and while tinned beans and peas may have been a poor substitute for turnips and parsnips, they didn't spoil the taste of this particular meat pie. Together with potatoes and carrots (fresh, from my own home-grown stock), it made one of the finest meals – no, *the* finest meal – I'd had in three years, and by the time we'd finished pudding – semolina and Prince Roly – we were all fit to bust.

I was at the head of the table for no other reason than that I'd left my jacket over the chair there, and on my right was Cissie, who wore a coffee-coloured, below knee-length evening dress, which was a mite too tight for her. Muriel was on my left and our conversation throughout the meal had been minimal – she was still edgy, probably afraid trouble might flare up between myself and Stern at any moment. Stern sat next to her, old Potter opposite him. Cagney was under the table by my feet, well fed and snoozing, content to be among friendly people again (although he'd given a small warning growl every time the German got too close), and at the far end of the table, facing me, was a strange, almost exotic creature, silent, unmoving, and black, with a pink napkin tied around its neck. Muriel had introduced me to it when we'd first sat down to eat.

'Meet Kaspar,' she'd said. 'He's our guest this evening because the Pinafore Room used to be used by members of what was known as The Other Club, a collection of, well, rather eminent people, and politicians – Winston Churchill was one of them. The politicians dined here whenever parliament was in session, industrialists and other powerful men joining them. You'll see there's seating for fourteen around this table, but whenever there was an empty chair and the number of people present was an unlucky thirteen, they brought out Kaspar the cat. They tied a napkin around his neck and served him every course.'

There was something I didn't like about the three-foot-high black animal. Maybe it was its down-turned head and pointed ears, or its sinuous, snake-like tail that looped round in an almost full circle, or its arched spine etched with scrawls that looked like esoteric writings. I couldn't figure out why, but as the evening wore on, I realized it was just the creature's dark, brooding presence that made me feel uncomfortable; there was something ominous about it, as if it were a portent of doom rather than a good-luck charm. Now, over coffee and brandy, and some fine cigars Potter had scrounged from somewhere, the seal of the box they came in unbroken, the conversation returned to Kaspar.

'We found it on a shelf at the back of the room,' Cissie was explaining. 'We thought it would add some dignity to the proceedings.' She giggled at Muriel, hand to her mouth like a schoolkid. She'd joined the menfolk in the brandies. 'D'you think it'll bring us luck?'

I reserved judgement and it was Stern who answered.

'I have never understood if the black cat means good or bad fortune to the English. Are you saying it is good?'

Potter piped up. 'Always said meself if a black mog crosses yer path, yer in for a spot of bad luck.'

'No, no, that's wrong,' argued Cissie. My grandad always told me a black cat was good luck.'

'Wasn't that only on one's wedding day?' put in Muriel.

'No!' Cissie and Potter cried together.

'There are only five of us around this table anyway,' I pointed out, stabbing the air with my cigar. Blue smoke drifted towards the ceiling.

'Well spotted.'

I shrugged at Cissie's sarcasm.

'We were just making up the numbers.' Muriel gave her friend a worried glance. 'I mean to say, we're hardly a crowd, are we? What kind of discussions do you suppose they had in this room? With all those important club members – ambassadors, dignitaries, newspaper owners and editors, as well as the politicians themselves – some very momentous decisions must have been made. No church people were allowed in, by the way. But the Prime Minister himself –'

'Don't matter, neither way.' It was out of character for Potter to interrupt Muriel; it'd been plain throughout the evening that he regarded her upper-class credentials with some respect, if not awe. It seemed too much whisky, wine and brandy had blurred the class division for him, and I, for one, was glad to see it. 'Don't matter how grand they was, how much power was in their hands, they come down with the plague jus like everybody else. 'Cept us. We didn't. Money couldn't buy it off, an nor could fame. Neville Chamberlain – the gerk, I mean berk – to Jessie Matthews, Ivor Novello to Herbert Morrison, Martin bloody Bormann –'scuse me, my dears – to Groucho Marx, all dead, see? Unless...' He waved his finger around the table. 'Unless they was like us, our blood thingy. We're special, see? All the others ... werl, all the others...' He seemed at a loss. 'Werl, they're gone. Finished.'

'Then why do you still patrol the streets, Mr Potter?' The German was leaning forward, a cigar between his fingers. 'If almost everybody else is gone, why do you continue with your work?'

The logic didn't please the old boy. 'I should give up me duty jus 'cos things've changed? Without orders to stand down? With the *Luftwaffe* still knockin ten bells out of London? You Germans never did understand us English, did yer?'

'And you English never quite understood we did not want war with your country. The *Führer* had a great...' he considered the right word '... affinity with many of your people.'

'Oh no, not very many.' Cissie looked about ready to toss her wine at Stern. 'What you really mean is he had an affinity with a certain type of Englishman. Some of our so-called ruling class didn't think Adolf Hitler was such a bad chap.'

'That is not quite correct,' Stern replied, as smooth as Conrad Veidt. 'A good number of the English common people understood the Jewish problem, for instance. And I think all classes accepted our right to play a major role in the governance of Europe.'

'Only other Fascists believed that.'

'Please let's not argue among ourselves.' Muriel obviously didn't like this turn in the conversation.

The German was quick to respond to her plea. 'I did not mean to cause disagreement between us, but you must understand that I, too, loved my country, and I have suffered as much as anybody in this room.'

I placed my empty brandy glass on the table and dropped the butt of my cigar into it. My hands remained on the tabletop, about a foot apart, fingers clenched. 'Oh yeah, we understand, *V*ilhelm. After all, you were a good German, weren't you? A good, fighting Nazi.'

He regarded me warily, trusting me not one little bit. 'All Germans are – were – not Nazis.'

'Hoke . . .' Muriel warned.

'Of course not.' I leaned forward. 'And you, personally, never really had the chance to fight us, did you? You got yourself shot down right at the beginning of the war, so we can't hate you, can we? You hardly had time to cause much damage, and besides, you were only a navigator anyway, so didn't *personally* pull any triggers or push any buttons.'

'That is certainly the case. I told you –'

'Yeah, you told us you were captured and interned in April 1940, isn't that right? So why should we bear you any grudge? Hell, you practically played no part at all in the war.'

I felt Cagney stirring under the table, his weight shifting against my foot. I thought he must have sensed the rising tension in the room.

'But you were lying, weren't you, *V*ilhelm? You didn't want us to think bad of you, not while you could use us. At least, while you could use the girls here.'

The colour – what scant colour she had – was draining from Muriel's face. She was beginning to realize the party wasn't going to turn out the way she'd planned.

'What' – *vot* – 'are you suggesting, Hoke?' Stern had placed his own brandy glass before him, although his cigar remained between his fingers. Was there a sneer on those thin, humourless lips, was there hatred behind those passion-less eyes of his?

Keeping my hands on the table, I rested back in my chair. My tight grin lacked any pleasure.

'I'm suggesting you're a lying son-of-a-bitch,' I informed him quietly.

'Stop this now!' Muriel was on her feet. 'It's time you grew up, Hoke. This bitterness against Wilhelm – and yes, against us – is utterly pointless. Even though we saved your life you still resent us, you still look on us as some kind of burden, a nuisance you could well do without. Do you honestly think –'

'Let him have his say, Mu.' Cissie's anger was suppressed, her interest centred on me. A low, rumbling growl came from beneath the table.

Stern's smile was like my own: no warmth to it. 'Why do you bait me like this, Hoke? Is it because you are a rather absurd and intolerant man who will not accept the idea that Germany did not lose the war after all? That in the jaws of defeat the German Reich snatched victory with a weapon so brilliantly lethal it irrevocably altered mankind's destiny? That the Americans, with all their sophisticated weaponry and manpower, and the British who, if we are to be honest, were merely a spent force hanging on the coattails of their overseas masters, could suddenly lose to an army they thought defeated? Is that why you hate me so and imply that I am a liar? And isn't this what you expect me to say, Hoke? Isn't this the kind of Fascist language you want to hear from me? Isn't this just your own idea of how a German thinks, talks?'

Muriel and Cissie were staring at Wilhelm Stern, shocked by his words. Potter, bleary-eyed and heavy-lidded, opened his mouth to speak, but nothing came out.

My smile had frosted and my thumbs were twitching against my fingers. 'No, Stern,' I said finally, 'that isn't why I'm calling you a liar. Y'see, you made a slip while we were down there in the tram tunnel. You told us you'd witnessed starving dogs roaming the bomb-blitzed ruins of Berlin.'

His expression changed when he understood his mistake – his very stupid mistake.

'Because, *V*ilhelm,' I went on, enjoying his discomfort, 'the RAF didn't begin their raids on Berlin until August 1940, four months *after* you told us you were captured and interned over here.'

I leaned forward on the table again, a fury inside me that was intense but as cold as his pale eyes stiffening every muscle. 'What *did* you do in the war, *V*ilhelm? I'm betting it was something pretty nasty if you had to keep it from us three years after the event. Yeah, there were plenty of your kind over here in England, pretending to be Polish, Dutch, Czech, Belgian, all kinds of runaways and asylum seekers, but in reality spies and saboteurs. Which were you, *V*ilhelm? Did you get to blow up any munitions factories? Maybe that's how you got those scars on your neck, not escaping fast enough once you'd set the explosives. How about that, *V*ilhelm? Saboteur or spy – which was it?'

I don't know where it came from, but the gun was in his hand in the blink of an eye, and it was pointed at me. I realized he'd deliberately kept one hand – the one holding the cigar – in view on the table while I'd been talking, the other one sneaking into a pocket for the weapon he must have picked up – from a police station, from the corpse of a serviceman, or even from somewhere in the hotel itself – during his hunt around earlier in the day, because I hadn't returned the one I'd taken from him yesterday. There was more movement by my feet, Cagney rousing himself. We all heard his bad-tempered growl.

'The gun is merely for self-protection,' Stern informed me. 'I have no wish to fight with you, Hoke, but neither do I intend to be harmed by you.'

More commotion under the table, the mutt pushing his way through legs and chairs. Cagney suddenly appeared about halfway down, his teeth bared, a deep snarling-growl coming from his throat. He wasn't watching the German though; he was facing the door at the end of the room.

While Stern was distracted, I leapt from my chair, twisting so that I was at the back of it, and reached into my jacket pocket. My fingers were curling around the pistol butt as the door Cagney was facing burst open.

14

MY FIRST THOUGHT was to shoot the German; my second –
and it was only a split second after the first – was to duck
the gunfire that came my way.

Fortunately, the Blackshirts weren't aiming to kill, only to
frighten us all into immobility, but it didn't work that way
with me, because I took a dive as the mirror behind me
shattered and the room erupted with the sounds of machine-
gun fire and the girls' screams. I kept rolling 'til I was behind
the thick central column as candles split in two, a lamp in
one corner exploded as if hit by a cannon, and splinters from
the wood panelling spat across the table. I came up on one
knee in time to see Cagney scooting into the room next
door. Good move, I thought as I peeked around the column,
hoping to get a clear shot at the Blackshirt who was causing
most of the damage. But he was waiting for me to show
myself again and he peppered the column and the space
next to it with a hail of bullets so that I had to fall back to
avoid a faceful of lead. The drapes over the windows were
shredded, the glass behind them smashed, as I cowered out
of sight, biding my time. The gunfire abruptly ceased – out of
ammo, I assumed – and then so did the shouts and screams. I
acted fast, whipping round the square-shaped pillar, gun
hand extended, searching out my target.

Smoke wafted across the room, with it the smell of cordite

and candlewax. And something more. The familiar stink of the intruders themselves, a kind of cankerous odour that they carried with them like some unclean aura.

Cissie was huddled over the dining table, Potter on his knees beside her, while Muriel had backed up against the wall, shocked rigid. Stern held his hands high in surrender, his pistol lying on the tabletop. Blackshirts crowded the doorway, their ragged midnight garb and the array of weapons aimed around the room a dispiriting sight. The only person still moving was the goon who'd done the most damage – he was clumsily trying to fit a new magazine into a Sterling submachine gun. Again I acted fast, realizing there was no point in trying to take them all on with one small sidearm; there was one chance for us and a slim one at that. I was over the table, scattering glasses and coffee cups, before they could make their next move, their disease-induced slowness my only advantage. I came up behind Stern and locked an arm around his neck, my .45 pressed hard against his temple.

'Hold it right there!' I yelled at them, trying to keep the shakes from my voice as well as my gun hand. I pulled the German against me, using him as a human shield.

Five or six Blackshirts had managed to squeeze through that doorway and now every one of their guns was focused on me. The goon with the Sterling finished reloading and lifted the weapon chest-high, his hands as unsteady as mine.

'The German's dead if any one of you so much as scratches an itch,' I warned.

Stern could hardly breathe, let alone speak, but damned if he wasn't gonna make the effort.

'Shut up, Kraut!' I hissed into his ear. 'I guess it didn't take much searching to find your Fascist pals today when you left the hotel.'

He tried to squirm free, but I held him firm, digging the gun barrel even harder against his head just to cause him more discomfort. The temptation to shoot him right there and then was almost overwhelming, but I needed him – *we* needed him – as a hostage.

'*Back off!*' I shouted as more Blackshirts pushed their way further forward. I was the one who backed away, bringing my protection with me. I didn't like the craziness in their dark-smudged eyes, but then maybe they didn't like the craziness they saw in mine, because they became still sure enough. We had a stand-off – or so I thought – and that was a slight improvement in the situation.

'One bad move,' I warned them, 'and your *Kraut* friend's brains'll be dripping from the ceiling.'

I'd made up my mind to drop the one with the submachine gun first, then the two mugs on either side of him, each of them packing two pistols. When the rest scattered for cover I'd deal with Stern. All else was in the lap of the gods, but I was damn sure I'd never let them take me alive. I got ready to change my aim and the German stiffened even more, as though aware of my intentions.

'By all means, Mr Hoke, shoot our alleged *Kraut* friend if it makes you happy.'

The voice drifted through the hallway outside the Pinafore Room and I knew whose it was, although I'd never heard the man speak before 'cept once on a BBC radio broadcast early on in the war. I hadn't realized he knew my name either and then it dawned on me that he'd obviously learned it just that day, and the informant was right here in my arms.

The Blackshirts at the door stirred again, stepping aside to let their leader through. Sir Max Hubble appeared, propped up by McGruder on one side and his thick walking stick on the other. What was left of the candlelight did nothing to soften his appearance and I heard one of the girls – Cissie, I think – utter a small, fearful cry. Hubble came to a shambling halt a few feet inside the room.

'Well, Mr Hoke, aren't you going to shoot this man?' His sharp, wheezy voice was mocking as if he were taking pleasure from the situation. Maybe he enjoyed bluffing.

Well I had nothing to lose, so was prepared to call it. 'Unless you all move out so we can leave, I'll do that.'

Stern tried to tear my arm away, squawking something into my shirtsleeve that I couldn't catch. I held him fast, half-choking him with my grip.

'I'll tell you what,' Hubble said, his bluish lips beneath the thin moustache managing to form a smile. 'We'll do it for you.' He nodded at one of his men, who raised his pistol and pointed it at Stern's head.

Yeah, sure, go ahead, I thought, and then I saw the man's finger tightening on the trigger. 'Jesus,' I breathed.

'No!'

It was Muriel who cried out and ran forward to stand between us and the Blackshirts. 'You said nobody would be harmed. You promised me.'

She was staring straight at Hubble.

I couldn't believe my ears or my eyes. The gun wavered in my hand as I gaped at her back. I caught movement in the corner of my eye and saw that Cissie was pushing herself from the table, watching her friend open-mouthed.

'It's up to the American,' I heard Hubble say. 'He has the choice of either laying down his weapon and surrendering to us, or forcing us to shoot the person he's holding, and after that, him. We have other blood now.'

Cissie's fist crashed down on the tabletop, nearly causing more than one gun to go off. 'You brought them here!' she shouted at Muriel. 'You betrayed us. My God, how could you?'

Even in the flickering light I could see Muriel's face whiten as she faced her accuser.

'Miss Drake's father and I were great friends,' said Hubble as, like Muriel, he turned towards Cissie, using his whole upper body to do so, as if his neck had lost that small function. 'Our principles, our ideals, were the same, so is it surprising that Lord Drake's daughter should share those same values?'

193

I have to admit I'd never gone much on small-talk and after three years of none at all, save for the last couple of days, I wasn't surprised to learn I still didn't. And anyway, why gab? I knew all I needed to know.

Shoving Stern aside, I shot a hole through pistol-man's throat – he'd had to be first because his trigger finger was already halfway to squeezing. I would've taken Hubble next, but Muriel was in the way and, as much as I despised her, good old-fashioned propriety wouldn't allow me to shoot her in the back; so I settled for the goon with the Sterling, who was about to open fire again. I only winged him, but it was still enough to make him screech like a barn owl and collapse into three Blackshirts behind him, spoiling their aim and creating enough disorder for me to slide back across the table towards Cissie. I nudged her aside so I could get off a few clear shots at the enemy.

She screamed a warning as more Blackshirts came pouring through the double doors of the Princess Ida Room, and that was when I realized we didn't have a hope in hell. The only thing in my favour was the gun in my hand and my speed, but I couldn't shoot them all and I had nowhere to run.

Something – Lord knows what – struck me hard on the forehead and I went down, poleaxed. The next thing I knew, boots were stomping me and rifle butts were jabbing at arms and ribs. The Colt was wrenched from my grasp, bright flares were bursting inside my head, and somewheres a long way off someone was screaming.

All I could do – and there was no choice to it – was retreat into my own private sanctum, those lights fading fast, giving way to total darkness. I liked that darkness, I liked it a lot.

15

A DULL BUT SUDDEN PAIN semi-roused me; the sting of the second – it might really have been the third or fourth – had my eyes opening. I wasn't happy at what was before me, so I closed them again and another slap, this one on the other side of my face, convinced me to keep them open. I had to blink them several times though, partly because the light hurt and partly because they couldn't believe what they saw.

The light was everywhere, shining from the massive chandeliers in the ceiling and the low lamps set around the great lounge area. Yet more brightness flooded through the glass doors and windows of the riverside restaurant at the end of the lounge, as well as from the direction of the foyer and main entrance. For a moment I thought I must be dreaming, that the grand old hotel had returned to its former glory only in my unconscious mind; and then I took in the rotted corpses, many of them still seated or slumped in elegant but dusty chairs, while others lay on the carpeted floor, pushed aside with the furniture so that there was a clear space near the vast room's centre. Blackshirts were still busy creating more space, pushing back low tables and easy chairs, upsetting chinaware and cake-stands, throwing more corpses into heaps near the mirrored walls, shifting those already on the floor with their boots, not caring if skulls crumbled and skeletal hands broke loose.

I looked up at the person who'd struck me and groaned when I saw his death's eyes, the dried blood around their darkened lids, caked like biscuit crumbs in the lashes, the ulcerations and cyanotic discoloration of the man's cheeks and jaw. He grinned down at me, exposing bleeding gums, and when I tried to strike out at him I found my wrists were tied to the cushioned arms of a high-backed seat, the kind of formally comfortable armchair in which patrons of the Savoy had once taken afternoon tea or pre-dinner drinks.

My senses started to come together more rapidly and when I saw that my shirt had been ripped away to expose my left arm and shoulder, I began to suspect what I was in for. Panic hit me and I struggled to break free, the goon just leering over me, tickled by my efforts. I stopped when I noticed Stern, Cissie and Potter on their knees not far away, a bunch of Blackshirts covering them with an array of dissuaders – clubs and knives, as well as guns. And there came Hubble, just arriving, being helped down the carpeted stairway from the foyer by McGruder and another man, his decrepit body about ready to fail him. His smile when he saw me was no more than a tight grimace.

'Aren't the lights wonderful?' he remarked as he approached, his red-flecked eyes gazing up at the ceiling. 'It's been so long since we've witnessed such splendour, so very long.' He paused briefly to regard the kneeling prisoners, and he nodded as if counting their heads one by one before continuing his shambling journey towards me. Behind him, descending the stairs, was Muriel and there was a phoney kind of proudness to her, as though it took some effort to hold her head high and avoid the accusing eyes of her friend, Cissie. She passed by the kneeling prisoners without giving them a glance, even though Cissie called out to her.

Hubble came to a stop before me, both hands resting

on his cane, fingers like blackened claws wrapped around its grip, the two aides standing close by in case he should falter. He had an old man's tremble – and an old cadaver's stench.

Still he peered around him, his bent torso twisting with each turn of his head, admiring the chandeliers before gazing across the huge lounge itself, his eyes half-closed as if to shut out the more gruesome elements.

'If one didn't look too closely it would seem the grand old days had returned to the Savoy,' he mused. His speech had a high-pitched sibilance to it that was as thin and frail as his bones, and standing there in his loose black uniform, bent over his stick, flesh hanging from his scrawny neck like an empty sack, and with 'carrion' strewn all around him, he reminded me of an ancient buzzard. He went on, delighting himself rather than me: 'The hotel's own oil-fuelled generator was so easy to get running again – it took my men, the ones who know about these things, less than twenty minutes, even after all these years of disuse. I'm surprised you didn't attempt to start it yourself, Mr Hoke; but then, I suppose the last thing you wanted to do was draw attention to yourself.'

Some of his words were hard to catch; it was almost as if he were speaking from another room. He deserved a reply and I gave him one.

'You crazy bastard –'

He raised a shaky hand to shush me and, I have to admit, it did. What the hell could I tell him that deep down he didn't already know?

Now he turned to me, his head leaning close, the odour making me want to gag. 'It's odd, isn't it?' he said between laboured breaths. 'All this time chasing you and never once a moment for conversation between us.'

'I didn't think we had much to talk about,' I replied, trying to avoid the foul air he was exhaling.

Muriel had joined us by now.

'You happy, Muriel?' I enquired, looking past Hubble.

197

'Betraying your friends to these third-rate Nazis give you some kind of thrill? Like father, like daughter, I guess.'

'My father would have gladly sacrificed his life for his country,' she snapped back, her remoteness giving over to anger. 'But he recognized the poison that was slowly crippling our land.'

'Ah yeah, the Jewish poison, right?' My head was beginning to clear, but that only made me more conscious of the throbbing pain in various parts of my body, results of the beating I'd received. Shit, I'd hardly got over the lumps and bruises from my last run-in with these people.

Hubble hadn't liked my sneering tone. 'Even England's abdicated king was aware of the Jewish threat, as were many others of influence. If our own government had not been in the pocket of Jew creditors and extortionists, and so fearful of the proletariat itself, which was forever whining, forever demanding, malcontents who despised the natural social order, then perhaps the world would have had a very different and glorious future.'

'Oh Christ . . .' I began to say.

'The Jews murdered Christ, Mr Hoke.'

Some life had returned to those dead eyes of Hubble's: they shone with a zealot's passion.

'The Duke of Windsor and others of nobility would gladly have aligned themselves with Adolf Hitler's wondrous vision for mankind,' he went on, warming to the sermon, his voice even notching up half a gear. 'And they would not have been alone. Many leaders and eminent people – academics, industrialists, militarists, too – would have joined the crusade to purge our civilization of its insidious corruption and degenerative breeding, and indeed, discreet negotiations between ourselves and Hitler's emissaries that would have benefited both Germany and the United Kingdom were well underway before that fool Chamberlain was tricked into declaring war on a nation that should have been our greatest ally.'

Something had occurred to me while he was ranting and once more I stared past him at Muriel.

'Didn't you tell us your own brothers fought against Fascism, one in the navy, the other in the airforce?' I said to her.

'It was their duty to defend their country.' Some colour had returned to her pallid skin, brought there by her own anger. 'It didn't mean they agreed with our government's misguided hostility towards Germany.'

There was probably some kind of screwed-up logic to her argument, but I wasn't in the mood to figure it out. 'Just tell me why you turned us in to this bunch of madmen? I thought they, at least' – I nodded towards the kneeling group – 'were your friends.'

'Isn't it obvious?' she replied, her rage controlled again, her coolness back. 'Sir Max has to be saved. The irony is that I recognized him on the steps of the National Gallery when we helped you three days ago, but there was nothing I could do, everything was happening so fast.'

Out of the corner of my eye I saw an emaciated-looking man approaching, one of his cronies helping him remove his black shirt. His eyes were huge and kind of haunted-looking, as if the dark-smudged lids had shrunk around them.

'The world, or what's left of it, has to find a system again,' Muriel was blabbering, 'and we can only find the right kind through leaders like him, don't you see that? Our lives are not as important as his.'

'So offer him your blood,' I suggested.

'There's no need when I can take yours,' Hubble pointed out.

He shuffled aside to let the thin man through and I winced when I saw the ulcerations and bruises that covered the newcomer's naked arms and upper body. His companions placed a small black case like a doctor's bag (maybe it *was* a doctor's bag) on the carpet by my feet and opened it. As another Blackshirt spread a dingy tablecloth across the floor by the chair I was tied to, the one with the bag drew out a thin length of rubber tubing with what appeared to be flanged steel needles at either end, and some metal clips.

'Don't you understand?' I appealed to Hubble. 'It's crazy. It won't work. You have to be matched with the same blood type for it to do any good. You'll just kill us both this way.'

Hubble turned back to me, that mad shine still there in his dark eyes. 'But I have nothing to lose, Mr Hoke. If the transfusion fails, it only means a different sort of death.' He might have chuckled then, or a small expulsion of blood might have gurgled in his throat, I couldn't tell. 'Besides,' he went on, pointing his stick, 'we will try the procedure on this noble volunteer first.'

The half-naked man, who was settling onto the tablecloth on the floor, gazed up at him like an acolyte at a god.

'He'll die,' I promised.

'He's prepared to do so. But really, Mr Hoke, aren't you aware that even centuries ago the South American Incas regularly carried out blood transfusions with far more primitive instruments than we have, and, so history informs us, most occasions proved successful. All we need to do is make two small punctures in the correct veins and allow gravitation to do the rest.'

Wilhelm Stern was close enough to be easily heard. 'But it was also outlawed in Europe in the seventeenth century because of the many deaths transfusions caused.'

I was glad of his intervention, but wondered if it was for my sake, or because he didn't like the idea of being the next guinea pig.

'Nobody knew about blood types in those days. To them, blood was blood and there were no differences,' he reasoned. 'Transfusions were successful only between people who, by chance, belonged to the same grouping. *Mein Gott*, they even used the blood from pigs and sheep at that time. Muriel

'– Miss Drake – you must make this man understand, you must explain that what he is about to try is impossible.'

'But I'm not a doctor. How can I tell him what I don't even know?'

Cissie's eyes were wide and pleading. 'You saw for yourself what happened at the sanatorium, you know how their experiments failed each time.'

'We didn't know anything at all! They wouldn't even discuss individual cases with us, they kept us in the dark about everything.'

'If different blood types could be mixed, then the doctors would have saved themselves!' Cissie reasoned.

Hubble, irritated by the squabbling, smacked the side of my chair with his cane. He got our attention.

'There is one thing I'm sure they didn't try,' he said in that creepy faraway voice of his. 'They did not take *all* of the donor's blood and transfer it into the recipient's *empty* system.'

It was breathtaking in its flawed logic and now I knew he was completely insane. I wondered if his mental state had always been shaky, or if the disease itself was rotting his brain.

'That's ridiculous, you fucking lunatic!' Couldn't help it, had to make him aware of my considered opinion.

This time his cane bounced off the side of my skull. The blow was too weak to hurt much, and I had the satisfaction of seeing him stagger, only McGruder at his side preventing him going down all the way. A chair was quickly brought over, and when they'd settled him into it, facing me, about two yards away, I noticed that every part of him – his hands, his legs, shoulders, head – was trembling. His chest was heaving as he tried to regain his breath.

'No, it is not ridiculous,' he insisted between gasps, as if I were the lunatic. 'The recipient's blood will be *slowly* drained as blood from the donor will be *slowly* used to fill the veins.'

I laughed. Maybe it was hysteria, but I honestly appreciated the humour of his twisted reasoning. It was so outrageously and brilliantly simple.

'You will kill both persons.'

For once I didn't mind the 'vill'. After all, Stern was speaking up for my benefit as well as his own. They'd kill me anyway, whether they carried out the transfusion or not, but I preferred a fast bullet to a leisurely bleeding.

'Your man will have died from blood loss before his body will accept the new blood.' Stern spoke quietly, authoritatively, a teacher explaining a difficult problem to a child. 'Conflicting blood types will not even be the cause: you will kill this unfortunate man just as surely as if you had slit his throat with a knife.'

'His blood will be replaced as quickly as it is lost!'

The shout set Hubble wheezing again and McGruder watched over him anxiously. The Blackshirt leader held a handkerchief to his mouth, his body doubled-up in the chair, his shoulders jerking as spasms ran through him. When he straightened and took the handkerchief away I could see it was specked with blood. He took in a long, deep breath and I heard a peculiar faint whistling sound from inside his chest. His eyes were blurred with dampness now, the lustre in them dimmed.

'We're wasting time,' he said weakly. 'Let's get on with it.'

Someone grabbed my shoulders from behind and the goon who'd been rummaging around in the bag on the floor held up both ends of the rubber tubing, a stupid grin on his face.

'Wait, wait a minute.' I was out of laughter and getting more desperate by the moment. 'Listen. There are only four of us with the right kind of blood to resist the disease, five counting the fink here.' I nodded towards Muriel, but she wouldn't even look at me. 'Don't you get it? Even if the transfusions did work, you could only save a handful of your people. The rest are gonna die.'

'Ah, then you admit the transfusions could be successful?' The notion seemed to please Hubble.

I shook my head violently. 'Not a chance in hell. I'm just applying common sense.'

He smiled at me. Bared his yellowed teeth and smiled. 'This first transfusion will be our test, and it will be successful. By our second or third attempt, the procedure will be perfected.'

I understood now why Hubble was prepared to wait: let any mistakes be made on the first couple of mugs, so that any problems would be ironed out by the time it got round to his turn. Maybe he wasn't so crazy after all.

'After that we will move out of the city into the suburbs and surrounding countryside where we will find others like you. Eventually every one of us will be saved.' He barked the order, eager to proceed. 'Attach the tube to him! Miss Drake, will you be so kind as to assist – I'm sure you must have learned something about transfusions during your stay at the sanatorium.'

I wasn't sure of the expression I caught in her downcast eyes as she leaned over me. Was it fear, or plain old-fashioned misery? Was she beginning to regret double-crossing her friends already?

'Listen to me,' I whispered as she turned my wrist beneath the rope, exposing the veins of my forearm. Our heads were close. 'Tell them it isn't gonna work. Think of us, Muriel, think of Cissie. D'you want her to be killed?'

Her voice was low too. 'She's a Jew, isn't she?' she said.

My head straightened, knocking against the high back of the armchair. I don't know why, I should've expected it, but I was shocked. Under that sweet veil of English genteelness beat the heart of a viper. And in the three days I'd known her, telling her of my folks, the reason I'd joined in the bloody war long before my own country had been forced to come off the fence, making love to her, sleeping with her, I'd never once suspected the hatred she nurtured for her fellow man, the prejudices that had twisted her soul so that she believed her allegiance lay with a Fascist bigot who had been prepared to betray his own country. And I realized she hadn't concealed a thing. The plain truth was that none of our conversations had ever drawn close to the darker side of her nature. I hadn't asked – and presumably neither had Cissie in all the time she'd known Muriel – her opinion of Jews, niggers, gypsies, of Adolf Hitler and his Master Race ideology, Fascism, Nazism, hadn't even mentioned it. And nobody had asked her if she'd be prepared to turn in her friends to the people who meant to steal their blood. You see, she hadn't lied. She just hadn't been honest.

And then I wondered again about the look I'd caught in her eyes. It was fear, not regret, I was sure of that now. So what did she have to fear? I suddenly had the answer.

'You realize it's gonna be your turn sooner or later, don't you?'

I'd kept my voice low, and I took pleasure in seeing her hesitate for a split second. I watched her push the unacceptable truth away, her expression hardly changing, just that remoteness returning to her eyes, and I knew there was nothing more I could do. I raged inside as she stretched the skin of my lower left arm, pushing the muscles aside so she could locate a particular vein.

Tin buckets were being brought in by other Blackshirts; they placed them close to the man lying by my chair, while the bag-man drew out a scalpel.

'One more question, Muriel,' I said to delay the inevitable. 'How did you find these people? How did you know where to look? All the years playing cat-and-mouse with these creeps and I've never known where they came from. If I'd had any idea where their HQ was I might have taken the battle to them.'

It was Hubble who answered for her and, despite his poor condition, he did it with some delight. 'One man against a fortress? I hardly think so, my bumptious American friend.

You see, while you had your palace, I had my castle.' He wiped moisture from his lips with his blood-flecked handkerchief. 'But Miss Drake merely used her common sense and returned to the place where she had first set eyes on us. The National Gallery is one of our control centres, you see – at least, it was in our efforts to capture you. Didn't you realize that some of my men had followed your mongrel dog to the palace? How do you suppose we finally located you? Fully aware of just how elusive you could be, we had vehicles waiting at as many main road junctions as possible, all controlled from the great gallery at Trafalgar Square. Miss Drake found several of my soldiers still at that control point just ten minutes after leaving this hotel. After that it was only a matter of waiting for the right moment, when you were relaxed with a good meal and perhaps a little the worse for alcohol. The plan worked very well, wouldn't you agree?'

I felt a sharp pain as Muriel drove the hollow needle into a vein. She put a metal clip over the rubber tubing as blood began to flow. The man on the floor suddenly shrieked as the bag-man cut into his wrist and held it over one of the buckets. Muriel released the clip and blood quickly filled the tubing to emerge in a thin stream from the point of the needle at the opposite end; confident no air bubbles would be carried into the recipient's veins, she pushed the needle into his arm.

'You're murdering me, Muriel,' I said quietly, but she just turned away.

'You can't do this to him!' Cissie had struggled to her feet, but one of the guards caught her by the hair and pushed her down again. Old Albert Potter was outraged by that and lumbered up to defend her, shoving the Blackshirt away. Wilhelm Stern also decided it was time to do something about the situation and grabbed the nearest guard's rifle, using it to lever himself off the floor. Another goon quickly stepped in, smashing his club hard against the back of

205

Stern's head; the German went down on one knee, his arms raised to ward off the next blow. Cissie wheeled round, despite the hold on her hair, and jammed her knee into her attacker's groin. He yowled with pain as he let her go.

But it was over in seconds. The Blackshirts swarmed over them, clubbing them with sticks and guns, knocking them down and kicking them as they lay sprawled on the floor. And there was nothing I could do to help my friends. As much as I struggled, I couldn't break free from the ropes that bound my wrists. But I could use my feet.

Muriel swiftly stepped aside as I kicked out and the man behind me, who had held my shoulders all this time, fought hard to pin me down. I dug my heels into the carpet, rocking the chair, more Blackshirts rushing towards me, pushing past Muriel, the big guy, McGruder, among them. My right hand gripped the end of the chair's arm and, as I jammed my heels into the carpet, I lifted, pushing backwards, the guard behind desperately trying to stop me. The armchair tilted, overbalanced, began to topple.

The guard did his best to hold it, but my legs were straightening, calves and thigh muscles straining. The first Blackshirt stumbled into me and his added weight sent the chair completely over, so that it fell backwards, tilting to one side because of the obstruction behind. We went down with a crash, landing on the half-naked man lying on the floor, and I felt something loosen with the jolt.

We lay there in an untidy heap, the man beneath the pile feebly trying to push us off. For a short while there was silence, as if everyone had been taken by surprise. My head was against bare flesh, my wrists still bound to the chair. I could see the tubing lying a few inches away, the steel needle missing, blood oozing from the open end. The Blackshirt on top of me was trying to disentangle himself, the reek of him and the one underneath me filling my nostrils.

I was almost ready to quit. Sick as these clowns were, their numbers were overwhelming. My body sagged, giving in to pain, giving in to despair. This time we really were sunk.

Then I heard a familiar noise. A kind of distant rumbling.

16

IT DIDN'T TAKE LONG for the German bomber pilot to find his target for the night – hell, he must have seen those hotel lights from twenty miles away. I lifted my head to see everyone staring up at the high ceiling as though the noise was coming from the rooms above. The chandeliers began to vibrate.

Then there was a deafening blast as the windows of the next-door restaurant blew in, glass and stone shrapnel roaring through to the room we were in, bringing with it more glass from the dividing wall. The whole building seemed to rock to its very foundations, the chandeliers waving in the wind the explosion caused, the walls and pillars around us trembling, shaking off dust. The tall mirrors cracked and furniture was swept forward as if carried by some invisible tidal wave. Brittle cadavers disintegrated, their various parts tossed into the air, and saucers and cups, cake tiers and lamps, withered plants and rotting napkins all flew towards us, carried by the storm, pulverized by the broiling gust.

Some Blackshirts dropped to the floor, hands over their heads for protection, others cowered where they stood: they were the unlucky ones, the force of the blast knocking them off their feet, sending them crashing into the furniture or pillars, their screams faint under the thunderous row. I was fortunate: I was shielded by the back of the chair I was tied to and the goon on top of me. Even so, chair, Blackshirt and I were pushed across the floor, pellets of glass and masonry tearing into the soft cushioning of material and flesh. The Blackshirt howled and rolled away from me, writhing as he tried to reach a glass shard embedded in the back of his neck.

One of my wrists was loose – it was the chair's arm I'd felt give a little when we took the tumble – and it didn't take much to tug it from its bindings. I was twisting round to work on the other one when another earth-shaking *boom* set the world spinning once more. The second bomb must've landed on the Savoy's roof, because the crashing, tearing noise continued as it dropped through the upper floors. The final explosion threatened to demolish the whole building. Great drifts of dust cascaded from the ceiling and lights, enveloping the lounge in a powdery mist.

Although dazed, the pain in my ears threatening to split my skull, I worked on the rope, blinking grit from my eyes and spitting more from my mouth. Frustrated, I got a foot against the chair's arm, then pushed against it, at the same time pulling the rope with both hands. The cushioned arm came away from the rest of the chair just as the third bomb hit another part of the building, this one falling on the other side, somewhere near the main foyer. The avenging angel of the night skies was making the most of this dazzling target and I knew he'd be banking already, turning sharply to get back over us again. I yanked my arm free as a section of ornate ceiling right above me began to crack. A chandelier crashed to the floor, followed by another, this second one demolishing a macabre tableau of mouldered corpses that had taken silent tea for the last three years in a discreet corner of the room. Two brown marble pillars in the same corner collapsed, bringing down a large section of ceiling with them, fire from the room above falling with the debris. There were shouts and screams from all around as Black-shirts tried to flee and I saw two disappear beneath a shower of rubble as another part of the ceiling broke away. A kneeling woman, her hair white with dust, her black uniform in tatters, was trying to pull a piece of glass, shaped like a long, curved scimitar, from her chest, and when it finally came free it released a cascade of blood that splattered onto the carpet. She fell backwards, her dark-fingered hands clawing the wound, and was drenched by her own blood.

A deep *whoosh*ing alerted me to more trouble to my right and as I turned my head a huge tidal wave of flame billowed through from the main entrance foyer, swallowing up everything in its path, burning carpet, walls and furniture. I fell back, drawing my legs up, head tucked in, arms folded over my hair, fearing the fire would not stop until it had swept through to the other side of the building. But I felt the heat instantly recede and when I looked up the flames were being sucked back into the foyer. I guessed incendiaries had been sent with the bomb, all exploding together, causing the firestorm. The fire still filled the top of the short stairway to the foyer, and it had left smaller blazes behind in its retreat. Shapes moved before it, figures rushing to and fro in panic, not knowing which way to go, which way to get out. As dark rolling clouds of smoke curled through, poisoning the air, stinging eyes and scorching throats, the lights began to flicker.

Only a few feet away from me Hubble lay on his side, his chair on top of him, and just for a moment, one brief wink of time, and in all that confusion, our eyes met. Now tiny needles of fire glittered in those dark eyes of his and I felt as if I were looking into the burning hatred that lived inside his soul. His mouth opened as he shouted something, but I couldn't hear what it was over the storm of screams, crashing masonry, and the crackle of fire.

I pushed myself to my feet and stood there, unsteady, half-crouched, my joints stiff and my head reeling, dust and smoke filling my eyes, a bedlam of sound filling my ears. As I raised my hands to wipe dirt and tears from my eyes I noticed the flanged needle was still sticking from my arm. I pulled it out and tossed it away, globules of blood oozing from the wound. There was no time to stem the flow – I had to make a break for it before the Blackshirts got over their panic and before the goddamn room collapsed in on itself. Instead I tore off the rest of my shirt and quickly dabbed at the blood before dropping the bloody rag to the floor. McGruder and another goon were on their feet and leaning over their leader, pulling away the chair that pinned him to the floor; Muriel was closer to me, on her knees, body crouched over, her silver dress torn, a flap hanging loose to expose her shoulder. I quickly searched the immediate area for a fallen weapon, figuring I'd kill all four before I took my leave, but suddenly an arm wrapped itself around my neck from behind.

In a reflex action, I fisted my left hand in the palm of my right, and shot my elbow back, as swift and hard as I could. Spittle dampened my cheek as my attacker huffed and doubled up. I spun round and kicked his legs from under him; he went down like a sack of bricks. Wasting no more time on him and forgetting about dealing with Hubble and his goons – but having to resist the urge to snap Muriel's neck as I rushed past her – I joined Cissie and Stern, who were struggling with their guards. The German was held by one Blackshirt, while another was beating him with his fists; Cissie was tussling with a black-garbed, crop-haired woman, who gripped both her wrists and was trying to force her back down onto the floor. First punching the Blackshirt in front of Stern in the kidney area so that his hands dropped to protect himself, I then belted him hard in the side of the jaw. His head snapped away from me and his knees buckled. Without waiting to see if he was out for the count, I wrenched the second goon away from Stern and drove my fist into his stomach, following through with a punch to the bridge of his nose (the best place if you mean business). His eyes crossed and Stern helped by chopping the underside of his hand against the man's neck, so that he fell without protest. I swiped the first man, who hadn't quite gone down yet, with the sharp point of my elbow and felt bone in his nose disintegrate. He might have screamed as he tottered back – his mouth opened and his neck stretched – but another explosion from a room somewhere close by drowned out all other sounds. The floor seemed to heave and more cracks appeared in the mirrors and walls as they shuddered. It was like being in an earthquake as other parts of the ceiling collapsed and pillars shifted their positions.

Cissie and the woman fell to the floor, the Blackshirt on top and still clinging to Cissie's wrists. It took two steps to reach them and I dragged the woman off Cissie, throwing her aside. She lay there screeching, but the fight had left her.

As I turned to help Cissie to her feet I noticed Stern stoop to pick up a discarded Sten gun, then aim it at someone rushing at him from out of the smoke. Just as the Blackshirt reached him, Stern jerked the weapon forward into his belly and pulled the trigger. The man did a little jog, his arms flapping, boots stamping carpet, as the bullets disassembled his innards.

A wave of heat engulfed me once more as the fire bloomed out from the broad staircase to the foyer and lobby area, gusts of air sucked in from the blitzed entrance exciting the flames. The grand old hotel was finished: it had survived the worst London air raids, wounded but always unbent, but now there was nobody to quench those flames and repair the damage; fires in other parts of the building would join with this one, making one huge conflagration that would only be extinguished when there was nothing left to burn. There was no more time to waste; we had to leave, and we had to leave now.

'Look out, Hoke!'

Cissie had screamed the warning almost into my face as a tall Blackshirt loomed up over my shoulder. When I wheeled round, his rifle was raised to smash down into my head. I started to duck, even in that split second aware there was no way I could avoid the blow, but gunfire rattled through the smoky air and the butt-end of the weapon wavered above me, only inches from my skull. Then it just dropped away, the goon holding the rifle falling with it. Stern joined us, a wisp of smoke curling from the Sten gun's muzzle.

He leaned close to my ear and shouted, '*We must get out!*' and I was dumb enough to nod my head at the obvious.

'*Through that way!*' I pointed towards an opening at the side of the big room which led past the cloakrooms and into the corridor where all the private dining rooms, including the Pinafore, were located. Although I'd been unconscious at the time, I knew Hubble must have brought us along that way into the lounge.

We started off in that direction, moving as one, Cissie clinging to my bare arm as if afraid to let go, Stern on the other side, Sten gun held hip-high, covering the ground before us. Once again, survival instinct had kicked in, helping me to operate despite a groggy head and some stiffness from the beating, and we dodged around figures who seemed oblivious to us as they rushed around in the swirling smoke, afraid the whole building was gonna tumble down on them. But if we had the idea that all of Hubble's Blackshirts had forgotten about us we were soon corrected: a whole bunch of them were suddenly standing between us and our intended escape route, pistols and rifles raised towards us, staves and short axes brandished by the few women amongst them. They wouldn't want to kill us, I knew that – we were useless to them dead – but they could incapacitate us easily enough; besides, they had another reason for negotiation, a hostage.

In all the commotion and anxiety to get out of there fast, I'd forgotten about Albert Potter. He was on hands and knees, one of the Blackshirts crouched over him, holding a blade to his plump throat.

The three of us came to a halt, Cissie calling out the old warden's name, her fingers digging into the flesh of my arm. Stern brought the Sten gun up to his chest and aimed it at the group. I could only spit more dust from my mouth.

It was a stand-off, smoke swirling between us, the flames from the stairway and other parts of the room licking everything orange. The electric lights flickered again, dulled, came back, the generator in the hotel's basement beginning to run slow, then picking up; either the bombardment had caused problems, or three years of lying idle had upset the machinery. I didn't care which, I just prayed for a total blackout. Sure, the fires would still provide some kind of light, but it would be unsteady as well as poor, and any edge was better than none at all.

Hubble was among the group holding us up, his ever-faithful goon, McGruder, by his side, supporting him. Hubble took an unsteady step forward, McGruder careful to go with him, making sure his leader didn't stumble.

'Don't make another move!' Hubble shouted in that weak, high-pitched way of his. 'If you do, this man will be killed instantly.' He pointed a shaky, dark-stained finger at Potter. The blade at the warden's throat pressed into the soft flesh, not enough to draw blood, but enough to make a furrow. 'His is old blood anyway and we'd prefer the younger, more healthy kind,' Hubble said, as if we'd appreciate his reasoning. 'Your kind, Mr Hoke. And your companions'. Good, vibrant blood.'

How long was it gonna take the mad bomber to make his turn and get back over target? He wouldn't let an opportunity like this go by without dropping every last bomb and incendiary on board. No, he'd douse those glowing lights with fires of his own making, and then he'd spit on the wreckage as he headed home to the Fatherland. C'mon, Fritz, knock this place out, gimme a chance.

I pulled Cissie behind me and scanned the immediate area for fallen weapons. Okay, the Blackshirts would go for non-fatal wounds, tricky for any marksmen. And they'd have to try for the kind that didn't bleed too much; off hand, I couldn't think of any. So: Dive for the nearest gun before they cut the legs from under you. Already tense, I tensed some more.

'Kill Hubble first,' I told Stern.

'*No!*' Cissie tugged at my arm. 'You can't do that, Hoke, they'll kill Albert.'

'They'll kill us all anyway,' I replied, still searching the floor. 'Do it, Stern, do it now.'

The German turned his head towards me, then looked back at Hubble. Something crashed in the foyer, beyond the wall of flame.

'Hoke, I cannot –'

'None of it matters!' I snapped, at last finding what I was searching for, a pistol lying close to an upturned chair on the littered floor. 'Shoot him now and let's finish it.'

'You're insane,' said Cissie over my shoulder.

I felt myself grin. 'Yeah,' I agreed as I judged the distance between myself and the fallen weapon.

Stern levelled the Sten at the Blackshirt leader, who suddenly looked less sure of himself. But the German lowered the submachine gun, then dropped it onto the carpet.

'It is senseless,' he whispered, as if to himself. It was as if not just his energy, but his spirit too, had drained from him. Then, to me: 'There has been too much killing. We must reason with these –'

A number of things happened before he'd completed the sentence: Hubble nodded at the goon with the long knife, who neatly slit Potter's throat; the lights surged, then fell almost to nothing; I went down, rolled forward and came up with the German's discarded Sten gun, finger already tightening on the trigger.

17

I'D FIRED TOO WILD and too soon, because McGruder pulled Hubble to the floor before I could take proper aim at him. The bullets caught a couple of Blackshirts who weren't quick enough to duck, while others in the group blocking our way scattered, some diving for the floor, others just scooting off, heading for cover. A mirror shattered on the far wall and splinters flew from a marble column. The lights brightened again as the generator below ground revived and I had the chance to pick out Hubble with the Sten gun. He was crouched on the floor, his loyal henchman's beefy arm thrown over his shoulder for protection, and he was watching me like a paralysed rabbit. His time was up sooner than he'd figured, and I was the gun-packing Reaper, both counts pretty hard for him to take.

I pulled the trigger and nothing happened.

Tried again, but it was useless. The gun was jammed or empty, God knows which, but it was all the same to me. I threw it away and went for the pistol I'd spotted earlier.

But even as I hit the deck it seemed to rise up beneath me, slamming into my body so that I turned over from the shock. The blast – heavy, thunderous, like nothing I'd heard before – overwhelmed all other noise, and the shell of the building juddered so violently I thought it must come tumbling down on us all. The Bomber King had completed his turn and was back over target. I guessed he'd dropped his whole bomb-load in his determination to blot out the beacon below. A great wind from the foyer swept through the lounge, carrying with it lethal shrapnel and fireballs, and I hugged carpet, pressing my body into its softness, riding the reverberations, sparks and burning cinders scorching my naked back and arms, pellets of masonry and splinters of wood raining down on me. My hands were over my head, but I heard more crashing sounds, then screams, shouts, and the floor beneath me continued to tremble. Although there were more close-set explosions, I decided it was time to be up and running again.

The broad stairway leading to the foyer and main entrance was totally engulfed in flames by now, and I knew everything beyond it – the reception area, reading lounge, and the staircase to Harry's Bar – would have been completely destroyed. Powdered glass and dust filled the air with thick smoke as other chandeliers broke loose from their fittings and hurtled to the floor, while whole ornamental mirrors fell from the walls and more pillars fissured as they shifted under the strain of the collapsing ceiling. But I was on my feet, looking round for Cissie and the German, swiping at the smoke with my hands as though it were concealing veils.

I soon found them both behind me. Stern was pulling bright red cinders from Cissie's smouldering hair, his face covered in blood. Cissie's nose was bleeding and I saw her lips were moving; she was shouting at me and pointing, but I couldn't hear a thing – my ears, and probably theirs too, had been deafened by the explosions. As Stern flicked away the last cinder, smothering the smouldering strands with his other hand, Cissie touched my face. Her fingers came away stained with blood and she showed them to me. I wiped my face with my own hands and felt no wounds or embedded glass and shrapnel, so was sure all I was suffering was a nose-bleed from the blasts and, from the look of her, that was Cissie's only problem too. Stern, though, had a deep cut over his brow and blood was streaming down into his eyes; he kept clearing it with his sleeve so that he could see, but still it poured out, blinding him each time. His clothes were ripped and I wondered if he'd shielded Cissie from the worst of the blasts, because her dress was relatively untouched.

Taking them both by the arms, aware they couldn't hear a word even if I screamed at them, I pulled them towards the opening we'd been heading for. I took time out to kick over a Blackshirt who was lumbering to his feet in our path and, although he went down fast enough, there were others all around, dark shapes looming up in the smoke mists like spectres in a graveyard. Something brushed my cheek, a sharp arrow of air, and even though I hadn't heard the gunshot, I knew someone had recovered enough to take shots at us. Pushing the girl and Stern on ahead, I paused only long enough to lift an upturned coffee table from the floor and hurl it at the murky forms closing in on us. Then I was running again, quickly catching up to the other two, who had almost reached the passageway, and it was weird, unreal, rushing through that silent chaos, slow-moving figures around us, the fires bathing everything orange, even the smoke, old corpses beginning to smoulder with the advancing heat. Then my ears suddenly popped and the full horror hit me with its sounds. Shots were being fired, people were yelling and screaming, and a terrifying low rumbling-grinding was coming from the building itself.

I couldn't see Hubble anywhere, but then I wasn't bothering to look for him. I only had one thought and that was to get through that archway into the passage before one of the bullets found a target. A hail of bullets ripped through a group of tables and chairs close by, shredding the husked corpses seated there, and sending fountains of splinters and broken crockery into the air. I ducked and swerved, managing to grab at Cissie as I went, bringing her down with me when I fell. I heard Stern cry out, saw him stagger as another wild volley was sent our way. He seemed to recover, stumbling on, and as he disappeared through the archway I was already pulling Cissie to her feet and pushing her after him.

We made it. We rushed into the wide passageway, the smoke thinner inside, the air more breathable, and we kept going, catching up with Stern, who was holding his shoulder as he ran. The three of us almost reached the turn in the passageway that led past the private dining rooms where a couple of hours ago we'd been enjoying a fine meal with rare wines and excellent brandies; almost, but not quite, because some of the goons had fired into the archway after us. Stern staggered again, this time into the closed door of the Gondoliers Room directly ahead of us, and I caught him as he bounced off it and started to fall. I dragged him round the corner and out of sight of the Blackshirts just as wood splintered from the door. Stern sagged in my arms, but I wouldn't let him go down; I kept him moving, even though he was crying out at the pain. I could hear footsteps pounding the floor-tiles behind us.

'Hoke, there's a stairway!' Cissie shouted.

The lights stuttered again, almost fading to complete darkness. They came back, but not to the same glory; I prayed for the generator to help us out a little by giving up entirely.

'Help me with him,' I said to Cissie, pulling Stern's arm over my shoulder.

She took the other side and we went down the stairs, moving as swiftly as we could, but taking care not to stumble. We heard shouts and more running footsteps from above and we tried to keep our descent as quiet as possible, shushing Stern when he started to groan. The further we went, the gloomier it became; not because the generator was failing, but because there were fewer lights in use down there when the machinery controlling them had originally shut down. That suited me fine: the more shadows to hide in the better. There were husks on the stairs, all dressed in faded Savoy livery, and it was over one of these uniformed corpses that I tripped, bringing both Cissie and Stern down with me. The German shrieked at the sudden aggravation to his wounds and as I clamped my hand over his mouth we heard more shouts, then footsteps on the stairs. I was up again as quickly as I'd fallen, bringing Stern with me, then bending his body with my shoulder, hoisting him in a fireman's lift. He was goddamn heavy, but I clenched my teeth and kept going, whispering to Cissie to go on ahead and clear the steps of other obstacles. Down and round we went, the sounds of our pursuers growing louder, closer. At the bottom of the staircase we found a narrow corridor and we hurried along it, the light in this basement area almost non-existent. My load was growing heavier and my limp decided to make a comeback after a day's absence. Another corridor, this one broader, rooms off it leading to boiler rooms, machine rooms and store rooms; there were thick pipes running along the ceiling, smaller ones running alongside them. The walls were of white brick tiles covered in dust and grime, and long cobwebs hung from the pipes; our own footsteps seemed even louder in this place, but still we could hear the Blackshirts drawing closer. We came to a heavy door and Cissie pushed it open: we were in a smart hallway, doorways on both sides, an ascending stairway directly ahead. I recognized where we were: the stairs led to the riverside entrance and behind the doors were the hotel's grand function rooms and banqueting halls. Tempting though those stairs were, I knew I'd never get up them fast enough carrying the injured man – I could hear our pursuers behind the door we'd just emerged from and they'd be bursting through after us at any second – so I grabbed Cissie's hand and pulled her into the open doorway on our right.

She realized where we were the moment we were over

the threshold and in the gloom I felt her go rigid in my grip. She began to back away, shaking her head.

'We gotta hide,' I hissed at her. 'Just long enough to shake 'em off.'

'Not here,' she whispered back.

But it was already too late to change our minds. We heard the door to the hallway open.

'Quick.' I pushed her ahead of me towards one of the curtained bunk-beds. Pulling the curtain aside, I unloaded the semi-conscious German onto the narrow bed, then ordered Cissie to climb in after him.

At first I thought she was going to resist, but voices outside the door took the choice away from her. She slid in after Stern and I climbed in after her, drawing the curtain closed behind us. Something softly broke beneath our bodies and in the darkness a powdery dust smelling of fossilized mushrooms rose up around us. Stern gave a feeble moan and I groped for his face, finding his mouth and covering it with both hands. He tried to twist his head away, but he was too weak to succeed; I held him there, hands clamped tight, and soon his body went limp. Afraid of suffocating him, I immediately lifted my hands an inch or two away from his mouth, ready to bring them down at the faintest murmur. Beside me, Cissie was trying to control her own breathing – I could feel the slow rise and fall of her chest within the close confines of the veiled bunk. Her fingers clasped my bare shoulder.

The sour odour of decay became almost overwhelming, giving us another reason to restrain our breath intake: it was difficult to shake off the notion that the foul dust floating around inside that enclosed refuge might poison our lungs. That smell and more soft crumblings beneath us confirmed what I already suspected and what I really did not want to know: we were lying on top of the crusted body of someone who'd crawled inside this darkened space a long time ago to escape the invisible killer thing that was in the air itself.

Cissie must have realized at the same time, because she made a sudden lunge across my shoulders, and only by twisting my body and pinning her to the wall with my back did I prevent her from tearing open the curtain and tumbling out. Her breasts heaved against my shoulder blades and for an uncomfortable few moments I thought she was gonna throw up all over me. She held on though, her panic giving way to a more controlled fear, her breathing slowing down; and soon I felt her tears on my back. Beneath me, Stern began to moan and I quickly eased my weight off him again and held a hand to his lips. Despite the pain he was in, I think maybe he was aware of our situation – or at least, that we were in danger – because he became quiet and lay still once more. In inky blackness we waited, and I wondered how many other rotted corpses lay about us in this reinforced tomb. Cissie had sensed them when I'd first brought her here, and I admired her willpower now; me, I was used to the decayed remains of the dead – I even collected them – but she was still learning to accept it all.

Voices tensed us.

'They're not in here,' someone said.

'How d'you know?' came a hushed reply. 'It's too dark to see.'

'They'd have gone up the stairs. There's a way out up there.'

'They didn't have time, we'd have seen 'em. They've ducked in here, or one of those doors opposite.'

Another voice joined in, quiet like the others, as if afraid of disturbing the dead. 'What's behind all them curtains?' it said.

'Looks like some kind of bunker in there. Probably the hotel's own Blitz shelter.'

Shuffling footsteps as they entered.

'Fucking hell, it's creepy.'

So they felt it too. Enough to make them change their minds about searching the place? Somewhere far off there was a muffled crash or explosion, I couldn't tell which.

'This whole place is gonna come down.'

'Sodding Germans.'

'Well let's get out before it does.'

'No, we gotta check. If Hubble found out we hadn't, he'd have our guts for garters.'

'Shit, I had a better time in the army.'

'He pulled us together, didn't he? Gave us all a chance. It'd be every man for hisself without Sir Max.'

'Okay, okay, let's get on with it.'

I swore under my breath. They were moving further into the room. I shifted my weight, got an elbow beneath me, and Stern gave a soft moan.

'D'you hear that?'

'What?'

'There was a noise, sounded like someone moaning.'

'I never heard it.'

'It came from over there.'

I parted the curtain at its centre, just enough for me to peek through. There were three of them, as the voices had indicated, their figures vague and shadowy in the poor light from the hallway. I was surprised, assuming more had chased us down here; then I realized the main group had probably gone straight past the stairway so they could search the private function rooms along the upper hallway, while these three had broken off to investigate the basement. I let go of the curtain and pulled back as the three men drew near.

'It came from behind one of these.'

Through the material of the curtains I could see the lights outside were fluttering again.

'Here, I don't want to be in this bleedin place if the lights go again.'

'All right, let's make it quick then.'

The swish of curtains being drawn back came to us. They'd started at the beginning of the row of bunks we were hiding among and were working their way along.

'Why don't I just put a burst through the lot of 'em?' came one of the voices.

'What, and kill the people we're looking for? We need 'em to survive, you bloody fool.'

'So Hubble says.'

'Yeah, well he's right. You saw the American and his friends – they all look healthy enough, none of 'em's touched by the disease. They've got the good blood and we need it. It don't take a genius to work that out.'

Another curtain was drawn aside, this one over the next bunk down. I heard Cissie gasp in a sharp breath.

The material in front of me ruffled, then dim light accompanied by a long-bladed knife (the same one that had slit Albert Potter's throat?) came through the parting. There seemed no point in *waiting* to be discovered.

I pulled back the curtain so smartly that the man on the other side shrieked in surprise. My other hand gripped the fist around the knife and pushed it upwards and back so that its point sank into the startled Blackshirt's throat. His shriek became a choking gurgle and rising air forced splatters of blood from the throat wound and his mouth. I felt its warmness as it sprinkled my face and shoulder, and I leapt out of the bunk, shoving the choking man away from me into the Blackshirt behind him. This second one's pistol went off as he staggered backwards and I ducked instinctively. The bullet hit the ceiling and the man fell to the floor with the weight of his knife-struck pal on top of him.

The thing of it is, and as I keep saying, these poor saps were not the men they used to be. The Slow Death had weakened their muscles and slowed their reactions, otherwise they'd have cornered and captured me way back. I was no superman, no *Übermensch*, as Hitler had liked to call his élite, but I was still pretty fit – working on the allotments and lifting bodies on a near-daily basis had taken care of that

– and living with constant danger had kept my wits sharp enough, so I had the edge on these characters. And knowing I was no good to them dead had always encouraged me to take risks, which was why I'd taken the fight to them at that moment and almost shocked them rigid.

The third man was still gawping at me as I started towards him. His weapon, a Thompson submachine gun, whose round magazine made him look like a hoodlum from one of those gangster movies that were all the rage before the war, was frozen in his hands. No Jimmy Cagney or Edward G. this guy, though, because I was already diving for his legs before he remembered to pull the trigger.

I was under the Thompson's stubby barrel so the bullets only ruined the floor as I struck his knees, unbalancing him and bringing him down on top of me. I kept rolling and came up behind him. Reaching over his hunched shoulders, I grabbed the submachine gun's warm barrel with one hand and its butt with the other, jerking the weapon upwards so that it cracked against his lower jaw, knocking what little sense he had from him. He clung to the gun though, but his grip was slack. I pulled it back against his windpipe, squeezing hard and, I guess, crushing or breaking something inside, because he suddenly went limp, all life gone from him.

I heard a scuffle and looked up to see Cissie's shadowy figure hurl itself at the second Blackshirt, whose pistol was aimed in my direction as he sprawled on the floor. He dismissed her with a backward slap of his hand and pointed the gun at me again. But this time it was Stern he had to contend with.

The German aimed a kick at the gun hand, but missed and struck the Blackshirt's wrist instead, spoiling the shot. I was already scrambling across the floor on all fours and before he got a second chance, I'd smashed my fist into his nose (never fails). The back of his head hit the floor with a sickening smash, but just to make sure he wouldn't be a nuisance any more, I snatched the pistol from his sluggish grip and brought the butt down hard on his forehead. His head slowly lolled to one side as Stern sank down beside him. Aware that the gunfire would have attracted the attention of other Blackshirts who were hunting us, I was on my feet in an instant.

'Stern, you okay? Can you get up?'

He swayed on his knees, head lowered, eyes downcast. 'With your help,' he managed to murmur.

A stain that could only have been blood was darkening his shirt collar and when I touched his shoulder I felt the slick wetness soaking through his jacket. Pistol in one hand, I reached beneath his arms and hauled him up, then held him there while I quickly looked towards the open doorway. Cissie pushed herself off the floor and skirted round the man with the knife in his throat, his hands still on the handle, his body quivering as his sick blood drained from him. She joined us and took Stern by one of his arms to help me support him.

'He's badly hurt, we've got to do something about his wound,' she said urgently.

'No time,' I told her as I ripped open his shirt collar, then pulled the fancy silk handkerchief from his suit's breast pocket. I tucked it under the shirt collar, feeling for the wound. 'Okay, hold it there, try to stem the flow as best you can.'

She pressed the already blood-soaked silk against his neck, both of us aware that Stern's wound needed a proper dressing and that he shouldn't be moving about.

'Hoke.' Stern had raised his head and was trying to see me in the gloom. 'Leave me the other weapon, the Thompson. I can hold them off for you, or at least take up some of their time.'

Don't think it wasn't tempting. But I said: 'We're getting out together, Wilhelm.' No V for the W, just a straight 'Wilhelm'. Despite his pain, he managed to clap a hand on my

226

shoulder. In the light from the doorway I noticed he'd even managed a faint smile.

'I was a spy, you know,' he said.

'Yeah, I know,' I replied. 'But it doesn't matter any more. Now, let's get going before the rest of 'em find us.'

Tucking the pistol into the waistband of my pants, I guided Stern towards the light, stooping to pick up the Thompson as we went. I took a quick peek out into the hallway while Cissie held the injured German steady.

'All clear,' I told them. 'The river entrance is up those stairs and it's the easiest and quickest way out.'

One of Cissie's arms was stretched across Stern's chest as she kept the makeshift pad tight against the bullet wound, and her other hand was wrapped around his upper arm.

'Can we really make it, Hoke?' she asked, her wide eyes studying my face for the truth. 'Won't they realize we'll try and get out that way?'

'Depends. I'm hoping those bombs have caused too much confusion for Hubble and his people to think straight. We got other choices – it's a warren of rooms and passages down here – but I don't think our friend would make it. The sooner we break out, the sooner we can fix him up.'

If I'd been on my own, or even just with the girl, it would've been a cinch. I'd taken time during my stays at the Savoy to locate all the trade and staff exits, every outlet from the basement area, as well as the quickest way to them; but now I had an obligation. Stern had saved my life – twice – and I wasn't about to let him down. Sure, he'd riled me with his arrogance earlier that evening, but he'd just been hitting back, mocking my expectations of him as a German. And it was *Muriel* who'd joined up with the Blackshirts, not Stern; *he'd* helped me fight them.

We were halfway up the stairs to the riverside entrance hall when we heard the trampling of many feet from somewhere over our heads. Stern was making a fair effort of getting himself up those stairs without relying entirely on me and the girl, but it was slow progress and I wondered how long his strength would hold out. Concentrating on each step, he seemed oblivious to the noise from above, but Cissie looked across him at me, her panic not far from the surface.

'Keep him coming,' I said to her, letting go of Stern and racing up to the entrance hall above.

I'd just reached the top when I saw the first of the Black-shirts beginning to descend the stairway from the first-floor foyer and I lifted the Thompson just as they set eyes on me. With cries of alarm they backed up, a couple of them turning to run, and I sent a hail of bullets after them. The Thompson submachine gun never was an accurate weapon, but it had a good effect, enough to hold the goons off 'til Cissie and Stern were stumbling past me towards the glass exit by the side of the revolving door. Another burst to give the Blackshirts something more to think about, then I was rushing through the exit behind them.

Glass shattered around us as the goons returned fire, sprinkling our hair, peppering my naked skin, and I turned in one last effort to keep them back, the muzzle of the Thompson already spitting flames. One of the bolder Black-shirts was halfway down the stairs when my gunfire raked his chest, knocking him over, his arms outstretched, rifle flying into the air. He started to slither the rest of the way down, but I didn't stay to watch: I was out in the open, running along the alleyway created by the zigzag barrier, quickly catching up with Cissie and Stern. I kicked away the plank across the entrance to the alley and then we were out into the night.

We stopped dead at what confronted us.

Lights still shone dimly from the Savoy's shattered windows, some of those lights a flickering orange, the glow of fires inside, and their reflections were thrown across the narrow roadway and park opposite. The moon lent its own illumination. All of it revealing the people gathered outside the hotel, their numbers scattered, some in small groups, others solitary.

They watched the burning building, upturned faces shimmering in its glow, and there was a strange emptiness in their staring eyes. Without counting, I guessed there were a couple of dozen of them, maybe a few more than that, some of them, obviously sick with the Slow Death, supported by healthier companions, most dressed in fine clothes, a few – mainly the single people – in tattered rags. There were children among them – a little girl, no more'n five or six, clinging to a woman I assumed was her mother (or maybe her adoptive mother); two boys, twins by the look of them, about seven years old, holding hands and standing close to a man and woman; a toddler, around two years, clutching a dolly and in the arms of a bearded man – and, unlike the adults, these children had a look of wonder on their faces as they gazed up at the lights and flames. Then they began to notice us, and soon all of them were looking in our direction.

Several backed away, as if in fear, but going only as far as the park railings. Others watched us with surprised curiosity, and maybe with hope.

'Hoke,' Cissie said breathlessly, 'who are these people?'

'Beats me,' was all I could reply.

Stern, leaning heavily against Cissie, looked at us both. 'Like moths attracted to a flame,' he said, his voice strained. 'In this case, to the lights, don't you see? Hoke, you must warn them.'

A noise from behind, a scuffling of hard leather on concrete, made me wheel around before I could say any more. The Blackshirts were filing along the alleyway, trying to move quietly now that they saw we were no longer running. I fired from the hip, taking out the first two, sending the others scuttling back. But that last burst had used up all that was left of the ammo and the Thompson was lifeless in my hands. I cursed as I threw it away – there should've been

229

fifty rounds in the drum magazine, but much of the ammo must have been used up earlier by the Blackshirt I'd taken it from – and drew the pistol from my waistband.

'Hoke!'

I turned at Cissie's cry and saw more dark figures rounding the corner from a side street further along, Blackshirts who'd found other exits out of the blazing building. They came to an abrupt halt when they saw the silent strangers standing in the roadway and on the opposite pavement. A shout went up when they spotted us next.

'Oh God, we're trapped.' Cissie had spoken to me as if I didn't appreciate the seriousness of the situation.

'No we're not. We can get through the park.' I pointed the pistol in the other direction where there was a small gate in the iron railings.

'But these people – we've got to help them.'

I took Stern from her, pulling his arm over my shoulder once more, keeping my gun hand free. 'There's nothing we can do for 'em, they'll have to take care of themselves!'

I moved off, slowed down by Stern, using the brick barricade as a screen between us and the Blackshirts who were outside the riverside entrance.

'Keep up with us!' I yelled back at Cissie as she hesitated.

'Run!' I heard her shout at the waiting people. 'Don't stay here! Don't let them take you!'

When I looked over my shoulder they were still standing there, confused, probably afraid, not knowing what the hell was going on. I fired a couple of shots over their heads to put some life into them, but although one or two started to run away, the rest cowered or sank to the ground.

'Cissie, come on!'

Reluctantly she began to follow and when shots were fired from the goons near the corner, she caught up fast. There were more figures loitering in this stretch of road and we tried to convince them that it was in their best interest to get away, but, like the others, they seemed too bewildered to move. Maybe they thought we were the villains, that those uniformed people were the only law the city had left; or maybe they thought they'd be shot if they did try to escape. I didn't know, and right then I couldn't help 'em: I was too busy saving my own and Stern's skin, and I guessed that Cissie was now of the same mind – she'd caught up with us and was taking some of the injured German's weight. We couldn't help them if they didn't want to be helped; we could only offer some hurried advice. And we did. Even with bullets whistling over our heads, we yelled and tugged at those closest to us as we made our way to the park gate; but it was no good, they just crouched low to the ground to avoid being hit. Of course, it was really the strangers who were helping us, because not only were the Blackshirts afraid of harming any part of this precious new consignment of healthy blood, but our rarity value had depreciated considerably.

Dodging through the space between two kerbside cars, we were soon at the park's entrance and I took one last look at the scene behind us. Blackshirts were already rounding up the onlookers, with only three of them chasing after us. Still supporting Stern with one shoulder, I took careful aim and brought down two as they ran. They both screamed, the first dropping to his knees, clutching at his chest, the second spinning across the hood of a car and slowly sliding to the ground. It was enough to discourage the third. He skidded to a halt, the metal toecaps of his boots scraping sparks off the roadway, and shouted something after us. He remained where he was though, neither retreating nor advancing, just loitering there, shaking a fist and cursing. I took a bead on him, but Stern placed an unsteady hand on my arm.

'Better that we just leave,' he said, his words tight, as if squeezed through a constricted throat.

I spat on the kerb, knowing he was right, that there really

was nothing we could do for these other people. Reluctantly we turned and I led the way through the thick shadows of the neglected park.

18

I TOOK THEM DOWN to the Embankment where the old river ran pure silver under the uncloaked moon, its waters free of human detritus, driftwood and loose craft the only blight. A short flight of stone steps over the river wall led us to a wooden jetty where I kept a small motor launch, tanked up and regularly serviced like all my escape vehicles. Soon we were heading downstream, the quiet throbbing of the boat's engine and the distant, fading drone of the Dornier, one contented *Kraut* bomber on his way home, the only sounds. We'd heard more gunfire behind us as we'd made our way to the jetty, but now it'd ceased, leaving us to wonder about those poor souls we'd found waiting outside the Savoy. How many had been shot or beaten for resisting the Blackshirts? How many of those suffering the Slow Death had been killed where they stood, eliminated because their blood was useless to Hubble and his parasites? And how many more of those pilgrims had arrived at the front of the hotel, at the shattered main entrance, attracted by the lights blazing through the night sky? Had they been captured too?

While Cissie cradled Stern in her arms and did her best to stanch his bleeding, I steered the motor launch close to the riverbank, keeping us under the cover of buildings and walls, checking over my shoulder to see if we were being followed, watching the grand old hotel burn. Its electric lights, sirens to the survivors, a beacon to the Dornier's pilot, were finally doused, but by then the flames had taken over, more than compensating for their loss. It was nothing new to me, this kind of senseless vandalism, but still it was a tragic sight and a heaviness weighed upon me. The Savoy had served as a resolute symbol of London's unbreakable spirit during the Blitz; by tomorrow it would be a gutted shell, maybe even reduced to rubble. It had survived the war almost intact and three years later it'd taken just one man, guided by a company of fools, to destroy it.

Cissie was quietly weeping, but there wasn't much I could do to comfort her. Nor could I help the wounded German – all my efforts had to go into getting us away from there. Rumpled barrage balloons drooped like small grey clouds over the blackened city, testimony to mankind's inventiveness and absurdity, and the river stretched ahead like a broad, metallic highway, taking us to a quieter part of the graveyard.

We journeyed into the concealing darkness of the river bends.

19

NO 26 TYNE STREET was at the very end of a long and narrow cobbled turning that looked like a cul-de-sac, but wasn't, just off Whitechapel High Street, Jack the Ripper territory, and we approached it through a covered alleyway that had a thin, waist-high post at one end – an ancient cannon barrel rooted upright in concrete, an iron cannonball fixed firmly into its muzzle – and a tall gas lamppost outside the other. Less than twenty minutes earlier we'd left the motor launch moored to a set of mossy stone steps that climbed from the river to a wharfside passageway. Between us, we'd carried the wounded German to the roadway where I soon found an open-top Austin Tourer in reasonable working condition and with enough juice left in its tank (gasoline had completely evaporated in many of these stranded vehicles) for the next phase of the journey. The three of us had crammed into it, Stern semi-conscious and moaning softly, Cissie through with weeping, but withdrawn and silent, and I'd driven past the old Billingsgate fish market – the worst of its foul stench had long since faded, but it was still bad enough to wrinkle your nose – and then carefully through the canyon streets of the City, once London's thriving financial sector, where the roads, sidewalks and doorways were littered with dark shapes, unrecognizable bundles that had once been the life-pulse of this glittering square mile. A glance at Cissie told me she didn't like it here – her eyes shifted uneasily, her head kept jerking as if she'd seen something in the road ahead, or in one of the doorways – and I remembered her nervousness when I'd first shown her the Abe Lincoln Room at the Savoy. She was perceptive to ghostly things, I guess, and the events of the evening hadn't helped her nerves any. Hell, I had to grip the steering wheel tight to stop my own hands trembling, and I was relieved when we were through the area. A few minutes later we'd reached our destination.

I'd parked the Austin outside a wash-house in Old Castle Street, a road that ran parallel to Tyne Street, then carried Stern over my shoulder through the little alleyway that connected the two streets. No 26 was three doors away from the alley and tucked into a corner facing *up* the cobbled street. Like the turning it was in, the house itself was narrow, with three floors squeezed on top of one another and a cellar, and it was in a strategic position (a prime reason for choosing it as a refuge) because nobody could enter from the high street without being observed from one of its five front windows. The dwellings at the top end of Tyne Street were gutted shells, bomb-wrecked, but in the middle it opened out to a tiny square before continuing towards No 26 with two-storey houses on one side and bigger, three-storey houses on the other, all of them joined and with defunct gaslights mounted at intervals along their walls. The London Docks were not far away and the *Luftwaffe* might have done Tyne Street's residents a favour by demolishing the rest of the houses during one of their hit-and-miss raids on dockland (as long as those residents weren't inside), because these places were slums and had been for a long time.

Behind No 26 and its neighbours were tiny, concrete back yards filled with mangles, bicycles, tin baths – all rusted now – piles of coal and outside lavatories, the yards themselves backing onto a bigger compound where some of the traders from the big bustling street market called Petticoat Lane kept their stalls and barrows. Sally had brought me here one Sunday morning, not ashamed of showing me a rougher part of her town, and I'd remembered Tyne Street and the usefully positioned No 26 after my first run-in with the Blackshirts when I was looking for safe havens. Sure, I had my pick of thousands of such places, but all my eventual choices had something to do with Sally.

The back windows of No 26 – and oddly, there were only two, both over the house's creaky wooden staircase that twisted up from the end of the short, ground-floor corridor to the bedrooms at the top – overlooked the yards, the lower one providing a handy exit should the enemy come pounding on the front door.

Most of the family furniture was packed into the ground floor's only room, making it the parlour/kitchen/dining room and (because it had the only sink in the whole place) bathroom. It was about sixteen feet square and its single window looked out onto the street. In one corner, close to the deep enamel sink with shelves overhead, cups and pans hanging from them, stood a cast-iron gas stove and, instead of a fireplace, in the wall opposite the window there was a huge black range built into the chimney breast, with ovens at the sides and a fire grate in the middle; an oversized kettle, more saucepans, along with a small camp cooker I'd brought here myself, cluttered its flat surface. Next to it was a lumpy armchair with frayed armrests, a flower-patterned sofa, where I'd dumped some of my clothes, taking up most of the wall on that side of the room; sitting on a veneered hardboard sideboard under the window was a Bush wireless set and a stoneware vase filled with shrivelled flowers I'd never bothered to throw out. Just behind the door to the corridor was a plyboard kitchen cabinet, its pull-down work-top closed, and nestled between this and the gas stove stood a tall lampstand with a tasselled shade, an arrangement imposed by jumble rather than design.

The wall here was nothing more than a wooden floor-to-ceiling partition separating the room from the corridor, painted cream and brown like the door, window frame and sill, and the mantelshelf (these days loaded with cigarette cartons) over the range. Deep brown, patterned linoleum covered the floor, almost worn through in places, and at the room's centre, with barely enough space between it and the surrounding furniture, was a steel Morrison shelter substituting for a table, the wooden chairs around it pushed tight against the wire mesh sides. All I'd found on it when I'd first entered No 26 were a half-empty jar of furry lemon curd, a split packet of dried Weston Biscuits, a can of Keating's bug, beetle and flea powder, and a yellowed copy of the *Daily Sketch* dated 24th March 1945, the very day the Blood Death rockets had fallen.

Mercifully, the house had been empty of corpses and it hadn't taken long to collect those on the cobblestones outside and transport them to the stadium; as Tyne Street was to become an occasional home I figured this was the least I could do for its dead residents. After that I'd moved in with my own comforts and weaponry (the bedroom above was stashed with canned food and guns, as well as a few hand grenades I'd picked up from a depot not too many miles from there, just south of the river). I didn't mind that this place didn't have the comforts of my other refuges; fact is, its shabbiness made it less of a target for the Blackshirts – they'd never expect me to hole up in a shack like this – and I'd always felt pretty secure here.

I kept the front-door key on the inside sill of the ground-floor window, the window itself left open a couple of inches, so while Cissie propped Stern up by the door I went and got it. She didn't make a sound as I pushed the long key into the lock, but I knew she was all in; even in the moonlight her face looked haggard, her eyes full of skittish nervousness and concern for the injured German.

Pushing open the heavy front door, I took Stern over my shoulder again and carried him straight to the end of the short corridor. The bare wooden stairs creaked and groaned under our weight, the sounds exaggerated in the close confines of the tall house. The bedroom door was open and moonlight streaming through the two windows helped me work my way through the boxes and stacked cans towards the bed. I laid him down carefully and even before I'd drawn the curtains and lit the oil lamp on the mantelpiece with matches lying next to it Cissie had removed Stern's jacket and was unbuttoning his shirt.

'I'm gonna boil some water,' I said to her. 'Use something to try and check the bleeding.'

She stopped me as I reached the bedroom door. 'Hoke. The bullet . . .'

I tried not to think about it. 'Yeah. It'll have to come out. That's why we need lots of hot water.'

'You'll do it?'

That's what I hadn't wanted to think about. 'Unless you want to volunteer.'

She didn't reply and I shrugged. 'I'll do what I can.'

I hurried downstairs and lit the camp cooker on top of the range. I'd never risked lighting a fire here, nor anywhere else unless out in the open, because chimney smoke could attract the wrong kind of attention, and I wasn't going to light one tonight. After adjusting the circle of flames, I worked my way round the Morrison shelter and pulled the curtains tight together, then lit the lantern on the makeshift tabletop. The room brightened, but the shadows became more intense. I drew the pistol and laid it next to the lantern.

Pipes clanked before water gushed in spurts from the tap over the sink and I had to wait for a steady flow before filling a saucepan; the pressure was weaker than the last time I was here and it took a couple of minutes to fill the container to the brim. Once the saucepan was on the burner I washed my hands with a rock of carbolic soap from the sink's drainer, repeating the process when I was done, and shaking them rather than use the stiffened rag passing itself off as a kitchen towel on a hook nearby. I needed a cigarette badly, but decided to wait.

Cissie's call came from over my head, followed by a loud thump on the ceiling.

Holding my hands close to my chest to keep them clean, I made my way back upstairs, glancing out the window opposite the tiny landing as I went by. There wasn't much to see through the weather-stained glass, save for shadows and the odd shapes of stalls and trestles down in the bigger yard, but I was confident that no one had followed us here. As I turned away I stumbled on the last step to the landing and my shoulder bumped the opposite wall; like the partition downstairs, it was made of wood and the cracking sound that came from it was like a gunshot. Through the open doorway I saw Cissie react sharply and I mumbled an apology as I approached the bed.

'Please help me with him,' she pleaded, the lamplight catching the glistening of tears on her cheeks.

Stern was almost on the other side of the double bed, pushing himself away as if to escape her caring hands. She knelt on the mattress and tried to pull him onto his back, but her efforts were too cautious, too gentle. The German shouted something in his own language and his hand thrashed out, striking Cissie on the shoulder. I quickly joined her and, forgetting about dirtying my hands, grabbed his arm and turned him. I winced when I saw the sheets were drenched with his blood.

'Take it easy,' I told him uselessly as I pinned him to the bed with as little force as possible. But he twisted again and for the first time I clearly saw the blood bubbling from the wound in the back of his neck. It ran through puckered skin and livid burn scars that spread downwards from his hairline, across his shoulders and towards the halfway point of his spine. These were old markings though, and my attention returned to the fresh wound: I thought I noticed something embedded there, a slight, blackish protrusion under the slick coat of discharging blood. I touched my hand to it to confirm my suspicion and felt a hard lump that I knew wasn't bone.

'The bullet's almost worked its way out,' I said, more to myself than the girl. 'At least it'll make things easier.'

Next I examined the wound in his arm, close to the shoulder, and grunted when I realized there were two punctures, front and back. The bullet had passed clean through, taking tissue and muscle with it but, s'far as I could make out, without touching bone. Straightening up, I noticed the blood-soaked rag Cissie was holding in one hand.

'His shirt,' she said.

'Christ. Okay, I'll find you something else.' I remembered the mildewed towels and sheets in a cupboard across the room; they weren't ideal, but they'd have to do. 'Keep him on his side, as he is. We'll deal with the arm wound first, try to stop the bleeding, then I'll get the bullet out of his neck.'

'The pain's too much. Don't you have anything to give him?'

'Pills'd be no good, even if he could swallow them. Tomorrow I'll get to a hospital, find some morphine.'

It was something I should have done a long while ago, in case of accidents to myself, but I guess I'd been afraid of having easy access to any powerful opiates; heck, booze was a big enough problem for me. There was something else, also: I hated those kind of places – hospitals and churches – because they were nothing more than huge burial vaults, crammed with the bodies of Blood Death victims who'd fled to them to be saved, either by medics or the Lord Himself. No, I stayed clear of those kind of charnel houses.

'I'll get some proper dressings and bandages as well as the morphine, but tonight we'll have to use what we got.'

'We need something to soak up the blood now, then something to keep pressed against the wound.'

'Gimme a minute. Just hold on to him, okay?'

I went to the cupboard set into the opposite wall and the

241

musty smell was strong when I opened its creaking door (although the coppery reek of fresh blood coming from the direction of the bed was stronger). Reaching in, I pulled out all the linen and cloth towels I could find – not many, at that – then took a thin pile of bedsheets from a higher shelf. I carried them back to the bed.

'Do what you can with these while I get the water,' I said, already heading for the door again.

The water was just beginning to come to the boil so I took time to rummage in the kitchen cabinet for a suitable instrument for some on-the-hoof surgery. The best I could find was a long, thin-bladed carving knife; it was a little big for the job, but the only one with a point strong and sharp enough to dig into flesh. Taking it over to the range, I lifted the saucepan and put the knife's blade into the small but fierce flames, slowly turning it over so that both sides and edges were sterilized without becoming blackened. I kept it in the heat for about two minutes, then replaced the saucepan with the knife's blade inside so that the water quickly came to the boil again.

I filled another saucepan and exchanged it for the one on the gas cooker and then, leaving the blade in the bubbling water, I carried the first saucepan upstairs.

Stern held out for some time before he started screaming. I'd had to probe deeper than I'd thought to get the knife's tip beneath the lump of lead, Cissie holding the lamp as close as she could while endeavouring to keep the German down with her other hand. Once, he rolled out of her grasp onto his back and I had to withdraw the blade quickly. When we got him on his side again, I went to work more ruthlessly, ignoring his screams and sliding the blade down through spurting blood and along hard metal while Cissie used her whole weight to pin him there. Twisting the knife and levering sharply and forcefully, I felt the bullet move. Stern's scream filled the room and probably echoed up the street as the bloodied lump fell out onto the stained bedsheet. I went limp thinking I'd killed him until I saw his chest still rising and falling. I saw there was blood on his lips.

Cissie finished up, cleaning and dressing both wounds while I went back downstairs to fetch more hot water. I brought it up and helped her change the bedsheets for new, if not fresh, ones, rolling the unconscious German to one side and covering the blood-sodden mattress with double layers of towels. I left her there to watch over him, wearily treading downstairs again to the jumbled front room, my bloody hands shaking so much it was impossible to light the cigarette I took from one of the cartons I kept on the mantelshelf; in the end I had to lean close to the camp cooker and light it from the blue flame. I sank into the armchair, rusted springs groaning under my weight, and rested my head back. I closed my eyes and filled my throat and lungs with smoke.

There was whisky in the kitchen cabinet, but I was too dog-tired to get it.

It was still dark when moans from over my head awoke me. I sat there and listened to Stern's agony, feeling pity, anger and helplessness. The pity was for Stern, something I never thought I'd feel for a German; the anger was against those bastards who'd done this to him; and the helplessness was because there was nothing more Cissie and I could do.

There were footsteps on the stairs – the whole house warned of any movement inside its walls with creaks and grumbles and even sighs – and then dread took a slow dive into the pit of my stomach when the shadowy form of Cissie appeared in the open doorway. I already knew what she was gonna ask me to do.

'Hoke, he needs medication now, something to kill the pain. Antiseptic, too, and fresh dressings and bandages to keep the wound clean. He won't last the night otherwise.'

Oh shit, I thought. Goddamn bloody shit. I hauled myself out of the armchair.

The enormous, Gothic-grim hospital was a mile or so away, along Whitechapel, its edifice forbiddingly bleak in the moonlight. I'd taken time only to wash away some of the blood and to pull on a grey sweatshirt, its sleeves cut away at the elbows, to protect me from the slight chill that had come with the early hours. Taking the pistol – I noted for the first time it was a Browning .22 – from the table, I tucked it back into the waistband of my pants and left the house. I ducked into the pitch-black alleyway, a hand running along the rough brick wall for guidance, and returned to the Austin open-top that had brought us here. The drive hadn't taken long, but I stayed in the car on the ramp outside the hospital's main entrance for a while, steeling myself to go inside. Only the thought that Wilhelm Stern had saved my life twice and the more I delayed the worse it was for him made me open the car door and mount the steps to the open entrance (those doors were open because old bones had jammed them that way).

Holding the lantern I'd brought with me shoulder-high, I went inside.

I still hate thinking about those wards and corridors packed with human debris, some of the corpses piled on top of each other as if their last moments had been spent struggling, fighting for attention maybe; now they were locked together in eternal strife, or at least until their bones collapsed. There

244

were smaller forms among them, the deteriorated bodies of children, but I refused to look at their little withered faces, treading through them carefully, my eyes averted, looking directly ahead. They were everywhere, those mouldering things that were once living, breathing people, in every space, every corner, as I'd known they would be, and I shuddered each time my foot brushed against something brittle and crumbly. The sour smell was everywhere too and I clamped my hand over my mouth and nose to mask the worst of it.

It took almost an hour to find the room I was looking for and still I hadn't toughened myself against the carnage around me: I was scared to my boots, and nausea was only a heave away. Even as I broke into locked glass cabinets and examined vials and jars, looked through cupboards for gauze and surgical dressings, then into drawers for pills and syringes, I kept looking over my shoulder, expecting to see something I really didn't want to see. I gathered up anything that might be useful, including sedatives, forcing myself to be calm, to take my time and collect essentials and maybe not-so essentials, loading scissors and safety pins, antiseptic creams and boxes of Elastoplast, anything that came to hand, into a laundry bag I'd taken from a storage closet. Only when I was sure I was done did I run from that place.

It was growing light behind the distant rooftops as I drove along the broad Whitechapel High Street and weariness was making my eyelids heavy and my hands like lumps of lead on the steering wheel. It didn't take long to find my way back to Old Castle Street, and I was soon hurrying through the alleyway, my legs hardly able to support me, then pushing open the door to No 26.

Cissie was sitting on the stairs at the end of the short corridor, dawn light pressing itself through the begrimed window overhead to flush her hair and shoulders with its grey mantle. From her muffled sobs I knew I was too late. Stern was already dead.

WE LAY SIDE BY SIDE in the bedroom at the top of the house, both of us still fully clothed, Cissie watching me, one hand resting in the gap between us. I was on my back, looking out the window at the brightening sky, cigarette between my lips.

I'd led her to this room – next door was a much smaller, single-sized bedroom – and waited for her weeping to end, aware that those tears were not just over the death of Wilhelm Stern, whose body was covered by a single clean sheet on the bed in the room below us, but also over her friend's betrayal and everything that had followed in its aftermath: the botched attempt at blood transfusion, the slaying of poor old Albert Potter, the bombing of the Savoy, our flight downriver from the Blackshirts, leaving those other wretches, who'd been lured from their hideaways by the lights, to the mercies of a dying madman. Her bewilderment at Muriel's treachery only increased her distress, because they'd become true friends – or so Cissie had thought – during a period of massive upheaval when the world itself had been stripped of civilized guidelines and robbed of most of its inhabitants. Despite their different social backgrounds, they had formed an alliance, each one supporting the other in moments of despair, their companionship helping them keep

246

their sanity. Until Muriel had discovered her own kind again in the form of Sir Max Hubble.

The guise she'd adopted in order to survive had fallen away like a cloak worn for warmth and not for taste, and that disloyalty – the choice Muriel had made – was something Cissie could not understand. The truth of it was – and I tried to make Cissie understand this – that the bitch *had* been loyal, but it was to her own class, to people of her own persuasion. Hell, Cissie had been there when Hubble had mentioned that Edward, England's abdicated king, demoted to dukedom, had aligned himself with the Nazi ideologies, along with certain others of the so-called British aristocracy. Before the war their persuasions were no great secret, according to other pilots I'd spoken with, and only the formal outbreak of hostilities had hushed them. Breeding above principles, was their warped philosophy. Their own ideals were more important to them than their own countrymen. It was a decadent and self-serving system, one that flourished throughout England's history, and something my own mother had been glad to leave behind when she made her home in America, even though she loved her birthplace, and these 'wrong-sorts', as she put it, were only a small minority. Muriel, I'd assured Cissie as I'd brushed her curls away from her grubby face, had only remained true to her own conditioning, and her double-cross amounted to little more than a natural alliance.

None of it seemed to help Cissie much, but maybe some of it eventually got through, because after a while she ceased her weeping, wiped her cheeks and nose with the back of her hand and started to talk . . .

'Wilhelm wanted you to know he was sorry.'

There was a hollowness to her voice in this bleak room, its only furniture the bed we lay on and an armchair with

247

wooden arms, a pile of boys' clothing – different sizes, so I knew they'd belonged to more than one – resting on its cushioned seat. I turned my head and her dirty face was not unlike a child's itself in the pale, morning light, only shadows beneath her eyes indicating the trouble she'd been through.

'He managed to talk?'

'Towards the end. I think the pain lessened, but because of that he knew he was dying.'

'Why sorry?'

'Oh, not for what he'd done. He said he'd only been fighting for his country during the war, carrying out his duty, just like us.'

'Yeah, his duty.' I dragged on the cigarette, then took it from my lips, hanging it over the edge of the bed, smoke curling up between my fingers.

'He was apologizing for Germany's final action, not for his role as a soldier.'

'He was a spy.'

'Soldier, spy – it was all the same to him. But he was deeply ashamed of what Hitler did to his own country and the rest of the world. He said Germany's inevitable defeat should have been accepted with honour. He didn't want you – us – to judge his race by the mad dogs who ruled them. Only the High Command had known about the rockets and what they were capable of.'

'What's it matter? Nothing can change what happened.' My eyes closed. Yet, weary though my body was, my mind refused to shut down: it was still buzzing with everything that had happened since yesterday.

'He just wanted you to know, Hoke, that was all.'

'I figured him right and got him wrong. I didn't trust him, but he saved my life.'

'Wilhelm understood that. He didn't blame you for your suspicions, Hoke.'

'Did he manage to tell you what his mission was over here during the war?'

248

'He found it difficult to speak towards the end – he was choking on his own blood. But he tried . . . oh, he tried so hard . . .'

I thought the tears would start again as she cast her eyes downwards, but she straightened, her mouth set tight.

'He wanted to set the record straight between you and him, something about honour among enemies. I think he wanted to die with your respect, Hoke, not your hatred.'

'He'd already earned my respect.' I lifted the cigarette again and held it over my lips for a moment. 'So what *was* he up to?'

'He told me his plane was shot down, but it wasn't over the East Coast, it wasn't a Heinkel, and it wasn't in 1940. It happened one night in '44, a few weeks before D-Day, and the aeroplane was a . . . what was it? . . . a Junkers. Yes, he said it was a Ju 188. It was gunned down over the Solent and the seven others on board with him were all killed. He managed to bale out before the burning plane crashed.'

Her gaze went past me towards the window and the oncoming day was reflected in her hazel-brown eyes.

'His clothes were alight when he jumped, and – absurdly, he said – he was more worried about the fire becoming a beacon in the night sky than burning to death. The rushing air put out the flames, though.'

I thought of the scars on the German's back and neck and wondered at his courage. To parachute into enemy territory in the middle of the night, then to hide himself while search parties scoured the countryside for survivors, badly burned and alone, well, that took a rare kind of guts. Another thought occurred to me.

'He told you there were seven others with him in the Junkers? That kind of bomber only carried a crew of four.'

'It wasn't a normal crew. They all had official papers on them giving them Slavic names, not German. If they got caught their cover story was to be that they were Polish and Czech freedom fighters who'd stolen the plane to escape

249

to England so they could carry on fighting with the Allied Forces.'

I clicked my fingers. 'Exbury Point.'

'What?'

'I remember hearing something about a mysterious German bomber crashing at Exbury Point, near the Beaulieu River where assault landing craft and barges were being made ready for the invasion of Europe. Rumours were that all kinds of secret activities were going on there –'

'Yes, that was it. He said German Intelligence had learned that pilotless rocket aircraft were being tested along the inlet from the Solent and it was his job to discover how far ahead the British scientists were with their experiments. Only three men on the Junkers were meant to parachute into the area – the rest were crew members, but with the same kind of papers as the spies in case the worst happened.'

'And it did.' The end of the cigarette glowed brightly as I drew on it. 'But how the hell did Stern get by after he'd jumped?'

'He hid for two days, then was able to reach his contact in the New Forest when the commotion died down.'

'But his burns . . .'

'He was a bit special, wasn't he?'

And some, I thought, guilt over my treatment of this war ace nagging at me. 'What happened to him?' I asked.

'Well, he stayed in the area feeding back information to his bosses until the invasion took place. He said it was important for you to know that he did very little harm to the Allied Forces' efforts down there, because once the counter-invasion of Europe had started – which was very soon after he'd arrived – his intelligence reports had hardly any value. All he could do was try and survive himself.'

I blew smoke and crushed the cigarette stub against the bare board floor, my fingers brushing against the pistol lying there. When I rolled back, Cissie was propped on one elbow, looking down at me. Her curls fell loose over her face again.

'Hoke?'

I didn't answer, just stared back into her eyes.

'We imagined they were all evil, didn't we? The enemy, the whole German race, I mean. We thought they were all the same.'

'They started the whole goddamn thing.'

'Hitler started it.'

'And the German people went along with him. People like Stern.'

'We bombed their city first.'

'Your country only retaliated for their first raid on London.'

'It was a mistake. The German bomber was off course. They hadn't meant to bomb civilians. And our own government knew that when they ordered the raid on Berlin. Hitler's answer was the Blitz on London.'

'Stern told you this?'

'He was dying, he wouldn't have lied. I never believed all the propaganda our government put out anyway, just most of it. Like everybody else, I suppose.'

My eyelids were beginning to feel heavy once more. Cissie had a point, but I didn't have the energy to agree or disagree. Either way would've meant more debate and I was just too beat for that.

'Hoke?' She thought I'd fallen asleep.

I murmured something, or maybe I just groaned.

'The last thing Wilhelm wanted you to know was that he didn't mean any of those things he said at dinner. He was just tired of your goading, he wanted to strike back and he regretted it. He despised the Blackshirts too. He said they aligned themselves with the worst of his countrymen, the bigots, the Fascist bullyboys. That's why he didn't join them last night. In fact, he said if he could live he would help you in your fight against them.'

'I'm not fighting the Blackshirts, Cissie. I've always run away from them.'

'Then why d'you stay here, Hoke? Why didn't you leave the city years ago?'

My mind was drifting and I found it very pleasant. 'Too much to do,' I mumbled, giving in to the creeping lethargy. The mattress beneath us may have been musty and full of lumps, but I seemed to be sinking into an overwhelming softness. Something was shaking my shoulder and I turned away from it. The voice persisted though.

'What, Hoke? Tell me what you have to do? Tell me . . .'

I was gone and soon, so was the voice. Mercifully, my sleep was dreamless.

I think it was the warmth on my face, the blaze against my eyelids, that woke me. My eyes opened and I turned away from the sun's rays, disturbing Cissie, whose arm had been curled around my waist. Our faces close, she blinked at me for a few moments; she didn't move away.

Everything came at me in a rush and I was suddenly alert, leaning on one elbow to check the open bedroom door, then turning towards the dirt-smeared window, squinting my eyes against the sunlight forcing its way through.

'What is it?' My reaction had frightened her.

I listened for a full minute before replying. 'It's okay. We're safe.' I couldn't really be sure of that until I'd taken a look outside, back and front of the house, but I didn't sense any danger right then and my instinct had always been reliable. I lay back on the thin pillow and realized I was aching in a hundred different places and hurting in a few more.

There was dried blood on my arm where they'd tried to bleed me last night, and the incision still throbbed a little. My shoulder was stiff, the dressing that had covered the bullet graze now missing, and various cuts and bruises reminded me of the hell I'd been through these past few days; even breathing too deeply caused a dull pain, but I could tell my ribs were only bruised, not cracked, otherwise that pain would've been a whole lot sharper. My ankle felt okay, although a mite sore, and I rotated it one way, then the other, just to test it: it complained sure enough – a sudden twinge, was all – but there was no swelling any more, so I knew I could get around okay. Anything else – cuts, gashes, sores and contusions – didn't matter: there was nothing to cause me serious problems.

The back of Cissie's hand brushed against my cheek. 'What's the diagnosis? You going to live, Hoke?'

'I reckon.'

Lifting my head from the pillow, I inspected the room, checking all was as I'd left it from my previous visit some months before. I hadn't had the chance before we'd fallen asleep in the early hours, and the room had been dim anyway; now I saw it was the same as always, the kids' clothes on the armchair, the fireplace full of cold ashes, the door to the corner cupboard that was stuffed with more clothes and only a few toys and comic-books still slightly ajar.

'How're *you* feeling?' I asked when I was satisfied nothing had been disturbed.

'My legs feel like they've run a couple of hundred miles and my arm's still sore from the grip one of those Blackshirts had on me, but otherwise, 'cept for some bumps and bruises, I'm fine. I think.'

As she followed me in scanning the room I studied her profile. Her jaw was good and firm, her nose neither dainty nor dominant, kind of just right, the thin scar across its bridge white against the dirt on her face. There was dust and glass in her singed hair and the evening dress was mussed up, torn in places, but like me, she'd suffered no serious damage.

'Who lived here before?' she asked, unaware I was watching her. 'Were there bodies . . . ?'

I shook my head. 'No, the place was empty when I moved

253

in. But my guess is that a woman lived here with three young sons.'

'No husband?'

'Mothballed suits in the wardrobe downstairs. And no shaving brush and mug by the sink.'

'P'raps he had a beard.'

'No men's underwear or socks either. The husband was either serving in the Forces, or the woman was a widow. I think when the final rockets fell she took her kids to the Underground station in the high street. That's probably where they died.'

Cissie gave a little shiver. Even after all this time and so much tragedy, the deaths of one poor ¡woman and her deprived kids still caused her grief. How much more difficult then, when the victim was someone you knew and loved. Oh yeah, that could lead to your own disintegration.

'Look,' I said, sitting up on the bed, 'I'm gonna make coffee, tea if you'd prefer. You rest up and I'll bring it to you. Then we'll think about . . .' I shot a glance out the window, judging the sun's position '. . . we'll think about some lunch.'

She rose too. 'No, let me do it. You must still be all in.'

I pushed her down again. 'I know where everything is. And I'd rather be moving around than letting my muscles stiffen up. So what's it to be – tea or coffee?'

'Tea.'

I swung my legs off the bed, but she caught my hand before I could move off.

'Hoke, those people outside the hotel last night . . . Who were they, where did they come from? Were they part of Hubble's organization?'

'You saw the surprise on their faces, and you saw how the Blackshirts reacted when they ran into 'em.'

'Then who . . . ?'

'Refugees, like us. Refugees from the Blood Death. At least nearly all of them were – they seemed to be taking care of the odd one or two who didn't look so good. I think they were a little whacky after so many years of hiding away and the Savoy being lit up like that, like some Christmas tree in a black limbo, well, I guess it drew them out, lured them away from their hiding places all over the city. The lights probably gave 'em some hope, made 'em think a part of the old life was returning, and they had to see it for themselves. They made a bad mistake.'

'What will Hubble do with them?'

'You already know.'

She lowered her head and as I watched, a single tear dropped into her lap.

I touched her shoulder. 'It takes some of the heat off us, Cissie.'

I left her there on the bed, staring after me, my meaning slowly dawning on her. Maybe it was a selfish remark, but there was truth in it: Hubble had all the decent blood he needed for now, so he didn't have to come looking for us. Okay, I was thinking only of our own skin, but selfish as the notion might have been, it gave me some passing comfort. Unfortunately I'd underestimated Hubble's hatred of me – or was it his *obsession* with me – after all this time. Yeah, I'd underestimated it badly.

21

ON THE TINY LANDING outside the top bedroom, I took time to stretch a leg across the winding staircase and rest my foot against the edge of the deep window sill opposite. It was an easy manoeuvre – the gap was less than four feet – and by leaning forward I was able to pull open the curtainless window. It swung inwards towards the adjacent wall, displaying a fine view over east London's rooftops, the white spire of Spitalfields church rising into the bright sky in the distance, its clockface forever frozen to one moment in time. It said ten-to-four, and I wondered what day, what month, what year it had stopped and how meaningless that very second must have been with no one around to notice. I don't know why, but it felt to me that this day was a Sunday – maybe it was because Sally had always brought me to the market here on Sunday mornings – and, judging by the sun's position, it was around noon. The month was July or August, I wasn't sure which, and the year was '48. Yeah, so call it a Summer's Sunday, 1948. It had no significance, and I had no idea why the muse had come upon me; unless some kind of order was slowly filtering back into my life. Was Cissie's presence doing that, this awareness that she'd be depending on me? Was having another life to consider going to bring about some kind of pattern to my own?

I snapped out of it and scrutinized the yards directly below, making sure no one was creeping up on us down there. A drop of maybe thirty feet below was No 26's back yard, half of it roofed over by several sheets of corrugated iron that was meant to keep the rain off the coal heap and rinsing mangle underneath; in the open section I could see a tap fixed to the wall and the door to the outside lavatory. All was quiet down there, as I'd expected, and I pushed myself straight, using the banister post on the landing to haul myself back.

The wooden stairs creaked as usual as I descended to the next landing, and I paused outside the door of the bedroom where Wilhelm Stern's cold body lay. I decided not to look in – what was there to see? The shrouded shell of what was once a very brave man? No thanks, not today – and went down to the ground floor, my left hand sliding round the thick central beam that rose from the corridor below to the landing at the top of the house. When I filled the kettle I noticed the water was running brown, something I hadn't been able to discern the night before. I shrugged and put the kettle on the gas cooker – boiling heat would kill any germs and we'd just have to put up with the taste. It was as I was reaching for the matches to light the canned gas that I heard the noise.

A scratching sound, coming from the corridor outside.

Mice? Rats? Tiny animals who were survivors like me? Creatures lurking behind the walls or under the floorboards? As I struck the match, the noise came again. And this time I realized it was coming from the front door.

Blowing out the flame, I made my way round the Morrison shelter to the window. I leaned between the withered flowers and wireless set on the sideboard and peered through the parted curtains. The street outside was empty.

The quiet yelp I heard next had me scooting into the corridor and drawing the bolts of the front door I'd locked in the early hours of that morning. Turning the key and without thinking, I pulled the door open and there was

Cagney sitting in front of the doorstep, his paw raised to scrape the painted wood again. He howled when he saw me, but it was a small, exhausted sound, and he tried to stand on all fours, his tail twitching in a feeble attempt at a wag. He almost toppled over with the effort and I saw that his haunches and back legs were covered in blood, the pavement underneath him sticky with the stuff. There were bloody stripes across his back and flanks, as if someone had taken a whip or thin stick to him.

'Oh Jesus, boy . . .' I dropped to one knee and Cagney tried to lick my face. 'What have they done to you?'

Opening up my arms to him, I leaned forward and he shuffled towards me, desperate for my comfort, the drool that sank to the ground from his jaw flecked with red. Bad thoughts surged through my mind just then, a deepening rage welling inside me that was only contained by my pity for the half-dead mutt that was my friend and companion.

'Cagney –' I began to say, when the doorframe beside me erupted into a powdery flurry of splinters.

I fell back into the corridor, the machine gun's roar and wood shrapnel shocking me off balance. The second burst of gunfire caught Cagney full-on and small explosions ripped open his back, lifted him, his agonized shriek piercing the air over the sound of the bullets.

This time I screamed his name, knowing when the last bullet tore open his head he was already dead. His quivering body slumped across the threshold and I had no choice, no matter how much I loved that dog, self-preservation taking over and instinctively making me kick him out again. With nothing to jam the door now, I kicked it shut.

Bullets pierced the thick wood, showering me with splinters, thin rays of sunlight penetrating the tiny holes to shine through the dim, dust-filled air like a dozen narrow flashlight beams. I heard footsteps on the cobbles outside and something slammed against the door, shaking it so hard I feared it might fall inwards. Taking a chance, I reached up for the key, twisting it in the lock, then I scrambled away from those beams of light, rising to a crouch as someone began to prise open the door's vertical letterbox. From the room beyond the partition wall came the sound of breaking glass.

I fled up the stairs, taking them three at a time, cursing myself for stupidly leaving the pistol beside the bed, reaching the first landing as furniture crashed over in the room below and more bullets bit into the tough front door, probably around the lock itself. Something smashed and I knew they were inside.

On the first landing I ran into Cissie, who was barefoot and – beautiful, gutsy lady – was clutching the gun I'd left behind.

'Back up!' I yelled at her, no time for explanations. Besides, I think she'd figured it out for herself.

Running footsteps and shouts along the corridor below.

Snatching the gun from her, I pushed Cissie up, barely giving her the chance to turn. She tripped, but regained her balance instantly, using her hands on the stairs above to help herself climb.

'We'll be trapped up here!' she shouted back at me, but I shoved her onwards, speeding her on her way.

I paused only long enough to lean round the stout centre post and shoot at the leading shadow below. The shadow's owner hesitated, reluctant to risk the next bullet, and it gave us time to gain the top landing.

'How did they find us?' Cissie cried, clutching at me. 'I thought they didn't know this place.'

'They followed Cagney,' was all I could tell her as heavy boots pounded the stairs. I realized the Blackshirts must have caught Cagney back there at the hotel, trapped him in a room, as likely as not, just in case he might come in useful. They'd beaten the poor mutt, half-crippled him so's he couldn't move too fast, and then they'd let him go in the hope he'd head straight for one of my sanctuaries. And Cagney knew my routine, even if I wasn't properly aware of it myself. Y'see, I always came here after the Savoy, it was a rut I'd subconsciously fallen into over the years. The palace, the hotel, downgrading to Tyne Street, from there to an apartment near Holland Park, back to the palace to repeat the process. It could've been natural instinct that had brought Cagney after me, but I figured it was more likely to be the set agenda, one he'd gotten used to. And of course, he'd used the alleyway to get to the house as we always did, a route I believed would be invisible to the enemy, bringing his trackers with him. Hubble had gone with his hunch, and it'd paid off. What I couldn't understand was why he'd gone to so much trouble now that he had a healthy blood supply.

Machine-gun fire sprayed the wall next to the landing window opposite us and Cissie screamed as she backed into the tiny bedroom with its single cot behind us. I caught her arm and hauled her back out onto the landing, firing four shots over the stout balustrade to give the Blackshirts something more to chew on. Their reply was another burst of machine-gun fire that smacked into the ceiling over our heads, dislodging plaster and fragments of timber.

It suddenly dawned on me. These lunatics weren't out to capture me – hell no, they didn't need my blood any more. This time they were out to kill me. Call it revenge, anger over the killing of some of their own by me and the dance I'd led them over the years, or maybe just plain envy because I had something they hadn't – good, wholesome, disease-free blood. These boys were out to nail me once and for all – and I guess that included anyone who was with me.

'Cissie,' I said, more calmly than I felt, 'we're gonna jump.'

She looked at me as if I were crazy. Then her gaze went to the open window and panic took over. She tried to yank her arm away.

'There's a roof just below,' I said quickly, holding her tight. 'We'll be okay. Just trust me.'

Bullets thudded into the plaster ceiling again and chipped

wood off the edge of the landing. Gunsmoke rose from the stairwell, its cloud mingling with the floating white dust. There were more excited shouts down there and one or two banshee screeches. Heavy boots clumping on wood, single, wild shots. They were coming up.

'Now, Cissie, *now!*'

She came with me, no hesitation at all, hopping across the gap onto the window's deep ledge, our figures blocking the light for no more'n a fraction of a second as bullets shattered glass and frame beside us. We were gone, dropping like stones through the air, falling in an eternity of dread that took maybe three seconds, possibly less, the corrugated roof rushing up to meet us.

We both yowled in terror as the old, rotted iron gave way beneath us, a neat section breaking off like a trapdoor. Our fall continued, but was soon over as we landed on the piled coals in the yard below. Like the tin roof itself, it broke our fall, saved our legs, maybe even our backs, from being broken. We rolled down the small hillock in an avalanche, then sprawled across the concrete floor of the back yard.

I sucked air, too numbed to feel pain just yet, my eyes unfocused, seeing only a spinning blue expanse of sky above. The weight on top of me was Cissie and I let her head rest on my heaving chest while the dizziness slowed down. The edge of the roof we'd fallen through came into view, then the brickwork of the house itself, rising impossibly high into the sky – or so it seemed lying there on my back with lumps of coal digging into me. The little landing window was about a mile away.

My senses, nudged by fear, returned fast. Any moment now there'd be gun barrels poking through that opening, aimed down at us. I pushed myself to a sitting position, bringing Cissie with me, my hands on her shoulders. She was blinking hard, trying to regain her own equilibrium, as I examined her face. But she got the question in first.

'Are you all right?' Her voice seemed distanced from the dazed uncertainty in her eyes.

Instead of replying I got a knee under me, then hauled us both to our feet. My gun was gone, lost when we'd crashed through the roof, and I swiftly scanned the yard. A stirrup pump stood in one dark corner and a two-handled zinc bath leaned against a wall; a dried heap of soiled clothing stood in a straw basket next to the rusted mangle; coal was scattered everywhere, making my search more difficult. But I found the Browning lying on the small drain covering beneath the yard's tap.

Grabbing the gun and quickly checking it for damage, I bundled Cissie towards the back wall as more noises came from inside the house, shouts and footsteps beating the stairs, growing louder as they descended. We had to be over the wall before they pulled the double bolts of the big back door and turned its stiff key. And before those weapons appeared at the top window.

Without a word, I tucked the pistol into my waistband and folded my arms around Cissie's lower legs. As I lifted her she reached for the top of the seven-foot high wall and dragged herself up, a final push from me helping her on her way. Then I climbed after her, toecap digging into the rough brickwork, elbows levering myself upwards. All this had taken a matter of moments, from leap to climb, and by the time I'd straddled the wall, Cissie had dropped to the other side. I took a swift glance at the landing window before following her.

Sure enough, the first gun barrel had shown up, a strained face looming behind it; I realized the Blackshirt was being supported by his cronies on the stairs below, because they hadn't figured how else to reach the window. It gave us an advantage, gave us a chance to skip through the long stallholders' yard at the rear of the houses before they'd worked out a decent way to take aim at us. Something crashed against the back door.

I knew it was dark at the end of the corridor inside No 26, even during the day, a small set of steps leading down to the yard door, another flight descending from there to the cellar, and because of the lack of light the Blackshirts were now scrabbling around for the door key and bolts and banging at the wood in frustration, all of which was allowing me and Cissie extra time. I decided to use it.

My left hand cupping the fingers of my gun hand, I took careful aim at the wrinkled-up face at the window above and gently squeezed the trigger with the pad of my index finger. The Blackshirt saw me though and his head plunged from view – now you see it, now you don't – as the gun spat flame.

I heard faint cries as he fell onto the men supporting him and hoped they'd all taken a tumble. Wasting no more time, I dropped from the wall, grabbed Cissie by the waist, and started running through the debris of rotting stalls and barrows, weaving around wooden packing cases and lumps of metal, old wheels and mouldering cardboard boxes, making towards the big gates at the end of the yard.

We were halfway there when Cissie tripped over wire sprung loose from a busted orange crate. She stumbled into another box and went down, with me sprawling over her. That fall probably saved our lives, because at that moment a round of bullets whined over our heads, breaking up a trestle and snapping a stall's wooden upright a few yards in front of us. Still on the ground, I aimed the pistol over my shoulder.

There were now two faces up at that top window, the Blackshirts' shoulders crammed together, elbows on the sill supporting their bodies. One was pointing a machine gun, the other a rifle, and it was the machine gun that was spitting fire. Below them, arms and hands were appearing on the wall as the goons who'd managed to open the back door tried to follow us. I fired at the window first, four or five rapid shots in desperation, praying my ammo wouldn't run out.

Even from that distance, the two holes that appeared on the forehead of one of those faces were neatly precise, but it was the shot man's buddy who screamed and disappeared from view; the dead guy just slunk away, slipping out of sight like someone sinking into quicksand. My next shots were at the head appearing over the wall, the bullets chipping brickwork; luckily it was enough to make our pursuers duck down again. The hammer clicked on empty with my next attempt to warn them off and I knew that was it – the gun wasn't jammed, it was empty. I tossed the useless piece of iron away.

Cissie and I rose together and we both realized we'd never make it to the end of the yard – once the enemy regained its nerve we'd be like targets in a shooting gallery. There was only one hope for us and there was no time for words: I pushed Cissie towards a nearby stall that backed up against a back-yard wall to our left. Leaping onto the stall's flatbed, I reached down and hoisted Cissie up after me just as the Blackshirts began clambering over the far wall again. We scrambled over and dropped down into another enclosed back yard. I almost whooped with relief when I saw the back door to the house was wide open. We rushed straight into the welcoming shadows and, once inside, I wheeled around and slammed the door shut behind us, praying the Black-shirts hadn't had time to witness our change of direction.

Cissie had sunk to her knees in the dim hallway we found ourselves in, but I didn't allow her to stay there. Just a tug did it, and she was in my arms, leaning against me, her breasts brushing my chest as she gasped for breath.

'We can't stay here,' I told her between my own harsh breaths. 'We gotta find someplace else to hide before they start searching all the houses along here.'

She drew away a couple of inches so I could see her nod in agreement. There was blood on her shaded face, a cut in her forehead probably caused by our fall through the iron roof, or by the stumble in the big yard. She opened her mouth, about to ask a question, but I pressed my fingers to her lips. For a long moment we looked into each other's eyes, hers wide and frightened, the whites grey in the gloom, my own probably the same, even though I was more used to the chase than her. I hoped she couldn't see how scared I was.

Without another word I led her along the hallway to the front door. Controlling my breath as if the wrong ears might pick up the sound, I undid the latch and peeked out. To the left, further down the road, was the lamppost that stood near the entrance to the alleyway leading into Tyne Street, beyond this and on the other side of the road, the Austin Tourer outside the wash-house. To try and reach it would be too risky – it would mean going past the alley – so I decided the opposite direction was the only way. We'd have to move fast though. Beckoning Cissie to follow, I slid out into the sunshine.

We heard more shouting and an occasional burst of gunfire – the goons shooting at shadows among the rubbish or just in frustration? – beyond the row of terraced houses as we stole along the street, keeping close to the windows and walls, Cissie limping worse than me. At the corner I brought her to a halt.

The side street here could be crossed in four long strides it was so narrow; but it led directly to the yard gates fifty yards or so along, and so it was a vulnerable point. Even though I knew those gates were locked, I was also aware that a hefty kick would open them easily enough. More voices, pretty damn close – near the other side of the gates, I guessed. They sounded kind of angry.

I had no idea how many Blackshirts had come after us, but their noise told me there was quite a crowd; soon they'd be spilling out into that little side street.

'You got enough juice left to go full lick?' I whispered to Cissie.

She set her jaw and nodded. 'Just watch me.'

'Okay. No clatter.' We both looked down at her bare, bleeding feet and I shrugged.

Then we sprinted.

We'd lost ourselves in the maze of market streets once known as Petticoat Lane, stopping to catch our breath only when we were sure we weren't being followed, or could hear no distant calls and crack of gunfire, moving on as soon as we'd got our wind back, searching for a safe haven. There were plenty to choose from, but only when we'd passed through an archway and found ourselves inside a courtyard overlooked by ornamental iron balconies did we pick a flat at random on the second floor. Its flaky door was unlocked and once inside we'd bolted it, only then collapsing onto its hallway floor.

After a while Cissie had roused herself and, without a word, crawled into my arms. I'd held her there, my back against the wall, legs spread across the hallway and touching the opposite side, my chin nestled into the singed curls of her matted hair. And she'd felt good to hold on to, good to keep close, and when eventually her hand reached up to my neck, her fingers curling round to caress me, well, that felt good too.

But, as time wore on and my strength returned, my anger began to burn.

22

CISSIE HAD PLEADED with me long into the night, insisted it
was insane. But I hadn't listened. I knew what I was going
to do.

'You're only one man,' she'd argued.

'Yeah, but *they're* dying. Nothing slows you down more'n
that.'

'Hoke, please ... let's just get away from here, out of the
city, me and you ...'

'I've done enough running. It's time to quit, time to bring
it to an end.'

I'd struck a match and lit the Woodbine I'd taken from a
pack lying on the kitchen table.

'Besides, others are involved now. Maybe I can save 'em
if it's not too late.'

'But where will you find them? They could be anywhere
in the city.'

'He told us, don't you remember?'

She'd looked at me curiously, slowly shaking her
head.

'When they had us in the Savoy, me trussed up like a
turkey, ready for some bloodletting. Hubble said something
like, while I had my palace, he had his castle.'

I'd exhaled smoke, creating a cloud between us.

'S'far as I know,' I'd continued, 'there's only one castle in London, right?'

I'd watched her steadily.

'Right?' I'd said again.

23

I TOOK A FINAL DRAG on the last Woodbine and dropped the butt onto the ground, for some reason – old habits? – grinding it into the concrete with the heel of my boot. It'd been a long morning. And it was only just beginning.

From where I stood near the top of the hill I could take in the whole north-west spread of the ancient fort and the great towered bridge looming beyond it. Wrinkled blimps, some lower than others, hung listlessly over the dockland wharves along the river's edges, while the jagged ironwork of tall cranes reached into the pale skyline like broken church spires. The bridge was raised, each side vertical, so that they almost scraped the two high walkways joining the twin towers: the tall ship they'd once opened for (it must have been something spectacular for the bridge to be fully raised like that) had long since drifted onwards to berth alongside some distant wharfside, its crew and passengers all dead, its cargo no longer needed, leaving the guardian of this stretch of the river frozen open behind it, the hands that had worked the bridge's machinery by now shrivelled to bone and gristle. A lone gull flew between the towers, then wheeled around in a swooping arc as if changing its mind, sensing this necropolis was no place to be; it headed back downstream, its white wings catching the early sun.

Squinting my eyes, I studied the castle, searching for signs of life. There were none.

Its centre keep – the White Tower, it was called – rose over the ramparts, a dishevelled flag drooping from the flag-pole on its roof, its walls and corner turrets washed grey by centuries of city dirt and weather grime, as were the bastions of its outer walls. Even so, speckles of white showed through like chalk on a cliff face as if to reveal the real glory beneath the dulled façade; and buttresses, relieving arches and tops of battlements were like bleached bones, as if someone had scrubbed them clean; but it was no more than the nature of the stone itself, this effect, and had nothing to do with care and attention. Part of the northern bastion had been demolished by a lucky strike from a *Luftwaffe* raiding party, and the surrounding walls and railings were nicked and scarred by near misses. Otherwise, the Tower of London stood proud and impregnable as it had throughout centuries of English history. On this summer's day though, in the year 1948, it had only a single invader, one who wasn't expected. And that would make all the difference.

I crouched to look inside the canvas bag at my feet, checking its contents, pulling its strap over my neck and shoulder as I straightened up again. Flipping open the button holster at my waist, I drew the Browning P-35 high power automatic and jacked a shell into the chamber. The double click as the slide came back, then returned, was a good sound, a satisfying sound. I'd chosen the P-35 because it was one of the best 9mm automatics around, if not *the* best, accurate and carrying thirteen rounds in its magazine (I had an extra mag in my left pocket and another in the bag). When the *Krauts* had occupied Belgium, they'd taken over the factory that manufactured these guns, which soon became a substitute service firearm for them; but what they soon discovered was that many were being sabotaged in production and were as likely to blow their hand off as stop an enemy. Fortunately, the one I had came from Canada, so I knew it was okay. I slipped it back into the holster. Leaning against the low parapet wall in front of me were three more weapons. I'd left it 'til now to make my final decision on which one I'd be using that day.

My first choice would've been the Bren gun, one of the best light machine guns of all time: reliable, pretty fair accuracy, steadiness in firing, and with a reasonably low rate of fire, which allowed a better aim without too much ammunition wastage. Also, it had only three kinds of stoppage factors (certain similar weapons had twenty-three, for Chrissake!) and I knew how to fix all three, and smartly at that. But now I nixed it, because even with its bipod folded forward the gun was awkward to carry if you intended to be moving fast – and before the hour was out I intended to be moving *very* fast.

So I turned to the Thompson, nicknamed the Tommy gun, lifting it and feeling its weight. It handled well and could be switched to single-shot if required; but this one, the military version, carried a twenty-round box that took only two seconds of automatic fire to empty (with the fifty-round magazine cartridges would rattle around like nuts and bolts in a tin box, which could be a mite embarrassing if you were sneaking up on an enemy position). It also had a 'spray' effect, which was fine for trench warfare, but not so hot if the good guys were mixed up with the bad guys. I needed more control.

Laying down the Thompson, I picked up the Sten gun that had been standing next to it. This would have to be the one. Its main advantages were that it was easy to carry, especially using a fitted sling, and it was simply built, so there were fewer things to go wrong. Another advantage was that the magazine fitted into the gun's left side so that it could lie across my forearm for additional stability and wouldn't interfere if I had to hit dirt and fire from the ground. It also had a thirty-round capacity which, with two spare mags inside the bag, should be more than enough for my purposes. Before

I'd brought this particular model along I'd been faced with another choice. During the war, commandos and raiding parties understandably had favoured silenced weapons, so a variation Sten gun had been produced with its own inbuilt silencer and canvas heat-resistant cover, and these particular versions were among the collection I was able to pick from. After a few seconds' deliberation, I'd elected the unsilenced MKY, a quality 1944 model with wooden stock, pistol grip and rifle foresight, deciding that today I'd want *plenty* of noise.

Removing the magazine, I shook it against my ear just to hear the slight but reassuring shift of cartridges, then slapped it back in. It entered smoothly, no fuss at all.

Satisfied with the 'artillery', I reached under the back of my sweatshirt and slid out the double-edged commando knife from the sheath attached to my belt. The thin, ridged handle was wrapped in leather and the tapering blade with its wickedly sharp point was coated in non-reflective black. It looked vicious and I hoped to God I wouldn't have to use it – I didn't want to be that close to the enemy. I put the knife away again, but left the handle protruding outside the sweatshirt for easy access.

I'd been lucky that in the early hours of the morning I hadn't needed to travel too far to find other items I'd be using that day, because when the *Luftwaffe* had turned its attention towards the Soviet Union back in '41, giving London's East End a breather from their bombing raids, quite a number of factories and firms in these parts had converted to war production, manufacturing anything from demolition charges to safety fuses, from dynamite to shells fitted with explosives; just across the river at Woolwich was one of the country's biggest armouries. For the hand weapons I'd paid a visit to a deep shelter transit depot I knew of only a couple of miles from where I now stood, a place where troops waiting to be shipped overseas had been billeted, equipment and all, until time to go. Unfortunately, the last lot hadn't gone anywhere – the Blood Death had seen to that – leaving the depot well stocked with all kinds of weaponry and tackle. It wasn't pleasant searching the stores down there, and only a deep seething rage that over-whelmed all else got me through it.

Oddly, I was no longer trembling. It'd been a bad night, I'd hardly slept thinking of what I had to do, and laying there in the dark, my hands had started to shake and my throat had tightened up so that it was difficult to breathe. My mouth had dried too, and there was a dread in my gut that felt like a physical lump. It was a relief to leave the bed while it was still black outside and set things rolling. And now, after a lot of hard work and some travelling, my hands were steady and my mouth wasn't at all dry. There was a grim determi-nation in me, a kind of dark coldness that had taken over from the rage to stifle any other emotion. Sure, I was scared, but for the first time in three years I felt I was in control.

With one last sweeping inspection of the old castle and its battlements, I moved out.

24

AS I WALKED DOWN the cobbled hill towards the castle's main gates I remembered the first time I'd visited the Tower of London. It was in '43 and, because this tourist attraction was closed to the public for the duration, I went along without Sally. The British government encouraged US and other Allied Forces to visit its country's historic places and monuments – it was a great exercise in public relations – and I was just one of thousands of American servicemen stationed over here to drop in on the Tower. I was among a small group of flyers, about half-a-dozen if I remember right, two of 'em English, and we had a guide – one of those scarlet-tunicked Beefeater guys – all to ourselves. He was thorough, enjoying his own country's history and traditions, but I'd forgotten most of what he told us, although I still retained a fair idea of the layout of the place and had a vague notion of its past glories (and infamies). Last night I'd been puzzled as to why Hubble and his not-so-merry band of blood thieves should choose the castle as headquarters when they had the choice, like me, of London's finest mansions or hotels – those still left undamaged by the Blitz and unchecked fires, leakages and gas explosions, that is – but I eventually came to the conclusion that the Tower of London, with all its historical associations and grandeur, suited Hubble's own vision of himself. His crazed mind considered himself the new overlord of civilization, the baron of rebirth, if you like, military master of the New Order – why else the martial uniforms and his sham, jackbooted army? – so what better centre of command than the fortress of England's most famous conqueror, William? Hubble had an acute sense of destiny. Besides, there were comfortable enough living quarters within the walls and I was willing to bet old Sir Max had claimed the best for himself. And that was where I hoped to find him this morning.

Carcasses and a few abandoned vehicles, some of them military, littered the road and broad pavements of Tower Hill, and halfway down I passed the remains of a carthorse still attached to its wagon's shafts, the body almost picked clean, the bones yellowed by the sun. The cart, laden with boxes, had its rear against one of the many short iron posts (small French cannon captured in the Napoleonic Wars, like the one at the end of the alleyway in Tyne Street, set upright in concrete and painted black) and I remembered being informed by that fancy-decked guide on my previous visit how the carters from Billingsgate fish market (just down the road and not far from where I'd moored the motor launch two nights ago) would back their wagon's tailboard against a post whenever their horse got too weary hauling its load up the hill. Of the driver there was no sign – had he been one of the lucky ones, or just a Slow-Dier? – but the fish boxes on the cart had obviously been attacked for their contents at some time in the past – the marks and scratches on the wood were aged – although they remained unbroken. Still walking, my gaze went back to what was left of the horse and I suddenly understood what had happened here: unable to get at the fish packed inside the sealed boxes, the birds – had to be birds, judging by those marks on the wood – had eaten the horse. But what kind of bird could strip an animal that size of all its flesh? I thought of the lone seagull that had flown through the bridge minutes earlier and wondered, but it was a distraction that disappeared when I drew nearer to the tall, bomb-scarred gates at the bottom of the hill.

I waited a few seconds before entering, looking around first, listening, searching for the slightest sign of life. Ahead of me was the stunted, twin-towered gatehouse, the royal crest cut in stone above its archway: this was the entrance to the Tower itself and I almost expected to find a sentry on guard there, ready to challenge me. I heard and saw no one. But then, who would Hubble expect to invade his fortress?

The Sten gun had been hanging by its sling over my shoulder, and now I took it off, holding it before me, muzzle pointing directly ahead. I went on, feeling exposed, vulnerable, passing through the gatehouse and wondering if anyone had a weapon trained on me behind those arrow slits in its walls.

The air was cooler inside the archway, but it scarcely chilled the sweat on my brow as I studied the stone causeway over the moat. The sturdy wooden gates of the larger, inner gateway towers across the causeway were wide open, but there was nothing inviting about them. I took a look over the low side wall at the dried-out moat below and frowned. During the war, this wide, grassed-over defence ditch had been full of allotments, Tower staff and soldiers digging for victory and supplementing their plain rations with their own fresh vegetables; those same vegetable patches were now unkempt and overgrown, parched by the hot summer. It occurred to me that if the Blackshirts really had taken up residence here, then why hadn't they maintained the allotments? They might be sick, but they still needed to eat. Suddenly I was doubting my own assumption. Had I got it wrong? When Hubble had referred to his 'castle' had he meant something else, using the word as some kind of metaphor for his own grandiose view of himself? So far there'd been no sign of life, no sounds to interrupt that awesome, dead-city silence, so had I made a big mistake?

And then I spotted something down there that made me

think again, a splash of red amongst the green and brown vegetation. Another, and still more. Different colours now, some of them easily camouflaged by the shrubbery around them. Most of those tones were faded, but the red was easily recognizable: they were the uniforms worn by the castle's keepers, the warders, the scarlet tunics of the Beefeaters. I understood instantly what had taken place here.

The inner wards of the Tower had been cleared of corpses by the new squatters, the Blackshirts themselves, those bodies dumped out of sight into the surrounding moat and left there to rot. The less visible carcasses were in khaki, the uniforms of regular soldiers, and the rest, I figured, were the forms of wives, kids and visitors on that fateful day, all dressed in wartime drab. The Blackshirts didn't give a cuss about the allotments and fresh vegetables, not when other food was so readily and easily available, so the vegetation was left to cover the mass grave.

So okay, the game was still on.

I stole from the cover of the archway and dashed across the causeway. Now I was inside the fortress itself.

Once through the next dim passageway, I grew even more cautious, sure I was drawing closer to the hub of things. To my left was a little road called Mint Street, where in the olden days the Tower had its own money-making operation going; there were quaint, tiny dwellings where the Yeoman Warders and their families lived, as I recalled. Part of the street was in ruins, another lucky bomb-hit. In front of me was Water Lane, its uneven, cobblestone roadway dangerous if you were in a hurry; I made a mental note to watch my step when things heated up later on. At the corner where these streets met was another tower, this one with a bell house jutting from its top, and the windows in its thick walls set me feeling exposed again – it was too easy to imagine marksmen watching me from inside, waiting for the right moment to shoot. I moved across the intersection in a crouching run, coming to a halt only when I was around the tower and flat against the wall on the other side. From there I made my way along Water Lane, keeping close to the wall, alert for any sound, any movement, not stopping again 'til I'd reached another archway opposite a set of steps leading down to the water-filled entrance known as Traitors' Gate, where criminals, political outcasts and dignitaries alike had been brought to the Tower by boat. Sunlight shone through the bars of the massive gate and the grille-work above it to pattern the still waters below, this grim pit partially roofed by a wide sweeping archway carrying a timbered building, whose windows overlooked my position. Yet again, I felt too vulnerable, so I didn't linger.

I scurried into the shadows of the passage beneath the Bloody Tower (yeah, that name seemed about right), going down on one knee at the end of it to survey the wide, open area laid out before me, re-familiarizing myself with the lie of the land before advancing any further.

A broad walkway with a couple of sets of rising steps stretched out ahead of me, the long overhanging branches of untrimmed trees from untidy greens on either side creating welcome shadows, the great square edifice of the White Tower, *the* tower of legend, looming at least ninety feet on the right of the final set of steps, the ragged flag I'd spotted from outside suspended limply from its roof. To my left was a high grey wall, broken by a narrow opening where steps led up to the next level. I knew that up there, beyond the wall, were two adjoining rows of Tudor houses and cottages, all white plaster and wooden beams, among them the Queen's House, the official residence of the Tower's Governor, and there, I guessed, was where I'd find Hubble.

I was about to make my way towards it when movement caught my eye. Keeping perfectly still, I let my eyes search out the disturbance (you never try and duck out of sight if any motion on your part might give away your own position), and then I saw them, sinister black shapes moving about the tall grass in front of the White Tower, creeping, it seemed to me right then, like dark assassins closing in for the kill. I released my breath when one of the creatures fluttered its wings – the same one who'd caught my attention a couple of seconds before – and flew to a post at the top of the timber stairway to the tower's entrance. The big bird sat there on its perch, its long beak stabbing the air. Another appeared on the side wall to the steps ahead of me, then another hopped across open ground in the distance, and it was only then that I realized that these were the Tower of London's legendary ravens. At least six of them had been kept here through the centuries by clipping their wings so they couldn't fly, the superstition being that any fewer meant the monarchy would fall. Obviously these birds had bred unsupervised after the Blood Death and, although it was common for other ravens to devour new eggs and some males might even kill off their own young out of jealousy, quite a few here had managed to survive. I guessed that this new breed, with no one around to clip their wings, stayed in, or always returned to, the castle grounds out of habit, or because of some kind of natural instinct passed from generation to generation.

Now I understood what had happened to the carthorse on Tower Hill, and was glad I hadn't examined any of the human corpses lying thereabouts. But with that thought, there came another, one that hit me so hard that my body sagged and my head lowered so that my chin was almost touching my chest. This thought was like a nightmare, one that was constant and came in waking hours as well as in dreams, an image I'd tried so hard to suppress, but one I could never forget. It visited me as fresh and horrific as its moment of reality, a harsh vision of Sally, my wife, outside the cheap basement flat we'd rented, lying in the stairwell, so still, so dead, her eyes gone, her . . .

The bitterness erupted and suddenly I could no longer see clearly, everything before me had become blurred, watery . . . My shoulders hunched over as I leaned forward on my knees, forehead inches away from the ground. But I fought it, I fought hard, forcing myself up again, shaking my head as if to loosen the sight trapped inside. The fingers of my free hand cleared my eyes and slowly, deliberately, I made myself think of what lay ahead of me that morning – after all, it was for Sally as much as Stern and Cagney and all those other victims, and it was for myself, it was especially for myself . . . And oddly, it was the thought of Cagney among all those others that brought me back to the present. Not because of what the Blackshirts had done to him, but because of those sinister black birds maundering around the castle grounds. What *they* had tried to do to him.

It hadn't been a couple of miles from this very location that the dog and I had first set eyes on each other, the time I'd been digging in the allotment to look up and discover Cagney watching and sniffing my lunch from a safe distance. The day Cagney had been attacked by ravens and together we'd fought them off. Those ravens had come from this place, I knew it as sure as I knew Hubble and his maniacs had set up camp here. My hands tightened around the Sten gun. I wanted to blast those evil, stinking predators into oblivion, blow every one of 'em into a puff of black feathers and shredded flesh, because I associated them with all the vermin that still roamed this world, human and animal alike. I thought of Cagney on the doorstep, his hind legs bloodied and crippled, and I thought of every victim of the Blood Death, not destroyed by some manufactured disease, but by the wicked intent of the corrupt few we'd once shared this planet with. And I thought of those malign bastards still left running loose to kill and maim, to take what didn't belong to them . . . Oh yeah, I wanted to kill those ravens and what they represented, and I even took aim at the one on the post; but the cold calmness came back to me before I could squeeze the trigger. Those creatures were not the real badness; they just looked like it to me at that moment. I lowered the weapon.

I got to my feet and, swiftly and quietly, I entered the narrow opening in the wall on my left and climbed the mossy steps. Before reaching the top, I knelt down and peeked round the low wall that overlooked another neglected lawn and the two terraced rows of Tudor houses and cottages. There didn't appear to be any life inside those dwellings, but I noticed two rusted water trucks parked untidily in front of them, and they told me all I needed to know. The antiquated waterpipe system of the old castle and its quarters hadn't been able to cope with the severity of the previous two winters, the pipes probably cracking, the system flooding, everything breaking down, so the residents here had had to bring in their own supply. I waited a few minutes before making my next move, and when I did it was almost a mistake.

The dark-garbed figure emerged from a concealed set of steps at the far end of the smaller houses opposite just as I came out from the cover of the wall. Whoever it was over there had obviously come from a rampart tower, whose entrance was on a lower level to the cottages and green, so that first the head appeared followed by the shoulders. I'd already dodged back behind the wall, disobeying my own rule of remaining still because I'd have been noticed anyway. It was a chance I'd had to take, and it seemed I was in luck – there were no shouts of alarm, only the distant scuffing of boots on concrete. The figure was marching – and I mean *marching* – across the courtyard, past the site of the Tower's notorious chopping block towards the castle keep, the White Tower itself. I stayed out of sight, peering over the wall only when I thought it was safe. But the marching figure was gone from view and I had to stand erect to catch a glimpse of it again. The dark-uniformed man was just disappearing behind the far corner of the White Tower.

Keeping low, I ran forward on the balls of my feet, making hardly any noise at all. In a clear area of the great yard I noticed a solitary machine gun on a tripod; it looked like a Vickers Mk 1 and I was relieved to see its fabric ammunition belt was empty. The gun had probably been left there by garrison soldiers and the Blackshirts had enjoyed themselves taking potshots at easy targets: a black sentry box near one of the cottages was a mess of bullet holes and splinters. Maybe Hubble took his military pretensions so seriously he insisted his followers keep up target practice. I wondered if he had them parade marching as well.

Leaving my cover, I crossed open ground to the corner of the White Tower, pausing there to scan the area. Across the yard to my left was a small chapel and directly opposite was a huge multi-windowed blockhouse, complete with elaborate battlements and gargoyles, an octagonal tower on either side of its entrance. I thought I heard noise coming from somewhere in that direction, but although I listened hard nothing else came. Sneaking a hasty look around the turret I was leaning against, I caught a flash of black uniform entering a second raised doorway to the White Tower.

So, was this it? Was this where the Blackshirts and their hostages were gathered? The rest of the grounds seemed deserted and it made sense for Hubble to keep his captives in one location. So what better place than the White Tower itself? There were large display rooms inside, the exhibits anything from cannon to armour, with plenty of space to hold prisoners. And plenty of room to ... I prayed to God they hadn't already begun the transfusions.

I knew I couldn't waste any more time. I slipped round the corner and raced towards the stone staircase leading up to the keep's doorway, at any moment expecting the Blackshirt to reappear; but it didn't happen, I had a clear run. Without breaking stride, I grabbed the iron stair rail and climbed, taking the steps two at a time, holding the Sten gun in one hand by its pistol grip, muzzle aimed at the doorway above, my hand sliding along the top of the rail to steady myself. I reached the small landing without incident.

The double doors to the keep were wide open, but there were no sounds from inside. I snuck a quick look, then pulled back again, allowing the impression of what lay beyond the opening to sink in.

The room was below door level, a vast basement chamber with archways and flagstone floor, helmets and breastplates mounted around its dingy walls and cannon of various sizes arranged in neat rows inside alcoves along its length on either side of the central area. Iron chandeliers hung from the high, dusty ceiling, but much of the light came from lanterns placed around the room, the rest from the big doorway itself, revealing a scene so horrific I really didn't want to take a second look.

Leaning back against the outside wall, my eyes shut tight, I fought the nausea that threatened to debilitate me. But it wasn't only the sight of those half-naked bodies down there, corpses of men and women sprawled in their own gore, rubber tubes still attached to some of their arms, the smell of excrement thick with the stench of blood, that caused the sickness in me; no, it was my own dread sense of failure as well. I'd let them down, left it too late. The Blackshirts had already carried out their stupid, desperate plan to purge their veins and replenish them with new blood, and those first volunteers had paid the price along with their victims, because they lay dead too in that terrible crimson flood. I prayed to God Hubble was down there among them.

I forced myself to take another look, hoping there might be some that were still alive, a few I could help before they bled to death. And I was curious to discover if Hubble really had been destroyed by his own lunacy. I guess I was curious to know about Muriel too.

Some of the Blackshirts were still slumped in wooden chairs, their 'donors' lying beside them; others lay curled up on the soaking floor, their hands curled into claws, mouths open as if in silent screams, as if the infusion of alien blood had sent their bodies into paroxysms of agony. I wanted to scream at them for their reckless stupidity, for the useless barbarity of it all. Why hadn't they at least waited, tried the transfusions one at a time so that when the first or second failed, they'd give it up? I guess I was underestimating their desperation – what the hell did they have to lose anyway? – as well as the damage already done to their brains and their unfailing belief in their leader. But the only pity I felt was for the victims; I felt nothing at all for the parasites.

I stepped inside and stood on the small platform over-looking the charnel house, ignoring its stink as I searched among the contorted shapes; unfortunately, several were face down, or on their sides with their backs to me, and others were half-hidden in the alcoves. To be sure that Hubble and Muriel were with them I had to go down there for a closer inspection.

As I went into that nasty hell-hole I began to realize there were not enough corpses here to account for all the Black-shirts and the people outside the Savoy, and that puzzled me. And the women and children – where were they? S'far as I could tell, there were no women here, and definitely no kids, yet two nights ago there'd been a whole bunch of them. I figured there were about twenty bodies that I could see, and Hubble's army alone must've amounted to triple that number, despite their losses in the air raid on the hotel and those I'd killed personally. I reached the bottom of the stairs and stepped over outstretched limbs, avoiding the worst of the blood lake, working my way along the alcoves, peering past the battered cannons into the dark corners, looking for more bodies, hoping to find some live ones.

I must've been concentrating too damned hard, because he was almost on me before I heard the first sound.

I hadn't forgotten about the man I'd followed into this place, my mind had just been distracted, is all. It was the splashing of his boots through the blood that caused me to wheel around in his direction. He must've been waiting inside an opening at the far end of the chamber, watching me all the time, and now he was coming at me in a rush, a mediaeval pike held out before him, its nasty-looking metal point aimed at my gut. In that instant I realized it wasn't a Blackshirt uniform he was wearing, but the navy blue day-duty tunic of a Yeoman Warder. His long coat was dusty, torn in places, the red braiding frayed, missing in places, and his unkempt hair hung in loose tangles over his crazy-man eyes, spittle glistening in his long, matted beard. Close as this, I could see two things about those wild eyes: they were leaking blood, and they were filled with a malevolent hatred that was just for me. Jesus, they almost rooted me to the spot, but my reflexes kicked in.

I stepped towards him instead of backing away, turning my body to lessen the target area. There was no time to shoot him (besides, I didn't want to alert any others who might be lurking in this place) so I looped the Sten gun's sling over the pike's metal tip as it skimmed past me, just inches from my stomach. The sling caught on the red and gold silk tassel between the point and wooden staff and I yanked the weapon towards me, twisting away from the demented warden, using the pole as a lever to knock him off balance. He fell to his knees as I completed the turn and he yelped like the crazy he was as I drove my left fist into the back of his neck. He went down hard, his face smacking against the wet floor. It'd been a smart manoeuvre on my part, but it worked chiefly because of the man's own slug-gishness; he had the sickness in him, same as the Black-shirts.

I pounced on him, my knee against his spine, the pikestaff still caught up in the gun's sling. I dug the fingers of my free hand into his matted hair and jerked his head up, then smashed it back down against the flagstone. He gave a small gurgling kind of scream, then lay motionless. He wasn't out though; a low moaning came from him. I was about to repeat the process, send him on his way for good – sure, I knew it wasn't his fault, his brain was as diseased as his blood, but I'd spent too long at war with his kind and there was no sympathy left – but I thought of the victims around us, innocents who'd been murdered because they were different, had something the bad guys wanted for themselves. And I remembered there might be others still alive, but waiting to die. I lifted his head again.

'*Where are they?*' I hissed close to his ear.

He wasn't so mad that he didn't know I'd crack his blood-drenched face against the floor again if I didn't get an answer. Through bruised lips and cracked teeth he managed to say: 'They . . . they took them.'

'*Took them where?*' I deliberately pushed my anger, allowing it to overcome my own revulsion at what I was doing. Tightening my grip in his hair, I tugged his head up another couple of inches. He got the message and mumbled something so fast I couldn't catch it.

I pulled his head back even further so that I could look into those terrible eyes. I winced at the leaking blood and the burst veins in his cheeks. The fingers of his hands spread out before him were blackened and swollen, smelling of gangrene. I wanted to choke.

'*Where?*' I spat out through clenched teeth.

I guess he didn't like the wildness in my own eyes, because his diction suddenly improved. 'They . . . they needed . . . God's help.'

I stared at him.

'Sir Max . . . Sir Max said God . . .'

His words trailed off in a whining moan, the saliva that drooled from his cracked lips turning pinkish as it flowed, becoming a deeper red by the time it reached the floor. His body began to convulse beneath me, gently at first, a trembling that became a shaking, and then a violent thrashing. He began to cry out, then to scream, and I had no choice, I had to stifle the sounds, stop him arousing others who could be anywhere inside the keep.

This time I put all my strength into smashing his head against the bloodied flagstone and the sickening thud it made was a hundred times worse than the soft groan that came from him. His body went limp and his head lolled sideways; on his bloody face was an expression of contentment, as if he were glad to be off somewhere else. At least, that's what I told myself to ease my conscience. I didn't know if he was dead – his body wasn't even twitching – but I guess I hoped so. Better for him, that way.

I untangled the Sten's sling from the pikestaff as I got to my feet. And it was then that I heard the strains drifting through the open doorway above my head. It was organ music.

I remembered the chapel across the great courtyard.

25

IT WAS A WEIRD, tormented sound that wafted through the warm morning air across the wide, open space between the keep and surrounding buildings, muted and agonized organ music that had more in common with Lon Chaney than religious adoration. It came from the little church tucked away in a far corner of the yard, an overgrown, weed-ridden green with untidy trees spread before it, a bell tower rising over its rough-stoned walls and slanted roof, the bell inside its open turret visible from where I stood at the top of the White Tower's steps. I took a deep breath, dreading what I might find over there, before descending those stairs and scooting across the courtyard, the soles of my boots sticky with blood, heading for the nearest cover, which was the grand neo-Gothic building opposite, expecting to be challenged at any moment.

Nothing happened though, no sudden challenge interrupted my flight across open ground, and as soon as I reached the opposite wall, I went down on my haunches, facing out, the submachine gun weaving left and right, ready for the slightest disturbance. Apart from the faint, creaky organ music from the chapel, all was quiet and still.

I caught my breath and moved on, keeping close to the wall like always, using all the cover I could get, and before long I was crossing the passageway between the blockhouse

288

tower and the chapel itself. Standing on tiptoe beneath the first of the five tall leaded windows, I peeped in, but the glass was too thick and too filthy for me to see anything clearly. All I caught was movement inside, although I heard other sounds over the organ music, voices shouting, others pleading.

Afraid my shadow might be seen, I ducked again and made my way along the row of windows, skirting round two big, lichen-covered tombs set on plinths along the path, searching for the chapel's entrance. I found the door around the corner, between the west wall and bell tower, a cart for carrying small boxes or sacks standing close by. The door was open a few inches and the droning music was bad enough to make me want to block my ears. I thought I heard a child's wailing as I crept closer.

Back against the door, I used an elbow to widen the gap, the Sten upright, close to my chest. I lowered the barrel as the door swung slowly inwards, turning my body at the same time towards the chapel's interior.

The aisle before me, a few feet wide, led straight to a small, plain altar, a gold crucifix at its centre, a decorative leaded-glass window overlooking it. Light from all the high windows was dulled by the dirty glass, and the ceiling beams of dark wood cast their own oppressive gloom. To my left was a set of high arches, inside the first an alabaster tomb-chest, a stone knight and his lady laid out on its surface; further along the covered area was a massive wood-carved organ with tarnished pipes; beyond that, at the end wall, another door.

Dust motes floated in the subdued rays of light that played on the heads and shoulders of the congregation and there was movement everywhere, bodies shifting on the benches, distraught children waving their arms in the air, Blackshirts patrolling the centre aisle, weapons at the ready. Some of these people were moaning, others could only cower in fear, but all were looking at the diminutive figure standing before the altar.

Hubble had his back to them, and the tall Blackshirt, the one called McGruder, was helping him remove his shirt, exposing a thin, bruised arm and a hand that was now darkened almost to the wrist. Hubble's bare shoulder was hunched and covered with nasty blemishes, the blood beneath the skin visibly thickened. It was an ugly sight, which stirred up the nausea I could still taste in my mouth.

He began to turn in my direction and I stepped behind the half-opened door in case he saw me.

With some effort, Hubble straightened himself. His chin jutted as he stood with one hand on his cane in a pose that he probably imagined made him look strong, invincible, a leader of men. But his sunken cheeks and the dark bruising around his eyes, the blueness of those tight-drawn lips, the sickly pallor of his skin, almost translucent now, so that the network of tiny broken veins beneath was clearly visible, his thin hair – once immaculately groomed, now straggly and brittle, falling forward over his waxen forehead – and the stubborn stoop of his shoulders, not to mention the palsied quivering of his limbs – all this only mocked the old image, reduced him to a hideous parody of the man who'd enthralled thousands of similar bigots with his Fascist oratory before the outbreak of the second – and last – world war, a man who'd marched at the head of a neo-Nazi army, subordinate only to Sir Oswald Mosley. Yet those bloodshot eyes still burned with a zealot's fervour and I realized he was more dangerous than ever: Hubble didn't have long for this decimated world but his dementia was driving him on, giving him the strength and the will to inflict even more misery.

I remained hidden behind the angled door, figuring out my next move.

The tuneless organ music finally droned to a wheezing halt when the Blackshirt leader raised a trembling hand towards the player, an obese, bespectacled woman with shorn hair, who wore the same black garments of terror as the men of Hubble's army. She twisted her bulk to face the altar, the effort difficult for her, and even from where I stood peering round the door at the far end of the chapel, I could see the marks of death on her loose-fleshed face. A couple of guards shouted for quiet, another striking out at hostages close to him, as Hubble began to speak.

'Almighty God, forgive our blindness in not seeking Your blessing and guidance . . .'

His voice was frail, almost quavery, yet it filled the small church, quietening the crowd more successfully than any threats from the guards.

'. . . and look down with favour on our poor mortal bodies and everlasting souls. We thank You for our deliverance and ask that You bless those here among us . . .'

His shoulders shuddered and hunched even more, and he coughed into a hastily drawn handkerchief, holding it to his mouth 'til the spasm passed. It was already bloodstained and when he took it away there were fresh, deeper blotches. His voice still had that peculiar distance to it, yet it was uncannily clear, and I wondered what this man's power had been like in the old days, when he was fit and able.

'Those among us . . .' he went on, as if nothing had occurred '. . . for their selfless sacrifice to the greater cause. Let their pure blood spill into our veins and replenish our sick bodies.'

There were cries of protest from the people packed into those benches and the Blackshirts sitting among them hit out, one of the patrolling guards even poking his rifle into the head of a skinny youth on an end seat. Their objections were quickly subdued.

'This we ask of You, dear Lord . . .'

Hubble's deranged eyes were appealing heavenwards, a martyr suffering for his God. My finger twitched restlessly on the Sten's trigger.

'. . . in the knowledge that we are Your chosen few.'

And there you had it. This crazy man sincerely believed – as had his all-time hero, Adolf Hitler – that God was on

291

his side, that he and his followers were the natural inheritors of the Earth by God's command. The fact that Hubble's blood was the wrong kind for survival barely made a dent in his twisted logic; that was just part of the hardship the righteous had to endure and finally overcome, all part of the great test. Hubble had gotten it a little wrong before, but now he'd seen the true way, so was seeking help from the Divine Saviour – something he'd foolishly omitted to do before – to make the transfusions successful so that his and his Blackshirts' reign would continue. He was too far gone to realize it wasn't simply goodwill he was asking of his Maker – it was a miracle! I was too disgusted even to smile. I edged the door open further.

It seemed Hubble had completed his devotions or supplications, whatever he considered them to be, and he made a sign with his hand. A Blackshirt on the front bench rose, dragging someone up with him. McGruder, standing protectively close to his leader as usual, beckoned the Blackshirt forward and I saw whose arm he clenched.

Muriel was no longer wearing the long, silver evening dress I'd last seen her in: she'd found, or been given, a man's black shirt a couple of sizes too big for her, which she wore outside grey slacks. (I caught this when she moved into the centre of the aisle just in front of the altar.) She seemed reluctant to accompany the goon – she kept trying to pull her arm away – and I soon began to understand why.

There was a chair by the altar, which McGruder helped Hubble into (it was odd the way the big man fussed over his leader and I wondered what Hubble had done for him in the past to earn such slavish loyalty) while the other Blackshirt pushed Muriel forward. Y'know, Hubble managed to give her a twisted kind of smile as he settled himself, like she was offering herself willingly and he appreciated the gesture. I noticed her back stiffen.

Something else I noticed right then: beneath the cross on

the altar was a tangle of rubber tubing, sunlight glinting off the attached steel needles and clips.

So that was the plan, and Muriel was to be the first. After all, to Hubble's unhinged way of thinking, she had the purest blood of all. She was healthy, beautiful, with a fine brain that was in tune with his own (what a bonus) – and most of all, this kid had the *breeding*. A lord's daughter, no less, a member of the aristocracy, the ruling class. Oh yeah, her blood would do fine. And Hubble knew he didn't have much time – hell, I could see even from that distance how much he'd deteriorated since a couple of nights ago. The transfusions in the White Tower had failed, but now they had appealed to God, asking for His forgiveness and guidance, and naturally Hubble (what did I say about his kind of people?) had chosen the best for himself. Hallelujah!

McGruder ripped open the front of Muriel's shirt, tugging one side over her shoulder and pulling her arm out of its sleeve.

'No, don't!' I heard her plead. 'You can't do this to me, Max. I helped you. We believe in the same things.'

He only continued smiling up at her like some old, benevolent uncle – a mad-as-a-skunk, depraved old uncle with lechery in mind. He didn't utter a word though, didn't even nod his head; McGruder knew what to do and was already making himself busy. Unlike for most of his companions, and certainly his leader, the Blood Death seemed some ways off for the big man: his movement was a little slow, but he still appeared powerful enough as he held Muriel with one hand while he reached behind for a length of transfusion tubing with the other. Several more pieces fell to the floor as he pulled one free and there was a cry from the side of the chapel. The fat, bespectacled organist was stumbling towards the altar, a wail of anguish coming from her open, blue-lipped mouth. On the way she pounced on someone sitting on the front bench, and when she held her thick arms aloft, she was holding a child, a small girl. (You see the

293

lunacy of these people? How much blood did the fat lady expect to get out of this kid? Enough to fill an arm?) She tried to carry the girl to the altar, but somebody screamed and a woman jumped up – the little girl's mother or guardian, I figured – and tried to snatch her back. Uproar followed as other hostages leapt to their feet and began struggling with the nearest Blackshirts. Women screamed, kids bawled, and the few men among the 'donors' started punching, all of them only too aware of what was in store for them even if they hadn't themselves witnessed the deaths of those others of the same blood. McGruder let go of Muriel and rushed towards the overweight organist, who was struggling with the hysterical woman, the child between them; but by now, other Blackshirts suddenly had the same idea as the organist. There were only a certain number of 'donors' left, much fewer than the number of Blackshirts present, and none of those goons wanted to be left out. Other guards began dragging victims towards the altar.

I saw one Blackshirt, a skinny guy who looked as if he hardly had the strength to carry his submachine gun, grab a female by the hair and attempt to pull her off a bench, but she fought back, giving him a shove that sent him toppling into the opposite row of benches. She turned and ran, making for the exit.

She was halfway down the aisle before she saw me in the open doorway, the door pushed wide now, the Sten gun chest-high, pointing straight at her.

Behind her I could see Hubble, on his feet again, his wizened face screwed up in a blaze of fury, his lips moving, mouth open wide, as if he were trying to bring some order to the party. McGruder was punching the fat lady to the floor, the mother had hold of her screaming kid again, and other goons were hauling resisting victims into the aisles, clubbing them with their fists and weapons, just sane enough not to shoot any of 'em. And maybe that fact had finally dawned on those hostages, that they were no good to the

Blackshirts dead, because they were suddenly putting up one hell of a fight.

It was bedlam inside that chapel, a madhouse of shrieks and shouts and warring factions, and through it all, through that pandemonium, Hubble finally clapped eyes on me. His anger turned to blank surprise. And then his pale, shrivelled face arranged itself into a trick-or-treat mask of sheer venom. Something more though, in fact a whole lot more, was in that expression: loathing, sure, but a kind of abhorrence too, as though the devil had arrived on his doorstep. I was the oddity, you see, I was the *abnormal*. Just like the ABneg types fighting his own men. The disease had rendered us the freaks of society (whatever society he imagined was left) and I was his No 1 freak. The problem was that no matter how loathsome I was to him, I had what he needed. And that made him hate me even more.

Yeah, well, I could live with it. I tucked the Sten into my shoulder and squeezed the trigger.

I'd aimed high for fear of hitting my own kind and the window above the altar shattered, the noise of breaking glass and gunfire suspending the action for a second or two. Heads looked my way, eyes were startled, and then the screaming started all over again. The pandemonium was worse than before when I fired off another burst. People ducked for cover as bullets spat into granite, dug into wood and smashed glass; I eased up so they could hear me yell:

'Get outta here, just run, get away, go!'

Muriel was one of the first to get the idea, even though my words hadn't been intended for her. Our eyes locked briefly and I saw the uncertainty in hers – she didn't know if my next bullets might be for her. But she must've decided I was a better bet than Hubble, because next moment she was breaking free of the brawl and heading my way. McGruder made a lunge at her, but I fired off another burst (I would've taken his head off if there'd been no danger of hitting innocent people), and he took a dive, disappearing behind a wall of bodies. Sustained fire caused the nose of the Sten gun to rise and I let it, shooting high into the walls, swinging round almost leisurely towards the windows on my right. They exploded one by one, creating the fresh panic that I wanted.

The woman who'd been the first to spot me in the doorway began crawling forward along the aisle, moving fast, her head down as if afraid to look at me again. Muriel wasn't far behind, but more people were tumbling into the aisle, blocking her path. She had pulled the shirt back over her shoulder and was clutching the material together over her breasts even as she struggled to reach me.

'*Come on!*' I yelled again. '*Time to go! Move it!*'

I only meant the hostages, but some of the Blackshirts had taken to the notion: they started running for the small door at the other end of the chapel. Hubble had had enough of all this. He stood on the step before the altar and jabbed a darkened finger at me, and even over the uproar I could hear his high-pitched voice shrieking orders. McGruder's head and shoulders appeared over the crowd and he grabbed two nearby Blackshirts, pulling them close around Hubble, forming a protective shield against any gunfire I might send his leader's way. I took aim anyway, but as I did I realized Hubble wasn't pointing at me at all; his finger was waving at Muriel as she fought her way down the aisle towards me. McGruder and one of the bodyguards started after her, knocking people aside as they went.

And that set me to revising my plan. Hubble wanted the girl as much as he'd wanted me when he thought I was the only healthy blood type left in the city – let's face it, her bloodline was a few grades up from mine (if you believed in that kind of thing, that is, and Hubble, just like his demagogue, Hitler, clearly did) and that thought gave me a second option. The original plan had been to snatch Hubble; now I realized Muriel might be an even better hostage, because she'd come willingly.

That first woman crawled past my legs and then was gone, out the door, making – I hoped – for pastures new. An older woman, grey-haired, wrinkled face, was climbing over benches towards me, a boy of about sixteen helping her. Then came the two boy twins I'd noticed outside the Savoy, hustled by a middle-aged woman. A young girl, no more'n fifteen, leapt from the benches and scooted in my direction, bumping my elbow as she went by. They'd all caught the drift, they'd seen their chance to escape. But I couldn't leave with them, not 'til Muriel was by my side. And not 'til Hubble had time to organize his men for the chase.

Bullets thudded into the wall beside the door, causing me to crouch, then return fire. More shouts, more screams – more gunfire. But the crowd before me was thinning, every-body scattering for cover. A man – a fleeing hostage – fell into me, knocking me back against the open door, and when he slumped to the floor, clawing at my clothes as he went, I saw the blood spurting from the holes in his back. A great crush of people surged towards me and I knew if I didn't get out the way I'd be trampled underfoot, gun or no gun. Muriel was close to the front, but somebody tripped in front of her and she and others behind her went down in a tangle of arms and legs.

Another burst of gunfire just to keep things hot and I stepped forward, reaching into the jumble for her, my fingers managing to close around her wrist. I pulled hard and she came up fast, crashing into my chest, her hands resting on my shoulder. I thought I heard her say my name, but there was too much clamour, too many screams and moans, to be sure. I took her with me, backing towards the doorway, watching the advancing Blackshirts among the crowd as we went.

One particular goon was too close for comfort and I knew I had to stop him. But nothing happened when I pulled the Sten's trigger. Without even thinking about it, I tossed the submachine gun into my left hand and reached for the P-35 with the other. I shot almost from the hip – no time for anything else – and the goon screamed as he clutched his belly and staggered. He fell to his knees, then went down as bodies piled on top of him. Others behind the heap hesitated, watching me warily.

I stepped away from the exit and waved at it with the pistol. *'Come on, get going!'* I shouted. *'I'm with you!'* The bolder ones among them believed me and ran outside.

By now Hubble's army had worked themselves into a frenzy and those with guns started blazing away at the ceiling, frustrated because they still didn't have a clear line on me. Blue smoke curled in the air and the uproar was deafening; I figured it was time to make my exit. At any moment those Blackshirts would be up on the benches to get a better shot at me, so I re-holstered the pistol and bundled Muriel out the door, breaking into a run as soon as we hit open air. I gripped her wrist to keep her with me and carried the Sten by its body. Those who'd already fled the church were scattering across the courtyard and I silently wished them luck, hoping they wouldn't quit running 'til they were on the other side of London. Muriel and me, we cut across the overgrown lawn, our steps high through the long grass, heading diagonally towards the broad stone steps and path that led to the passageway beneath the Bloody Tower. The lane beyond it led to a wooden bridge, which crossed the moat to the wharf road, and if the Blackshirts didn't cut us down before we reached it we had a chance. We were running on a prayer, but that was nothing new for me.

We passed the empty Vickers machine gun, so far, so good, and kept going; if we could get to the path below the steps we'd be out of sight for a stretch, maybe even long enough to get under cover of the passageway before they opened fire on us. But wouldn't you know it, it was at that point that Muriel decided to take a tumble. I tried to hold her, but her shoe just slipped from under her and she went sprawling, squawking as she rolled over.

Instead of minding her I whirled around, pulled out the used-up magazine and inserted a fresh one from the bag I carried, my hand slipping into the Sten's pistol grip as I faced them. What was left of the black army was pouring round the corner of the chapel, still a few hostages among them, the Blackshirts too interested in us to bother with them. No doubt Hubble's orders were to get Muriel and me, the others could be rounded up later, and that was fine, that's exactly what I wanted. I gave them a short burst of fire, just enough to slow 'em down but not to make them lose interest. A peculiar sight then, one that would've had me screaming with laughter at any other time: that two-wheeled cart I'd noticed outside the chapel door came into view, McGruder pushing it, Hubble crouched inside like a big kid being taken for a ride. I shook my head, assuring myself this was really happening, it wasn't just another stupid nightmare after an evening hitting the booze. Nope, I wasn't dreaming, the bullets chipping concrete in front of me told me so.

I sent a spray of bullets of my own back and had the satisfaction of seeing the cart swerving and Blackshirts hitting the deck. I heard a groan from Muriel and threw a quick glance her way. She was half-sitting, nursing a bleeding elbow that peeked through a hole in her shirt.

'Are you hit?' I yelled.

She gave a quick shake of her head and regarded me with some fear. She was scared all right, and not just of the Blackshirts: I guess she thought I might turn my weapon on her.

'Okay, get up. You know what your new pals want from you, so start running again. I'll cover you.'

'We'll never get away.' She spoke breathlessly, her small exposed breasts heaving, her frightened gaze sweeping past me towards the mob. 'There are too many of them, we can't outrun them all.'

Yeah, I thought. Too many of them. Too many to kill with

only bullets. And I wanted every damn one of 'em accounted for. I scuttled over to her and leaned close. 'Just get on your feet and haul out.' I yanked her up with one hand and pushed her towards the steps. She was unsteady at first, fastening a couple of shirt buttons as she went, then she broke into a run that started the Blackshirts surging forward again.

I followed close behind, but backstepping, gun trained on our pursuers just to keep 'em at bay. Timing was everything, y'see; I had to get this exactly right. Luckily they were smart enough to slow down, 'though they kept coming, watching my every move, playing me out. I took a swift head count and figured there were around forty or so of them left and that surprised me. Even if there were some still inside the chapel, the Slow Death had claimed a whole mob of 'em since the Blackshirts and I had first become acquainted. Well, it didn't cause me any grief – the less I had to deal with today, the more chance I had of coming through in one piece.

Hearing Muriel's shoes clattering down the steps, I did a turnabout and made a dash for them myself. A roar went up from the crowd as I disappeared from view and I knew we had only a few seconds to get into the passageway. Quickly catching up with Muriel, I took her arm again to help hurry her down a second set of steps and she cried out in protest, afraid we were both gonna break our necks. Ravens on the green in front of the White Tower flew into the air in alarm, their shrieks – that harsh, croaky kind of *kaa* – sounded like cursing to me, as if they were warning us off, intruders unwelcome, and I was of a mind to blow one or two of 'em out of the air just for the hell of it. But I kept going, landing on the path with Muriel, dragging her onwards, the short, dark tunnel opening up ahead.

More shouts, more gunfire. Bullets spattered the ancient wall of the Bloody Tower, warning shots telling us we'd better stop running or else ... We plunged into the cool shade of the archway as more bullets ricocheted off the cobbled path, their sound growing louder as they beat a line towards us. I pushed Muriel against the wall and the bullets pounded on past us, their impact thunderous in the confined space. I held her there, waiting for the row to stop, the echoes to fade, my face pressed into her hair and our bodies tight together as chips of stone spat up at us. I caught the faint whiff of faded perfume, felt her softness against me and, stupid though it was under the circumstances, remembered her nakedness beneath me, her arms curled around my waist, pulling me into her. I remembered how afraid, how vulnerable, she'd been that night at the hotel. And then I remembered how she'd betrayed her friends.

I pushed myself away from her then, and with an almost contemptuous side-swipe of my arm sent her reeling towards the other end of the short tunnel. As the Blackshirts spilled down the steps I went back to the entrance, showing myself to them. They hesitated yet again, some cowering on the steps, others trying to run back up them, as I raised the submachine gun. I took careful aim and pretended to squeeze the trigger.

When nothing happened they raised their heads or stopped where they were and looked at me. Surprise turned to glee as I tossed the weapon away and disappeared back into the shadows. One of 'em even laughed aloud, thinking the Sten had jammed.

They came after us then like hounds after a wounded fox, baying for our blood – yeah, literally.

Out in the open on the other side of the archway, the sun stinging my eyes for a moment, I held Muriel by the wrist again and we fled, sweet Jesus, how we fled, the uneven roadway doing its best to trip us, the howling mob behind us giving us all the encouragement we needed. The bridge over the dry moat wasn't far, but my chest was beginning to burn and my breath was scorching my throat. As wild gunshots whined through the air I could feel Muriel starting to slow down, dragging on me, her pace becoming awkward.

'You gotta keep going!' I yelled at her.

'We can't make it!' she croaked back.

'We can. They're slow, don't you see? We just gotta keep ahead of 'em!'

We reached the archway exit and pounded across the wooden bridge, and now that we were outside the old fortress, Muriel's energy seemed renewed: she picked up speed and her movement became more controlled. Before us was the River Thames, ancient cannon set in a row all along its edge, pointing south across the water as if fearing an invasion from London's other half. A wartime concrete pillbox stood among them, solidly square but useless against the enemy's last invisible weapon. To our left, Tower Bridge rose high and proud, its bascules frozen open for all time, the river beneath flowing clear and pure in the sunlight.

Me in the lead, we headed towards it.

26

SHE DIDN'T UNDERSTAND when I pulled her round to the stairway.

'The docks,' she gasped as she tried to break away. She drew in quick, sharp breaths. 'We can lose them easily in the docks.'

She had a point. The road under the northern span of the bridge led straight into dockland – or what was left of it after the fire-bombs had done their worst – where there were plenty of side streets, alleyways and ruined buildings to get lost in. Sure, it would've been easy to shake off the Blackshirts in that labyrinth, 'cept that wasn't any part of my plan.

'We're going onto the bridge,' I told her, trying to catch my own breath. Sweat trickled down my back and my throat felt burned dry.

'You're insane. The bridge is raised – we can't get across!'

'We can use one of the walkways at the top.'

She looked at me as if I really was crazy, but there was no time for argument, so without another word I pushed her into the covered stairway. The lead Blackshirts were about forty yards away, and for now they'd given up shooting, no doubt confident they'd soon catch us. Coming up the rear was Hubble, pushed by McGruder in that ridiculous perambulator, waving his arms and bitching orders as he bumped over the cobblestones. With one last look, Muriel scuttled up the steps.

At the top of them, a short tunnel led back under the bridge's roadway, and another flight of stairs went up to the bridge approach itself. Our footsteps echoed around the damp walls together with the sound of our own laboured breathing and even before we'd reached the second flight of stairs I heard pounding feet and shouts coming after us. By now we were running on adrenaline – my old ally – and I could only pray it'd sustain us for a little while longer.

Up the stairs we scrambled, both of us using the iron rail set in the brick wall to pull ourselves forward, my other arm clamping the canvas bag against my side to stop it bouncing around. We burst into bright sunlight again and the bridge's north tower loomed over us, battleship-grey suspension girder-chains on either side of the roadway rising away from us in great, swooping slopes towards the upper reaches. With its stone cladding, arched windows, mouldings and niches, turrets at each corner, the tower resembled some sinister Gothic castle straight from a creepy Grimm's fairy tale. Fairy tale? Hell, with its shallow balcony near the top and spires and finials around the roof, it felt as if we were making straight for Bela Lugosi's town house. Bloodsuckers on our tails, a virtual mountain to climb ahead of us, I closed my mind and kept going.

Through the great archway at the base of the tower where traffic once flowed onto the bridge itself we could see a huge concrete wall plugging the gap. Rusted buses, trucks, and automobiles still queued before it as though waiting for the bascule (that concrete wall was the raised bridge section itself) to lower so they could continue their journey into the city's southern sprawl. On the other side of the bascule was a sheer drop to the river below and directly opposite was the underside of its sister bascule, this one also raised and standing erect against the south tower.

Beside the archway was a narrow flight of stone steps

leading up to an inset doorway, and this was the entrance into the tower, which I wanted to be inside before the mob got too close. Once there, it meant a long haul to the fourth level where the high walkway that spanned the river, joining both towers, would take us across. Although it would be a tough climb for us, I knew it would be even tougher for those unhealthy freaks on our tails.

Along the approach we raced, traffic that would never move again on our left, a thick, ornamental iron rail to our right, howling Blackshirts hard on our heels, and blue skies and dead city all around. Somehow it felt as though I were taking it all in for the last time: the battered, broken rooftops across the city, those wrinkled balloons sagging in the sky, buildings that used to be thriving warehouses now empty shells along the river's edge, bent and crumpled cranes, boats and barges still moored to quaysides, stirring in the drift. Three years I'd remained in this open mausoleum when survivors with more sense had fled, three years of tidying the streets and getting nowhere. D'you still remember the point of it all? the familiar sneaky little voice inside my head jeered. And if you did, was it still worth the effort? Forever hunted by sick people turned to vampirism, hiding away like an animal, killing just to stay alive, always vigilant, always afraid, carrying on the war when it should have finished with the Blood Death genocide. Did it make any sense at all? No, 'course it didn't, none whatsoever. Sally was gone, she knew nothing of this even though your obsession was because of her. Her and ... well, you know. You're crazy, Hoke, crazy like the human leeches chasing you now. Have been since you lost the world. And you know it. But at least it's coming to an end, this madness. Yeah, another end, and this time you'll probably be included. You should've listened to Cissie, Hoke. *She* told you you were crazy too ...

Bullets whistled over our heads again, interrupting that sly, taunting voice inside my head, a voice that was my own good sense, snapping me back to the here and now. Fact was, I had no choice anyways: my idea had progressed too far to call it off. Those Blackshirts were still trying to frighten us into stopping, but their shots only encouraged us to make a final spurt onto the pier that ran around the base of the tower. The bridge's control cabin, protected by sheaths of steel plating and sandbags, nestled beneath the tower itself, and I noticed its green signal was still raised to allow non-existent ships through. Out of sight underneath the pier were the cogwheels and accumulator tanks that helped operate the bascule on this side of the river.

'Up the stairs!' I ordered Muriel as I wheeled around to check on the hounds. Hell, the first goon, who was just about one of the healthiest-looking specimens in a black uniform I'd seen for a couple of years now – healthier even than McGruder, I'd say – was only ten yards away. I could've dropped him easily with the Browning, but I didn't want to discourage the crowd from following us into the tower, so instead I turned my back on him and skipped up the steps after Muriel. She'd already pushed open the door at the top and we went through almost together.

'Keep going,' I said to her, pointing to the rising stairs inside, and without even glancing at me she did as she was told. Her shoes clacked on the iron treads and her breaths were now emerging in short, sharp cries. I waited in the shadows behind the door, listening to the approaching footsteps outside. They grew louder, broke as the Blackshirt leapt the first few steps, then resumed, coming closer.

Waiting 'til the last moment, I slammed the door in the goon's face and heard a muffled shout, then a series of yelps as he bounced back down those steps again. I'd busted the door's lock in the early hours of that morning, so I couldn't shut the Blackshirts out and give myself a chance to get a good head start on them up the stairs before they broke in. I raced after Muriel, taking the steps three at a time and soon catching her up.

Like I said, a long haul to the top, two hundred and six

steps in all (I'd counted them some hours ago), the hydraulic lifts naturally out of action, bullying Muriel all the way. Pounding footsteps followed us up, the occasional, useless shot ringing out (we were well protected by the solid staircase as long as we kept two flights ahead of the pack), our hearts thudding faster, our legs growing heavier, and our lungs heaving painfully with each step. Oh Jesus, we were never gonna make it, we didn't have the strength. But still we went on, every turn a sweetener to reach the next. Although there were plenty of windows, the glass was filthy, so seeing our way was another problem. Quite a few times one of us tripped, but when it was Muriel I just lifted her again and pushed her onwards, and when it was me I cussed and used the thick wooden handrail to pull myself up. The higher we went, the more exhausted we became; and it was getting harder for both of us to draw breath. To make matters worse, the commotion below seemed to be growing louder, the pack drawing closer and closer. Impossible, I kept telling myself, those people were in worse condition than us, we were still way ahead of them. If only I could've believed myself.

Some of the Blackshirts, I began to realize by sound alone, had taken the other staircase – there were two inside the tower – and they seemed to be making better progress than those behind us. We caught a glimpse of this bunch as they poured onto one of the spacious landings below, and a roar went up when they spotted us too. Muriel almost collapsed in front of me.

'They . . . They've got us, Hoke,' she stammered, her chest and shoulders heaving. 'We can't make it.'

So much for the Bulldog Breed. 'We're nearly there. One more flight, that's all. We'll be okay up there, I promise you.'

I stepped alongside her and grabbed her by the wrist. Her whole body was shaking and she seemed to spasm with every breath she drew, but I half-carried her with me, using whatever strength I had left to keep her moving. At first, she weighed on me, but when she saw the staircase opening out onto the top landing, some of her strength – and her spirit – returned and she began to climb by herself. The gloom brightened too and, I guess, in some foolish way that gave her more hope. She stumbled on ahead of me.

We virtually dragged ourselves up those last few steps, using our hands on the higher treads, our knees on the lower ones. And then we arrived at a wide area with windows overlooking the river and city on three sides, the sun piercing the grime and lightening the room with broad dust-swirling shafts. There was no time to rest and though Muriel's legs were giving way and dry retching noises came from her throat as she sucked in air, I forced her on, taking her to the half-glass double doors across the room from us. There were other doors here, cupboards or doors to private offices, as well as tables and chairs, cleaning equipment and all kinds of clutter, but the important thing for us was those wide double doors – we had to get through them before the mob reached this level.

And we managed to, staggering onto the long walkway that stretched across the River Thames, running parallel with its sister footbridge a short distance away to join the north tower with the south. We were a hundred and forty feet above the water here and a coolish breeze drifted through the open iron latticework of its side walls, ruffling our hair, brushing our skin, helping to revive us. We drew in deep gasps of clean air, filling our laboured lungs with its sweetness, our eyes closing at the sheer pleasure. Yet still I wouldn't let Muriel linger.

'Down to the other end,' I told her wearily, heading that way myself. The noise of the approaching Blackshirts was muffled by the double doors that had swung closed behind us, but it was growing louder by the moment.

'Yes,' she said meekly, breaking into a stumbling run. Her face was racked with exhaustion, but there might have been a smile there, a faint glimmer of relief showing through.

There was a chance now, she was thinking, a chance if we can just get through those other doors at the end of the long span. Most of those people following were in poor condition and they'd be in even worse shape than us after the climb. Once on the other side of those doors it would be easy to descend, we'd easily get away from them, and then out into the south side of the city, losing ourselves in the streets there. Oh yeah, I could see her thinking all that and, although she was dog-weary, she was already beginning to pick up speed as she avoided debris and piled boxes along the pedestrian bridge, hurrying past equipment covered by tarpaulin that protected it from the elements, stuff that might have been stored there since the walkways had been closed to the general public at the outbreak of the war. Shadows were already falling on the glass section of the double doors as I followed her, the room beyond becoming crowded.

The walkway was wide enough to allow at least five pedestrians to walk comfortably side by side along its length and enjoy the spectacular views of London through the intersecting iron girders; those girders sloped inwards so that the ceiling was narrower than the floor below, and rising above the opposite footbridge I could see the slate roof and spires of the south tower. Across the gap, inside the sister walkway, an anti-aircraft battery had been installed and I remembered thinking more than once about coming up here one night and waiting for the stubborn German bomber pilot to fly his Dornier along the river – like the *Luftwaffe* before him he always used the Thames as a guide into London and the docks – then blasting him out of the sky as he went by. Nice idea, 'cept I knew as much about heavy artillery as I did about knitting cardigans, so I abandoned the idea. But the thought, inspired by my first privileged tourist visit here, had always kept Tower Bridge in my mind, and last night, knowing Hubble and his black army were garrisoned in the nearby castle, a different notion had come to me.

I passed a corpse wearing the dusty blue uniform of a

custodian or maintenance man precariously perched on a straight-backed wooden chair halfway along the footbridge and I had to skirt around the covered boxes it seemed to be watching over. The jacket was loose over slumped skeletal shoulders and the dead man's shrivelled eyes were cast down at the concrete floor; strands of white hair on the naked scalp were too brittle to be stirred by the breeze. Avoiding more boxes, I went after Muriel, who was almost at the end of the walkway by now.

We both heard the double doors behind us burst open and the yattering rabble surge through, but neither of us bothered to look. I began to slow down though, popping the flap button of my holster as I did so.

Muriel made it to the doors, almost crashing into them in her eagerness to get through. She was sobbing as she grabbed the vertical handles on each side and pulled. I heard her cry out in dismay when nothing happened. She tried again, yanking the double doors with all her might, rattling them in their frame. Still they held tight.

She looked over her shoulder at me as I drew near. *'They're locked, Hoke!'* she almost screamed. *'Oh my God, they're locked!'*

I came to a halt and turned to face the advancing mob, drawing the pistol from its holster in a smooth, easy movement.

'Yeah,' I said to her. 'I know.'

27

SHE STARED AT ME as though I'd finally flipped and I guess my grim smile confirmed her suspicions.

'We're trapped,' she said incredulously between hard-fought breaths.

'So are they,' I remarked, nodding towards the small army of Blackshirts, which was now beginning to slow down to a stroll as they realized our predicament.

S'far as I could tell, most of them were on the walkway now – a few were probably still climbing, but they'd be here soon – and their unhealthy faces were filled with weary triumph. Some were unsteady on their feet, others were being helped along by their buddies; one or two were holding on to the iron girders for support and sucking in great lungfuls of the high fresh air. They filled the footbridge, a shabby band of sick bigots and hopeful (and hopeless) parasites, stealing forward, coming to a halt when they saw the gun in my hand. Weapons were raised towards me.

I waved the Browning in the direction of Muriel and said, 'She'll be no good to you dead. And neither will I.'

Even the dullest of them got the message. They stopped shuffling forward.

'Don't shoot.'

I recognized the feeble, high-pitched voice easily enough,

311

but wondered if Hubble was talking to me or his rabble army.

'We have them now, they can't escape.'

The crowd moved aside as he was helped through from the back, McGruder and another Blackshirt supporting him by the elbows. That pleased me a whole lot. Hubble had made it, and that had been my main concern.

Muriel had come away from the locked doors to stand closer to me and Hubble frowned at her.

'Keep away from him, Miss Drake,' he warned, fixing her with those fanatical eyes of his, the dark tints around them making him look like the villain in one of those old silent movies. He tried to straighten his body, an effort that was only partially successful, as if to assert his former power. 'This man is a savage, but he won't harm you. That's right, isn't it, Mr Hoke? You wouldn't shoot such a fine young lady.'

'I guess not,' I replied, and pointed the gun at his forehead.

His unwholesome smile withered and he lost his grand pose: his body sagged to its old lines. He glared at me.

'You can't kill us all, fool,' he hissed through his grimace. 'One shot and my men will tear you to pieces.' His eyes sought Muriel again. 'Step away from him. Join us again, your friends, your true kind. I was desperate before, otherwise I would never . . .' he left it unsaid, still smart enough not to spell it out for Muriel. 'We have this one now, we . . . I . . . can use his blood . . .'

Unbelievably, Muriel took a step towards this degenerate. But she looked around at me before going any further, confused and uncertain.

'Go ahead,' I said, weary of the game. 'Join them if that's what you want to do. But he'll bleed you, Muriel, he'll steal your blood and leave you dry.'

'But what else can I do, Hoke? How else can I survive?' She looked beaten, her strength gone, her breathing still unsteady. 'They'll kill us right here if we don't go with them.'

'My dear Muriel, of course we wouldn't do that.' Hubble had dropped the 'Miss Drake' in favour of a more paternal address, and there was something obscene in the wheedling tone he mistook for charm. 'We're the same, you and I, and your father was a valued friend. Whatever your decision, I promise you'll not be harmed in any way.'

And if you believe that, Muriel, I thought to myself, you deserve all the hell you'll get from this ghoul. But the banter was okay, all this talk was giving the stragglers time to reach the walkway. Raising my head, I looked past those in front and saw two Blackshirts stumbling through the doors at the far end. They had to be the last of the pack judging by the numbers here. Okay. Time for the finale.

I lifted the canvas bag from my neck and flipped it open. Four steps took me to the girders on the inner side of the footbridge and, using a diagonal strut for support, I pulled myself up onto the handrail that ran along its length. Over their heads I could see a shadowy figure beyond the glass half of the distant doors. Good. Cissie had left her hiding place and was sliding an iron bar through the handles on the other side of the double doors, locking them good and tight. She wouldn't have done it unless the stairs were empty, so I silently wished her God speed on her journey down.

The Blackshirts were watching me uneasily, unsure of what I was up to and waiting for their chance to rush me; I kept the pistol levelled at Hubble, hoping that would hold them back.

'You got a choice, Muriel,' I said, much calmer than I felt and keeping an eye on the crowd rather than looking at her. 'Come with me, or stay with this vermin and die.'

That confused her even more, but there was no time for explanations. McGruder let go of Hubble to take a couple of steps towards me; the gun redirected at his head gave him second thoughts.

'It'd give me great pleasure,' I let him know, and his agitation settled. He was still too close for comfort though, and

I decided it was now or never. But it was my turn to be surprised when Hubble began to make odd gagging noises, as though something was stuck in his throat.

He clutched at his neck, his black fingers shivering, pulling open his shirt, his body starting to convulse. His eyes looked as though they were about to pop from their sockets, and they were bleeding from the corners; blood was pouring from his ears also, and then from his open mouth. He stooped even more as McGruder reached for him, and then began to squeal, an awful drawn-out sound that was more animal than human. His hands grabbed at his chest, then his stomach, then a shoulder, his body contorting as he tried to touch the pain. His black pants were drenched as liquid poured from his lower orifices, and I knew it was blood that was soaking them, that blocked arteries inside him were bursting, discharging their dammed-up load; soon other, smaller veins were breaking, discharging their flow, and we could see the darkness spreading beneath his sallow skin. His muscles cramped, major organs began to falter, then fail. The moment he had dreaded and had known was approaching fast was finally here. It was time for Hubble to die.

His squealing became a high, keening scream that ended when a fierce gusher of blood exploded from his mouth to splatter the floor and those close to him. His dying was violent and it was horrific, and we watched as if mesmerized. That is, we watched until I decided that no person, no matter how twisted, how evil, deserved such an agonizing death. I shot him between those leaking eyes and he dropped without another murmur.

Everything happened fast then, and I moved like a jack rabbit to keep ahead of it all. A howl went up from the crowd and McGruder went down on his knees beside Hubble's blood-oozing body. Others hurled themselves at me and by the gleam in their eyes I could tell they wanted to drag me down and tear me to pieces with their bare hands. I lashed out with my foot, kicking one in the jaw – that same, healthy-looking guy whose face I'd slammed the door against down-stairs – sending him reeling back into the mob and giving me time to pull something from the canvas bag hanging loose from my shoulder. Holding it in my left hand, I took careful aim along the walkway with my right, my elbow looped around the iron strut, the extra height on the rail giving me the angle I needed. I pumped three rapid shots into the blue-uniformed corpse on the chair surrounded by covered boxes.

Those shots did two things at once: the noise stunned the Blackshirts enough to paralyse them momentarily, and the corpse tumbled over sideways onto the floor, releasing the lever of the hand grenade it had been sitting on – I'd carefully pulled the pin earlier that morning, y'see. I had a few seconds to get off the walkway before the grenade exploded and set off the dynamite inside those covered boxes.

One more thing to do before I left the scene: I dropped the pistol, shrugged off the bag on my shoulder, drew the pin of the grenade in my left hand and tossed it into the crowd, close to the disguised explosives on the other side of the walkway. Then I was gone.

Dizziness hit me as soon as I'd squeezed through those struts and was on the outside of the footbridge. The river and south pier below seemed to leap up at me, the sudden vast *emptiness* around me nearly making me lose balance. But I fought against it and quickly slipped down through the gap between the walkway floor and outer ornamental rail, my foot finding the top edge of the raised bridge just below. Those few seconds I'd needed to escape had passed and I wondered if the grenades were going to blow – there was no way of knowing what those years in storage had done to their mechanisms – and I had time to look up and see Muriel's white, frightened face peering down at me through the girders, then someone scrambling past her before I ducked under the footbridge.

The explosions came and the world around me erupted, the first boom mingling with the second. I clung to the great bascule as it shuddered beneath me, and the air thundered with the blasts, the roof above my head juddering wildly, threatening to collapse on top of me, now another blast joining the first two, the sound alone almost sending me reeling into the waters so far below. Flames shot out from the footbridge, only the thick concrete a few feet above my head protecting me, and huge balls of fire rolled into the sky. I screamed against the noise and my own horror, aware that Muriel's body had been carried ahead of those flames, narrowly missing the opposite walkway to fall away through the air, only one arm outstretched, the other one missing, her clothes torn from her but her skin burning. It was a fleeting glimpse, but one that was fused into my brain, a sight I knew even then would never fade – *if* I lived through this. I shut my eyes, but the image was even stronger.

I began to slip, the trembling of iron and concrete beneath me increasing, so that I had to open my eyes again to find ridges, projections, anything I could cling to. Debris of all sorts – bits of wood, fragments of iron, pieces of bodies, whole bodies – was flying outwards, tumbling almost leisurely to the river below, and smoke, fire, and dust billowed into the air. The top of the bascule was wide enough for me to lay on, and metal ridges and holes containing bolts that locked both sides together when the bridge was lowered helped me cling there while the entire structure shook and groaned. I was afraid the whole bloody thing would come down because when I'd hidden the dynamite along the walkway in the twilight hours of dawn, Cissie helping me haul it all up those tower stairs, I'd no idea how powerful it was or how unstable. Like the grenades, it'd been in storage a long time, so it was unpredictable. Well, now I was finding out, and I was scared as hell.

Massive black smoke-clouds darkened the sky and the bascule continued to vibrate like a vast tuning fork. I began to pull myself towards the other side of the span, only too aware of the long drop on either side and soon I was at the rail that ran by the roadside, the thick, ornamental balustrade that would serve as a ladder to the' pier below. And as I lowered myself over the edge, biting into my lip, terrified I was gonna lose my grip and fall, I looked up to see McGruder, his face black and scorched, hair burned off his blistered scalp, crawling towards me along the top of the bascule. I just had time to remember the figure I'd seen climbing past Muriel through the girders, when the world lurched away from me once more.

Both of us slipped, McGruder managing to fling an arm over the wall that was the vertical roadway, me linking an arm through the decorative end of the rail as I slid down. We held on to the bridge as it began its rumbling downward journey. But it abruptly juddered to a halt and I was almost thrown off again. My legs swung free and I clawed desperately with my other hand as the arm through the hole was nearly wrenched from its socket. I grabbed another part of the patterned rail and my feet found a hold further down. Still deafened by the noise of the explosions, the world a strangely silent place around me, I hung on for my life, happy to stay where I was 'til my nerve came back.

But there was a further movement. A trembling ran through the ironwork, and I realized the bridge hadn't stopped at all, that it was slowly, ponderously, continuing its descent. The machinery controlling its operation had been disturbed by the blasts, cogwheels and pressure points released so that the bascule's own weight was bringing it down. A quick glance across the river to the opposite bascule told me only this side seemed to be affected – the other bridge didn't appear to be moving at all. I wasn't sure how it was possible – the big engine room that controlled Tower Bridge was on the Thames's south side, far away from the explosions – but guessed it was the levers or braking system inside the control cabin on the south pier that had been

317

disturbed, along with the bascule itself, the balance shifted, with nothing to hold it in check. The cogwheels could only control the fall.

I pulled myself tight against the rail, prepared to ride it all the way, hoping the bridge wouldn't level out with too much of a jolt. I might have even enjoyed the trip, knowing my game plan had panned out, I'd fought the battle and won, if a black-stained, raw-scalped, red-eyed head hadn't appeared above me. McGruder hadn't been thrown off when the bascule had shifted – hell no, he'd hung on and then crawled along the apex to get to me. And now he was a spit away, gaping down at me with hate in his eyes and murder in the sick thing he called his heart.

His clenched fist struck my forehead, almost dislodging me. He tried again, reaching over as far as he could, but this time I dodged. With his next lunge, he'd grabbed my hair and was hauling me up. Tears blurring my vision, I gripped his wrist and forced his hand away, some of my hair going with it. My feet slid from their holes in the rail and I was hanging by one hand, my legs kicking empty space while he took full advantage, clambering down the other side of the rail, using its openings and decorative swirls as a crude ladder as I had. Then he was leaning round, trying to break my grip on the rail, pushing at my shoulder, tugging at my other arm, all the while the bridge continuing its sluggish, lumbering descent. My ears suddenly cleared and I could hear the straining of metal against metal, the groaning of rusted machinery forced into motion after years of suspension. And I could hear McGruder's frustrated grunts too as he tried to tear me loose.

I swung out over the river, the bascule at least a third of the way down by now, and dizziness nearly overcame me again as the river spun beneath my feet. From that height, I knew hitting the water would be like striking concrete.

A searing pain shot up my arm, the one poking through the rail's fancy ironwork, and I yelled hard and loud, my neck stretched as I tried to see the cause. On the other side of the rail McGruder had his teeth sunk into my bare flesh.

I swung my leg, managing to get a toehold on a metal lip above a line of rivets, then, with the added support, I began to hoist myself back up. Ignoring the pain, I made sure I was secure before pulling the arm that was under attack from McGruder's teeth out of the hole. Blood – that precious ABneg stuff those leeches cared so much about – streamed from the deep wound and somehow the sight of it renewed that old rage. I guess I'd spent so long protecting my own life's liquid that the thought of this bloodsucker gorging himself on it – yeah, I know, he was only trying to make me lose my grip, but I wasn't exactly rational by then – while I was busy doing other things sent me a little crazy myself. Scarcely realizing my own actions, I was suddenly hauling myself over the rail, that anger stirring up whatever last reserves of strength I had (yeah, more *last* reserves). I jumped down onto the steep road on the other side and pounded McGruder's upturned face with my fist.

Keeping an arm linked around the top of the thick rail, my feet braced against the slope, I slugged him again and again, showing no mercy, giving him no chance to strike back. His body slid under me, only one of his hands maintaining a hold on the ironwork, his back against the stone slabs of the tilted kerbside and for a moment – just one fleeting moment – I thought I had him licked. But he came up with all the power I'd known he had, sickness or no sickness, almost defying gravity for a split second by lifting his back from the stone and shoving me away from him with both hands. I swivelled round, my spine striking the rail with a jarring thud, almost losing my grip, and as he began to slip down the incline, he wrapped his arms around my lower legs, checking his descent, his weight weakening my own grip. And he was chuckling, he was holding on and twisting and tugging to make me let go of the rail, and goddamn chuckling while he did it. I brought my free fist down on his head and neck, but it seemed to have no effect on him, none at all. He only laughed all the more, grinning up at me so that I could witness the full extent of his madness. And then he did something even more peculiar: he twisted his neck and deliberately looked down the slope, the movement so exaggerated I knew he wanted me to follow his gaze.

I did. And I understood his intention.

At the bottom of the ever-decreasing hill, where the bascule joined the tower's approach span, was a long dark trench stretching across the road. Inside there, inside the pier itself, were the cogwheels – the quadrants, I think they were called – that helped raise and lower the bridge on this side of the river. I had no idea what other machinery was inside the black hole, but knew McGruder wanted to take us both sliding down into it. What the hell, he didn't mind a quick death, so much better than a slow one. I hit him harder, turning my own body to shake him off, but it was no good, it was as if he didn't feel the blows. Without warning, one of his hands shot up and grasped my wrist, the one holding on to the rail, and he started to tug at it, trying to pull it away. My fingers began to open, the strain on them too great; soon only the tips were around the ironwork.

My other hand found his throat and I squeezed, my thumb pressing into his windpipe. His grin only broadened as my boots began to slip on the concrete. My hold on the rail was almost broken, my fingers almost straightened.

And then I remembered the knife.

Letting go of his throat, I reached round to my back and drew the dark blade from its sheath. It slid out smooth and easy, and I plunged it down hard between McGruder's shoulder blades, just beside his spine.

His eyes bugged in shock, their tiny veins almost embossed on the whites. Whether it was because of the sudden pain, or it was intentional, his arm clamped even more tightly around my legs, causing me to jerk upright, my hand releasing the knife. But he lost his grip on my other wrist and his grin vanished, his eyes took on a distant look. The pressure on my legs slowly lessened, and then he was slipping away from me, his fingers clawing their way down my leg.

But when his hand had almost reached my feet, the fingers suddenly wrapped themselves around my ankle, jerking it from under me, so that I fell flat on my back. Sheer reaction made me grab a lower part of the rail again as I started to slide, but it took all the strength I had left – and there wasn't much – to hold myself there as my body stretched, dragged down by McGruder's weight.

My arm trembling with the strain, my back flat against the stone, my spine feeling the vibrations rumbling through the groaning bridge, I raised my head to look down at McGruder. He was on his stomach, the knife angled into his back, and both of his hands were now clenched round my ankle as he tried to drag himself back up the incline. There was no expression on that blackened face now, even though his eyes still stared into mine.

He pulled himself upwards, using my leg as a rope, his shoulders quivering with the effort. And as his head drew level with my knee, that sick, lunatic's grin returned. Oh the eyes were still distant, kind of glazed over as if his mind was off in some faraway place, but those blistered and cracked lips were spread wide, the blood-smeared teeth bared in a grin that was just for me. I raised my other foot and smashed the heel of my boot into his nose.

Blood – bad blood, diseased, coagulated blood – burst from his nostrils like lanced poison, and his hold on me relaxed. Then he was falling away from me, slithering towards that long black narrowing gap at the bottom of the slope, his last gaze fixed on me all the way. I turned over and scrambled upwards, reaching for the top edge of the bascule, dragging myself up onto the apex. I slumped there, riding the summit, one leg and arm roadside, the other half of me over the edge, and I watched McGruder as his fingers raked the roadway and his legs slid into the thinning gap.

His chest rose from the concrete and I realized the bottom of the bascule was angled to join the underside slope of the roadway itself when the bridge was level. The rest of his body was too bulky to go through.

It was terrible, but I couldn't turn away, I couldn't close my eyes to the horror. McGruder screamed and screamed as hundreds of tons of concrete, iron and lead crushed his hips and legs, the sound abruptly cut off by the thick explosion of blood that squeezed through his body to erupt from every opening in his head.

The gap closed completely and the bridge was down. And I was falling, shaken off my perch by the sudden fierce bump as the roadway levelled, tumbling over and over 'til I hit the cool waters thirty feet below.

28

CISSIE WAS YELLING at me and pumping my chest at the same time, and I'm not sure if it was the pain or her shouts that brought me out of my stupor. I retched river water and tried to turn onto my side. She helped me and began thumping my back. I started to protest, but more water belched from me. I could only moan and gulp in air between heaves, my head jerking off the soaked concrete with every spasm.

'Why?' she was yelling at me, her voice ringing off dank cavern walls around us. 'Why didn't you listen to me? Why did there have to be more killing? You bloody, bloody fool! You nearly got yourself blown to pieces, just like I said you would!' She began to sob, her blows becoming more feeble. 'You never listen and you never talk. I still don't even know why you stayed in this bloody awful city, living with corpses, always on the run, killing just to stay alive!'

She babbled on, weeping and cursing, pounding water from my lungs and generally giving me hell 'til I started to laugh. My chest and shoulders lurched as though I were having some kind of fit, but the laughter expelled the last drops of water I'd swallowed in my swim across the Thames to this tiny quayside underneath the bridge's northern span. Luckily for me the shock of falling into the river had helped put some life back into my exhausted body, just enough to get me fighting again, kicking water, keeping myself afloat on the currents. I knew I'd drown if I didn't make the effort, and that seemed pretty silly after all I'd been through, so I struck out for the shore (the currents had already carried me close to the north tower), swimming through debris and human flotsam thrown from the high walkway by the explosions. I clung to the pier for a while, fingers digging into the cracks between its stone blocks, getting my breath back and working up some strength for the rest of the journey, then inched my way round, every so often my numbed hands slipping off the concrete's slimy surface and my whole body shivering from cold or shock, probably both. On the other side I could see the stone steps leading up to the covert landing stage tucked beneath the first span, and where once they probably dragged suicidal bridge jumpers from the river; it didn't seem so far and, goddamn it, I was gonna try for it. What choice did I have? I kicked off my boots, unbuckled the gun holster, and headed for shore.

I think I went under two or three times – it's hard to recall just how many – but on each occasion I'd pop up again, thrashing out with more vigour for a few strokes before settling into a weary but steady rhythm. When I thought the game was up, only yards from that little hideaway dock, and began to sink, my feet touched something solid underneath me, something I could push against to get me back to the surface. Another couple of strokes and I was able to stand; I could walk – I could stagger – up the long, sloping ramp towards the two sets of steps leading to the landing stage and, when the water was only waist-high, there was Cissie running down those steps, calling my name. She'd jumped into the river and waded out to meet me, tucking herself under my shoulder, and helping me reach safe ground, weeping and babbling on about how she'd watched me fall from the bridge, knowing it was me even from that distance because I wasn't wearing black, and how, when she'd searched for a boat, she'd found the tunnel leading to the concealed landing stage under the approach road. She had to drag me up those slippery steps and that's when I'd buckled and she'd begun pounding my chest, afraid I was going to drown on dry land.

She didn't understand I was laughing – she thought I was choking – and she beat my back even more, shouting at me not to give in, that I was going to pull through, and please, please, *please*, don't die, Hoke, don't *die*. I lifted an arm to ward her off, but I was too weak.

'Cut ... cut it out,' I managed to gasp, and she quit immediately.

'You're all right.' She seemed stunned.

'I guess,' was the best I could do. I didn't have the energy to laugh again, but I stoked up a grin.

She just wailed. She just threw herself on top of me and blubbered. Pretty soon I was blubbering with her.

And eventually, when our tears had dried and we both sat shivering in that gloomy, damp, brick cave, my arm around her shoulders, holding her close, I told her why I'd never left the city.

29

THERE WAS NOTHING left for me here any more. Nothing left for me to do.

I eased the military truck through the paralysed traffic as the huge column of smoke and fire rose up over the rooftops far behind me, the funeral pyre only a gesture, a symbolic mark of respect for the passing of so many, those thousands of burning corpses representing the millions that had perished in this city. I'd never had the chance to visit Wembley Stadium in wartime, but now and again, when I'd been unloading all those carcasses I'd collected from the streets, I'd heard – I was *sure* I'd heard – the ghost-echoes of cheering masses, voices raised in praise of human skill and endurance. They'd never frightened me, those spectral ovations; no, they'd only deepened the sadness, made me even more aware of my own isolation, my own loneliness.

Some miles back, I'd stopped the truck and leaned out the side window to watch the fire, maybe just to make sure it was effective. The blaze was awesome. Giant black clouds, edged with gold and crimson, curled up to the heavens, the flames that drove them violently beautiful as they consumed the heaped legions of fuel-soaked corpses below. I could do no more for the deceased citizens of that once-great place and Cissie had been right when she'd said that the rest would turn to dust in their own time.

And she *had* finally understood why I'd never left the city.

Under the bridge, huddled together, my strength slowly returning, I'd told her of my love for Sally, how we'd met at Rainbow Corner, a club for US servicemen in Piccadilly, she with girlfriends from her office, me with a couple of pilot buddies from another squadron, how one hello, one dance and one light kiss had meant instant love. We were married less than six months later, both of us sure of our feelings, realizing the risk that came with the war, but that same risk making us see there was no time to waste . . .

I hadn't even known she'd been pregnant when I came searching for her three weeks after the Blood Death rockets had fallen; she hadn't told me, I guess, because she hadn't wanted to burden me with another worry, at least not 'til there was no way of disguising her condition. I wasn't allowed to leave the airbase when the country's population started dropping dead, because all pilots still breathing were kept under guard in case the enemy launched a grand attack now that they'd knocked out our defences. Hah! It was all so laughable, so insane, none of us knowing what had really happened, communications with the outside world kept tight by our surviving commanding officer, who was carrying out his last orders to the letter. And before long, everyone on the base had gone down with the disease, everyone 'cept me. I was alone and scared out of my wits, but I was finally the only one left alive. That's when I'd fled to London and the real nightmare had begun.

I was already traumatized by the time I found Sally lying outside on the steps leading down to our basement flat, and the sight of her nearly finished me. Her eyes were missing, her flesh torn open. The rats had eaten into her belly and ripped the foetus of our unborn child from her womb. They'd left it on the step, close to her outstretched hand, half-eaten, almost unrecognizable. I'd known what it was though and I'd given in to the hysteria right there beside them both, my wife and our baby, given in to the madness that had sustained me for at least a year afterwards. Maybe not all that madness had left me yet.

All I could do – all I could *think* of doing – was burn what remained of their poor bodies. There was nothing there to honour, you see, nothing recognizable to pray over. That wasn't Sally lying on those steps, and it wasn't our baby next to her. They were just pieces of discarded meat. Leavings. Waste. Not my family.

I took them inside the house and set fire to the curtains. Within an hour, the whole row of houses on that side of the small street was ablaze.

And the madness drove me to gathering up other exposed and vulnerable dead ones, hundreds, *thousands*, of them, and taking them to a suitable burial ground so that they would not just be fodder for the surviving vermin that now openly roamed the streets, to an enclosed place where eventually I could lend some dignity to their passing. Even when the craziness wore off – the bitterness never did – I couldn't give up. It gave my life some small purpose, I'd told Cissie, it gave me a reason, no matter how senseless, how hopeless, to carry on.

Like I say, Cissie had understood.

But now it was over, burned from me. I think I even smiled at the thought.

She was waiting for me with the others at the corner of Westminster Bridge, just under the statue of Boadicea. I could see them up ahead as I turned the corner from Whitehall, smaller figures among them, the kids and adults I'd set free in the old castle. We'd rounded up fewer than a dozen women and children when we'd returned to the castle grounds, only two men with them, one middle-aged and in poor condition, the other hardly more than a kid himself. Oh yeah, and we'd caught sight of two Blackshirts scurrying away, trying to hide from us; but that didn't worry me – how long did they have left anyway?

One of the kids saw me approaching and began jumping

up and down, tugging at the skirt of the woman closest to him and pointing in my direction. They all started waving, the two boy twins and some others even running forward to meet me. Cissie stayed where she was though. She was unmistakable in her new blue frock, one hand raised in greeting, the other on her hip. Even from the truck I could see she was smiling.

I passed the battered Houses of Parliament, Big Ben tall and looming, and carefully drew the vehicle to a halt, wary of the kids rushing forward in their excitement.

'You ready?' I called from the open window, returning Cissie's smile.

'It's done?' she said in reply.

'Can't you see?' My thumb indicated the huge cloud of smoke darkening the horizon behind me.

She nodded. 'I hope it burns the whole city. We don't need London any more.'

The women, helped by the two men, were already lifting the children into the back of the truck.

'Sit up front?' I asked Cissie.

She strolled over and opened the passenger door. The sun was behind her, shadowing her face as she leaned in, but I could still see the whiteness of her smile, the fine little scar running across her nose. She climbed up, flopping purposely into the seat beside me.

'You needed to ask?' she said.

'Guess not,' I replied. 'Ready to roll?'

She banged on the screen behind us. 'Everybody set?' she called.

A chorus of yeses came back, followed by a few muffled giggles.

'We're ready,' Cissie declared. She looked ahead through the dusty windshield. 'I always fancied the Surrey hills.'

'I always liked the sea.'

'Does it matter?'

'Not one bit. There're plenty out there just like us.'

329

I pushed the stiff lever into gear and pulled the truck away from the kerbside – funny how they'd all been waiting safely out of the road – and we rolled onto the bridge. As ever, the river beneath us was silver with specks of dazzling gold.

For no particular reason – old habits again? – I glanced into my wing mirror and my foot almost slipped off the accelerator. Without saying anything to Cissie, I stuck my head out the window, looking back. I wasn't sure what I was searching for at first, it seemed so, well, so out of place. Then I grinned. It was, it really was.

The zebra – yeah, four legs and a whole lot of black and white stripes – was ambling across the broad road some distance behind us, heading, I figured, for the overgrown green in Parliament Square. I ducked back inside the cab again, just in time to swerve round a Ford parked in the very middle of the bridge.

'What are you grinning at, Hoke?' Cissie was still smiling herself.

'Nothing,' I told her. 'Nothing at all.'

And maybe that zebra was nothing. It set me thinking though. And hoping too. Although I had no idea what I was hoping for.

AUTHOR'S NOTE

'48 required a great deal of research into World War II and conditions in London around that time. Where possible, I've stuck to the facts, but in instances such as the escape along the Tube line between Holborn and the Aldwych, which was in truth closed down during the war years, I've allowed the story to stretch the actuality. There also appears to be some confusion between the experts as to whether trams were allowed to run through the tunnel beneath Kingsway during those dangerous years, so again I've opted for artistic licence (or not, whichever the case may be). Most other details should be accurate, but please forgive any mistakes I'm bound to have made and certain elaborations used for the sake of dramatization.

JAMES HERBERT
Sussex, 1996